T0321303

NEVER KEEP

CAROLINE SUSANNE
PECKHAM VALENTI

BOOKS BY CAROLINE PECKHAM & SUSANNE VALENTI

Solaria

Ruthless Boys of the Zodiac
Dark Fae
Savage Fae
Vicious Fae
Broken Fae
Warrior Fae

Zodiac Academy
Origins (Novella)
The Awakening
Ruthless Fae
The Reckoning
Shadow Princess
Cursed Fates
The Big A.S.S. Party (Novella)
Fated Throne
Heartless Sky
Sorrow and Starlight
Beyond The Veil (Novella)
Restless Stars
The Awakening: As Told by The Boys (Alternate POV)

Darkmore Penitentiary
Caged Wolf
Alpha Wolf
Feral Wolf

Sins of the Zodiac

Never Keep

A Game of Malice and Greed
A Kingdom of Gods and Ruin
A Game of Malice and Greed

Age of Vampires
Eternal Reign
Immortal Prince
Infernal Creatures
Wrathful Mortals
Forsaken Relic
Ravaged Souls
Devious Gods

Caroline Peckham & Susanne Valenti

Interior Formatting & Design by Wild Elegance Formatting
Map Design by Fred Kroner
Endpaper Artwork by Ignacio Perez Meana
Cover Artwork by Rudy Duca

ISBN: : 978-1-916926-27-1

Never Keep/Caroline Peckham & Susanne Valenti – 1st ed

This darkly romantic tale of fantasy, wonder and woe is dedicated to all the wandering souls of the world, seeking refuge between the pages of books and wistfully dancing through make-believe lands that call to you all the more deeply than your own.
Here, in this new and twisted magical realm, you will find gothic halls to creep through, beautiful libraries to peer into, and characters who will steal your heart and refuse to give it back, keeping a piece of you in this story forevermore.
Once touched by the magic woven through these pages, you cannot go back. So are you ready to step into The Waning Lands, dear one? Because fate is calling your name...

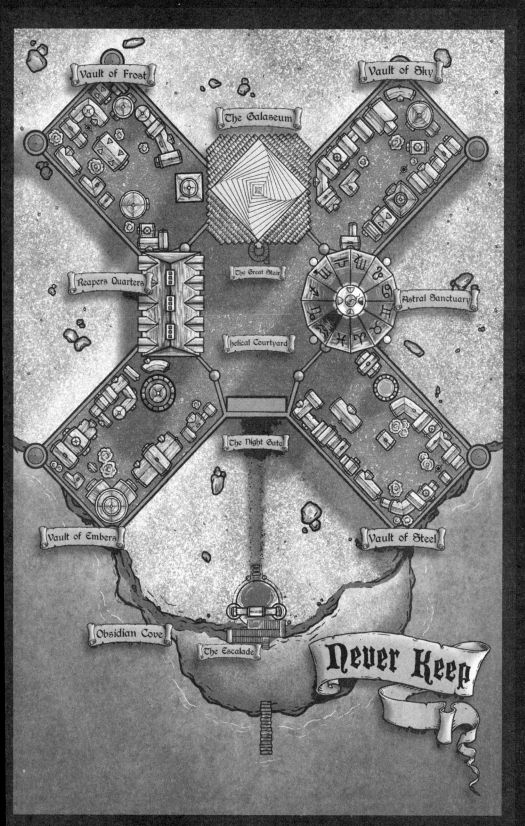

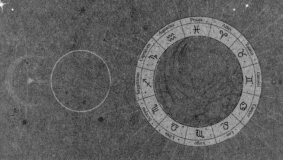

EVEREST

CHAPTER ONE

Misfits forge the most remarkable paths - my mama had told me that.

"Better to be on the outside looking in, than on the inside looking out, Everest."

It was a little harder to believe in those words when a group of assholes were throwing rocks at you.

"Get her!"

I ran as fast as my legs would go, and a rock crashed against my back, making me hiss through my teeth in pain. But I didn't stop, taking a route into the trees, following a path up the hill which was little more than an animal track winding through the prickly brush.

At least the night offered me cover, though the moon's silvery light would betray me if I strayed from the shadows of the scrappy woodland. All the way out here on the verges of my hometown, only the sky would hear my screams.

Thorns tore at my bare legs and arms, the heat of my land calling for as little clothes as I could get away with, the air thick with warmth even in the dead of night.

The crash of footsteps told me they were following, my half brother, Ransom, no doubt leading the charge with his pack of bloodthirsty allies in tow. By the ocean, I hated him. I hated him so ferociously that sometimes I thought it would eat me alive.

Another rock whistled past my ear, and my heart lurched as I ducked. Eské - *fuck* - I wasn't losing them.

The dry ground rose beneath my bare feet, the dusty hill climbing ever higher until my breaths were labouring and I prayed to Delphinus to offer me a drop of luck tonight. The stars ruled this world, and the water constellations were above all others when it came to the land of Cascada, home of the Raincarvers who claimed dominion over the elemental power of water. Pisces, Scorpio and Cancer were the highest of celestial deities to my people, but the lower constellations were steeped in power too, all of them able to change the fates of worthy Fae – or curse them in the name of petty contempt.

My thick, curling, brown hair swung forward in the wind, so long it tangled around me, and I had to sweep it back from my face to see again. Mama said my hair was only second in its wild nature to my heart, neither tameable, both beasts of their own free will.

I finally crested the hill, turning left, disoriented in the dark, and I only realised my mistake when an intense crackle of magic made the hairs on my arms stand on end.

I was heading toward The Boundary; the wall of power that kept enemy Fae from entering our lands, the other Elementals. Fire, Earth, Air. This barrier marked the end of Cascada's borders on the eastern part of our territory, looking out towards the dreaded Crux. The vast, desolate crater where the corners of the earth, water and fire lands met.

The barrier kept our adversaries out, and the elders said it would destroy any Fae who tried to leave without permission too. It would have been as good as a death sentence to go out there anyway. There were things in that wasteland, wild, monstrous, magically-altered creatures placed there by us and our foes alike, waiting to feed on any Fae who was dumb enough to try crossing the wilds. Put simply, it was inaccessible and suicidal to attempt entering. Meaning I was running straight towards a dead end.

A crack came from the trees to my right and my throat thickened. The footsteps of my pursuers had fallen quiet, so perhaps it was just an animal. Maybe they'd lost my trail and turned back.

With that hope in mind, I headed closer to The Boundary, a feeling of eyes on my flesh making me turn to glance wildly through the gloom between the boughs, but no attack came.

I kept going, and the temperature began to drop, every step I took plummeting me into a colder and colder world. I never came up this way, it was forbidden for un-Awakened Fae - those of us who weren't yet old enough to harness our magic and the ability to wield water - to be this near to The Boundary.

Those who had their magic Awakened by the stars, unleashing the elemental power that lived in their veins, held certain privileges in Cascada, such as the right to voice their own opinions in matters of our homeland. At the age of twenty-one, every year, Fae were sent to Helle Fort to unleash that magic in them and to face assessment for their calling in life. There was no calling as esteemed as that of a warrior selected to train and fight for the army of Raincarvers who fought in the Endless War against the other nations. An army I was determined to qualify for.

The call of battle had whispered my name since the moment I could hold a sword. And despite the contempt of my half-brother and his adoring fans, I was determined to see my destiny unfold at Never Keep, the fortress where all great warriors learned to harness their element under the guiding hands of the star-chosen prophets known as the Reapers during six months of magic instruction.

Competition for a place at Never Keep was fierce, but I had set my heart on claiming one. Those who survived the gruelling training at the Keep and made it home again were changed, their souls tainted with unknown horrors, blood well and truly on their hands since claiming their warrior birthright. That would be my fate soon enough. I'd turn twenty-one in under a year's time, a Pisces with Aries rising, and when that time came, I would be shipped off to Never Keep alongside my vicious half-brother and all the other water elementals who came of age with us to be assessed for a position fighting for my land.

Snow had been cast ahead of me with magic, and I shivered, wrapping my arms around myself as goosebumps spread across my skin. I was used to balmy air and the warm swells of the ocean where I could ride the waves using my wooden tiderunner, not this frigid tundra where the world seemed so still, so utterly unwelcoming.

Water could be deadly in all forms, but it was also the greatest life giver in The Waning Lands. I'd been raised on tales of the revered warriors who had died in the first battles of the Endless War so long ago that the stories about them had become legends, always a little different every time I heard them.

Hazarar the Fierce had supposedly turned a whole faction of Stonebreakers - who held the power of earth - to ice and crushed them all with a giant hammer made from the tempestuous waves of the ocean.

My people were deadly, but so were our enemies. And one day, I would face them on the battlefield and shed their blood with as keen a hunger as they sought to shed mine. It didn't unsettle me, I ached for somewhere in this world where I belonged. And I had the feeling it would be there, at the heart of the chaos.

The trees here were heavy with snow, bowing under the weight of it all, the branches woven together above me. It was too dark to see much further, so I slipped a hand into my pocket, taking out the everflame I kept in a little jar, shaking it to brighten it up.

I'd be in serious trouble if I was found carrying this thing around, but it had been a gift from Mama, a trinket she'd acquired in her line of work at The Forge. It was only meant to be used in work such as hers, forging weapons and wielding our enemy's fire for our strength, and I shouldn't have been carrying it around for my own needs. It was a miracle which I secretly coveted even if I did hate the Fae who had created it – a fire which never went out, burning eternally, creating a light that needed no fuel and persisted without end.

My mother had been selected as a Provider long ago, birthing children from the ruthlessly powerful Commander Rake who had been assigned to her, and though she had never fought battles, she wasn't one to flinch at death either. I was glad my features resembled hers over his, from my warm brown skin to my large bronze eyes and wide lips that my mama had said were made for smiles. Though I hadn't had many chances for those. This small life of mine was forged under the weight of a brutal war, and I was born to be a cog in the machine that drove our nation toward greatness.

Mama had told me stories that had set my blood chilling when

I was just a child, of a time when the Flamebringers - who held the power of fire - had marched into our land and burned a path of death right through the heart of our nation. She had taken up a sword, cutting down those who sought to kill her loved ones, and victory had been claimed after a bloody week of carnage. Those tales had always lit me up instead of making me cower. As if the streak of wildness that lived in her, lived in me too.

I made it to The Boundary, the air sparking with energy and a ripple of deepest blue light shimmering before me, the unearthly glow making the snow glitter at my feet. There was a steep drop beyond it, a slippery slope of ice plummeting down, down, down into the wild valleys where nothing but a grisly end awaited any sorry soul who went out there.

I was fascinated by the idea of all that danger sitting so close to the borders of our land, miles of unimaginable horrors waiting for a foolish squadron of Fae to try their luck at making it across The Crux into our territory.

In the distance, Pyros - the land of the fire wielders - loomed, nearly lost to the darkness at this time of night. I wondered if somewhere on the far side of the distant boundary beyond the wilds, a Flamebringer might be peering this way too, my enemy so close and yet neither of us able to reach the other. All the four lands had defensive magical barriers like this running along the borders that faced The Crux, though they were hardly needed when crossing that wasteland was a death sentence.

An eerie, blood-curdling shriek carried from far out in the wilds, and I shuddered, taking a step back from the crackling magical boundary.

My heart lurched as my back knocked into a hard body, and I

knew my quarry had found me.

Strong hands crashed against my spine, shoving me hard, and I lost my footing, my knees hitting the ground and the everflame jar slipping from my grasp, landing in the snow with an incriminating thud.

"By the ocean, Ransom, your freak of a sister has her own fire," Alina Seaman accused, and I glowered up at her as she stepped forward to stand beside my half brother. She was tall, strong, with hard features that were a likeness to her powerful warrior aunt, her long, black hair so silken it was as if it had been woven from the night itself.

"*Half* sister," Ransom corrected coldly.

My brutish half brother was all muscle, clearly the one who'd shoved me. He resembled our father in all ways, his skin far lighter than mine, his height towering, shoulders terribly broad. He was built for war, my father's perfect heir with his natural bloodlust and obvious power. His hair was russet brown, perfectly kept, and his eyes were a slick of mud that always held so much arrogance. An arrogance well instilled by our father. The barbarous commander favoured him, hailing him as his latest prodigy. He praised and doted on him in a way he had never even attempted with me. To him, I was a runt, a pointless endeavour to be dismissed, while Ransom was his budding warrior who would soon be ready to be honed into a fearsome weapon.

To make his esteem all the greater in my father's eyes, Ransom had recently Emerged as a Merrow – the very same Order my father happened to be and, of course, in his opinion, the greatest Order in existence. They were a ferocious breed; jagged, serrated blue scales coating their body like armour in their shifted form, remaining mostly Fae in appearance apart from the spines that ran the length of their backs and the sharp spikes that extended between the knuckles of their hands. In water, they could shift their legs into a tail and carve through waves faster than any other Order of the ocean, their throat producing gills that allowed them to breathe underwater too.

All Fae held an Order; the ability to shift into a creature of scales or fur. Some only partially shifted, such as Centaurs and Harpies, but others transformed entirely into Werewolves, Nemean Lions, Pegasuses and the like. Every Order form had gifts of their own, a type of magic unique to their kind such as the Sirens' ability to influence emotion or the Medusas' gift to paralyse their enemies with a single bite from the snakes in their hair. Each Order had a particular way of recharging their elemental magic once it was Awakened too. Merrows drew their magic from the turning tides, Pegasuses flew through clouds to bolster their power, and Werewolves ran beneath the moon.

I, much to my father's disgust, was yet to Emerge into my Order form, meaning my abilities and the powers I might be able to use in battle were still unknown. I ached to Emerge with a desperate kind of need, hoping to prove myself powerful once the truth of what I was had been revealed but, so far, I was still waiting. Most Fae had long Emerged by my age – which was just another reason my father had to dismiss me.

More of Ransom's band of merry fuckwits moved forward from the shadows, baring their teeth at me like wolves who'd found a lamb to prey on. A few of them had shifted into their bestial forms, a huge Nemean Lion baring his teeth at me, his golden fur rippling in the wind, his size terrifying and his teeth as large as knives. Maria was smirking cruelly in her Centaur form, stamping a hooved, brown leg. I hoped that when I gained my own form, I wasn't something half Fae, half beast. I'd prefer to shift entirely or not at all.

I tried not to show my fear, but it was tracking along the inside of my veins, eating away at me. I'd been pushed into the dirt beneath them all my life, my nose bloodied countless times, but there'd been a change in them since we'd reached our teen years. Their bullying had turned more vicious, more cruel, and I knew where it ended if I couldn't escape again.

"I question every day how I could be related to such a *thing*. Look at what she's wearing," Ransom sneered.

My heart twitched with hurt as they took in my clothes, the shift I'd made by hand, blue with little seashells stitched across the material and lacquered with etzia oil to give it a constant rainbow shimmer, along with the armour I'd made to fit over it. A gleaming breastplate painted metallic blue with matching wrist cuffs.

"Why are you dressed like an ugly sea urchin?" Alina jeered, and anger flooded through my chest. "Do you think that armour will actually protect you from us?"

My cheeks scorched as they all laughed, mocking me, and as much as I wanted to scream a retort back at them, my tongue wouldn't curl around the words. Everyone in this land told me to *tone it down, stop being so odd, try to fit in, don't stand out, keep your head down, play it small.*

There were only two people I knew who encouraged my differences. One was my Mama, though I didn't always tell her the truth about why I often came home bruised and bloodied. The shame of it was just another dent to my already poor reputation. But I always *did* come home to Mama, and I couldn't let her down by not making it back tonight. I would never be the daughter she was the most proud of, not with six older sisters already graduated from Never Keep with plenty of battles to their names and too many accolades to count. But

I *could* make it home.

With a surge of determination, I shoved to my feet, snatching the everflame into my grasp, holding it out in front of me and making Alina nearly fall on her ass as she stumbled away from it.

"She's trying to wield fire," she gasped. "Look at her. Rejecting her own lineage. It's foul."

"Would you rather be a flame fucker, Everest?" Ransom growled, stepping forward, his dark eyes lighting under the glow of the everflame. "Do you think you'd fit in better there? Because I don't think any of them would want you either."

He clearly wasn't afraid of the everflame, even as I turned it his way, my foot sliding out behind me as I took up a fighting stance. I counted six of them, easily enough to beat me in a brawl, but I could probably break at least three noses before I went down. I may have been scrawny and outnumbered, but I was feisty and knew how to fight, courtesy of my training. Every citizen was taught basic combat, even if we didn't all make the cut for Never Keep's warriors when the assessment came. We had to be able to defend our land regardless.

"I'm no flame fucker, but you will be when I shove this everflame up your ass, Ransom," I spat to try and rattle him, making some of his little friends gasp. It didn't do much to ease the frantic pounding of my heart.

"Grab her," Alina encouraged my brother, a growl in her throat that was more worthy of the Werewolves than the Order she actually possessed. Cyclopses held mental powers that could sift through your memories and pick through your thoughts. She had gotten inside my head one too many times since her Emergence and I was determined she wouldn't do so again. "Make her eat that fire. Make her pay for scorning the ocean."

Ransom came at me, his large hand reaching for my throat, and I ducked it, making a bid for freedom, but he caught hold of my waist, hurling me onto the snow, my back warming with the heat of The Boundary. The energy it emitted was thrumming through the air, making my ears ring with the magic it held.

My heart thrashed with fear at what would happen if I touched it. Maybe I'd melt there and then, or turn to ash, or my lungs would burst and I'd bleed out at Ransom's feet.

Kaské - *shit* - I needed to get out of here. *Fast.*

I popped the lid off of the jar, throwing the whole thing at Ransom's face in a furious attempt to defend myself. He cried out, raising a hand, batting the jar aside, and the everflame went tumbling over my head.

My lips parted in shock as it hit The Boundary and exploded on impact, the wall of magic destroying it so quickly that the glass was shattered into tiny pieces, scattering across the snow. There was nothing left of the everflame, as if it had never even existed.

"Woah," Ransom cooed and some of his friends shared excited looks.

"Do you think that would happen to her if *she* touched it?" Alina whispered to him keenly, and my blood ran cold.

"Only one way to find out." Ransom rushed forward and I scrambled to evade him, but he had me trapped. He caught my thick, brown curls in his fist, shoving my head towards The Boundary, and a scream of terror pitched from my lungs.

A flash of memory seared across my mind of a boy's lifeless body crumpled at the feet of my father, Commander Abraham Rake, put there by a gang of bloodthirsty kids who were glorified for their strength.

"Good," Father had praised them. *"The weak must fall so the great can rise."*

It was dog-eat-dog in this land, always had been, always would be, and it was actively encouraged too. Runts didn't make it to adulthood, because runts made the spine of Cascada weaker. I'd made myself a target when I'd refused to go along with the crowd, when I hadn't found ways to fit in and create a group of my own. They called me different, unusual, an outcast. And no one would flinch if I was killed now, except perhaps Mama and my one friend in this world. Harlon Brook. He'd taken me under his wing long ago, one of the strongest Fae of our generation, but he had never been one to go along with the pack either. He'd stood at my side through thick and thin, but he wasn't here now. I was alone, facing the murderous look in my brother's eyes, wondering if he might just kill me this time.

This cut-throat barbarity was the way of our kind. There was no place in this callous world for rejects.

I clawed at Ransom's arms, drawing blood, thrashing, kicking, fighting for this life of mine that no one else would fight for. It was survival in its purest form, and my soul was screaming for another day in the sun.

"Goodbye, Everest. I'd love to tell you that I'll miss you, but Father would scold me for lying. He will praise me greatly for unburdening him of his failure though. Of all his children, you are the tar on his name. But not anymore." Ransom threw me at The Boundary and Alina cried out in excitement while the others cheered, the Nemean Lion releasing a roar.

The warmth of The Boundary rushed over me, and terror carved its name into my very essence as the magic ran across my skin, consuming me.

Yet somehow, impossibly, I *wasn't* consumed. I wasn't burning up in its terrible power, ripped to pieces by the magic. Instead, The

Boundary let me through.

My relief was painfully short-lived as I started falling, slamming onto the steep ground of the icy slope, trying to grab anything I could for purchase, but it was already too late.

Ransom's brown eyes widened in surprise as I went skidding away down the sheer bank and a horrified scream left me as I fell, sliding down the plain of ice, crashing over sheets of compacted snow, unable to get a hold on anything at all.

My knees were ripped raw against the ice and my body was badly bruised as I began tumbling like a ragdoll, losing all control of my limbs as I gained momentum down the hill.

My shift tore in places, seashells ripped from it, scattering away from me with clinks and jingling that sounded like bittersweet music. My breastplate took a bashing but stayed firm, protecting me from some of the bigger rocks I slammed into, but it likely wouldn't be enough to save me from the violent impact that was coming at the bottom.

I clasped my head in my hands, curling in on myself, trying to protect anything vital, the moon a blur of silver above me as I rolled over and over.

My spine hit hard ground with such a forceful collision that I was winded in an instant, spluttering and coughing as I tried to draw breath where I lay in a pile of crushed seashells.

"Skyforgers!" Alina shrieked from far above me on the hill, and I blinked to try and right my thoughts, that word striking fear into my soul even as I fought to make sense of it.

Cries carried out all across our town, far beyond The Boundary, and I stared up at the thick clouds that were rolling in above the wilds, searching them with a frantic terror crawling up my spine. They parted like a veil and the moonlight glinted off of the giant slab of land which was revealed within them, an entire island travelling in the sky, descending on our people like wraiths in the night. The air elementals were here, and they had come for blood.

A nightmarish shriek carried from the wilds, driving terror through my heart as I pushed up onto my knees, still staring at the horrifying sight of the hulking sky island as it passed overhead, blocking out the moon entirely.

It didn't matter that I was still breathing, or that The Boundary had let me pass through unscathed, because my death would either seek me here in the wasteland or it would come at the hands of the sky warriors descending on us from above. But I would rise to meet it, like always. Because I was born for war.

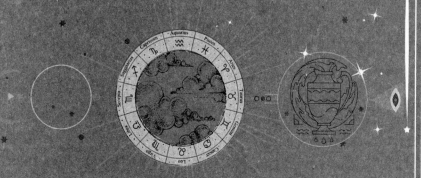

VESPER

CHAPTER TWO

We were all weapons.

Every single one of us birthed and forged in the flame of war, a nation of monsters and heathens.

Every gift we were born with was honed into an advantage, each more deadly than the last.

And my beauty was my sharpest weapon of all.

I snorted as I looked at the cherry blossoms dancing in the breeze that whistled through the narrow slip of land beneath me, highlighted by the shimmering moonlight. Such fragile, fleeting flowers. Beautiful, innocent, soft. I may have been compared to them by the brute who had claimed my allegiance, but I was only one of those things.

And there was nothing soft or innocent about me. Not anymore.

I ran the sharp tip of my thumbnail along the curve of my bottom lip, tasting blood as I sliced into the skin. The wind tossed a lock of pale pink hair before my eyes, softening the world with its pretty colour, my lie branded on me in those small ways, my appearance sugar sweet from a distance.

But there was a reason my true name had been forgotten. There was a reason they all called me by the title that was hissed in my wake and screamed upon my arrival.

Sky Witch.

And oh, what a witch I could be.

"Do you think we'll ever tire of hearing that sound?" Dalia asked on my right, her wicked smile clear in her tone as the Raincarvers in the outpost town of Castelorain far below us screamed in anticipation of our arrival.

"It grows repetitive," I replied with a shrug, my gaze fixed on the lights beneath us which were blinking out one by one as magic was snuffed and the Fae cowering beneath the massive slip of land we rode upon tried to hide in the dark.

Moraine snorted her amusement from my left and I glanced her way, the edge of my lips curving as I took in her broad smile, her long silver hair remaining in place thanks to the braids which secured it, while mine instantly took the opportunity to sweep across my eyes as I turned my head. She had shifted into her Harpy Order form, her silvery wings a match to her hair, both a sweeping contrast to her warm, brown skin. The armour her kind coated their flesh in for battle covered the lower portion of her body, her legs and waist in metallic scales which gave way to the black battle leathers that protected her chest and arms.

I pursed my lips at the pang of jealousy her wings roused in me and focused back on the panicking outpost we were closing in on.

Beyond it, The Crux scarred the land, a crater fifty miles wide and carved so deeply into the earth that none had ever dared explore its depths – not that anyone would be likely to get close enough to try with fire, water and earth territories all bordering it. It was no man's land, a void caught at the heart of the Endless War, and as we drew closer to it on our flying island, we only added to the threat by placing a fourth nation at its border.

"He's coming," Dalia murmured, and I straightened my spine, turning to look as Prince Dragor emerged from Echo Fort at our backs.

The building was designed for war, squat and strengthened against damage with countless shields imbued in its sandstone walls. War machines were mounted on its turrets, catapults and projectiles loaded with iron bolts and heavy stones awaiting an attack from any flying Orders such as Manticores, Griffins or Pegasuses foolish enough to try and strike at us in our domain – the sky.

Barracks consumed the flanks of the building but at the heart of it, the prince held rooms as grand as any of those in his palaces back in our land of Stormfell to the far north. Not that he spent much time in them; he was far more interested in roaming the front lines and seeking new targets for our warmongering – hence the position of the fort at the tip of our travelling mass of land. Prince Dragor wanted to look our enemies in the eye as he watched them die beneath us.

Dalia raised her chin, the short strands of her close-cropped black hair dancing in the breeze as she stood to attention, her grip tightening on her windrider at her side. The shaft of golden metal was a near mirror to my own, though the slim magic turbines mounted on either side of hers were more angular than my rounded design where the runes carved into the metal buzzed with the power imbued in them.

I turned my back on the landscape far below us, the heels of my boots scraping against the gravel and sending some of it tumbling from the sheer edge behind me. My pale pink hair instantly billowed forward over my shoulders, surrounding me and narrowing my line of sight down to nothing beyond the approaching prince and his convoy.

Dragor's cold eyes looked beyond me as he strode closer, taking in the terrain below, his expression calculating, his strong jaw locked in what seemed to be a displeased expression, though honestly, even after all of these years, he wasn't easy to read. I wasn't certain if it was because his moods could shift as abruptly as the wind or if he was simply so good at concealing his true emotions that gaining a lock on them was never going to be possible.

He was pale, everything from his ice-white hair to his chilled blue eyes and the pristine white battle leathers that clung to his muscular frame and defied all logic. To look at him now, most Fae might assume that he never got his own hands dirty, but I had seen that white stained in blood more times than I could count. The blood of his enemies, the blood of traitors, even the blood of those he had claimed for his closest companions – because true loyalty could withstand a little bloodshed after all. His jaw was a hard line, his cheekbones even sharper and I couldn't help but stare a little every time I got close enough to do so, his hold over me unlike any other.

Dragor was the oldest son of King Aquila, ruler of the air kingdom of Stormfell and the most likely candidate to take the throne when his father passed, though his sister and two brothers were also in the running. He was in his early thirties and spent most of his time at war where he had carved out his brutal and ruthless reputation despite his youth, leaving the scandals and politics of court life to his siblings.

He may not have been looking at me, but I watched him without pause. Sometimes I felt like my very existence was so entwined with that of the Prince of Storms that I would simply cease to be were he ever to fall in battle. I was his creature, his creation, his shadow in the darkest of places and my every move was calculated by his desires.

"The clouds kept us hidden above the sea," Prince Dragor clipped, his voice a rough and jagged thing that sent my pulse skittering.

The Wind Weavers stationed close enough to hear him all straightened their spines with pride, though I knew it to be little more than an observation on his part. Had they failed, then he would have had far more to say on the subject. Success was expected. Failure punished.

He stalked closer, the weight of his presence settling over me as he moved to stand by my side and Dalia stepped back to make way for him, the toes of his boots sending more gravel down towards the panicked Raincarvers below. No doubt there were warriors down there – more than enough to hold the line against the fire and earth lands which stood so close at hand, but they couldn't hope to stand against the might of Ironwraith when our island sailed overhead.

I turned to look across the dark landscape below, our island blotting the light of the moon and making it harder to see, but I spotted The Forge which had been named as our target all the same. I wetted my lips, tasting the blood that coated them, a surge of power rolling through me as I tapped into the Ether and grounded myself in the magic which roamed wild throughout every piece of The Waning Lands and beyond.

Few Fae knew the dark arts of wielding Ether, only those willing to risk their souls for the power it offered were bold enough to try and claim a hold over the deadly magic of it. But I had long since realised how much of myself I would need to sacrifice to carve a place out in this world. Even those willing to learn blood magic weren't all selected to do so, the Sages of Stormfell only willing to take on the most promising apprentices. Fortunately, I had made myself a worthy candidate for that position.

"You won't disappoint me, Vesper," Dragor breathed, his hand skimming my spine, fingertips pressing against my battle leathers just hard enough to let me know how easily he could push me from the ledge.

"I won't," I agreed, trying not to react to his nearness, neither to tense or lean into him. Instead, I recited all that I was inside the confines of my own head and made certain my breathing remained just as it had been before his arrival.

They call me the Sky Witch. Bloodborn Aquarius of the greatest nation of them all. My birth took place in the eye of a storm while battle raged around us and my mother's screams were met with those of men dying in the fields of glory beyond. I am yearning. I am lust. I am the greatest desire of all who fall prey to my power, and I am lethal in more ways than can be counted. I am Fae. I am Air. I am master of blood and bone. My name holds no power because it is not what I am.

My true name is War.

Dragor increased the pressure on my spine, his mouth dropping to my ear and an involuntary shudder spilled through me.

"Then go."

I snatched the windrider from its position beside me and leapt from the edge a heartbeat before he could push me.

Wind whipped my hair back from my face, gravity made my heart leap up into my mouth and the wildness of the air surrounding me made a throaty laugh tumble from my lips.

I let myself fall, my grip tight on the metal of my windrider, the runes carved into it raised beneath my palm as I ran my fingers over them, activating them. The magic coiled within its twin wind turbines roared to life as the air rushed through them and I almost lost my grip as it jerked upward, changing my trajectory.

I hoisted myself up, throwing my leg over the smooth shaft which made up the saddle, smiling darkly at Dalia and Moraine as they swooped into formation on either side of me. Moraine beat her silver wings hard, not needing the magical contraption to remain skyborne while Dalia rode her own windrider at my side. In a little over a year, the three of us would claim our places at Never Keep and our air magic would be Awakened at last, allowing us to navigate the skies with the power of our element, but I wondered if I might still prefer the rush of my windrider even then, the exhilaration I felt speeding through the sky on it second only to the rush of bloodshed.

Blasts of ice and water shot for us as our enemies took aim from below and we fell into a deadly dance to avoid them while rushing for the ground at a furious pace.

There was nothing in this world which compared to flying like this, the air ripping through my hair and stinging my cheeks as I tore through it in a bloodthirsty charge.

"The Sky Witch!" a man screamed in warning from beneath us as we drew close enough to the ground to be seen clearly.

I didn't even have my elemental magic Awakened yet, but they already feared me for my mastery over sword and blood magic alike, my reputation on the battlefield earned over six years of savage victories.

They knew what hell approached on this foul wind, and as the sky filled with more and more of our warriors at my back, I knew the dawn would run red with the blood of Cascada.

EVEREST

CHAPTER THREE

I'd shed my breastplate, using it as a wedge to slam into the ice and haul myself up the sheer slope, but my arms were roaring with effort, and I'd only made it ten feet.

My thoughts snapped onto a low growl that carried from the shadows behind me, but I didn't look back, even when a guttural, mechanical noise clacked through the air too.

I shuddered, gazing up at the impossible climb and digging my bare heels into the ice. My teeth were gritted and my arms shook, but I wouldn't let go. Determination lived in my bones, its meaning carved into my soul, and I wouldn't falter at the sight of ruin.

I jammed my foot into a small dent in the ice, then released a growl of effort as I yanked the breast plate out of the ice wall, my stomach dropping as the wind tugged at my hair, pulling me back towards the deadly chasm. Then I drove the metal plate into the ice as far above my head as I could reach and dragged myself higher once more.

"Eské tamin, Koe morden mas ocil harbrin," I gritted out in Cascalian. *Fuck fate, I make my own tonight.*

The heavy shadow of Ironwraith, the island of the sky, had descended over the outpost of Castelorain and the sound of battle carried to me from afar. Ransom and his friends were long gone, likely off to prove their mettle, leaving me to my fate in this Scorpio-forsaken valley of death.

A whirring of metal sounded beneath me, a scrape of jagged claws tearing through the ice and that horrid growling sound set the hairs rising along the back of my neck.

I glanced down, knowing I'd regret it and proving myself right as my gaze fell on the monstrous beast below. It was wolf-like in its gait, its body a mixture of sharp metal and powerful flesh, its face a twisted creation that resembled an ape's. Its mouth was full of curved silver teeth that were so sharp they could strip the flesh from my bones in seconds and the desperate hunger in its eyes promised that fate to me.

The monstrous creature sliced its claws into the ice, climbing after me with far more ease than I could possibly match. Fear carved through my chest as I drove my heels into the ice once more, finding enough purchase to rip the breast plate free and force it into the frigid surface above.

I scrambled higher as the beast swung a metal paw at me, its claws raking through the ice and carving a huge chunk out of it. My heart thrashed as I fought to hold onto the plate, my feet skidding against the ice as I hunted for another foothold.

A rumbling noise sounded beneath me and I chanced another look, finding a bright orange glow blazing between the monster's jaws. Magic sparked and crackled within, and I could see my death staring back at me as that pulse of power exploded from its mouth.

With a cry of fright, I swung myself sideways, abandoning my breast plate just before the shot of power tore right through it. I hit the ice wall and went skidding down it at a wild pace, finding myself slamming back to the bottom of the slope as that blast of power crashed into the top of The Boundary. Parts of the bank shattered under the impact and my lips parted in alarm as huge slabs of jagged ice came crashing down the slope towards me.

I raced for cover, diving behind a boulder just as the first slabs smashed to the ground.

A great wrenching of metal and a guttural roar made me chance a look beyond my hiding place and I found the beast crushed under the impact of the ice, two of its limbs torn clean off, metal sparking with magic and wet with blood as the monster struggled beneath the ever-mounting weight of the ice. I'd been raised on spine-chilling stories about the beasts that roamed the wastelands down here, their creation designed to stop anyone from crossing the barren space between nations, the metal magically forged to flesh with twisted blood magic that stopped them from dying of hunger, but left them forever famished, desperate to fill their bellies yet unable to ever do so.

My breaths skittered past my lips, my gaze locking on the severed front limbs of the beast as the avalanche eased.

I broke into a run, an idea locking into place inside my head as I grabbed one of the metal legs, heaving the heavy thing into my arms and whacking it against a rock to break off the clawed foot. My lip curled at the blood which oozed from the flesh still moulded to it, but I repeated the process with the other limb, then used two thick pieces of wire from the body of the beast to tether them across my hands, binding the metallic claws tight to my skin.

I gazed up at the icy wall with a newfound resolve, locking my sights on the places the rock had been exposed where the slabs of ice had fallen. Moving to the base of the slope, I drove the claws bound to my right hand into the ice above me, the sharp metal sliding into place far easier than my breast plate had. As I tried my weight on it, the claws locked tight and offered a perfect grip.

"Hia kaské." *Holy shit.*

I laughed a little manically at my creation, reaching up to lock my left claws in place too. Then I was climbing, moving far faster than before, and after an ascent that left my feet frozen and my body numb, I found myself scrabbling over the top of the cliff and rolling onto my back in exhaustion.

The Boundary crackled beside me as I shed the metallic claws from my hands, tossing them back down into the canyon. I eyed the wall of magic with trepidation, all I had known about this magical barrier now turned on its head. I'd passed through it with ease. And I didn't know why.

I reached for it, the clash of war only growing, and one look upwards showed a battalion of Skyforgers sweeping down upon wings, air magic and machines alike. My pulse ratcheted up at the sight of battle descending, the cries of my people igniting a bloodlust in me to defend this beautiful town of mine.

A roar of challenge sounded from the warriors of Castelorain, this outpost where weapons were forged. This northern corner of our land was tasked with defending against any Stonebreakers who worked to form land bridges across The Crux and the wilds, or Flamebringers who tried to come at us from the sea. A legion of our finest warriors were placed right here, and they were a hellish force to be reckoned with.

It wasn't the first attack I had witnessed, and as sure as the tide, it wouldn't be the last. But it was one I would be ready to prove myself in, to defend this land which was made by the courage of the Raincarvers, which was rich with the blood of our people who had fought and died to protect it.

If there was one thing I had known since I was young, it was that my life would likely end in bloody carnage, and I had been taught to seek the honour of such a death so that I might earn my place beyond The Veil instead of my soul being cast to ash at the hands of the stars.

Gritting my teeth, I stepped through the barrier, facing the possibility of my demise as I fixed my focus on my mother and Harlon. They were out there in the thick of the bloodshed, and I knew Harlon would have taken up arms already, proving his place as a warrior in this world. I longed to join him and demonstrate that I was no runt. Perhaps I'd have my father's gaze fall upon me with pride by the end of this night.

The magical barrier let me through, the crackle of energy over my skin nothing but a tingle of static, despite how fierce I knew the magic to be. A lie. We had been told a lie. That stepping through this boundary would equal death. But why?

Of course, to protect fools from finding themselves in the jaws of the beasts in the wilds.

I sprinted off through the snow, the dark even thicker now that Ironwraith was shading the moon. The terror of that island hanging overhead coiled in my gut – it only remained in the sky thanks to the power of the Fae casting the magic to hold it there, and I hoped our forces could overpower their wielders and hurl it into the depths of the hungry sea.

I forced myself not to consider what would happen if it fell upon us instead. Ironwraith had been haunting the skies along with the other battle islands of the Skyforgers for hundreds of years, and though its shadow cast a chill of dread down my spine, I would not yield to fear.

My toes were so numb I could hardly feel my feet as I padded through the tracks of Ransom and his allies, finally making it to dry, warm land as I made it off the hill. And there at its base, chaos reigned.

The town clung to the hillside, made of closely packed streets which wound between the pale stone houses with red-tiled roofs. The roads were steep, falling away towards the shore where the ocean glinted silver under the moon, winking at me in promise of victory. Or at least, that was what I hoped.

Raincarver warriors were spilling between the buildings, racing to meet the Skyforgers as they descended from above like a tempest of destruction. Water magic blasted them from the air, shards of ice impacting with our foes and bringing them to the ground with bloody savagery. They tore our enemies from the sky, the Raincarvers casting shots of pure, ruinous magic that collided with the Skyforgers' shields and blasted them to oblivion.

The Skyforgers responded with magical attacks of their own, and as I raced between the streets, my mind fixed on making it to the armoury at the nearest watchtower. Without magic, I couldn't simply dive into battle, and I longed for a blade in hand so I could take up my place at the side of my people.

I made it to the town square, the cobblestones spreading out ahead of me, the fray of the fight centred right here. A Skyforger blasted a shot of air right between the eyes of a Raincarver warrior in front of me and my gut lurched. He hit the ground with a wet thump, blood splashing my legs and hardening my heart with hatred for the air folk who had come here to reap their bloody harvest.

"Everest!" a familiar, deep voice barked, drawing my attention to a man as familiar as my own heartbeat as he came running for me across the square which had turned into a battlefield.

Harlon looked right where he belonged; in the thick of battle with one huge sword in hand, bright purple magic pulsing along its edges. His muscles pressed against his dark blue battle leathers with the coiling sea serpent insignia of Cascada blazing silver on his chest. The look of them were too tight, like he had already outgrown his latest set once again. He was likely bigger than Ransom now, a fact my half-brother despised, even more so perhaps than the way he matched him in combat. It must have been partly to do with his Order, because since he had Emerged as a Monolrian Bear shifter, Harlon had been growing by the year. He had sun-kissed skin and his brown hair was lighter than mine, with a streak of gold through it that coiled against his cheek, and his eyes were two dark coins that stole my breath like usual.

Harlon had always made me feel safe, and even now amidst the turmoil of war, he became a steady focal point that settled the furious pounding of my heart. There was something about him that spoke of control, his movements decisive and his mouth set in that familiar vicious slant which said he could have the world if only he wanted it enough.

I raced to meet him, and he gripped my arm, looking down at me in concern. "What the fuck happened to you, Ever?"

"It doesn't matter," I said fiercely, knowing my torn clothes and bloodied knees were the least of our concern. "I need to get to the armoury."

"No." His grip on me tightened, his growl a firm command. "Your mother needs you. I saw the Sky Witch; she's headed straight for The

Forge. I can't leave this fight, but you can. Go to her. And go quickly."

"The Sky Witch?" I echoed in horror.

That creature was nothing but a monster wrapped in a beautiful veil. She wasn't even Awakened yet, only twenty-years-old like me, but battle hardened over the last six years beneath the rule of the Storm Prince Dragor who cast children into war like pieces on a chessboard. She fought without air magic, yet the rumours of her control over Ether and the vile blood magics linked to it were as renowned as her prowess with a blade.

She had become a nightmare, whispered about behind locked doors; the girl with the face of a deity and a soul drenched in sin. She had murdered so many of my kind that the numbers were lost to legend, the tales of the deaths she reaped meaning that her title alone brought a snarl to my lips.

"Go, Ever," Harlon urged, that single golden lock swinging forward into his eyes. Those damn eyes which I could never resist when he looked at me like that. But of course I would go to my mama regardless of his orders.

"Stay alive," I demanded and he stepped back, swinging his sword as he searched for his next opponent.

"I always do," he said, tossing me that crooked smile which was so wild, it set a fire blazing in my soul.

I turned and ran across the courtyard, my bare feet no longer numb as they struck against the warm cobbles, moving as fast as possible. My mama could handle herself, but if I could get to her before the Sky Witch made it there, I could save her from the evil headed her way. So with hell raining down on me from above, my body battered and my limbs still burning from the climb out of the wilds, I made a bid for The Forge, to protect the woman I loved more dearly than anything in this world.

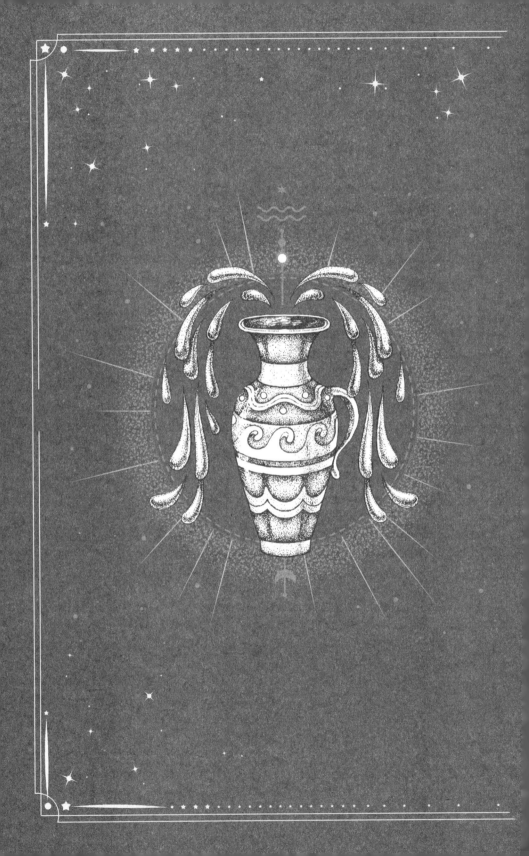

VESPER

CHAPTER FOUR

I wound through the sky on my windrider, dodging blasts of ice and water, dropping below a blue Pegasus who charged through the sky with his horn dipped low towards me and whirling around to hound after him instead. The horse-like creature kicked out with his hooves and his feathery wings beat against the violent storm of wind that twisted around us.

My blood lit with the thrill of the hunt as the Fae in Pegasus form whinnied in alarm, the woman riding him shifting in her saddle and drawing back a bow.

She balked as she met my stormy gaze, recognition flaring in her expression before she let her arrow fly.

I jerked aside, the arrow skimming my cheek so closely that I felt the brush of the feathers lining its shaft as it carved through the air past my ear. I drew a dagger from my belt and flung it, catching the rider in the throat and grinning wickedly as she clutched uselessly at the wound.

She began to topple sideways and I shoved to my feet, balancing on the thin body of my windrider and urging it to move faster.

I leapt from the saddle, crashing onto the Pegasus's back and causing him to neigh furiously as I lunged for the rider, catching her hand just before she could fall from the sky towards the chaos of the fighting below.

Her eyes widened, some form of gratitude forming there even as she choked on her own blood, dying at my hand. I reached out and snatched the blade free, yanking it sideways and letting her blood spill over my hands and the flank of the Pegasus before releasing my hold on her and thrusting her from me.

I tipped my head back, breathing a prayer to Aquarius in thanks for the offering of blood before reaching for the hum of Ether which flowed through all things in this world and beyond.

The raw power of the universe spilled through my bones as I formed a connection to it, a heady breath rattling my lungs as I offered up the blood I'd spilled as sacrifice. Power consumed me, the rush of dark magic sinking into my veins, making me ache with the need to release it.

I spun the dagger in my grip, my other fist tight on the saddle as the Pegasus bucked and thrashed beneath me, throwing himself into a roll through the air in an attempt to knock me free.

I clung on, bracing a boot on his wing as he spiralled and raising the dagger again.

I drove it down, aiming for the space between his ribs where I would find his heart, but he shifted before I could land the blow, his wild whinnying becoming a stream of curses as he returned to his Fae form, naked and wild with fury.

We plummeted through the sky, our bodies colliding, his fist slamming into my jaw and wheeling my head aside with a ferocious strength.

I swung my knee into his side, my hair whipping around me in a cloud of pale pink, the strength of our collision forcing us apart as the ground rushed nearer.

"Eat dirt, you unholy bitch," he snarled, shifting twenty feet from the ground, his Pegasus form returning and his wings snapping wide so that he could catch himself on an updraft and save himself from death.

I threw my arms out, whistling sharply, my life racing down in a count of seconds before the roar of my windrider filled my ears, the magical contraption bound to me, linked to my magical signature - the essence of who I was as a Fae - and chasing me through the sky.

I slammed into it, cursing as my grip slipped and the breath was driven from my lungs by the hard metal of the contraption, but I held on, throwing my leg over it once more as I directed it towards the stars again.

My head whipped around as I locked my focus onto the blue Pegasus, now charging at a legion of Skyforgers as they descended from Ironwraith and I hurled my dagger after him, striking him in the flank.

He whinnied in agony, wheeling around, and I fought to keep my gaze locked on him as my veins burned with the flood of blood magic which was still desperate for a point of release.

The wound became a target, his blood a magnet for my dark power of Ether. I threw my hand out, drops of the blood I'd spilled flying from my fingertips and speeding across the sky towards him.

The moment they met with the wound on his flank, my breath stilled in my lungs, my connection to his power complete and his end written in the stars themselves.

I coiled my fingers into a fist and pulled, power rushing through my ears like a building storm which only I could feel, his blood halting in his veins, heart racing in panic as its chambers emptied out until, with a violent crack, his lifeforce was wrenched from him and was sent careering into me.

The rush of pleasure that spilled through me at his demise was blinding, a moan of ecstasy rolling up the back of my throat as power resounded through my bones before slipping away again.

I blinked, forcing my focus back to my target, my gaze snapping to The Forge ahead of me just as Dalia and Moraine sped through the warring Fae in the sky to re-join me.

"That's it?" Moraine asked, beating her powerful wings, the silver feathers now splattered with blood.

"That's it," I confirmed, leaning low on my windrider and urging it to speed between the bloodshed towards our destination, my bloodlust sated and the point of my mission clear.

Dalia dropped low, a bottle in her hand and a wicked smile on her red lips as she tipped it up and let it fall over the Raincarvers below, soaking them in a highly volatile concoction of faesine and wicker oil before blowing a flame from her lips and letting it fall into the flammable concoction.

She threw me a wink over her shoulder, knowing I was scowling at her without needing to check because I'd told her in no uncertain terms to contain the gifts of her Order form before setting out on this mission.

"If Dragor sees-" I snapped, but she only laughed as my words were cut off by a tremendous explosion as her flame met with the faesine mixture and a cluster of Raincarvers were torn to pieces.

"Dragor sees what he wants to see, *Vesper*," she called, taunting me with that name, clearly having heard him growl it into my ear. "You should know that better than anyone. Besides, it's not as if he doesn't know I'm a Chimera – breathing fire doesn't make me a Flamebringer."

I ground my teeth, glancing up at Ironwraith, the enormous mass of land floating far above us, blocking out the sight of the moon and the stars alike. There was no way of spotting any of the Fae who might be watching us from its jagged cliffs, yet in my soul, I felt Dragor's eyes following us.

No. He was watching *me*. Always waiting for me to fail, for my weak blood to show itself. But I never had before, and I wouldn't now.

I focused on The Forge and pushed my windrider to its limit, dodging through the battling Fae and leading my unit of three towards our target. The Raincarvers had made a mistake in stealing from us and I was here to make sure they never forgot it.

An explosion of ice magic nearly knocked me from my windrider but I swerved, riding the blast of power before lurching back on course and dropping from the sky like a falling star.

Moraine tucked her wings, speeding for the ground, racing me to our destination and cursing as I beat her to it, my heels digging into the dirt to force my windrider to a halt.

I dismounted, Moraine landing beside me, shifting so that her wings disappeared in a pulse of silver light just before Dalia caught up to us, skidding to a halt too.

My two friends drew close either side of me, Dalia brushing the strands of her short, black hair away from her eyes with tattooed fingers before tossing her windrider skyward with a long whistle.

I followed her lead, commanding my windrider to shoot away from me and setting my attention on the looming brick building before us.

The doors were barred against our entry, guards clustered around them, bearing weapons and urging us closer with jeering taunts.

"That's the Sky Witch?" one of them sneered, his gaze fixing on me as I slowly unsheathed my sword and began walking towards them at the front of our group of three. There were ten of them, pity I didn't have time to indulge in a fair fight – it might have been fun. "She's five foot nothing and about as terrifying as-" His mouth fell slack as I stepped into the glow of the bobbing amber Faelight cast above their heads, illuminating my features and forcing his eyes and those of every other Fae surrounding him onto me and me alone.

Lust was such a stupid, fickle thing.

I ran my thumb over the hilt of my sword, feeling for the inverted Laguz rune, shaped something like a number seven, though the angle was far sharper. *Madness, confusion, despair.* This was my favourite sword for a reason. One cut, one taste of blood for the Ether in payment for the magic and insanity swiftly followed.

"Be mine," one of the guards grunted foolishly, the power of my Order making him dumb with lust. It was the truth of me and yet it wasn't at all – simply what I was beneath the confines of my flesh. Yes, my face was something to behold, my body a model of seduction, and yet none of that should have made Fae stupid with desire. The power which caused their minds to fog was all in my blood – the blood of a Succubus, a master of temptation.

I smiled at him, a pretty, wicked smile which I followed with a savage swipe of my sword the moment he took another step.

The spell broke like shattered glass, the Raincarvers flinching out of their stupor, but I was already among them, swinging my sword and cutting them open. Two fell dead instantly, three more took wounds which began to fester. I called the dark magic of Ether to me again, feeding the taste of their blood to Laguz, the rune drenching itself in the sacrifice I offered and turning them against themselves.

I lurched back as an axe swung for my throat, ducking beneath the blow and swiping the legs from beneath a female who screamed like a banshee as she fell.

The sharp hiss of three arrows flying in quick succession announced Moraine's involvement in the battle, three Fae falling dead before knowing what had killed them. And then Dalia was there as I threw myself onto the Fae I had taken to the ground.

She drove a punch into my side, hard enough to make bones crack, and I hurled my forehead into the bridge of her nose, shattering it with a spike of victory. She swore wildly, hot blood spraying us where Dalia danced between the Fae standing over our battling forms, cutting and slashing with her blade, carving them open and moving too fast for them to return the wounds.

One fell as the Fae I grappled with struck me again, his blood splattering me, though I didn't flinch.

I dropped my sword, my opponent too close to make use of it, her fists driving into me with brutal efficiency.

She threw her weight to the side, rolling us as I snatched a dagger from my belt. Her fist collided with my face, cracking my skull back against the ground, but my dagger had made it to her chest in the same moment.

More bodies fell around me as the Raincarver blinked down at me in horrified realisation of her own demise, her life slipping from her in a breathy exhale while I watched the light fade from her eyes.

"So slow tonight, V," Dalia taunted, grabbing my forearm and heaving me upright, the body of my kill toppling to the dirt with the rest of her unit.

I scoffed lightly, pushing to my feet, reclaiming my sword and turning to the entrance to The Forge. One of the guards I'd cut with the power of Laguz was throwing his head against the heavy door with a series of sickening thumps, the madness sinking deep within his bones.

I stalked towards him, grasping the back of his fighting leathers and whirling him around to face the fighting Fae at our backs.

"Go kill something," I purred, pointing at the closest unit of Raincarvers. "There's a good boy."

I shoved him away from me, not bothering to see if his insanity had accepted my suggestion as I shoved my blood-slick hair away from my face. I shouldn't have left it down for the battle, but I was addicted to the feeling of the wind racing through it and I didn't care for much else in this wretched world.

"Is he here?" Moraine asked, stepping forward to work on the door.

"Yes," I replied, lifting a hand to the vial of blood which hung from my neck, the few drops warm within my fingers, urging me on. The spell I'd cast on it would lead me directly to the man who had bled to fill the vial and there was no doubt in my mind that he was contained within the bowels of this building now that I stood before it. "The tip off was good."

I ignored the relief which settled over me at that fact. Dragor's fury would have been beyond compare if the Fae we sought wasn't here after all of this effort had gone into retrieving him.

"Wait," a male voice called out from behind me, and I turned, my sword raised for a fight, though I lowered it a fraction as I found a Skyforger hurrying to join us. "Prince Dragor said you were in need of my help."

The man was brutishly tall, his body powerful beneath the tight-fitting battle leathers, dark hair falling forward into his eyes which blazed with a darkness that instantly put me on my guard. He was dangerous in all the ways that counted, and I immediately disliked him as he spared me little more than a glance before looking to Moraine and Dalia. There weren't many Fae who could dismiss me so easily on first sight and though sometimes I loathed the way idiots fawned and panted for my attention, I found I disliked it more when my allure failed to draw a reaction at all.

"We need no help," I sneered, bristling as he drew closer, his height imposing, presence domineering.

"No offence, but I don't answer to the Sky Witch," he scoffed, the title I'd earned in fury and bloodshed sounding like a joke on his lips. "I answer to the prince."

He finally looked to me again, turning his head so that the glow of the Faelight still blazing above us illuminated his features and I blinked at the sharp cut of his jaw, the strong brow, the blazing, honeyed brown eyes which seemed to grab hold of me and lock me in place.

My lips parted on a jagged gasp which I cut short with a force of will, blinking again as I reminded myself that a face was only a face. I, of all people, knew that beauty should be nothing to covet for beauty's sake alone.

"What are you?" I spat, my eyes roaming over his features, hunting for flaws that weren't there. He was...breath-taking.

His gaze skimmed over me briefly before turning away again.

"Not interested," he replied, and my cheeks burned at the flippant dismissal. He hadn't even paused when seeing me for the first time – a feat not many Fae could claim, thanks to my nature.

"I mean your Order," I snarled, suspecting an Incubus because what other than a creature designed for sex and lust could look like this god of a man?

"Well, that's classified, sweetheart," he replied, stepping forward to take over from Moraine who had drawn her blade and abandoned the door.

"The fuck did you just call me?" I growled, tightening my grip on my sword.

"Who are you?" Dalia demanded, and he offered her a dark smile before throwing his weight against the door and smashing the damn thing open.

"Cayde Avior," he replied, his name ringing a bell, though I was certain I'd never laid eyes on him before. I wouldn't have forgotten.

"Well, *Cayde*," I snarled. "This is *my* mission, not yours, and I don't need your fucking help." I shouldered past him and he let me, a low laugh following me into the darkened interior of The Forge.

"Just following orders, sweetheart. Go ahead and pretend I'm not here if it makes you feel better."

I was really fucking tempted to stab him for daring to use that pet name with me again, but a resounding boom sounded from within The Forge, jerking my attention back to my task.

This asshole wasn't worth me risking Dragor's wrath, and if the prince felt the need to check up on me, then I wasn't going to give him the satisfaction of finding me lacking.

"Done," I growled, jerking my chin at Dalia and Moraine so that the two of them fell into position on my flanks, and I swept away into the warmth of the building, leaving Cayde to follow or fall back. I didn't care which.

I ground my teeth as I fought to ignore the sting of anger which nagged at me while Cayde's footsteps trailed us into the darkened building.

I paused at the sight of a set of large, double doors to our left which clearly led into the main portion of The Forge but as I wrapped my fingers around the vial of blood at my throat, I found myself drawn right instead.

A narrow staircase stood there in the shadows, the pull of my blood magic telling me that the Fae we sought was down them.

I took the flight of stone stairs which curved away below the building, delving beneath the workspace which I assumed lay through the doors on the left.

Cayde's presence was like a nagging wound to my pride which I fought to ignore as he continued to hound us through the shadows. Dragor hadn't shown this level of mistrust in me for years. What had I done to make him doubt me?

I chewed on my tongue, my fist so tight around the vial of blood which hung from my neck that it was a wonder the damn thing hadn't shattered. But the magic held true, my footsteps unfaltering as I descended the stairs. It was so hot in here that it became harder to breathe, the blazing furnace of The Forge leaking heat into the walls and thickening the air to the point of stifling. The lands of Stormfell to the north were never hot like this and I found myself missing the crisp air of my homeland as we moved further into the muggy space.

"This way," I muttered, a shriek echoing up from the dark passage which ran beneath The Forge, urging me on.

The walls were tightly packed, the thin corridor only wide enough to allow us to walk in single file, metal doors marred with rust lining the wall on our left.

Dalia and Moraine moved into tight formation at my back, and I refused to so much as glance around at Cayde as he continued to follow us into the dark, though I could feel his eyes pinned on me.

I halted sharply at a door which was almost impossible to spot in the gloom, nodding to Dalia as I hefted my sword and braced for a fight. She threw the door wide, and I spat a curse at the sight revealed in the greyish light of the room beyond.

There was Ford – the asshole I'd been sent in to retrieve, covered in blood and strapped to a table like a fucking slab of meat.

"Dead?" Moraine hissed, her fear only apparent to me because I knew her so well.

If we had failed in retrieving him then Dragor's wrath would be swift to follow our return.

I swore, sheathing my sword and striding into the room, sparing a glance for the vials and vials of venom which had presumably been taken from Ford before he'd died. Basilisk venom to be precise, potent and deadly, a biological weapon coveted by all sides of the war.

He was one of ours, but he'd been kidnapped almost a month ago, our spies unable to locate him until now.

"Fuck," I cursed, reaching the near-naked Fae and pressing my fingers to his throat so I could be certain.

My gut coiled with a fear I refused to admit to myself as I thought of what Dragor would do when he found out I'd failed.

"Warm," I gasped. "Thank Libra – he's alive!"

"No shit," Dalia breathed, hurrying over to help me cut him free.

Ford groaned as I rolled him over and slapped him hard enough to force his eyes open.

"We're here to get you out," I growled, making him look at me. "You'll be alright."

One look at the wounds carved all over his body made me think that wasn't so likely, but all I needed was for him to stay alive until we made it back to Dragor. The Reapers could fix him if they agreed to do so, and the prince held enough sway with them that there was a good chance they would.

"The pain," Ford hissed, reaching out and grabbing the front of my fighting leathers, his eyes not seeming to really see me. "I need the pain."

"I know," I replied tersely.

Basilisks replenished their magic through pain and they needed magic to produce venom, so it wasn't hard to figure out what had happened in this room.

"They milked me dry," he wheezed, clinging to me so hard that his weight threatened to topple me. "Teats and teeth and cock."

"Gross," Dalia said, and I shot her an irritated look.

Yes, it was fucking gross, and he was currently hanging from my neck like a star-damned necklace.

"You," I snapped, turning to glare at Cayde who was casually leaning against the doorframe, watching our interaction. "Put those muscles to use and carry him."

"Are you going to say please?" he drawled, not moving an inch.

"How about I carve your balls off and make you eat them if you refuse?" I hissed, jerking free of Ford and drawing a dagger.

"Now, now, play nice, sweetheart," Cayde said, his tone anything but threatened and I bared my teeth at him, taking another step his way.

"V," Moraine murmured, so low it was hardly audible, but I heard the warning.

I didn't make idle threats, but this asshole was here on Dragor's command and I *did* answer to the Prince of Storms.

Cayde stalked past me, a breath of amusement slipping from him before he hauled Ford's half dead body into his arms.

"The teats," Ford whimpered, clutching at his nipples and making my upper lip curl back with distaste.

"Let's just get him the hell out of here," I commanded, turning my back on all of them and striding into the corridor once more.

I almost slammed straight into a figure who lunged from the darkness, a black mask pulled low to conceal his face, pitch black eyes widening in surprise as he jerked away to avoid the collision. I swear there was a glint of red in them for a moment too.

"Raincarvers," I barked, informing the others who were still trapped in the room at my back, unable to make it around me as I raised my sword.

"Wrong," the man growled, recovering faster from the sight of my face than most managed and swinging a blade at me so quickly that I almost didn't parry it in time.

"Is that the Sky Witch?" another male groaned from beyond him, but I couldn't spare the moment it would take to look away from my opponent as he swung for me again with another savage strike of his blade. "I'd fuck her so good that she'd never look at another-"

I flung a dagger, hitting the stupefied asshole in the thigh and making his declarations fall away to cries of agony while the bastard fighting me swung for my head with enough force to rattle my bones as our swords collided again.

The corridor was tight, too narrow to allow either of us the room we needed to fight effectively, and I was forced to block and parry far more often than I should have liked. This motherfucker was one hell of a fighter, a true challenge that I relished meeting.

Dalia, Moraine and Cayde with the barely conscious Ford in his arms made it into the corridor as I forced my opponent back, but there was no room for them to join the fight.

I twisted beneath my attacker as he swung for my head again in a furious, brutal strike, using my momentum to slam my boot into his chest and sending him crashing back into his companion who let out a wild curse.

I expected him to lunge for me a second time, but instead he backed up further, yanking something from his pocket and twisting it sharply in his fist.

My gaze caught on it for just a heartbeat but that was all I needed to recognise it.

They weren't Raincarvers. That was a Flamebringer weapon. And I knew exactly what happened when it detonated.

"Run!" I bellowed, turning and sprinting back towards the stairs, the others following my command without question, racing ahead of me as the Flamebringer hurled the device straight at us.

It hit the wall, clattering across the stone floor, the seconds ringing in my ears, the knowledge that it wouldn't be enough time to escape pounding through my skull as I sprinted as fast as my legs would carry me.

"*Shift*," Cayde's rumbling voice barked ahead of me.

Dalia and Moraine had made it to the stairs, and my eyes widened as a tiny black snake hurtled through the air after them, launched from Cayde's fist in their direction – Ford in his Basilisk form. It was the smallest size he could take, but I'd seen Basilisks on the battlefield and they were monstrous, as large as a building when they wanted to be.

Moraine caught him, her wild eyes meeting mine as she paused for all of a breath, halfway up the stairs where she might have a chance of survival.

"Go!" I bellowed, my death racing for me, but they didn't have to suffer the same fate.

I was out of time, my fight having drawn me too far in the wrong direction, but they could make it.

Pain ripped through her eyes before Dalia caught Moraine's arm and yanked her away. My one salvation in the face of my death was that the only people I had ever cared for in this forsaken land of war and ruin would survive this.

The device bounced against the floor at my back for the final time and I couldn't help but look around as it exploded, fire tearing from it, filling my vision, the last thing I would ever see-

Strong arms banded around me and then there was nothing but black as I was thrown to the ground, a huge body covering my own, a heated breath against my neck.

The scent of him overwhelmed me, the feeling of his flesh driving mine into the ground awakening every piece of my being. I met his honeyed brown eyes as fire exploded around us, the wild glow of it lighting the corners of my vision, but it couldn't reach us, the darkness that enveloped us somehow shielding us from the power of the blast.

I blinked up at him in shock as I found my heart still beating – racing now as he held me tightly in his grasp and I realised that I wasn't dead. I wasn't even injured.

"What are you?" I demanded for the second time and his lips tilted in a hint of amusement.

"A Drake. Meaning my wings can't burn," Cayde replied dryly. "I guess it's not so classified after all. But you're welcome – you know,

for the part where I saved your life."

And without another word, he released me, letting me fall back to the cold, stone floor as he stood and strode away after the others.

I pushed myself to my feet, snatching my sword from the ground and staring at the heaped rubble which now blocked the passage beneath The Forge. I supposed I should be glad that the Flamebringers had only used a conduit filled with a small amount of fire magic – no doubt a larger explosion would have brought the building down on all of us.

"You're marked!" I yelled at the heaped rubble, knowing the Flamebringers would hear me from the other side of it. "Death will find you the next time our paths cross."

"I look forward to proving you wrong – witch!" one of the bastards called in reply, his laughter haunting me as I turned and ran after the others.

We had retrieved our package. Whatever business the Flamebringers had with the Raincarvers, I wanted nothing to do with it. All I knew was that their arrival in this place couldn't be a coincidence and it couldn't equal anything good. So it was time to get the fuck out of here.

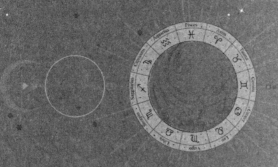

EVEREST

CHAPTER FIVE

I raced into The Forge through a backdoor, the sound of the roaring furnace that was used to make the blades spilling out into the cavernous space. I'd heard the explosion coming from the far end of the building and my fears were climbing as I sought out my mama.

The heat of this place was stifling combined with the balmy weather. The water elementals who worked here had the power of ice to cool themselves, but I held no such gift yet, and I found it hard to breathe in the oppressive air.

The blast which had echoed through the building appeared to have taken place elsewhere as I spotted no clear signs of damage to the structure surrounding me. I just hoped my mama had been nowhere near it.

I wasn't foolish enough to call out to her, certain our enemies could be close by. The Sky Witch might be here alongside her vile allies already, and at that thought, I hefted a newly-made blade into my grip from a row of barrels, the dagger sharp and wicked, marked with the sea serpent emblem of Cascada.

It wasn't as fine as some of the weapons my mama had taught me how to make at home, her skill so great it was a tragedy that all of our people couldn't wield her creations. I grew better at it with each passing year, but I wasn't sure I would ever match her prowess, her weapons something truly magical to behold.

I crept deeper into The Forge, my footsteps silent, my movements graceful as had long been my way. Mama believed my Order would reflect this part of me, and I wondered if I was destined to Emerge as light-footed as her form, a Teumessian Fox. But I hoped I would get an Order that was more powerful than even Ransom's Merrow form, then maybe I would be seen as strong, capable like he was. Perhaps then my place training at Never Keep would be secure - if only I could claim such a fate. It was the sole dream I'd had in my small life that had sparked a sense of purpose in me, and if I failed in that ambition, I didn't know what I would do.

I grasped the blade with an easy hold, comfortable with it, though it had little personality. No kiss of magic in the steel, just an empty vessel ready to be wielded for bloodshed. Mama's blades all had their own feel, their individual essence, like each was imbued with a little piece of her soul, and I wished I could have one of them in my hand now instead. But this would have to do.

The scent of smoke carried to me and as I passed the giant furnace built for forging and headed on into the brick corridor that led to the main entrance. I found no one, heard no one either, and I started to grow anxious about the whereabouts of the workers. They shouldn't even have been here tonight, but Mama had been called in for extra shifts to finish up some new weaponry they were working on.

I didn't make it far before I found my way blocked by debris, the recent explosion having torn down half the roof here. There was no passage on and I turned back, quickening my stride and wondering if my mama had already come to blows with our enemies. Or perhaps she had made it to safety and I was wasting my time hunting when I could be in the thick of battle, fighting for a place of respect among my kin.

Shouted orders reached me from down a corridor and I quickened my pace, hope binding itself to my soul. I raced towards the sound, running through a chamber filled with piles and piles of metal barrels that were labelled with the symbol of a Basilisk. Mama had told me about the terrible power of that venom before, but I had never known we held such vast stores of it here.

At the far end of the chamber, the workers were gathered, hurrying to seal up a room with ice.

"Mama," I called, spotting her among them and she swung around with a look of relief. Her dark hair was braided down her back and her brown eyes blazed in fear as she found me there.

"It's not safe for you here, Everest," she gasped.

"Nor you," I said urgently. "The Skyforgers are coming."

"It's sealed," a man in a grey uniform boomed. "None of our enemies will get their hands on the weapons in there."

"We'll take up arms and join the fight," Mama said fiercely. "No Skyforger will triumph over us."

I nodded, keen to do just that as I hurried with Mama and the workers back in the direction I'd come.

Mama grabbed my hand, halting abruptly and I turned as her grip tightened on my hand, her gaze fixing on something to my right.

I glanced that way, finding two masked men stepping out of a door in the shadows with fiery blades in their hands, standing close to the rows and rows of metal barrels that were full of Basilisk venom. This had to be to do with that new weaponry they had been working on, the sight of it making my breath catch.

I raised my blade, my gaze fixing on the Flamebringers, the plain black masks on their faces making them appear more monster than man. They must have used the distraction of the Skyforgers' attack to sneak into our land, but their purpose here wasn't yet clear.

The largest of the men struck his two swords together and fire bloomed from the metal, pouring away from him, spilling across the floor and hungrily embracing the barrels.

"No," Mama gasped. "The Basilisk venom!"

The one who had set the fire looked our way as if noticing the gathered Raincarvers for the first time, the other Flamebringer cursing and shoving his comrade back toward the door. The fire took root, racing for the barrels several feet in front of them and The Forge workers cast water in a desperate bid to try and douse it. But the terror in Mama's eyes said it was too late.

She threw herself at me, forcing me to the floor and covering her body with mine while the entire world ripped in two.

My head cracked against the floor and I was dazed, staring after the Flamebringers as they raced into the doorway, the one who'd lit the fire losing his mask as it fell from his face to hit the ground. He glanced back, eyes of purest sin meeting mine, like a spill of oil mixed with hellfire. His face was brutally beautiful to look at, the slash of his eyebrows carving over those wicked obsidian eyes and the slant of his cheekbones like two cuts of glass driven beneath his skin. His black hair was as sleek as feathers, wayward and tumbling more to the right of his face than to the left, and there was a hint of deepest red to it, like a slick of blood glossed through it.

The boom of the explosion was all I could hear, and in those few seconds of life I had left, I clung to my mama and tried to make her roll, tried to shield her from what was to come. But she bound my limbs in ice, coating us as she tried to protect us both from the blast, her whole body working to shield mine while the raining spill of Basilisk venom came pouring down among the rising flames.

The workers screamed and my mama screamed with them, her body taking the brunt of the scorching venom. It could burn through flesh in seconds, devouring Fae like a demon reaping death.

I screamed too, but mostly in terror for her, my heart thrashing with an aching kind of dread that drove so deep into my bones, it cracked some piece of my soul, shattering it with the force of an anvil driving into me.

Mama wailed and writhed, but she never stopped casting ice, freezing me in place beneath her, my legs tucked under hers, refusing to let me move even a single inch. Her own arm lay over my left one, but my skin was partly exposed, my palm face-up as more of that acidic venom came splattering down on us. I screamed bloody murder as it splashed across my hand. If I was in pain, it was nothing to what my mama must have felt and tears of horror slid from my eyes as our gazes remained on each other's, freezing against my cheeks as they met with her magic.

She was shuddering, convulsing, yet trying to hold on as she shielded me with everything she had while the blast of venom and fire slowly halted.

The screams were quietening, death a whisper now in the wake of its roar.

Mama blinked, gazing down at me with blood bubbling from her lips. I tried to speak to her, only to find my mouth was sealed shut with ice, so thick and impenetrable, I couldn't even tell her that I loved her in the moment of her death. Because that was what this was, I knew it with such certainty that I was choked by it, crushed in the fists of the stars and forced to face the horror of it without escape.

"Find who did this," she rasped. "Never rest, Everest. Until they pay for what they have done."

I tried to answer, to promise her I would as I accepted the fading light in her eyes, knowing I couldn't refute it. Though I wanted to with every fibre of my being.

Blood was soaking through the ice encasing my body, her blood. Thick and warm, and enough to start to thaw the freeze that had been cast upon me.

I barely felt the pain of my hand through the agony of her loss, and as her eyes glazed, I prayed to Pisces, Scorpio, Cancer, Cetus, Delphinus, Hydra, and all the water deities that lived among the stars to let her pass beyond The Veil and find peace.

She had died for me, a heroine's death, but was it enough to earn their favour? The possibility of her being denied the passage was too horrible to consider, and I shuddered beneath the brittle weight of her, trying to gain enough strength to break the ice still binding my limbs. A noise of utter grief tore through my throat, locked there by my sealed lips.

After an unguessable amount of time, a shadow in my periphery made my heart lurch and Mama was pulled off of me. I expected death to find me in the form of an enemy, a Flamebringer or Skyforger come to finish the last of their quarry, but it was Harlon I found instead.

"Ever," he croaked in relief, pulling me from the floor and lifting me against his chest. "I heard the explosion; I came as fast as I could but...I'm so fucking sorry I didn't get here in time to stop it."

Heated pain flared in his eyes for my mother, but he carried me from the wreckage, leaving her broken body behind. As my eyes fell on her, a whimper of torment finally cracked the ice on my lips and I stared at her burned body, her entire back destroyed by the venom which had eaten into her bones.

"Harlon, go back, I can't leave her," I begged, clawing at his chest as I tried to shake off the rest of the freezing ice, but I was still in the grip of my mother's lasting magic.

"I have to get you to safety first. But I'll come back for her, I swear it," he vowed, looking down at my injured hand as I curled it against my chest.

There was fear in his eyes over the reality of what that wound could mean. The skin was ravaged, and if there was one thing I knew about Basilisk venom, it was that there was no healing its scars. Healing was a rarity of its own, the gift of such knowledge belonging to the Reapers alone, though they didn't offer it out too many. And there was one injury worse than any other in this world, the loss of a hand was as bad as it could get in terms of my ability to fight with magic. If I couldn't cast with this hand, if it was too broken to mend, then my hopes of being accepted into Never Keep had just dwindled to nothing. But that knowledge barely managed to find its way past the abject grief that clutched my heart in an unforgiving grip, never to release me from the agony of my mama's loss.

The roof above had been cleaved open by the blast, the great gouge in the metal giving a view of the hulking form of Ironwraith overhead, and a burning kind of rage settled in my soul over their hand in this.

But it wasn't them I hated most. It was the dark-haired man with the soulless eyes. The monster who had set that fire, who had watched as it swallowed us whole. But it had not consumed me as he had hoped.

That crack in my soul deepened to a fissure which changed me irrevocably from the Fae I had awoken as this very day, twisting me into a vengeful creature that would offer him no mercy. And I made an oath upon the ocean and all the stars in the heavens that his death would soon be *mine*.

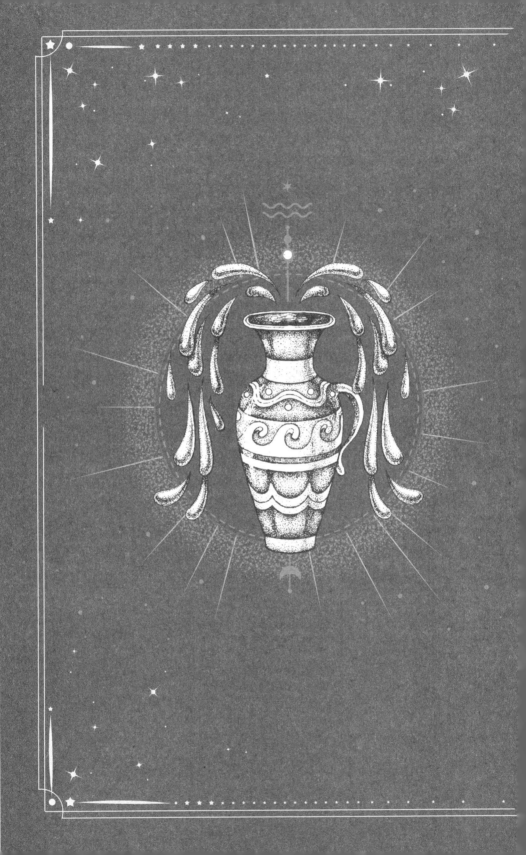

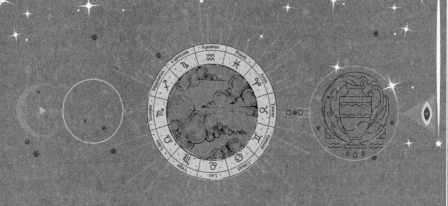

VESPER

CHAPTER SIX

The sky was alive with motion as we tore through it, weaving between battling Fae in and out of their Order forms. Moraine flew ahead of us, beating her powerful silver wings and firing arrows at any who blocked our path as we raced back towards the floating island overhead.

Cayde flew behind us, partially shifted still, his leathery wings the only piece of his Drake Order form on view. I worked hard to ignore his presence, the sting of having him sent to join us on our mission biting into me and making a cold fury spill through my veins.

I pressed a hand to my pocket, feeling the coiled body of the Basilisk shifter within and trying to calm myself with the fact that we hadn't needed Cayde's assistance anyway. At least not to retrieve the package – so far as the saving of my life went, I planned on dealing with that debt later.

"Watch out!" Dalia cried, swerving to the left and I followed without hesitation, twisting my neck to look back just as an enormous spear of ice cut through the air right where we would have been. It sped towards the sky then crashed into the outer edge of Ironwraith, blasting a chunk of the island free from the rest. The screams of the Fae standing on it filled the air as they fell.

I cursed as huge lumps of rock and earth tumbled from the sky, flattening myself to my windrider and urging it to move faster as the debris spilled down from above.

Moraine cried out as a jagged lump of rock collided with her wing, a sickening crunch sounding as it snapped.

"No," I gasped, wheeling my windrider around as she began to fall, weaving between the mass of Skyforgers who were scrambling to escape the plummeting lump of land.

Moraine's eyes met with mine as she fell, her silver braids tangling in the air before her, and I gritted my teeth, racing back towards the ground after her.

Dirt and bodies fell through the space dividing us, but I ignored them all, giving no notice to the lumps of rock which smacked against my spine or the rain of gravel which threatened to blind me. Moraine was my sister in arms. If she fell, I'd fall too. She was my strength when I found myself lacking, my spirit when my own threatened to break, my comfort when the horrors of war pressed close in the darkness of the night. She and Dalia were all I really had, and she would *not* fall alone.

A Griffin bellowed as it charged for me, its eagle's beak clacking menacingly as its sharp talons reached for me, meaning to pluck me from my windrider and feed me to the wrath of gravity.

I hurled a dagger at it, barely sparing a glance to make certain my blade found its mark and dropping into a roll as the beast's claws ripped across my shoulder. Its talons caught in the fabric of my leathers and jerked me backwards, but I threw all of my weight into my roll, forcing the enormous beast to move with me before kicking my boot against its lion's ass and propelling us away from each other.

Moraine was tumbling towards the ground even faster now, her broken wing curled uselessly across her chest while the other flapped feebly in an attempt to catch the wind and slow her fall.

I dove faster, tearing through the sky and looking at nothing but her, my arm outstretched as the ground rushed nearer, a unit of Raincarvers spotting us and turning their wrath our way.

Moraine threw her hand out and I caught it, her weight almost yanking me free of my windrider and we lurched precariously to one side. I snarled with determination, digging my heels into the sides of my windrider, refusing to fall free of it, hauling her up onto it instead.

Dalia tore past us, hurtling straight towards the unit of Raincarvers and scattering them as she aimed her windrider right for them and hurled more cocktails of faesine down on them too, causing their attacks to go wide, missing us with their blasts of water and spears of ice.

Moraine cursed in pain, her thighs clamping tight around the windrider and arms banding around my waist while her broken wing hung limp beside us, the pain clearly too sharp to allow her to shift them away.

The magical machine wasn't built to take two, but I was smaller than most riders, our combined weight surely no more than a large male, and she wasn't going to fall prey to this battle.

A resounding boom marked the lump of falling land hitting the ground at my back and I ducked my head as debris pelted in every direction and Fae screamed as they were crushed or wounded.

I didn't look down, setting my gaze on Ironwraith once more and leaning low against the windrider as I aimed for the floating landmass.

Dalia sped ahead of us, cutting through any who got in our way, and Moraine drew her sword to ward off attackers from the rear, but we were lucky; the lump of falling land had caused a void in the fighting where Fae had scrambled to escape being crushed.

We tore through the open space, a flash of beating black wings in my periphery letting me know that Cayde was still close, but I ignored him resolutely as we tore through the sky.

Dalia led the way, my windrider moving far slower with two onboard but still, we made it through the warring Fae and swept over the cliffs which marked the edge of Ironwraith.

I aimed for the open ground in front of Echo Fort, my eyes raking across the Fae who remained there, hunting for Dragor among them. I was both relieved and disappointed to find the prince absent and I swallowed a lump in my throat as we hurtled down to land, my boots skidding against the packed dirt as we came to a halt.

Dalia landed to our right, the three of us dismounting hastily and I met Moraine's dark eyes in silent question. She raised her chin, letting me know that she could withstand the agony of her injuries for a while yet and I nodded.

"Report," Imona sneered, and I looked around at the General as she stalked towards us, her narrowed gaze pinned on me.

She was a tall woman, all sharp angles and brutish attitude, her black hair cut severely to her chin. I didn't think I'd ever seen her break a smile and she certainly wouldn't dream of offering me one. Her trust in me was about as thin as spider silk and no amount of proving myself would ever change her opinion on the matter.

I was crossborn after all – birthed too early under the wrong sign. My mother had been waterborn and I had been planned for a Pisces birth, but the stars had intervened, bringing me to the world early and marking me as a child of Aquarius instead. It was why I had been sent to war at fourteen, why I had been tested and trialled more than any other I knew – though of course my sisters in arms had been placed in a similar position, but their shame was the work of their airborn parents – Dalia's father having failed in a mission which cost the Skyforgers a battle and Moraine's mother shaming her bloodline by being captured by the Stonebreakers. Yes, shame marked us all, and we had all been named as Sinfair – those whose reputation bore a stain which only glory in war could blot out - but they would never bear the weight of having weak blood.

"We retrieved the package," I replied, taking Ford from my pocket and holding the tiny snake out before me.

Imona reached for him but I withdrew my hand, ignoring Cayde who came to land on my left as if he had any right to stand with our unit.

"I have orders to deliver him to Prince Dragor myself," I said, placing the Basilisk back in my pocket and ignoring the tension which rolled through Imona as I denied her. But I had long since learned that this woman would never respect me, would never offer praise for my wins and would only ever hunt for my failures. It didn't matter – she wasn't the one who ruled here. I had fought with tooth and nail to draw the eye of the prince, to prove to him that I was worthy and earn the right to follow no command but his.

"Your windrider isn't designed to take two," Imona snapped, finding the failure she was so desperate for and proving my point. "Eight lashes for breaking protocol."

Dalia and Moraine bristled beside me, but they knew better than to try and intervene on my behalf. I fought my own battles in this place and I wouldn't stand for them getting involved.

Cayde released a low growl from my right and I shot him a dark look, not knowing why he was still here, let alone why he was involving himself in this. I dismissed him instantly, my gaze snapping back to the general.

"That's fair," I replied, though every piece of me screamed that it wasn't, that breaking protocol to save the life of one of our most loyal and ferocious warriors seemed more than worth it to me. "Now? Or after the retreat?"

General Imona sneered at me again, her contempt ripe in the air.

"After. You must report to Prince Dragor first. But once we are clear of the battlefield, I expect you in the garrison yard, stripped to the waist and ready to receive your punishment."

"I look forward to making amends for my failure," I replied, offering her an insolent smile which no doubt only made her hate me more.

Imona narrowed her eyes at me, jerking her chin towards Echo Fort and dismissing me without a word.

"Do you want us to report with you?" Dalia asked once we had moved far enough from Imona to speak privately.

"No," I replied, eyeing Moraine's broken wing with a lump in my throat, though I turned my thoughts sharply away from that path. "Go see the medics. I can handle Dragor – I'll petition for him to get you a healer," I added, and Moraine's brows pulled together.

"You don't have to-"

"You're one of his best fighters," I replied firmly. "What sense does it make to have you unable to fly for the next six months while it heals when the Reapers hold the power to fix it in an instant?"

Dalia and Moraine exchanged a look and I knew they were thinking as I was – the chances of Dragor getting a healer to take a look at her were slim to none, but that wouldn't stop me from trying.

Moraine nodded, the closest thing I would allow to thanks, and the two of them departed, leaving me to stalk towards Echo Fort alone.

No. Not alone – I still had a fucking shadow.

"Why are you still here?" I barked, whirling on Cayde who to my utter frustration didn't even bother to stop and answer me. He just kept walking towards the huge gates which led into the fortress without even pausing to say a word.

My fist curled around the pommel of my sword and I ground my teeth as I watched him go.

The ground shuddered beneath my boots and I looked around at the edges of the floating island where the Wind Weavers were now powering the turbines which moved Ironwraith through the sky, directing air magic through them and guiding us away.

I dug my heels into the ground, giving myself a moment to adjust to the motion beneath my boots as the wind tugged at my pale pink hair and tangled in the matted blood which now stained it.

"Answer me," I barked, stalking after Cayde and having to practically jog to catch up with his long stride.

He continued to ignore me, so I snatched a dagger from my belt before grabbing his arm and forcing him around, pressing the tip of it to his side in a perfect position to spear a kidney – not entirely fatal but it would hurt like a bitch. To my utter fury, he replied in kind, though his dagger rested firmly against my throat.

"Violent little thing, aren't you?" he said, giving me a look which was about as far from fear as physically possible.

"Killing an ally is punishable by death," I replied scathingly.

"Removing an organ or two will probably only earn me a whipping or a week in the brig, either of which I'm willing to suffer for the pleasure of making you scream. How about you? Is my life worth yours, because you've chosen a particularly lethal place to cut."

Cayde narrowed his eyes at me, leaning closer. "Don't tempt me, sweetheart – I've heard that Succubae bleed black and I'm all kinds of interested in finding out if that's true."

I scoffed, shoving him away from me before slicing my thumb open on the tip of my blade, red blood pooling in answer to his question. "Looks like I'm a disappointment then."

"You said it." He took off again.

I had to fight the urge to hurl my dagger at his back, sheathing it instead as the island began to pick up speed and the sound of battle faded in favour of the bellowing wind.

The shields would go up to drown out the sound and block the worst of the frigid wind soon enough, but I assumed there were still units returning from their fight with the Raincarvers, requiring them to stay down for now.

I held my ground, counting to twenty, forcing my blood to settle and my temper to still. Facing Prince Dragor while wearing my emotions so close to the surface of my skin was never a good idea and I needed him to be impressed by me if I had any hope of him summoning a healer for Moraine.

I watched as Cayde disappeared into the fortress, my dislike of him festering and my irritation over him saving my ass growing. I didn't want to owe him anything. In fact, I would make it my priority to save his sorry life as soon as possible to make us even again so I could go back to not knowing he existed.

I closed my eyes, releasing a heavy breath and forcibly ignoring the honeyed eyes which peered back at me from the confines of my mind while fire flared around us, and strong arms held me close.

I sheathed my dagger and strode towards Echo Fort with my head held high, reminding myself that I had been victorious once again. The Basilisk in my pocket proved my worth and the Flamebringers had even been kind enough to destroy every drop of stolen venom that the Raincarvers had taken from him.

The huge wooden doors which led into the fort stood open and I ignored the guards standing either side of them as I passed. I stepped into the main hall which looked out through stone archways onto the garrison yard where formation exercises and punishments took place.

I bit my tongue as my gaze fell on the whipping post in the centre of the sandstone yard, knowing I would once again be making its acquaintance before the day was done thanks to General Imona.

I turned to my left, heading away from the barracks and deeper into the building, following the curving hallway as it rounded the garrison yard until I made my way to the stone stairs at the furthest end of it.

There was no sign of Cayde and I hoped that meant he wasn't meeting with Prince Dragor after all. I wanted to demand an answer for the need to send that asshole to check up on me, but demands didn't tend to go down well with the man who owned my allegiance.

More guards lined the doors to the prince's private chambers, eight of them scowling at me as I approached, their dislike clear even if several of them were painted with lust too. I could feel it, that crawling appreciation, the eyes which peeled me apart and spoke of sinful thoughts, it was power but that didn't stop my contempt from rising at the touch of it.

I ignored the guards, striding between them, my skin prickling as the wards placed over the entrance to Dragor's private quarters reached out and tested my magical signature, checking my identity and letting me pass.

My boots thumped from hard-wearing stone to the pristine runner emblazoned with our kingdom's coat of arms; a crowned eagle, wings spread wide within a swirling vortex, a lightning bolt caught in its talons.

I kept my head high, refusing to cringe at the mess I was leaving in my wake. I had my orders. Prince Dragor was clear that I was to report to him alone when the task was complete.

The opulence only grew the deeper I moved into the prince's quarters, passing heavy wooden doors which punctuated the sandstone walls, each of them closed to refuse me so much as a peek within. Tapestries depicting the most celebrated victories of our nation hung in the spaces between the arched doorways, the warriors represented in them watching me pass with silent judgement in their eyes. I fought so hard to be counted among them, yet sometimes, I doubted there was anything I could achieve which would cast the tarnish from my name. I was Sinfair and I always would be to anyone who counted.

The long corridor opened up into the prince's reception room where several of his advisors stopped talking abruptly as I rounded into their presence. A table heaped with refreshments; wine, fruit, bread and countless baked delicacies lay behind them, ignored. Several richly-crafted chairs remained unoccupied while the advisors chose to stand lumped closely together in the centre of the room.

"You were successful?" Tobias asked, peering down his long nose at me with expectation.

"I was," I agreed because the fact that Ironwraith was moving made it plain that I'd either failed or succeeded anyway.

He exchanged a look with the three others, silently communicating something which I didn't care to interpret.

"Casualties?" Vernon demanded, his red hair windswept and battle leathers splattered with what looked like mud up the side of his leg, letting me know he had been out there for at least part of it.

The others wore the tailored, impractical clothes which marked them as aristocracy, making it obvious they had not seen battle today, though that didn't surprise me. Skirmishes like the one we had just taken part in were mostly fought by the infantry with several colonels risking their necks alongside us and a few generals barking commands.

"I'm not here to make a full report," I replied.

"You have the package?" Amoria asked, the aged woman easily the smallest among them yet still a good head taller than me, her greying hair braided into a coronet on top of her head.

Any answer I may have given was interrupted by Tobias who chuckled, gesturing at me with the silver wine goblet clasped in his many-ringed hand.

"Is that a Basilisk in your pocket, or are you pleased to see me?" he boomed, sloshing some of the wine over the rim of the goblet and staining his fingers with it.

I was saved from responding to that remark as the doors to Dragor's office were thrown open, a wild breeze gusting past us and revealing him within the lavishly decorated space, leaning against his desk to the rear of the room.

"Release Ford from your protection, lieutenant," Prince Dragor said, not bothering to raise his voice and I hurried to take the small snake from my pocket before placing him on the rug before me.

Ford shifted without needing to be commanded, and from the corner of my eye, I saw his pasty skin, marked with countless lacerations and oozing wounds, his ragged breath scraping through the air like a drag of fingernails through my ears. But I didn't look at him directly. Prince Dragor had my full attention now.

He didn't blink, didn't flinch at the state of his prize, merely glanced at him then beckoned me into the office with the curl of a single, elegant finger.

I stepped over Ford, leaving the advisors to deal with him, muttered curses passing between them as they assessed his condition and lifted him between them using their air magic. I heard them departing as I strode into Dragor's office, but I didn't look back, my gaze set firmly on the prince and his icy blue eyes which tracked every step I took into the room.

The doors slammed behind me, his cast so subtle that I hadn't even noticed him moving his hand, but the air from his magic billowed around me, hurling the lengths of pink hair over my shoulders to dance across my face.

Dragor lifted a silver pocket watch from the desk beside him and glanced at it. "Fifty-eight minutes," he commented.

I remained silent, uncertain if the time it had taken me to complete the task he'd set pleased or disappointed him.

The watch hit the desk with a thump as he tossed it aside and my heart leapt, though my features remained utterly motionless.

"You're wounded," he added.

My brows pinched together in confusion – I couldn't recall sustaining any relevant injuries during the battle but he pushed to his feet, towering over me as he advanced, taking my hand in his.

My throat worked on a rough swallow as his skin met with mine, his fingers gently turning my filthy palm in his grip, lifting it as he ran his thumb up the length of mine before pressing down on the cut which I'd carved there myself to prove a point to that asshole, Cayde.

"Self-inflicted," I confirmed, raising my eyes to his, daring to meet the icy blue of his gaze.

Dragor lifted my hand to his mouth, smiling at me in the way a wolf might grin at a lamb before pressing his lips to the bleeding flesh, placing a kiss against the sting of the wound. The way he held my hand meant my fingertips brushed the sharp line of his jaw and I stilled, the temptation to flex my fingers and test the softness of his skin warring with the icy coldness in his expression.

"The venom was destroyed," I said, remaining utterly still, picking my words with care. "Flamebringers snuck into the battle - I think they sought to remove the weapon from both us and water but-"

"But you managed to extract Ford before they could end his life alongside the destruction of the venom," he finished for me and I blinked, uncertain what he thought of that.

"Yes."

"General Imona informs me you have earned a lashing," he went on, his words spoken against the sting of my thumb, my blood staining his lips and forcing my eyes to fall to them even as bitterness coiled in my gut.

Of course Imona would have sent a message ahead of me, eager as always to point out my failings. My gaze fell from the captivating torture of the prince to the desk behind him where a note bearing the tell-tale signs of having been folded into the shape of a bird was written in the general's scrawling script. No doubt she'd shot it directly to him using her air magic while I'd been caught up bickering with the trained dog the prince had sent to check up on me.

"Moraine was the one who got Ford out," I said, snapping my focus back to the prince, knowing he wouldn't appreciate any hesitation. "It was due to her that we succeeded. I earned my punishment for saving her when her wing was broken, but I believe I did the best thing for the interest of Stormfell. She is a ferocious warrior and sacrificing her when I was able to save her made no-"

"What was the priority of the mission?" Dragor asked coolly, his grip on my hand tightening the smallest amount, though I stilled as if he'd struck me.

"To retrieve Ford," I replied.

"And where was my asset when you dove from the sky to save your *friend?*"

"Moraine is my comrade, not my friend," I protested, knowing I'd said the wrong thing the moment the words spilled from my tongue.

"Ask it," he growled.

I raised my chin, steeling myself as I flexed my fingers against his jaw, hoping that was what he wanted, wondering if I'd ever be able to figure him out the way I did most men. I made no attempt to wield my Succubus Order gifts though – I wasn't a fucking fool.

"She needs a healer," I said, refusing to let my voice waver. "The medics can bind her wing, but it will be months before the bone heals well enough for her to fly and-"

"There it is," he breathed, withdrawing so sharply that I stood with my hand raised before me for several seconds as I took in the fact that he was no longer inhaling my oxygen, no longer touching me at all.

I bit my tongue against the words which ached to follow, dropping my hand then remaining still as his assessing eyes roamed over me, the silence stretching. I wanted to demand a healer for Moraine. I wanted to ask him why he had sent Cayde – why he had decided that I was incapable of fulfilling the task he'd set me? Why-

"Are you going to tell me why you reek of another man?" Dragor asked as he moved to my right, circling me like a hawk above a rabbit.

"I don't," I growled, knowing he could smell nothing on me but blood and death, totally thrown off by the unexpected question.

"So you haven't been embroiled with a winged Fae who was described as – what was it? – Oh yes." Dragor lifted Imona's note from his desk before circling behind me as he read her description of Cayde. "Bloodied from battle and exuding a level of arrogance fit for the company he kept – she isn't a fan of yours at all, is she?"

I said nothing. He was the one who had sent Cayde after all. What did he expect me to say of him? Was this some test? Another trial I'd been set up to pass or fail without knowing he was once again assessing me?

"So tell me why you saw fit to include a new member in your squad?" he pressed.

"He was very insistent," I ground out. "And we didn't have time to waste arguing over-"

"Did you catch him in your snare, little demon?" Dragor asked, his presence so close behind me that I couldn't help but turn my head, just enough to see him at my back, looming over me, his shadow consuming me entirely.

"No," I said truthfully. "I made no use of my Order gifts and he wasn't even stunned when first laying eyes on-"

My words cut off abruptly as Dragor's hand wrapped around my throat, his chest slamming to my back, his mouth dropping to my ear as he bent low to growl into it.

"And how did that feel?" he asked, amusement and malice equally ripe in his voice.

"Odd," I replied honestly.

I had met enough Fae who could resist the pull of my kind to know it wasn't impossible, though admittedly uncommon when looking upon my features for the first time, but Cayde's flippant dismissal of me had been new.

"I've warned you not to rely so heavily on your pretty face, haven't I?"

"I don't," I protested.

Did I use my lure to distract my opponents? Of course I did, just as all Fae used the gifts of their Order forms in battle, but I didn't rely on it and I was more than a match for those I met on the field without the need for tricks.

Dragor breathed a laugh which crested the shell of my ear and made my hair flutter against my neck. His free hand closed over mine where I had gripped the dagger at my waist the moment he'd grabbed me, and I felt his smile as he moved his mouth to my cheek.

His white battle leathers had to be getting filthy pressed so tightly to mine, but he didn't seem to care about that as he held me captive in his grasp.

"You did well," he said finally, and I exhaled slowly past the grip he maintained on my throat. "Though not well enough to save you from that lashing."

"I wasn't asking you to-"

"No. You never do," he said in a low voice which had my skin prickling as his hand slipped from my throat, fingers trailing down the sensitive skin until he was lightly clasping the neck of my leathers. "You just ask me to call upon the Reapers to help your...comrade."

I said nothing. Pleading him to help Moraine certainly wouldn't help.

Dragor stepped back, my body flushing with heat as he released me, leaving me uncertain if I craved his return or relished the freedom. He moved his hands to my shoulders and slowly, deliberately, ran them down my spine, his thumbs scoring the lines of my shoulder blades in a way which had me biting back the ungodly sound that rose in the back of my throat.

I shut down the thoughts which rushed for me, the memories, the yearning, the fucking raw need-

"One day," he murmured, almost to himself as he withdrew, leaving me trembling from the possessive touch. "You and I will stop dancing around this and-"

The ground beneath my feet lurched so suddenly that even my sharply-honed reflexes couldn't stop me from staggering forward and falling over Dragor's desk. His weight collided with mine a heartbeat later, a furious bellow escaping him as we clutched the desk which was thankfully bolted to the ground and held on as the world tipped beneath our feet.

The screams came before the bells began to toll – the familiar rhythm clanging out a pattern which let every Fae on Ironwraith know precisely who was attacking us.

"Stonebreakers," I spat in surprise as Dragor shoved himself off of me and stalked to the arched window behind his desk, throwing it wide.

"We'll conclude this later," he snarled before leaping from the window and letting the air snatch him into its grasp.

He was gone by the time I lurched to the open window, my fingers biting into the metal frame as I looked out over the view offered by the position of his office on the fourth floor of the fort. Sunlight speared the sky as it punctured the horizon ahead of me and I squinted against it, holding up a hand to look out over the landscape far beneath the outer edge of our flying island.

I couldn't make out much of the rugged landscape but as another echoing boom rocked the entire island, almost hurling me from the window and marking a second harpoon's impact with our land, I found myself not caring. This was war and that was all I knew. My blood hummed with power as the Ether of the world called out to me and I released a sharp whistle, hoping to Aquarius that an air wielder had recharged my windrider, because today's fighting clearly hadn't come to an end.

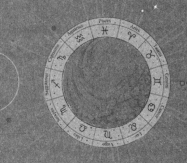

EVEREST

CHAPTER SEVEN

Harlon's scent of lime and sea air was all I focused on as the clash of battle rang out around us. He held me a little tighter to his chest as he threw a kick at the door of an Astrologist's store, the lock shattering under the impact before he carried me inside.

My thoughts were in a haze of grief as he sat me on a table, knocking aside a display of tarot cards and crystals as he did so. He took hold of my injured hand, gently turning it over to inspect it while I laid down the blade that I'd taken from The Forge, my breaths coming in slow, uneven exhales. She was lost…gone.

"Fuck, Ever," Harlon exhaled, and my eyes tracked over his distressed expression, my tongue empty of words as he hurried off into a back room.

Bloody screams and the chaos of war clashed like a faraway din in my ears, even though the battle was so close it could have spilled in here at any second. I tried to get a grip on my mind, the roiling grief that was cleaving my chest apart and the numbness that had my body in a firm hold. If a fight followed us here, I couldn't be found like this. I had to make a stand for Cascada.

"You're in shock," Harlon said as he returned with a bottle of aura cleanse which was pretty much all water, but it had a gleaming amethyst crystal at the bottom of it. He held a cloth too and he took my hand again, taking in the blazing red burn across it.

"This will hurt," he warned, then he tipped up the aura cleanse and it splashed against my wounds, jolting me violently out of the numbness and into purest pain.

I threw my good hand to my mouth to stifle my scream, biting into the back of it as he washed the last of the venom from my skin then dried it with the cloth.

I lowered my hand from my mouth, my eyes watery from the agony, and Harlon gripped my chin to make me look at him.

"This doesn't break you, Ever, do you understand me?" he said firmly. "You have a soul crafted by the hand of the ocean herself. You hold the strength of the tide in your blood, so you will not fade, you will *fight*."

I found something to hold onto in his words, the strength of them washing through me and wrapping my heart in steel.

"Domerna sil oceania," he growled, his copper eyes flaring with all the injustice of what had happened to me. *Tame the ocean.* Those words were spoken in our native tongue, the one we were encouraged not to speak in favour of speaking the Universal Language. Words we had called to each other time and again while out in the surf, riding the waves upon our tiderunners. But they meant so much more than that now.

"Domerna sil oceania," I whispered.

"Louder," he commanded.

"Domerna sil oceania," I said fiercely, and he stepped back, letting me drop to my feet.

I snatched the blade and, as if guided by the hand of Pisces herself, my head turned. I found my gaze falling upon two men racing along the cobbled street beyond the building, avoiding the clash of war between water and air. The Flamebringers. The men who had caused my mother's death.

My gaze fixed on the one without a mask, the back of his head to me as they took a right down a back alley. I ran, no other thought present in my mind but vengeance as I sprinted through the door to take chase. I was light-footed, fast, and I knew I could catch that monstrously beautiful killer if only I didn't lose sight of the next path he took.

"Everest!" Harlon barked, taking chase at my back, but I spared him no attention, my teeth gritting as I sprinted on, turning down the alley my enemies had taken.

There, at the end of the darkened passage, I saw them turning once again, left this time, disappearing into the shadow of the night. But I was only moving faster, tearing after them with a fury that lined my limbs and had me moving with all the power of Cetus in my muscles.

I made to lunge out of the alley, to catch the man who had taken my beloved Mama from me, but a hand banded around my wrist and yanked me back. Harlon flattened me to the wall, his hand clapping over my mouth, stifling the words of rage that poured from me.

"Not like this," he hissed as I struggled furiously against his hold. But he was bigger than me by far, his bulk immobilising my limbs.

"You are not nearly trained enough to take on a Flamebringer. Those men have likely been killing since they could hold a blade. Do you know how they raise their warriors in that place?"

I did know. The rumours were rife. Children were wielded as weapons and nothing more, honed and crafted just as the metal at The Forge. Only their nobles were regarded as true Fae, and it made me hate the Flamebringers all the more. But if my mother's killer was nothing but a machine created for slaughter, then all the more reason to make sure he was destroyed.

Harlon lowered his hand from my mouth as I spat a curse at him. "You dare take this decision from me?"

"Never," he said, a dark kind of fury in his eyes that spoke of how much he despised those Flamebringers too. "But you're not prepared to take them on."

I glanced out of the alley in desperation, my eyes just picking out the two men as they raced for the woodland that climbed the northern hill. They were making for The Boundary, and a sudden realisation hit me.

"They're un-Awakened – they don't have their fire magic yet," I gasped. "That's how they got through The Boundary. Ransom pushed me through it tonight and I was unmarked by its power."

Shock marred Harlon's face, but he didn't waste time questioning me on that. "Then they are only as strong as the weapons they carry," he said, a gleam of malice in his gaze.

I glanced at the simple blade in my hand, accepting it wouldn't be enough. "Step back and follow my commands."

Harlon's eyebrows arched, then he conceded, surprising me as he retreated to let me go. "I know you need this," he said in a gruff voice. "So command me at your will. I'll have their heads tonight if it's what you ask of me, Ever."

"You can have one of them, but the maskless Flamebringer is *mine*," I growled, taking off out of the alley but veering to the left back towards the roar of battle in the heart of the town.

My bare feet hit the warm stone street and I lifted my blade in preparation of what we were about to face as we rounded into the town square.

Skyforgers were being ripped from the sky by ice and water magic as they raced for the hulking mass of Ironwraith. It was now retreating from battle, the giant island already halfway out over The Crux as its warriors made a passage through the air toward it. I didn't know whether we had forced them to turn tail or if some other tactic was in play on their part, and I didn't have time to figure it out as a giant Caucasian Eagle tore from the sky, its talons reaching for my head and a musical cry breaking from its razor-sharp beak.

I raised my blade with a yell, swiping at the beast and cutting its foot clean off, making the shifted Fae shriek in pain and fly for the heavens. But as my eyes narrowed and my upper lip peeled back with hatred for the Skyforgers' hand in my mother's death this night, I knew I couldn't let it escape.

I threw the blade with all the strength I possessed, the dagger wheeling end over end before finding a home in the Eagle's chest. It shrieked as it died, slamming down to the street before us in a heap of twisted brown feathers. I snatched the blade from its chest as I leapt over its corpse, running faster while Harlon followed in my wake.

We made it to the town square where the battle was still raging, and my gaze fell on Commander Rake, my father taking up centre position among a group of soldiers wearing the dark blue armour of Cascada. His Merrow Order was out in full force, his thick, muscular arms covered in sharp navy scales that protruded from his skin like razorblades. They crawled up his neck, over his chest and legs, the spines on his back curved and lethal if anyone was driven into them. His brown hair was a tangle of curls that fell to the nape of his neck, brushing against the thick beard that coated his chin.

His hands were raised, water spewing from them in great whips that caught Skyforgers by the ankles and tore them from the air, throwing them to the cobbles with sickening cracks. His soldiers ran forward to finish any the commander brought down, and blood washed across this beautiful place. Even the central fountain was running red as several bodies lay face down in the water, their wounds spilling blood into the once sparkling blue. The sapphire eyes of the twisted sea serpent that spiralled up at its heart reflected the flash of magic in the air, as if it was truly laying witness to the massacre and my pulse thumped a rampant tune of death inside my skull.

Townsfolk had taken up arms and were battling around the square with the Skyforgers, trying to kill as many as they could while more of the air wielders retreated to the sky.

"Go that way," I ordered Harlon, pointing him down the narrow street to our left. Steep steps dropped away towards the glinting moonlit ocean in the distance, and along that path lay my home. "Fetch my mother's ice sword and meet me on the corner of Galatea Street."

A flash of hesitation filled Harlon's eyes, but he nodded, placing his faith in my reckless plan.

With him on a safer path, I took a direct line across the square, knowing I was risking my neck, but I couldn't waste any time. The Flamebringers would be closing in on The Boundary, and there was only one way we could catch them now.

Strong hands gripped my hair from above and a cry of alarm left me as I was yanked into the air by a Harpy with brown wings. I brought my blade up as my scalp screamed with pain, swinging it at his leg, but it only swiped across the metallic armour that coated his body with a screech of metal.

He carried me higher and the square dropped away below me, my heart thrashing at the sight as he flew over the tiled rooftops. I reached up again, latching my hand around his waist and getting just enough purchase to look up and hurl my blade at his face. He cursed, his head whipping sideways to avoid it and he released me, a scream tearing from my lungs as I went tumbling out of the sky.

I hit a red tiled roof, slamming into it and rolling in a blur of motion, bruises blossoming across my skin and my knee splitting open again. As I went flying over the edge of the roof, I threw my arms out, somehow catching the gutter by nothing but a sheer miracle, and a breath of thanks passed my lips for the luck of Delphinus gracing me.

I glanced below me as I hung onto the tiles, spotting a balcony just to my right. With a swing of my legs, I managed to launch myself that way, landing lightly in a crouch with the nimbleness that my mama had often praised me for.

At the thought of her, my heart wrenched painfully and the shock of the Harpy's attack fell away in favour of my keener focus. Vengeance. It called to me with all the wrath of the stars and I would answer its call this very night.

I lowered myself over the balcony's edge, letting go and dropping to the street, hitting the ground running. The flight with the Harpy had brought me closer to my destination, and as I wheeled around another corner, I found the cavalry stables waiting for me.

The gates were bolted, but it didn't take me long to find a place where I could climb the brick wall, heaving myself up and over it then dropping onto the other side.

The horses were stamping and whinnying nervously in their stables, scenting smoke in the air. But the one horse that seemed unaffected was the one I had come for. Karkinos. My father's war horse. He was a white stallion with a black braided tail and mane, his size imposing. His bridle hung waiting by the door and I grabbed it, unlocking the bolt that kept him contained, and he snorted at me, eyeing me with suspicion. Only my father was meant to ride him. If he knew what I planned, I would have been on the heated end of his ire, and that was a place no Fae ever wished to be.

"Easy boy," I said, offering the bit to his mouth and he reluctantly accepted it.

I patted his soft nose as I fitted the bridle in place then guided him from his stall. He trotted after me as I took off at a run for the gate, yanking open bolts and levers before shoving it wide. I led Karkinos to a low wall across the street, stepping up on it then leaping onto his back. I cursed as the reins grazed against my injured hand, and I released them, holding on with only my right. Without a saddle, he was a little harder to ride, and I was more used to the narrow waist of my mama's work pony. I kicked his sides to get him going and I got him quickly into a gallop, gathering the reins in my right hand and racing up the hill in the direction I'd told Harlon to meet me.

Karkinos was faster than any horse I'd ridden, the warm wind sweeping over me and making my long hair fly out behind me. I guided him through the winding cobbled streets then pulled to a halt at the corner of Galatea Street, where the trees dotted the hill ahead of me.

Harlon was there with my mother's gleaming sword strapped to his hip, and his eyes widened at the sight of my father's war horse.

"Ever," he gasped. "This is suicide."

"You don't have to come," I said, not wanting to drag him down this path I was on, but my grief was cutting too deep for me to see anything beyond what I had to do. If I paused for even a second, I'd crash and burn in the agony of my loss.

"As if I'd let you go alone." Harlon leapt up, heaving himself up behind me, and I kicked Karkinos to get him moving again as his arms closed around my waist.

His hooves thundered across the street, then up the dirt path into the trees, tearing through the brush as I spurred him into a gallop. Harlon's arms tightened around me and I clenched my teeth as I urged the horse to go even faster, fearing the Flamebringers might have made it into the wilds by now. But at that possibility, I didn't balk. I knew I'd follow my mother's killer there. So long as I had a path to him, I'd be following it.

We scaled the hill, meeting with the thick snow that caked the edge of Cascada, and as The Boundary came into sight, I guided Karkinos to the right, following the line of it and hunting for the men who couldn't be much further ahead.

My gaze was drawn to the huge land mass in the sky where it floated above The Crux. It was so large, its shadow straddled the two-mile-wide gap that parted us from the earth-ruled land of Avanis, and as we broke out of the trees, I realised the Stonebreakers were springing an attack of their own. Huge harpoons were wedged into the far side of Ironwraith and the floating island was tilting as the Stonebreakers fought to drag it from the sky.

"Ever – watch out!" Harlon barked and Karkinos reared up as fire suddenly bloomed along our path.

We were thrown from his back, my fall cushioned as I fell against Harlon, and he wheezed a breath from the impact.

Karkinos turned and bolted into the trees and the two of us scrambled upright, finding the Flamebringers standing beyond the fire with their flaming swords the clear source of that fire.

The one without the mask was standing beyond The Boundary, looking to his friend who was dangling upside down from a tree, toying with his sword. He swung from the branch, flipping over and landing lightly on his feet, cocking his head to the side, his eyes brightest green behind his mask and his messy dark brown hair hanging wayward around it.

"Come on, North," the maskless one spoke, and I drew my mother's sword from the sheath strapped to Harlon's hip, stalking straight for him despite the flames that were licking their way between us and them.

Harlon drew his own sword from the sheath across his back, the metal glinting as it reflected the flames.

"I'll take the tree climber," he muttered. "Claim your vengeance."

"I have two fresh kills to make first," the one called North said, his voice a taunting drawl that echoed from behind his mask.

I raced forward, slamming my mother's sword into the earth and ice shot away from it, freezing a path right through the heart of the flames. I sprinted through the gap and Harlon followed, tearing past me to clash with North, their swords clanging as they collided.

I raced towards The Boundary, my gaze fixed on the brutish man standing just beyond it, watching me with a cool indifference. As if I was nothing but a butterfly hovering in the wind.

The power of The Boundary crackled over my skin as I charged through it, raising my sword and swinging it with a cry of hatred spilling from my lips.

The Flamebringer casually lifted his own sword, parrying my blow with such strength that I went stumbling back a step.

His eyes were as black as death, so empty it was as if he held no soul at all. His brows were drawn low, shading those sinful eyes, and his lips were tilted in a downward turn, no part of his features engaged with shock, intrigue, anger.

I swung at him again, the power of ice scoring out from the sword in a blast of shards, the magical power imbued in the blade. He twisted his sword so fast, a swirl of flames was all I could see along its edge as it melted all of those shards before they even got close.

I ducked low, slashing the edge of the sword at his legs, but his own blade was already there, blocking the blow and sending me stumbling back again from the power he used. Though he barely seemed to move, as if he was hardly using the strength he clearly possessed. He was big, taller than Harlon, and every part of him was built like a unit made for battle.

"North, let's go," he commanded, barely raising his voice, no real urgency there, like he wasn't capable of feeling even that.

I swung at him again, rage tearing through me at how little he acknowledged me while I threw everything I had at him. I went for his head this time, swinging the sword high, but his own came up to stop it.

I drove my heels into the ground, trying to force my way past his sword, but I only sent mine scraping down the length of his. My left hand screamed as I clung to the hilt, the wound from the venom bleeding against the metal and a stream of curses spilled from my lips.

"North," my opponent called again, shoving his weight into his sword and sending me flying backwards so fast I almost lost my footing.

"Just as soon as I've killed this giant sea urchin," North panted, clearly more stretched by Harlon's fight than my opponent was by mine.

My assailant glanced towards Ironwraith as it tilted more violently towards Stonebreaker territory across the wilds, absorbing the sight as if he was taking stock of it more than being affected by the view. I pressed the advantage of his distraction, swinging the sword with all the strength I could muster, striking straight for his heart with my mother's face burning through my mind. What he had done was too terrible to truly register, my thoughts still jarring with the reality of what this man had taken from me. My heart was a ragged, bloody thing in the wake of his attack and I despised him viscerally, to the core of me and beyond. This hate was pain, it was poison and it could easily destroy me, but not before it destroyed *him.*

His sword was there without him even looking my way and his foot came out, wrapping around mine and sending me tumbling to the ground.

I hit the snow with a growl, my breaths coming heavier as I shoved to my feet once more, determined to make him pay.

"You could have let them live," I spat. "You could have let us walk out of there before you set that fire."

The Flamebringer looked to me, recognition crossing his features at last. I didn't give him a chance to speak, if he was even going to bother saying a word. I swung for his neck and he sidestepped, throwing a foot out to send me crashing to the snow again. I tried to get upright, but his boot slammed down on my chest, his eyes flashing red with some dark, roiling power that had my breath catching in my lungs.

"Your desperate need for vengeance makes you predictable," he said, his voice dripping with malice. "Your death is inevitable, Raincarver."

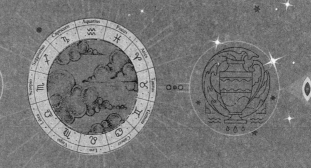

VESPER

CHAPTER EIGHT

My windrider hadn't been given the magical boost it needed and the pommel vibrated angrily as I directed it over the turrets which lined the outer wall of Echo Fort, forcing me to drop into a gut-lurching dive.

The magical contraption roared then fell terrifyingly silent beneath me, dropping like a stone for the last ten feet. I was reminded forcibly of the time I'd been dumped into the Altian Sea when my last windrider had burned through its power source after I'd been made to take a detour during a scouting assignment around the Zenhyr Peninsula off the coast of Pyros. But I wasn't going to hit water now.

The windrider sped towards the ground, still racing forward thanks to its momentum, and I dug my heels into the dirt, kicking up sand and grit while slowing my movement enough to be able to launch myself free of the magical vehicle.

I rolled across the dirt as the windrider crashed to the ground, flipping over twice and causing a Minotaur to moo indignantly. I bared my teeth at him in reply and he dropped his head in deference, turning to look over the cliff edge. I shoved myself upright and my boots pounded the ground as I ran on.

A blur of sliver made me throw myself down into a crouch, snatching a dagger from my hip which I drove into the dirt to make an anchor about three seconds before the enormous harpoon collided with the island.

Fae screamed as they were knocked free of the cliff by the resulting tremor, that same Minotaur mooing in alarm as he tumbled out of sight. Most of them would catch themselves with air magic before hitting the ground, but any of the Sinfair like me, too young to have been Awakened yet, would be meeting the ground below at one hell of a pace.

When the tremors subsided enough to allow me to regain my feet, I ripped my dagger from the ground and stood once more.

Generals were barking commands, Prince Dragor's army was rallying, units re-forming and preparing for battle, awaiting their orders before diving from the cliffs with air magic launching them through the sky.

I caught sight of General Imona to my left, her sharply cut black hair swinging forward for a moment, thankfully hiding me from her sight. I may have answered directly to the prince, but that didn't mean I wouldn't be forced to follow her commands if she found me here without orders in place from him to override her.

I hunted for the prince between the crowded bodies, shoving people aside and putting my back firmly to Imona.

The ground lurched violently and I grabbed the nearest soldier by the arm, steadying myself and possibly contributing to the fact that she lost her balance and crashed to the dirt, but I had no time to waste on her. My heart had just leapt into my throat, my skin prickling with unease because Ironwraith had started moving again and we were no longer headed south.

The land beneath my feet groaned and quaked as it began to tilt, Fae screaming all around me as those closest warriors to the cliff tried to run back to the fortress.

Between the fleeing bodies, I caught a glimpse of white just before Dragor launched himself into the sky on a column of air.

"Cut those lines!" he bellowed, but as I shoved my way between the packed bodies and took in the three gigantic harpoons which were imbedded in the bedrock of our island, my hope for that plan shattered like falling glass.

The lines which were dragging us towards the ground were thicker than the largest of tree trunks and woven entirely out of glimmering silver metal. We were fighting against the earth warriors of Avanis whose power over the element was as tremendous as our control over the sky. There was no way we would be able to cut through those lines before we were dragged to the ground by them.

The island continued to tip, the roar of the wind turbines which kept us aloft filling the air and blotting out the screams as our Wind Weavers poured every scrap of their magic into the turbines that held us in the sky, trying to rip us free of the tethers.

What had been flat ground was now a hillside, the angle growing steeper by the second and anything which hadn't been bolted down was now tumbling from the cliff edge towards the unforgiving land below.

I looked around, hunting for a windrider to hurl me into the air and finding a Fae readying to launch a skyglider instead. The contraption held no power like a windrider did, the wide sail using the air currents to transport a single Fae through the sky while hanging from the bar beneath it. They were mainly used by the Awakened forces who could use their air magic to manipulate the direction they took while silently spying on our enemies from far above, but they worked with or without the magic.

I ran for the Fae who was readying to launch, calling out to draw his attention and pushing into my Order gifts enough to make him blink stupidly at the sight of me, his mouth falling slack as he stared, his lust rising in the air. I took hold of the desire he felt, ignoring the compliments he blurted as I raced for him and setting my sights on the prize he still held ready to launch.

"You're more beautiful than the rising sun," he gasped, reaching for me.

I shoved him into the dirt, snatching the skyglider from him and throwing myself from the precariously tilting landmass in the same movement.

Ironwraith gave a violent jerk as it was wrenched further east and the soldier whose glider I'd just stolen tumbled away beneath me with a cry.

"Let me touch your haaaaaaaaiiiiir!"

He would probably be fine – he had air magic after all.

An up-current caught beneath the triangular canopy of the glider and I cursed as I was hurled skyward, clinging to the bar beneath the thing and cursing my hot-headedness for not pausing to strap myself in.

Ironwraith retreated beneath me, the sprawling mass of our moving island revealed as I sped higher. It was tilting horribly, the usually flat landscape now at a forty-five degree angle to the ground, our forces launching from it in droves while supplies and equipment tumbled to the earth far below.

I dropped my gaze from the island, taking in our position. We hadn't completed our retreat from Cascada yet – Ironwraith now straddling the gulf of space which created the no-man's land between earth and water, its shadow touching both territories just south of The Crux itself.

The Raincarvers hadn't given up their fight with us, their forces rushing to attack as they saw the advantage of our predicament and moved to make the most of it.

To the east, Avanis, the lands of the earth wielders, spread away from us, those three enormous cables dragging Ironwraith towards them foot by foot, but the rising sun made it almost impossible to see what awaited us on the ground when they brought us down. Because Ironwraith *was* falling. The truth of that impossible fact hit me like a winter storm as I looked to our warriors who were fruitlessly trying to carve through the cables which were dragging our land from the sky.

I threw my weight to the right, forcing the skyglider to turn and tilting it downwards so I could get closer to the battlefield, the sound of clashing blades and screaming Fae a chorus I knew well. My place was in the depths of the bloodshed, not high above it in the safety of the clouds. But as the glider pitched downward, its canopy shielded my eyes from the blazing sunlight which was cresting the eastern horizon, giving me a clear view of what awaited us in Avanis.

My lips parted as I took in the endless ranks of soldiers thirty miles in the distance, at least twenty thousand of them – a full force, not a skirmishing party like ours. They surrounded three enormous contraptions which secured the harpoons to the ground, slowly cranking them and winding us in.

I called out, looking for a general, colonel, or even better, Prince Dragor, but the updraft had dragged me far above the battlefield and the skyglider was descending too fucking slowly.

We couldn't let them drag us down. If the Stonebreakers forced us to crash near that army, they would overrun us in a matter of hours and Ironwraith would be lost.

I looked around desperately, not bothering to keep calling out as my voice was stolen by the wind. I needed to get down from here and I needed to find the prince.

A hundred feet below me, a squad of six waterborn Pegasuses were flying into battle, charging for the Skyforgers who were battling to dislodge the harpoons.

I yanked a dagger from my belt, reaching out for the Ether that surrounded me and opening up a channel within myself for its dark power. When I was fourteen, I was sent to war for the crime of having been born in a land other than my own. I was given seven years to prove myself worthy of a chance to enter Never Keep and unlock my air magic. I'd been trained to fight since I could hold a sword and had torn my way upwards from the very bottom of the pecking order.

I'd known that my early deployment, just like all Fae born with the weak blood of our enemies was designed to carve us from their ranks. They wanted us to throw our lives away on the battlefield and rid them of the tarnish of our company. But I wasn't the kind to bow to fate. I'd known I would be facing bigger, stronger, well-seasoned warriors on the battlefield and I'd known that I needed every edge I could claim for myself. Which was why I'd offered up a piece of my soul and risked my life to learn how to wield Ether and perform blood magic. The knowledge of the practice was openly available, but the

Oracles who taught it only deemed a few worthy of their teachings. I'd proven my worth to my Sage, Moya, and she had given me access to the power I'd needed to survive. The key to it was balance – sacrifice for gain. You only had to be willing to give up whatever it demanded, and I was always willing.

I smeared blood from the cut on my thumb across the blade of my dagger, roughly marking out the rune Teiwaz, in the shape of an upwards pointing arrow for authority, then I picked my mark and hurled the dagger.

The purple Pegasus beneath me whinnied in pain as my blade sank into the joint between its wings, the horse-like creature rearing from its position and beating its wings rapidly as it looked around for its attacker.

I tugged on the Ether, a rush of power hurtling through me as the blood I'd offered up met with the blood of my prey. Within moments, I had hold of him, forcing his body to go rigid, a wild neigh rolling from his throat as he lost control, his wings frozen on either side of him.

I muttered a prayer to Gemini and released my hold on the skyglider. I fell like a stone through the air, my muscles tense, pulse rioting as I forced myself to focus on nothing beyond my target.

The Pegasus was locked in place, his wild panic making the rest of his herd turn for him, and my hands began to shake as the blood magic threatened to cease. I had seconds before I lost him, seconds in which I could force his blood to fall to my command and end his life, but that wasn't my purpose just yet.

I slammed onto the Pegasus's back and rolled, his wild whinnying filling my ears as the sudden addition of my weight almost knocked him from the sky.

I grabbed a handful of purple mane, jamming my boot against his feathered wing and almost dislocating my fucking shoulder as I was nearly thrown free.

The blood magic shattered and he began to beat his wings, bucking and thrashing beneath me as he climbed back towards his herd who had all wheeled in the sky to face me.

I scrambled upright, yanking my dagger from his flesh and sheathing it before drawing my sword.

They were on me before I could fully take the measure of them. I ducked and swung, blood spraying as my blade carved into a powerful neck then ripped along the belly of another who was forced to wheel above us. They fell from the sky and the others flew around to come for me again, the sharpened points of their horns aimed directly for my heart.

Through the clash of colourful bodies, I'd spotted one of our own – a Manticore with the body of a lion and leathery wings like a bat, charging into the fight to assist me.

Roars met with whinnies, the beast I stood on threw himself to the side, my blade cut through flesh and then I was falling again. Bodies tumbled around me, the Pegasus herd dead or dying, screaming to the wind which wouldn't save them, and then the Manticore was racing for me.

I held my sword away from him as he came, diving beneath me then tucking his wings, but just as I was about to land, a bolt of ice speared through the sky and took him in the chest.

My eyes widened in panic as the beast was hurled away from me and the sickening sight of the ground rushing closer became the only thing I could see.

I threw myself into the Ether, hunting for a target, using the blood of my enemies as an anchor but it was happening too fast, the world whipping by and-

Strong arms banded around my waist, jerking me back into the sky and I choked down a breath as I turned in my saviour's grip and found Cayde looking at me with an eyebrow raised.

"Do you always need saving this regularly?" he asked, his powerful wings beating at his back where he remained shifted only partially so that he could make use of them.

"I never needed rescuing before I had the displeasure of meeting you," I snarled, the press of his muscular chest against mine a disconcerting sensation as we soared through the air.

"Are you certain? Because I'm getting the impression that your reputation was exaggerated."

I bit back the retort I wanted to offer him, instead taking in the battlefield once more, my fingers gripping his forearms as if I were going to shove him back, though we both knew I couldn't.

The Skyforgers were making no progress with destroying the harpoons and the Raincarvers were forcing us to engage with them while we needed to be preparing to take on the Stonebreakers waiting for us in the distant field.

"Take me to Prince Dragor," I demanded, hunting for him among the warring Fae and coming up empty while Cayde soared back towards Ironwraith, carrying me above the melee to the relative safety of the flying island once more.

"I have my own orders to follow," Cayde replied dismissively. "Find him yourself."

I opened my mouth to demand his cooperation but he hurled me away from him before I could so much as call him an overbearing ass.

I bit my tongue on the yell which threatened to escape me as I hurtled towards the tilting landscape of Ironwraith, refusing to give him the satisfaction of hearing me scream at his brutish behaviour.

I hit the dirt before the gates to Echo Fort and rolled to absorb my momentum before regaining my feet once more.

The gates were open before me, Skyforgers racing out in their battle leathers, every one of them armed to the teeth and looking furious, but it wouldn't be enough if the Stonebreakers managed to get us to where that ambush lay in wait.

We were losing altitude, the roar of the wind turbines a ferocious cry that was pitching towards a whine as they were pushed to their limit in their efforts to resist the harpoons.

A flash of white hurtled from the sky and my heart leapt with relief as I found Prince Dragor coming in to land on the battlements above the gates to Echo Fort.

I took off at a sprint, diving into the ranks of Skyforgers, shoving my way through them, using my elbows and fists where necessary. I had to get to him before he engaged the enemy again. I had to tell him what I'd seen.

Figures closed in around the prince as his generals and advisors all clustered to him, no doubt discussing tactics and receiving their orders. I'd seen the same thing play out countless times and I knew I didn't have long. The prince was decisive and ferocious with his battle tactics and he could easily be gone again within minutes.

I made it to the base of the fortress, craning my neck back to look above the enormous wooden gates which led inside. I couldn't see the prince or his advisors anymore but I hadn't seen him take to the skies again either. The route through the fortress and up onto the battlements would take too long to navigate so I sheathed my weapons, took a running jump at the wall and grabbed the closest window ledge.

I began climbing quickly. My training had gone beyond brutish warfare and combat; I had been crafted into a weapon with countless sharpened edges and I could creep through the shadows, scale buildings and execute assassinations just as proficiently as I could halt the blood in my enemies' veins.

Up and up I clambered, using cracks in the mortar as often as the ledges beneath windows to scale the sheer wall. There were four floors between the ground and the battlements above, but I kept my gaze firmly on my destination, not once wasting time on looking down. A drop could only kill me if I was fool enough to fall.

Ironwraith lurched violently as a fourth harpoon collided with it and I cursed my own arrogance for tempting fate as I almost fell from my precarious handhold. The world rattled beneath me and more Fae were flung from the cliffs.

Through some miracle and maybe a favour from the stars, I held on, gritting my teeth as I continued to climb.

I was breathing hard as my fingers clasped the top of the battlement at last and I heaved myself up onto the parapet, ignoring the four swords which swung my way as the advisors surrounding Prince Dragor were startled by my arrival.

I disregarded them entirely, my eyes locked on the prince whose white battle leathers were now stained with vibrant splashes of red, his icy eyes pinning me with violent expectation.

"The Stonebreakers are drawing us into a trap," I panted. "I took a skyglider to a point way above the clouds and on my descent, the canopy blocked the blinding rays of the sun, revealing a host of twenty thousand awaiting our collision with the ground where those harpoons are mounted."

The advisors, now all dressed in their own leathers, burst into speech at once, Tobias and Varnon bellowing to try and outmatch each other's voices while Amoria eyed me sceptically.

"Silence," Prince Dragor hissed, his word enough to have them stopping mid-sentence.

He stalked to my side, gripping the battlement and glaring out into the blinding light of the rising sun. He raised a hand to shield his eyes, and I followed his lead, but the dazzling sunrise made it impossible to confirm my claims.

He turned to me and I raised my chin, meeting that chilling, penetrating stare as he weighed my worth and made his choice.

"Command the Wind Weavers to cease powering the turbines," he barked, pivoting to look to his advisors once more, and I supressed the grin which itched to fill my lips as General Imona glowered at me furiously. "If those dirt lovers think they can force us into a trap, then they have severely underestimated us. We won't be dragged to the ground at their whim – we shall crash where we are and rip the harpoons from Ironwraith's belly with the force of gravity to aid us. All un-Awakened Sinfair who have not already been deployed, injured parties and any warriors whose power has been depleted in battle are to board a Skimmer and evacuate before we make contact with the ground. Everyone else is to take to the skies – they have five minutes and no more."

"We're directly over the wilds!" Tobias protested and a chill ran through me at the thought of that magical wasteland beneath us and the monstrous creations which roamed it to maintain the borders between the warring nations.

"We are still straddling it," Varnon contradicted. "We will collide not only with the wastelands but will touch down on both Avanis and Cascada."

"Good," growled Dragor, his fist curling with anger at his side. "We will carve off the lump of stone which has been captured in the grasp of the harpoons then replenish what we have lost from our enemies' precious lands in payment for what we will be forced to abandon to the wilds."

"You mean to claim new land?" Amoria questioned, her silver hair the only thing which seemed utterly unmoved by the wind that continued to whip around us. "The king hasn't sanctioned-"

"You answer to me, not my father," Dragor sneered, though to my surprise, Amoria didn't wither beneath the cold contempt in his expression. "And I assure you, the king will not question my choice in the matter when we return to the homeland not only with our target but with new lands claimed against our enemies."

"We'll inform the Wind Weavers," Imona said. "The Crossborn can assist-"

"The Sky Witch will remain with me," Dragor growled and the shiver which rattled down my spine made me uncertain whether I was pleased by his intervention or not. "Prepare the Carvers. Inform the rest."

The advisors left in a rush of air magic, each of them using it to hurtle themselves towards the various sides of the island where the Wind Weavers were working furiously to keep us aloft and battle the pull of the harpoons.

"If this fails then we will likely all die in this place," Dragor said once we were alone, his gaze moving to The Crux and I followed the line of his attention, looking down at the scarred and destroyed hunk of land which marked the only place in all of The Waning Lands where three nations met. The ugly destruction of that blackened, desecrated ground was achingly perfect to me in its ruination. It felt like I was looking at the heart of our continent, the truth of the rot the Endless War had caused. The reality of what we all fought over so eternally – what so many of us gave our lives for in the end.

"I won't die," I replied because it felt like the truth. I wasn't going to let my bones fall to rest in this hellish place, surrounded eternally by hatred and more death. "None of us will," I added as I felt the prince's eyes studying me from far too close for it to be safe. "We have you."

I looked to him as I said it, inhaling sharply as I found him leaning into my personal space, his cold eyes peeling me apart and inspecting me too closely to ever find me worthy. When he looked at me like that, I felt as though he could see the blood running through my veins, the weakness which I had been born with, the truth which no action of mine could ever truly banish.

I swallowed and he tracked the movement, his attention trailing to my mouth then back to my grey eyes once more.

"What loyalty you preach," he said softly, though his words sounded like a bellow as the turbines chose that precise moment to go quiet, the magic falling silent and Ironwraith plummeting from the sky.

Dragor didn't react but I lurched for him, gripping the front of his battle leathers and holding on for dear life as we fell in a rush of motion, Fae screaming in the distance, the wind a tumultuous roar. My pale pink hair whipped around me, my heart remaining in the heavens far above as we fell and fell.

Dragor smiled slowly, stepping close to me and taking hold of my waist between his large hands, bending down to keep his eyes locked with mine.

"You are my creature," he said, his words a demand which I

somehow heard above the roaring of the wind and the screaming inside my own skull.

"I am," I swore because he was the one thing which could offer me a true place in this world and if being his weapon, his assassin, his monster meant that I belonged, then I would become whatever he demanded of me.

His magic wrapped around us like the fist of a giant and he launched us from the parapet a moment before Ironwraith collided with the ground.

A wave of dirt and debris exploded in every direction and I could have sworn the Wind Weavers hadn't even slowed our descent at all. Though the fact that Echo Fort and all the other buildings which clustered across the expanse of Ironwraith still stood proved that they must have done so enough to protect the integrity of our land.

Dragor lifted me above it all, the dazzling light of the sun blinding me as I looked out towards the earth lands of Avanis. His grip on me was firm, possessive and unyielding, the hard planes of his body crushed to mine so tightly that I was certain he could feel the pounding of my heart against his.

The Fae of Cascada were screaming, running, crying out in horror as a huge portion of their town was crushed, no doubt wiping out many of their people. More cries drew my attention to the other side of the island where Ironwraith had collided with Avanis, land of the Stonebreakers where a single warrior screamed in a grief so pure that the sound of it pierced my cold heart and made a chill run through my veins.

I looked down at her, somehow seeing her clearly through the cloud of dirt and warring bodies, my eyes locking with hers and the pain of her loss washing through me so vividly that I was certain she had to have some form of psychic ability.

I opened my mouth to point her out to Dragor, uncertain why I had even noticed her between the clashing masses which surrounded us but before I could speak, an arrow streaked through the air and struck her in the throat, silencing her cries.

A burn flared in my chest as I watched her fall, something in me twisting uncomfortably as I wrenched my eyes from her corpse.

"We need fifteen minutes to carve the land struck by the harpoons from the island, sire," Varnon called, shooting towards us through the sky on his own pillar of air magic, his red hair flying back from his face as he moved.

"I want a square mile carved from each nation before we depart," Dragor snarled, a need for vengeance colouring his tone.

"Yes, sire," Varnon agreed, his eyes taking in the way Dragor held me before snapping away just a fast. "But there is a problem – the beasts which roam the deadlands approach Ironwraith from the north and south. Perhaps we should opt for haste instead of-"

"You have your orders," Dragor sneered. "My warriors can handle a few beasts of metal and flesh."

Varnon nodded his understanding, then shot away.

"Come, my Sky Witch," Dragor purred, hurling us through the air towards the destroyed landscape of the no man's land where ranks were forming to face whatever horrors now converged upon our island. "Let me see how prettily you dance among the monsters."

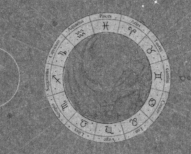

EVEREST

CHAPTER NINE

The earth was still trembling with the aftershocks of the impact of where Ironwraith had struck Castelorain, crushing part of my town. A flurry of terror and panic had cried out from my people and my heart twisted with the destruction besieging my homeland. But despite the disorder ripping the air in two with the magnitude of what had just happened, I still didn't turn my eyes from the man I was intent on laying to ruin.

"You'd better kill me now or I'll hunt you for the rest of your days," I snarled at the Flamebringer who had killed my mother.

After he'd gotten apparently bored of parrying my attacks on his legs, ankle and a few sharp jabs at his cock, my enemy had taken his boot off my chest to observe Ironwraith falling from the sky and slamming into Avanis across The Crux before striking the edge of Castelorain too. I'd gained my feet and forced his attention back on me even when the ground had quaked from the violent impact. We had been in a back and forth since of me striking while he lazily parried my blows, barely offering me the courtesy of looking at me as his gaze trailed to his friend, North, and Harlon's fight. I couldn't spare a moment of my attention to them, leaping from the snowy ground again and stabbing straight for my enemy's chest.

He knocked me away with his blade, flames skittering across it to hiss against the icy metal of my mother's sword. He hadn't even bothered to draw his second blade, and I got the feeling I was boring him as I threw all of my power into my next attack.

I swung my sword high then dropped it, catching it with my injured hand, carving it low instead at the last second as a hiss of pain spilled between my teeth. His sword was somehow there again to take the impact, his movements so fluid it was like he was an extension of his weapon. I'd never seen swordplay like it, and no matter how practised my movements were, I couldn't get past his guard.

"Fools dig their own graves," he said, the barren, deep tone of his a weapon of its own, plunging straight into my heart.

"Cut the fucking poetry," I snarled, my ire digging deeper as I struck at him again.

He swept his fiery sword around in a circle, the force of the blade driving against mine making the hilt score into my bloody palm, but I willed the agony away and demanded my focus to sharpen. With a skilled twist of his blade, he forced the sword free of my grip and it landed in the snow at his feet. I lunged for it with a gasp, but his knee came up, driving into my face and making me stagger back as pain bloomed through my mouth, blood wetting my tongue.

"What will you do now?" he asked, as if he couldn't actually care less what I did. He crouched down, taking my mother's sword and weighing it in his free hand. "It's a good thing you didn't ignite the magic in this blade before stepping through The Boundary, or it would have been turned to ash."

"Give that back," I demanded, lunging at him and he swung both swords wide, allowing me beneath his guard then driving them into an X at my back, caging me within his muscular arms.

I was so close to him that I could smell oak and cinders on his skin, the perfect concoction of villainy. The tinge of danger in his calculated movements told me I was half a second from my body being cleaved apart on the edge of both swords, but he had let me too close to him. He believed me so insignificant that he had actually drawn me into this vulnerable space, and my hand snared the hilt of the short sword still sheathed at his hip.

I drew it fast, slashing it against his skin, scoring a diagonal line from his hip to his shoulder, blood spilling from the vicious cut that should have had him roaring in agony. But instead, all he did was part the swords at my back and kick me so hard that I was thrown to the ground beyond The Boundary. I didn't care about the pain of his strike, a savage smile of victory lifting my lips at what I'd done.

He took stock of the wound, his blood red fighting leathers torn apart by the strike and blood dripping down to stain the snow crimson. His dark eyes fell on me, his boots marking a passage my way as he raised his swords with the intent to kill. And I swear the sky shuddered as it acknowledged the demon stalking toward me.

Ironwraith was climbing back into the sky beyond him, dominating the view as the sunrise bled into the sky.

The ground began to quake, first a gentle rumble then an almighty roar of noise as great lashes of air magic came tearing down from the Skyforgers' island. I threw myself to the right to avoid the blast as a ferocious wind hit the ground, scoring through the earth like a knife, carving its way through the hillside and off towards the ocean, slicing our town in two, and we stood on the very cusp of the land the air wielders were seeking to steal.

I gasped as the ground jolted violently, turning to look for Harlon and finding him on top of North, their swords discarded in the snow and his knuckles turning white as he worked to choke his enemy to death.

North was turning blue and my own assailant turned from me, setting his sights on Harlon instead, swinging my mother's blade in one hand and his fire sword in the other.

"Harlon!" I shouted a warning as the earth was ripped skyward, my stomach bottoming out as we sailed up towards Ironwraith at a ferocious pace.

The Skyforgers were doing what they did best, stealing land from other nations and claiming it for their own. But as we rocketed towards the island in the sky and the wind pressed down on me, a gigantic hand built of the ocean itself reared up and slammed down on the far edge of the chunk of land, tilting it violently downward.

There was no doubt it was the brutal, beautiful work of my father.

I skidded down the slope along with the others, Harlon thrown off of North by the sudden decline and slamming into a tree. He fought to hold onto it as screams sounded out across the lump of land and I went careering towards him along with the Flamebringers.

We had to move, had to get free of this land before it joined with Ironwraith where the Skyforgers would be waiting to butcher anyone left clinging to it and hurl our bodies to the ground far below.

Harlon caught my arm before I could tumble past him and I held on tightly, hauling myself up to cling to the branch.

A hand locked around my ankle and I cursed as the full weight of my enemy hung from my leg. I kicked hard, forcing him off me and he caught the branch of a tree just below, while North went sprinting away down the tilting island with a cry of alarm, nearly losing his footing at every step.

My enemy glared up at me from the branch below and I kicked at his hands, trying to force his grip from it while Harlon clung onto me. The bastard had managed to sheathe my mother's sword at his hip, but his fire sword was lost to the carnage as boulders the size of houses went crashing down the hill towards the water hand.

Whips of air struck at the fingers of the water hand, breaking its grip and then we were tilting violently back the other way, falling from the tree that now stood upright once more. We let go, hitting the ground, and the Flamebringer did the same, sprinting for the far edge of the land.

The water hand was reaching up once more, its fingers tearing into the ground and forcing the earth to tip sharply toward it once again.

"We have to jump off this land," I gasped.

"Jump? We'll fucking die," Harlon said in refusal, but I grabbed his arm and forced him into a run.

"Trust me," I insisted, watching the place those giant fingers locked around the edge of land again and charging straight for them.

The world tilted and I nearly lost my footing as the snow slid beneath my feet, but instead I kept running, speeding along the ever-increasing descent to dry, warm land, passing between brush and rock then meeting the streets of the town I knew so well.

The water hand was right at the end of the next alley, the smooth stone beneath my bare feet making it harder and harder to stay upright. But somehow we did, and then we collided with that watery hand, diving straight into it as I pulled Harlon after me. It was like jumping straight into a whirlpool, and I was flung around in the churning saltwater, unable to see anything, unable to breathe or swim as I lost my grip on Harlon's arm.

I was plunged into darker water, kicking and kicking, swimming for the surface, hoping Harlon was close on my heels.

I broke the waves, finding myself out in the ocean where the arm of the hand stretched up and away from us. Harlon surfaced beside me, gulping down air and we stared in horror as the hand's grip was broken by more whips of air and a chunk of our town at least a mile in diameter was stolen away into the sky.

In the distance, I could just make out another hunk of land being torn from Avanis, dragged up to join the hulking mass which was Ironwraith as the newly-grown island launched itself towards the heavens once more.

I glowered at the dark, rocky underside of the island as it sailed higher for the cover of the clouds, the lump of land which had been held by those harpoons now carved off and left to rot in the wasteland between our two nations.

My gaze locked on movement by the shore as two figures dragged themselves from the water, the dark clothes of the Flamebringers telling of who they were.

I started swimming, furious they'd survived that fall and determined to finish this fight once and for all. But as they darted into the torn-apart earth and rocky boulders where the land had been ripped from its roots, I lost sight of them among the shadows. Still, I didn't stop swimming, my mind set on that single goal as the grief came for me again in a rolling wave of agony.

By the time I made it to shore, my limbs were trembling from exertion and all I found waiting for me was Commander Rake striding along the beach with his warriors grouping together, Ransom and Alina close behind them.

"The Flamebringers were here," I said urgently, running to my father, hoping he would send a battalion of warriors with me to hunt them. "They killed Mama. I ran to The Forge to warn her of the Skyforgers and was there when the blast was set. I-"

The commander's gaze dropped to the blood that was beginning to swell again on my left hand and he snatched my wrist, staring at the red skin that would surely scar beyond repair. His brown beard was blood-flecked, and the scales of his Merrow Order still on show, though the spikes between his knuckles had slid back beneath his skin. In the wake of battle, he looked even more terrifying than usual. The strike of his back hand came so fast that I had no time to even flinch before I was thrown into Harlon's hard chest.

"You failed her. And now you have destroyed one of the only worthwhile pieces of yourself," the commander said in a cold tone, his words cutting deep.

Harlon's arm came around me protectively. "She fought to kill the Flamebringers. We chased them to The Boundary."

"So where are their heads?" Father growled.

"They got away," Harlon admitted in a mutter, and my failure was crushing.

"I'll find them. They're heading for The Boundary again, there's still time," I said, pushing out of Harlon's arms, and my father stared down his crooked nose at me.

"You will do no such thing," he hissed, then snapped his fingers at two of his guards, sending them off to take the path I ached to follow myself. "From now on, you will be a shadow in our land. A creature akin to rats and foxes, and you will be treated as the useless vermin you are."

He turned his back on me, directing his warriors to their post-battle duties while I stared after him, finding the sniggering faces of Ransom and Alina glancing my way before they scurried off after the commander.

"Wait," I gasped, ready to try and make him see that I held some worth. That I wasn't useless, that I could still fight, still walk the path of a warrior. But the words died on my lips as the warriors marched away up the beach, because what proof did I have of that? I'd failed in rescuing my mother, I'd failed in ending her killer.

Harlon rested a hand on my shoulder as my soul fractured a little deeper, my father's rejection cleaving me apart.

"He's wrong, Ever," he said quietly, shifting closer behind me, the warmth of his body calling to me. But I wouldn't seek solace in his arms. A divide had just been drawn between me and the rest of this town, and Harlon deserved more than being caught on the wrong side of it.

"No, Harlon," I whispered, my voice hoarse with the raw agony of the loss of my mother. "This time, he's right. I couldn't save her. I couldn't even avenge her."

Harlon turned me to him, his brow drawn low as he knocked his knuckles under my chin. "It's not your fault."

Never rest, Everest. My mother's parting words to me carried to me as if upon the back of the ocean breeze. I inhaled them like a toxin, letting them fill my lungs and bind themselves to the shattered remnants of my soul. And I felt them taint me with a dark kind of strength, one that twisted and altered me, shaping me into something sinister.

"It is," I said, looking up at him with a newfound strength gilding my words. "But I won't rest until I have her killer's heart."

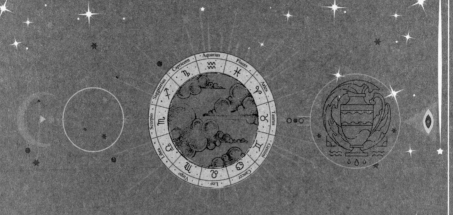

VESPER

CHAPTER TEN

The shadow of Ironwraith withdrew overhead as I remained locked in combat in the depths of the no-man's land which divided the lands of Avanis and Cascada. I bared my teeth as I spun beneath the swiping metal claws of a beast which looked to have once been a bear, its bulk towering over me, its jaws parted in the maddened fury of the twisted creations that roamed the wilds.

Long ago in some madness or genius now forgotten to the dredges of the Endless War, Fae had taken wild beasts and experimented on them, melding their bodies with metallic contraptions imbued with magic. The idea had been to create more warriors to throw into the countless battles, but the reality had been these horrifying beasts which were impossible to control.

They were driven mad by the magic forced into their bodies, unable to die thanks to the potions and spells cast on them with dark magic and the twisted manipulations of Ether. There was no way of utilising them in the war without risking them being unleashed on the armies who deployed them, but somewhere along the line, someone had come up with the idea of placing them in this desolate slice of hell.

They were left to roam this broken wilderness between the lands, a law unto themselves, starving and feral with an insatiable hunger. The Boundaries which marked the edges of the nations they bordered stopped them from crossing thanks to their magic, but in this place, they acted as a further line of defence against any Fae foolish enough to try and attack directly across the borders.

The air kingdom of Stormfell wasn't free of their burden; our lands in the distant north shared a border with the fire-ruled land of Pyros, the chasm parting our nations holding its own share of monstrous creations. I had seen them before, but until now I'd never been forced to face one head on.

All around me Fae were launching into the sky, their air magic hurling them away from the battle with the beasts as they heeded the call for retreat, the bells of Ironwraith ringing to signal us home. But without my windrider, I had no hope for retreat and I had seen no sign of Prince Dragor since he'd dropped me into this mayhem.

I spun out, my sword clanging futilely against the metallic armour which coated the beast's belly and a curse spilling between my teeth.

I was forced to dive beneath it as it lunged for me, rolling across the barren land, the bones of small creatures crunching beneath me where they littered the crusty soil.

I threw myself to my feet then danced away as the bear hunted for me on its far side, having lost sight of me for a moment.

My gut dropped as I looked for the remainder of our troops and found only three warriors still standing in the field with me.

My eyes met those of the closest soldier as he kicked a beast which appeared something like a tiger in the side and knocked it away from him. His gaze hardened as he looked at me, no remorse showing at all as he launched himself into the air and shot away, abandoning me to my fate.

I committed his pasty face and the whisps of white beard to memory, marking him for later and trying not to flinch as the two remaining warriors abandoned me too.

Sinfair. Crossborn.

The words haunted me like the curse they were.

The bear rounded on me and I ran to meet it, bellowing a roar in reply to the one it offered me. I'd been fighting it for long enough to have picked up on its style and as it swiped at me with those lethal claws, I jumped. My boot landed on its forearm, giving me the leverage I needed to propel myself even higher and I fisted my hand in the fur behind its ear as I launched myself onto its back.

A cry escaped me as I swung my sword in a double handed strike, throwing all of my considerable strength into the strike and decapitating the beast with a blow that made my arms echo with the force of it as it toppled to the ground.

I leapt away from it as the other beasts all whipped around, the too thick, too dark blood which pulsed from the bear's severed neck drawing them all to it like the rabid creatures they were, and they forgot me as they fell into a frenzy of feeding.

I set my gaze on the retreating form of Ironwraith and broke into a run, my feet pounding across the uneven ground, arms pumping, breaths heaving. I wouldn't be left behind. My reputation wasn't unfounded.

A single cable still hung from the island, the only harpoon to have snapped in its crash to the ground and I fixed my eyes on it as I ran. Faster and faster, my muscles screaming in protest, my lungs burning, eyes watering from the sting of the dank air. I sheathed my sword, managing not to impale myself through some small miracle and leaving my hands free as I ran faster still.

The island was rising, Ironwraith heading for the clouds, turning away from Avanis in case more harpoons lay in wait. The cable no longer dragged across the ground but now swung a foot above it. Two feet. Three.

My blood isn't who I am. My weakness doesn't define me. I carved my place in their kingdom. I made them notice me. I earned my own name among them. I am just as they all whisper; black-hearted, ruthless, unstoppable, and above all else, un-fucking-killable.

The cable whipped upward, six feet off the ground and climbing rapidly, already above my head, but I was jumping, my hands grasping and then the cold metal was biting into my fingers and I found a purchase on it.

I smiled grimly as the beasts howled and feasted below, digging my fingers into the woven metal cable which was a thick as the trunk of a hundred-year-old tree. My boots scrambled against it, but I gritted my teeth and kept climbing.

Up and up. The wind was biting, chapping the skin from my cheeks, blasting my hair all around me as the island retreated into the clouds.

I couldn't see a thing as the frigid fog engulfed me, my handholds growing slick as I continued to climb. My arms trembled with the effort it took, my boots slipping out more than once, threatening to pitch me right off of the cable and hurl me into the unknown below.

It didn't matter. Nothing mattered beyond the next hand hold, next heave of my arms, the brutal clench of my thighs. Until finally, my fingers met with rock and dirt, the familiar stone and sand of Ironwraith welcoming me home.

I released a ragged laugh, using the prongs at the top of the harpoon to pull myself from the cable and then I was clambering over the stony cliff face on the rear side of the island.

Scaling the cliff seemed easy in comparison to that whip of metal, and before long, my arm was hooking over the top edge, my right leg following.

I dragged myself to my feet on the six inches of space before the giant air shield which had been erected to surround the moving island, protecting us all from attack and the elements.

I took a dagger from my belt and drove it into the air shield with a savage strike, causing a spiderweb of cracks to form all over its surface.

Fae on the other side whirled to face me, drawing weapons and crying out in alarm. Pure fear lit the faces of many, including the asshole who had left me to die down in that slice of hell.

But my focus, every single piece of it, was captured by Prince Dragor who had fallen utterly still before the gates of Echo Fort, his light eyes widening just a touch as I gave him my most wicked smile.

And as he smiled darkly in return, I knew that my reign as the Sky Witch wasn't anywhere near over.

It had only just begun.

ONE YEAR LATER

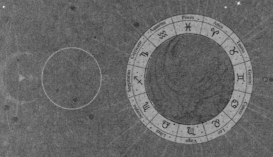

EVEREST

CHAPTER ELEVEN

I leaned over the wooden table where all my forging tools lay in haphazard chaos, while I rubbed oil into the hilt of my newly finished dagger. It was ready. And it was a beautiful, deadly thing that had not only been created in my mother's forge at the back of this very room but had been imbued with all the vengeful rage that simmered in my soul.

I'd spent months and months practising my craft to be able to make a blade such as this. I'd even used some of the metal from the blown apart Forge roof in town along with a piece of the mechanical armour worn by the dead beast I'd left down in the wilds that day.

I'd retrieved its claws long ago, crafting them into gauntlets that could be worn to climb in and out of the wasteland too, tools that had come in handy more than once. Whatever metal was used to imbue those magical beasts was strong as kaské. It had been hard to work with, but I'd gotten there in the end. And now my creation was finished, all for one thing.

The place on the hilt I was polishing was bare, a gap left purposefully in the engraved decorations. Flames curled around the spot, but they were being doused by a roaring wave, and the space between them was waiting for the day I learned the name of the man who had murdered my mother. Once I held that knowledge, I would etch it into this very place and send a prayer to Pisces to bless the blade with all the fury of my star sign and grant me favour in my quest to destroy him. This blade, which was blood red at the hilt, paling to a perfect silver at the deadly tip, would soon pierce my enemy's heart.

The door that led onto the alleyway was flung wide and I squinted out at the blazing daylight glinting off of Harlon's bare shoulders. His head was cocked and his expression stern as he stared in at me, one eyebrow arching. He was naked from the waist up, barefoot too, and his tanned muscles gleamed under the morning Cascalian light.

I hissed at him like a wildcat, wincing away from the stark brightness as my eyes adjusted to the sudden change. All the curtains were closed in here, and the whole place was a mess courtesy of my influence. My mama's house was a simple structure, this room the only living space outside the two small sleeping rooms and latrine.

"Ever, get your ass out in the sun," Harlon insisted. "And when did you last eat?"

I looked to the bowl of watery oats I'd picked at a while ago. Or was that last night?

"I'm working," I insisted, glancing down and taking stock of myself in the humbling light of day. My hair had grown in the humidity of the night, my unruly curls taking on a life of their own, each of them headed in their direction. My leather work apron was sticking to my skin, and I recalled taking off everything but my undergarments beneath me somewhere around midnight last night. Was my ass sticking to the seat a little? Perhaps. But if anyone had seen me undone by the obsession of my work enough times to have grown used to the sight, it was Harlon.

"Fuck work. The surf's good, let's get out there. It's our last chance to visit Undashine Shore."

My ears pricked up at that, the ocean calling to me like it so often did. And Harlon was right. We were going to be shipped off to Never Keep in a few hours. This would be my final opportunity to swim in warm waters with my friend for a long time. From what I'd heard, the surf around the island where Never Keep was situated had a lot of power in its waves, but the water was as cold as a polar bear's tits.

I slid the blade off of my work table, trying to subtly slip it into a drawer, but Harlon noticed, stalking through the room, rolling back his broad shoulders. My eyes made a passage down the hardened planes of his chest, perfectly defined in every way, a man fit for war.

"Have you finished at last?" he asked, and my gaze snapped back up to meet his.

"Yes. Maybe. No." I slipped the dagger into the drawer, but Harlon pounced, his muscles having grown muscles of their own this past year. He slammed into me like a fucking boulder, but I ducked down, taking the blade with me and moving so fast, he never saw me coming. I was behind him in a heartbeat, pressing the dagger to his ribs.

I smiled my victory, but he spun around fast, his hand snatching my wrist while the other locked in my hair and bared my throat to him.

"Yield," he purred, and the deep tenor of his voice sent a shiver rolling through me. The kind that shouldn't have been born between friends.

Harlon was made for succeeding in all his endeavours. Between his cocky, easy manner and his good looks, he drew plenty of women to his bed. I would have been blind not to have noticed him now, but in all honesty, I'd noticed him when he was a scrawny kid picking me up out of the dirt and wiping the dust off my knees. He had fixed up my bloody noses, sprains and even a broken wrist once after Ransom and his friends had sprung attacks on me.

Somehow, I'd always gotten away, and Harlon would invariably find me at Undashine Shore licking my wounds. He'd tend to my injuries, cleaning and binding them while I cursed out Ransom and swore I'd beat him next time. Harlon had offered to be my escort a thousand times, but I'd refused to use him as a shield, facing my fate like a Fae and working to come out on top. It didn't matter that Ransom moved around with a pack of heathens and I was severely outnumbered, because accepting Harlon's help felt like failing. And I wouldn't offer any more reason for the assholes in this town to call me weak.

I slammed my heel down on Harlon's foot and he cursed, his grip easing just enough for me to throw a hand up, jamming it into his wrist to force it out of my hair. I snatched the blade from my snared hand and held it to his heart instead, the tip pressing into that tempting golden skin of his.

He boomed a laugh, the sound filling up the room, his presence dominating the space. "You're good. But you're not that good, little fish."

"Yonla i pishalé," I hissed.

"Tut, tut," he scolded. "You should be speaking the Universal

Language not Cascalian."

"But calling you an asshole always sounds so much prettier in the old tongue, Harl," I said with a smirk. "The U.L. has no pizzazz."

He jabbed my bare back with something sharp and I glanced down, finding he'd somehow unsheathed his own deadly little knife.

"I reckon I'd survive that easier than you'd survive a skewered heart," I said, fluttering my eyelashes as my lips lifted in a twisted smile.

His gaze dipped to my mouth then back to my eyes, a frown lining his brow as he shifted minutely closer. For a second, I was frozen, unsure what he was about to do but having the sense that I wanted him to do it. There'd always been something between us, and it had grown sharper when we'd reached adulthood. But even when Harlon snuck into my filthiest of dreams, I'd never crossed that line in real life. Our friendship was far too valuable to risk on the sake of a relationship that might just end up in shattered pieces. Then I'd lose him forever, and that wasn't an option. He was my lifeline in the dark, the one who had gotten me through the greatest depression of my life.

After Mama's death, I'd spiralled. Hard. My hand had taken a long time to heal, but he had been there to tend it day after day, soaking it for me in aloe and rike leaves when I couldn't even muster the will to leave the house. Eventually, something had shifted in me. The grief I had been drowning in had transformed from a jagged, agonising kind of torture to a hard, impenetrable fortress of vengeance against the man who caused my pain. My heart had been hardened, strengthened by my loss and made anew. What I was now held little innocence, my eyes wide open to the cruel, unforgiving world, but so long as Harlon was there to keep enticing smiles from me, I wasn't wholly lost.

Which was all the more reason that I couldn't ruin what we were. I would never sate the desires of my flesh in him. When it came to sex, I'd sought release in the arms of some truly ruthless men. The type fresh home from war, warriors who needed the heat of bare skin to wipe the horrors of battle from their minds. The ones who drank too much and indulged too hard, men who were scarred, vicious and had no idea of the life I led here in Castelorain.

At eighteen, I'd found myself captivated by a man who went by the unfortunate yet apt name of Ruckus, following him to one of the taverns that lined Brissale Beach. I'd walked up to him wearing a hand-stitched green dress with little gold fish embroidered into the fabric and a necklace made from spoons swinging around my neck, then I'd laid my hand on his cock through his britches and raised an eyebrow.

Me and subtle didn't exactly belong in the same sentence.

It hadn't been in any way like Alina's first time which she had loudly regaled to her friends after a training session in the Sunserl Courtyard, speaking of a Fae who had brought flowers to her door every night before taking her virginity in a thrall of passion and gentle love.

Me? I had found myself with a firm, rough hand sliding around my wrist and a man called Ruckus leading me into a back alleyway behind the tavern. There, pinned between a hard wooden wall and a man twice my size, my dress half pulled off me in his need to get to my skin, I had been fucked with the brutality of a warrior who had known nothing but violence in however many years he had served in battle.

Yet between the bite of pain his thick cock had caused while driving inside me and the bruising kisses he'd laid on my lips as his stubble rubbed my skin raw, I had found something to like in the frenzy of his lust.

It wasn't the sweet, romantic pleasure Alina had spoken of, but it was something equally rare to me. The way that man ached for me with such simplicity was something foreign in my life, the whispers of my beauty passing his lips in heavy pants such a stark contrast to the taunts or ridicules I was used to. I had reduced that powerful man to a singular want, and that want was me.

After that, I'd occasionally wandered to the taverns, looking for him at first, but once he had returned to battle, I'd found others who had been just as willing to worship me with that same kind of rough delight.

It wasn't something I spoke to anyone about, not even Harlon. He didn't go into detail about the women he bedded either. It was an unspoken rule between us, like deep down, we knew that the other wouldn't like to hear about it. Though sometimes I wondered how Harlon was with the girls he laid his affections on. Was he as rough as the men home from war? Or was he gentle like Alina's first boyfriend had been?

Harlon's gaze fell on my blade as I lowered it from his chest and he swore, the tense moment falling away between us, lost just as it should be.

"Ever, this is…" He took the dagger from my hand, and I reluctantly relinquished it into his hold, my lips pressing tight together as I prepared to get his opinion. The only opinion I gave a kaské about these days.

"The tip could be sharper," I said quickly. "And I still need a name to fill the blank spot on the hilt. It won't be finished until then."

He twisted the dagger in his grip, admiring it from every angle, from the Pisces fish swimming along the blade, to the very same constellation etched onto the other side.

"It's perfect. Perhaps even better than your mother's work," he commended.

I snatched it back, scolded by his words.

"I could never match her talent," I growled.

"Don't take offence, little fish," he said, smirking in that way that always had women falling at his feet. But I wasn't like them.

Harlon and I were an echo of each other's souls. He had lost his parents in a bloody battle with the Stonebreakers from Avanis, and his upbringing here in Cascada had been anything but easy. His carefree smiles hid it well, but I knew about the farrier who had taken him in and had raised him with a cruel hand. I knew about the whippings which had left the scars that still tinged my friend's flesh when the sun shone on them just right.

He was a man on a passage to war now, but once he had been a boy that had well known the scent of his own blood. It was why we'd bonded. He'd catch waves on his tiderunner to escape the farrier for a while and that was how we'd met. The two of us chasing freedom at Undashine Shore, a beach that had been a refuge for both of us. Our secret escape that not even Ransom and his friends bothered to make the arduous trek to.

Today was our last chance to claim a ride upon the ocean at our sacred hideout before we were shipped off to Never Keep for our assessment. I knew from that point on, I would be on a path of revenge that wouldn't end until the man who had killed my mother found a just and wicked death. From guessing his age, and knowing that he couldn't have been Awakened as he had crossed through The Boundary, I knew he would either be at war by now or perhaps about to become a neophyte at Never Keep. And the only way I would find him would be by walking in his footsteps.

Regardless, the battlefield was the destination I was seeking. I had dreams of visiting Castelorain decorated in medals, only to find my father's attention turning from Ransom to me, praising me and me alone.

It was a petty dream, but one I quietly hung on to. If only I could be seen as *more*, as a powerful warrior with an endless list of deaths to her name, then I wouldn't be shunned from society. I might even be revered.

I wasn't allowed to fight in battles before my training at Never Keep by law of Cascada, but ever since I'd discovered that I could slip beyond The Boundary into the wilds, I'd returned there regularly to test my strength.

After one particularly bloody encounter with Ransom, I'd taken my mother's sword and stalked into the wilds, determined to prove myself. I'd returned with the flesh and metal head of one of those vicious beasts, the thing still wrapped in a sheet now and stuffed beneath my bed. I'd peeled off some of that metal for use in forging weapons, but it was still mostly intact. A trophy that I'd shown no one but Harlon.

He was the keeper of my secrets, and I his. We held plenty of crimes to our names, but not even Harlon had stepped into the wilds. That was a place only I dared to venture, a place where I thrived in the disorder.

Harlon had warned me time and again not to go there, especially after I'd come back with blood dripping down my leg and a jagged piece of metal sticking out of it one night. He'd had the job of stitching that wound while I bit down on a piece of wood in the bathing tub and did everything in my power not to wake the neighbours with my screams.

All traces of my passage beyond The Boundary had to remain

hidden, but even after I'd recovered from that particularly nasty incident, I'd eventually found my feet padding back there in the dead of night. If only I could be stronger, could push myself harder, could stretch myself a little further. Then maybe I'd ensure I secured my place at Never Keep.

Harlon didn't need to accompany me into the wilds to train anyway – not that I'd ever invited him. He was still enrolled in the daily training classes for un-Awakened Fae which my father had banned me from attending last year.

Harlon often put Ransom on his ass during their spars, and I'd seen him do just that from the tiled red rooftop that sloped down towards the Sunserl Courtyard.

I watched, even if I wasn't allowed to attend, learning all I could from sight alone while perched in the shadow of the statue of Typhon, the giant sea serpent which represented our land. Its spined body coiled up around a trident and the marks of Pisces, Cancer and Scorpio decorated its brow, its legend well-known by the people of Cascada.

The tale claimed that Typhon had been so beguiled with the ocean from his place perched up in the stars, that he begged the three signs of water, Pisces, Cancer and Scorpio, to let him down from the sky so that he might bathe in the moonlit waters.

His wish was granted upon the condition that he would carve a new land from the ocean floor and drive it up to the surface where Fae with water magic flowing through their veins could be protected by the giant serpent. Typhon agreed to be their guardian and drove Cascada from the water after his descent to the ocean, giving birth to our land and blessing it with the grace of the element of water. I didn't know how true it was, but I liked the pretty picture it painted in my mind all the same, and I especially liked the shade his statue offered me from the midday sun on that rooftop.

Harlon had made a point of sparring with me after every session at the Sunserl Courtyard, and we'd become accustomed to the routine. I'd lurk somewhere along the rocky cliff path that led to Undashine Shore and pounce on him, trying to tackle him to the ground. I was successful about half the time, especially when I used ropes to bind his ankles. But he was quick to adapt to every technique I came up with.

I'd taken my training to the extreme this past year. I'd even created wearable weights I could tether to my arms and leg when sparring with Harlon, pushing my body to its very limits, always with the soulless Flamebringer in mind.

I often thought of him, that cruel, sharp-edged face haunting me in my nightmares as deeply as when I was awake. It was an obsession that only intensified with time, never lessening. I would become the greatest warrior I could be, great enough to defeat him when I one day tracked him down. It would be my crowning glory, my moment of redemption, and if I was blessed with the luck of Delphinus, it would be in public too, so that all those who had doubted me before would revere my power.

It was a goal that drove me in every waking hour and every unconscious one too, my hatred ever-growing, mutating into a demon of its own. One that whispered wicked wants in my ear.

"Hello?" Harlon waved a hand in front of my face. "You've completely spaced out."

I blinked, coming out of my murderous reverie, my mouth lifting as I refocused on my friend, the one steady thing in my chaotic life.

"The ocean calls," I said, stepping past him and running for the door.

"Er, your ass is kinda out," Harlon called, and I came to a skidding halt, remembering the leather apron and undergarments combo I was sporting right now. I liked my clothes to be interesting, but this was bordering on a level of unusual even I couldn't accept. My cheeks flushed a little as I realised Harlon had a full view of a lot of bare skin.

I twisted around, a forced kind of laugh leaving me before I ran for my bedroom, slipping inside and pulling off the leather apron. I tossed on a feather-light dress that was palest yellow, little pink feathers I'd gathered from a raygull's nest dangling from the hem and tickling my legs. With a burst of excitement at the thought of meeting with the ocean again, I ran back into the living room, shoving past Harlon and flying out the front door.

I left my shoes behind, still miserably gathering dust since the last time I'd worn them. My feet kissed the warm cobblestone alleyway beyond the door, the alley sloping down steeply towards the sea. I could scent the ocean from here and hear the soft cry of gulls calling my name. *Ever, Ever, Ever.*

Harlon muscled past me so hard, he nearly knocked me on my ass, and then he was off, racing down the hill with a taunting laugh trailing back to me.

"Pishalé," I cursed him in the Cascalian tongue. *Asshole.*

With my gaze set on the sea that glinted between the narrow streets, I sprinted after him as he started a race he'd given himself a head-start in.

The warm wind rushed against my skin, and freedom filled my lungs as I inhaled the taste of the ocean. My truest home, a place I belonged which no one could take from me.

Our tiderunners awaited us in the makeshift shelter we'd built from palm leaves at Undashine Shore along with the two-piece costume I'd made for swimming. I'd used gold whelk leaves to give it a shimmer akin to sunshine and stitched a line of seashells along the hips in the shape of sea turtles.

I couldn't wait to slip out of my shift and walk into the waves, letting them welcome me into their arms. There was magic in those waves, as old as the moon and as ancient as the hill Castelorain was perched upon. And if there was anywhere that could sweep away my fears about today's journey to Never Keep and what lay waiting for me on that island in the north, it was the ocean in all her glamour and beauty.

As I made it to the end of the street, I looked left, my feet slowing as I took in the edge of the town where it had been sheered in half by the Skyforgers a year ago. The Raincarvers had started rebuilding, but this part of Castelorain still held an echo of that day. A house was carved right open, giving view into someone's personal space, a half-finished painting still sitting in its easel. Most haunting of all was that the painting showed a landscape that no longer existed in our town, the once familiar street now lost to the Skyforgers.

I ran on, my thrill in the race dampened by the sting of the past. So much had been taken from us that day. And as I veered away from that ragged piece of Castelorain, I saw my mother's face in my mind, her lips moving, forming the words that were burned into the recesses of my soul.

Never rest, Everest.

"Recite the plan," Harlon encouraged as we filed towards the ship that would take us to Never Keep, the weight of my pack a sturdy reminder of all my most prized possessions perched so simply upon my shoulders.

Harlon had told me that bringing the head of the beast I'd killed in the wilds was one step too far, but I had managed to fit all of my mother's weapons in the pack along with my clothes, my smithing tools and my sewing kit.

I'd swapped my yellow dress for fitted red britches with blue pockets in the shape of scallops and a tunic that matched, cut short to reveal my navel. It was a more comfortable outfit for travel, though it wouldn't keep me warm once we reached the northern seas. It would be a few days before that though. The trip would take ten days in total, our passage across the waters made simple by the gifts of the Awakened Fae of Cascada.

Which was why we held the greatest armada in the four nations. The other nations would take varying amounts of time to reach the northern waters where Never Keep was located. The Skyforgers would travel upon one of their sky islands, the journey perhaps five hours or so from the land of Stormfell by air, and while the Flamebringers were closest to our destination in the north, they held no power over the waters as we did so their journey across the seas would be slower, but the Stonebreakers would take the longest so would likely be underway already.

"Be a badass and downplay the dodgy hand." I saluted him, but he didn't smile at my joke.

"Ever, go through it properly," he growled. He'd opted for brown trousers and a white shirt for the occasion, his sword sheathed at his hip and his pack even smaller than mine.

I fought an eye roll at his tone, trying to deny the way my body reacted to it too. I was pretty sure the rebel in me got a kick out of defying his commands, but at some point in the past few years that kick had turned into a thrill laced with a sinful kind of heat.

I looked beyond the heads of the un-Awakened Fae who were queuing along the boardwalk towards the grand ship that was bobbing at the end of the dock, its white sails glinting in the morning sun. The sea serpent, Typhon, was carved into the prow, winding around it with its large, open jaw reaching from its end, sharp teeth poised as if to bite.

"I've got this," I promised. "I've spent the last year training for this day."

"Then why are you fidgeting like there's fire ants in your undergarments?"

"Maybe I stuffed a few in there for good luck," I said, trying to win that smile from him, but dammit he was grouchy today. And that was rare when it came to him. Harlon Brook could be chest deep in a river of shit and he'd still take a moment to enjoy the sunrise. He had a habit of tilting my chin up to see it too, so things must have been really bad if he was grilling me now.

"Do you doubt that I'll get accepted?" I asked my greatest fear.

My own doubts, I could handle. But his? They would be devasting.

His faith in me was often the foundation of *my* faith in me. Without him, I'd be alone in this wretched world which had been so very unwelcomingly to me.

"No," he said firmly. "But I know the importance of this day to you, I don't want you to just pass the test, Ever, I want you to crush it into oblivion. I want every Raincarver in our land to take note of you as I have. I want them to see your strength, I want them to stop dismissing you. Life's been a piece of shit to you, and I know it's not fair, but you're going to have to work ten times as hard as any

other Fae to earn your place, not just at Never Keep but in society."
He rounded on me, gripping my shoulder, and the flare of passion in
his eyes made me inhale sharply. "This is your path to greatness. The
world will rue the day it turned its back on you, and I'll be there to
cheer to the damn stars when it does. So don't just succeed, conquer."

"Harl," I sighed. "I fucking love you sometimes."

"What about the other times?" He dropped his hand from my
shoulder, smoothing it through his floppy brown hair. My gaze flicked
to a group of Fae who were glancing his way appreciatively. Some of
them offered me filthy looks, the fox hanging out with the hound not
to their taste apparently. But despite my father's public declaration of
my out-casting last year, Harlon had never turned his back on me. He
didn't step away when people looked too close, in fact, if anything,
he moved nearer.

The commander didn't like it, but Harlon was one of the most
promising warriors of our generation, and even my father couldn't
help but dote on him. I'd heard him refer to me as Harlon's pet more
than once, and it wasn't the worst thing he'd called me, even if it was
pretty fucking degrading.

"I'm semi-tolerant of you the rest of the time," I taunted, casually
ignoring the sneers people were offering me. Most of them ignored
me like I was nothing more than a foul scent on the wind, but a few
couldn't help but wrinkle their noses. It was surprisingly easy to
ignore them these days. I'd realised it was simpler to reject people
just as they rejected me.

My walls were high and impenetrable, the only one with access
the man standing before me now. But I did have a quiet fear that
continued to burrow into my brain in the quietest of moments. Once
Harlon was at Never Keep, he'd be bunking with other Fae, I might

not even share quarters with him at all. He'd find new friends, ones who didn't tar his name with a pariah's brush. How long would it be before he drifted from me, claiming the golden life of a celebrated warrior that he had always been fated to earn?

"Oh to be semi-tolerated," Harlon pretended to swoon, only drawing more attention to himself as he mock-fainted, knocking into a stocky man ahead of him.

The guy smiled when he realised who had stumbled into him, waving him off while Harlon clapped him on the shoulder and was drawn smoothly into conversation with the stranger. I watched him for a moment, fascinated by the casual interaction, wondering what that was like. To be so...accepted.

"My boy," Father's booming voice made me turn and my heart knotted as I spotted him marching through the crowd. The un-Awakened Fae scattered in deference of his position, making a path from him all the way to Ransom who was a few paces back in the line.

Father's hand clapped down on my half-brother's shoulder, offering Ransom a wide, prideful smile that made my stomach twist with jealousy. What it must have been like to be Ransom. A silver spoon stuffed in your ass at birth and your great destiny laid out before you, sprinkled with hand-picked roses and drops of fucking starlight.

"It is a joyous day indeed," Father boomed, so all could hear. "My latest prodigy heading off to Never Keep, following the footsteps of his decorated father and so many of his sisters and brothers. How many accolades will you come home with after your first season in battle, eh?"

"As many as I can possibly earn, Father," Ransom said, lifting his head, looking as smug as a rat in a larder.

"Here." The commander slammed a weighty pouch of coins

into Ransom's chest, and my half-brother grabbed it with a gasp of excitement. He peeked inside, the glint of gold lighting his brown eyes with a greedy hunger. "I'll send you a pouch of karmas every month that you continue to impress the Reapers at the Keep."

"I'll make you proud, Father," Ransom gushed, and the commander drew him into a fierce embrace.

"You already have, my boy, you already have," he said, leaving me with a bitter expression curling my lips.

"Forget them," Harlon said in a low voice, trying to turn me away from the sight, but my feet were rooted in place. For once, I had boots tethered to them, and I already missed the steady warmth of the earth, but mostly the kiss of the ocean.

Father's eyes snapped onto mine and my cheeks flushed hot at the scrutiny that blazed within them. I averted my gaze, looking anywhere else, but sensing his dominating form making a path my way.

He had spoken directly to me so rarely since his dismissal of me that I had no expectations of him doing so now. I waited for him to walk by, but his shadow fell over me and I could no longer pretend I was preoccupied with watching people board the ship.

I turned, my head tilting back to look up at his face, his towering form like a beast in human flesh, an echo of his Merrow Order form.

There was another bag of coins in his hand, smaller than Ransom's by far, but there they were, hanging from his fingers and tempting me to dream of their intended destination. Could he really mean to offer me such a gift? I hardly dared hope it, but my heart lifted with that possibility all the same. A pathetic want, I knew, but there it was, like a starved dog hunting for scraps from the very owner who had turned it out into the street.

"I have decided, after great consideration, to offer you a suitable endowment in the name of your mother's honour," he said tightly, clearly still no fan of mine, but this had to be a positive.

"That's generous of you," I said, throwing a glance at that tempting bag of karmas hanging from his scarred fist. I was going to Never Keep with a sum total of thirteen silver kismets to my name, all of them earned by fixing up the armour of the warriors home from war.

I'd spent the bulk of my earnings on food, then the rest on new materials for clothes, tools and metals for forging. I needed that gold more than I wanted to admit.

"I've trained hard for my position at Never Keep. I think…I hope I can make you proud, Father," I said. Ergh, I could hear it. The pathetic want in my voice, the neediness, the beggar in me who longed for this man's approval. She was a vain creature, always hunting for scraps of praise like a lowly wretch.

Commander Rake's lips twitched with some emotion I couldn't place, and I felt Harlon stepping closer at my back, the hairs prickling along my neck telling me that something wasn't quite right.

"Never Keep," he scoffed, looking me over with a hint of disgust sliding across his harsh features. "You will not place."

"But I-" I started in confusion, and his voice boomed out for all to hear.

"I have put in a good word for you with the Providers whose great honour and duty it is to offer up their wombs for the creation of the next generation of warriors, so that they might pair you with a man of great esteem. A man who has served this land for many a year. Quentinos Wavellion is-"

"What?" I gasped in horror, cutting over him. A circle began to form around us as people were drawn to our conversation, their eyes wheeling from me to the commander. "He must be at least twenty years older than *you*, his battles long won and that wound of his still festering. He's ancient, besides, I'm no Provider. I won't ever take that path."

"You will take the path that most fits you!" Father roared, taking no consideration for how much attention he was drawing. "Your womb may still bear good fruit, despite the spoiled vessel it's housed within."

Those words ricocheted around my skull, scraping against my mind like sharp nails. *Spoiled vessel.*

The crack in my soul widened, splintering and fragmenting a little more.

A manic kind of laughter rose in the back of my head, and suddenly my fist was snapping out, flying towards his crooked nose. Harlon caught my wrist half a second before I could land the blow, dragging me forcibly back a step.

I blinked out of the momentary madness that had taken me hostage, finding the commander's eyes widening with utter fury.

He snatched me from Harlon's arms, his hand fisting in my hair and his face twisting into a sneer.

"Strike at me, will you weakling?" he hissed in my ear, wrenching on my hair so hard that my toes almost left the ground.

"It was instinct," I blurted, my hands fisting as I weathered the pain in my scalp, not letting myself fight back against him. "I'm a warrior, see?"

"Insolent brat," he snarled, throwing me away from him so I hit the dirt at his feet, my pack clattering as the weapons inside it were jostled.

Father's eyebrows raised at the sound and he planted a kick to my side that sent me sprawling onto my front. He ripped the pack from my shoulders and I rolled over, staring up at him as he unbuckled it, tugging it wide and taking note of the contents.

"I have long waited to wield your mother's fine creations," he said, his tongue slicking over his lips and his brown eyes gleaming greedily.

"They're mine," I gasped as he wrenched two of her sheathed blades out of the pack along with the beautiful crossbow she'd made.

"Yours?" he spat, tossing the bag to the ground as he unsheathed one of the daggers, the blue metal practically singing as the sunlight hit it. The handle was etched with a coiling representation of Cascada's sea serpent, looking so real it wouldn't have surprised me if it had come to life and bit the hand that held it. "You are not entitled to anything that belongs to my Providers. You should be thankful I let you live in your mother's dwelling, but all of her worldly possessions passed to me the moment she died."

"You can't take them." I lunged from the ground, reaching for the blade in desperation, but that very knife came up to press to my throat, my father's threat starkly clear.

"Be thankful I do not cut out your tongue for your impertinence, runt. For your behaviour, you will make the journey to Never Keep below deck and in irons." He sheathed the blade, strapping each of his new weapons to his belt with links of magic-made ice, then stalked away through the crowd with the coin pouch still swinging from his fist.

I stared after him with my heart climbing into my throat, anger racing through every piece of me over the loss of those weapons.

Commander Rake made a path for the admirals who were directing people onboard, but before he made it to them, he slowed in front of Alina Seaman, smiling warmly at her. They shared a few words, then he pressed the coin pouch into her hands.

A wild kind of injustice filled me at the sight. She wasn't even related to him. She wasn't blood. She was just Ransom's little pack mutt.

Harlon lifted my bag, dusting it off and sliding it back onto my shoulders while I stared after my father. People were chattering about all the drama, sniggering at me and not caring that I noticed.

"Look at me again and I'll cut all of your noses off and feed them to a fucking dolphin," I snapped at a group of women who were giggling at my expense. The back of my neck was too warm and I didn't know if I wanted the ground to swallow me up or if I'd prefer to start swinging my blade at anyone who was laughing at me.

They shrank away as I drew the dagger that had been forged for vengeance, turning their backs on me. At least my father hadn't taken this weapon from me.

Harlon squeezed my arm, drawing my attention back to him.

"Breathe," he said.

"It's just – those are *my* blades – and that fucking coin purse, how dare he give it *her*? – and Quentinos!? Is he kidding me? – *Me*? A Provider? Is he insane?" I growled in rage, flicking my dagger from hand to hand and spinning it between my fingers, jabbing at the air intermittently. "I'll chop *Cunt*inos's dick off and shove it in his festering wound if he puts it anywhere near me."

"Breathe, Ever," Harlon repeated. "You're doing the muttering thing."

"I'm just so – *argh* – you know? He took those weapons to hurt me, I know it. And I have to be in chains now? Below deck! And what if – oh for the love of Scorpio, I'm not even going to get to see Never Keep from the ocean when we arrive. It's not fair, *he's* the one who riled me. Who wouldn't throw a punch after hearing an ancient wrinkle dick was being optioned for their womb?" I jabbed at the air again and Harlon let out a noise of anger.

I glanced up at him, finding a tense line on his brow. "That's not going to be your fate."

"Yeah," I agreed, sheathing my blade as I finally took his advice and breathed.

I turned my left hand over, eyeing the pale, scarred skin that contrasted with the deep brown hue of my natural tone. My mind fixed on what it signified, on what really mattered when it came down to it: killing the man with the black eyes who had stolen my mother from me.

Pisces would guide me to him. I'd earn a place at Never Keep. I had to. Because the alternative was simply not an option.

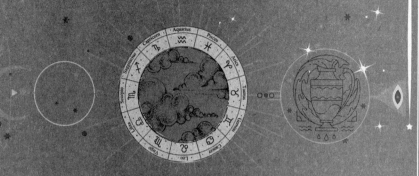

VESPER

CHAPTER TWELVE

My boots thumped heavily against the polished white tiles which lined the grand entrance hall filled with the esteemed company of the Wrathcourt. The sprawling palace of Wrathbane was where the air kingdom's royal family held their seat in the far north of The Waning Lands in the air ruled nation of Stormfell.

"Here we go again," Dalia muttered from her position a step behind me to my right.

"I'm getting a strong sense of déjà vu," Moraine agreed, rustling her silver wings in a way that I recognised as both a warning and a sign of her amusement.

"No one is forcing you to accompany me," I pointed out, tightening my grip on the grisly trophy which swung from my left fist, dripping blood across the floor.

"Bullshit," Dalia scoffed. "You're forcing us to accompany you through the simple fact that this scandal will be all anyone is speaking of for the rest of the month – we're hardly going to miss out on that."

The corner of my lips twitched, tugging at the swollen, aching slash which had been carved into my right cheek from temple to jaw. It would leave one hell of a scar when it healed, but I wasn't certain that was a bad thing – my face could do with a little less symmetry.

We were late which didn't bode well, and our blood-splattered, battle-worn appearance wasn't exactly out of character, but it wouldn't meet the expected dress code either. And on the first occasion when we had actually been intended as guests of honour too. Though, in all fairness, that was likely an exaggeration. The ball we were about to interrupt was being held to celebrate the most promising candidates of our birth year finally turning twenty-one and being sent off to complete six months of training at Never Keep where the secrets of our elemental magic would at last be revealed to us should we secure a place – which we would.

Almost all of those who had been offered an invitation to this event were aristocracy, regular members of the Wrathcourt and well used to these kinds of social events. The three of us had actually *earned* our invitations rather than just passing into this world via the appropriate womb which of course was the only way a Sinfair could ever hope to set foot among high society.

I supposed the king might regret that choice now. Then again – he might be thrilled. Honestly, it was difficult to judge, but I was almost certain Prince Dragor would approve and he was the one who owned my allegiance, and the one with the most power in the kingdom if everyone was being totally truthful with themselves.

The king was old and bored of war; he had long-since divvied out the rule of his land among his children and Dragor was the heir who had risen highest and claimed the most. Not that his brothers or sister were likely to admit to it.

Guards stood to attention on either side of the doors to the ballroom where the lilting sound of an orchestra playing a waltz rang out and at least a hundred people chattered and gossiped over glasses of wine which probably cost as much as a battleship. But who cared? Air kingdom was flush with wealth and rife with power, so of course they flaunted it whenever they could.

One of the guards opened his mouth, taking a step towards us as if he might protest three bloodstained heathens intruding upon this lively event while touting the head of an enemy like it was the latest fashion. Another guard slapped her hand to his chest, shoving him back into position by the door, lowering her head and hissing beneath her breath to remind him who we were.

"The Sky Witch answers to none but the royals," she breathed and again, a smile threatened to crack the jagged wound open on my cheek.

At first no one noticed us as we stalked into the opulent space, the ceiling opening up above us beyond the upper terraces where more courtiers tittered and looked out across the party.

The entire room was decorated in shades of white and gold – the colours of our nation – elaborately carved stone archways giving way to a wide, glass roof which domed overhead, allowing the stars to shine down on us.

The scales of Libra were carved into the stone above the glass doors which led to the outer balcony on the far side of the grand space and to my right, the face of Aquarius peered at me over his bucket of water as he poured it. The twin faces of Gemini observed from the stone to my left too, beautiful mirrors of one another, their wisdom on offer to all who sought it.

The royal table stood beneath the scales, raised on a dais to give the king and his children a view above the rest of the room. The dancefloor occupied much of the central space, swirling skirts of varying metallic colours swishing around the legs of the women who moved to the practiced steps and their partners who held them firmly.

In the spaces to the left and right of the dancefloor many round tables were taken up by aristocrats who discussed anything from the state of the war to the weather, to marriage arrangements and business deals. It was all so predictable – at least until they noticed us.

"For the love of Gemini," Cassandra Bluster snarled as her eyes fell on me, her golden skirt whirling around her legs as she jerked to a halt mid-dance. She was the picture of a Wrathcourt aristocrat, her golden hair coiled artfully in a design which likely took hours to perfect, her bronze skin unblemished and unmarked by war despite her being trained for combat – I guessed daddy knew a Reaper or two he could call in healing favours with. Her partner, who was one of the Effelbrand heirs – though I could never remember which – scrunched his nose up as his gaze fell to the severed head swinging from my fist.

"Trust in the Sky Witch to turn up bloody for every event," Cassandra scorned, looking to her preening friends and acting as though I couldn't hear her every word. "No doubt it's her barbarian blood – I've heard they roll in the dirt and fuck like beasts in Cascada. That's probably why they failed to plan her conception better-"

I stopped in my tracks, Dalia's sharp breath of excitement catching in my ear as I swung the severed head in Cassandra's direction, flicking blood over her and her companions then smiling darkly as a drop struck her directly in the mouth.

Ether rushed for me as I opened myself to the twisted power of it, the blood I'd spilled in claiming this head more than payment enough to offer me what I wanted.

Cassandra jerked violently as my connection to her blood formed and I took hold of her body, forcing her limbs to lock and her eyes to bulge with terror.

"What's wrong Cassandra?" Dalia purred, stepping around me and closing in on the terrified courtier. "Cat got your tongue?"

Cassandra's friends backed away, even the Effelbrand heir released her, none of them willing to intervene on her behalf.

My grasp on Cassandra's body let me feel every straining muscle, from her twitching fingers to her straining tongue as she fought to speak – no doubt to beg – and the rush of power had me fighting down a moan as it consumed me.

"More like a demon has a hold on it," Moraine laughed, reaching out to grasp Cassandra's chin, her dirty fingernails pressing into the courtier's skin as she forced her jaw to move. "I'm so sorry," she said in a simpering voice which was such a good likeness to Cassandra's that I broke a laugh and my hold on the blood magic shattered.

Cassandra wrenched herself away from Moraine's grip, causing my friend's nails to gouge lines in her skin as she threw herself back into the crowd of dancers.

She was babbling something inane which may well have been an apology, but I had no interest in whatever it was.

Prince Dragor had just gotten to his feet and the look of cold fury in his eyes made the smile fall swiftly from my face.

I jerked my chin towards him and silently led the others through the dancers who scattered to allow us to pass, the trail of dripping blood now weaving across the pale floorboards too.

The music never faltered and the swish of skirts told me the dancers continued to move across the floor behind us too. Nothing rattled a Skyforger after all. But I could feel the eyes of the crowd glued to me, their curious whispers adding a soft hiss to the ambiance which hadn't been there before our arrival.

Prince Dragor sat at the high table directly beside King Aquila in the position of honour at his right hand. Princess Laurina was positioned on the king's other side and the two remaining princes, Roarson and Evard had places set for them bookending the line-up, though they weren't currently present.

I moved to stand before the king, though my eyes met Dragor's and stayed there as I dropped to one knee, the connection only breaking when I bowed my head low in deference.

We remained as such while the swish of skirts and pulse of music continued to fill the air, the seconds ticking into a minute, then two.

Only the sound of Dragor's chair legs scraping across the tiles told me that the royal family remained before us. My knee began to ache where it was pressed to the cold floorboards, my fingers cramping where they were knotted in the hair of my kill but I didn't so much as lift my head, waiting on their command.

"Rise," King Aquila growled eventually and we did, my sisters in arms standing with me. "Out with it then."

I nodded to the king, my eyes tracing over his long white hair, which had been pulled back into a neat tail, the colour of it only a few shades lighter than his son's. His weathered face was fixed in a bored expression and the way he leaned back in his chair may have seemed casual on first glance, but I sensed a heavy exhaustion clinging to him. There had been whispers that the king was dying for years now, and despite the small clues which might signal a decline in his health, he remained with us, holding onto the throne through pure determination if nothing else.

Dragor had once told me that his father refused to die until he saw the war won, and though that had to have been a joke, sometimes I wondered if there was truth in it.

I stepped forward, reaching for the empty plate intended for Prince Evard and placing it between the king and Dragor before depositing the severed head on top of it facing the two of them.

"Do you expect me to recognise this mangled corpse?" the king grumbled, scowling at the head as though it offended him – not because he was disgusted by it but likely because it wasn't singing its own secrets and saving him the bother of having to listen to me.

"That," Dragor murmured in a dangerous tone. "Is my advisor, Tobias Stern." His pale blue eyes snapped to me, his jaw ticking. "Do you care to tell us why you have murdered one of the most powerful and influential members of our court? Tobias's family hold lands which stretch the length of the Valborn Plains and provide much needed food to fuel our army - not to mention the six towns within his province which send yearly recruits to bolster our-"

"Tobias was a drunk and a coward," I sneered dismissively, causing Princess Laurina to drop her fork with a clatter as I dared interrupt her brother's tirade, but I had been dancing this line with Dragor for long enough to know that he preferred a point to be made rather than pranced around. "He was a valuable asset because of his family holdings but he was greedy and sloppy – no doubt if he had spent more time in recent years keeping his training sharp, I wouldn't have managed to take his head from his shoulders."

"He hid from the fighting at Crathguard," Dalia added in a bored droll. "I saw him skulking behind the armoury while the rest of us dove into battle."

"He was also a traitor," I added as if it were an afterthought.

Dragor's eyes brightened and though his expression remained just shy of livid, I could have sworn he was entertained by this interaction.

"Proof?" the king demanded, spearing a potato with his fork and shoving it into his mouth.

"We were sent to Pyros to remove a player from the board," I said, uncertain how much the king even knew about the assignments his son gave me.

Memories of that dark and oppressive land pushed in on me, the stench of burning and soot staining the walls as we crept down dark alleyways and avoided the watchful eyes of the street thugs who ruled there. All of them were headed by the violent ruler known as The Matriarch. She was a brutal creature born of the ganglands, her cohort of sinners stoking a plague of death in her name, and all who crossed her found themselves meeting a bloody end.

We'd been disguised as Flamebringers of course and had moved among them without too much trouble, allowing us to locate the gated mansion where our target lived.

The husband had died quickly – he was no great warrior and I'd caught him by surprise right as I slipped in through a rear window, Dalia and Moraine remaining outside to guard the exit and make sure our retreat was clear. But the real effort had come when we navigated our way to the enemy General's office. She was an important piece of the Flamebringers' hierarchy and removing her would create an opportunity for our forces to press forward at my prince's command. Of course, I hadn't expected her to be meeting with a traitor.

"I found Tobias deep in conversation with the Flamebringers' war chief, General Kalfire, who I was there to assassinate. I draped myself in shadow and listened while he spilled secrets about our movements, telling her details about the next planned Ironwraith raid as well as giving information on the layout of the estate of Lord Darcoid who I assumed The Matriarch plans to strike against in one way or another."

"His lands are rich with coal," Prince Dragor murmured thoughtfully, but Princess Laurina slapped her hand down on the table, making her food bounce on her plate.

"Enough," she spat, looking at me like I was something she would dearly like to scrape from the base of her shoe. She was an imposing woman, her features sharp in every way from the crisp triangle of her nose to the razor slashes of her cheekbones and defined point of her chin. Her hair was a deep ebony which contrasted brutally with her pale skin – the only one of the king's children not to have inherited the pale blonde hair of their father. "I won't sit here and listen to these accusations from a dirt born creature of hellish reputation. You allow this beast too much leeway, Dragor. I appreciate the fact that her Order form makes her appealing, but if you want to fuck her then just do it in private – the rest of us shouldn't be subject to her violent tendencies and lack of decorum. If there is truth to these accusations-"

"I swear on the scales of Libra that every word I have spoken is the truth," I said, forcing myself to bow my head to her in deference despite the keen desire which rose in me to pounce across the table and see how uncouth she found my sword when it was plunged between her ribs.

"If what the Sky Witch says is true – and I remind you that doubting her word is akin to doubting my own judgement, sister," Dragor said in rough growl. "Then we need to act against these nefarious plans and make certain to send more forces to Lord Darcoid's estate in preparation of an attack. Not to mention changing our plans for the deployment of Ironwraith and likely several more of our upcoming strategies as Tobias was privy to many of them."

"Your judgement is in question either way, dear brother," Laurina purred. "Tobias was *your* advisor after all."

Silence fell as the two glared at one another and I almost didn't notice the king leaning forward to peer at me from between them, ignoring the volatile atmosphere as if it were as inconsequential as a summer breeze.

"You'll submit to a Cyclops reading?" he grunted, and it sounded like a question, though of course it was a command.

"I will." My vow was echoed by Dalia and Moraine but as they hadn't been present to overhear Tobias's treachery, the truth would be torn from my mind by the psychics, turned over and digested, picked apart in hunt of a lie. I didn't relish the prospect of the king's Truth Sayers rooting around inside my head, but I knew it was necessary. All five of the Cyclopses would take their turns slipping into my mind and memories, untangling my thoughts and motivations before making individual reports which would then be compared to ascertain the accuracy of them. But I had nothing to hide.

"Good. Enjoy the festivities first – it is your last night among us for a while," he said, waving me away dismissively as though I hadn't just exposed something so potentially catastrophic that it would change the course of the war itself. "Dragor, take care of whatever needs doing to stifle the impact of these claims for now. No doubt you will need to question the rest of your inner circle as well."

The prince got to his feet and stalked away without another word to me, the roiling cloud of his displeasure so thick that Fae scrambled to move aside for him as though they could feel the foul touch of it.

I bowed to the king once more, turning to leave but Laurina

flicked a finger, casting a whip of air to strike me in the face, splitting open the ruined skin there once more and causing blood to run freshly from the wound. I stilled but didn't flinch, looking directly at her and obediently awaiting whatever it was she had to say to me.

"You will clean yourselves up before indulging in the festivities," she snapped, her blue eyes flashing with contempt. "And if you spill so much as one more drop of blood on our floors, I'll have you scrubbing them clean yourself while the revellers step on you as they pass."

I nodded my understanding, tearing a chunk of fabric from the edge of the tablecloth before her and pressing it to my cheek to make certain I didn't make any more mess of her precious floors.

Dalia chuckled darkly as I led my two friends away, the burning pressure of the princess's ire never once lifting as she no doubt glared after us until we had left the ballroom behind once more.

"I guess we'll see you back here in…well I was going to say thirty minutes but I think it will take you closer to an hour to scrub the sin from your skin this time, V," Moraine chuckled, her dark eyes sweeping over me appraisingly.

"It's bone deep by now," I assured her. "But I can polish the exterior to hide it well enough."

"You can't hide it, asshole," Dalia snorted, turning away from me. "It's just that everyone else is too terrified of you to point it out."

I smirked after their retreating forms as they headed for the palace gates so that they could return to their rooms in the city barracks, letting my hand fall from my cheek, the balled-up fabric of the tablecloth now stained red with my blood.

I started walking in the opposite direction, heading deeper into the palace grounds towards the apartment Prince Dragor had given me to make use of here, away from the barracks. He had claimed the special living arrangements were in part to reward me for my accolades in war and in part to save the other recruits from the torture of my nearness – keeping them from the temptation caused by my Order form. I had never quite decided if I should feel honoured by the gift or insulted. Was it truly a reward or just a way for him to keep a closer eye on me?

Contemplating the prince's trust in me - or potential lack of - was never a particularly enjoyable state of mind and I scowled at the darkened corridor ahead of me as I started along it. Wide archways stood open every twenty feet or so, allowing patches of glimmering starlight into the space along with the frigid polar wind which was so common at this time of year, whispering tidings of turning leaves and snow to come before long.

I rounded the farthest reach of the walkway and turned towards the guarded doors which led into the east wing – Prince Dragor's quarters. Though as his wing was made up of over two thousand rooms, many of them dedicated to housing his staff and most celebrated warriors, it wasn't as though I was actually living in his personal space.

Once again, the guards let me pass without hesitation, though there was a new recruit on duty who took a double take as I drew nearer then fell to his knees, throwing himself into my path and prostrating himself on the stone floor.

"My Lady, please allow me to assist you with your wounds," he begged. "I will do anything I can to aid you. Let me wash your linens, massage your feet, compose a poem about the way you smell of death and-"

One of the other guards kicked him to silence his babbling and I paused, arching a brow.

"I smell of death?" I questioned in a low voice.

"Forgive Reg, your...erm...Sky Witchness," a guard said, looking at me, then away, then at me again like he didn't know which was the least likely to raise my ire. "He was warned about your beauty and allure but it is quite something else to behold, the startling wonder of your features and the way your eyes sparkle brighter than all the stars in the-"

"Enough," I grunted, knocking him back and placing a foot on Reg's spine as I stepped over him, causing him to groan in an overtly sexual manner.

I continued past them without another word, upping my pace in case they were tempted to follow. My gifts had done this before – flaring more powerfully than usual when I was injured, encouraging those who laid eyes on me to offer all kinds of desperate pleas to assist me.

I kept my eyes firmly ahead as I crossed through decorative courtyards and grand halls meant for entertaining, each space hung with lavish paintings and detailed mosaics either depicting the stars, representations of the three zodiac symbols which were born to air magic, or the violent acts of war which were committed by our most prolific historical monarchs and their best warriors.

My apartment was located on the ground floor to the far east of the sprawling palace and by the time I made it within the confines of the heavy wooden door and locked it, I was so tired that I wished for nothing more than to lay down in my bed and sleep.

However, the prince's intentions for me were clear the moment I looked around at my rooms. A fire had been lit in the hearth, a copper tub filled with heated water set before it and draped over my bed, a silver embroidered dress had been laid out for me.

I tossed the blood-soaked cloth into the flames, knowing only too well how easily blood magic could be used against me should someone else get their hands on it.

The ball was well underway and time was short, so I leaned my sword against the copper tub within easy reach then removed the rest of my weapons and stripped out of my battle leathers in well-rehearsed movements.

I glanced down at myself, taking stock of the vivid blue and green bruise across my ribs, pleased to see it was improving at last. Ink coiled through the bruised skin, a pattern of twisting clouds filled with hidden runes and words of prophecy in the language of the stars. Words of power and strength, protection and fortune. I'd worked my blood magic into the decoration on my flesh and though very few Fae ever saw the ink which spanned my back and crept around my ribs, I couldn't help but think of it as the most honest pieces of me. My Order meant that everything about me from my face to the curves of my body had been designed to seduce and command desire, but those swirling lines of scripture mixed with the representation of the power of air spoke more truthfully about who I really was.

I groaned as I sank into the water, letting myself drop right beneath the surface. Blood from the wound on my face tainted the liquid surrounding me, the cut stinging in protest but I ignored it, needing the grit from our travels to wash free of it if I wanted to avoid infection.

I counted to fifty before I let myself scream, all of the frustration, anger, shock and grief which surrounded me daily pouring free in my tiny underwater haven. It was a ritual I couldn't even remember starting. I simply shoved every scrap of feeling, every hint of humanity deep down inside me day after day after day and then when I was alone, beneath the surface of the water, I gave it that one point of release. I let myself picture the faces of the Fae I'd killed in my most recent battles. I let myself acknowledge the tremble in my limbs where the blood magic I'd used had carved a price from my soul. I heard every veiled or outright insult, every slander against my blood, every muttered insinuation that I had earned my position on my back instead of on the battlefield thanks to my Order. All of it rushed out of me as I screamed until I was void of breath and was forced to emerge above the surface once again.

Panting, I grabbed a washcloth and made quick work of scrubbing the grime from my skin then took the bar of fragrant soap intended for my hair and worked to clean that too.

I was out of the water and stepping into the dress within minutes.

The garment was stunning; clearly intended for someone of far greater birth than me and I swallowed against the sense of gratitude which rose in me, reminding myself that this wasn't some petty gift – I had earned it.

The style was the latest design, a pale white coated in silver embroidery, the fitted bodice and billowing sleeves traditional enough but the skirt cut just below the knee, the voluminous fabric encouraging it to twirl around the legs, revealing more skin and clearly made for dancing. It was a perfect fit of course, clinging to my curves and cinching tight around my waist, though I couldn't reach the ties to secure it at the back.

"I thought it would be more lavish." A rough voice had me whirling for the door, a dagger snatched into my grasp as I bared my teeth at the unwelcome guest.

"How did you get in here?" I demanded as I took in Cayde leaning against my doorframe, his features cast in shadow by the flickering light of my fire. He hadn't actually crossed the threshold but he had opened my door without knocking. A door I was certain I had locked behind me.

"Believe me, I have no interest in coming to your room," he drawled, glancing around at the bare space, the only décor my collection of weaponry which hung against the far wall.

"And yet you're here." I turned the dagger in my grasp, pinching the end of the blade between my thumb and forefinger.

"I was tasked with bringing you this." He raised a small jar with a waxy-looking poultice inside it, shaking it at me in explanation.

My cut cheek tingled as if in recognition, fresh blood slowly dribbling from the wound and I was forced to slash my hand across my chin to stop it from falling onto my dress.

"You aren't housed within the east wing," I said firmly because I knew I would have noticed his arrogant swagger strutting about the place if he was.

"And you are fond of pointing out obvious facts. Are you going to take this from me or will I be required to stand here all evening?" Cayde glanced away as if desperate for something else to claim his precious attention, his profile offering me the opportunity to study his chiselled features for a moment without him studying me in turn.

There wasn't any motive that I could think of which might have drawn him here beyond delivering the poultice, but I had good reason to mistrust him.

In the year since I had been unfortunate enough to make his acquaintance, Cayde Avior had become the most infuriating thorn in my side. He was one of us – the Sinfair whose shame clung to us like a second skin, though luckily for him he wasn't born of weak blood like me. No, from what I had gathered by asking about him – purely because he was in my way so fucking frequently – first his mother had lost an entire legion to a raid on the earth lands of Avanis. Then his father and older brother had gone seeking revenge, taking five thousand Skyforgers without permission from those in a position of true power, leading them all into a trap which had ended every last one of them.

Before then, nothing much seemed to have been known about the younger Avior brother, and when the Stonebreakers had attacked his home and killed every soul in sight, his survival had seemed something of a miracle - though all he had really done was Emerge at the opportune moment and use his newfound Drake form to fly for sanctuary. The royal family needed someone to punish for the failings of his family and as the sole surviving member, Cayde had appeared from within the woodwork and been named a Sinfair like me.

Clearly, he had decided that becoming the most celebrated Sinfair of our army would win back his favour with the royals. But there was already someone who had claimed that position. Me. And I'd be damned if I'd let him take my place.

"Give it to me then," I demanded, holding my free hand out for the poultice but Cayde only arched a brow as he looked back at me.

"No thanks? No please?" he questioned, lowering his hand and dropping the jar into the pocket of his brocade suit.

I hated to admit it, but the thing looked good on him. He had precisely what I lacked – aristocratic blood. And where I felt out of place in the dress the prince had gifted me, Cayde looked just as at home in the deeply embellished blue suit with its golden stitchwork as he did drenched in the blood of his enemies and clad in battle leathers. Just another thing to hate about him.

"If the prince sent you then you have your orders. So stop dicking about and hand it over," I growled in a voice which made most people shit their trousers, but not him. Of course not him.

Cayde scoffed lightly, turning to leave as if he didn't give a damn about following orders or not. I hurled my dagger, catching the sleeve of his suit and pinning it to the doorframe, forcing him to a halt.

"Your aim is either impeccable or terrible," he commented, reaching for the dagger while I gave up any pretence of patience and stalked towards him, my teeth bared.

"You know which," I hissed, shoving him against the doorframe and pinning him there with my forearm against his chest.

Cayde's lips twitched with amusement - like I wasn't the deadliest creature in this place - and I snatched the jar of healing poultice from his pocket.

I shoved away from him, causing the dagger to tear the fabric of his suit further and taking a grim satisfaction in that small victory as I moved back into my room.

"Your dress is open at the back," he commented.

"Well don't go thinking this is some cliched bullshit where I ask you to fasten it for me. If I wanted your hands on my body, I could achieve it in a far less convoluted way." I dropped into the chair before my desk, unscrewing the lid and sticking my fingers into the jar.

The poultice smelled of honey and lavender, the other herbs mixed within it creating a fresh undertone and even inhaling the scent of it made my aching body feel better.

True healing magic was the closely held secret of the Reapers who only offered out their abilities when they were petitioned to do so and felt moved to oblige, but there were potions, spells and poultices such as this one which helped with most wounds.

I took a dagger which I'd been using to mark my place in a book and angled it in the light so I could see my reflection, albeit a warped version of it, then carefully applied the poultice to my wound.

"You have a lot of scars," Cayde commented from his position by the door and I turned to glare at him, finding him toying with the dagger which he had now pulled free of his jacket.

"I've fought in a lot of battles," I deadpanned. "Why are you still here?"

"I was referring to those caused by lashes," he pushed, his tone darkening as if my inability to follow all of the rules laid out before me was somehow infuriating to him.

"I'm sure you are aware of my bloodline," I ground out. "So it should be no surprise to you that I come under scrutiny far more often than someone as used to privilege as yourself."

"You seriously think I'm privileged?" Cayde growled, that infuriating calm finally cracking.

I got to my feet, stalking back over to him and gripping the door in preparation to fling it closed in his face.

"I was raised in a waifhouse, told from the moment I was placed there that I was not worthy of my star sign, that my blood would out and prove my weakness time and again. I have been looked at with scorn and disgust every single day of my wretched, wicked life and everyone surrounding me was simply waiting for me to fail. In fact, they *wanted* me to fail. I have fought for everything I have, from the food in my belly when I was four years old and they told us that there would only be enough for the strongest to eat, to the right to even offer myself as a candidate for battle training. Which, by the way, I earned by brawling with boys twice my size when I was eight years old and winning. Every time I prove myself worthy of note, the bar is raised higher, making me reach for it once again. But you, poor, self-pitying heir to a line of fucking fools who brought shame down on their family and left you to shoulder the weight of it, only have to prove yourself less foolish than your parents and the world will once again bow to the whims of your airborne bloodline and you will return to the place of privilege and entitlement which was squandered by your dumb fucking fami-"

Cayde moved so fast that I almost didn't get my guard up in time, my forearm striking his and knocking the dagger from his grasp before it could make contact with my side. But I should have seen it for the distraction it was. His other hand made it beneath my guard, wrapping tight around my throat as he whirled me around and slammed me into the door, pinning me in place and snarling right in my face. A jolt of pure exhilaration sparked through my veins as the beast in him rose up and lunged for me. This was what I fucking lived for.

"That's enough," he hissed, but if he thought I was done just because he was choking me then he really hadn't been paying attention in all the time he'd spent trying to steal my crown.

My foot snaked around his and I had him on the floor in the next heartbeat, the two of us scrambling for the upper hand, rolling across the pale tiles.

We struck the edge of my bed and jarred to a halt, his weight bearing down on me, his hand still locked around my throat.

"I should snap your neck," he snarled, and I laughed because he thought he had me beat, the poor little Sky Witch trapped beneath the big bastard with the eyes of sin.

I threw a solid punch to his kidney, forcing him to curse, his grip slackening just enough and my forehead collided with the bridge of his nose, the loud crack confirming the break.

Cayde didn't slacken his hold again, his fingers digging in, cutting off my air supply as his weight pressed down between my thighs, his blood dripping onto my face.

My heart was galloping in my chest, my eyes pinned on his and suddenly the tension between us felt so much more potent, like a promise of something far more decadent than death.

"What precisely am I interrupting?" the cold voice fell over us from somewhere beyond Cayde's bulk, but I didn't need to see him to know precisely who stood looking at us now.

Cayde's weight was pinning me to the floor, his hips between my thighs, my skirt bunched up and bodice slipping from one shoulder where it hadn't been tied in place. No doubt this looked far more compromising than it was and a cold dread rushed through me at the thought of the prince seeing me like this.

I shoved Cayde back and he submitted, getting to his feet and pinching the bridge of his nose to stop the bleeding, a soft crack sounding as he realigned the bone I'd broken.

I scrambled upright, hoisting the sleeve of my dress back over my shoulder and looking to Prince Dragor, keeping my chin high despite the pure venom which glinted in his ice blue eyes.

"It was a poor choice of venue for a spar, your highness," Cayde grunted, not bothering to wipe the blood from his face and I had to admit that he looked even better than usual when he was bloody from battle. Though perhaps that was just the thrill of me knowing I'd broken his nose.

Dragor didn't even look at him, his eyes fixed firmly on me, trailing to my throat where I no doubt had Cayde's handprint lining my skin, then taking in my unfastened dress. I knew better than to speak.

"The ball awaits, lieutenant," Dragor said softly, dismissing Cayde with a flick of his fingers and I couldn't help but look to the asshole as he bowed his head obediently then left the room. His gaze struck mine for a single moment as he exited, and I braced myself for the fresh wave of hatred before it even hit. His fury was like an anvil to my chest, but there was more to the dark look he offered me in parting, a silent promise that this wasn't in any way close to done.

Good. I wasn't done with him either.

The door snapped shut as Dragor stepped over the threshold and I jerked my focus back to my prince as the air was filled with the wild tempest which was his presence.

"They say that to fuck a succubus is to ruin yourself for all other lovers," he said, stepping towards me and making me blink at the topic he had landed on. "Do you think there is truth to that, my little Sky Witch? Do your lovers trail after you in desperation, begging for another taste of your sweet poison?"

He took hold of my chin and I frowned at him. "I don't get much time for lovers," I replied dismissively while his eyes hunted mine for a lie.

It was the truth. Though I couldn't pretend I hadn't taken anyone to my bed. Usually when the need arose in me, I simply found myself a hall of sin and took pleasure from the unknown bodies who sought it within. Memories of broken kisses trailing my flesh, of mouths and hands exploring my skin, of writhing bodies and wanton moans rushed through me. I had even used the full force of my Order gifts in those places a few times, allowing myself the freedom to come undone in the darkness where all of my most debauched desires were celebrated and explored.

"War takes its toll on all of us," Dragor said. "But it is no reason to deny your flesh the reward of pleasure when it is offered."

I looked between his icy eyes, my heart pounding both from the collision with Cayde and the danger which coiled in the room surrounding this beast of a man before me. I should have been cowering at the look in his eyes and yet this fear, this terror was what I lived for.

I took a step forward while most would have stepped back.

Dragor arched a brow at me and I stepped closer again.

"You have caused me many issues this night," he growled, his posture rigid as I moved so close to him that I was inhaling his air, the sweet thrill of danger rolling off of him.

"I did what I was asked and rooted out a traitor for good measure," I replied resolutely, because if I was going to be punished for something then I wanted to be certain my worth was understood.

"Tobias was my friend since childhood," he ground out.

"Perhaps you should keep his head in a jar in your office then. That way you won't miss him so dearly," I suggested, my muscles tensing for the blow I knew would follow, my reckless tongue always urging me towards danger instead of saving me from it. But I stood by what I'd done. I had even attempted to take Tobias alive and got my face split open for it as thanks.

Dragor scowled for a drawn out moment then barked a laugh, causing me to blink in surprise.

He shook his head, turning from me and moving to look out of the small window which stood above my desk. As my apartment was on the ground floor and at the farthest end of the eastern wing, the view beyond it showed only a small walkway followed by the outer wall of the palace.

"Come here. Tell me what you see." Dragor didn't turn to check whether I was obeying the command because of course I was.

I stepped close to him and looked out at the dim view, a shrug lifting my shoulder.

"A wall."

"Yes. A wall which surrounds this place. A wall which I want you to take with you to Never Keep. One I expect you to maintain surrounding yourself at all times. Whenever you think to release some of the tension of battle, whenever you imagine you need an outlet, you shall remember this wall and remind yourself that you alone stand within it."

"I don't-" I began but Dragor's hand clasped the back of my neck and he shoved me down over the desk, my hands flying out to brace myself against it as my pulse leapt in alarm. I knew every move I needed to free myself from the position, but he was my prince. I couldn't strike him.

"You have worked very hard to get my attention for the last five years," Dragor growled, leaning down over me so he could speak in my ear. "And now, at last, you have it."

Seven years, but I supposed I'd failed during the first two if he only counted five.

My lips parted but I didn't know what I was supposed to say to that and the silence pressed down on me while he waited on my response.

"I...I'm only aiming to please you, Dragor-"

He yanked me back upright, his hand remaining locked to the back of my head as he jerked me around and pulled me against the solid planes of his battle-hardened body.

My breaths came faster, my fingers curling at my side with the knowledge that I would have drawn a dagger on anybody else who tried to hold me captive like this.

"Tell me who you serve," he breathed.

"You," I answered instantly.

"Not the king?" he pushed.

"You," I affirmed.

"Not the great kingdom of air, Stormfell herself?"

"I'm yours," I swore because for so long now I had known that to be the truth. I had pledged myself to this beast and given up so much of my humanity in the pursuit of pleasing and impressing him and finally finding my own place in this ravaged world. No one was ever going to offer me a position of power, but I had sworn to carve one out for myself and I had chosen a place at the side of this heathen to claim it.

Dragor almost smiled, his hand falling from the back of my head and skimming down my spine where the unfastened dress left my skin exposed.

My chest rose and fell heavily, the dress threatening to slip and expose my body to him as his fingers pushed lightly at the open back.

My gaze fell to his mouth, that wicked slash across his strong jaw and I let myself imagine what he might taste like as he stepped against me, turning us slightly so that the backs of my thighs pressed to the wooden desk.

This was dangerous. In all the ways Moraine and Dalia warned me that vying for the attention of the prince was dangerous and even more so than that because this was a line we had never crossed before. I'd thought him immune to my allure when we had first met, his attention slipping over and beyond me like I was no different to any other warrior in his army. I had looked at him with his power and his title and I had seen my chance to prove myself, but he hadn't seen me at all.

Even after I had gained his attention by winning my way through countless battles in his name and earning the whispered reputation that had first seen me called the Sky Witch, he had never once looked at me the way most men did.

But I had looked at him. I had seen the power which clung to him, the respect that all those surrounding him offered up so easily, the loyalty he inspired through word and action alike. And now, at last, I felt as though he were seeing me too.

Through either bravery or madness, I reached out to touch his face, my fingertips tracing the line of his powerful jaw as I kept my eyes pinned on his mouth, afraid to meet his gaze in case I'd read this wrong.

"Careful, little witch," Dragor growled, stepping forward so that his knee pressed between my thighs, and I was forced back onto the edge of the desk, almost perching on the thing. "If you follow this path you'll become my creature entirely, bound to me in every way. I won't relinquish you once I've had you, so be certain you know what it is you're claiming because once you've fallen for the sin of me there will be no repenting, no undoing it. If it is true that you will ruin me for all others then you will take on the full weight of that. You will be mine in every sense. So tell me. Is that what you want?"

I lifted my gaze to his at last and for the first time I found the ice in them heated, his expression unchecked, his control slipping.

The only thing I had ever wanted was to belong and his offer sounded a lot like that. Would I become his creature? Wasn't I that already? All things considered, belonging to the prince of air didn't seem like such a very hard choice to make, even if he did terrify me as surely as he haunted my desires.

"Yes," I breathed, condemning my soul with that one little word.

His mouth met mine with such force that I was driven right back onto the desk, my thighs parting to make way for him to step between them, his tongue sinking between my lips in a brutal claim that had me undone.

My fingers found the lapels of his jacket, curling into fists around them as I pulled him closer, sinking into the sinful taste of his kiss and moaning into his mouth. He was everywhere, this force of nature taking hold of me, capturing me and binding me in the cage of his solid arms as he laid his claim right down to the marrow of my bones.

My dress slipped from my shoulder, freeing my breast so that my hardened nipple grazed roughly against the golden brocade of his suit.

His mouth devoured mine, his hand moving beneath my skirt, skimming the inside of my thigh before pushing my undergarments aside so that he could feel my wetness.

Dragor growled his desire, biting down on my bottom lip and sinking two fingers into the tightness of my cunt. I arched against him, moaning loudly, my spine tipping back, my fists tight around his lapels as he drove his fingers in and out of me, his thumb finding my clit and making me cry out louder.

He kissed me harder and I fell prey to the sin of his fingers inside me, the utter devastation of his touch, the taste of his tongue invading my mouth.

I rolled my hips against the movement of his hand, my body tensing, my grip on his jacket so tight I could feel the stitches straining in protest.

Dragor's mouth fell to my neck, his teeth grazing my skin and drawing a ragged gasp of his name from my lips as he worked his way lower.

My open dress gave him access to my breast, his tongue rolling over my nipple before his teeth sank into the soft skin and I gasped at the rough worship, my gifts flaring as my body gave way to his commands.

His desire surrounded me, the force of it writhing through my veins and making my heart race with all the secret fantasies I had indulged in about this man who was power itself.

His fingers drove into me with more force, his thumb riding my clit in the most delicious way which had my toes curling and body thrumming with pleasure.

I tugged on his lapels hard enough to pull his eyes back to mine, the light in them flaring as he pushed his fingers in deeper, watching me fall apart beneath him.

I claimed his lips again, his kiss hard and unforgiving, demanding my surrender and though it went against every part of my nature to do such a thing, his want for it and my want for him had me giving in.

Prince Dragor had been my obsession for so long it seemed that my need for his eyes on me was as intrinsic to my survival as my need for air to breathe. The rush of holding him captive with my lips, of having his hands on my body after craving him for so long had me intoxicated.

I could feel the hard length of his cock driving against my inner thigh, the size of it making my pulse riot, the longing to feel every inch of him consuming me.

The force of his desire made my head spin, his want for my flesh, his rampant lust, the carnal need all filling the air around us as my gifts opened me up to the power of them. But there was a need even greater than all the rest, a ravenous desire for control in all things, for possession and dominion and right now, he was testing the control he wielded over me.

His fingers brought me to the edge of ruin, pumping in and out, his thumb rasping against my clit with every thrust of his wrist, my world narrowing to the feeling of his fingers inside me as oblivion rushed closer and my moans filled the air.

Dragor broke our kiss, leaning back to look at me as he brought me to the point of ecstasy beneath him, his cold eyes roaming over me like I was something to devour.

"It's the power that gets you off, isn't it?" he purred, watching me writhe beneath him, his hand an expert in sin, taking complete hold of my body. "I've watched you for a long time. I've seen the way you light up when you outshine your counterparts, when you prove your mettle, when you *kill*. I've seen the way your blood sings for violence, and I knew you'd be wet from the moment I found you pinned beneath that brute when I arrived in this room."

I sucked in a sharp breath, my head lifting, lips parting on some protest or defiance but he drove his fingers into me again, curling them within me while pressing down on my clit and forcing a climax from me that had me crying out instead as pleasure rushed through my body in a wave of rapturous bliss.

Dragor tugged his fingers out of me, clasping my face in his hand and pressing that same thumb which had just driven me into oblivion down on the ragged wound which marked my cheek.

He leaned in, close enough to kiss me again, but the words which brushed my lips were no sweet caress.

"I'll have you perfect or not at all," he growled, his eyes moving to the wound as I bit down on my cheek to halt any sound of pain which might have threatened to escape me as he continued to press against it. "The Reapers will fix this. Now get up and make yourself presentable for the ball. You have one night left to prove you are more than a simple savage to the people of the Wrathcourt before you head to Never Keep. I expect a creature of mine to present herself properly. Do you understand?"

"Yes," I bit out, though the agony in my face made it hard to even take in the words but I couldn't help the flare of indignation which rose on Moraine's behalf – she had suffered through months of slow recovery with her broken wing while the prince refused to ask the Reapers to assist her with magical healing. Yet now he intended to get them to squander their gifts for the inconvenience of a scar on my face?

He released me and stepped away, leaving me to right my dress as he straightened his own suit then strode from my apartment without another word.

I swallowed against the lump which had risen in my throat and counted to one hundred as I bent my arms at an awkward angle and forced the dress to fasten at my spine. With each number I passed, I locked away a little bit more of the ragged creature who had just offered herself up to a monster to devour. I knew better than to have let my guard slip like that. I knew better and I'd done it anyway. For a moment, when I'd been in his arms I'd been-

I shut that thought down as I reached one hundred, smoothed out the rumpled skirt of my dress, carefully applied more of the poultice to my cheek then raised my chin and swept from the room.

I was the Sky Witch. I did not bend and I certainly did not break. If Prince Dragor demanded perfection, then he would get it. First at the ball and then at Never Keep. Tomorrow, I would set out to unleash my air magic at last, and when I finally claimed that final piece of my power, I would be certain to wield it well enough to win back his fickle favour.

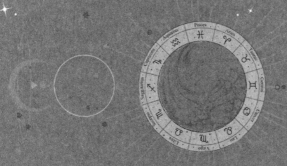

EVEREST

CHAPTER THIRTEEN

I slammed into the boardwalk on my back, the breath shoved out of my lungs from the force of the impact, gazing up at the motherfucker of an admiral who had tossed me over the side of the docked ship.

"Pishalé," I wheezed at him. *Asshole.*

My upper half was bound in thick chains, my arms unable to move, my fingers flexing towards the padlock, but I couldn't reach it. Pain echoed down my spine and I cursed as a chorus of raucous laughter carried to me from the onlooking admirals.

"Hey!" Harlon barked from up on deck and the sound of an argument broke out.

The air was frigid here, this small, rocky island off the coast of Never Keep a sacred place where all magical Awakenings in the four lands were held. We were in the polar circle, the air frosty and what little I could see of the landscape was barren, made up of black volcanic rock with deep green moss clinging to it in swathes.

I couldn't see much of the surrounding island beyond the iron grey walls of the fortress from this position, and I hadn't been allowed to come up on deck to see it from the ship. Those pieces of shit had followed my father's orders to a T, and apparently it wasn't over because they hadn't spared me the thought of a key to unlock the heavy padlock hanging from my chains.

An admiral cried out in fright then came crashing down beside me on the boardwalk. One look up showed me Harlon leaning over the side of the ship, gazing down at me with wayward hair and a protective look in his eyes.

"Give me the key," I demanded, lunging at the fallen admiral, managing to get onto my knees and biting his hand like a rabid animal.

"Ah!" he wailed. "She fucking bit me. Here – take it, you psycho." He tossed the key at me and it went pinging across the decking, tinkling its way along, the sound like the mocking laughter of a fucking pixie as it dropped away between one of the gaps in the boards.

"No," I gasped, lunging after it, but it was far too late, the sound of the key hitting the water with a parting splash.

"Fetch it, drip," the admiral said, shoving to his feet and flicking a finger. A torrent of water shot from his hand, slamming into me and sending me flying over the edge between the boardwalk and the ship. I splashed into the freezing abyss with a cry stifled by the icy sea as it claimed me and the weight of the chains dragged me under.

The water was clear and I could see the hulking ship rising up beside me, bobbing precariously and causing a current that forced me deeper. My back hit the rocky seabed and I thrashed against the chains, kicking to try and swim back to the surface.

My pulse climbed when I didn't rise so much as a foot, and I reminded myself not to panic. No good ever came from panicking. The legend of Quazin the Wavewanderer was testament to that after his ship had been punched full of holes by the Stonebreakers upon a stormy sea. In a frenzy, he had been so focused on weaving the water away from the holes in his ship that he not been prepared to defend himself when the Stonebreakers had stormed his ship and cut his head from his shoulders. The moral of that story had been hammered into us in combat training, *"A hole in a ship is less deadly than the swinging blade of your enemy."*

The tale was intended to force our minds to calculate the risks of a situation, to notice which forms death was taking and pay attention to the one that loomed the closest. Drowning wasn't my greatest threat yet, these chains were.

I twisted on the rocky bed, hunting the sea floor and finding a couple of fish eyeing me irritably like I was disturbing their tranquil little slice of ocean. A stream of bubbles slipped from my lips as I noticed a flash of silver beneath them, rolling towards it and snaring the key between my teeth. Which was about as much good to me as gripping it between my ass cheeks, but here we were.

A shadow cascaded down from above and Harlon's furious face came into view within the gloom. I jerked my chin up, showing him the key, my lungs starting to make it clear they would be far happier above the surface now.

Harlon swam powerfully down to me, taking the key from my lips and driving it into the padlock. Within seconds, he had the chains torn from my body and I swam fast for the surface while he rose with me.

My head breached the water and I gulped down a lungful of freezing air, more laughter sounding from the admirals on the ship. I heaved myself up onto the boardwalk and Harlon dragged himself out too, taking my hand and helping me to my feet. I immediately tugged my hand out of his, looking to the admirals with a glare, not wanting them to see me as some distressed damsel who needed rescuing. The one who'd tossed my key was now back on deck, casually twisting my beautifully crafted blade in his hand, his blue eyes glittering at it as if he had already decided it was his.

"You'd better move fast," Harlon said in a low voice, swiping a hand through his hair to wring the water from it. His pack was sitting on the boards, but mine was still nowhere to be seen, and I knew exactly where to find it.

"I'll be five minutes," I said quietly, glancing back at Helle Fort as more and more Fae from Cascada poured off of ships in the port. We weren't the only ones here either. The hulking mass of an island peeked from the clouds above, telling of the Skyforgers, and not all of these ships belonged to Cascada. There were more far out in the water too, un-Awakened Fae arriving in their droves from all four lands, travelling to this neutral territory for the age-old tradition of our kind, set in place by the Reapers long ago.

All four lands respected and revered the Reapers, following their teachings of the stars. Helle Fort was sacred just as Never Keep was, and bloodshed between the four warring nations was forbidden here, punishable by execution at the Reapers' hands. It wasn't just the threat of that fate that stayed the blades of our enemies and ours alike, this was proclaimed by the will of the stars, spoken to the Reapers directly from the source of our creators. Among their ranks were Seers, those who possessed The Sight, a hallowed gift that gave these honoured Fae glimpses of the future and helped the Reapers guide us all in leading lives of worth and honour.

If any Fae here today held such a gift, they would be taken into the fold of the Reapers to claim a venerable and highly envied position among them. That wasn't the only path into their ranks though, for Fae who were Awakened with more than one magical element would be taken by them too, hailed as an acolyte – a Reaper in training. Our star signs may have been linked to the elements of our lands, assuring that we would Awaken with the elements of our homelands, but sometimes the stars selected Fae for such a destiny, gifting a Raincarver with water and air, or a Flamebringer with fire and earth and so forth. I imagined what my father would think if I happened to be gifted in that way, and the thought of his simpering appraisal had my pulse elevating with the possibility, but then I realised that would mean me giving up my dream of being a warrior and I balked against the possibility.

I kicked my sodden boots off along with my socks then nodded to Harlon and padded away down the boardwalk towards one of the thick, taut ropes that was tethering the ship to the dock. I tested my weight on it then pushed up onto my toes and quickly scaled the rope, my arms lifting either side of me for balance. It was easy. I'd long been adept at climbing trees, scaling buildings and passing between rooftops, but the hard part was what came next.

I sprang over the edge of the ship, landing lightly and slipping away below deck down a steep stairway. Silently, I hurried to the storage room I'd been kept in, finding my bag tossed beside a barrel of oranges and I snatched it up, stowing a few fat oranges in it for good measure then shouldering it and racing back the way I'd come.

The cold was biting as I made it to the top deck again, my wet hair plastered to my cheeks and my thin, soaked clothes useless against the icy wind. I'd known it would be cold here, but I'd underestimated that knowledge. The few clothes I'd made for this winter climate were clearly not going to be good enough, and with the few coins I had for supplies, I didn't know how I was going to afford to get anything better.

I slipped quietly along the deck towards the admiral who had now sheathed my dagger at his hip. He rested his elbows on the rail, directing the last Fae off of it, and thankfully his friends had disembarked to help guide the masses towards Helle Fort.

I slinked up behind him, silent as I went, reaching for the hilt of my dagger and holding my breath. With a nimble move, I yanked it from its sheath and he swung around, his eyes widening as they landed on me. Swinging my blade to distract him, I unhooked the sheath from his hip and snatched it away while he staggered back from my feigned strike. I leapt over the edge of the ship before he could do anything to stop me, hitting the boards hard, stumbling into a run as a blast of water wheeled past my head.

"Harl – go!" I cried and I heard him racing after me as I tore along the boardwalk, hitting the black sand of the beach and burying myself in the crowd, ducking my head low and pushing between the throng of Raincarvers.

Harlon wasn't far behind me, his bulk cutting a path more slowly and making people curse him as he went, but he wasn't the admiral's target.

I didn't stop moving until I'd forced a passage almost all the way to the front of the crowd that was closing in on the giant gates to the fort.

I surreptitiously slotted myself in behind two chattering women and glanced back, finding Harlon bustling his way forward, offering out winning smiles and words of thanks to those who let him pass.

Which they did of course, breaking smiles and sharing jokes with him, their ire forgotten in an instant.

Harlon finally joined me and offered me my boots, dangling them in front of my face with my socks jammed into them.

I realised he must have changed his clothes back on the boardwalk, because nothing but the damp strands of his hair spoke of the dip he'd taken in the ocean. I, however, was going to freeze my tits off if I didn't get out of these wet clothes soon.

As we stepped into the shadow of the arching gateway, I ducked into an alcove to the side of the moving crowd, dropping my pack while Harlon followed, tossing my boots down beside it. I stripped down fast, and my friend moved to stand in front of me, shielding me from any prying eyes.

I didn't have much in terms of clothing options and plucked out a sand-coloured one-piece with tiny turquoise stones stitched onto the material in swirling patterns. It would leave my legs bare along with my arms and would be about as useful against the cold as tossing a napkin over my tits. But it was that or nothing, and walking into my trials naked was hardly going to show respect to the Reapers. They might just cut my head off there and then.

I pulled on some fresh undergarments, made from a soft pink satin I'd acquired from a local merchant in Castelorain, not exactly the sort of thing I'd planned on wearing for my assessment, but I shimmied into them anyway and pulled on the outfit. The material was stitched between my legs, so at least I wouldn't end up baring my ass to the Reapers, but this really wasn't ideal. As I pulled on an armoured plate over my chest and strapped my blade to my hip with my belt, I figured I was just going to have to suck it up.

I put on some dry socks, but had to slide them back into damp boots, grumbling as did so, then I balled up my wet clothes and stuffed them into my pack before shouldering it.

"Okay, let's move." I stepped past Harlon, slipping into the crowd again and he jogged after me.

"That's what you're wearing? You'll freeze," he balked.

"Yeah, well it's this or risk hypothermia in my wet clothes," I said. "At least I'm dry. Ish," I added when I noted the way my long hair was dripping a path behind me on the large stones.

Harlon kept fussing, but I stopped hearing him when I took in the giant drawbridge that led its way across a vast moat towards a set of open wooden doors. The grey walls of the fort stretched up high towards a swirling cloud where the Skyforgers were disembarking from their floating island onto the high cliffs. A waterfall spilled over it in a turbulent cascade of white froth, blasting into the river that wound out around the fort to create the natural mote and heading on to greet the sea.

A dark kind of hatred swept through me at the sight of the Skyforgers, the memory of the attack on Castelorain always so keen in my mind. My mother's screams echoed in my skull and I dropped my gaze from my enemies, my hand tightening into a fist at my side. I was finally on the path I'd been dreaming of walking ever since that day. My vengeance awaited me beyond these walls, and out towards the great isle where Never Keep was said to tower like a titan upon its shores. My place was waiting for me there, my magical instruction promising me the skills I needed to secure my revenge on the Flamebringer who was responsible for my mama's death. He was my goal, my sole focus now.

We passed over the drawbridge and through the iron gates, the huge courtyard of grey stone with a gate in each of the four walls and a stone stairway in the middle, leading down into the dark. Banners for each nation fluttered in the breeze above them. To my left, the white banner of the Skyforgers pictured an eagle holding a lightning bolt in its talons; to my right, a snarling bear swatting at a falling star glared at me from the dark green background of the Stonebreaker's banner, and directly ahead of me a tiger roared among a swirl of fire on the Flamebringer's red banner. Above me, the sea serpent of my nation was depicted on our blue banner, rising from a stormy ocean.

The un-Awakened Fae of the three elemental lands were entering through their own gates and tension snapped through the air as we took in the cut of each other. We held obvious differences, the clothes of our lands contrasting. The Skyforgers were clad in black battle leathers and had a generally pristine appearance, like they were striving to resemble the nobility that ruled their lands. Perhaps some of them were aristocracy, destined for positions of power, Fae who would one day give orders that might result in the deaths of the other elementals gathering here. They were ferocious in their self-importance, regarding the rest of us as if we were utterly inferior on every count.

My gaze moved to the Flamebringers, taking in their own fashions. Some wore button down shirts peeking out from beneath leather jackets, or fine cloaks paired with battle straps, armoured plates and decorated sword sheaths. The result was something terrifying, or perhaps it was the look in their eyes that really ignited the violent air about them. Like they had seen more bloodshed than most ever should, that they were right now picturing me cleaved apart and would delight in the prospect.

The Stonebreakers had a barbarous look about them, from the ink lining their skin to the fact that they all seemed to be enormous, thick with muscle and intimidating in sheer size alone. They watched the opposing Fae with something akin to a pack of predatory animals, everything about them screaming of instability and an impending attack. Their clothes were a mixture of furs, leathers and cotton, all in neutral tones and there was a sea of battle axes and long swords sheathed on their backs.

My people had thinner clothes that were generally more colourful than the other nations'. We favoured the blues of the ocean, turquoises, azure and cyan, or the colours of a sunset, like ambers, pinks and yellows. Our hair was adorned with braids, and most of our armour was a range of metallic blues and silvers.

Us Raincarvers were slowed by a group of Reapers in their gold cloaks who directed us into a line before the stone stairway that led below ground. All four groups of elementals were urged into lines too, and a chilling kind of quiet fell over the fortress as we assessed each other.

Our enemies. The next generation of Fae who we would meet on the battlefield and equal each other's deaths.

I scoured the faces of the Flamebringers, seeking the man whose name was waiting to find its place on my dagger just in case there was a chance fate had decided to present him to me now. But I found only strangers glaring back at me, their eyes dark and full of loathing. I just hoped my target still lived, and no other Fae had claimed his death from me, because I would hate to be denied the privilege of his end.

A clamour of muttering and several curses drew my attention back to the Skyforgers as a trio of women shoved the others in line aside, moving to claim their positions at the front of their queue.

"Tie me up and whip me raw!" a man yelled and the woman with short, dark hair at the right of the trio threw her elbow into his gut hard enough to make him double over with a harsh wheeze.

The one leading their group was shorter than the others, the crowd surrounding me making it hard to see much aside from a glimpse of pale pink hair as I craned my neck to see what was happening.

Pink among a sea of black leather. Ice trickled through my limbs as I realised who was here. That hair whispered of the truth of her Order. It was just one of the many things that Fae spoke of in tones of reverence about her, even when those words were laced with hatred.

Her name was hissed through the crowd as others took note. The Sky Witch.

She'd been there that fateful day when I'd lost my mother and my town had been torn in two. My jaw locked tight as I sidestepped the big asshole in front of me and I fell still as I found myself looking straight at her across the cobbled courtyard.

My breath stalled in my lungs despite knowing what she was and having tried to prepare myself for it. I blinked as I worked to fight off the daze I felt upon seeing her perfectly proportioned features, focusing on the brutal, jagged wound which had been carved into her right cheek, though somehow it did nothing to diminish her beauty. She looked like a painting, ethereal, unreal. No wonder she thrived so viciously in battle if this was what happened when Fae laid eyes on her. Even a few seconds of hesitation could equal death in battle and by the looks of all those surrounding her, she could have gutted ten of them before one so much as regained their composure.

I glanced at Harlon behind me, finding him watching her closely, his copper eyes tracking over her face before falling on me and remaining there. I looked back at the Sky Witch, my hand curling into a tight fist, fingernails biting into my palm as I reminded myself of who and what she was, of the fact that she had been there to attack Castelorain, making it possible for the Flamebringers to slip through our borders and end my mama's life.

The allure of her shattered as I focused on that, though there were many Fae who seemed entirely lost to it, calling out declarations of desire, lust, and proposals of love while The Sky Witch simply glowered at them. Her two companions, both terrifying in their own right, moved to block anyone foolish enough to try and approach. But I didn't get the feeling the Sky Witch needed their protection; more that they were protecting the Fae who had fallen for her allure from what might happen if they got too close.

"Fae of the four nations," a Reaper spoke, his voice amplified by magic as he touched his fingers to his throat. He was an elderly man, long grey hair sleekly hanging down by his shoulders.

We all fell silent reverently, the four nations united in this one thing: our worship of the stars beneath the guiding hand of the Reapers who were blessed with the words of the deities themselves.

"You will be called forward one at a time to meet with your appraisers and be assessed in magic, mind and body for your place in the world. Those of you hoping to attain a position at Never Keep, wishing to take up the fight started by the four nations in a time lost to legend when Layetta, Rishan, Alrier and Kiana walked the world, their conflict casting The Waning Lands into the Endless War. Head down the steps when you are called and may the stars bless your fortune."

I assumed he had done this speech several times already today because plenty of our nation and many Fae from the other lands had passed this way already.

There was a sudden hesitation in the women heading the line just ahead of Harlon and me, and as the one at the front turned back, I realised it was Alina Seaman. Her gaze locked on me and she caught my arm, shoving me to the front.

"Runts first," she hissed, jabbing me in the back, and before I could grapple with her, the grey-haired Reaper locked eyes with me and beckoned me forward.

I swallowed a curse, glancing over my shoulder and meeting Harlon's gaze. He quirked an encouraging smile at me, and I gave him a nod that said I'd see him soon before throwing an icy look at Alina and moving forward.

"Why's she dressed like that?" A snigger came to my right and I didn't bother to look at the Stonebreakers as a few more taunts carried to me from the onlooking Skyforgers and Flamebringers too.

Alina was whispering with her friends, a ripple of giggles sounding from them before the Reapers glanced their way and silence fell once more.

I steeled myself, trying to ignore the eyes from all around that were peeling me apart as I approached the Reaper.

"Do you wish to try for a place at Never Keep where you might earn the right to join the ranks of warriors who battle for the supremacy of your nation? Or is your calling for another path?" the Reaper asked me, his wizened voice a scrape across my ears.

I raised my chin, my father's suggestion that I claim a place as a Provider ringing through my mind, striking rebellion and defiance through my soul.

"I wish to place at Never Keep," I replied firmly and though I didn't turn to look at her, I somehow felt the Sky Witch's attention on me as I spoke those words, like I had just made myself into a true opponent of hers.

"Raise your right hand," he ordered and I did so. The Reaper swept forward, taking a glittering crystal from within his robe and holding it against my palm. It glowed as it brushed my skin then he nodded. "Your magical signature has been recorded. Please take the path to my right where the Combat Trial awaits," he instructed, pointing me to the steps and I descended into the dark.

I touched my fingers to the dagger at my hip, its presence reassuring as I met the bottom of the deep stairway, finding myself in a long tunnel lit by flaming sconces. Paintings were scrawled across the walls denoting the four elements, trails of fire, water, wind and leaves following me through the dark. If possible, it was colder down here than above ground, and goosebumps crept along my skin as I worked to draw my attention away from that sensation. But I was used to warm waters and long days in the sun. This was a kind of cold that had teeth, sinking into me like an invisible beast.

A light grew at the far end of the tunnel and I stepped into a chamber where a shaft of sunlight cut right down from a circular hole in the high roof, shining directly onto a stone table. Weapons were laid across it; a dagger, sword, axe, bow and spear, each of them made of pure gold. They were beautiful, stunning creations that looked to be forged with near-perfect skill.

I admired them as I stepped closer, and a booming male voice filled the air, though no Fae was in the chamber with me.

"Lay your wares in the chute and select one weapon. If you step into the Combat Trial with any arms of your own possession, you shall not place at Never Keep."

I shed the pack from my shoulders, taking the dagger from my hip and tucking it safely inside before buckling the bag up tight. Then I moved to the hole that lay beside the stone table - which I guessed was the chute - hesitating as I hung my pack over it.

"I'll get this back, right?" I asked the bodiless voice.

No answer came and I huffed out a breath as I said goodbye to all my worldly possessions and tossed them into the chute. They disappeared into the dark and I stepped closer to the table, deciding which weapon to take.

I was adept with each of them, but I favoured the blades, so I took up the gleaming sword and weighed it in my grip.

"Is your selection final?" the voice echoed out again.

"Sisca," I affirmed in Cascalian, then quickly said, "Yes."

A grinding of stone scraping against stone sounded ahead of me and I found a door opening in the chamber wall, a sandy passage appearing beyond it.

I walked that way, raising the sword and passing more flaming sconces as I followed the trail of sand. Sunlight spilled out ahead and I quickened my pace, finding a wide arena spreading out before me. Five Reapers sat high up on a ring of stone seats, their faces tilted down within the golden hoods of their cloaks, their gazes assessing as they watched me walk to the centre of the arena.

I swallowed thickly. In Castelorain, we didn't see many Reapers aside from the two who reigned over the Astral Sanctuary and they rarely left the confines of the place of worship. Even when I attended the sanctuary to pay homage to the stars, I was always positioned to the rear of the building, the eyes of the Reapers never falling on me from their place at the front.

I regarded them with awe and trepidation as I found all of their gazes locked on me now. The Reapers were the best of Fae kind – those destined for a fate far greater than the call of war, hence their position outside the authority of the four nations. They were blessed by the stars, the magic that was Awakened within them not constrained to the single element of their birth. Some of the conscripts who had come here today would hear not only the call of the magic their star sign had assured them, but that of another element, or perhaps even three, or occasionally all four of them. It was rare, but when a soul was blessed by the stars and marked by this claim of superiority, they were at once welcomed into the fold of the Reapers and trained to become an acolyte of the stars themselves.

Despite my pretty daydreams of finding myself among their ranks by the end of the day, it was so rare that I seriously doubted it. Besides, no element except the ferocious power of water had ever called to me. I couldn't imagine a fate where I would claim dominion over air, fire or earth alongside it.

"Begin," one of the Reapers spoke and a bellowing roar made me wheel around in alarm.

A cage stood in the shadows, the door flying open as a giant beast burst from within. It was just like the creatures from the wastelands, this monster part animal, part magically imbued metal. It looked as though it had once been something akin to a crocodile, but its legs were longer, its movements quicker as the beast came tearing towards me with open jaws.

Magic glittered against the shell of its armour, and I set my gaze on the green scales of its neck between the plates, racing to meet it and swinging my sword as adrenaline swept into my blood.

Its jaws snapped at me, its teeth a mixture of metal and enamel, its snout coated in armour too. I rolled to avoid the strike, gaining my feet beside it and slashing my sword towards its neck, my instincts alive and burning. It moved at the last second so my sword hit the armour instead, the blow denting the metallic plates, but there was no way I'd be able to cut through it.

The beast's tail swiped out, slamming into my legs and throwing me from my feet. I hit the sand, rolling again as the creature wheeled around, coming for me at speed, its jaws wide and ready to take my head from my shoulders.

Instead of escaping the oncoming death I could see in its reptilian eyes, I leapt upright and rushed to meet it, my sword driving into that open mouth and sinking in deep before slicing up into its skull.

Flesh and bone shattered from the impact and the beast shuddered, dying just like that as I wrenched my blade from the back of its throat and turned to the Reapers with a victorious smile twisting my lips. *Too easy.*

My heart thrashed, the thrill of the win setting my soul on fire. But I found no such excitement in the Reapers' eyes, just a simple nod from the evident leader and a single finger pointing me towards a door that was sliding open in the wall to my right.

"Praise to the stars." I bowed my head in acknowledgement of them and hurried off through that door.

"Praise to those who tread their destined path," the Reapers replied in unison, the words making my skin prickle. Their power was absolute, touched by the stars themselves and I could feel their strength crackling in the atmosphere.

The sword was wrenched from my hand and I glanced back as it went flying away across the arena on a magical wind and the door closed behind me.

I found myself in a smaller chamber with a single Reaper standing there, her face impassive, her eyes seeing me yet entirely void of emotion. She raised a single hand, urging me closer and I cautiously approached.

The Reapers were gifted with the great and divine knowledge of our makers, and each of them held a presence that spoke of that extraordinary power, setting my pulse skipping in delight at being so close to them.

She laid a cool palm to my forehead and her two eyes slid together into one, bulbous eye, revealing herself as a Cyclops. I hadn't had great experiences with their Order thanks to Alina, but I trusted the Reapers implicitly and no fear found me at her touch.

She breathed a single word, "Open," and I knew exactly what to do.

I relaxed the boundaries of my mind and let her fully into my head, the rush of her Order gifts sliding over me and making me weak from the tumult of magic.

She sifted through my thoughts, seeking what she needed, sorting one memory from the next as she weighed and measured the cut of me.

I urged memories of the wasteland to my mind, letting her see the creatures I'd slain, showing every moment of strength I owned.

But she pushed past them, discarding them as if they were nothing, and my heart crushed as she found the memories of Ransom, Alina and the others chasing me, beating me, belittling me. The words 'runt', 'freak', 'outcast' echoed through my head and my father flashed into my mind. His sneers, his dismissal.

Embarrassment coated my skin and I willed her elsewhere, trying to show her more, the better pieces of me. But she only rooted deeper, finding the truth I feared most of all. My mother laying over me while Basilisk venom rained down from above, my left hand burned and scarred beyond repair. I saw the Flamebringer's face so clearly that all the hatred which lived in me for him scored a passage through my chest, and as the Reaper withdrew herself from my mind, I realised I was screaming.

I clapped a hand to my mouth, fighting away the cruel memories of that day and the wound in my heart that had never truly healed over the loss of my mama.

"I'm more than what you saw," I rasped, trying to find a hint of something in this woman's gaze. Her Cyclops Order retreated and her one eye returned to two. But her expression was blank. She gave no hint of whether she had been moved at all by what she'd seen.

"You are not a Seer," she stated. "You hold no power to speak with the stars, no gift of visions or fortune telling."

"Okay," I exhaled, not surprised by that. "But listen, what you saw, it doesn't define me, it doesn't mean-"

"You may now progress to your Awakening," she said in a bland tone, another stone door opening at her back.

I remained rooted to the spot, needing to know if what she'd seen of me meant I had just lost my chance at placing at Never Keep.

"I'm more than that," I pressed, and her eyes dropped from me, her interest lost.

"You may now progress to your Awakening," she repeated.

I nodded, accepting her words, not wanting to disrespect her.

"Praise to the stars," I murmured automatically.

"Praise to those who tread their destined path," she replied.

I walked past her with anxiety warring in my chest, unsure if I had made the cut, or if the single fact of being who I was, of the dark truths that were etched into the fabric of my past, had just cost me everything I'd ever hoped for.

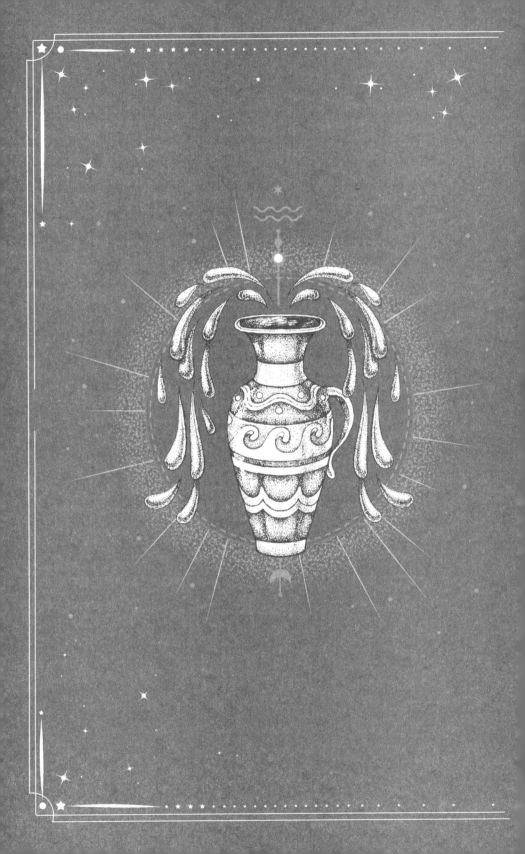

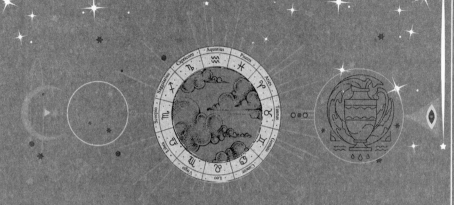

VESPER

CHAPTER FOURTEEN

My Combat Trial had been laughable. The magically-altered beast I'd fought had looked to have been an ape at some point, but fighting it was nothing compared to the true chaos of war, the bloody fight for survival and clash of steel and death which I was so accustomed to. I'd stalked from the assessment chamber without even bothering to wait for the Reapers there to confirm that I had achieved the necessary judgement. I hadn't even used the golden weapon they'd given me to kill it, showing them what I was capable of with brute force and my bare hands instead. If that was their idea of battle preparation, then I was glad I wasn't receiving any physical combat training for war in this place.

The Reaper whose cold and clammy palm had pressed to my forehead while invading my mind with their Cyclops power had actually snatched his hand back after delving into some of my most brutal memories. I'd done things in the name of Stormfell which apparently made even the servants of the stars flinch. I'd given him a sweet smile as he ushered me out of the assessment, confirming I had no Seer abilities either, his pallor decidedly paler than when I'd begun.

I strode out into a wide courtyard where all those Fae who had passed their Combat Trials before me were either pausing for a break or heading to join the long lines which rose up the distant pathway clinging to the mountain ahead of us.

The setting sun was still shining brightly and I closed my eyes, tipping my head to the sky and bathing in the feeling of our closest star offering out its blessing.

There were eyes on me, many watchful eyes, plenty of them hostile, though I held little fear of them acting on their hatred here.

I released a long breath then opened my eyes again. Reapers stood all around the courtyard, lining the pathways which ran up the mountain too. Their gold robes made them stand out starkly among the sea of battle leathers and war regalia. There was something about the holders of the faith which always unsettled me, and even when the hoods of their cloaks were facing away, I felt their attention prickling at me like they knew things the rest of us didn't. Perhaps their placement closer to the stars than the rest of us gave them a higher level of understanding, or perhaps they just believed it did and so soaked up the feeling of supremacy.

Many of the Fae now awaiting their Awakening would be hoping for the blessing of the stars to call them into the service of the Reapers and gift them a gold robe of their own.

It was a sign from the stars themselves that they were to be lifted above the position of warrior for their born nation and instead elevated into the ranks of the Reapers who stood apart from the ties of blood and calls of war.

I couldn't think of anything worse. I was a born warrior and the call of the air kingdom sang in my blood despite my stained heritage. I had been created to fight and nothing more. Being selected to stand apart, to reign beyond, sounded like its own personal slice of hell to me. I was no Reaper and if by any twist of bad luck I felt the call to wield an element in addition to air, I planned to reject it or, at worst, hide it because my place in this world was on the battlefield.

A shiver darted down my spine, instincts honed in battle snapping my head around and my eyes meeting with the steely gaze of a man who looked so out of place that for a moment all I could do was stare at him.

He was tall; even in this place of Fae and beasts, he stood a head taller than most and clearly dwarfed me. His curling hair hung to his chin, clinging to the deep brown skin of his sharp jaw and the dark clothing he wore, made of layered fabric which wrapped around his frame yet hung loose enough for free movement, marked him out as different. Even if everything else about him hadn't screamed it for all to see.

Danger had long since called my name and I didn't balk at the hungry look he gave me before parting his lips in a feral smile.

Shock jolted through me, though outwardly I didn't react at the sight of the fangs he now bared in clear warning. Or...no, that wasn't a warning, his eyes sparked with excitement and if I wasn't mistaken, I would have to say it was desire in his expression – not for my body but for my blood. No doubt the wound marring my face, still bloody and raw only made him hunger for it more.

Vampire.

I pursed my lips in distaste. Of course I knew all about the Vampire covens who had stolen great swathes of the wastelands to the far east of The Waning Lands for their empire, but never before had I come face to face with them.

In fact, as I let my gaze trail behind him, I found four shadows clinging to his back, more of his kind come to seek their newest recruits.

Upon the Awakening of our elemental magic, any Fae whose Order form was a Vampire would Emerge, their fangs snapping out and an insatiable desire for blood consuming them instantly.

We were a continent at war and yet there was one exception to that immovable truth – the Vampires were a law unto themselves. They didn't care what elemental magic a Fae held in their veins, they only cared for their own kind. And the rest of us had long ago learned not to interfere with their way of life.

The Vampires formed covens among themselves, the groupings so powerful when united that none could stand against them in battle. They moved with inhuman speed and fought with unnatural strength, running rampant at will and snatching unsuspecting victims to feast upon up and down the borders of our lands.

I sneered openly at the group who had clearly come to claim any Fae who Emerged as one of them, glad to know that I wouldn't be risking that fate, having already Emerged as a Succubus and knowing my own Order form.

"Nice," Dalia purred from behind me, and I tore my gaze from the fixed stare of the Vampire to look at her. "Do you want to share him?"

"The bloodsucker?" I sneered. "I've heard that their debauchery extends further than even a Succubus can comprehend. Besides, I don't much like the idea of being bitten while taking my pleasure."

"Hmm," Dalia sighed. "Pity we have other plans – I think I could give the biting a go if there's any truth to the fact that they only fuck as a pack."

I glanced at the group of Vampires again, watching as they stalked away up the path, their unusual clothes billowing and their volatile reputations making certain that no one got in their way.

"Interesting," I said, but my mind wasn't really focused on the idea of fucking Vampires; my attention had shifted to the line which wound up the mountainside towards the cavern marked with the symbols of the air signs.

"Where's-" I began but I cut myself off as my gaze fell on Moraine who had just emerged from her own Combat Trial, shoving several Fae aside when they failed to move fast enough and knocking one of them into the dirt.

"Miss me?" she cooed, the sun glinting off of her silver, braided hair.

"Like a pain in the ass," I replied sweetly before turning towards the path and leading the way up it.

My gaze trailed to the right where the conscripts from Pyros were winding their way along their own route, offering up a wicked smile as some of the Flamebringers noticed me, hissing my name to each other on the wind.

"This is weird," Dalia commented. "They're right there, practically within striking distance and yet we're just…leaving them alive. Letting them draw breath. My palms are itching for my daggers and my mind is spinning endlessly with all the ways I could carve them up into little lumps of coal but I'm not acting on any of it. I feel so malcontent."

I snorted my amusement but didn't waste any more time looking to Pyros's warriors. My focus was fixed on the cavern at the very top of our pathway.

We reached the back of the line but I simply shoved the closest Fae aside and barked a command for the rest to move.

Some dared to grumble. One asshole actually stepped out of line and made to draw his sword, but my fist collided with the back of his hand, forcing him to drop it right before my elbow jerked up and caught him beneath the chin, knocking him on his ass.

I stepped over him and Moraine definitely stepped *on* him, but after that, the rest simply got out of our fucking way.

Sky Witch. Sky Witch. Sky Witch.

The name echoed on whispers as our arrival was announced ahead of us, necks craning, the odd idiot groaning, one or two throwing themselves towards me with declarations of love or desire.

I ignored them all, letting my sisters knock back any who got too close, though for the most part, the other members of the line restrained those who were completely lost to my allure. I didn't dislike what I was, but I had to admit that it grew tiring to endure the blurted declarations of lust and devotion whenever I was forced to move among strangers.

We made it to the front of the queue, the girl who had been about to step forward to take her turn at her Awakening quickly retreating and offering us her position.

I looked up at the three symbols which had been carved into a plate of white stone above the yawning entrance to the cavern, Aquarius, Gemini and Libra each represented in simple, clear depictions.

The cool air within the pitch black of the cavern washed over my face and the Reapers who stood to either side of it gestured for me to enter.

I glanced at Moraine, offering her a faint nod then to Dalia whose short hair had fallen forward into her dark eyes. Her lips lifted with anticipation and excitement. I almost smiled in reply before turning and heading towards the pitch black of the cavern.

"Actually, I think I might go first today." Dalia reached out, grasping my elbow and trying to shove her way ahead of me.

I caught her wrist in mine, my knee colliding with the side of hers and I knocked her back into the wall with a feral snarl.

"Down girl," I hissed, smirking at her while my forearm crushed her windpipe and her dark eyes sparked with amusement.

"Bitch," she rasped lovingly.

"Asshole," I replied in kind, pressing a kiss to her cheek before shoving away from her and heading off into the dark.

The two of them sniggered like a pair of alley cats who had just goaded a lioness, and I shook my head at their nonsense while trying to concentrate on what was ahead of me.

I knew roughly how this went – I needed to pledge myself to the will of the air signs and beg they offer up their power to my unworthy soul. Then some kind of sparkly star shit would take over, unlock my ability to wield air magic. After that, I simply had to channel it with enough force to pass my Magical Trial and then I'd place at Never Keep.

The dark pressed in on all sides, the passage before me twisting downwards, my own instincts keeping my feet on the path despite the lack of visual aids.

The fading sunlight from the entrance to the cavern was swallowed as I descended beyond its reach and my footsteps began to echo dully, the air growing colder as it swept through my hair. Despite my blindness, I got the impression that there was a drop opening up on either side of me and an equally huge space yawning overhead.

My boots met with stairs but I didn't falter, heading down them one at a time, a deep pressure surrounding me as the magic of this place reached out and took stock of me. I felt rather than heard whispers from all around, the sigh of a hand brushing my cheek, the taste of blood gracing my tongue. Were the stars watching me now, leaning closer to place judgement upon my war-bound soul?

A tall door creaked open before me and I squinted into the golden light which emerged from it, hesitating as my eyes adjusted, my gaze roaming over the carvings on the wooden frame. There were the usual symbols for air magic mixed in with runes which spoke of power and the will of the land.

I crossed the threshold with my chin raised and my skin prickled from the kiss of magic on the air.

Before me, three huge statues awaited, the twins of Gemini represented as glorious queens with wings that glimmered with golden light in a way which made them seem aflame. The scales of Libra were balanced perfectly on my right with the water bearer for Aquarius looking at me over his upturned bucket, his eyes spearing me right to my core.

No one else stood in the room, though something told me I was being observed and I lifted my head, squinting into the golden light and finding the open sky far above me, the stars glimmering in the darkening sky as they looked down on this place of spun fortunes.

My heart leapt as a deep chanting started up from the gloom beyond the shadows. It sounded like a hundred male voices all moving to a precise and powerful melody, spoken in a language I had never heard before.

Take the hands of Gemini, a voice breathed on the wind and I swallowed against the unearthly aura which wound its way around me momentarily before sweeping away once more.

I had never been one to hesitate, so I strode forward, my gaze locked on the outstretched hands of those warrior queens.

I reached for them, my entire hand only managing to encircle a fingertip on each of the immense statues, cold stone skimming across my palm.

I looked up into the faces of the twins as the chanting grew louder then bit down on a curse as something reached inside of me and *pulled.*

The taste of dirt washed over my tongue, threatening to choke me as a power so solid and immovably *wrong* rushed through me, making me fight against the urge to cry out in pain and scream for it to stop. The seconds dragged, my hands seemingly fused to the statues as that rough presence tried to tear something out of me which I was utterly unable to give.

I spat as the taste of mud slipped from my tongue, panting against the discomfort of that foul magic before screaming in earnest as water rushed into my lungs and I found myself drowning.

I heaved and coughed, jerking against the hold the twin statues had on me, my body convulsing violently as the acidic water burned its way through me.

But no, that hadn't been burning at all because as I finally managed to cough the water free of my lungs, every piece of me caught fire. Sparks flashed before my eyes, the stench of burning flesh engulfing me, my body thrashing and quaking as I fought to free myself from its unending torment.

Just as I thought I would surely die from the ravaging flames, they fell away, my chest expanding on an inhale of the purest breath I had ever taken. It was crisp and clear, a rush of tumultuous energy which sped not only through my aching lungs but into my blood, my flesh, my soul.

A breath of laughter spilled from my lips as the power embraced me and I embraced it in turn, relishing the rush of raw magic, letting it engulf me and awaken some part of my being which I couldn't imagine ever having been without. It was a part of me, intrinsically bound to every piece of who and what I was. The power built and built, my fingers trembling with the desire to unleash it and suddenly I was stumbling away from the statues, a wide and pure smile lighting my entire face, tugging at the aching wound on my cheek.

I barely even noticed the door that opened beyond the statues, my feet carrying me through it as I revelled in the power, its sweet caress lighting me up from the inside out, begging me to set it free.

I moved across a wide outcrop on the northern cliff of Helle Fort, the line of Fae moving aside for me as I practically ran towards the Magical Trial arena. I shoved my way through the wooden doors to the hulking arena before an idiot who started babbling nonsense about the beauty of my face and I barely even glanced at the Reapers who stood congregated to watch my trial on a balcony above the wide space.

"You must exert control over your element and prove-"

"Stop talking," I growled, not caring that it was a Reaper I spoke to, or what their fucking rules on what I was supposed to do with my newfound power might be.

I placed my feet firmly in the heart of the arena, barely glancing at the targets and barriers which had been placed all around me in order to test my strength. This power needed an outlet and I was desperate to sate that need.

The stone doors banged shut behind me and I let it all tear from me at once.

A storm of air exploded from me, Fae crying out from their positions on the balcony above the arena as every target, every barrier and even great chunks of the arena walls were ripped apart in the ensuing blast.

A tornado tore from me, lashing my hair against my face while I remained firm in the eye of the storm, the shattered remains of everything in the arena now swirling around me in a chaos of unbridled power. It was brutal, raw and wild, everything I was at my core, and I let it tear from me in an endless torrent of pure power until I had nothing else left to give.

I panted heavily, my hands on my thighs as I peered up at the Reapers who stood clustered above me on a balcony, protected from my outburst by an air shield which itself had cracked, great spiderwebs of damage making their features unfocused as I looked out between tangled strands of pale pink hair.

I blinked in surprise as I found another face among them. Prince Dragor's pale eyes were bright with a possessive fervour that made my heart race powerfully.

"You have been deemed a worthy warrior for the great and noble kingdom of air," one of the Reapers announced, his gaze roaming over the shattered remains of the targets that had been laid out in the arena. "You have placed. Welcome to Never Keep."

I sank into an imitation of a curtsy which was too full of arrogance to really be considered respectful, my arms swinging wide to pull out the sides of my imaginary skirt.

Prince Dragor watched me with a dark thrill in his eyes which caused me to grin at my boots before I schooled my features and straightened again.

I turned and headed from the arena, my legs trembling slightly with exertion and a dull ache left in my chest somewhere close to the thumping pulse of my heart where I was certain my magic should reside.

I frowned at the strange new feeling, lamenting the loss of my new power and trying to focus on what I needed to regain it. Every Order of Fae recharged their magic in differing ways; Nemean Lions had to lay in the sun, Sphinxes needed to read, Vampires, somewhat obviously, had to drink the blood of others to steal the magic they required. Then there were Werewolves who had to run beneath the moon, or Pegasuses who had to fly through the clouds. Standard magical recharging actions for standard Orders, but I was something uncommon.

My power was subtle, my gifts both physical and intrinsic and to recharge I needed to embrace the desires of those around me so I could syphon their magic directly from them and into myself. Yes, it could be sexual which was the assumption made of my kind - mostly due to the obvious physical attributes we claimed. Our startlingly attractive appearance, the unnatural, attention-grabbing colour of our hair, the allure which rolled from us so easily and encouraged many Fae to attempt to gain our favour.

But when I was sixteen, my Sage Moya, the Oracle who had deigned to train me in the ways of blood magic and the control of Ether, had gifted me a book. The diary was old and damaged in places, but it had been written by a Succubus who had dedicated her life to unfurling the mysteries of our kind. The secrets I had uncovered within those tattered pages were ones I kept so close to my heart that I had never even shared them with Dalia and Moraine.

Sexual desire was the least of what I could obtain from those who fell under the sway of my allure. I could see the shape of their truest wants and desires, be it wealth or glory, greed or power, love or lust. I could sway those desires too with enough will and time to work on them. I could twist them into something darker, more desperate, or simply more inviting. And if I helped them to act on any part of those wants then I could drain the magic right from their bones and steal it for my own power.

So in war, I could urge my enemies to hunger for my death even more than they did on first sight, stealing their magic from them with every strike they made at me, powering myself while weakening them. And now that my elemental magic was unlocked, I would be free to exploit that power to my fullest capabilities at last.

There was more to what I was, more which I knew I would be able to unravel and unlock with my air magic at my fingertips and I was anxious to explore every piece of it.

Prince Dragor stepped out in front of me and I almost flinched, glancing at the staircase that had been carved into the rear of the arena, no doubt giving access to the platform where he had observed my assessment.

"This is Andol," he said, no word of praise on my achievement, just a curt gesture towards the Reaper who had followed him down the stairs. "He has graciously agreed to repair the damage to your face."

I bit my tongue on the retort I wanted to give, not caring one lick about the wound to my face or the scar it would likely leave. This was intended as a gift. Or at least I might have seen it that way before last night.

I schooled my expression, dropping to my knees before the Reaper and murmuring some bullshit about being unworthy for such an accolade.

"Hush, keen warrior, your praises should be directed to the stars. I am merely their vessel," he murmured, his paunchy hand cupping my cheek, perspiration making his palm clammy.

He wasn't gentle, pain flaring through the wound as his fingers probed at it, but I remained unmoving, uncertain what to expect from this sacred magic. The secrets of true healing were one of the most closely-guarded gifts that the stars had bestowed upon the Reapers. They could perform feats of magic so powerful that they could return a Fae from the gates of death itself, mending their body entirely and remaking them no matter how grave the wound or illness. It defied all except the power of the stars, and I swallowed thickly as a tingle of magic began to wash against my skin.

It felt as though a thread had formed between me and the Reaper who held me, his magic pressing into me invasively, probing around inside my own as though taking account of my soul itself.

My skin buzzed with magic but so did patches on my arms, legs, back and stomach, every piece of me which held a scar earned in battle or punishment blazed with the simmering heat of his power. I gasped as it rushed through me, every dull ache of a long-healed wound, every mark of stupidity and bravery alike simply wiped away as if my entire body was a slate now prepared for a new beginning.

I blinked up at the Reaper wordlessly as he withdrew his hand, my own fingers travelling over the perfect smoothness of my cheek in wonder as I found the injury healed.

"Praise to the stars," I breathed, the words never having felt so pious on my lips before. Because surely that was the power of the heavens themselves and nothing less. It was…miraculous. No story told of it could ever encompass the feeling of it rushing through my veins.

"Praise to those who tread their destined path," the Reaper replied, his hand landing on Dragor's shoulder, squeezing tightly as they exchanged a loaded look.

I barely stifled my gasp as Dragor dropped to his knees in deference to the Reaper, bowing his head and murmuring his own words of worship too.

The Reaper headed back up the stairs and I stilled as the prince curled his hand around my bicep, tugging me to my feet.

"I will see you into Never Keep," he said roughly, taking the pack I had placed into the chute before my Combat Trial from the ground behind him and holding it in his fist. "And as we travel, you will recall your vow to me. You will remember that wall which now surrounds you."

I looked at his sharp profile and he turned to face me, his arm moving to encircle my waist.

"I remember," I said, my gut lurching as he shot us into the sky with his air magic.

The isle which held Helle Fort shrank beneath us and I couldn't help but stare down at it from the dizzying height before Dragor directed us away from it, heading further north over turbulent, iron-grey seas.

Night had fully fallen and the clouds were thick but the chill in my bones wasn't due to the frigid wind. Dragor's fingers dug into my waist, his mouth dropping to my ear, his lips brushing against the soft flesh and making me shiver as he inhaled deeply.

"What a dark and forbidding creature you are, my Sky Witch," he breathed where only the wind could hear us and, despite myself, I turned to look into his icy eyes.

"I thought…" I began then stopped because what was I going to say? I thought you were angry? Jealous? Terrifying? Done with me?

Did any of that make sense? Had the unease and anxiety which had kept me from sleep last night held any real basis?

"That is where you were mistaken." Dragor clasped my jaw in his grip and turned my head so that I could look out over the sprawling isle which housed Never Keep and my eyes widened as I took in the enormous structure.

Walls built of black, volcanic rock rose up above the sheer edge of the cliff face, the turrets crowning them in jagged, unwelcoming peaks and towers which glared out over the roiling sea.

A port lay at the foot of the cliffs leading to a cove with black sand marking the beach, a sheer stairway cutting back and forth along a narrow cliff path seeming to be the only way to access it.

At the apex of the stairs was a jutting ledge of stone before a pair of iron gates big enough to admit a Dragon shifter – though no Dragons remained in The Waning Lands to test such a theory.

The keep itself was shaped like a jagged X, the four long structures known as the vaults all spreading out away from the central area which housed the common grounds where Fae from every land would be forced to cohabit for instructions in wielding the cardinal magics and praising the stars in the Astral Sanctuary.

I stared over the rugged rooftops, the black stone well-weathered from the tempestuous climate this far north and out to sea. A central triangular courtyard lay open at the heart of each of the vaults and I caught glimpses of effigies and idols, the symbolism in every elemental sector a brazen announcement of pride in the lands which each one represented.

Dragor released his hold on his air magic and we plummeted from the sky, my pulse ticking with adrenaline as the rough pier of stone before the iron gates sped closer. Never Keep looked like the broken tooth of some immense beast from above, the open gates its wide jaws, ready to swallow me whole.

The prince jerked us to a halt before letting our feet touch down on the stone, making me the first of this year's conscripts to arrive at Never Keep and take up my place as a neophyte within its walls.

Dragor gave the iron Night Gate, carved with the phases of the moon, a sweeping glance then turned to me, grasping my hair in his fist and arcing my neck to make me look at nothing but him.

"You will be the best," he growled, his eyes two chips of ice, the command rough with possession.

"I already am," I replied with a sneer.

Dragor tightened his grip on my hair to the point of pain, leaning in to speak against my mouth.

"Your arrogance will be your downfall," he swore, the words ringing with a sense of prophecy to them which stilled the blood in my veins before his mouth took possession of mine.

The kiss was a brand against my lips, a mark of his villainy which stained me to my soul and reminded me of my place in this world, at his utter beck and call.

I stumbled as he released me, his presence gone in a rush of wind which sent my hair into a spiral and revealed his absence in its wake.

I turned from the temptation to hunt the skies for him, picking up my pack from where he'd dropped it on the ground then I placed my hand upon the hilt of my sword as I strode through the iron gates, determined to exceed all expectations, including my own.

EVEREST

CHAPTER FIFTEEN

Water magic stirred in my veins like a rippling pool, and I only had to call on it to transform that pool into a tempestuous sea storm. I had always felt a connection to the ocean, and whenever I bathed in her warm waters, I knew it was where I belonged. But now that my magic had been Awakened, it was as if I carried her with me, from her turbulent, destructive fury to the gentle flow of a meandering river.

Water was the greatest element in this world, needed by all, and without it, every living thing would perish. Now that power was a part of me, but I still hadn't tried to cast it.

My feet tracked heavily into the arena made specially for the Raincarvers' Magical Trials, a wide, still pool filling most of the circular place. Six Reapers gazed down at me from their positions on a balcony perched high enough to observe me. This arena was an echo of the one I had taken my Combat Trial in apart from that mirror-like water. Wooden targets were perched upon the walls, and effigies of wooden creatures stood around the pool too.

"You must exert control over your element and prove yourself worthy to become a warrior of Cascada," a female Reaper spoke up from the middle of the group. "You are required to cast water into existence, but you may also wield that which lays in the pool. All targets in this arena must be destroyed upon completion of your Magical Trial and in doing so, you must show prowess and potential for growth if you are to succeed in placing at Never Keep. If you do not still wish to follow the path of a warrior, simply kneel and you shall be returned to your homeland."

"I won't kneel," I growled.

"Then begin," she directed, taking her seat once more.

My chest tightened as I raised both hands, flexing the fingers of my left one, feeling the scar tissue there and praying to Scorpio that he would ensure I could cast despite it. The fear of this moment had haunted me for too long, the nightmares of failing to cast with both hands hounding me into the dark. It would mark me as lesser, weaker, useless. Just as my father had branded me.

Guiding magic to my fingertips was all too simple and my breath caught as the current of pure power twisted into something volatile.

Water blasted from my right hand, scoring out across the arena and slamming into one of the wooden creatures. It shattered into a thousand pieces, but my heart stuttered as no magic came from my left hand. Not a shimmer, not a drop. Heat flamed along the back of my neck, and I schooled my features, lowering my left arm with a casualness that I hoped would go unnoticed, pouring all of my energy into my right. Water tore through the room, smashing targets everywhere, my control over it growing keener with each passing second. A voice in the back of my head was declaring me useless, but I couldn't acknowledge it. If I did, I'd fail this trial, and so long as I could cast at all, I still had a chance.

My connection to the power was instinctual and as I willed the water to chill, it turned to blades of ice. At a twist of my fingers, they flew in every direction, crashing into the last targets and leaving them in pieces. My power blasted out more furiously and I realised I was barely tapping into my reserves, this wild ocean in me flooding forth endlessly.

I focused on the pool in the room, connecting to it with ease and drawing it up into a spiralling whirlpool that I could spin like my fingers were connected to it with invisible threads. It was a writhing mass of deadly power and I sent it crashing out in every direction, slamming into every wall along with the magical barrier that protected the Reapers from my cast.

Water dripped from me, and I gathered it all up again, pulling on every drop in the room, dragging it toward me and starting to bend it. I gritted my teeth, focusing on how to move it, managing to shape it into a giant cylinder, and with a force of will, I made it move like a snake, trying to forge jaws into one end, but before I could figure out how, the central Reaper stood up and barked, "Please cast with two hands, candidate."

The water came crashing down in a tumbling wave that rocked the stone beneath my feet. I stood, soaked and freezing as the adrenaline wore off and my blood turned icily cold.

"I destroyed the targets," I called. "Aren't I done?"

"You will not be finished until you have completed what we require," she clipped.

My pulse pounded in my ears and I lifted my left hand, looking down at the scarred skin there, a wave of fear and sharpest rage scoring through me. I saw the face of my mother's killer, felt the burn of the Basilisk venom that had caused this scar, and I realised he was about to take more from me again.

"I can't," I rasped, forcing my tongue to curl around those words.

The central Reaper cocked her head. "Excuse me?"

I walked forward, around the pool, close enough to be standing right beneath them and held up my left hand for them to see.

"Basilisk venom," I explained thickly. "It left a scar on me long ago. I cannot draw magic from this hand. But you saw my power, I broke the targets, I can make up for-"

"Silence," she cut over me. "You will return to your homeland. You have not passed your Magical Trial. You have not placed at Never Keep."

The air stalled in my lungs, her words like a knife slamming into my chest. I shook my head, refusing that fate even as it fell upon my shoulders. I couldn't go home. I couldn't return to Castelorain to be forced into the company of Quentinos Wavellion. My father would make me take the path of a Provider. He would give me no choice.

"I destroyed the targets!" I barked. "I did what you asked and more besides."

"It is a kindness," the Reaper said softly. "The stars are protecting you from the tides of war. It is a blessing, young one."

"Hykaské!" I cursed in Cascalian. *Bullshit.* "You've said nothing of my power. Would I pass if I'd cast the very same magic with both hands?"

"Of course – your magic was astounding. To have such control upon your first casting-" a male Reaper piped up, but the leader shot

240

him a glare that made him bow his head and mutter an apology to her and the stars.

I stared at her in disbelief. "So I'm to be rejected on what grounds?"

"You have a clear disadvantage," she said firmly. "A flaw that cannot be fixed. Not by our hands or any other. Basilisk venom leaves scars not even healing magic can repair. The stars have deigned this your fate, you would do well to bow to it gracefully. Now please make your way from the arena and return to the dock."

My boots felt rooted to the ground, the rage in my veins climbing with every passing second, the drip, drip, drip of water from my hair like the ticking hands of a clock. This path could not be denied me. I was going to Never Keep. I was not going to be turned away and sent to my homeland to become a womb to bear the next generation of warriors. But I was part of *this* generation. I belonged at the Keep. And no Reaper, no star, no hand of fate was going to stand in my way.

A blast of absolute power ripped from me, wielded by my right hand as I directed it at the magical barrier that protected the Reapers from my casts. A roaring wave of water slammed right into it, and a bolt of energy connected from me to it, like a twisting, writhing darkness inside me, spilling out of my chest and fuelling that wave. It crashed into the barrier and a blast of light ricocheted across it before it fizzled out with crackles and sparks of magic. I gasped as the wave went crashing over the Reapers, soaking them through.

They all scrambled out of their seats with cries of shock, staring down at me in disbelief and the lead Reaper looked to me with intrigue colouring her expression.

"How could she do such a thing with just water magic?" one of the Reapers hissed to another, and they shook their head in awe.

I glanced between them, unsure if I should be turning tail and fleeing right about now, but something in the lead Reapers' expression kept me rooted there.

"Her water power is great indeed," she mused to the others. "It is a great pity she cannot wield it with both hands."

"High Reaper," the male who had stood up for me earlier shuffled over to her, whispering to her in a voice I could definitely hear. I noticed he had two stars marking the breast of his cloak and the woman he spoke to held three stars, signifying their rank. "There are no specific rules declaring a one-handed caster cannot place at Never Keep."

"There are only so many places to bestow, Reaper Jaspin, and we cannot waste one on a gamble," she hissed back.

"It won't be a waste," I called, vowing it down to the essence of my soul. "And if it's about room, then board me in a fucking broom cupboard for all I care. I'll sleep with the mops and buckets. Just let me train."

"She has passion," one of the other Reapers said thoughtfully, stroking his neat black beard. "Why not take up her offer? Place her wherever she will fit and she can have a room once one becomes available."

I knew what that meant. When someone at Never Keep died, because that was the kind of brutal place it was. Not everyone made it through their magical instructions.

"A wildcard," the High Reaper mused. "Do the stars seek to surprise us this day?"

"Yes," I said quickly, not caring what reason they had for making this decision only that they *had* to make it. "In fact, I had a dream just last night of such a thing. The courage of Pisces guiding me into Never Keep and promising me challenges untold. She said I would come to

Helle Fort and astonish the Reapers," I lied, trying to convince them that my place here was destined and hoping the stars forgave me for my blasphemy. I'd be sure to leave an offering in the Astral Sanctuary as thanks if they allowed me this one chance.

"There you have it," Reaper Jaspin announced. "The stars have spoken."

The High Reaper considered that, then sighed, looking to me. "You have placed at Never Keep. Your room is undetermined. I will send word to you soon." She took a pin from her gold cloak, sending it to me upon a pillar of water and I took it. "Keep this, it will guide a Reaper to you when it is time."

"Thank you," I gasped, a stone door opening to the side of the arena, and I raced for it, tearing outside into the moonlight.

The stone plaza outside was thronging with Fae, and steep steps led down the mountain towards a dock where wide wooden boats were ferrying those who had passed their trials to Never Keep. There were four ports, each one marked for water, air, fire, and earth, not even our passage to the Keep united, each dock lit by a tall iron lamppost. Reapers waited on the boats, directing people onto them and using magic to guide the vessels away across the dark ocean.

I looked at the silver pin in my hand, taking in the emblem of the Reapers, a star with an elemental symbol on four of the points. My gaze fell on piles of bags and I hurried over to the one closest, tossing bags aside as I searched for mine. I noticed couriers in black robes wheeling some away in carts, the items inside carefully placed, and I guessed some people had paid for the privilege. But I was left to root through the mountain of shit that the less affluent assholes like me had brought with them. When I finally located my bag, I pulled it from the heap, double checking all my belongs were accounted for then securing my dagger back at my hip.

Two big hands grabbed me from behind and I wheeled around, thinking of Ransom and readying to strike, but finding Harlon there instead.

"Well?" he demanded of me, his expression tense.

"I placed," I said, a big ass smile lifting my lips.

He yanked me into a tight embrace and held me against him. "I'm so fucking happy for you, Ever."

"And you got in, right?" I asked, knowing the answer already, but as he drew back, I found him looking anxious.

"Everest, I…"

"Don't bullshit me, Harl. I know you got in," I said, jabbing him in the pec.

"Yeah, I did, but-"

"Hell yes. Maybe I can sleep on your floor then because I'm pretty sure I'm going to be shoved in a broom cupboard, but it doesn't matter because we're *in*."

"A broom cupboard?" he balked.

"I'll tell you about that if you tell me where your 'but' was going." I gave him a pointed look and his shoulders dropped, a dejected expression falling over his features.

"I got two Elements," he said tightly. "Water and earth."

I stared at him, floored by those words. It should have been good news, great fucking news actually. Two elements meant you were destined to become a Reaper, and that was a path which was revered across all four nations, but Harlon had always been so clearly a warrior that the idea of him as some spiritual, robed star whisperer just refused to make sense in my mind.

"They train us separately," he said, dropping another heart-rending truth. "I'll be at the Keep, but…from what they said, I'll hardly see the warriors. Maybe not at all."

"Oh," I breathed, trying not to let my smile fall, but my heart was sinking and reality was closing in.

We were going to be separated, sent off on two fates that might not easily cross in future. The Reapers resided in their own quarters within the Keep so far as I knew, a place the rest of us were not permitted to enter. And once his training was complete he could be sent off to any of the four nations, serving in an Astral Sanctuary or as an advisor to the leaders of the differing lands, perhaps working as a healer, but likely not in Castelorain.

"It's a great honour to be a Reaper," I said, trying to muster some excitement into my voice, but I didn't think I managed it. "And two elements? Shit, Harl, you've got it made."

His brow only creased more and he stepped closer to me, the throng of movement around us becoming a blur as he took up the entirety of my view. "This isn't the path I wanted. I don't want to leave you."

"This is bigger than us," I said, but the words were heavy on my tongue. "The stars chose you for this."

"Stop it," he growled, stepping even closer. "Speak your mind, don't spin a web of bullshit for me. Who knows when we'll see each other again? I don't want lies to be the last thing you say to me."

"It won't be the last thing I say." I grabbed his shirt in my fist, drawing him even closer, unsure what I intended to do only that letting go of him now felt like a goodbye. "We'll see each other at the Keep. We'll make it happen."

He pushed his hand into my damp hair, pulling me to him and I went, letting myself melt, my hand sliding up his chest to rest on his shoulder.

"I'll find you, Ever," he swore, then his mouth was on mine and I was crushed to him as his arms went around me, forcing me onto my tiptoes so I could meet the ferocity of his kiss.

My mind sparked with all the fears I'd had about crossing this line, but they were shoved away by the heat of him surrounding me and the way it felt when his tongue pushed between my lips. My hands slid around his shoulders, pressing myself flush to the firm, muscular planes of his body and kissing him back. This man who had seen me when no one else had, who had had faith in me without cause, who'd met me in the ocean. But now we were about to separate upon a new shore.

Our lips parted and my heart rioted from the burning contact of his hands on me, his forehead falling to rest against my own and his warm breath meeting with mine in a rising fog, chasing away the icy air.

"I've waited far too long to do that," he said in a low tone as my skin continued to buzz and spark from that kiss. "And now I realise how much time I've wasted thinking I would always have you, thinking there was no deadline on us. But I didn't want to break what we have. You're my friend first, Ever, but I have to lay an offering of more than that on the brink of our parting, otherwise the regret will feast on me from the inside out. But I want you to train first, to chase your desires and land within the fate you have long been owed, and then and only then, will I ask you to be mine."

He started walking away and I noticed a line of Reapers guiding a group of Fae towards a smaller, though far grander boat upon the shore. He was leaving. The time was upon us before I was remotely ready to say goodbye.

"Wait," I gasped, but he didn't wait, he turned to join the Reapers and let them draw him into their fold, leading him onto the boat.

I stood alone among the crowd of Fae who were making their way down the steps to their own boats, and I felt more lost than I ever had in my life. Without Harlon, I was truly solitary. He was my rock, the one who knew exactly how to hold my broken pieces together. With him gone, I feared I'd shatter in the loneliness of it all.

His ferry took off from the shore and was soon swallowed by the pressing darkness of the night, only the faint glow of a lantern swinging from the prow marking his passage.

I lifted my gaze to the hulking form of Never Keep on the edge of the dark horizon, a low mist shimmering on the water around it, highlighted by the moon. Something solidified in my chest, a darkness that was gilded in grief, the promise I'd made to my mother's ghost to find her killer rising sharply inside me. That was what mattered. The trail to that fate lay before me, and though I hadn't expected to walk it alone, it wouldn't stop me from following it.

I'd find Harlon on that island regardless, even if we wouldn't be learning to wield our water magic together as I'd expected. He would still be close, and I had to let go of my own selfish desire to keep hold of him and let him go on to greater things. It might not have been the place he had expected to claim, but it was one revered across all the four nations. He would rise among the Reapers, learn knowledge and powers untold. I had to try my best to be happy for him, even if the knot in my chest ached with how much I already missed him.

That kiss already felt like an illusion, a dizzying moment of reality colliding with my dreams. He desired me. Truly. As I desired him too, and now he was gone and I didn't know what to do with the turmoil of confusion inside me. I wanted him, yes, but I feared what that want would do to us. How it might change the precious, mutual, uncomplicated love we'd held for each other for so many years.

I started down the stone steps, heading toward the boat that was waiting to take a group of Raincarvers to the Keep, lost to the beautiful torment of my thoughts. Alina was among them, and though I wasn't surprised to find she had placed, a bitterness still coated my skin as I joined the growing throng of my people.

Most of their faces were those of strangers, and I relaxed as I realised they didn't know me, that a fresh slate awaited me here. I was only an outcast in Castelorain, but perhaps Never Keep would be different. Not that I took easily to people. My guard was firmly up and honestly, I preferred my own company over most Fae's, but I wouldn't be a pariah here. Maybe I could find a few kindred spirits.

A familiar, muscular arm wrapped around my shoulders and I jerked away, unsheathing my dagger and pointing it at Ransom.

"Relax, sis," he crooned, and I scowled. He had never called me that in his life. "Seriously, Everest. You placed at Never Keep, I never thought it would happen, but I can't deny your ability now that it's pointed out so clearly to me. Besides, we're going to be comrades in battle soon enough. Shall we leave the past in the past?" He held out his hand for me to take, offering me the sort of smile I had only ever seen him pass out to his vile friends.

I stared at his outstretched palm like it was a rotten fish, recoiling from it with a hiss passing between my teeth. There had always been something deeply animal about me, and Mama had been certain it was a sign of my Order, but I wondered if it was more to do with the fact that I'd been chased from street to street all my life like unwanted vermin.

"You think I'll just forget the way you treated me?" I snarled, insulted by his casual offering.

"No," he said, stepping closer and tipping his head down. He looked so much like my father in that moment that it only set my hackles rising further. "But how about an apology for it?" He still had that offending hand held out in offering. "Come on, Everest. A truce at least. It's going to be us and them in there. I'd prefer if my enemies weren't lurking in my own ranks. Surely you feel the same?"

I hesitated, seeing the sense to his words, even if I still doubted them. I was trying to tread a new path here, and if Ransom really was willing to back off and leave his harassment of me in the past, it would be all the easier for me to focus on my magical instructions.

Reluctantly, I sheathed my dagger then slid my hand into his, laying my faith in the hope that maybe the light of Scorpio had made him see sense. His fingers closed around mine, his palm far bigger, crushing it in his grip. His smile tilted into a wicked sneer and I didn't even have time to curse myself for the foolish mistake I'd made before he wound a loop of rope around me, binding my arms to my waist and cinching it tight.

"Now!" he cried and I was hauled backwards, a cry leaving me as some of his friends yanked on a length of the rope behind me and I was dragged off my feet.

I hit the boardwalk with a snarl parting my lips, hauled along the wooden slats and trying to wield my element to save myself. But I didn't know how to control it properly and only managed to cast a line of ice beneath me that sent me skidding along quicker. The rope was tossed over the top of a lamppost and Ransom crowed excitedly as I was dragged skyward. Alina tied off the rope on a post at the edge of the dock, leaving me hanging there.

She shrieked a laugh and my cheeks flamed as I thrashed, trying to get to my dagger, but my arms were bound painfully tightly to my sides.

"Everest Arcadia is a freak from the gutters of Castelorain!" Ransom boomed and the sizeable crowd of elementals all looked at me. From here, right across the three other docks, to all the Fae exiting the arenas. Most of them were drawn to the show.

"Any who take pity on this pathetic runt can join her in exile and face the wrath of me, Ransom Rake, son of Commander Rake." A ripple of mutters broke out at that name, my father's bloodthirsty reputation well known throughout the four nations, and it looked like Ransom had just earned himself a position of respect before we'd even stepped foot in Never Keep. I wasn't worthy of taking my father's surname like my half-brother was. Only Father's 'true heirs' were bestowed with that accolade. I preferred my mother's name anyway, and at least I wasn't called Alina Seaman.

Ransom twisted his fingers and water spurted down my legs, soaking through my undergarments and shift, making it look like I was pissing myself. The laughter grew to a crescendo that crackled against my ears and made my anger turn to a wave of utter embarrassment.

Alina's cackling laughter reached me along with many other unfamiliar laughs, carrying across the docks and echoing over the water. The Reapers did nothing, simply waiting on the boats and directing the Fae to file onto them, and Ransom marched onboard with a bunch of Fae running after him, clapping him on the back.

Eyes were on me from all directions and as the first boat sailed away with my half-brother's laughter still carrying back to me across the water, punctuated by Alina's high-pitched giggles, I fought even harder to get down.

My mind was sparking with fury, my chest tight with rioting anxiety, but I took a breath, realising my panic was making this harder than it needed to be. I focused on my element, the ocean stirring inside me in offering and I ripped through Ransom's rope with a blast of ice shards and went falling towards the boards of the dock.

I landed with a crash, my knees splitting open on the wood, but I shoved upright, snarling at the closest Fae whose smiles withered at the ferocity they found staring back at them. I sent a blast of water out in every direction, knocking several of them into the sea, then I took up the front of the line as another boat pulled into the dock, ready to ferry us to the island.

"Hey - water freak!" a Flamebringer called from the next dock over and I ignored him, my back prickling with tension as my muscles bunched up. "Come on, pole-pisser, look over here!"

I glanced back for one reason only, a ball of ice forming in my right palm as I found the asshole sniggering among his friends. I threw the ice with all my strength, hitting him dead between the eyes and he crashed into the deck so hard, the boards cracked from the impact. He groaned, muttering furious curses as he lay there in a daze.

"Move it," a girl snarled from behind me and I was shoved forward, stumbling and quickly grasping the edge of the boat.

A Reaper produced a glittering crystal, just like the one that had read my magical signature before, and she touched it briefly to my arm before nodding and letting me pass over the gangplank. I made my way for the front of the vessel, wanting to put some distance between myself and the Raincarvers who were still tossing jibes my way. *Pishalés – assholes.*

It wasn't long before the boat was full and it took off across the water, the Reapers working their power into the ocean so we carved a fast passage across it.

My embarrassment ebbed away as Never Keep loomed out of the dark, the star-speckled sky standing out starkly behind the cavernous black rocks that jutted up like the spires of a demon's crown. Lights twinkled in the towers beyond the rising turrets of the high walls, but I could see little more of the place I would now reside in for a full year.

The boat soon docked upon a black sand beach, and I took in the sheer steps cut into the rock wall, climbing almost vertically up towards the Keep, jutting back and forth at sharp angles across the cliff face.

A Reaper stood waiting at their base, a ball of light glowing above him and illuminating the way on. I was first to disembark, leaping off the prow of the boat instead of filing onto the boardwalk and making my way up the dark beach.

"Welcome to Obsidian Cove," the Reaper said in a voice which carried over the crashing of the waves at our backs. "To reach the Night Gate, the entrance to Never Keep, you must first master The Escalade." He indicated the intimidating stairs which were carved into the cliff, and I craned my neck to get a look at the dizzying climb before us. "Come."

The Reaper wordlessly turned and led the way up the dangerous climb, one slip upon the wet stairway promising a deadly fall.

The ascent was brutal, but my thighs were well used to hard work. Between the tiderunning I did almost daily in the ocean, climbing the rooftops of Castelorain and traversing the rising hills of my land, I was well prepared for this. From the huffing, panting and groaning sounding behind me, it seemed not everyone was though.

At the cliff's peak, the Reaper silently led us to the high black walls of Never Keep, the towering structures as sheer and smooth as glass. The Reaper led us to a vast entrance set into the walls, the wrought iron gates carved with the phases of the moon standing wide open and awaiting our arrival.

We followed the gold-cloaked man through the gates, stepping onto giant flagstones as we emerged in a courtyard big enough for several thousand Fae to occupy at once – no doubt a place where the entire year's worth of conscripts might gather together. Starlight glimmered overhead, illuminating the carved walls where the sky was reflected in images of constellations and elemental magic.

"This is a sacred place of learning where you are expected to put aside your warring and focus only on the study of the power which has been bestowed upon you this glorious night," the Reaper called, his voice amplified with magic to carry back across the group. "Of course you will harbour animosity to those from the other lands and will not be expected to bunk with them. The neophytes from each nation have access to their own Vault – one of the four arms of the Keep where only those from your own nation will be allowed to step so that you might sleep and study in peace. The Vaults intersect at the very centre of the Keep where we now stand and run diagonally in opposing directions, maintaining your separation outside where possible. You will, however, congregate for your instructions in Cardinal Magic – the power which you can now all command regardless of element - which take place up the Grand Stair to the Galaseum at the heart of the Keep. You will also take meals in the refectory located beneath the Galaseum and you will attend Astral Sanctuary together with the other elementals too." He pointed to a wide door, intricately decorated with representations of every star sign which stood to our right and I made a mental note of it, knowing it would be all too easy to get lost in this sprawling place.

"To your left is the Reapers' Quarters where my brethren reside and it goes without saying that access to our private residence is forbidden."

I glanced to the door directly opposite the Astral Sanctuary, thick wood, entirely unadorned in contrast to its counterpart greeting me with steely defiance as if the thing itself had been created to seem as unwelcoming as possible. Had Harlon taken that door when he'd arrived at the Keep? Was he somewhere beyond it, perhaps settling into his new quarters, meeting the other acolytes who the stars had chosen for greatness?

I tried not to let jealousy carve its way into me at the thought, but as I stood a little apart from the other Raincarvers, my crotch still wet from Ransom's attack, I couldn't help but wish the stars hadn't seen quite how special Harlon was and had left him to the fate we'd both dreamed up together.

"The Vault of Embers lays here in the south." The Reaper pointed to an archway wreathed with carvings of fire and destruction which stood behind us to our left, a wide hall opening up beyond it leading to the private chambers of the Flamebringers.

"The Vault of Steel is to the east." To our backs, but on our right, another imposing archway led towards the space allocated to the Stonebreakers, the walls decorated with real, twisting vines and blooming flowers, the scent of earth and life whispering from within.

"Come." The Reaper led us across the courtyard and through a wide door where the enormous structure he had referred to as the Great Stair dominated the internal space. It was wide enough for ten Fae to climb it abreast, the white marble it had been carved from at odds with the black volcanic stone which made up every other wall of the Keep.

Once again, the Reaper paused, giving me a moment to take in the doors behind the Great Stair which stood open to the refectory, revealing lines of wooden tables laid out with benches on either side of them in preparation of a meal, though sadly for my grumbling stomach, no food appeared to be present.

"The Vault of Sky is to the north east." The Reaper pointed to the archway marked with swirling effigies of air magic on our right where the sounds of someone whooping and hollering in excitement echoed back to us. "And the Vault of Frost lays to the north west." Muttering broke out as we all swivelled towards the archway on our left, the stonework marked with roiling waves and whirlpools. "You are strictly forbidden from entering all Vaults other than your own."

He continued on, and we followed him into the cavernous passageway, my gaze moving from the grey flagstones to the flaming candelabras above. Constellations were glittering in the ceiling between them, marked there in silver and catching the light of the candles.

It was a long walk down the wide hall into the depths of the north western Vault, but we were finally led into it through a blue metal gateway with glimmering sea creatures marked into the walls around it. A guard stood either side of it armed with large swords and dressed in dark armour, and they praised the stars as the Reaper passed them by.

The sound of running water and burbling pools reached me as we stepped into an entrance hall that spanned at least a hundred feet. The humid air immediately chased away the cold which had been clinging to me since arriving in the Keep, and I took in the place in awe.

A giant pool lay at the centre of the chamber, surrounded by lush vegetation, the familiar palms and ferns of my homeland leaning over the water. There were many different levels, stairways and ladders climbing to smaller pools, and waterfalls trailed from one into the next. Three towering effigies stood at the peak of the cascading pools, water spurting from the scorpion tail of Scorpio as well as the two mouths of the fish for Pisces, and the claws of the crab for Cancer where they stood at the pinnacle of three waterfalls.

"This is the Poseidon Spa." The Reaper barely gave us any time to take in the tempting room before leading us through an arching doorway to a glass staircase that spiralled away above us. Water trickled within the glass, moving in a constant rise and fall of glittering droplets.

"There are four towers in the Vault of Frost, each holding sleeping quarters for the neophytes," the Reaper explained. "There are many beds to be claimed in this one, so you make your way skyward. There are a few private quarters, but most are communal. Beyond here, you will find the courtyard where your elemental instruction shall be held, as well as the Library of Frost where books can be found for private study. As it is late, you will now retire for the night, but you may explore your Vault more thoroughly come morning."

I made to step onto the stairs, but the Reaper caught my arm, drawing me aside and allowing the rest of the group to sweep by, chattering excitedly as they disappeared into that tantalising tower.

"I believe you bear a token," he said and I frowned, reaching into my pocket and taking it out. The Reaper took it from me then turned on his heel, his gold cloak sweeping out behind him. "Come."

I followed him, leaving the glass stairway behind with a sinking disappointment, but I had wanted to be placed here, I didn't need the frivolities that went along with it. Even if they did look seriously fucking frivolous.

The Reaper led me down a stairway which I almost didn't spot in its shadowy corner of cobwebs, this one a plain grey stone that went down, down, down until I didn't think there could possibly be anywhere deeper inside the Keep, nor anywhere colder.

But apparently I was wrong, because we went deeper still, and he finally led me into a dank corridor that had a brutal chill to it. He guided me through a wooden door where the sound of clunking pipes and the churning slosh of water made me frown.

"Here we are," he announced, and I took in the chamber which had literal ice crawling up the walls.

"Um, not to be dramatic, but I might freeze my ass off and die if I sleep in here," I said, a shiver wracking through me.

The Reaper chuckled. "We would not leave you without warmth, neophyte." He charted a path across the room and I looked up, realising the ceiling was made of glass with water sloshing back and forth inside it, a low blue glow sparking intermittently through it.

"What is this place?" I muttered.

"It's a cleansing chamber," he said. "All the water that is pumped through the Vaults cycles through a cleansing ritual, passing by runes imbued with power by the Fae who work tirelessly to keep this sacred place of learning in pristine condition to ensure it is of the purest quality. It is then heated as it rises by runes imbued with fire magic as it returns to the pools and tubs of the Fae housed in Never Keep. You are actually one of the rare few to ever see this place. It is a great honour."

"Oh, I feel honoured alright," I said dryly, but he didn't seem to catch the sarcasm as he moved to a large iron grate in the wall. He reached into it and flames blazed to life within, making me flinch a little at the casual use of the element. But the Reapers somehow seemed beyond the burning hatred which simmered within me for the Fae of the other nations, like accepting their role as a voice of the stars truly meant they could put aside the prejudice, hatred and animosity that we were raised with. Would that happen to Harlon? Would he somehow forget to hate the Flamebringers even after they killed my mama? Would he find a way to make peace with the Skyforgers after they had killed countless Fae from our town? I couldn't imagine it, yet this Reaper showed no sign at all that he looked at me with anything even close to hate.

Despite my mistrust of the Reaper's fire magic, I couldn't deny that I needed it and I hurried towards the heat of the flames with my hands outstretched to warm them.

"That is an everflame – you can stoke it or allow it to simmer as you need but it will remain lit eternally for your needs. I had a meal and some items of comfort brought here for you," he added, gesturing to a couple of folded blankets, a pillow and a plate of bread, cheese and grapes. "There is also a map of Never Keep and a schedule for your perusal. If you need the bathroom, you may use the servants' latrines just down the hall from here, the third door on the left. But I am afraid there are no baths on the lower levels. You will have to use the communal bathhouse within your Vault, which you can locate on your map. Praise to the stars."

"Praise to those who tread their destined path." I replied automatically, bowing my head to him and he strode away, taking his Faelight with him and leaving only the roaring flames of the fire. At least the chill was beginning to lessen, but that churning, sloshing noise seemed to be growing louder.

On the bright side, if I could gather the materials, it would be simple enough to make a forge in that fire – assuming I could figure out how to remove the grate. But honestly, bright sides were pretty dim right now, and as I rolled out my blankets and sank down onto them, hugging my knees to my chest, nothing but heaviness pressed in on me. Harlon was gone. Ransom had ensured the Fae here saw me as a reject already, and my living quarters left a lot to be desired.

There was a hole ripping open in my chest that spoke of old wounds, my mother's death seeming so fresh that it was as if I was caught in that Forge again with a rain of hellfire and venom pouring down on us.

I blinked away the dark thoughts, taking my blade from my hip and focusing on the glint of firelight upon the metal as my heart rate slowly steadied. My plan of revenge seemed so very far away despite me claiming a place at Never Keep.

I felt like something other, an unwanted creature to be hidden in the bowels of the fortress, and despite how much I was used to living on the outskirts of society, I'd not considered how quickly my past would chase me into my future. Perhaps the stars had always meant for me to be solitary, perhaps I would be greater because of it one day. But right now, I was nervous of what the dawn would bring, because something told me I was going to need to lean into my most ruthless inclinations if I was going to survive the wrath of Never Keep.

VESPER

CHAPTER SIXTEEN

The Vault of Sky was comprised of a series of buildings which all towered around a central triangular courtyard designed for us to practice our fighting drills and master our elemental magic away from the prying eyes of our enemies. Some of the rooms in the enormous network of chambers were dedicated to mastering the various uses of air magic, others designated for the living space for this year's neophytes. There was a library bigger than the ballroom at some of the lesser palaces in the air kingdom and a bathhouse which made the copper tub in my apartment at Wrathbane look little better than a bucket filled with slop.

There was one tower in this section of Never Keep, the eight floors having been assigned as sleeping quarters for around twenty, but I'd claimed it along with Dalia and Moraine, demanding that anyone wishing to join us bested me in combat to claim their space.

So far, there had been no takers. We'd tossed the beds we didn't require out into the hallway for the Fae who were now left without anywhere to sleep to brawl over, though Moraine had kept a spare in case she wanted to sleep with a different view.

I cared little for the sport of taunting those too weak to demand their own quarters, but Dalia and Moraine had made a game of rushing through the corridors and scaring the shit out of them while they tried to claim some rest in their poor excuses for beds.

I'd spent my evening arranging my room on the very top floor of the tower to my liking, drawing the four poster bed across the chamber so that I would have a clear view of the door as well as one out of the eastern window. I liked waking with the sun, but I knew in this northern slice of the continent that the winter nights were far too long to hope for that.

In that way it was like Wrathborn, the daylight lasting a matter of hours in the winter then sprawling across most of the day and night throughout the summer months.

With snow already on the ground, I knew we would be lucky to enjoy eight hours of full sun a day for the next few months, less once we reached the deepest part of winter. It was one thing I didn't enjoy about our kingdom and one of the more selfish reasons I had for joining the raiding party aboard Ironwraith when I had first been given the option after my enlistment. The battles sought out from the voyages of the wandering islands were the most dangerous but joining them meant seeing the world too.

Once I had the furniture where it was best positioned in case of an attack – including moving an armoire close enough to the door to drag it in front of it while I slept – I had tended to my weapons.

A warrior is only as sharp as their dullest blade. The old mantra from my early battle training hummed through my thoughts as I tested my swords, daggers, the spear I didn't often use but loved like an old friend, and each arrow in my armoury.

My windrider sat beside the window, ready to launch me into the sky at a moment's notice should the want or need take me. Technically, I would be able to move through the air without it once I had mastered my air magic sufficiently, but I was confident I would continue to use it all the same. From the back of the windrider, I could speed through the sky firing on my enemies without needing to focus on the magic which was propelling me through the air. I would also be able to imbue the runes which powered it with magic of my own now, meaning there was no limit to how long I could stay airborn anymore.

I slept well enough, my bed comfortable if unfamiliar, but I had long grown accustomed to sleeping in new places and forcing my body to shut down to claim the rest it required. No nightmares had escaped the locked box of horrors which I shoved to the farthest reaches of my mind and when I woke, I felt ready to face whatever the day had to offer.

I padded across the cool flagstone floor, favouring the deep red rug when I could and tossing a new log onto the fire to stoke the dying embers.

A copper tub sat in the corner of the room behind an engraved privacy screen, but I hadn't seen any servants about the place to ask them to bring heated water up to fill it for me. I paused as my gaze landed on the matching copper basin which sat beneath a gilt mirror, a bent pipe positioned over it with a round knob on the top of it carved with what looked like an imbued rune; the same kind as stored power in my windrider. But Laguz was the rune for life energy, imagination, dreams…water.

Last night I hadn't been able to puzzle out what the thing was intended to do but my skin chilled as I considered the dark magic my Sage had warned me of. The wicked power she had trained me in was used for many things, some of which were rumoured to command power over the elements. To seek that knowledge was a blasphemy which would earn a swift execution for anyone foolish enough to attempt it, but when teaching me about the runes and their varying meanings, she had once whispered which of them had the potential to affect the elements aside from air.

I glanced over my shoulder at the still firmly closed door, reaching for the brass knob and closing my fingers around the cool metal. The thrum of power contained within the rune seemed to confirm my guess that it had been imbued with power and if my understanding of Laguz's potential meaning was correct then...

I sucked in a sharp breath as I twisted the knob and a jet of water burst from the spout beneath it, splashing into the basin and beginning to fill it quickly.

My skin prickled and I checked the door again, but this wasn't some hidden relic I had discovered and tampered with. It was simply an item in my room. An item which stored water magic.

The basin steadily filled until it threatened to overflow and I gritted my teeth, grasping the knob again and rotating it in the opposite direction, disabling the rune and stopping the flow of water.

I stared down at my rippling reflection for a moment then dipped a finger into it.

The water was cool and crisp like fresh mountain run-off. My throat was parched and I swallowed thickly, considering whether this might be some trap. But it seemed far too convoluted for that.

I raised my finger to my lips, inhaling deeply, hunting for the scent of poison before sucking the water from it. The taste was as clear as the liquid looked and I swallowed thirstily but refrained from taking more. I would wait to see if my body developed any adverse reactions before risking a further drink. I knew my poisons well, but there were a few which defied the clues of scent and even taste.

A deep ringing sounded from somewhere further into the Vault and I made quick work of dressing in my battle leathers, secreting six daggers about my person. We'd been told we weren't allowed to carry weapons when summoned to the common areas, but I'd be damned if I wouldn't attempt it. There were several rules in this place which the Reapers enforced, the most notable of which was that we couldn't kill the other elementals despite our feud, upon punishment of execution. But another was that there would be no leaving the Keep and surrounding island until our graduation.

There was only one exception to that rule, and I, as Sinfair, was it. If I was called to battle, I would be allowed to answer that call, but if anyone other than us left the Keep, their place here would be revoked. It was the intention of the Reapers to bless us by the stars during the six months that we were bound here, to ensure we all held equal chance in this unforgiving war, but there was no true equality in such things. Each nation prepared the strongest of their un-Awakened Fae for battle both before their time at the Keep and after, their tactics secret and ever-adapting. But only the kingdom of air sent those who hadn't completed their training at Never Keep into battle – and it was only the Sinfair who faced that fate. The crimes of our blood, be it by birth or relation to a Fae who had brought down such punishment on their future generation, we were the only magic-free combatants to ever set foot on the field.

I left my room and descended the curving staircase which carved a hole through the centre of our tower, making my way to the ground floor where Dalia and Moraine lounged on two of the deep blue couches that furnished the somewhat cosy space. There were rugs and tapestries, two huge fireplaces and a well-worn oak table with seating for twenty at the furthest end of the stone chamber. Clearly it was intended as a common area for the full unit this place was capable of housing, but the empty spaces suited me far better than the inane chatter of countless idiots.

"It's cold as a gnat's ass in this place," Dalia grumbled from her position with her legs slung over the back of the couch and her head hanging close to the floor, her short black hair brushing the dusty flagstones.

"Colder than that," I replied. "No gnats could survive this icy tundra."

Dalia sighed, flipping over and landing on her feet like a cat, which I supposed as a Chimera she technically was, at least in part.

"You look good, V," Moraine said, her assessing gaze roaming over me suspiciously, making it clear that was no compliment. "There's all kinds of innocent vibes clinging to you."

"I'm the picture of purity," I agreed with a shrug as though I had no idea what she was referring to.

"I count three," Dalia purred, flicking my forearm where I'd strapped a dagger out of sight beneath my leathers.

"Then there's bound to be more," Moraine accused but I scoffed dismissively and led the way out into the corridor beyond the tower.

A cold wind swept along the stone passageway, making the flames in the iron braziers flicker with a threat to go out.

It was too early for the sun to be up, but the eerie blue light caused by the snow coating the ground outlined the few windows we passed.

I took the lead, striding purposefully towards the Heart of Never Keep where the four nations would be forced to cohabit for meals, worship and instruction in the cardinal magics – the power which all of us had claimed alongside the use of our element.

We passed through the Vault of Sky, taking the most direct route and crossing through the lavishly decorated courtyard which held countless statues, idols and carvings dedicated to our zodiac signs and element, but was also so big that we would be able to practice both battle and magical tactics within it.

The archway denoting the exit to the Vault of Sky which led into the heart of the Keep was carved from a stone so pale it appeared white, a stark contrast to the black walls of the Keep. There were guards standing to attention around it just as there were no doubt guards barring entrance to the other Vaults too. We weren't allowed to kill each other here but obviously the real rule was that we couldn't be caught doing so. I had my list of targets from Dragor. I simply had to see them eliminated in ways which couldn't possibly tie back to me.

Most of the air conscripts had arrived ahead of us, the deep chiming of the bell still clanging away somewhere overhead as we all filed towards the Great Stair which sat at the very centre of the Keep.

Moraine barked a warning to those who hadn't noticed our approach and a pathway appeared to allow us through the masses.

A tense silence hung as we climbed the stairs, a line of Raincarvers marching up them at the same time, a foot wide division between us and them.

I kept my gaze ahead, ignoring the stares of our enemies while keeping my senses sharp and tasting their desires with my gifts so I would know if any of the bloodlust aimed my way spiked in preparation of an attack. The Raincarvers were a fierce people, their warriors cunning and known for their unpredictable natures.

The ceiling opened up above us as we stepped through the wide doors which led into The Galaseum and I allowed myself a glance up at the vaulted glass spires overhead which offered a view of the dark sky above.

A glimmer of green and pink announced the presence of the northern lights and I had to force myself to look away from them before I was captivated by their beauty. The Sky Witch didn't stare at pretty lights in the sky. At least not in public.

The diamond-shaped room descended away from us, a wide, flat space taking up the base beyond a banister of carved white wood. Stone benches rose away from it, creating an amphitheatre with four defined sides, the corners arranged to leave a clear gap between each of the warring nations.

Most of the seats were filled already but that made little difference to me. I led the way down towards the banister where the view of whoever planned to address us would be clearest, moving through the ranks of Fae in black fighting leathers which marked out the Skyforgers.

I didn't even have to say a word as I came to a halt before the three warriors who had already claimed the best position for themselves; they got to their feet despite their imposing statures, making way for our trio of beasts.

"I would trade all the gold in my family vault for a taste of your lips," the woman in the centre of the group said in a seductive voice, leaning in to grasp my arm.

Moraine had a dagger to her throat before I replied. "I'd suggest you unhand the Succubus," she warned while I gave the warrior a cursory glance. She was beautiful, I'd give her that, her lips full and figure fuller. I might have even been tempted if she wasn't so blinded by my allure and I wasn't now bound by my vow to Dragor.

"Another time," I purred, brushing my fingers against the satin skin of her cheek and feeling the rush of her desire as it stoked the furnace of power within me, a heap of her magic becoming mine just like that.

The man with her grunted an apology, dragging the woman away and I settled into her seat with a contented sigh.

"If you're looking to get laid then warn me, will you?" Dalia grouched as she took the seat to my left, Moraine dropping down beyond her. "I don't need to get caught up in a whiff of your seduction when you switch it on like last time."

"I'm well aware of the way you pounced on me like you'd been possessed by the spirit of a horny goat," I assured her, remembering how she had lunged at me and half gagged me with her tongue a few years ago.

"You turned that shit on while I was feeling vulnerable."

Moraine choked on a laugh. "Vulnerable? Your emotional range swings from bloodthirsty to murderous. You're about as vulnerable as a rabid wolf."

"And I didn't 'switch it on', I was wiping guts from my knife at the time," I pointed out, wondering if I should confide in them about the deal I had made with Dragor. "I guess that's just what gets you going."

"Well it certainly did more for me than your knuckles colliding with my jaw did," Dalia grumbled.

"I was saving you from yourself. I know I'm not your type."

"Yeah. Your cock is too small," Dalia agreed.

I barked a laugh but it fell flat as a shadow loomed over me, forcing my eyes up to find Cayde lingering in the spot before me like he might actually be considering trying his luck in making me move.

"You really want me to show you up in front of all the other elementals?" I asked because I may have been pointedly ignoring the fire, water and earth conscripts so that they knew how little I was concerned by them, but I was well aware of their presence.

"Relax, sweetheart, I'm saving you for dessert," Cayde replied dismissively, hauling the guy on my right out of his spot and dropping into it smoothly.

His wings were out for some obnoxious reason and the thick leather of the one closest to me knocked against my arm as he made himself comfortable.

"Back off," I hissed at him.

"Worried your fan club will get the wrong idea about us?" he taunted, jerking his chin at the Fae who sat across the open space from us.

We were opposite the earth wielding Fae from Avanis, the Stonebreakers' rugged appearance indicative of the brutal existence carved out by the nation of war lords and ruffians. They were big bastards, not one among them even close to my small stature as I let my attention sweep over them. There were bulging muscles, thick scars and plenty of heavily-inked skin, marking their bodies with stories of their accomplishments if the rumours I'd heard were true.

Even in this place I could see the subtle divisions within their ranks, the scattered loyalties to the various crowns they coveted, meaning their alliance against the rest of us was never as cohesive as it should have been.

Likely it was why Avanis hadn't won the war already, because even I could admit they held the most ferocious warriors, their battle-hardened armies a force to be reckoned with. But it was their fractured leadership and chaotic governing system that let them down. They wasted time on infighting when they should have been utterly united against the forces beyond their borders, not squabbling like miscreants and costing themselves precious lives and land.

The front row of their section was made up entirely of male Fae, one of whom was drooling as he stared at me transfixed, the others caught between blinkless staring and gawping.

"I guess they don't get many Succubae in Avanis," Moraine sniggered.

"I wonder how susceptible they are to my power then," I mused, pushing myself forward and resting my forearms on the railing before me.

I smiled slowly, sinking into the depths of my power and focusing on the Fae opposite me as I reached out with my gifts and took hold of their mounting desires. Lust was beyond apparent and it was so easy to manipulate. I tugged, urging those emotions to heighten, encouraging them not just to lust after me but to hunger for a taste of my skin, to need me with a desperate yearning.

Several of them pushed to their feet, one knocking another onto his ass, curses rising angrily from their lips. I met the gaze of one of the biggest assholes towards the far end of the line and very deliberately winked at him as if we shared a secret.

The Fae who had been so set on staring at me descended into a chaotic clash of swinging fists and furious claims of my affections as their desire quickly turned to jealous rivalry and violence.

I sat back, smiling to myself as the Stonebreakers fell into a wild brawl just in time for the door at the base of the amphitheatre to swing open and six Reapers to emerge from the passage beyond. The Stonebreakers' desire for me, for glory, for the win, all fuelled my power until I was burning with the glow of it, my fingers tingling with the desire to unleash it once more.

"Fucking idiots," Cayde grumbled beside me and I gave him a heartbeat of my attention before looking diligently back to the Reapers.

"What is the meaning of this?" a cold voice echoed up from below, loud enough for all of us to hear but only because the Reaper had amplified his voice with magic, not because he had raised it.

Several of the Stonebreakers scrambled to disengage themselves from their brawls but a few of them seemed too far gone to even try and stop. It was rather entertaining.

A rush of magic struck the Fae who continued to fight one another and they dropped to their knees, clutching at their chests and throats, eyes wild with alarm, glaring over at the Skyforgers as if we were to blame for whatever was happening to them.

"If one cannot breathe, one cannot brawl," a female Reaper said serenely, her eyes sweeping around the room at the thousands of conscripts who peered down at her. Those at the back of the enormous amphitheatre were practically lost in shadow.

"She did it!" one of the earth warriors yelled, pointing at me where I sat innocently in my chair, a picture of composure and decorum.

"Did what?" I drawled.

"Marry me!" a man from water screamed, drawing the attention of the room to my right.

Dalia cackled delightedly but I didn't react in any way.

"Please suck my dick," another begged and then he was choking too, several others who had looked like they might be tempted to make declarations of their own falling back in their seats or from their chairs, panicking as the air was stolen from their lungs.

Tittered laughter and jeers broke out from the Skyforgers behind me, some of them praising the power of the Sky Witch, others simply sneering at the fools who had fallen for my power. Though they were no more immune to it than those in the surrounding tiers of seating.

"I wanna lick your toes," some asshole panted in my ear, his face pushing though the strands of my hair from behind.

My fist snapped up, driving into his throat with enough power to knock him back into his own seat and the Fae either side of him hastily yanked him away from me. I supressed a shudder and cast a furtive glance over the Reapers to make sure they hadn't seen me do it.

"Ah, so it isn't all sunshine and orgies then?" Cayde asked, his wing brushing against my side in that infuriatingly distracting way.

"Enough," a Reaper growled from the heart of the group, pushing back his gold hood and I noted the four stars on his cloak marking his high rank. A true hush fell at last as every Fae in the room dropped their eyes to the ground.

"Praise the fading light," thousands of voices hissed as one, mine included. I hadn't expected a Grand Maester to be among the Reapers tasked with instructing us, his rank far superior to most of the Reapers I had encountered here so far. And by the horrified gasps and soft pleas for forgiveness, I had to assume no one else had either. It was sacrilege to disrespect any of the servants of the stars of course but Grand Maesters were said to converse directly with the creators of our fate and disrespecting one of them was tantamount to spitting in the eye of the heavens themselves. The only rank above theirs was that of the Cardinal Reaper himself who was practically a deity in his own right and leader of their order of worship to the stars.

"Those of you who prove to be so weak of will as to succumb to the Order gifts of those surrounding you will not make the cut for elevation beyond the walls of Never Keep," he sneered, his dark skin holding something of a papery quality to it, his vibrantly blue eyes blazing with accusation as they scoured every Fae within the room.

"Praise the fading light," many voices repeated as he finished but my lips had fallen still and I was simply watching the Grand Maester from beneath my lashes and between strands of pink hair.

"Enough of that. If you praise the light every time I utter a sentence then we will likely never progress beyond your basic induction. You are here because you managed to place at Never Keep – you passed the trials and claimed your elements and now tread the path all warriors before you have so faithfully followed for the countless years in which the Endless War has been waged. As you know, we have rules. You will not kill within these walls."

Muttering started up again but was quickly silenced by the sharp gazes of the Reapers in their pristine cloaks.

A few of the Stonebreakers who'd had the air stolen from their lungs collapsed as they lost consciousness but no one moved to help them and more continued to pass out as the Grand Maester went on.

"Today is about understanding the path. Tomorrow you will be tasked to walk it. So, back to the rules. Beyond the point of midnight, all conscripts shall return to their allotted Vaults. On the first day, third day and fifth day, of each week you will attend Astral Sanctuary. Instructions on the cardinal magics – meaning the use of your power without the interruption of your element such as silencing shields, concealment, amplification, etcetera will take place here in the Galaseum. Meals can be taken in your vaults, but if you require hot or freshly prepared food then you will attend the refectory here in the heart of the Keep where you will again cohabit with Fae of other elements. I repeat – you will not kill within these walls. This is a place beyond the sway of war, a sacred sanctuary and to besmirch these blessed stones with the blood of your enemies is akin to spitting in the eyes of the stars themselves."

I glanced over to the Flamebringers who sat rigid and silent in their uniform rows, their clothes emblazoned with the tiger insignia of their people. I gave myself to the count of twenty to search their faces in hunt of the first name on my list, though as I only had a copy of an old portrait to go off of, I wasn't surprised I didn't spot him.

"Today, as so many of you have proven that you need improvement on the subject, we will focus on mental shields," the Grand Maester finished and I supressed a groan, wondering if I might be able to excuse myself. That wasn't even real magic – any competent Fae would have a solid mental shield in place already and have had plenty of prior training in how to erect and maintain it against the work of psychically gifted Orders such as Sirens, Cyclopses or Basilisks.

My gifts hadn't slipped past mental shields anyway, they weren't a psychic ability so couldn't be stopped in that way. It was strength of character and self-control that held Fae back when falling under my influence. If they weren't easily tempted into action by the presentation of their desires, then they wouldn't be swayed by the kiss of my influence.

I gave the rest of the instructions only enough attention to be able to answer any questions which I might have been called upon for, and to make sure I looked attentive. In reality, I spent the following hours scouring the mass of enemies who surrounded me on three sides, weighing and measuring each of them and hunting for my prey.

My eyes fell on the Raincarver girl who had headed into her

Combat Trial first yesterday, her wild hair and wilder clothes making her stand out even from her position in the back row where the shadows clung to her. She was easily noticeable among the bland masses of Fae who were dressed to match their comrades, and I found I liked the uniqueness she offered among a sea of sheep.

She met my gaze and didn't flinch from it and I offered her the hint of a smirk as I noted her mettle before moving my attention on to hunt the rest of the faces surrounding her.

Dragor had a list after all. I wouldn't disappoint him by making him wait on its fulfilment.

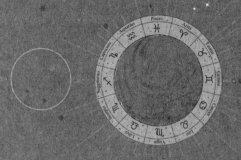

EVEREST

CHAPTER SEVENTEEN

There had been times during the night that the whirring and clunking of the pipes in my so-called sleeping quarters had sounded like screams. It had woken me time and again, leaving my eyes raw with tiredness today. Our first instruction on mental shields had been simple enough, but most of our practise was intended for personal time. It had been followed up by a morning learning about casting silencing shields – a magical barrier that could stop anyone from overhearing you speak to others, or to close yourself off to outside noise entirely. I had a feeling the second use was going to be more important to me in the loud cleansing chamber I had to call home, but the Reapers had warned us the magic was complex and needed ample practise to master.

We weren't going to be spoon fed our magical instructions here; the knowledge was imparted, then it was up to us to learn how to practice it well. There was a library in each Vault where further research could be done on the magics discussed, but there was no reading list or guidance as to what to look for. It was a test in itself, I suspected. A way to weed out the lazy from the ambitious, and I wasn't going to be caught on the back foot. The moment I had a chance, I'd visit the library in the Vault of Frost and collect as many books on mental shields as I could carry back to my quarters.

For now, we had a free hour to get some food from the refectory and there was an optional visit to something they called 'Wandershire' where we could buy supplies. Despite the fact that I'd dried off my warmest outfit, the freezing air in the Galaseum had left my fingers numb, and I'd resented the Flamebringers who had been coaxing flames to life all around them. I'd studied each of their faces, hunting for the one whose death belonged to me, but the chamber had been so vast, there had been no possible way to search them all. I'd decided my focus should belong to the Reapers anyway. I didn't want to miss a crucial piece of information and cost myself some knowledge; it would only make me less capable of taking down the man I planned to kill. Every skill I gained now could be an advantage to me in that fight, especially if I learned it faster and better than he did.

Still, as I walked through the cold, cavernous passages of Never Keep, trailing at the back of a long line of Raincarvers, I couldn't help but steal glances at the faces of the Flamebringers who passed me by.

They openly sneered at my people, curses passing between them while I let my gaze flick from one face to the next. They were a ruthless people, their clothes made for war, but there was a touch of finery to them too. A show of gold swinging from their necks or glints of astrological watches on their wrists, and shining emblems representing their gangster ruler, The Matriarch, - a magpie with a skeleton hand gripped in its talons - gleaming proudly on cufflinks, broaches and pins. Their look was a mixture of raw brutality and highest nobility, though, from what I knew of them, their land of Pyros held nothing of the latter. It was ganglands to its core, their ranks earned through bloodshed between their own people and by the selection of The Matriarch herself.

I had spent some time researching their land in hopes of it giving me an edge when I found my Flamebringer – alright, a fuck load of time. The Matriarch – Mirelle Brimtheon – had risen to power at the young age of eighteen after she'd publicly beheaded the previous ruler who had been a tyrant in their land. She won the love of the people and during her reign so far, she had led countless victories in war between the nations, the bloody fortunes she secured revered across Pyros.

She had a habit of adopting the orphans born from the losses of war, raising them as warriors branded with her name, only to send them out into the very wars their forebearers had died in. It sounded like brainwashing to me, and from what the Raincarvers said of her, she was a conniving master of death, and one of the most dangerous Fae in the four lands.

I'd already grabbed some fruit from the refectory and had eaten it quickly before heading for the shore where the tradesfolk were said to be. I hoped the few silver kismets I had would be enough to buy me some material to make some gloves. I still had a small tin of rare glimlock lacquer I could coat them with which would make them permeable to magic, letting through my power without having to remove them. I'd acquired the stuff from a drunk, sweaty warrior home from war who had told me I could have it if L promised to kiss him. I'd made that promise and slipped it from his fingers, then swiftly made my exit. Technically my promise still held, and technically I had no intention of ever fulfilling it.

The stuff had been used in the forging of my dagger – after a lot of experimentation, I'd realised I could bond it to the metal and if my estimations were correct, it would be far less easily damaged by magical attacks. Magic should slide right through that permeable barrier on its surface and keep it safe from damage. It was yet to be tested, however, but now I was Awakened I would try it soon enough.

"Look at this sea urchin," a Flamebringer drawled at me, and I decided not to respond as he pointed me out to his friends. "She's got seashells on her clothes – did you stitch those there yourself, urchin?"

I glanced down at the pale blue dress I wore that had a row of delicate seashells around the waist and lacy sleeves. The thin pink trousers I'd put on underneath it didn't do much to keep out the cold, but the warmest items I had were currently soaking in a tub of suds in my quarters. I'd put on my sea-glass neckless too, the chunks of different colour pieces hanging down over my chest. *And I look perfectly perfect, thank you assholes.*

"I think they've crawled out of the sea and are licking the sea slime off her," another asshole joined in.

I flexed my fingers, willing the floor beneath their feet to turn to ice, but I used a little too much power and sent a blast of it sliding away under all the Flamebringers in the passage. People went flying, skidding over and hitting the flagstones on their backs. The one who'd called me a sea urchin cast flames to try and melt the ice at his feet, but instead set his friend's ass on fire while another lost control of his Order form and shifted into a Centaur, his hooves flying out in all directions as he tried to stay upright on the ice.

"Hey!" he barked at me, but as the Raincarvers turned to laugh, I slipped away between them, quickening my pace until I was running along with a smile lifting my lips.

I made it out to the Heliacal Courtyard where the large iron Night Gates were standing open with Reapers posted either side of them. I bowed as I went, muttering the words of respect, "Praise to the stars," and heading for the steep Escalade that led down to the beach.

I descended the sheer stairs as quickly as I could, joining a crowd by the crashing waves where they stood on the black sand of Obsidian Cove, all of them looking around in confusion.

Several Reapers stood by the shore, and four obvious groups divided on the beach as we banded together with our own. There were a few hundred Fae who had come to the shore for supplies, but I couldn't see any sign of tradesfolk or stalls.

The Reapers were gazing out to sea expectantly, and I weaved my way to the front of the Raincarvers to get a better look, the black sand shifting beneath my boots.

I checked the faces of each Fae, hoping Harlon might have come, but there was no sign of him, and I wondered what his first morning here had entailed. Was he enjoying his training? Had he made new friends already? Knowing him, he had. He was easy company to keep, and most Fae couldn't help but like him. With a small knot of jealousy in my chest, I accepted I was no longer going to be his regular companion. But maybe I could find a way to see him soon at least. That kiss between us had been playing on my mind, my thoughts ripped into two camps on the matter. It had felt so fucking good to breach that gap between us and to know he wanted me like that, but the other half of me retreated from the idea of putting our friendship on the line. I'd already lost him to the Reapers, losing him completely was unthinkable.

"What are we waiting for?" a Stonebreaker called from her group, her arms bare despite the wicked cold. My gaze tracked over the ink on her skin and the shaved side of her head, the other side a long mane of deep brown.

The earth wielders looked at such a contrast to the Raincarvers, our brighter clothes hinting to ocean life and the days we spent basking in the sunshine. I *maybe* took that look a bit further than most, but since Mama had taught me to create clothes, I'd never seen the point in making anything that looked just like everybody else's. It may have been one of the reasons Ransom and his friends had to mock me, but even when I'd gone through a phase of trying to fit in more, they'd simply found other reasons to taunt me. So I'd refused to cut out pieces of myself to please someone whose opinion I didn't value anyway.

In truth, if I had access to more materials, more metals, I would have taken it further still. I had visions of fish-scaled armour, paired with swords that held distinct shark fins curving up from the hilt. I'd stitch turquoise silk into my leathers and detail Typhon, the sea serpent of Cascada, upon them along with any other image I desired.

"Make way, Wandershire approaches," a Reaper called, and I frowned, following her line of sight across the ocean where the peaks of Helle Fort climbed up from the dark water. Not even the sun's light seemed to penetrate the ocean here, like she rejected her rays, brewing in her own turmoil.

A flash of movement caught my eye and I pivoted toward it, my breath stalling at the sight of the strange, hulking thing approaching across the sea. At first, it looked to be a ship, but its shape didn't fit that structure, and as it drew closer, I saw chimneys spewing smoke, a clock tower rising at its heart with golden hands, its roof sloping up to a tiled steeple. It stood between a crush of buildings, built of wood and stone, an entire town perched upon a vast platform.

To either side of it were rotating fins, metal and magic united to make the structure move through the water with the fluidity of an ocean creature without so much as a sail to guide it. Catapults ringed the structure, visible between a savage metal fence that circled the entire town with spikes topping it. They had enough blood staining them to confirm that something or someone had tried to scale them on multiple occasions.

The Fae on the beach retreated as the town closed in on the shore, and those twisting fins changed into something new, splitting apart and turning into eight, giant metal legs. The town rose upon them and crawled up the beach like a monstrous spider before coming to an abrupt halt and sinking down into the sand. A whirring filled the air and steam plumed out from a network of pipes that ran beneath the structure, my eyebrows arching as I took it all in.

Two golden gates stood high above us, the base of the town still ten feet in the air, but they were flung open in the next second and a beautiful stone stairway was crafted into existence by the Stonebreaker who stepped out.

It seemed this man was as much a fan of unique fashion as I was because his long fur coat was white with black splashes, hanging open to reveal bare skin, a spill of golden muscles and a cluster of amulets swinging from his throat. His pink trousers rode low on his hips and his army boots were strapped up with strings of wire and daisies. He wore a top hat which he took from his head in respect to the Reapers, springing down the steps to land heavily in the sand before them, taking a bow.

"Wonderful fucking day, ain't it?" He stood upright, his dark blue eyes wheeling across us all. "But fuck me, there were a lot of monsters out along Grimvale Passage today. Do you lads and lasses ever clean up the ocean or are you the ones placing those beasties out there?" he asked the Reapers who gave him cool looks.

"Get on with it, Mavus," the closest female Reaper said. "The Grand Maester has allotted you two hours, and you have already squandered fifteen minutes of your time."

"That's rich, ain't it?" He held a hand to his chest as if wounded. "I come all the way out here, a humble trader seeking to make a livin' and I have to skewer ten beasties to even make it to this stars-forsaken place. There ain't no one else in these dangerous waters who would bring you your wares, but here I am, risking me own neck to do it."

The Reapers said nothing, and he sighed heavily, turning to us. "Forgive me, I ain't even introduced myself yet. I'm Mavus Angelico, Mayor of Wandershire, and I have the rare and highest honour of being a neutral party in your four-way war. You've probably heard of me."

"My father said you made a blood-tie with him to heal his gout but his foot fell off last year!" a girl piped up angrily among the Skyforgers.

"Blood-ties?" Mavus gasped in offense, looking to the Reapers. "I don't make blood-ties, me. No, I'm just here to make an honest trade with these fine folk. Your father shouldn't be makin' blood-ties, doll. That's the work of vagabonds and lowly cut-throats, that is. Nothing like you'll find here in my lawful town." He threw her a stern look then shot a winning smile at the rest of us, talking louder when the girl tried to argue. "Now here's my sweet Wandershire." He moved to pet the metal leg of the town and I swear the whole structure shivered a little.

There was magic in that thing unlike anything I'd ever witnessed, and this man was somehow the key to it. How was he allowed to roam freely like this? I'd never heard of traders who were neutral parties in the war. What allowed him such privilege?

"She's sweet to those who are sweet to her but invoke her wrath and you shall find her an unwelcome place indeed," he warned, his eyes glinting with darkness and his smile a little too wide as he looked between us, something manic about him that set the back of my neck prickling. "Please, step aboard. I accept gold, karmas and kismets if you've got 'em, item trades and blood- er bloody great tales of war too." He threw a sideways glance at the Reapers who gazed icily back at him in warning.

"You know the punishment of making blood-ties with any Fae of Never Keep," a male Reaper growled. "Your neutral rights will be revoked."

"Indeed, indeed, I weren't gonna say nothin' about blood-ties," he scoffed. "You Reapers always look for the bad in me, but I ain't never done anythin' but bring you fine wares from the four nations." He bowed to them, then gestured for us to move forward. "Climb aboard, dogs and dolls, my keepers shall greet you in the many trade stores and provide you with all your worldly needs for study and recreation alike." He winked, beckoning us closer and I moved with the crowd, intrigued as I climbed the steps and passed through the golden gates into Wandershire.

The narrow street ahead was paved in mottled bricks, winding off into the throng of tightly-packed buildings, all of them strangely tall and too thin. I eyed the many store fronts, passing by window displays of quills and inkwells, parchment and all the study supplies I could ever need. I still had enough of those items, so I passed them by, gazing up at the high chimney stacks that topped many of the slanted slate roofs, the smoke drifting away into the sky.

I turned left and right down the narrow alleys, and soon found myself alone, falling to a halt as I reached an armoury. The weapons in the window display were beautiful pieces, and my gaze lingered on a double-bladed sword with a red hilt that looked as though it were crafted from Dragon scales. Unlikely, considering there hadn't been a Dragon shifter seen in years. It was a mimicry etched into the metal probably, but without being able to touch it-

"Beautiful, ain't she?" Mavus's voice made me jump and I unsheathed my concealed dagger, turning sharply toward him. He ignored the blade, moving closer and sliding an arm around my shoulders as if we were old friends. "I got her off a battlefield in Avanis. Fuck me, the smell of the dead went on for miles, you shoulda been there. Real place of rot and decay if ever I saw one. I prefer the battlefields of a Flamebringers' victory. They scorch up the bodies, see? You can't smell nothing but cooked flesh, and that don't smell half as bad as you might think."

I jerked out from under his arm, my blade still raised. "So this weapon is stolen," I accused, glaring at the Stonebreaker who dared address me like a friend.

"Stolen?" he gasped, getting that wounded look about him again. "The dead don't own nothin', doll. Weapons ain't no use to them when they're rotting on a battlefield. My wares might be taken from dead fingers, but I ain't never stolen a thing in my life. Except a few hearts." He smiled brightly like we were having a casual conversation and maybe that was how he saw it. But what he'd said was pretty fucked up.

"If I died and my weapons ended up here for anyone to claim, I wouldn't be happy about it," I insisted, and I noticed his gaze lingering on my dagger for a moment.

"That's the thing about dead people, doll. They don't feel nothin' about anythin'," he said grimly. "Death's just a deep black sea, not a glitter of starlight in sight as some fools would like to believe. What say you on that?"

I deliberated my answer, unsure how much I wanted to say to this Stonebreaker who I was alone with down here. "I think the worthy find a place among the stars beyond The Veil."

"The worthy," he tasted those words in his mouth. "I've been around a fair time and I can't say I've met anyone fitting that description. Even the sweetest of grandmamas have a taste for blood on their little ol' lips. I've seen it. I've lived it."

"You don't look that old." I glanced him up and down, placing him maybe in his late twenties, early thirties at most.

"I'm ancient if you count your days by how many horrors you've witnessed," he said darkly, and the glimmer of past traumas hung heavily in his eyes before he blinked and smiled again. "Now, what's your name, doll? And what are you here for?"

"Why do you care?" I asked, taking another step away from him.

"Suspicious little creature, ain't ya? But alright, I'll tell you the truth as to why I followed you."

I stepped back again, my dagger raised a little higher and magic caressing the fingertips of my right hand. The cry of seagulls sitting on a nearby roof and the chatter of Fae in the next street over made the atmosphere calm enough for this situation not to brew a storm of concern in me, but I wouldn't be taking any chances. I'd been cornered before by wolves as savage as this asshole looked, and I'd lived to tell the tale.

"I have an eye for those in need of something a little more... unusual, shall we say? I make trades in all kinds of wares, lass.

Anything you need, your heart's desire can be answered between the streets of Wandershire."

"Well your eye is wrong," I said. "I'm looking for material to make gloves. That's all."

"Ah, that's all, she says," he mused, his gaze falling to my dagger again. "That's a piece of something I'd like to see closer. I know special when I see it, doll. That's no ordinary dagger." He held out his hand and I scoffed.

"As if I'd hand you my weapon."

"You're a conscript at Never Keep. Do you think I'd be welcome back upon the shores if I made a habit outa gutting the neophytes?"

"I'm still not going to hand you my blade," I said simply.

"Hm…" He considered me. "Material, you say? Right this way then, doll." He gestured for me to walk ahead of him, but I did no such thing and he tittered a laugh before leading the way. I'd be turning my back on this guy right about never.

He guided me into a busier street, gesturing to a clothmaker with stunning material draped across the window display. Mavus led me inside and my lips parted at the sea of materials hanging from wooden racks and pouring out across circular tables.

I stowed my blade, rushing towards a swathe of darkest blue fabric that was both soft and durable. It was textured too which meant it would still keep a good grip on a blade when it was made into gloves. A notice beside it claimed it had been waterproofed by the magic of the clothmaker with a lifetime assurance. Then I saw the price and quickly snatched my hand away from it.

My heart sank as my gaze flitted from one notice to the next, the amount of karmas I'd need for these materials far more than I had. Even if I started offering weapon and clothes repair services out to my fellow Fae, it could take months to earn enough to be able to make purchases in this store. I felt Mavus's eyes on me and slowly did a circle of the place, pretending I was interested and nodding to the red-haired woman behind the counter.

Then I headed for the door, but Mavus swept into my way, his hand slamming against the wall so his arm extended across my path.

"I thought you were seeking material, doll?" he purred and something in his tone sent adrenaline sweeping into my veins.

"None of this is what I need," I said lightly.

"Horseshit," he said, holding up something in his hand and jostling it.

I cursed, realising it was my coin purse. He had somehow stolen it from my pocket.

"Give me that." I swiped for it, but he held it out of reach.

He casually poured the coins out into his palm, thumbing through them, his fingers clad in silver rings. "Ah, I see." He frowned. "This all you got, doll?"

I shrugged, but it was answer enough.

He slid my coins back into the purse and handed it over, my suspicion of him only growing as I pocketed it.

He caught my arm, pulling me closer and speaking in a low voice just for me. "I know the feel of light pockets. Which is why my trades extend beyond coins, doll. Let me take a look at that dagger of yours. A look, that's all. And I'll gift you any material you want from here."

"Any material?" I asked in surprise, the tantalising offer too tempting to deny.

"How much do you need?"

"A yard of the blue," I said quickly, pointing to it. "And another yard of fleece if you have it."

He boomed a laugh. "A woman who knows what she wants, a rarity indeed. And a deal you have, my dear." He offered me his hand and I slid mine into it, gasping when a clap of magic rang between our palms. I'd heard a bit about the magic of star promises, but I was only capable of making them now my magic was Awakened, our vow to each other bound by the power in our veins.

His smile widened and I didn't feel all that happy with this part of the deal as I slid my precious dagger free of its sheath and passed it over.

"Bless Cassiopeia," he murmured. "And the sweet song of Cygnus. This is a fine, fine thing. Where did you get it?"

I sensed he was digging for a truth he already suspected, his eyes glimmering with the sheen of my blade.

"I forged it," I said.

"There, see." His gaze snapped up, landing on me and looking at me in that same way he'd looked at the blade. As if pricing me up in his mind, figuring out my worth and how he could make use of it. "I knew you were special."

"Not the word of choice in the town I'm from, but I'll admit I prefer it." I held out my hand for the blade but he spun it around, testing it in his grip then flicking his nail against the tip to make it ring. Finally, he gave the blade back with a sigh.

"You give me that dagger and I'll give you any material you want in this store. Indefinitely," he said and the woman behind the counter hiccoughed as she overheard.

"I'll compensate you, Sally, don't you worry," he called to her.

"No deal," I said, sheathing it fast.

He frowned, running his thumb over his chin as he considered me. "You've got a story to that blade. A meaning behind it."

I said nothing, looking to the blue material across the store. "I kept my end of the bargain, am I about to learn you don't keep yours after all?"

"I made a star deal with you, doll. Don't you know what it means if either of us break it?" he asked, snapping his fingers at the woman and pointing to the material. "A yard of that and a yard of fleece," he directed her.

"No," I answered his question. "What happens?"

"Seven years' bad luck, is what," he said, smirking at me. "The stars will curse you for it, and in this forsaken land I don't need any more things going against me. I hedge my bets, see?" He gripped the cluster of amulets at his throat. "I pray to them all, every last one of those pretty little bastards in the sky. I may be earth born, but I'm loyal across all constellations, all elements too."

Shock rolled through me at the admission. "But you back earth in the war surely?"

"Like I said, doll, my loyalty lies up there." He kissed the amulets and pointed to the roof, meaning the sky I guessed. "I'm a neutral party."

"Why do the nations allow it?" I whispered, stepping closer to him and feeling as though this conversation would earn me the severest of punishments back at the Keep if it was ever heard.

"It's all about value." He looked me over, taking in my handmade clothes. "You can have anything in this world if you know who to offer your value to. But be careful, lass. If you're not prepared, then you'll find yourself licking the soles of the sovereigns of this world, begging for a mercy they won't ever grant." His eyes told of some terrible, wicked thing in his past that almost made me warm to him. I knew the taste of ruin and it seemed he knew it too.

"There we are," he announced brightly, stepping away from me, all light again instead of dark. He took a paper bag from the storekeeper's hand, passing it to me and I could hardly believe I'd just been given what I needed for free.

"This was...odd. But thanks, I guess," I said then headed for the door.

"What's your name, doll?" he called after me, but I didn't answer, slipping out onto the street and taking a few quick turns in case he was following again. I was appreciative of the strange deal, but I didn't like the way he looked at me. It left a shudder in my skin that wouldn't shift.

I opened the paper bag, gazing at the beautifully crafted material inside, my heart lifting at the sight, my mind already crafting the gloves I was going to make from it. Mavus Angelico might have been unsettling, but I wasn't going to complain about the gift he'd offered me.

I walked straight into a solid body and went stumbling back a step, my eyes lifting as the huge guy turned around, glancing down at me and making my lungs crush in my chest. I knew those eyes, black as nightshade and as empty as the open sky. I had seen him in every dream, every vengeful wandering of my mind. And now I was abruptly and irrefutably eye to eye with him, caught so off guard that I didn't even have my blade in hand.

"*You*," I snarled, unsheathing the dagger that was intended for his heart and dropping my bag in favour of focusing on this fight.

My mother's killer. He was standing there, turning to me with a casualness that said I was about as important to his day as an errant fly buzzing around his head. And one swift bat of his hand was all it would take to send me on my way.

His leather jacket hung open, and the magpie emblem of The Matriarch was stitched into a diagonal battle strap across his chest, following the exact line that I had cut him with my blade. If possible, he had grown even bigger this past year, his height more intimidating than I remembered, and those eyes, so penetratingly dark that they seemed to eat into my soul. They flashed red for the briefest moment, some hint of what lay beneath his terrifying exterior, something perhaps even more monstrous than his outer skin. I sensed it had to do with his Order, but what it was, I couldn't guess.

I was so stunned to find him here that it took me a second longer to remember to strike at him. A cry left my lips as I swung my blade for his throat, intending to slash it right open and paint myself in his blood. But his hand came up, snatching my wrist in a bruising grip, his fingers as hot as hellfire against my skin. The burn bit deep, but I didn't release my blade, snatching it into my left hand instead and stabbing low, aiming to stick it in his gut.

But before it could land, a magical force hit me, the horrid, oppressive power driving into my skull and taking hold of my mind. My simple mental shields shattered from the impact of whatever wicked spell he had placed upon me, and I gasped as my hand came to a shuddering halt, the tip of the blade just grazing his stomach, his mind wielding my body with the unholy power of whatever Order he had claimed. His eyes were darkest red, and he was all I could see as he bent me to his will, that terrible power making my hands return to my sides, my fingers working to sheath the dagger.

There was a sound of growling at my back and I swear the sky turned red above him as he pushed that power deeper inside me until my knees were buckling to his command, his magical possession wracking through my limbs and forcing me beneath him.

"Name," he commanded in a rough tone.

That voice that had haunted me for so long, the one I had pictured twisting into a scream as I reaped my vengeance upon him, but instead, it had my own tongue curling to its order.

"Everest Arcadia," I rasped, some part of me fighting against his power still, but with every passing second, his claws curled deeper inside my mind.

I was forced to look up at this brute of a man while he stared down at me, his ruggedly handsome face impassive and cold. His hand shifted to beckon something and three, blood-red hounds coiled into existence beside him, the snarling, savage-looking creatures setting my heart thumping painfully hard.

My enemy's fingers were inked with the tail of a bird that disappeared out of sight up his right arm, and a gold signet ring adorned his little finger marked with the magpie of The Matriarch, the name Kaiser Brimtheon curving beneath it.

"Is that your name?" I managed to force out, despite his hold over my tongue, shock jarring through me. *Brimtheon.* He was one of The Matriarch's spawn, her orphan warriors.

He frowned, his mental power slamming harder against me and closing my lips. He forced my head to turn and look at the huge red dogs, their bared teeth aimed right at me and making my throat thicken.

My fingers twitched for my blade, but I couldn't make a move toward it, and no magic would come to my fingers either. I was his puppet, my mind linked to him by strings of his creation, forced to move to his will.

"Do you know what I am?" Kaiser asked, his tone a low drawl that held no taunt or much life at all.

I shook my head in answer and sensed Fae moving closer at his back, his friends watching on, but my eyes were fixed on Kaiser.

"Is that the Raincarver who scarred you, Kai?" one of them asked in surprise, and I recognised the voice as the Flamebringer who went by the name North, the one who had fought with Harlon all those months ago.

A twisted smile lifted my lips at his words. So my strike had left its mark, and Kaiser clearly wasn't privy to the Reapers' healing magic as I'd heard The Matriarch was. She apparently didn't care to seek aid for her soldiers.

Kaiser's eyes flashed wickedly and the hounds stopped growling, moving together as one and shifting into something else. Terror and pain wracked my bones as they changed into my mother then threw themselves at me, knocking me to the ground on my back. The world altered and suddenly I was pinned beneath my mother's weight, her screams pitching up to the sky as Basilisk venom rained down on us. My limbs were frozen by her power. I couldn't move. Fear spilled through my flesh and my own screams joined hers, the true nightmare of that day brought to life in an instant. And with a jolt of clarity I *knew*, in the depths of my bones, what Kaiser was. A creature of legend, a rarity among Fae, possessing an Order so terrible it was said few survived the cruelty of their wrath.

"Fury," I gasped as the vision of my mother turned into one of those snarling, dark red dogs instead, the beast pinning me down and its master leaning over it to glare at me.

Only Kaiser didn't really glare, it was emptier than that, this hollow monster seeing me suffer and drinking in the power I fed him through my dread. The well of my magic drained in my chest as terror shuddered its way through my body and I fought off the sensation of my mother's weight, the most awful moment of my life reborn.

Furies fed on fear, their magic recharged by the terrors of others, and his gifts could form monsters such as these hounds with nothing but a thought. He could sense every Fae's nightmares and bring them to life before their eyes, exposing them to their greatest terrors over and over, all the while taking possession of their bodies and minds, forcing them not to fight back. The strongest of his kind could bring true memories back to life in his victims' minds, just as he had done with the memory of mother's death.

He was a thing of horrors, and perhaps that was why it seemed no soul lived in his eyes.

"You seek to kill me," he stated. "But you cannot fight off the power of my possession. So how will you ever lay a hand on me, silka la vin?"

"I managed it once," I gritted out, unsure what those final words meant. It must have been spoken in the old tongue of Pyros. "I'll do so again, and I won't miss your heart this time."

"I didn't even have to possess you before. And in all the months that have passed, still you haven't trained well enough to lay a scratch on me."

"Why didn't you kill me that day?" I hissed, my tongue my own again as he focused his Fury possession on keeping me still on my back beneath one of his vicious hounds. The question had kept me awake more nights than I could count as I replayed my fight with him in my head. He could have driven a sword through my chest, he could have thrown me into The Crux.

"Your death wasn't worth the time it would have taken to clean my sword," he said hollowly, and something about the lack of taunt was worse than the way Ransom sneered at me. Like I was literally nothing to this man.

"Yon eskindo pishalé," I spat at him.

"A fucking asshole, am I?" he drawled and I gaped at him, shocked that he knew the Cascalian language. "I know all the tongues of my enemies. It makes it far easier to spy on them."

"We're technically not on Never Keep grounds," North chimed in keenly. "Kill her and toss her body in the ocean."

"Like I said," Kaiser replied as a cold chill crept over my skin. "She's not worth my time."

"I'll clean your sword for you," North offered, and a titter of laughter sounded from more Flamebringers behind him, but I was so firmly pinned to the street that I still couldn't see them.

"Do you still carry my mother's sword?" I demanded, but he didn't answer. "Of course you do." I sneered. "It's made far better than any fire blade you wield. I bet you've tried to disguise it as one of your own." I assessed the hilts of the two swords strapped either side of his hips, noticing the glint of the less-worn metal on the one on the left. "That one." I jerked my chin at it. "I'll retrieve it soon enough when you lay dead at my feet."

His Fury hound snapped at my face and I winced, but no bite came.

"Your words may pacify your longings for revenge, but they will not become actions," Kaiser said darkly. "No Fae in Never Keep could claim my death."

He turned his back on me, his hound stepping off of me to follow at his heels with the other two beasts, but his possession still kept me bound in place.

"Says the man who bears a scar of my making," I called after him.

He stilled, his back to me as if he was reconsidering walking away, and my heart juddered at the prospect of him returning. My vows were true enough, but the fact was, I was pinned to the street with no way of fighting him off if he decided to drive a sword into my chest.

Kaiser kept moving, the group of Flamebringers parting to let him lead the way forward, proving his position among them. North glanced back at me, his dark brown hair sticking up in all directions and his grin a malicious thing as he ran his finger across his throat in a promise of my death. But I didn't care for idle threats, I'd faced plenty of those from Ransom and I was still here breathing. No, what I cared for was the plan forming in my mind, the way I was taking stock of everything I had just learned about my mother's killer. Every free moment of my time would be spent reinforcing my mental shields and learning how to block out the power of his Fury gifts until I'd perfected it. And in the meantime, I had a name to etch into my dagger.

Kaiser Brimtheon.

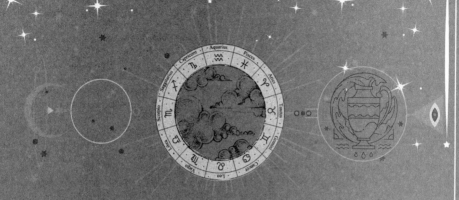

VESPER

CHAPTER EIGHTEEN

Sweat slicked my skin as I swung my sword with wild fury, the clash of steel on steel echoing around the triangular courtyard in the heart of the Vault of Sky. The frigid air was a welcome respite from the stifling heat of my own flesh as I pushed myself to the limit, facing off against both Dalia and Moraine at once.

"Don't drop your shoulder," I barked at Moraine, slapping the flat of my sword against the side of her neck where she'd left herself open.

Dalia twisted behind me, aiming to strike at my back while I was distracted by berating our other sister in arms, but my sword clashed with hers before she could land the strike.

I kicked out at Moraine, forcing her back as the two of them tried to trap me in a pincer movement, then I threw my head back so that Dalia's blade swung past me instead of landing a blow.

I lunged at her in the space she'd left open beneath her outstretched arm, my forearm clashing with hers as she tried to drive a dagger at me in her other hand and I collided with her hard enough to put her on the ground.

My sword pressed to her throat as I pinned her beneath me and I threw a dagger at Moraine who tried to lunge for me while I was occupied with my win.

She deflected the dagger with her sword, but I met her gaze while I held a second blade pinched between my finger and thumb, both of us knowing I could have thrown it already and struck her between the eyes.

"Asshole," Moraine grunted, tossing her sword to the ground and I grinned through the blood staining my teeth thanks to the split lip she'd managed to give me somewhere amid the rampant fury of our combat practise.

"You know you love me," I taunted, pushing to my feet and offering Dalia a hand up.

She slapped my palm aside, spitting curses against my name as she scrambled upright unaided, forever the poor loser.

"The stars favour you with gifts of prowess as well as beauty, it would seem," a man commented from behind me and I turned to look at him, ignoring the press of the other eyes which had been present for the last hour, watching from the shadows.

"You're one of Cassandra's posse," I commented, taking the measure of him quickly and finding him likely to be lacking.

"I'm not sure I'd put it like that," he replied, carving a hand through his smooth, blonde hair and eyeing me curiously.

I reached out with my gifts. He wanted something from me, but it wasn't lust he was hungry with.

"How would you put it then? There is a certain smell to your breed and I don't often mistake the reek of it."

"I'm not as well-bred as the Blusters or any of the other sycophants Cassandra claims for her closest companions. But I have an uncle who is a High Reaper so I think she seeks influence by trying to draw me into her cabal."

I paused in the act of turning away, my interest piqued despite my usual determination to stay well clear of court politics. But I had often wondered whether the family members of the Reapers were given certain privileges with the stars. Were they given the gift of foresight? Would the prophets of the heavens deign to look into their futures for them? Or would they perhaps be offered a few snippets of wisdom from the stars which the rest of us weren't deemed worthy to receive?

"And would her efforts at recruitment pay off were she to earn the accolade of your friendship?" I asked curiously.

"Perhaps. But I seek connections with Fae who have proved their worth in actions rather than bloodlines. Which was why I was thinking we might form some kind of…understanding?"

I looked him up and down. He had been out here training for over an hour and was sufficiently ruffled and breathless to suggest he at least took his part in the war seriously. But I didn't much like striking bargains with anyone, especially the kind spun in the murky waters of the Wrathcourt.

"What is it you want from me?" I asked and I didn't miss Dalia and Moraine lingering close enough to eavesdrop while pretending to check their weapons for damage.

"Nothing. I'm simply offering the hand of friendship in a court of snakes," he said easily. "I'm Ogden Breeze."

I didn't take the hand he offered.

"Tell me what privileges your uncle affords you and how they might be of benefit to me," I replied, moving towards the water barrel and dunking a cloth into it so I could wipe the blood from my face as he answered.

"If I give you the truth, will you use it to ruin me?" Ogden asked, taking a cloth of his own and mopping the back of his neck with it.

"No," I said honestly. "I couldn't give a fuck about the Wrathcourt and I care even less about you. I doubt I'll remember your name after this exchange unless you can prove you have worth."

Ogden released a nervous laugh and I dunked a ladle into the water barrel, taking a drink from it. "Okay. The truth is…my uncle is so obsessed with ideas of his own superiority that even if he was able to offer out tips or whispers from the stars to his kin, I doubt he would. Besides…"

He trailed off but that hesitation was the most interesting thing that had happened in this conversation, and as I tasted his desire to rant about whatever it was that was stalling on his tongue, I tugged at it.

Ogden didn't seem to notice my interference in his desires, the words spilling from him in a rush as if he simply couldn't help himself.

"From what he has said, and the way he danced around the subject of proof and the questions I have asked about the will of the stars, I can't help but find reason to doubt in their superiority altogether. I mean, we just have to believe that people like my uncle are better than my father or me just because they can command additional elements? Think about it. Why are we even celebrating that? I'd say it's a sign of failure not accolade – imagine the shame of having dirt run through your veins alongside air. I'd have a mind to find the nearest cliff and hurl myself-"

I didn't hear the rest of Ogden's tirade because I walked away before he could finish it and Dalia and Moraine kindly stepped between us to stop him from following me.

"Fucking idiot," I muttered as I crossed the courtyard, reaching out to brush my fingers over the water carrier's bucket as I passed the huge statue in the shape of Aquarius, mentally apologising to him for listening to even a minute of that bullshit.

Ogden was little more than a jealous, petulant child, raging against the stars and the Reapers because he and his father weren't deemed worthy to join them. He could offer me nothing in the way of access to his uncle and I certainly had no interest in aligning myself with his non-believer bullshit.

I slipped behind a tall pillar which was the first of a line of them to the west side of the courtyard, sheathing my sword as I went in hunt of my shadow.

Those watching eyes lost me as I travelled through a throng of Fae discussing the upcoming instruction in air magic which we were all about to attend. I pushed through the closely-packed bodies until I made my way around the courtyard and came to a halt behind the asshole who had been watching every moment of my training.

I took up a position leaning against the wall, kicking my right foot up to press to the cold stone while he peered left and right, clearly in search of something. A something which I was pretty certain was me. The why was the issue.

I took an apple from my pocket and bit into it loudly, the beast before me stilling and slowly turning to look at me.

I arched a brow and Cayde frowned.

"Care to tell me why you were watching me fight?" I asked.

"What's to say I wasn't watching Moraine or Dalia?" he countered, moving to lean one shoulder against the pillar he had been skulking behind for the past ninety minutes while he'd observed me.

"The hateful look in your eyes," I replied, not bothering to swallow my mouthful of fruit first. Cayde was aristocracy after all and manners were bred into them like a second layer of blood. If there was one thing I knew about getting beneath the skin of assholes like him then it was that reminding them of everything they hated about me usually worked a treat. "And the way they've been pinned to me tirelessly. If you simply wanted to fuck me then I could feel it, but you want more, don't you?"

His ambition, desire for power and hunger for recognition all hummed in the air between us and I was left with little doubt that our rivalry was the cause of it. There couldn't be two prizes of the Sinfair. One sin-stained miscreant rising to greatness was an anomaly. Two was a whisper of change in the air. And the Wrathcourt didn't like change.

"I'm searching for your weaknesses," Cayde said, stepping closer to me and I grinned as I took another huge bite from my apple.

A bell tolled throughout the courtyard, calling us all to attention and I straightened my spine, excitement over our imminent instruction burning through me.

"Let me know if you find any," I said, slipping around him as the bells continued to chime. "It's been twenty-one years and I've still only managed to count one. And really, what does a little weak blood matter when you're the Sky Witch?"

"You're so fucking full of yourself," Cayde muttered at my back.

"Look who's talking," I replied, pushing into the crowd and leaving him behind.

If he wanted to skulk in the shadows and obsess over ways to outshine me then that was his prerogative. I had bigger goals in mind.

I joined Dalia and Moraine who were standing by the exit to the courtyard where an iron door was set into the stonework which marked the wall leading to the desolate landscape outside of Never Keep.

So far, the door had remained firmly locked, but today we were due to head through it for the first time and move onto the icy tundra beyond where we could practice our air magic without need for constraint.

The door was drawn open as I reached it, a trio of Reapers, cloaked in gold as usual, awaiting us on the frosty landscape beyond.

I tossed my apple core into the hands of some ogling idiot as I passed him, shuddering in disgust as he began licking it and groaning my name.

My sweet hellions swept in to flank me as I led the masses through the door, Cayde appearing like an unwanted stench on the air beyond Dalia too.

I ignored him, my eyes on the Reapers as they beckoned us after them onto the rocky plain and our boots crunched over ice and gravel as we followed.

To our left, the Vault of Frost extended into the unwelcoming terrain, the angle of the long buildings creating a V as they converged at the centre of the Keep. We moved away from both Vaults, walking for around ten minutes and spreading ourselves out as the Reapers instructed us to do so.

"Elemental magic is, in ways, the purest form of power any of us possess," Reaper Tessa called, her red hair vibrant where it spilled from beneath her golden hood, her green eyes lined with age and wisdom. "Today we will work on nurturing the natural connection you feel to your air magic, using that bond to unleash the fullness of your power. Then the hard work will begin. It is easy to blast down a door with brutal strength but the subtleties of picking a lock with a whisper of magic is something much more refined. The most potent power comes in the form of the unexpected."

My lips lifted as I listened to her, my own views on power so very like her own. After all, I was a woman of small stature born at the wrong time and cursed with the blood of my enemies, but I had forced the kingdom of air to sit up and notice my power regardless.

I inhaled deeply as I fell into the eternally shifting purity of my air magic, and as Reaper Tessa began instructing us on how to feel for the flow of it and let our will work alongside it instead of pushing for domination over it, I found that made a beautiful kind of sense.

My magic was something I wanted to work alongside, not force beneath my heel. And as I raised my hands to cast a breeze into the air, I could have sworn I felt the power within me smiling as it met with a kindred spirit and we began to learn the art of working as one.

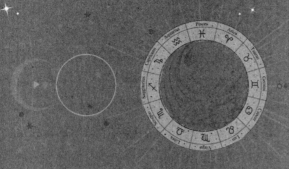

EVEREST

CHAPTER NINETEEN

I had never experienced a storm such as this. Even the most ferocious of sea storms that had blown across the coast of Castelorain didn't compare. Me and the other Raincarver neophytes were out bobbing in the frantic, churning waves of the furious ocean off the shore of Never Keep, and it took all my energy just to keep my head above the water. My legs kicked, my arms fighting the push and pull of the waves that were sweeping around us, clashing together like colliding anvils.

I was caught more than once between those waves, the wind their puppet master, twisting and churning the sea until she was frothing at the mouth, trying to drag us into a watery grave.

The booming voices of the Reapers cried out to us from above, riding upon the crests of high waves that went sweeping by, their bodies shielded by bubbles of air magic, keeping them in a pocket of calm away from the roaring wind, pummelling rain, and frenzied ocean.

"Part the rain, rise upon a wave and carry yourself to shore," Reaper Pavros called as he went sailing by, his black curls perfectly dry, not a single touch of rain wetting him.

The skill in their magic was enviable, their gazes impatient as they watched us thrash in the sea, fighting with our own element.

Casting water was one thing, but taming a feral beast such as these stormy waves was another entirely. It took all my focus just to try and stop the water from smashing into me and sending me spiralling down towards the seabed.

We'd been given swimwear that clung to our bodies like a second skin, but it was too thin, too simply made to really keep out the frigid cold. My fingers were numb as I flexed them to cast, but the rest of my body was warm enough thanks to the burning in my muscles while I treaded water endlessly.

As I tried to wrangle another wave headed my way, I managed to push my will into it, preparing to guide myself onto its prow. But the monstrous thing reared up then crashed into me, making me lose my grip on my magic and sending me spinning into the black depths.

I kicked hard, fighting my way to the surface and guiding water behind me to push me to the air above quicker.

I came up close to Ransom, finding his features twisted in concentration, his brown hair plastered to his cheeks. A wave slid under him and he rose with it, accidently bringing me too but as I tried to swim off of his rising wave, the water bucked and sent me flying into my half-brother, knocking him off balance.

He fell on top of me and we went crashing into the ocean together, our limbs colliding as we fought to get to the surface again.

As we made it above the sea, his fist swung for my face and I swerved it, his knuckles slamming into my shoulder instead, giving me a dead arm.

"You caused that," I snapped, shoving him in the chest.

"Bullshit," he snarled, swinging for me again, but I swam underwater to escape the blow, finding a group of glug fish staring at me from the murky sea.

The Reapers had warned us about them, their long, tubular grey bodies and gaping mouths not looking like much of a threat, but if they latched onto one of your limbs, they had a poisonous bite that would hurt like a bitch for at least a day.

I kicked away from them, breaching the surface further from Ransom so I could focus on wielding again. The water around me was just as volatile as ever and the rain pelted me like shrapnel as I turned towards the horizon where more violent waves were headed for us.

"Connect with the essence of the cresting wave," Reaper Pavros called out as he went sailing by upon a wave of his own creation again. "Sense the roiling fury at its heart and urge it to do your bidding. You are one and the same. Water is water. It lives in you as it lives out here in the tempestuous sea."

"Domerna sil oceania," I said between my teeth, thinking of Harlon and all the days we had spent dancing between the waves of Castelorain. *Tame the ocean.*

This might not have been the sun-soaked waters I knew so well, but it was still the same beast, just in a wilder form.

I focused on the wave that was coming for me, starting to swim for the shore while keeping one eye on it over my shoulder, just as I would have if my tiderunner had been beneath me now.

I pushed my magic into the ocean, not letting it take any form, just connecting to the pulse of the water and listening to what she had to say.

At once, my magic attached to that roiling wave and it didn't feel like an oncoming enemy anymore. It was my kin, and I only had to ask it to do as I wished and it would be more than happy to oblige. In my other training sessions, I had taken to casting magic with my right hand in such a way that it seemed I was casting with my left too, keeping my weakness secret. But here between the frantic water, there was no need to pretend, because no one was watching closely enough to notice anyway.

The wave rolled under me and screams rang out from the other neophytes as they fought to rise upon it. I didn't look their way, my attention honed on my connection with the water as it pushed me up and up until I was standing on the frothing edge of the coiling wave.

A smile lit my face as I went riding in towards the shore, but Reaper Pavros swept in front of me, his youthful face twisting in alarm as he guided his wave away from mine and I started chasing him towards the obsidian beach ahead.

He glanced back at me, a cheer leaving him as he spurred me on. "That's it!" he cried. "Now part the rain!"

I turned my attention to the pummelling raindrops, trying to push them away from me, and my heart lifted as they swept aside. Pavros continued to cry encouragements, lowering on his wave to step off onto the black sand beach. I was closing in on it by the second, about to be the first to achieve this goal. But then water crashed into me from behind, hitting me so hard I was thrown forward off of my wave, slamming into the sea before the wave curled over and swept me under it in a violent vortex.

I kicked hard, rising to the surface with a splutter, finding Ransom sailing past me on the following wave, a smirk on his lips which told me he had been the one to drive water into my back and knock me from my perch. He sailed smoothly onto the beach, stepping off beside Reaper Pavros who clapped him on the shoulder and heat flared in my veins.

A snarl left me as more and more Fae made it to the beach, Alina among them, tossing her black hair away from her face and running to embrace Ransom in celebration. It had been robbed of me. My victory. My moment of glory. *I* should have been the one to make it there first.

As Reaper Pavros directed them all back into the sea to practice, a wild fury coiled in my chest that brought a growl to my lips. A shiver of movement in the water drew my attention to my right and I dipped my face under the surface, finding a group of glug fish bobbing there.

I lifted my head, treading water and glaring at Ransom as I sent water blasting beneath the ocean, driving those glug fish right for him as he waded back in up to his waist with that smug fucking look on his face.

But the smugness faltered as my glug fish crashed into him. He looked down in shock then a cry of fright left him as he yanked a hand out of the water, revealing one of those tubular grey fish latched fully around it, suckering its way over his wrist and moving higher still.

"Ah!" he yelled, trying to shake it off, then snatched his other hand out of the water, revealing another glug fish covering it. "Reaper Pavros!" he yelled, backing out of the water as Alina gazed after him in shock.

As Ransom made it to the shallows, he screamed and fell down on his ass, his legs rising from the water to reveal two more glug fish, one on each of his bare feet.

A wave slammed into the shore, slapping him in the face and sending him rolling across the sand past Reaper Pavros's feet. Ransom thrashed like a beached dolphin, trying to shake them off then screamed higher still as he looked down at his crotch, finding a glug fish burrowing through his swimsuit to latch right between his thighs.

"My cock!" he wailed and a manic laugh left me, echoed by the neophytes on the shore. "It's eating my cock!"

He smacked the glug fish between his legs with his fish-bound fists and Alina came racing out of the ocean, diving to her knees between his legs and grabbing the long fish that was suctioned onto his dick.

"Calm down," Reaper Pavros gasped, moving to help. "Just relax."

"Relax?!" Ransom roared. "It's trying to eat my dick!"

Alina yanked on the offending glug fish, pressing her bare foot to Ransom's chest as she pulled and pulled.

"No - stop!" Ransom shrieked. "Ahhhh! You're gonna pull my cock off!"

The glug fish released his dick at that very second and Alina went flying back onto the sand, the glug fish slipping from her grip, slapping wetly onto her face and suctioning over her lips. Her scream was muffled by the fish as she scrambled backwards in the sand in panic, trying to pull it from her face in desperation and I lost my shit, laughing wildly as I watched.

Ransom's dick was exposed where the glug fish had ripped through his suit, his cock botchy and red, a ring of teeth marks in it speaking of the venomous bite it had given him. He wailed, trying to clutch it with his fish-covered hands, rolling back and forth while Reaper Pavros looked between him and Alina, stunned as he decided who to help first.

He ran to Alina, gripping the glug fish on her mouth and casting water over the fish's mouth and hers to pull it off, leaving her with swollen lips.

The bells began tolling back in Never Keep, signalling the end of the lesson and as a wave came up behind me, I connected my magic to it, determined to do what I'd come here to. I rose upon it, sailing smoothly onto the beach, parting the rain and stepping off of it onto the shore with a grin as I looked to my half-brother and Alina.

"The swelling will go down in a few hours and the pain will stop in a day," Reaper Pavros said, and I found him patting Alina on the shoulder as she sobbed, her lips five times the size they had been before and looking puffy as shit.

A few more Reapers had come to shore and had removed the glug fish from Ransom's hands and feet, tossing them back into the ocean. They offered him healing magic and I scowled as he panted in their wake, the swelling going down in an instant as he cupped his dick in his hands, trauma lining his expression.

"Can I be healed?" Alina asked in desperation through her lips which were so big and puckered they were starting to resemble a giant cat's asshole, still swelling with each passing minute.

"Commander Rake's son has been offered the privilege of the stars this once," Reaper Pavros explained. "You will be well again in a day."

He walked off, leaving her there with a sob breaking through her puckered lips which sounded more like a strained fart.

I burst into laughter and her eyes swung onto me in rage as Ransom joined her, his hands locked around his bare cock and his cheeks paled from the ordeal.

It was a shame they hadn't left him to suffer with a puffy cock, but of course my father's precious prodigy would be given privileges in this place. As Alina glared at me, I turned and headed for the Escalade, dripping wet with the cold wind biting into my skin.

The burn Kaiser Brimtheon had left on my right wrist stung in the frigid air, but nothing could dampen my mood as I started the climb back to Never Keep. Not when I'd succeeded in harnessing the sea and had gotten some sweet revenge on my least favourite people in the world for good measure.

I had a book on wielding the power of water tucked inside my notebook, the little tome fitting in it snugly. *Technically*, I wasn't supposed to take books out of the Library of Frost into the heart of the Keep, but eating in the refectory was pretty much torture when no one would sit with you.

I preferred the company of a book over most Fae anyway, and I wasn't going to sit staring at the wall while I ate, counting bricks. Fuck no. This beat that and the little tome had an engaging way of describing the connection between water elementals and their magic, keeping me occupied.

Though occasionally my gaze strayed across the Fae further down the bench where Ransom was loudly regaling the tale of the creatures that had 'attacked' him at Obsidian Cove. The glug fish sounded far more like ferocious sharks that he had ruthlessly overpowered in his version, and irritatingly, the Fae around him seemed to be eating it up. Some of them had literally been there watching on the beach, but now they were buying his bullshit like it was nectar to a bunch of mindless bees. There was no sign of Alina, and I guessed she'd decided to take her dinner in her room, feeding it through the pursed hole in her ass lips. I kinda wished I could be there to see that.

My gaze moved to the Stonebreakers, taking in some of the most dangerous-looking bastards among them and picking out anyone who might pose a real threat on the battlefield someday. My usual scouring of the Flamebringers' table lasted longer than any other, seeking the face of Kaiser Brimtheon, but I couldn't find him among them. The burn on my wrist was red enough to show the mark of his fingers where they'd gripped my skin, and hatred simmered in my blood as I ran my thumb over them.

Beyond the Flamebringers, the Skyforgers were eating by the long row of windows and my gaze paused on the Sky Witch. I felt the allure of her, but forced myself to stare at her until it was easier to detach myself from the seduction of her features. Then I returned to reading my book, eating a mouthful of vegetable stew that was a little too salty for my liking. Or maybe I was the salty one, my emotions the real stew inside me; the ache of missing Harlon, the vengeful rage I felt towards Kaiser, and the ever-persistent grief of my mother's loss.

Never rest, Everest.

I thought of her so often, her smiles, our moments together in the sun. She had loved me and my sisters dearly, but the eight-year age gap between the youngest of my elder sisters meant I had never been that close with them. They had shown no interest in me, perhaps because of the age difference or maybe they had seen me just as everyone else had. A runt. A daughter born to a Provider who they had assumed was done providing after so many years without producing a new child.

I didn't understand why my father had spent eight more years trying for another heir from my mother's womb. Was there a time frame designated by the Magistrine – the government of Cascada - in which she was meant to keep providing? I didn't know. I should have asked. Why hadn't I asked her more about what she'd been through? What it had been like to be assigned to a ruthless man like Commander Rake to birth warriors for our land? Had she ever loved him? And if not him, then someone? Anyone who had treated her with the adoration and affection she had deserved?

I sighed, returning my attention to my cooling stew and the book that could distract me from the questions I would never get an answer to.

By the time I was done eating, I'd finished the tome, flicking onto the last page and finding the emblem of Cascada sitting beside the prophecy I knew by heart. My mama used to recite it to me while brushing the salt and sand out of my hair before bed, and the memory of that pained me as I read it now.

War of the four, divided and torn asunder.
Flame, sky, rock and sea collide,
While the stars bless the valiant souls of battle.
Seek the void, for it shall guide the victor to their glorious
path,
A weapon of purity, and the gift of null.
In a web of lies and cruelty, fate will favour the cresting wave
of destiny,
And a bountiful empire shall be reborn under one all-powerful
rule,
Garnering the fortune and favour of the almighty sky.

The prophecy had been spoken by a legendary Seer who had lived when the Endless War began and knew the four instigators of our conflict. The suggestion of a 'cresting wave' being favoured in the war had confirmed in the hearts of Cascada's rulers that we would win the war. I hoped our generation would be the ones to lead them to that victory, and I would be among the heroes who brought the news of that triumph home. I could see myself now, standing on a battlefield with a sword held high and starlight gleaming off of my armour, marking me resplendent in their eyes.

An elbow jammed into the back of my head, knocking me out of that daydream and I hissed as I turned to look at the offending Fae. Ransom was walking by with his pack of sheep and he didn't look back as I glowered at him, my hand moving to the butter knife beside my bowl.

I let it go, figuring the Reapers keeping watch would punish me if I started a brawl. Instead, I gathered up my things and headed for the door, planning to get some more magical practise in tonight. My mental shields were improving, but the real test would be when I came face to face with Kaiser Brimtheon again. I couldn't let him gain possession over me twice.

Before I made it to the exit, an argument broke out in front of me, a male Skyforger with sleek blonde hair hurling his plate at the head of a red haired Flamebringer.

"What did you say to me?" the Skyforger barked, and the girl cursed as she ducked the plate and it smashed on the flagstones, drawing everyone's attention.

"I heard what you said in the Astral Sanctuary today. You were scoffing at the Reapers," the girl hissed, flames sparking in her hands. "You're an arrogant, waste of space Skyforger, and now you've shown what the aristocracy of your kind really think of our almighty prophets, Ogden Breeze. I heard your uncle is a Reaper. Fucking rich that is."

Ogden's cheeks pinked as he shot a sideways glance at the Reapers standing by the exit and my heart raced a little as they gave him narrow-eyed looks.

He thrust his chin up, looking back at the girl. "I have a right to question the world around me. Fae who accept it as it is are fools with minds easily bent to the will of others, fire harlot."

I glanced at the Reapers, my pulse quickening a little as I wondered if they were going to reprimand him for that. Although, he had a point in all honesty.

"My name is Kala Emberthorn," she hissed. "And the only fools here are the ones who scorn the stars' desires. The Reapers are practically gods among us, and you dare question them?"

"I stand for questioning all rules laid upon us, not just those of the stars," Ogden lowered his voice, clearly not wanting the Reapers to hear him, but I was sure they could. "Your small mind could never understand that, clearly." He turned away from her, marching to the exit and my eyebrows lifted at the fact that he hadn't offered the Reapers the words of respect when he'd passed them. He should have said 'praise the stars.'

Muttering broke out and I walked after the Skyforger, offering those words to the Reapers myself.

Two of them spoke to me in reply. "Praise to those who tread their destined path."

I headed back to the Vault of Frost, then down, down into the dark where my quarters awaited me. It was there, as I entered the cold room and willed the everflame back to life beyond the grate, that I heard an echoing scream. Stilling, I listened, straining my ears as I moved to the low-hanging pipes where I was sure the sound was coming from.

Some dark, twisting sensation in my chest set me on edge. The scream didn't sound again, but it wasn't the first I'd heard in here and though I tried to convince myself it was just the groaning of the pipes, my gut told me I would be a fool to believe that. But here in the lonely dark, I had no one to tell.

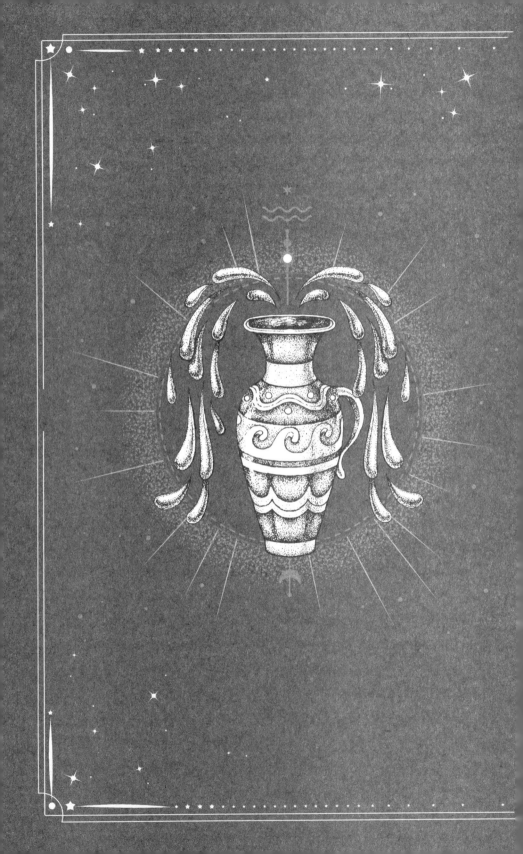

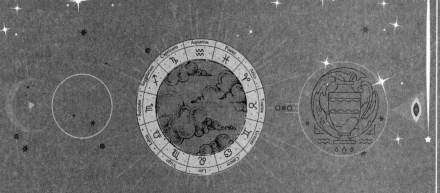

VESPER

CHAPTER TWENTY

A month at Never Keep was long enough for me to have learned most of the hidden ways between the sections of the sprawling fortress that I was allowed free access to. But it hadn't done much in the way of allowing me into those I wasn't.

The low chanting of the Reapers washed over me as I knelt, pious and observant at the Astral Sanctuary, worshiping from the front row of conscripts, the picture of the favoured top tier neophyte which I knew Dragor would expect from me.

This part of the ritualistic prayers to the stars always used to have me battling sleep, but in this place, it left me tense in the vulnerable position with so many of my enemies close at hand. My palms were flat against the cold stone, outstretched on either side of me, my forehead touching down on the ground too. It was the one place where I had taken to braiding my hair back, simply so I could see out the corners of my eyes in case any of the bastards skulking nearby thought to strike at me.

This main worshipping chamber was arranged in similar fashion to all the Astral Sanctuaries I had visited during my life, an echoing dodecagon-shaped space with twelve walls encircling it, each one decorated in worship and celebration of the star signs in order of rotation. Today, with the shifting of the moon, we had finally turned away from the watchful eyes of Virgo to direct our prayers towards the justice offered by the scales of Libra.

There had been a few mutters of malcontent from the Stonebreakers and overloud praises from the Skyforgers, but I remained silent as always in this place, observing the strict rules of worship, showing no favour to one star sign above another, though of course we all favoured those of our individual elements.

Silence reigned as we remained in place, the scent of stone and sweet incense filling my nostrils while the Reapers slowly paced the outer edges of our enormous congregation, chanting in that low, rumbling tone.

I was supposed to be opening myself up to the stars in hopes that they might deign to speak with me, but twenty-one years of receiving nothing but silence in these places had made me rather cynical about the entire debacle. If the stars wished to converse with me, I doubted they needed me to prostrate myself in silence before a stone effigy.

Minutes rolled into an hour and finally the twelve doors set into the twelve walls groaned open, revealing the offering chambers beyond.

"Waste of fucking time," someone muttered several rows behind me, and I stilled as a strange desire prickled against my skin. A Fae there wanted something with a keen desperation and my gifts were so in tune with the wants of those surrounding me, always in hunt of a source of magic, that I had instantly picked up on it.

I turned my head slowly, seeking the malcontent but finding a sneering Flamebringer too close to me for comfort. His desire was all too clear, bloodlust and…well, he would certainly have enjoyed the chance to kill me in private.

I met his eyes, simmering with the raw power of fire, my head tilting back because he was all kinds of tall – though in fairness there weren't many Fae I didn't have to look up at. It was a fact that had bothered me once. But I'd since realised that the only time it mattered to be looking up at someone was if you happened to be bleeding out at their feet.

I knew this Fae. He called himself The Cobra because he had a reputation for striking without warning and using lethal force. Not particularly impressive to me, but he was on my list and this was the closest I had managed to get to him.

The knife carefully bound within the confines of my waistband itched against my skin, but I couldn't strike at him like that here.

I gave a contemptuous scoff, wrapped my gifts around his desires then turned away, and strode towards the door which opened beyond the roaring visage of Leo, depicted as an enormous Lion mid-pounce, sharp teeth bared and eyes wild.

Soft muttering broke out at my chosen destination – we were encouraged to show devotion to each of the star signs, but no one had yet taken the opportunity to enter the temple of a sign which wasn't linked to their own element.

The Grand Maester looked to me as I approached, my position in the front row of worshippers making me first to select a temple to lay my offering in, and he smiled approvingly.

Such a good little witch, so pious in my devotion to the stars.

With every step I took, I tugged on The Cobra's desire for blood, more, more, more. His hatred was a truly vile thing, I could feel it coiling around me, could taste the sadistic pleasure he gained from killing. He wasn't just a soldier – he was in this war for personal gratification and a free reign to explore his own twisted desires.

I reached the door to the Temple of Leo and gave up on any pretence of subtlety, bolstering his desire for my blood until I was certain he would combust with the force of it.

"No!" The Cobra snarled, his voice echoing in the eerie silence of the sanctuary. "No air vermin should step foot in there."

"The worship of all star signs - and indeed all celestial beings - is not only encouraged but demanded by the heavenly deities which govern us," the Grand Maester replied in a low tone, and I continued into the temple without so much as glancing back.

A small, dark, stone corridor led deeper into the bowels of the sanctuary, guiding me down a tightly curling stairway with only a single torch bracketed on the wall to light the way.

At the base of the stairs, an archway opened into the Temple of Leo where countless depictions of the star sign cluttered the space, lit in a deep orange light by the fires which burned behind grates lining the walls. Statues, paintings, wooden carvings, tapestries, idols and metallic symbols. So many lions that, had this been a den of living beasts, I knew my meagre body wouldn't have come close to sating their hunger.

Shouts had broken out above me, The Cobra seeming to have lost all sense of himself in this holy place. I bit my tongue to keep from smirking, knowing there were Reapers close at hand even if I couldn't see any.

No doubt he would be placed in the iron gibbet, the cage barely big enough to hold a Fae warrior, suspended from the refectory ceiling for several days. It served as both punishment and a warning to others what they might suffer for rule breaks.

I had found several clandestine ways to reach the refectory from my tower in the dead of night and was confident I could make his death seem like a freak accident – a result of some underlying heart defect that would only be discovered at breakfast time - which I would be certain to attend late enough to avoid all suspicion that might have been aimed my way.

I made it to the largest of the stone statues in the room, placing my hand against the nose of the lion and leaning in close to offer it my prayer.

"I thank you for your ruthless nature, I claim it for my own. May the world feel the sharpness of my claws just as they do yours," I breathed.

I withdrew my hand from the cold stone, raising two fingers to my mouth and painting the six-pointed shape of the star across my lips while allowing my eyes to fall closed, in a gesture of worship to the stars.

I had expected the sanctuary to have grown quiet again by now, but there were still shouts and cries echoing down from above, more voices raised, not in anger but…something keener.

Releasing a slow breath, I moved on, trailing my fingers over the various idols and relics, making my way through the temple towards the exit where the stifling heat of the room gave way to the hint of a fresh breeze.

"I hadn't expected this until the blood moon," a rough voice muttered somewhere to my right and I stilled, concealed behind a wooden carving of Leo which was so large that it blocked the view of the shrine surrounding the exit.

"You think the Grand Maester will act?" a more feminine rasp replied.

"You seriously think he might not?"

Silence followed for several seconds but my instincts held me in place.

"The neophytes won't be coming through here now. Let's witness it for ourselves," the male voice suggested, and I inched to my left just far enough to spy the gold cloaks worn by the Reapers.

Their hesitation was brief this time.

"Yes. I'll lock the doors."

Her footsteps scuffed my way and I ducked down, flattening myself to the flagstones and rolling beneath the belly of the carved beast before shuffling into the shadow of a towering statue behind it.

I watched as the gold cloak of the Reaper whipped past my hiding place, her feet slapping against the ground before the sound of a door closing heavily and a bolt being drawn across followed.

I waited until she'd passed me again then smoothy rolled out of my hiding place, curiosity driving me after her.

The other Reaper locked the door which led to the exit from the temple, and I watched from the shadows as the two of them withdrew into a dim corner where a lacklustre tapestry hung against the wall.

They slipped behind it and I forced myself to wait for a count of ten before following. This was insanity. If I was caught spying on the Reapers, then who knew what the punishment would be? They were beyond the laws of Stormfell, beyond the laws of any but themselves. And yet my feet continued to whisper across the flagstones, my breaths silently fluttering between my parted lips.

The Reapers made no real attempt at silence as they continued through the narrow passageway, but they had a good lead on me and were no longer conversing so I had to focus on every thump of their feet against the floor. I didn't want to get too close to them but neither did I want to risk losing them in this network of passages. I'd already passed two branches in the tunnels that the Reapers hadn't taken, and I had no idea how many more there were.

I moved silently, years of training with the cut-throats who moved through the shadows in Stormfell paying off as I slunk through the darkness like a wraith.

A soft grunt alerted me to the Reapers far closer than I had expected and my hand met with cold stone where the passage should have continued. There was no real source of light in this place between places, only the odd glow seeping in from the rooms outside this passageway, small vents and holes between the mortar, nothing substantial enough to give me a real view of what surrounded me.

I stilled, uncertain of my path, disoriented in the dark but then I heard the grunt again and my head snapped up. I ran my hands over the cold stone walls that surrounded me, reaching out until my fingers brushed against a wooden rung. I curled my hand around it, testing it with my weight before silently heaving myself up and reaching higher still before finding a second rung. A ladder.

I smiled to myself and began to climb, hauling my body onto the ladder then scaling it quickly, hurrying after the soft scuffs of fabric and muttered curses sinking down to me from the Reapers above.

Light grew around me, dull at first but growing to a lighter grey which I recognised as the dulcet tones of dawn that Never Keep welcomed most mornings, the light growing against the snowy backdrop before the sun crested the horizon itself.

I tipped my head back, watching as the Reaper clambered off of the ladder and slipped into a passageway to the left of its peak.

I hesitated, the growing light meaning I was no longer shrouded within the shadows.

A distant sound of voices echoed up to me from below, urging me on and I continued to climb, moving faster now, my pulse picking up.

I made it to the lower edge of the precipice where the Reapers had climbed free of the ladder and eased myself up to look over the edge.

A long passage expanded away from the two figures who had paused half way along it, leaning towards the righthand wall where a series of star-shaped holes had been carved into the brickwork in a pattern which ran the entire length of the passage, allowing the light to shine through them freely. I recognised that pattern, the carved stone reflecting what I had taken for little more than decoration in the Heliacal Courtyard at the centre of the Keep beyond the training amphitheatre.

Voices were hissing through the space outside, a clamour of noise which could only be made by a thousand neophytes whispering at once.

"Are we too late?" the female Reaper rasped, pushing her face against the stone as she peered out.

A scream of agonised pain ripped through the air and I stilled, my instincts barking at me to move, to draw a weapon, to do anything at all other than cling to this fucking ladder and wait for them to find me. I dismissed the urge, my gaze flicking to the holes in the wall, but from my angle I couldn't see anything.

"Come. The spectacle won't last long," the male Reaper said, a hint of urgent excitement to his voice. "If we hurry we can make it to the vestibule before them."

The voices were growing closer beneath me and I cursed internally as I looked down into the shadows below, knowing I would be seen all too easily if another Reaper arrived to climb the ladder.

The two in the passageway hurried on and I forced my pounding heart to steady as I slipped over the edge, silent as a summer breeze, my eyes fixed firmly on them in case they looked back before turning down another passageway.

A second scream came from the courtyard beyond this hidden passage, a collective gasp colouring the voices of the mostly silent crowd. What could be taking place which might shock a group of Fae who had been raised in bloodshed?

The Reapers took a left at the end of the passage and I hurried to the closest set of holes in the wall.

The backs of a few thousand neophytes blocked my view so I moved on, the light from outside casting stars across my skin as I moved from one hole to the next, checking both the higher and lower vantage points and finding nothing but turned backs until-

I fell still, my eyebrows arching as I took in the sight of The Cobra suspended with air magic high enough for the entire crowd to see as the Grand Maester drove bolts of iron through his flesh and another Reaper cast chains of flames to burn the skin from his bones. The Reapers had been clear that execution would follow for any Fae who murdered another in this place, so had The Cobra killed someone in the sanctuary? Certainly the brutality of the execution suggested the Reapers were beyond incensed and I imagined spilling blood in the sanctity of their place of communion with the stars would achieve that. Even so, I couldn't help but be shocked by the barbarity of the pious Reapers as it played out. They had always seemed so above the bloodshed of war, but this proved they were creatures just as capable of it as the rest of us.

The Cobra screamed in agony as a third bolt sped for him, hitting his chest and causing him to cough up blood as it punctured his lung.

One look told me the wound was fatal, but the Grand Maester wasn't done. A fourth bolt tore through the air, then a fifth, sixth-

I looked away from the brutally slow execution, knowing precisely where it was headed without needing to witness every drawn-out moment.

Perhaps I should have felt something at the prolonged screams which were fading now into pleas for it to end, but I simply ticked the first name off of Dragor's list in my mind and gave my attention to the Reapers once again.

I had lingered too long. There were muffled sounds drawing closer from the ladder and the pair I'd been stalking through the dark would be gaining too much of a lead by now.

I broke into a run, pausing briefly to check around the corner they had taken then slipping around it myself. Of course the tunnel forked within a handful of steps and I cursed myself as I fell still, straining my ears to listen for him.

The Cobra's screams were echoing all around me, making it impossible to discern anything else so I took a guess and headed right, moving further from the sanctuary towards what I had already discerned to be the living quarters for the Reapers.

If it was forbidden for me to enter the other Vaults then this was bordering on sacrilege, but unless I could find a way out of these tunnels, I had little choice. Besides, I always had been a curious creature.

The light dimmed again as I hurried on, taking turns and once having to double back on myself when I heard the thump of footfalls approaching from ahead. I left The Cobra's screams behind, or maybe they fell silent with his death, either way, I should have been able to hear some sound of my quarry if they were near, but all was silent in the dark.

I pursed my lips, considering defeat and wondering how I might find my way free of these cursed passages when the sound of grating stone made me fall still.

"Heal him," a deep voice commanded, and I flinched from the closeness of it, afraid for a moment that I had been discovered, but it came from beyond the wall to my right. "Just enough to slow his passage."

I edged along at the sound of footsteps, a low groan giving way to a cry of agony just as I found a faint crack in the mortar and pressed my eye to it.

Six Reapers stalked along a long hallway lit by flickering torches, The Cobra suspended with air magic between them, his blood dripping to the ground as they moved.

I watched them go, their route leading them away from me in the opposite direction to the passage I hid within.

I hunted around for a way out, my fingers grazing the rough stone as I moved until finally, I grasped the edge of a wooden frame. The sound of the group was growing faint. I gave in to the risk of exposing myself as I heaved the frame aside and found myself looking into the passage from behind an ornate portrait.

I leapt from the hole, landing in a crouch and taking a moment to replace the portrait before breaking into a run and darting across the wide hall where blood still stained the floor.

I passed the open door the group had entered through, sparing a glance for it and thanking the stars that the Reapers standing guard there had their backs to me.

I hurried along the passageway, taking in the opulent drapes which hung in deep reds and golds from the arching ceiling, seven pairs of them in total, the first six tied open, the last closed but swaying slightly where the group had passed through.

I made it to the thick red velvet and moved to the right, peeking out from the corner of the heavy fabric instead of the centre.

My lips parted as I found myself looking into a room which had likely been as grand and opulent as the previous passage in some past time but now stood in a state of almost complete ruin. The extravagantly carved stonework was cracked and blackened as if by flame and yet it didn't appear to be scorch marks, more like some stain which had seeped into the stone itself.

Rusted shackles hung from the roof, the group of Reapers now clustered around them as they lifted the limp and panting body of The Cobra and secured his wrists into them.

Footsteps sounded behind me and my heart leapt, the only action available to me to push through the curtain.

There was a stone pedestal holding a glimmering golden dagger and a bronze goblet filled with some dark liquid to my right. I flung myself behind it without a second thought, crouching in the narrow cover it provided and holding my breath as I waited for the call of alarm to come. But nothing happened aside from the arrival of more Reapers entering through the curtain, several others already clustering on the far side of the chamber.

I chanced a look around the stone pedestal I was hiding behind just as they finished securing The Cobra and they all backed away from him, pressing themselves to the walls.

They had stripped his shirt from him, marks now scrawled across his skin in his own blood – marks which had to be runes and yet didn't look familiar to me at all.

A narrow window stood open behind me and I glanced at it, noting the route of escape and wondering how long I could risk lingering here before taking it.

I should have been leaving already. Whatever foul ritual this was clearly had nothing to do with me and everything to do with the Reapers, but curiosity - or perhaps insanity - had me hesitating where I was, wanting to see what would happen.

The Grand Maester stepped forward, a stone bowl clasped in his palm, his fingers dipping into it before he scattered something dark and glittering across the floor beneath The Cobra's dangling feet.

He was begging, his eyes wild and pain still written into his features as he hunted the hooded faces around him for some sign of mercy. But I didn't think they had healed him because they had any intention of allowing him to live. No, his death was imminent, but what purpose it would serve perplexed me.

"I call upon the dagger blessed by the sun," the Grand Maester rumbled.

I stifled a gasp as he whirled to face me, uncertain if I had made it behind the cover of the pedestal in time.

The golden dagger lying on top of the pedestal that I had chosen for my abysmal hiding place shot from its position as he claimed it with a whip of air magic.

I didn't dare peek out again to see what he was doing with it, but The Cobra's strangled screams gave me a fair idea.

"I call upon the blood of the fallen," the Grand Maester said loudly over the pleas of the dying man and the goblet shot away from the pedestal next.

Again, I didn't dare move, but as The Cobra choked and spluttered,

I could only imagine that he was being forced to drink whatever the fuck had been in that goblet.

"And so our offering is made. And so your feast is prepared."

Something changed as those words faded from my ears, something in the very air I breathed and the weight of the atmosphere surrounding me. There was a heaviness to the world which hadn't been present until that moment and a cold sense of dread seeped right into my soul.

My breath began to rise in a fog before me, my fingers trembling where they had curled around the hilt of my concealed dagger. Never, in all the years that I had been at war, had my hand shaken like that.

I realised that The Cobra hadn't been screaming before. No, the sounds issuing from his lips in the moments leading up to this one had been akin to laughter in the face of what tore from him now.

The noise he released was pure agony laced with a horror so deep that I couldn't even begin to imagine what level of hell he must have been enduring.

I couldn't move. Shit, I couldn't fucking breathe and yet...I had to know, had to *see*.

Somehow, I forced my limbs to cooperate, forced myself to turn, to grasp the edge of the pedestal as though it might somehow prepare me for whatever it was that I was spying on.

But as I looked out from my position secreted in the corner of this hall of nightmares, I found myself unable to see. Or...no...I could see but all around me was a darkness so impenetrable that nothing but the screams of the Fae trapped within it could escape it.

There was movement, power, that terrible weight in the air and sounds which were altogether too much like something...feasting.

Instinct, the need for survival, or fuck it – maybe it was *fear* – had me sprinting for the window and launching myself out of it without a second thought for whether any of the Reapers might have been able to see me through that living shadow or not.

The frigid air assaulted me, my fingers grasping at a black drainpipe to the right of the window and hauling me upwards. I hardly noticed the immense drop beneath me as I climbed, or the roar of the waves far below. I paid no attention to the yawning hole which stretched away between the black rock walls of Never Keep, not caring that it made no sense for it to be there, not wondering if the pressure of the water slamming into the rocks beneath might explode upwards at any moment and rip me down into it.

I climbed faster than I had probably ever climbed before, my fingers tearing open on the sharp volcanic stone, but I neither felt it nor cared.

The brutal wind threatened to tear me right off of the edge of the Keep and hurl me to the mercy of that drop, but I clung on and kept climbing until I made it to the grey tiled roof.

I broke into a run without even pausing to catch my breath, racing across the rooftops of the gothic building, avoiding spires, gargoyles and the openings punched through the architecture to make way for the courtyards until I made it all the way back to the tower which I had chosen for my sleeping quarters.

My boots slipped against the stone as I lowered myself from the roof, but I kicked the window wide and hurled myself through it.

I rolled on the hard floor, stopping on my hands and knees and panting as I caught my breath.

The creak of a floorboard had me reacting before I'd even fully taken in the damage to my door frame out the corner of my eye.

I ripped the dagger free of my waistband and flung it as I rolled, the rough curse and clang of metal on metal letting me know I'd gotten close, but my opponent had managed to block the strike.

I threw myself beneath my bed, grabbing the short sword which I had concealed beneath the frame and launching to my feet just as the bastard leapt onto the mattress.

A clash of metal, two weapons skittering across the floor, a flash of dark hair and my back collided with the wall as a heavy body drove against me.

"What the fuck are you doing in here?" I snarled up into Cayde's too pretty face, practically spitting at him as his forearm crushed my chest.

"Maybe I'm trying to figure out your weaknesses so that I'll be ready to kill you when the time comes," he taunted.

"It's probably time you realised I have none and give me up for a bad job then," I hissed.

"Where were you?" he demanded darkly.

"Precisely where my prince needed me to be as always," I replied stonily.

"We're supposed to be allies," he insisted. "You need me."

I scoffed, relaxing my body so that he could think himself the victor if he was dumb enough to do so.

"You know nothing about what I need," I replied scathingly.

"Not true. I pay attention."

"So do I."

"No you don't. Not really. Not to the things that are closest to you or which you deem to be no threat. You only look at me when I have a knife to your throat or if I happen to get within striking distance. I watch you when your guard drops. I watch you when you think you are nothing but shadow and I see those truths you hide so well."

"Oh please don't tell me you've discovered my secret knitting club."

"Where were you?" Cayde repeated, refusing to so much as snort at my jibe.

"I thought you watched me?" I taunted. "Or did you lose focus for a moment or two?"

"I've been tasked with staying close to you," he growled in a low voice and I balked at the suggestion of that.

"Liar."

"Not about that. My orders are to get as close to you as possible. And I don't like losing track of my target."

"Target?" I echoed but mostly I was just buying myself time because why the fuck would the prince assign Cayde to watch over me when he had made it more than clear that he had thought...

I swallowed thickly as I considered the position I had once again found myself in with this bastard, remembering how Dragor had reacted the last time I'd gotten myself into a compromising situation with Cayde like this. Was this some kind of test? Did Dragor think I wouldn't keep to my vow?

I narrowed my eyes then shoved Cayde with enough force to knock him off of me, snatching my sword from the foot of my bed and unsheathing it with a jerk of my wrist before levelling it at him.

"Speak and maybe I'll find my own tongue loosening," I growled.

Cayde looked me up and down in a way which felt utterly invasive and yet somehow unravelling at once.

"You're important," Cayde sneered. "I don't have to like it to admit that it's true. You matter in the war and you matter to the prince. This place is more dangerous than all the battles you have fought in purely because it is nothing like any of them. There are snakes in every corner and enemies at each turn. It's important you don't fall prey to any of them. You matter, Vesper."

I blinked at the use of my name. No one outside of my closest friends and the prince himself ever used that name. So far as I knew, no one even remembered it. Yet there it was, rolling from his silken tongue and wrapping itself around me like a claim of something far more personal than I would have willingly offered.

I considered him for a moment. He was arrogant, infuriating, outwardly hostile and irritatingly good at being all the best kinds of bad. Yet I could admit that everything he had ever shown me of himself right down to our ongoing rivalry was simply honest.

"Fine," I grunted, sheathing my sword and tossing it aside, letting our quarrel end for the moment. "I was somewhere I shouldn't have been and I saw something I should not have witnessed. The kind of thing which could very well result in your assignment failing."

"The Reapers?" Cayde guessed and I narrowed my eyes at him. He was right, he did see too fucking much.

"I don't think they saw me," I said, not denying or admitting to anything.

Cayde considered me for a long moment then sighed. "When you're willing to trust me with the rest of it then you know where to find me. In the meantime, if there is any question as to your whereabouts for the last hour, I will swear on all the stars in the sky that you were training in swordplay with me."

He moved towards the door and I watched him go with narrowed eyes. "Why?" I demanded before he could slip away.

"Because despite how the two of us might feel about one another, sweetheart, we're supposed to be on the same side of this war. So let's at least play the part of allies – until the role of nemesis becomes too tempting to deny."

He left without another word and I turned over everything he had said as though trying to puzzle out a riddle to which there was no answer. Cayde Avior wasn't really the biggest problem on my plate though, so I shoved him from my thoughts as I focused on my main meal, leaving him there in case I found myself hungry for dessert.

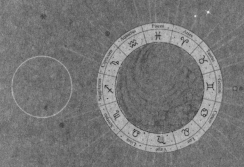

EVEREST

CHAPTER TWENTY ONE

There was a wild and furious storm battering the keep again tonight. I floated on my back in the highest pool in the Poseidon Spa, the towering stone effigy of Scorpio curling around the basin that held the water I lay in. Above me, a glass roof gave a view out to the dark sky and I worked on casting raindrops with my magic, letting them cascade down over me in a mimicry of the storm. My mind kept slipping back to the memory of that Flamebringer, The Cobra, being so brutally executed in the Heliacal Courtyard. He had killed a Raincarver during the fight he had started at the Astral Sanctuary. Though I hadn't known the girl who had been killed, a bitter kind of hatred had found me at knowing The Cobra had murdered one of my people. But watching the vicious execution hadn't brought me the satisfaction I'd expected.

Instead, I'd felt sickened by the display, and found myself

thinking about my own death. If I killed Kaiser Brimtheon between these halls and was found out, a terrible kind of execution awaited me too. But despite knowing that to be the case, I couldn't find it in me to make the sensible choice and halt my pursuit. Who knew when I would be in this close proximity with him again? I may never get such an opportunity again in my lifetime. It might be now or never, so it would be now. Just as soon as I felt trained enough to face him.

The bathhouse was quiet this evening, the conscripts all peeling off to rest after another day of cardinal magic instruction followed by a brutal session of elemental training out in the ocean again. This pool was a favourite of mine in the Poseidon Spa, a place few other Fae ventured to even during busier times.

From what I'd heard of the sleeping quarters in the Vault of Frost, they held grand tubs akin to pools. When that Raincarver girl had died, a room had opened up, but I hadn't been quick enough to seize it. A herd of Pegasuses had spread out their things, claiming it as part of several rooms they shared. Next time, I wouldn't be so slow to act.

Plenty of friendship groups spent time in each other's spaces during downtime. Talking, laughing. I caught snippets of it all whenever I moved through the passages here, catching glimpses of smiles and casual touches.

In the month that I had been at Never Keep, I had not been touched. Actually, I had barely been addressed. Instead, I haunted the keep, a creature that moved among the masses, going unnoticed for the most part. But when I *was* noticed, it was with disdain, sneering lips and occasional taunts thanks to Ransom's efforts in making me an outcast.

I was used to being solitary anyway. I preferred to walk my own path, but there were tugs in my soul that longed for Harlon; no one else had ever made the cut. Realistically, I was probably half of the problem when it came to making friends. I didn't exactly attempt to talk to other Fae, and my face was often fixed in the kind of scowl that warned people not to approach me. But when your hand had been bitten by the dogs you tried to pet as a kid, it kind of left its mark on you.

"Hiding, Ever?" Harlon's voice from the past drifted through my mind. It was a time when I'd been just a child with scuffed knees, sitting in the warm sand of Undashine Shore.

"I'm not hiding, I'm relaxing."

"Here between the dunes with nothing but geckos for company? You look like you're hiding to me."

"I prefer to be alone."

"Then I guess I'll go."

"No, wait," I breathed, looking to the boy with the sand in his hair and the ocean in his eyes. "Stay. I don't want to go back home."

He stepped closer, that protective look crossing his features. I had never really understood why he aimed it at me.

"A lot of the people in Castelorain have small minds and closed hearts, Ever. The whole world isn't like that. You'll leave this place one day and find somewhere you're seen for what you are."

"But there's nothing to see."

"Not true. Anyway, it doesn't matter where you go, I'll be there. You'll always have me."

"Swear it?"

"I swear."

"You broke your promise, Harl," I sang into the rain I'd cast from magic, though no real anger found me. I just missed him.

I'd asked several Reapers where to find their trainee acolytes, but had been dismissed time and again, told there was no coalescing between battle conscripts and Reaper conscripts. But I'd be damned if I was going to give up on seeking him.

The only place in Never Keep that seemed likely for him to be housed was the Reaper Quarters, and considering I was forbidden from entering that place upon pain of punishment, I was going to have to risk getting in there and being caught or give up on him. And the second choice wasn't an option.

So idle plans formed in my mind while I floated in the embrace of the warm water, feeling a rising swell inside my chest. My magic was recharging. And despite the fact that my Order still hadn't Emerged, I had this single clue about it now. I'd realised it during my very first week here, soaking in a tub in the bathhouse - showers weren't good enough, I had to be submerged at least partially to restore my magic. The trouble was, there were several Orders I knew of that recharged using water, but none I could pinpoint specifically to bathing.

Heptian Toads needed the rain, Merrows needed the turning tides, and Calypsos needed to swim under the moon, so none of those Orders were really lining up for me.

My thoughts turned to stealing a gold cloak from a Reaper to help me sneak into their quarters, then moved to my other plot. Kaiser Brimtheon.

I knew the rules better than ever now; I couldn't kill other neophytes and I was forbidden from entering the other Vaults too. But that assumed I got caught. If I laid a plan well enough, covered all bases, perhaps I could pull it off. I'd been training tirelessly in mental shields and all the cardinal magics the Reapers had imparted to us. The elemental and combat practise that was held in the Vault of Frost was proving I could do this. Perhaps not yet, but soon.

One of my greatest challenges in practise with the other conscripts had been disguising the fact that my left hand did not cast magic. I had to focus hard, but I could weave magic around it from my right hand and make it seem as though I was casting with both. As of yet, it seemed, no one had figured out my dark secret and I didn't plan on them uncovering it either. It would only be more ammunition for ridicule. A one-handed caster making it as a warrior was pretty laughable, but so long as I hid it well enough, none of my comrades would ever learn of my weakness.

A low chirruping sound made me jolt out of my thoughts and I found a small blue lizard crawling between two ferns. It had tiny wings, a flat sort of head and large eyes, like a little dragon. It chirruped again, cocking its head to one side, seeming friendly enough. I didn't recognise it as a Fae Order, but the thought made me hesitant as I moved towards it through the pool.

"Are you Fae?" I asked suspiciously and the creature chirruped again, observing me with dark, reptilian eyes.

"Oh boy, it's good up here. Yes, I like it here, I do."

I turned sharply at the male voice, finding a Raincarver stepping into my pool. He was a huge guy, his skin paler than was usual for the people of Cascada and his hair lightest blonde, just a smooth sheen of it cut short. His eyes were blue and he had freckles across his cheeks, his face round and a smile easily lifting his lips.

I glanced back to find the lizard gone, but before I could wonder where it had gotten to, a wail of utter pain carried through the pipe that curved over the tub and spewed warm water into the pool, making my heart lurch in shock.

"Did you hear that?" I gasped, swimming towards the pipe and listening for it again.

A tingle of magic stirred beneath my skin, something dark and potent writhing through me, but then it was gone, and I didn't know if it had come from me or that pipe.

"I hear the sloshing of the water, swishing and swirling," the newcomer said. "I like that sound."

"No, it was a scream. A man, I think." I rounded on him, finding him leaning back against the pool's stone wall, looking relaxed.

"Water does not scream," he pointed out as if I was a fool.

"I know," I muttered, straining my ears as I listened for it again, but all I could hear now was the rushing of the water.

"Pipes do not scream," he added.

"I know," I hissed. "What did you say your name was?"

"I did not say it."

"Well? What shall I call you?"

"People call me Galomp." He smiled then looked to the pipe. "You could fit inside that pipe and slide down to your screamer, wee, wee, wee all the way into the belly of the Keep. Oh boy, what fun that would be. Pity I would not fit."

"Yeah, except I don't have a death wish," I said, frowning as that scream lingered in my mind. I'd been hearing more and more sounds like that, disturbing me in the night, waking me and setting my blood chilling with the ruckus. Male and female, the different tones to their wails making me wonder if a host of lost souls were lurking in the depths of the isle where Never Keep stood.

The Raincarver servants who worked down in the passages had assured me there were no levels lower than the one where my quarters were, and I was undecided as to whether to bring it up with the Reapers. What if they thought I was losing my mind? What if they dismissed me from the Keep? What if they punished me and locked me in that horrible iron gibbet in the refectory, accusing me of lying or besmirching their names?

"And what shall I call you?" Galomp asked brightly, clearly not disturbed by mention of screams in the pipes. "I have heard people call you lots of things. Runt and freak and sea urchin. Which is your favourite?"

"None of them," I snarled, but at his wounded expression, I softened my features a little. He didn't seem to be aware that those names were insults. Or at least, he didn't seem to think I'd mind being called them.

"Oh no. Oh dear," he said quickly. "I do not want to make you sad. Did I make you sad? Sometimes I say things that are not meant to be bad, but they are bad."

"No, it's fine, Galomp," I said with a sigh. "My name's Everest."

"Oh boy, what a name. I do like it. Miss Everest. Ever. Rest. Ever, ever rest. Never ever rest."

"Stop it," I gasped, my mother's lasting words to me circling in my mind. *Never rest, Everest.*

He flinched a little. "I've gone and done it now. Really gone and done it." He hit his own forehead with the palm of his large hand.

"Don't worry about it," I muttered, moving to the edge of the pool and climbing out. It wasn't like he could have known what those words meant to me.

My dagger was on the stone surface hidden within my clothes and I guided the water off of my skin. It took a few tries, but when I managed it, I let it fall back into the pool, leaving myself perfectly dry. I left my swimwear in place, my favoured black and gold two-piece sitting snugly against my skin as I pulled on my red cropped shirt and matching red trousers with the blue seashells on the pockets. Then I picked up my dagger, running my thumb over the newly-etched name of Kaiser Brimtheon on its hilt, slipping it into the secret fold I'd sewn onto my trousers to conceal it at my hip.

"Are you going somewhere fun? Can I join you? I do like fun," Galomp said eagerly, standing up in the pool and revealing his full height. He was enormous, well over six feet.

"I-" My words fell still on my lips as I spotted that little blue lizard again.

It was hovering on its wings down at the bottom of the pool house near one of the stone walls. It landed on the stone, slithering away into a crack, then appearing a moment later out of another one a few feet away. The creature did it time and again, appearing from crack after crack and I might have been crazy, but I could have sworn it was painting a shape there. Something just big enough to be a door.

I made my way down the steps and ladders that led to the ground floor, my bare feet hitting the warm flagstones at the bottom. Breaking into a jog, I pushed through the leaves of a giant fern and found myself in the private space behind one of the pools. The lizard was no longer there, but I could see it now, that subtle shape in the wall, following the lines of the grey stones.

I stepped closer, thinking of those screams, knowing I shouldn't follow a path that wasn't meant to be found. But I'd never been one for turning from danger.

I placed my palm to the stones, pressing my weight into it and pushing hard. It didn't move and I pursed my lips, stepping back to assess it as I drew on my magic and thought on how I might unlock it. A rustle of leaves made me twist around, my pulse rising and my right hand ready to cast, but I found only Galomp there in his long blue bathing briefs with water gathering in a puddle at his feet.

"I can help you, yes I can." He strode past me excitedly, throwing his weight into the hidden door, but it didn't move.

A dark, roiling sensation in my chest made me frown as I stepped closer to the door, pushing it while Galomp continued to shove it too. A sense of magic slid over me then fizzled away at once and a grinding of stone sounded before the door crashed open.

"Shit." I glanced back through the ferns, fearing someone had heard that, quickly casting a silencing shield around us, though it was a bit late for that.

Galomp turned to me, gesturing to the open door with pride, but I was fairly certain I'd been the one to unlock the magic securing it, I just had no idea how I'd done it. "This way, Miss Everest."

"Just Everest. And you should stay here. No point in both of us getting punished if this goes to hell."

"Oh bother, but I would like to come. I do like secrets. This can be ours." His shoulders dropped in disappointment, and I stepped past him into the dark passageway, the low chirruping of that little lizard sounding somewhere within the shadows.

"Alright, but if we're shoved in the gibbet for this then don't go blaming me," I whispered.

"Oh boy, oh boy." He raced into the passageway.

"Can you close the door?" I asked, not liking the idea of shutting ourselves in here, but it was a dead giveaway if a Reaper stumbled across that open passage.

Galomp heaved the door shut, the heavy stone slotting back into place and blotting out all light. Thankfully, I had been practising casting Faelights this week and I willed one into existence now, the glowing amber ball of light rising above my head to brighten the passage. The Reapers had instructed us on this illumination magic in the Galaseum, and I'd worked hard to master it quickly.

The tunnel was narrow, damp and cold, winding away into the nothingness and promising only bad omens. I unsheathed my dagger, always feeling steady with it in my hand, keeping it tight in my left palm and leaving my other hand ready to cast. I was naturally right-handed, so training my left to work a blade as well as my right was a challenge, but every day the muscles grew stronger from the drills I put myself through. My quarters were now a disarray of roughly-made targets and every evening I worked on my throwing and fighting skills, forcing my left hand to train harder than my right.

That low chirrup sounded again and I hurried down the passage, the floor beginning to slope sharply downwards beneath my bare feet, the rough, cold stone biting into my skin.

A glow appeared up ahead and I realised the lizard's tail was alight with a reddish gleam, curling up and over its body to light the floor in front of it. It glanced back with a clicking sound in its throat and I steeled myself as I followed, the sound of Galomp's heavy footfalls echoing my near-silent ones.

Following strange creatures into dark passages probably wasn't the best idea I'd ever had, and when we rounded into a narrower tunnel, I was even more certain of that as a distant scream echoed out of the dark.

I fell still, glancing back at Galomp, his eyes shining with the reflection of my Faelight as he came to a halt too.

"Tell me you heard the scream this time?" I whispered despite the silencing shield around us.

"No screams, Miss Everest," he said, shaking his head sadly like he was more upset about disappointing me than the potential horrors that awaited us at the end of this passage.

The lizard disappeared around another corner, taking the light of its glowing tail with it and I clenched my teeth, forging on. I had to know what lay down here, what was causing that sound. Maybe it was just the wind entering through a sea cave, the sound distorted, making me think it was something more ominous than it really was. But that thought held little weight, especially when it seemed I was the only one who could hear it.

Maybe my mind really had cracked at last, Galomp and the tiny blue lizard just a figment of my imagination along with those screams. But then I heard another high-pitched wail and I quickened my pace, knowing it was real. Something terrible was happening and I had to find out what it was.

The tunnels sloped ever lower, winding deep underneath Never Keep until I was sure we must be deeper than even my quarters. Just as I had suspected. Either the servants had lied to me, or they didn't know about this place. I had the feeling that whatever lurked down here was the kind of secret that would swiftly see me executed if the Reapers ever discovered I knew it, and I shuddered at the memory of those bolts being driven into The Cobra's body.

I glanced back at Galomp again, finding him smiling around at the place in wonder instead of fear.

"You should go back," I urged. "Nothing good can come of this if we're discovered. I don't think you realise the danger we're in and I don't want to be responsible for walking you to your death."

"I am not afraid, Miss Everest. I like danger. It is quite fun. It makes my heart go ba-bomp."

"It will make your heart go ka-splat if we're caught and skewered on the end of a Reaper's sword," I hissed, trying to get through to him, but he just shrugged his big shoulders and kept walking.

I moved into a jog to stay ahead of him, wanting to at least face whatever was coming first if I was accidentally luring this guy to a grisly end.

We caught up with the lizard and its eyes burned brightly at me before it slipped away into a crack in the floor. I cursed, dropping down and lowering my Faelight to figure out where it had gone, finding a wide iron grate set into the stone floor. I wrapped my fingers around it, pressing my silencing shield over it before tugging and forcing it up. The sound of rushing water reached me from below and I sent my Faelight down into the dark, unable to see the lizard's glowing tail or anything of much at all through the gloom.

My Faelight illuminated a huge underground cavern, a river coiling through its heart and a large wooden boat bobbing on its surface, tethered to a dock. My heart thrashed as I recognised that boat as the one Harlon had taken with the Reapers. He had come this way. He could be close. But then…those screams. Had some of them come from him? The thought made my skin prickle with horror, but I forced the idea away. Why would the Reapers hurt their own? It didn't add up. It had to be something else.

A vague glow disappearing into another tunnel beyond the dock told me where the lizard was heading, and I focused on my water magic. We had been working on casting ice in the past week, shaping it into platforms out on the wild sea, so this should be simple enough. I frowned as I worked to make a slide out of ice, the straight, flat expanse of white shimmering into existence and I smiled as I completed it. It was wide enough for me and Galomp to use, and I glanced back at him to ask whether he was up for this. His big ass grin said he was, so I didn't question him again.

"Close the grate behind you," I instructed, and he nodded.

I sat down and let myself fly down the slide, crashing into the icy river and losing my breath from the shock of it. I kicked for the surface, a huge wave slamming into me as Galomp hit the water crying, "Wa-hay!"

Drenched and shivering, I climbed up on the rocky bank by the dock, quickly gathering the water from my body with my control over the element and sending it back into the river. Galomp did the same for himself as he came stomping out of the water, and I melted my ice slide so there was no sign of our passage.

"Come on," I urged, falling into a run as I chased after the lizard, thinking of Harlon and wondering if I might just get to see him at long last.

Galomp jogged after me as we entered a fine passage with paintings of the zodiac constellations on the golden walls. There were statues of each sign set into alcoves, little shrines to each one lit with everflames at their bases.

The stone floor changed to white marble tiles and I slowed my pace as we reached a tall metal gate in the wall ahead. I gazed through the gaps into a dark tunnel beyond, resting my hand on it and pushing, already knowing it would be locked, sensing a magical barrier holding it in place. I cursed, resting my forehead to the gate and gripping the iron bars, trying to see into the gloom beyond, the faintest flicker of the lizard's tail telling of where it was. But I couldn't follow.

The magic that hummed through the iron was powerful, far stronger than the magic that had been sealing the door shut in the Poseidon Spa. Despite having managed to shatter that somehow, I had no idea how to do so again. It had probably been a fluke.

"Our game is over," Galomp sighed in disappointment.

"Yeah," I whispered, thinking of Harlon and hating how much it felt like I was letting him down. If only I could reach him, to see he was okay, then-

A shuddering wave of power echoed through the gate and it clunked, swinging forward with such suddenness that I went stumbling through it.

"By the ocean," I gasped, turning to look at Galomp in case he'd had anything to do with that, but he just stepped through, looking around keenly.

"The game continues," he said eagerly. "Oh boy. What a day."

"Was that you?" I demanded.

"Was what me? Oh bother, did I do something wrong? Did I make you mad, Miss Everest?" He flinched like he thought I might strike him.

"No, the gate. Did you open the gate?" I pushed.

He shook his head quickly.

"Perhaps the magic permits neophytes," I murmured, unsure why that would be true but unable to come up with a better explanation.

I forged on down the dark tunnel, no daylight finding its way here, and the fire sconces were unlit. But there was a light growing up ahead, a dim blue glow that flashed intermittently. I extinguished my Faelight, not wanting to draw attention if anyone came this way and darkness fell over us.

A terrible, blood-curdling scream came from ahead and fear ripped through my chest before I starting running, toward it instead of away. Because I had to know, I had to see what was happening.

I rounded into a chamber where a group of gold-cloaked Reapers stood with their backs to us and Galomp's arms closed around me from behind. I grabbed my dagger, alarm racing through me and magic flaring in my veins before he placed me down again beside the arching entranceway out of sight.

"Hide and seek," he whispered in my ear, though our voices were still hidden within my silencing shield and I was thankful I hadn't stabbed him. He'd just saved my ass from being seen. "But I hope they will not seek."

I shifted closer to the archway, peering into the chamber where a huge glass altar stood at its centre. A man was lying on it, completely naked with runes carved into his skin, blood dripping from them and some potent power making him writhe within its command. My heart juddered as I recognised him. He was a Stonebreaker, one who had been declared dead, his body found in a passage in the heart of the Keep and the murderer still being hunted. But here he was, alive and...not well.

The Reapers began chanting, a low rumble rising to a crescendo and making the man writhe harder still. A scream pitched from his lungs and he reached for something above him that I couldn't perceive, like he was seeing something beyond this plane of existence, or perhaps he was just fucking hallucinating because of whatever power they had imbued in his skin with those runes. Why had the Reapers lied about his death? Had they been keeping him here ever since his murder had been announced? And what the fuck were they even doing to him?

As I watched, the nothingness above him shifted and writhed. It was just a thickening of darkness in the air, but as it coiled towards the man, he screamed like never before and horror rocked through me as I watched, having no idea what I was seeing, and before I could figure it out, Galomp tugged me back.

I turned to look at him, finding him pressed to the wall. "We should not look in there. I have a bad feeling. I do not want to look."

The sound of the Reapers' chanting came this way and I grabbed Galomp's arm as my heart lurched, dragging him back the way we had come, running as fast as possible.

I reached the iron gate which had swung shut, gabbing hold of it, but it was locked once more. And this time, it wouldn't shift. Panic rose in me as I rattled it hard, glancing back and hearing that chanting coming toward us. We were fucked. So fucking fucked.

A chirrup made me look around and I found the blue lizard lighting a path with its tail down a passage to our left which I hadn't even noticed in the shadows. I raced after it and Galomp followed, placing my faith in the strange creature and chasing it up to a stone sculpture of the Libra scales set into the wall. The lizard jumped into one of the scales with a clicking sound in its throat and the scales tilted, a hidden door suddenly opening in the wall to the right.

I grabbed the lizard, running into the passage with Galomp in tow, and shoving the door shut behind us, keeping the noise within my silencing shield.

We were in a narrow spiral staircase and I ran up the steep stone steps at speed, up, up, up in a never-ending whirl that had me dizzy and panting hard by the time we reached their summit. There was nothing but a wall in the darkened space at their peak, the space here so narrow that Galomp was pressed right up beside me as he reached the top of the stairs huffing and puffing.

I held the lizard towards the wall hopefully, its tail igniting with that red glow and its wings spreading as it launched from my palm. It landed on the wall, moving up it and slipping through a crack, proving another door lay there.

I pressed my palm to it, that same potent magic rising then falling away at my touch and I shoved hard, trying to budge the door, and it swung wide. We went stumbling out into a storage cupboard, rows of wooden shelves filled with dusty crystal balls, scrying bowls and decks of tarot cards filling the space around me.

Galomp screamed and I wheeled around in terror, thinking of that horrible nothingness above the man on that altar, but finding him batting away a cobweb along with the spider inside.

"Fucking hell, Galomp." I held my heart, laughing uneasily as he flicked his hand to get the last of the spiderweb off it.

"I do not like things with eight legs," he said, shuddering.

"You went down there in those stars-forsaken tunnels and a spider is what you're worried about?" I said breathlessly.

He shoved the stone door shut and shrugged his big shoulders. "It was not so bad."

"You saw the Reapers, right? And what they were doing?"

"I did not look."

"You didn't see the altar, or that man on it? That Stonebreaker? The one they said was dead just a few days ago?" I pushed in desperation, trying to remember the man's name, but I couldn't recall it.

"I did not look," he repeated, then glanced around the storage space and I dropped the silencing shield around us as disappointment rattled through me. "It is nice in here. I like it a lot. Except for the spiders."

"We have to tell someone," I said, marching for the wooden door that surely led back into Never Keep. But I had no idea where.

I glanced around for the lizard before exiting, but there was no sign of it, so I slipped through the door, recognising the bright passage as part of the heart of the Keep.

Galomp followed me out of the room, and of all the Fae to be discover me here with Galomp in his bathers, why did it have to be *them?* Alina shrieked and pointed us out, slapping Ransom on the shoulder while their friends looked between us eagerly. "Look, the freak and Galomp! They were fucking in that cupboard!"

"Shut up, Alina," I snarled, turning and heading away from them, needing to find someone to tell about what we'd discovered. But who? How was I going to tell anyone about this? The Reapers had been down there. They were involved in whatever I'd witnessed. They were covering up that Stonebreaker's death so they could strap him to an altar and do…fuck even knew what to him.

"What did she just say to me?" Alina snapped, but I didn't turn back.

I made it into the Heliacal Courtyard where groups of Fae were milling around in their separate elemental groups, glares passing between them.

I looked between them, trying to find a face I could trust, someone to confide in. But even the Raincarvers shrank from me and Galomp, clearly wanting nothing to do with us.

A blast of ice crashed into me from behind, sending me flying and I hit the flagstones hard, skidding across them and landing in the centre of the courtyard.

Laughter echoed out from the those around me and I shoved myself upright in anger, raising my hands and sending shards of ice flying back at Alina. Ransom threw up a shield of water that was warm enough to melt them on impact then dropped it with a vicious look twisting his features.

I was just that odd girl again, being hunted throughout Castelorain, forced to face the wrath of him and his friends time and again. They grouped around me now and Galomp looked from me to them, scurrying forward to stand at my side.

"Don't make enemies out of these assholes, Galomp," I muttered, readying for their next attack. "Go back to the Vault."

"I will stay here, Miss Everest," he insisted.

I noticed the Sky Witch standing with her two demonic looking friends near a stone fountain that was set into the wall, her gaze trailing over me then to my opponents before falling back on her companions, our fight clearly of no interest to her.

Alina's two eyes slid together into one bulbous orb, her Cyclops Order awakening and my pulse quickened at the sight. She stepped forward, her psychic power slamming into my mental shields and I worked to keep her out of my head, but Ransom began casting at me alongside his friends to jolt my focus.

Blasts of ice and shots of water pummelled me and I fought to shield, hardening my skin with ice as a protective layer, but their strikes only grew more harsh.

Galomp engaged some of their friends, blasts of power tearing between them and I worked to defend myself from the furious blasts of four Fae as they combined their power against me.

I knocked two of Ransom's friends flying with blasts of water, their cries of pain echoing through the courtyard as they hit a wall. Ransom used the distraction to cast a whip of water around my ankle and I wasn't fast enough to break it, slamming down onto my back.

Alina pounced, coming down on top of me with a victorious smile. I threw my fist into her kidney over and over as I fought to get her off, but her palm slapped against my head and her Cyclops power drove into me so furiously that my mental shields cracked and splintered.

I battled to keep them up, desperate to shove her out of my head as lashes of water snared my arms and forced me to lay still beneath her. Ice snaked across my chest and I didn't know who was casting it but that terrible power slithered into my chest and coiled around my heart. My entire focus was honed on melting it away and freeing myself from its threat, my pulse rioting as I tried to escape. With my attention on my mental shields wavering, Alina got in my mind, her big eye all I could see as she dominated my thoughts and demanded truths from my lips.

"Why were you and Galomp in that cupboard? Were you fucking each other? Were you Galomping with Galomp?" she laughed loudly, all eyes in the courtyard on me now as the truth came out of my lips. I struggled to keep it back but she urged it on, her power thick and terrible inside my head, and I couldn't find a way to force her from my thoughts.

"The Reapers are doing something terrible beneath the Keep. They had a Stonebreaker down there – he was marked with runes and some awful nothingness was creeping closer to him," I cried and silence fell as everyone heard me.

Alina stared at me in shock then whipped her hand back from my head, her mental power snatched away from me in the same moment. "She's crazy – her mind is addled. Ergh, it's *disgusting*." She reared away from me, moving back to Ransom's side and my half-brother laughed openly at me.

Plenty of others joined in and I shoved myself upright, sending a blast of ice shards at Alina's head. They would have hit had Ransom not moved quickly enough, throwing up a shield, but several of my shards scored down his arm and made him snarl.

Galomp was still fighting with Ransom's friends, huge blasts of water tearing away from him and as I watched, he charged at them, slamming into them full force and sending them flying with the strike of his body alone.

Everyone around me was laughing, muttering or sniggering and my eyes met those of the Sky Witch for a moment, the only one in the courtyard who seemed moved by what I'd said. In the depths of those storm grey eyes, I saw a river of belief, like perhaps for some unknown reason she accepted my truth.

Heat rose in my veins as the laughter grew and a burning sensation poured through my veins, rage mixed with embarrassment. It coursed through me like an inferno, and suddenly my body was shifting, a ripple of energy rushing down my spine and my form changed at once.

I landed on four large white paws, my clothes hanging loose around my new form, and a hiss of surprise left my lips. I'd Emerged, my Order was here and it looked like I was some kind of large cat. And in the puddle of water over the flagstones, I saw my reflection staring back at me. A leopard of some sort, a Relic Leopard perhaps, though their fur was tanned, not white like mine with these dark black spots, and I was smaller than one of them too. They could grow as big as horses, but I was closer to Fae-sized.

"What is she?" Alina muttered to Ransom.

"A fleabag cat by the looks of it," Ransom sneered.

Galomp came lumbering over to me, leaving his opponents nursing their wounds on the floor then scooped me into his arms and carried me away with impossible ease despite my size, petting my head. My claws dug into his shoulders a little as shock bound my limbs and I simply let Galomp carry me away towards the Vault of Frost, finding myself in a brand new body with no real knowledge of what my Order was, or if it would be something powerful enough to gild my name with my father's pride.

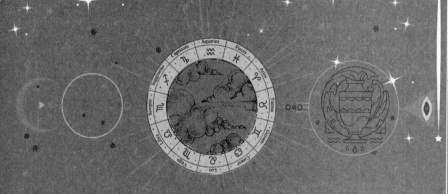

VESPER

CHAPTER TWENTY TWO

My boots sank into the powdery snow with every step as we charted a path across the tundra towards the distant Pinnacle where our air magic was finally going to be tested to its fullest.

In the last two months, our time taking instruction on our air magic had been focused on control, limiting our power and reigning it in. There had been more than a few grumbles heard within the ranks of the air conscripts, but I had fixed my attention on mastering every precise movement the Reapers had informed us about, every tiny action, each whisper of the wind across my skin and between my fingers. Until I was able to perform tasks with my magic in as much complexity as if I were using my own hands to execute them.

Within the first few weeks I could braid my own hair and turn the pages of a book or place a log on the fire.

Then I had honed that control until I could unlock doors by shaping my power to mimic a key or pluck a single piece of hay from a haystack.

My eyes ached from reading late into the night, my chest always hollow with the emptiness of expending all of my considerable power before I slept. It meant I had to steal magic from the other Fae come morning, tempting their desires to the forefront of their minds and sometimes making them act on them too.

It was utterly exhausting and yet the most exhilarating thing I had ever experienced. I was used to owning my power – used to thriving in battle and bloodshed and shining within the heart of chaos and pain, of drawing on ether and paying the price for wielding it but that was simply me harnessing the raw power of the world. Nothing compared to the flood of power which lived within me, utterly my own. It was a wild, lawless beast, a reflection of my own unfettered soul and the freedoms I had always yearned for with such desperation. It was raw and brutal and mine to command, and there was nothing in this world which would hold me back now that I had claimed it.

The subtle control of my magic which I could now wield with enough precision to thread a needle on the far side of my bedroom was a beautiful thing. But as the days had passed, I had found myself repeatedly looking from the windows of my tower to the east where an icy tower called my name.

The Pinnacle sat a three mile hike from the training courtyard in the Vault of Sky at Never Keep, the rocky mountain pass making it only accessible via this one route. Most days, when the fog rolled in, the snow tumbled from the sky and the clouds hung low and thick across this barren and unforgiving landscape, it was impossible to even see it from the Keep.

We were headed inland, and though I had purchased a set of thick furs to stave off the worst of the frigid cold, my cheeks were still chapping and my fingers were growing stiff.

"If it's much further I might have to gut someone just so that I can warm my hands up with their innards," Dalia muttered from my right, drawing a smile to my lips.

"Best do it fast before they freeze through then," I replied.

Dalia cast a look around at the Fae who stalked behind us. Cayde was of course keeping pace with us several feet to Moraine's left, his silence almost as offensive as the sound of his voice - should he ever deign to use it. We led the pack as always and behind us trudged an army of neophytes, each looking as disgusted with the weather as I felt. But I didn't let it show on my face.

Ahead of us, four Reapers hung suspended above the ground, floating towards our destination and setting a punishing pace for those of us forced to forge through the snow. They wore only their gold cloaks as usual, though as they had contained themselves within a shield of air magic, I supposed they were protected from the biting wind.

This week in our Cardinal Magic instructions we had been taught how to power share, meaning we could combine our power with that of others through physical touch. It required full trust to open the channels of magic between one Fae and another and very few of the other conscripts had been able to manage it but Dalia, Moraine and myself were bonded more closely than many true siblings. We had taken to it like ducks to water. The rush of combining our power was one of the best I'd ever had and we had been practicing it ever since, creating powerful shields or blasts of magic which would be capable of ripping our enemies apart in combat. My mind was full of fantasies about our next battle and I was jolted out of them as Moraine spoke.

"My cousin in Wrathbane wrote me this morning," she said, changing the subject. "The royals are hosting a huge party from the western tip – do you know of the Collingsdales?"

"Coal miners," I grunted, my studies on the aristocracy of Stormfell as proficient as necessary to not appear entirely like an uneducated waifhouse stray when I was among them.

"More than that," Dalia added. "I heard they found diamonds in their mines a few years back and are arguably wealthier than the royal family now."

I scoffed but a glance at Moraine confirmed it. To my irritation, Cayde was watching me from beyond her, clearly eavesdropping on our conversation. I considered throwing up a silencing shield to cut him out but honestly, nothing we were saying was particularly interesting and I refused to give him the satisfaction of knowing he had irritated me.

"And why are the oh so wealthy Collingsdales visiting Wrathbane?" I asked, trying to summon some intrigue even though I hated discussing court bullshit.

"That's the thing – no one knows. But the entire palace has been scrubbed from turret to cellar in anticipation of their arrival and decorated for some grand event. Apparently it's all anyone can talk about."

"Thank fuck we aren't there then," I drawled, gaining a laugh from my sisters.

A cry came from behind us and I glanced back, finding a neophyte on her knees in the snow, teeth chattering and face blue with cold. Huge swathes of the air kingdom was capped with snow for the winter so most of us were used to these kinds of conditions, but I assumed she hailed from somewhere to the south of our lands.

I sneered at her in disgust – if we were deployed into battle then we all knew what happened to those who fell behind so I made no effort to help her up. She'd either find the strength in her bones to forge on or would remain there and freeze to death, proving herself unworthy of serving the mighty sovereignty of air.

"This is fucking ridiculous," I muttered, looking ahead again, the snow billowing from the clouds and making it impossible to see much of the Pinnacle ahead of us but a darker shape was forming within the haze of white, denoting it.

I took my hands from my gloves, inhaling deeply as I called on the well of power within me before releasing it in a furious blast which cleared the snow from our path.

"Last one to the peak goes without pudding," Dalia challenged, breaking into a sprint without waiting for our agreement.

I exchanged a look with Moraine, the two of us clearly considering whether or not we would play this childish game before giving in to the competitive natures that had thrust us to the forefront of the Sinfair.

I shoved her and she danced away before throwing a wall of air magic up between us and allowing her to break free.

I called her a host of wildly unpleasant names, digging my fingers into the solid wall of air and forcing my power against it until it shattered. Then I was running.

The wind toyed with my hair and the sound of thousands of boots thundering after us made it clear that we had started a charge.

I didn't look back; my gaze was locked on the two women I loved most dearly in this world with the singular goal of seeing them fall.

They were both far taller than me but I was fast despite their longer strides, my physical training paramount even in this stone fortress of frost and ruin. I never took a day off, never allowed myself a rest, never took the chance that I might dull the edge I had worked so hard to gain. Every day I spent two hours before dawn training in combat with Moraine and Dalia – Cayde often watching from the shadows while refusing to join us. Then I made time to fit in a run and my strength training too. I wouldn't slip. I couldn't.

I barely even noticed the stone tower as it was revealed through the snow, perched upon what appeared to be a glacier, though I imagined stone must lie beneath the ice and snow. Great spires struck out towards the sky, stone balconies jutting from them at ever increasing heights until the tallest of them disappeared into the low-hanging cloud.

Moraine was the fastest of us, her silver braids slapping against her spine as she charged after Dalia who was laughing wildly, lost to the thrill of the game. I'd bet she'd have run even faster if there had been some prey for her to catch.

I twisted my wrists, tangling a knot of air magic between my fingers like a whip before throwing it out ahead of me. I hooked Dalia's ankle into my grasp and yanked her off of her feet so violently that her chin struck the ground and she spat blood at my feet as I passed.

"Bitch!" she cackled and I raised my middle finger at her over my shoulder, racing after Moraine who was closing in on the Reapers where they clustered on the steps at the foot of the tower.

I tried to lash Moraine into my grasp but her own air magic cracked down, slicing mine in two and leaving me with nothing but her goading catcalls to chase after.

She was almost there, mere feet from the steps and a petty glory which I refused to allow her to claim. I skidded to a halt, air magic rising within me like a tempest as the thundering feet of all those at my back drew nearer.

I raised my hands to the sky, sensing rather than fully knowing what to do and yet this power was so intrinsic to me, to who and what I was that it made sense to bend it to my will this way.

I drove my hands towards the ground and a wall of air slammed into place before Moraine, the sickening crack of her crashing into it at full speed reaching me even from this distance.

She was thrown to the ground and I broke into a run again, sweeping my arms out behind me and blasting the Fae on my heels back blindly.

A victorious smile burned across my face as I sprinted past Moraine who was clutching her bleeding nose on the ground while simultaneously kicking snow at me.

The Reapers watched us with assessing, calculating expressions, giving nothing away but I knew they would at least see that I had beaten every other Fae to this-

"Bastard!" I yelled, magic crackling in my fingers as Cayde dove from the sky on those obnoxious black wings and landed in front of me a heartbeat before I could reach the bottom step.

"Such a big mouth, and such little legs," he mocked, his gaze dripping over me, daring me to strike him.

I stepped up to him, glaring into his honey brown eyes, promising him all kinds of torturous endings before smiling sweetly instead of enacting any of them.

"Congratulations," I purred. "You proved you can win a race against unshifted Fae by using your Order gifts. How impressive. Would you by any chance like to see what I can do when I unleash the monster in me?"

The roiling tempest of my Order form rose to the surface of my skin, my shoulder blades burning as I held his gaze, the taste of his desire coating my tongue as I took measure of him. Oh, he wanted power. He hungered for it with a desperation which was likely only rivalled by my own. He wanted to be seen, he wanted to wrap his hand around my throat while sliding the other beneath my-

"Enough," Reaper Tessa commanded and I blinked, forcing my focus back to myself, vaguely noticing the Fae who had thrown themselves at me while drawn in by my power. They'd met with an air shield which it seemed the Reaper herself had erected to keep them back.

Cayde's hands were gripping my waist, his mouth hovering over mine so that I could almost taste the intoxicating-

I shoved him back with a snarl. "Down boy," I mocked, flicking my fingers at him and using air to push him several more steps away.

"Lemme tug your tatas," a huge guy begged, his words squashed together by the crush of his face against the air shield.

"I need a banana," a girl wailed. "I need a fucking banana!"

"Someone skipped breakfast," Dalia snorted, but her eyes kept skipping over me in a way which gave away her own reaction to my power.

"I would like you to play me like a harp," another asshole yelled and I was forcibly reminded of all the reasons I had to keep the full extent of my power locked down most of the time.

"Anyone unable to control themselves will face a week of reparations," the Reaper said firmly before dropping the air shield and allowing the conscripts to decide their own fate.

Hands reached for me and I stiffened, my fingers curling into a fist, but only one actually dared touch me, the woman's gentle caress brushing my sleeve before she hastily withdrew, apologising.

"You have mastered the basics of air control," the Reaper called, no longer paying any heed to my gifts. "So now it is time you test the strength of what you have claimed. The Pinnacle is designed for one reason only – to practice launching yourself into the sky and maintaining control over your magic whilst doing so. There are many levels in the towers at my back, each of which holding balconies where you will be expected to jump and take to the sky. The lowest of these, for those of you not yet confident in your ability – meaning all of you as it stands – are only twenty feet from the ground. With this level of snowfall, failure won't be fatal. But we expect all of you to be leaping from The Spear by the end of your six months at Never Keep. Understood?"

She jerked her chin upward to make her point more clearly and either by magic or intervention of fate, the clouds parted, revealing the jagged towers to their full extent. There were ten in all, each of varying width and size but the one in the heart of the group stood far taller than the rest, its peak so clearly resembling a spear that there was no doubting her meaning. Just below the tip, I could make out a stone balcony when I squinted and my heart pounded with a mixture of fear and excitement as I took in that challenge.

"Begin," Reaper Tessa commanded when no one raised any questions and I stalked ahead of the flood of Fae as all of us headed for the collection of towers. I'd taken a moment to read my tarot cards this morning and hadn't foreseen my death in them, so I was going to stick with the self-assurance which generally served me so well in my attempt at this.

"Where should we start?" Moraine asked sardonically, as though it hadn't been obvious from the moment those clouds had parted. She'd wiped the blood from her nose with the back of her hand but all that had really done was smear it across her mouth. At least it appeared to have stopped bleeding.

"I want the full force of my magic in my hands before attempting it," I replied, looking around the assembled Fae and selecting a target from them. I could sense the weight of their power on the air itself, those of lesser quality also of lesser appeal but this Fae was strong, I could practically taste his power.

"You!" I called, pointing at the red haired male who had been casting me subtle looks instead of heading into one of the towers.

"Me?" he questioned, glancing around.

"I can't see any other dense assholes lingering close by – oh wait, Cayde is still here so I apologise, but I've already had a taste of him and I found him indigestible," I said dismissively, not looking at the Drake who had gone suspiciously quiet since falling prey to my gifts.

The tempestuous nature of the power I had syphoned from him was making my blood pump faster, the weight of his magic an unwelcome distraction which I certainly didn't need any more of. This Fae before me, though powerful, looked as bland as a dry biscuit and that was precisely what I needed to settle my rampant pulse.

"What do you need, my...Sky Witch?" the man asked, taking a tentative step closer.

"Simply tell me what you'd like to do to me," I purred, beckoning him and smiling so sweetly I almost got toothache. My gifts coiled around him, his desires whispering to me as I began to tug at them, drawing his magic into me.

His eyes moved from me and landed on Cayde though, the lust which had been somewhat dormant ramping up considerably.

"Oh, even better," I said, offering him my hand. "Let's hear what you'd do to the brooding bastard with the wings if only he'd loosen up enough to try it."

The male took my hand, wetting his lips as his lust for Cayde grew beyond measure at the contact, his desire filling my magical reserves while his restraint came tumbling down.

"I'd lay beneath him while he stood naked over me with those wings out," he breathed, power slipping from him and into me. "I'd watch as his muscles flexed with every pump of his fist over his rigid cock."

"Are we thinking Cayde here has a big cock or did the stars deign him one as lacking as his personality?" Dalia asked innocently and I snorted a laugh while Cayde took the opportunity to stalk away from us like the haughty bastard he was.

"Big," the Fae holding my hand near moaned. "He'd fist my hair in his hand and drive it down my throat. I'd come close to choking on it but I'd take it, every inch-"

I snatched my hand from his as that image forced itself into my mind, except *I* was the Fae on my knees before Cayde, my body burning with lust as he used me for his own pleasure and I loved every fucking second of it.

"Enough," I snapped, shoving the Fae away from me so hard that he almost fell with the shock of being released from my hold. I ignored him, leading my sisters towards the central tower with a jerk of my chin.

"What was that about?" Moraine asked in a low voice as we stepped through the stone archway which might once have held a door but now simply stood open, allowing the base of the tower to fill with snow.

"My gifts," I muttered, trying to force away the image of Cade's cock in my mouth, the taste of him, the way my body blazed with heat. "They're stronger since my elemental magic was Awakened. I feel what the Fae I'm draining feel and apparently now I see it too."

"Seriously?" Dalia asked with glee. "You can just slip right into other people's fantasies? So how big *was* Cayde's cock?'

"His *fantasy* cock – that asshole had never actually seen him naked," I reminded her but she shrugged like that was irrelevant.

I rolled my eyes, dismissing her far more easily than that image.

The cold seemed thicker as we stepped inside the shadow of the tower, the snow tumbling over the toes of my boots while the wind whipped up small flurries which banked against the outer walls.

"Come on. The climb is going to take forever."

Dalia sighed dramatically, leading the way across the empty space and stepping onto the black stairs which coiled out of sight in an alcove by the far wall.

I followed with Moraine, taking up the rear, more speculation about the mysterious event at court falling from her lips as we began to climb the twisting stairs. I leaned over the stone balustrade, looking up through the hole in the centre of the spiralling staircase but the top of the tower was lost to shadow in the dizzying expanse above.

"Something is happening at Never Keep," I interrupted just as she got started on a guess that there might be a circus appearing in Wrathborn – we all knew the king wouldn't have ordered the palace scrubbed for a bunch of carnival folk who wouldn't even be allowed to step within its walls.

"Did you hear about that too?" Dalia asked, looking back at me, the strands of her short black hair tumbling over her forehead before she swept them away again. "About the water guy who was caught with an icicle lodged so far up his ass that it took two Reapers and a dog to-"

"Dalia your stories are the most ridiculous heap of bullshit," I snorted.

"They spread like wildfire through the refectory though," she replied, smug as shit about the ludicrous rumours she'd been spreading about the conscripts from the other elements. "Besides, at least half of them are true – or only mildly embellished. For example, there may not have been a dog."

"No shit? There wasn't a dog in this barren place where I haven't seen hide nor hair of a single creature for the last two months outside of shifters?" I replied.

"The dog adds the kind of juicy detail which makes the rumour fly," Dalia replied stubbornly.

"Was there really an icicle then?" Moraine asked.

"I swear on the shiny ass of Venus herself that I witnessed it. The idiot was yelling something about slipping while practicing his magic, but why were his trousers bunched around his ankles then? And that's some pretty precise aim for an accident."

"That's a real choice spot for frostbite," I muttered.

"This asinine conversation began with you telling us that something was happening at the Keep," Moraine prompted as we slipped towards silence again, the heavy trudge of our boots against the stairs the only sound.

I glanced around. We appeared to be alone on the stairs but doorways opened off of them, leading out into rooms with balconies at lower levels and you never could be certain if a rat was lurking nearby. Especially in this place, surrounded by our foes.

With a twist of my fingers I erected a silencing shield around the three of us, making certain that our conversation remained private.

"I should have told you about it before," I began. "But in the

Keep I always feel like there are too many ears listening in. Besides, knowing this might be dangerous. In fact, I know it's dangerous."

"And yet you still hogged all the fun of that knowledge for yourself," Dalia chided. "You really are a selfish creature, V."

I shook my head, knowing I really should have expected that answer. Of course danger would never deter my beastly companions.

"The day that fire asshole was executed in the Heliacal Courtyard after Astral Sanctuary," I began.

"You mean when you enraged him by choosing to enter the Temple of Leo and he lost his shit, pulled a knife and stabbed the closest Raincarver to death while you conveniently slipped away?" Moraine clarified.

"Six karmas to me, Moraine," Dalia chipped in. "I told you she'd offer up the truth before we were forced to ask."

"Took you a month though, V," Moraine accused and I had the decency to feel a little shitty about it.

"Yeah, that day," I agreed because we didn't do apologies, we just smacked each other around when we got emotional about things and unless one of them was about to throw the first punch, there was no need for me to comment any further on my lack of forthrightness. "Well, I may have followed the Reapers into their private passages beneath the Keep and trespassed on this fucked-up ritual they were performing."

Moraine and Dalia listened attentively as I recounted all I could, describing whatever the fuck had been in that room in as much detail as possible. But truthfully I hadn't gotten a good look at it and I was reluctant to admit how fucking terrified I'd been. We didn't go for piss your pants bullshit in the Sinfair.

"Have you found out any more since?" Dalia asked when I was

done, not wasting time on questioning my account of things no matter how insane they sounded.

"No," I grunted.

"You've been out sneaking around every night," Moraine commented and I scowled.

"You weren't supposed to have noticed that. I thought I was subtle."

"Sure. As subtle as a Succubus scuttling past our doors two times a night," Dalia said as if that were some turn of phrase and not pure nonsense.

"That. And I laid magical threads across the hallways which let me know when someone passes through them. I keyed them to recognise your magical signatures so that I wouldn't have to leap out of bed with a knife in hand every time one of you goes sculking off somewhere you shouldn't be," Moraine added.

"That's fucking smart," Dalia said, raising her brows at me.

"It is," I agreed. "You'll teach us how to replicate it."

"If you insist," Moraine replied lightly but she knew that was some clever, sneaky shit and she knew we'd want in from the moment she'd figured out how to do it.

"So you're assassinating targets for the prince *and* investigating the Reapers?" Dalia confirmed.

"You're not supposed to know that the prince asked me to-"

"Oh come on, V," Dalia scoffed. "Like it wasn't obvious – Dragor must have had you all alone at least four times on the flight to the Keep and he hand delivered you to the doors. If he wasn't tasking you with an assignment then you were definitely fucking, and as much as I know you pant over him, I haven't picked up the smug bitch vibes I think you'd have been glowing with if you'd actually been riding his cock, so-"

"I hate you," I said flatly and she cackled obnoxiously.

"And what possible assignment could he have given you to carry out while at Never Keep?" Moraine asked lightly. "It was either espionage or assassination and since that fire asshole lost his shit so spectacularly in Astral Sanctuary and then that wet fish from water went and fell down the stairs right after you'd gone to take a piss-"

"Tell me you only figured that out because you bitches are so deep into my business and not because it was actually in any way obvious," I groaned.

"Don't worry, V, it was entirely because we're so obsessed with you. So unless any other fucker has been stalking you, I very much doubt they could put it together. But I don't think the stairs shit will go unnoticed twice," Moraine said.

"It was too easy," I sighed. "I'd only been following her to get to know her movements a bit more and then suddenly, we were all alone on the stairs at the same time – I don't even think she knew I was behind her. She was toying with her wet, splashy shit and made a puddle on the floor and before I knew what was happening, I'd just snapped her neck and given her a shove." I shrugged innocently. "Honestly I think she was only a target because she was due to inherit some title or something. She certainly wasn't well trained or particularly threatening."

We fell into a discussion about the things I'd seen the Reapers hiding but neither of them were very keen to investigate it further. Moraine was of the mindset that the Reapers had nothing to do with us, while Dalia was secretly a pious little twat and actually believed that whatever it was the Reapers were up to could only be because they were following the guidance of the stars – something us mere single elementals couldn't possibly understand. I loved her but her blind faith in the stars to guide our fates drove me batshit sometimes.

As we finally reached the top of the stairs, I let my silencing shield fall away and pushed between my two sisters in arms as we found ourselves standing in a wide space with open stone archways offering a view out of the land all around us.

A pointed roof covered our heads, keeping the worst of the snow from settling inside the tower but frost still clung to the pale brickwork, small snowdrifts accumulated beneath the arched windows.

We took a moment to catch our breaths, gazing out over the view of the barren, stunning landscape. Everything was coated in a thick layer of snow, Never Keep to the east like a black stain before the iron waters of the sea.

The clouds had lifted entirely now, a pale blue sky offering a view of the rugged mountains to the north and endless flat, snow-covered plains to the west. I could just make out a pool of bright blue water in the distance – the hot springs which I knew lurked in this volcanic terrain. It was breathtaking in its beauty, the arctic wind doing nothing to lessen the thrill of standing here at the top of the world and breathing it all in.

"Fuck, that's a lot of snow," Dalia cooed.

"Are we doing this then?" Moraine asked, heading for the widest of the archways and the only one which fully reached the floor where a balcony protruded from the side of the tower, no handrail in place to save you from a fall.

"Keep your wings away," I told her firmly. "You use your magic or you go splat – just like me and Dalia."

"Technically-" Dalia began but I gave her a dark look and she bowed her head in deference, dropping it.

"Fine," Moraine sighed dramatically like I was such a pain in her ass. "Splat it is."

We stepped out onto the balcony as one, striding forward until the toes of our boots protruded from the edge and the wild wind threatened to pitch us straight off of it.

I reached out and took each of their hands, the three of us smiling at one another like the pack of heathens we were. We may have been shunned and shamed, forced to fight harder than any others for our place in this war and given nothing from anyone else to aid us, but we had this. Each other. It was brutal, and bloodthirsty, built perhaps from necessity rather than a desire for companionship or love but it had become so much more than any of that. We were family. A fucked-up family who cussed each other out and beat each other up and yet a family all the same. The only one I'd ever known.

The wind tore my pink hair back from my face and I smiled into it as we stepped from the balcony as one and fell into the void beneath the tower with clasped hands and matching raucous laughter rolling from our throats.

I had to release my hold on them to cast, the magic inside me rising up into a tempest before bursting from me like a flood from a dam. It spun me around, hurling me towards the stone wall of the tower for three terrifying seconds, and then I wrenched it under my command and launched myself towards the sky with a triumphant whoop.

I twisted around from my pillar of air magic, my gut swooping as I dipped and bucked within the maelstrom, figuring out how to control it to its fullest. Relief filled me as I found Dalia spinning through the sky to my right and Moraine speeding over the rooftops of the lower towers beneath us.

I tipped my head back to the sky and howled like a beast as my magic pulsed around me, offering up a taste of a reality which I had dreamed of so many times that I had lost count. I was flying. And I would never again be confined to a life rooted to the ground.

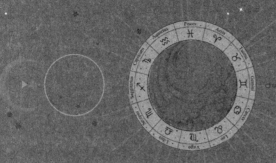

EVEREST

CHAPTER TWENTY THREE

Illusion magic was one of my least favourite practises because my useless left hand made some of the more complex casts difficult, meaning more times than not, I ended up frustrated as shit. They may have been easier to cast with two hands, but that didn't mean I was giving up.

"Again," I growled at Galomp who stood opposite me in the triangular courtyard in the Vault of Frost, pushing myself to my feet after being upended by his last attack.

We were occasionally paired up in practical Cardinal Magic classes and I had quickly learned that he was one powerful motherfucker. He cast with such casual ease that it was impossible not to admire the six illusions that stood around him, all in the perfect mimicry of himself. The trick was figuring out which one was the real him.

The courtyard was alive with shouts of attack, Fae clashing as they used illusions to confuse their opponents before landing strikes with their water element. A group of Reapers were moving between the ranks of conscripts, offering out sharp corrections as they went.

We never trained practically with the other nations, and I guess it was in an effort to stop us accidently murdering each other. Or not so accidentally.

Reaper Lily moved toward me, her thin mouth a harsh line and her eyes as cold as winter. "Begin," she instructed me.

Galomp and his illusions moved together into a group, trading places, side-stepping and making my eyes dart left and right as I worked to notice any flaws in his casts. I blasted water at the one lurking behind another, but the illusion fizzled away and was reborn to my right. I whirled away from it, casting water at another, then another, but the water crashed through each one and Galomp remained hidden among his decoys.

"Your hesitation will see you dead on the battlefield," Reaper Lily said simply.

I snarled, sending more and more shots of water out with my good hand, working to make it seem as though I was casting with my left hand too. My concentration was split and the disadvantage was showing with every failure I made.

"She has a head like a hot potato," Galomp said, all of his illusions speaking it at the same time. Damn, he was casting voice illusions too, able to project it with a skill I hadn't mastered during our instructions and all of our practice sessions since.

I blasted water at three more Galomps, failing to find him still as they all reshuffled themselves somehow keeping him hidden.

"What would you do in battle?" Reaper Lily demanded.

Those words struck something inside my head, realisation dawning on me. I was running drills just like I did back in my quarters, acting as if each target was its own opponent, giving them my attention one at a time. But if this was a fight to the death, I knew exactly what I'd do.

Water poured from my hand in a swirling vortex, slamming into all of the Galomps at once and triumph snared me, certainty filling me that I had surely found him now. The illusions all fizzled out in front of me, leaving no Galomps at all, and I stared at the empty space in shock.

"Galomp is behind you," he said and I spun around, finding him laughing in his low chuckling way, his shoulders heaving up and down with every guffaw. "I have been behind you this whole time, Miss Everest."

Reaper Lily shook her head at me then stalked away into the crowd muttering, "She's the next one they'll be scraping off the floor in the corridors."

My blood chilled as I stared after her.

The fact that a Reaper thought so little of me at this point, after all my tireless training was like a punch to the gut. I could defend myself, I'd proved it in these practical sessions time and again. Illusions were still new magic to us and it was hardly fair I be dismissed so easily after one defeat.

"That no-lipped, snake-eyed dick, how dare she?" I hissed to myself. "I can fight. I can kill. I can *win*. Stupinti tiska." *Stupid bitch.*

I thought of that naked, rune-covered Stonebreaker in the depths of the Keep wondering if Reaper Lily had been there that night. If more Fae were being tortured in that horrible place, I didn't know how to help the poor bastards. It made me think of Harlon though, fearing the secrets of the Reapers and what they might be doing with their acolytes. What if they were forced to take part in strange rituals like that? Would Harlon stand idly by? I couldn't picture it. That wasn't him.

The death toll in Never Keep had already climbed to twelve, though the Reapers only acknowledged it to say they were still hunting for the culprits. Then it would be a swift and bloody execution, but no killers had been caught as of yet and I had to wonder if any more of the supposedly 'murdered' Fae had ended up in that awful place under the Keep.

Not enough Raincarvers had died for me to claim a room in the Vault of Frost, but I was growing used to the quiet sanctuary of my quarters, and I might have grown to like it even more had those screams not continued to haunt me in the night. It wasn't my place to question the Reapers on their dealings, but what I'd seen didn't sit right with me. And whatever dark entity had been in that chamber with them had left a sliver of dread in me since.

"You are pacing," Galomp pointed out as I stalked back and forth in front of him, my Order form rising to the surface of my skin and begging to come out.

After I'd shown the Reapers my Leopard Order, I'd been tossed into Order Enhancement sessions with the Relic Leopards despite the fact that I clearly wasn't one of them. They had decided I was a 'smaller, white version of a Relic Leopard' which sounded a hell of a lot like being called a runt, and I was so fucking tired of being written off as that. I was meant to learn the ways of my Order from my kind so I could use my Order gifts in battle, but when all the Relic Leopards gave you one look and ran off every time you showed up to their meetings in the west wing of the Vault of Frost, you kind of lost motivation to go.

Instead, I'd been doing my own research in the Library of Frost. But the problem was, most of the books there detailed battle tactics and magical study. There weren't many tomes that covered topics outside of those subjects, so I was pretty much left to figure out my Order gifts alone. So far, I'd discovered very little besides from the obvious. I could climb even better than I'd been able to in my Fae form. My fur was so warm that I'd taken to sleeping in my Order form, curled up by the fire, and I had a lot of sharp teeth and claws that could likely do some real damage in a fight. That was…it. And maybe that really was all my Order had to offer. Not every Fae Order held magical gifts, but I'd hoped I'd have at least one that would strengthen me for battle. Perhaps something rare that my father would be forced to take note of and admire. Maybe something he'd praise out loud, regale to his friends, hail from hill to hill. Was a little hailing from hilltops really too much to ask for?

I was re-paired with another Fae for the next round and was glad when I managed to get her on her ass and win the fight. By the time the session was over, I'd won around half of my fights and I was getting better at both spotting illusions and destroying all those in my path. I also didn't forget to check behind me again thanks to Galomp's move. Whenever it had been my turn to cast them, I hadn't done it well at all, but I wasn't going to focus on how bruised my ass felt from being knocked over and forced to yield during those particular brawls.

The sky above had darkened to deepest obsidian, the stars glittering beautifully and making my gaze flit from one sparkle to another in fascination. I let the crowd sweep me inside, my thoughts turning to my favourite pool in the Poseidon Spa, then to that mysterious hidden door Galomp and I had ventured through all those weeks ago.

I'd tried it several times since, but whatever magic held it in place would no longer budge, and I wasn't sure what my plan would have been if it did. I'd not seen any sign of that strange lizard which had led us down into the depths of the isle either, and honestly the whole thing seemed like a fever dream now.

Galomp and I hadn't spent much time together since, and when I'd tried to bring the subject up with him, he just laughed and called it 'our little adventure' then lumbered off. He hadn't seen the monstrous things that I'd seen, and he wasn't woken in the night by those bloodcurdling screams that carried through the pipes. Even when I cast a silencing shield around me to try and block it out, I'd wake hearing it regardless, my shield having fallen while I slept. My heart would be racing, and I'd often think of Harlon, fearing what had become of him, of what the Reapers might be making him do.

The only thing that kept me calm was the thought that the Reapers wouldn't hurt their own. Multiple elementals were rare and they would be trained well to take up their positions as Reapers. Perhaps I didn't understand what I'd witnessed anyway. The Reapers were guided by the hands of the stars. Maybe what I'd seen wasn't as terrifying as it had appeared. But the knot in my chest told me those were just pretty lies I was trying to sell myself. The truth, I feared, was that Harlon was in trouble.

Despite the longing in my bones for bathing in hot water, I forced my legs to head for the refectory, exiting the Vault of Frost and making my way for something even more tempting. Food.

Since arriving here and claiming three meals a day, I'd lost my scrawny look, my body filling out how it should have. I had real curves to my hips now and my tits had never looked better, but it was the way my ribs didn't have that pokey look anymore that was my favourite thing about this new form of mine. Mama had fed me well enough growing up, but after my sisters had been sent off to war, her Provider stipend had mysteriously dried up. A fact she had tried to hide from me, but I'd overheard Mama begging my father, Commander Rake, to send word to the Magistrine that she still had one last warrior to raise. But the words he had spoken that day were still branded onto my soul.

"If you cannot feed yourself, boil the leech that ails you."

I'd started eating less after that, sliding some of my meal onto Mama's plate whenever she wasn't looking. I didn't want to be anyone's burden.

My father had made enough comments about the government's resources not being wasted that I had put two and two together. He was the reason Mama's stipend had stopped coming. As one of the finest warriors in Cascada, his word held power in the Magistrine. If he had decided I wasn't worth nurturing, then it was done. He had likely thought I'd die on the streets of Castelorain long before I made it to Never Keep, tossed at his feet by his pride and joy, Ransom. Part of why I was still here was definitely down to spite. I might not have had a full stomach back then, but spite was a fuel that knew no bounds. People could do great things in the name of proving assholes wrong.

The refectory was busy this time of night and my eyes roamed warily over the Fae of other elements, moving through the open space with its exposed rafters and grey walls to where a buffet was laid out on a vast wooden table that spanned the length of the room. I grabbed a bowl, piling it up with stew, a couple of bread rolls and a small iced bun before moving to perch at the end of a table claimed by the Raincarvers. They didn't acknowledge me, but it was better than the scowls and wicked sneers thrown my way by the other elementals –

expressions which I offered back in kind.

My skin prickled as my gaze landed on North Brimtheon milling by the buffet table with a couple of women. I'd surmised that he was another of The Matriarch's orphans, sharing Kaiser's name, but they were of no real blood relation. I did a quick scout of the area, but Kaiser wasn't in sight, and I shot a glance over my shoulder just in case he was pulling a Galomp.

"Party starts at nine," North said to the pair of Fae who were looking at him like he was something to eat. "Here."

He offered them two plain black masks and a chill raced through me as I recognised those very masks from the night my mother had been killed. North and Kaiser had been wearing them.

"He is coming right?" one of the women asked, taking a mask and shooting a hopeful look at her friend.

"Of course. Kai wouldn't miss one of my world-famous fuck fests," North said with a smirk. "Clothes are optional by the way."

The women only seemed more excited by that prospect and North leaned in, whispering in one of their ears, making her laugh riotously and slap him on the shoulder.

"Where is it?" the other one asked keenly.

"South tower, tenth floor," North said. "Don't be late or someone else might catch my eye. And Kai's an impatient fucker."

"How about the four of us spend some time together when we arrive?" one of the girls purred, running a hand down North's chest.

"Deal," North agreed with a dark grin before heading off down the buffet table, leaving them chattering excitedly together.

My heart pounded a little harder and I shot a silent thanks to Scorpio for setting this up for me. It had to be fate. I had a time and place where Kaiser was going to be tonight. Sure, it would be in the

Vault of Embers and *sure,* I'd be risking serious punishment if I got caught over there – and execution if I pulled off the kill. But maybe the stars were aligning tonight, and as I thought of my mama, I knew I couldn't pass up this opportunity.

A flash of pink in my periphery made me glance back and I noticed the Sky Witch lingering close to the Flamebringers a little further down the buffet table. She stalked right up to the closest woman, plucked the black mask from her back pocket and slipped away again without ever being noticed. Except by me.

As I watched her go, a plan rolled together in my mind, one that was ripe with danger. But that happened to be my favourite kind.

The rooftops of Never Keep were as welcoming as they appeared from the ground. They were made up of sharp tiles that were slanted and slippery as shit. But even with the ice and snow clinging to them, I made quick work across the Vault of Frost in my Order form with the hilt of my dagger clamped between my teeth in its sheath. Then I headed south around the sloping roof of the heart of the Keep and the glass spires of the Galaseum.

I sprang from one place to the next then leapt across to the roof of the Vault of Embers, landing lightly and padding onward on silent paws. My tail swept along behind me, covering my tracks and my claws helped keep me from slipping as I traversed the sloping roofs, paying little notice to the deadly drop on my right that overlooked the snowy land between the Vaults.

I could see well at night with the eyes of my Leopard, picking out every movement in every window I spied in the tower ahead. I raced toward it, reaching the high wall of the south tower and beginning the vertical climb. It was all too easy, my claws finding gaps in the bricks and my body made for this kind of agility as I moved ever higher, counting the floors.

When I made it to the right one, I shimmied around to a window, peering in at the dark corridor beyond to check it was empty. I rested the dagger on the sill, clinging tight to it then shifted back into my Fae form, leaving me naked. I slipped on the ice, losing my footing in the shift and I bit my tongue as I grabbed onto the sill for support.

My heart juddered as I caught myself and heaved myself back into a balanced position, pressing my hand to the glass pane. The crackle of a magical barrier told me my way forward was blocked, but I had something of a plan. I cast a silencing shield around me and the window then let ice spread from my palm, spilling over the glass. Throwing my magic into it, I tried to break it along with the magical barrier.

The glass shattered, pouring inside onto the floor while my silencing shield kept it from being heard. But the magical barrier held firm.

I cursed, reaching my magic toward it and trying to work out the intricacies, needing to unravel it. But I simply didn't have the skill, or at least, I thought I didn't until a twist of magic in my chest and a strange, roiling power slid from me into that barrier and it fizzled out of existence.

"Hia kaské," I exhaled in disbelief, unsure what I had even done to achieve that. But I didn't have a moment to question it, my time here already running dry. I had to get in and out.

I picked up my dagger from the sill, but before I climbed inside, a flash of movement in my periphery made me glance back at the rooftops.

For a moment I could have sworn I saw a glimmer of pink, but all was still. My guard was up though and I waited a few more seconds before climbing inside, careful to avoid the glass on the stone floor.

I slipped behind a statue of Aries by the wall, the ram standing proud with curling horns, then I held my breath and waited. As I suspected, a Fae appeared at the window and my pulse quickened as the Sky Witch climbed inside, leaping over the shattered glass and landing lightly beyond it.

She jogged away down the passage and I twisted the dagger in my grip. My enemies were everywhere tonight, and it looked like at least one of them knew I was here. But she was out of bounds just as I was. And whatever she was after, I doubted it had anything to do with me.

I waited a few more seconds before heading off down the corridor, the warmth of flames carrying through the stone and heating me despite my lack of clothes. The sound of music carried from somewhere close by and as I reached a turn in the corridor, I shot a glance into a large chamber beyond.

It was a grand common room with five roaring fireplaces set into the walls. Black armchairs, chaise lounges and sofas were filled with half naked Fae, all of them dressed for the occasion of North's so-called fuck fest. A few of them were already taking that name literally, one girl splayed out on a couch with two guys feasting between her legs and her moans lost to the classical music filling the air.

Seemingly centre stage at the party, North was spread in a wingback chair in the middle of the room, his chest bare and the tight muscles of his abs revealed as he lazed there watching a group of women dance for him. But my gaze didn't linger on him long, moving to the more imposing creature beside him in a chair of his own.

Kaiser Brimtheon had a formidable look on his face, one arm

hanging loose over the side of his chair. His black tunic was long-sleeved and he seemed to be the most clothed person in the room, even his boots in place, done up tight over his dark trousers. He had a look of sin about him, his black eyes moving from one dancing girl to the next like he was seeking out sustenance instead of sex. They were the only two at the party not wearing masks, perhaps their reputation too well known to bother trying to conceal their identities.

A woman in an ebony corset and high heels came sauntering my way and I shrank back behind the doorway. As she stepped out of the room, I lunged. My hand slapped over her mouth and froze her lips shut before she could scream and I sealed her eyes closed so she couldn't look at me. She grabbed hold of my arm and flames burned me, but I didn't let go, gritting my teeth against the pain and forcing her through a door to my left.

We stumbled into a broom closet and I kicked the door shut, sending my water element out in a blast that drenched her and sent her flying to the floor. Then I started to freeze it, her limbs becoming stiff as she shivered beneath me in fear.

I began stripping the clothes from her body before she froze completely, pulling on the black shorts that rode up to reveal a lot of ass cheek before strapping the corset onto myself and cursing as I struggled to do up the laces at my back. I glanced at her high heels and figured fuck that, grabbing her mask and placing it over my face. The burn on my arm was red but it wasn't blistering at least and I ignored the sting of pain in it.

I threw a silencing shield around the woman in case she got the ice to melt around her lips before I was done here and I slipped out the door, sealing the lock with ice too.

I strapped my dagger sheath to my hip as I walked into the party, lifting my chin and acting like I belonged. There were plenty of Flamebringers carrying weapons here, so it would go unnoticed easily enough.

My gaze slipped to Kaiser and I wondered how I was supposed to get this soulless being to go somewhere alone with me. I was acutely aware of the fact that I was standing in a viper's pit about to try and charm the biggest, baddest snake in the room to follow me to its death.

"He's spoken for," a girl with blonde hair sang as she moved to my side. I could only see the bottom half of her face beneath the black mask she wore, her lips painted red and pursed at me.

"By you?" I asked.

"By them," she said, jerking her chin at the four women who were dancing for North and Kaiser. "They fought for the privilege to win their eye in the Courtyard of Embers tonight, weren't you there?"

"I took a nap," I said and the girl breathed a laugh.

"Well it was vicious. One of the women they took out had to go to the Reapers to see if they'd heal her fucked-up arm. It was broken in three places apparently."

"What if North or Kaiser wants someone outside of their group? Don't they get a choice?" I asked.

"North likes them to fight for it, he encourages it," she said. "He says it's his Alpha Werewolf nature."

"And Kaiser?" I asked, mentally taking note of North's Order. Werewolves could be as vicious as they could be cuddly. And I got the feeling North spent far more time in the first category than he did the second.

The girl blew out a breath. "Surely you know what he's like."

"I don't spend a lot of time outside my room," I said. "My father encourages my studies. This is my first party."

"Shit, girl. You need to get out more," she laughed. "I'm Tyrine by the way."

"I'm Ella," I said quickly.

"Well, Ella, Kaiser Brimtheon is not your regular, everyday psycho. And the women he takes to bed come back scorched."

"Scorched?" I whispered.

"Burn marks," she clarified. "They wear them like trophies, it's pretty fucked up if you ask me. Although…I wouldn't say no." She eyed Kaiser appreciatively. "But I don't think his brand of fucking is for the faint of heart."

"My brand of fucking won't be either if I get him to choose me," I said. *Because it involves driving a dagger into Kaiser's black heart.*

"You really wanna catch his eye?" she asked, intrigued.

It felt strange having a Flamebringer talk to me with ease like that, the guise I wore veiling all lines drawn between us.

"Maybe. What does he like?" I asked.

"Hard to say. He usually just picks one when the moment strikes him. Or two. Or three. Depends what mood he's in."

The woman with the two guys licking her pussy let out a high-pitched moan that said she was coming and a few people cheered. One sweeping glance around the room said the party was starting to descend into something of an orgy. One man was sucking another guy's cock in the chair to my left and his grunts of appreciation were echoed by the moans of two women who were caressing and licking each other's breasts beside them.

North got to his feet, drawing my gaze to him as he stepped into the middle of the dancing women and pulled one towards him by the back of her neck, sinking his tongue between her lips.

Kaiser still seemed unmoved, but with the orgy growing more

heated I might not have much more time before he selected someone. Or multiple someones.

My eyes tracked over the cut of his jaw, those demonically perfect features of his, from the deeply etched lines of his cheeks to the heavy set of his eyes. He was a dark kind of temptation for anyone daring enough to try and draw his attention, but I scowled at the allure of his face. I was no prey of his. It didn't matter what he looked like, seducing my mother's murderer made my skin crawl, but I had a job to do and I wasn't going to fail at killing him again. If I had to catch his eye, then I'd find a way to do so.

I started towards him, my pulse thundering in my ears, telling me to stay away from this hollow monster, but there was no turning back now. Before I made it to him, however, one of the dancing girls peeled off from the group and raced in front of me.

She leaned over Kaiser, pointing her ass at me and I was forced to stop and wait while she ran her hand down his chest. Running kisses down the side of his neck, she moved ever lower, and his gaze fell on me as she sank to her knees between his thighs. My jaw tightened and I wondered if I was going to have to stand here while she wrapped her lips around his dick, unsure how to draw his attention away from her before that happened.

She caught hold of his shirt, pushing it up over his abs and I noticed a ring of scars on his side, like some beast had clamped its jaws around him and left its teeth marks there. Her hand lowered, riding over his cock, but Kaiser snatched her arm, forcing her away from him with a movement so sudden that it made my heart jolt.

Fire blazed beneath his palm but the woman moaned instead of whimpered, leaning into him instead of away. And I got the feeling that was a bad, bad idea.

He stood up so abruptly that she was knocked onto her ass and I wasn't remotely prepared as he came striding right for me.

Kaiser Brimtheon was a desolate soul housed within a body built for power. He towered over me and I was consumed by his shadow as he lifted a hand to grip my chin between his forefinger and thumb, jerking my head up to look him in the eye.

"Here or in private?" he asked in his dark, flat tone and I couldn't believe how easily I'd managed to gain that offer from him.

"Private," I answered, adding a husky kind of purr to my voice that spoke of how much I wanted him. Which I did. If wanting him dead counted as wanting him.

He ran the pad of his thumb over my lower lip, his skin so hot it was near molten. His hand dropped to take mine, curling around it possessively and sealing my fate. I let him guide me through the common room towards a spiralling iron stairway that led down through the tower, feeling eyes on me from all around, angry, jealous curses falling from the lips of the women who ached to take my place. But none would claim it after tonight because Kaiser would be left bloody in my wake.

His hand was rough against mine, his touch a sin in itself and I wondered if any woman he desired had ever denied him. But choosing me would be the end of him tonight.

The iron stairway led down several floors and he guided me along it, passing doors where moans and sighs of pleasure carried from beyond. He walked me to the one at the furthest end, away from all the rest and the door opened at his touch, his magical signature allowing him access.

I stepped into the grandest room I had ever entered. An iron railing ringed a firepit at the very centre of it and beyond it, large stained-glass windows rose up at least two floors where Leo, Sagittarius and Aries were depicted in red and amber tones. There was a balcony opposite them where I glimpsed a gothic lounge, but my gaze fell from it to the enormous four poster bed Kaiser was leading me toward.

We were alone now, but his guard likely wasn't down enough for me to strike. I doubted I could defeat him if he brought out his Order again, or if it came to a physical fight. So I had to make sure he was disarmed, caught off guard right before I plunged my dagger into his chest.

"On the bed. Take off your clothes," he commanded, releasing my hand.

"What? No foreplay?" I scolded, unable to bite my tongue. "The great Kaiser Brimtheon doesn't even warm up his women first. Note taken."

He paused, turning back to face me with eyes like two slivers of the night sky. "Most women just say yes sir and get on with it."

"You didn't ask most women to your bed tonight," I said, stepping toward him and hesitantly placing my hand on his chest. His heart thudded hard against my palm, slow and steady, unaffected by me in any way. Mine was the opposite, thundering with the prospect of what was to come, my bloodlust rising and the heat in my skin igniting. "So why did you choose me?"

I glanced up at him through the mask, a shiver of anticipation rolling through me at how close I was to my goal. I had dreamed of this moment so many times and I hoped when my blade ripped into his skin, his eyes were no longer empty, but full of terror for his end. This statue of a man who was so unmoved by the world and all its torturous reality would finally be moved by something. And it would be his death.

"Why?" he mused, something akin to intrigue crossing his features for once. "I fuck to feel something. That's what you'll provide me."

I frowned, sensing a lie in his tone, seeing the truth of him all too starkly in that moment. "No, you don't. You fuck to *try* and feel something."

His brow creased ever-so-slightly and he stepped closer to me. "Enough," he said blandly then caught my waist and pulled me all too near.

The heat of his skin melded with mine and I felt him everywhere despite the fact he had hardly touched me. But his presence was so thick, I could feel the weight of it in my lungs. I couldn't blink as I took in that face, angled down toward mine, close enough to count the dark eyelashes framing those villainous eyes.

An ounce of fear found me as he loomed over me, his hand sliding up my back, deftly starting to unthread the corset. His mouth came down on mine and my shoulders stiffened, his kiss anything but sweet as he forced my lips apart and took a taste of me while I refused to return the favour, leaving my body thrumming with the touch of him. Fuck. My skin was starved of contact and little shivers ran through my flesh in rivers, awakening to this cruel man instead of flinching.

He tugged my lower lip between his teeth, biting almost hard enough to draw blood, and my hand pressed hard to his chest between us while my other closed around the hilt of my dagger.

"I don't normally kiss the women I bring here," he said against my mouth. "But I'm curious about how far you plan on taking this."

"What do you mean? I want it all. All of you," I said, a little breathless from the taste of a killer on my lips, my heart rioting with fear. I felt too hot, my skin itching with the need to feel more, to have someone caress and kiss and want me. But it would never be him I allowed that privilege. I had just gone too long without skin-on-skin contact. It was instinct, nothing else, and it made me hate him all the deeper for eliciting such sensations from me.

My hand tightened on the dagger as I carefully drew it at my side, my pulse wild as I prepared to strike. To rid him from this world at last and secure my revenge.

"I can taste your fear, silka la vin," he said darkly, and a cold river of dread trailed down my spine at the use of those words. The same thing he had called me in Wandershire.

In a flash, I struck, driving my dagger up, but he shifted left so it stuck in his shoulder instead of his heart. He didn't even flinch, his hands snaring me and throwing me onto the bed with force, making a true kind of terror spill through me. He was on top of me in the next second, my dagger now in his grip, held to my own neck and his powerful weight forcing me down.

Rage crashed through me, tearing me apart at how easily he had disarmed me, how surely I had failed my mama. It ripped through the centre of my being and awoke that mysterious, dark power inside me, making it rise and rise like the roaring of the ocean. It blazed with an intensity that ricocheted through the edges of my skin, a power like no other burning out of me and driving into the hellion on top of me. But nothing happened, he wasn't thrown off of me or impacted in some way that I could tell, though his brows drew down like he had felt *something*. But whatever it was, it wasn't enough to save me.

"You think I didn't know it was you from the moment you stepped into the room, bare footed and as lost as a lamb in a slaughterhouse?" he snarled, rage flaring in his eyes.

Suddenly it seemed he *could* feel, and all that lived in him was anger, floods of it twisting his features into the most frightening of expressions. I started punching him, coating my fists in ice, trying to force him off but he pressed the dagger tighter to my throat in warning.

He stared down at me, teeth bared and eyes blazing, then he faltered, a gasp slipping from his lips. His weight left me as he knelt up, my dagger falling from his hand to lay by his knees and he held a hand to his chest, then looked to me in utter confusion.

I lunged for my dagger, grabbing it in my right hand and stabbing it at his chest with savage abandon, but he caught my wrist, crushing it in his grip.

"What did you do to me?" he rasped.

I tried to drive my weapon forward, my fingers tight around the hilt, frost sliding from my palm to rush over the blade and a snarl slipping from my lips. He had to die. I had to finish this.

"What did you do to me?!" he bellowed again and growling started up in the room, his Order gifts spilling into the air and bringing his three blood-red hounds to life.

Fear jarred through me and I could feel Kaiser feeding on it, starting to drain the well of magic in my chest and replenishing his own power reserves. I didn't know what I'd done but the way his aura was snaking into the room and those vicious hounds were drawing closer had me trapped in a vice of terror.

"Out," he said in little more than a whisper, and when I brought up my left hand to strike him, he roared it at me. "Get out!"

He swung me off the bed by my hair, dragging me to the window and hurling it open. I screamed as he launched me out of it, my knees slamming into the roof tiles of the Vault of Embers below the tower and the ice clinging to it sending me slipping away toward a deadly drop.

With a curse, I drove my dagger into a gap between the tiles to stop my fall, willing the ice around me to melt as I tried to get purchase with my feet.

Kaiser stared out from the window, glaring at me for two long seconds, his eyes dark as pitch and filled with all the wild, unbridled fury of a madman. Then he slammed the window shut. Huge icicles broke from the jutting edge of the tower roof far above, sailing toward me at an alarming pace. I raised my right hand, clinging to the dagger with my left and melting them at the last second so icy water splashed over me instead.

I shifted, letting my Order take over, my Leopard body tearing the corset and shorts off of me, but my sheath remained tight around my waist. I snatched the dagger in my jaws then raced away across the rooftops, needing to get back to the Vault of Frost as fast as possible.

The Sky Witch launched herself out of a window ahead of me and screams sounded behind her, her hands coated in blood and her eyes alight with murder.

"He's dead – someone killed him!" a shout came from inside and she glanced at me, grinning wickedly like we shared a secret of death and revelry, before taking off fast across the rooftops, aiming for the Vault of Sky.

My heart thundered as I overtook her, making it to the roof of the Reapers' Quarters then running across it and landing on the tiles of the Vault of Frost. One glance back showed the dark shadow which was the Sky Witch making her way east to the Vault of Sky and I knew she wouldn't speak my name to the Reapers – if she even knew it. Because I would speak hers in kind if she did. But that wouldn't save me from Kaiser's wrath if he decided to offer me up to the prophets of the stars for punishment.

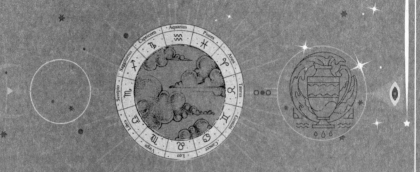

VESPER

CHAPTER TWENTY FOUR

Winter drew in closer with icy fingers wrapping tight around the black walls of Never Keep, making even the most weather-hardened of us shiver as we strode through the echoing corridors and moved between our enemies.

Only the Flamebringers seemed wholly at ease in the Keep at all times, their magic warming their blood from the inside out. Those of them with the most power flaunted their use of the skill by dressing as if for summer with bare arms and shirts left half buttoned, swathes of flesh exposed in a taunting manner while the rest of us suffered the bite of winter.

"Fucking heathens," Dalia muttered as we prowled up the Grand Stair towards the Galaseum, the wide, curving stone steps now as familiar to me as those of the palace at Wrathbane.

"I don't mind it so much," Moraine disagreed, eyeing a group of male Flamebringers who had taken to claiming the front benches of their congregation, clearly the strongest among their ranks just as we were among ours. "All the easier to cut their throats."

One of the males turned to glare at us as he overheard her, baring sharp teeth as a growl rolled up the back of his throat. Wolf. Or maybe a Bear. Both bled out as easily as the other so I didn't much care for the details.

"Threatened?" I asked him sweetly, not pausing in my stride, my gifts shivering across the narrow slip of air which divided us from them. Yes, we climbed the stairs in unison, our feet moving from step to step as one, but a river of emptiness remained in place between our ranks and theirs always. Neither of us wanting the taint of the other to get too close.

Blood lust. *Lust,* lust and…a whole shit load of nothing beyond him.

I tilted my head to gain a look past the snarling ruffian at the man striding half a step ahead of the others, his hair dark but for a sheen of deepest red which clung to the strands, above eyes which held a void of utter nothing in them.

"Keep your attention to yourself, whore," the first Flamebringers sneered, spitting on the step I had been about to place my foot on.

Every person on the stairs slammed to a halt, the heap of blazing trash whirling towards us as the air neophytes tensed with fury.

My gifts snapped from me, snaring the brown-haired, green-eyed asshole in my grasp, seeking out his every want and desire, picking them apart like a stack of straw in my fist. He was predictably bloodthirsty, pathetically hungry, ambitious to the point of jealousy, the rot of which speared out towards the Flamebringers who all gathered around him, particularly the one with the soulless eyes.

That could be fun to toy with, but I was feeling all kinds of petty and preferred the call of humiliating this piece of shit for the amusement of all those around us, so I went for sexual desire and smiled wickedly as I let him fall into the trap of my kind.

"What was it you called me again?" I breathed, my words a low threat as I built his desire to an ache which had him groaning, stumbling closer to me and staring as if utterly enraptured.

"You are the most beautiful creature I've ever laid eyes on," he moaned, trying to move closer but his friends grasped his shoulders to hold him back.

"Stay away from her, North," one of them growled. What a simple name for such a simple creature.

North tried to jerk free of them then fell to his knees, reaching for me and looking as pathetic as a whipped dog.

"Please," he groaned, reaching for me. "Let me touch you, let me sniff you, I need to lick your boots, brush your hair, explore every perfect inch of your flesh. Anything. Everything…"

Dalia sucked in a sharp breath at my side, her body going rigid and eyes widening at some vision the rest of us couldn't see.

"Release him," the unreadable one growled, taking half a step closer to me, but leaving that void in place between his kind and ours.

I let my gaze roll over him, sneering openly while trying to get a sense of what he wanted, to find a way into that blackened soul which peered out from within his hard expression.

Dalia released a breathy sound which was almost akin to a whimper and Moraine took a knife from her sleeve, baring her teeth in warning.

His name was scrawled across the face of a gawdy signet ring on his finger as if he needed the reminder of what it was. Kaiser Brimtheon. So he was one of the many orphans who had taken that name. I hadn't heard of him but then again, I knew little of the names of the Flamebringers – they didn't have high families in the same way our aristocracy did and beyond The Matriarch and a few key players, the rest seemed fairly interchangeable. He wasn't on my list either, luckily for him.

The seconds dragged as I tried to get a hold on him and I blinked as I felt the ragged brush of something against my soul as I did so – he was trying to get a hold on me too.

I smiled darkly as I realised neither of us could penetrate the mind of the other, wondering what measure of beast he might be.

North panted from his position on his knees, and I loosened my hold on him a little while studying the more worthwhile opponent before me, allowing him to reclaim some semblance of himself while my focus honed in on his friend.

"It's been a long time since air met fire on the battlefield," I cooed. "I think I'll enjoy our reunion when we make it there."

"Pyros strikes at your southern border daily," the possible Wolf, North, replied angrily, as if I'd been talking to him, though clearly the adults were speaking and the child had not been invited to join. "Just last week we took out a garrison you'd stationed at Pomair."

My lips twitched with amusement. "I'm sorry – I wasn't referring to the way your army nips at our ass like fleas on the tail of a Dragon. I meant real warfare – such as the battle of Osciron where I believe we flattened some silly little shrine you had built to the power of the flame and killed - what was it, Moraine?"

"Eight-thousand of their finest soldiers," she said coolly. "I recall we surrounded them and used the superior element of air to turn their own flames against them and burn them all ali-"

The Wolf lunged, some howling nonsense about his dead brethren pouring from his lips and my smile widened as his pack of mutts dragged him back again.

The Reapers were close. It didn't matter how much we might have all liked to kill each other – this wasn't the place.

Dalia released a noise which was almost a whimper and I stiffened. Whatever this Kaiser asshole was doing to her needed to stop.

I tugged on my hold North, reminding everyone that I had one of them in my hold too and he groaned as if he was coming in his trousers. "I need to touch you," he begged.

"Touch yourself," I suggested innocently and the Flamebringers who were fighting to stop him from lunging at me all cried out as they fought to stop him from unveiling his clearly rock hard dick in the middle of the corridor instead.

"Fight it, North!" a girl cried in anguish. "Don't let her reduce you to this!"

"How long until your friend breaks under the weight of her own terrors, I wonder?" Kaiser asked, his eyes never leaving mine, the threat there clear.

My jaw ticked.

"I will very much enjoy cutting your throat on the battlefield one day," I promised him.

"We'll see," he replied, not seeming remotely concerned about the target I'd just place upon him, but that would change when he tasted the point of my blade.

I snorted dismissively, looking to North who had managed to shove his hand into his trousers despite the four assholes trying to wrestle him back. I released my hold on his lust and shifted my attention to another desire which was plaguing him, yanking hard and making him piss himself before sweeping away up the stairs with Dalia's arm in my grip to make her move too.

She took in a shuddering breath as whatever had incapacitated her fell away, her eyes wild in a way I'd never seen before as they swept over me and then back to the Fae who had attacked her.

"I will rip his guts out and make him wear them as a necklace when we meet on the field," she snarled and neither of us commented on the way her limbs were trembling from whatever he had just done.

Moraine met my eyes as she subtly took Dalia's other arm and we made our way to our place in the Galaseum. She said nothing but we didn't need words. We'd finally taken note of our enemies and were simply adding their names to the ever-growing list of those who would need to die for our kingdom to claim its rightful victory in the Endless War.

The day passed in a long and arduous fashion, our instructions in the Galaseum focusing on physical illusions today, meaning the magic had to be good enough to make someone actually feel the presence of whatever we had created and not just see it. It had been challenging to say the least, though I felt I had grasped the mechanics of it by the time we were dismissed.

The refectory was no longer a source of contention between the rival elements. Each of us had selected a quarter of the room to claim for our own and the days when some jumped up water idiot or earth asshole tried their luck at sitting in our chosen place were over. Of course we had claimed the quarter of the room closest to the windows where we got the best view and didn't have to be too near to either the latrines beyond the Flamebringers or the line for the food by the

Raincarvers.

"Have you heard the news from Wrathbane?" Cassandra cooed from her place at our table.

Though it was endlessly tempting for me to demand the entire bench for the sole use of myself and my sisters, I had grudgingly been forced to accept that claiming twelve places at mealtimes for the three of us alone might have seemed like a lack of unity within our ranks to the watching enemies. The obvious downside being that I was forced to endure the inane prattling of those who chose to dine with us – all too often the high born heirs to aristocratic titles who were looking to gain the favour of the Sky Witch, even if they did so while muttering about my low birth and weak blood behind my back.

"Perhaps it's been confirmed that her mother really did fuck a wild Wolf thinking it was her father while they were running beneath the moon in shifted form," Dalia pondered, not bothering to lower her voice.

"Excuse me?" Cassandra snarled, her fingers strangling her fork as she glared around at us.

"Everyone says your mother fucked. A. Wolf," Dalia said more loudly this time, drawing focus from around the room. "As in an actual wolf, not a shifter. She just went full bestiality one night and then claimed she'd thought it was your dad after the rest of the pack saw her."

Cassandra's mouth opened and closed multiple times while her face turned a deep red.

"There is no such rumour about my mother," she snarled in a low tone.

Dalia just shrugged and speared a potato onto her fork, shoving the whole thing into her mouth and chewing obnoxiously.

"There isn't!" Cassandra insisted, louder this time while several others sniggered and a few of her friends exchanged looks which said they weren't sure what to believe.

I hid my laughter in a bite of my own food.

"Well," Dalia muttered in a voice just for me and Moraine. "There is now."

"You're evil," Moraine said, clearly delighted.

"I try," Dalia agreed.

Cassandra spent several more minutes trying to argue her mother's innocence before changing tactics and rotating back to her original topic.

"There's going to be a royal wedding," she said loudly, raising her chin. "My family have of course been invited to attend and I'll be taking two days' leave from Never Keep to do so. The Reapers have allowed it for those of...worth." She shot me a smug look as though already knowing that I wouldn't have received any such invitation even if I was the best conscript of our birth year.

But I didn't give a fuck about some poncy invite to a fancy event full of aristocratic assholes like her. No, my throat was thickening on a far bigger question than whether or not I was to be invited to the event of the year.

"Which royal," I hissed, my knife lodged so deeply into a carrot that it clearly held no hope of recovery.

"Oh, I'm so sorry. Were the lower class members of our gathered warriors not granted this news already?" Cassandra preened, trying to claw back some kind of respect from the others at the table.

"V," Moraine said in a low voice.

Dalia's hand grasped my knee beneath the table in warning.

I'd already thrown my knife though.

Cassandra shrieked, hurling herself backwards from her chair as her plate cracked in two, my knife piercing it dead centre and impaling itself in the table, carrot and all.

I was on my feet, kicking cups and plates aside as I strode straight over the dining table, not giving a fuck that every head in the room was turned my way, my fork clasped in my fist like a sword.

I jumped from the table, landing with my boots either side of Cassandra's head and making her release a scream of pure terror as I reached down and grabbed a fistful of her blonde hair, yanking her up just far enough for her to be looking my fork dead in the eye.

"What a pointless way to die," I breathed, holding her there on the cusp of death. "Finding yourself impaled upon a piece of cutlery simply for being an insufferable cunt."

"Prince Dragor," Cassandra gasped, clearly not stupid enough to make me wait any longer. "He will marry the Collingsdale heir a week tomorrow with the rising moon."

Ice slid down my throat, coating my spine and racing for my toes. I blinked. A single moment passing as those words struck me. I was his. He'd made me swear it.

But he had never promised to be mine.

I dropped Cassandra, tossing my fork down on her chest and stalking from the room, ignoring the thousands of eyes which were watching me go, not even caring that the Reapers appeared to be making their own moves towards us.

I'd done nothing other than climb across a table and toss some cutlery around. There were no fucking rules against that.

The silence in the refectory burst like a dam the moment the door swung closed at my back, but I didn't care. I kept going, the pain in my chest this thundering beat which seemed to be racing towards a climax I couldn't control.

I was walking at first but then I was running, my breaths sharp and jagged like they were stabbing my heart with every choked inhale. I didn't see the hallways or walls, stairs or carpets but then my hand was on the door to my room, my fingers fumbling the lock until I was falling through it.

A ragged cry escaped me as a rush of wind erupted in my ears and this prickling, burning sensation tore at my eyes.

I grabbed the closest thing - which turned out to be the rack containing most of my weapons - and hurled it to the ground with a snarl of utter fury.

Something wet splashed against my cheek and I fell still, my fingers pressing to the drop of water just as a second fell, rolling down the back of my hand.

I blinked furiously, my chest rising and falling in deep, broken breaths as the ringing in my ears just got louder and louder.

The door banged open behind me and I whirled around, a dagger flying from my free hand while I scrubbed my face clean with the other.

"Get out," I snarled, my knife hitting the doorframe beside Cayde's too calm face and he arched a brow at me.

"I don't think you mean that."

"You don't know shit about what I do or don't mean," I hissed, stalking for him, my hands colliding with his chest as I tried and failed to shove him from my room.

"I do," he countered, his hands wrapping around my wrists and caging my palms against his chest. "I know that if you'd meant it that dagger would have struck my heart, not the door frame."

"I've told you – you're not worth the headache of hiding a corpse and-"

"I saw you," Cayde interrupted, his grip almost bruising as he leaned down to speak into my ear, his breath caressing my neck.

"Oh, you have functioning eyes? Good for you." I jerked my arms back, meaning to dislodge his grip but he didn't release me. "This dance grows tiresome," I hissed.

"Let me be plainer then," Cayde replied, leaning closer and dropping his voice, his mouth caressing the shell of my ears with his words. "I saw you with your thighs parted as you perched on your desk in your room back at Wrathbane and Prince Dragor made you come for him with his fingers buried in your cunt while accusing you of being wet for me."

I blinked at his words, twisting my neck to meet his steady gaze, the revelation jolting through me and leaving me scrambling for a moment before I dredged up a waspish retort which came a beat too late to be delivered with the scathing dismissal I was aiming for.

"What's the matter, Cayde? Are you jealous?" I taunted.

"That's the funny thing," he said, dragging me closer still so that I couldn't see anything beyond the honeyed gold of his eyes. "Because I think I am."

He released me so fast that my fingers almost didn't fist in his leathers quick enough to stop him from withdrawing. I tightened my grip, my gaze falling to his ruinous, hateful mouth before pushing up onto my toes and capturing his lips with my own.

Cayde stilled, the heat of his mouth against mine a traitorous burn as I crossed the wall I had so faithfully promised to build around myself. But as his hands closed around my waist and he stepped into me, backing me into the room, I couldn't find it in me to care.

The door banged behind him as he kicked it shut, his tongue invading my mouth, his kiss stealing the sting of reality that the news about Dragor's wedding had set searing through me.

I moaned against his lips, tugging him towards the bed while he steered me for it, the two of us always in this battle for domination, control, supremacy.

I fell back onto the bed, never once letting our mouths part, the length of his cock driving against me through both of our leathers as his weight came down over me and I parted my legs to better accommodate him.

His fingers unclasped the buckles securing the shoulders of my battle leathers, tugging them open and revealing more of my flesh as this rampant heat built between us, this need to banish the months of tension which I had so adamantly denied existed with me and him.

I wanted him to claim me, to make me forget any oaths or promises I had been so foolish to agree to and to force my flesh to forget this aching wound which was peeling open inside me.

My hands made it to his belt, fingers caressing his cock where it strained against the material beneath it before I started to loosen his waistband, wanting nothing more than to feel him sinking inside of me, breaking my oath and serving Dragor with a taste of his own betrayal.

But as I tugged his belt loose, Cayde's hand fell over mine and he pulled back, breaking our kiss, looking down at me with unconcealed want as we both panted in the absence of that connection.

"Not like this," he growled, seeming to be convincing himself more than me. "I don't want you because you're hurting over him. I want you when you've fallen for the trap of me and ache for no hands on your flesh barring mine. I want you in my cage, little lamb, begging me to take you because there is no other who could satisfy the ache between your thighs or the desperate needs of your lonely heart. I'll have you all. But not while he can still claim you as his creature. I need you to be mine."

I frowned at him, the words so at odds with the constant rivalry that flared between us and the hatred that invoked, nothing spilling from my lips as he forced himself to withdraw.

I sat up, resisting the urge to tame the tangles his roaming fingers had knotted into my hair or wet the lips which had been bruised by the passion of his kiss. I said nothing at all as he buckled his belt, ran a hand over his face and exhaled heavily, as though doing this came at some great cost to him when it was me who was now suffering a second bite of rejection in a single hour.

He left, the door snapping closed and the heavy fall of his boots retreating down the stairs.

I looked at the girl in the mirror across the room, her leathers peeled open, her features written for poetry, body designed for temptation, and I hated her. She was as empty as the vast expanse of the sea. Just as brutal, just as powerful, just as easy to ignore when your feet were on dry land.

My shoulder blades itched as if that old wound couldn't help but be counted in my failings, in what I lacked.

I didn't cry again. Crying was for those who had something left to hope for, something to yearn for or strive for, even if it seemed beyond reach. I was simply being reminded of precisely what and who I was. A tool for a prince, a fantasy for a passing moment, an echo of a girl and a shell of a Fae.

I stripped out of my leathers and dressed for bed in silence, nothing but the wind and snow rattling my windows to break the monotony of nothing that surrounded me. Not until the door cracked open again while I lay in my bed in the dark and two shadows slipped into the room.

I feigned sleep as Dalia and Moraine climbed into the huge bed with me, my fingers coiling tightly around Dalia's as she took my hand in hers, my head falling to rest against Moraine's shoulder as she wrapped me in her arms.

We said nothing. It required no words anyway. Because we three were the shadows without affection, the weapons forged for war, and no one outside of this room cared for us beyond that use. But we forever had each other. And that was always enough.

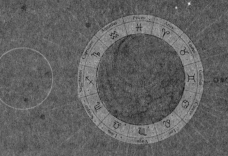

EVEREST

CHAPTER TWENTY FIVE

"D ance with me."

"I have two starfish for feet, Harl," I laughed, a little tipsy on the ale we'd stolen from the tavern.

The whole of Castelorain was out celebrating the summer solstice, praising the stars and the ocean for their bounties. Harlon and I had taken a barrel of ale right off the back of a wagon that had been pulled up in the town square ready for the celebrations, then we'd rolled it all the way up to the woodland on Sunfern Hill. Harlon had shifted into his big brown Monolrian Bear form to push it, and I'd mostly just ridden on his back and enjoyed the view while carrying his clothes. His fur was almost gold when the sun hit it right, and it was as soft as feathers. I could almost forget he wasn't just a big teddy bear until I glimpsed the size of his claws and teeth. It had been a full month since he'd Emerged and part of me was a teeny bit jealous that I didn't have my Order form yet. Still, playing with a giant bear in the ocean and riding him about the place sure was fun.

From the top of the hill, we could see all the way back across the sloping town that dropped away toward the ocean. The sun still glimmered on the water, its rays turning the liquid to molten gold as it made its descent towards the horizon. The townsfolk would be up until dawn – or at least the ones who hadn't drunk themselves into a stupor already. Music carried across the red-tiled rooftops, the band in the square playing drums and organettos to sound out the last day of spring.

The heat of the day was thick in the air and the cicadas came to life with the coming dusk, singing louder as if they wished to celebrate the change of seasons too. Ahead of us was a baking summer, long days that ended with sandy feet, sun-touched shoulders and salty hair.

Our combat training wouldn't cease and it would be far more gruelling in the thick summer heat, but it was still my favourite time of year. Cascada was made for sunshine, but if the warmth ever grew unbearable, the Awakened Fae would gather on the shore and bring a rainstorm down upon the scorched earth, settling the dust and soothing the burn in our skin.

Harlon took my hand, refusing to let me deny him a dance as he tugged me off the ground and swung me around, making me follow his moves. He was no longer a scrawny boy, but the makings of a man. At sixteen, he was bigger than most of the other boys our age and bigger than some even older. The farrier who had taken him in all those years ago might have been an asshole, but he didn't let Harlon skip meals. It was out of the purely selfish desire to produce our generation's greatest warrior, but so long as Harlon was fed, his intentions didn't matter.

Today, Harlon had brought a whole feast wrapped in cloth and laid it out here for us to gorge on, and though I'd questioned him about whether the farrier knew about it, Harlon had waved me off and refused to give me a good answer, demanding I eat lest he hurl himself over The Boundary into the Crux.

Days like this didn't come often, so I'd fallen for his mischievous smiles and let myself indulge for once.

The music pulsed around us and Harlon drew me closer as the sun fell away to the west, painting its goodbye in a display of ambers, yellows and sugary pinks. Harlon's hand came to my cheek, our smiles wide, our feet slowing as a headier tune started up in the distant square. He was still reeling me closer, our bodies touching, breaths heavy and heat crackling against my skin like a livewire.

"Summer calls," he murmured.

"Then winter beckons," I sang.

"Ever the pessimist," he accused, a smirk lifting his lips.

His body was so hot against mine, it rivalled the sun. He was brighter to me than that celestial body too, my guiding light. Always. When things were bad, Harlon made them good. It was his nature.

Smiles came easy to him even when the world was at its darkest. He found a way to enjoy each moment, capturing them like Faeflies in a jar. If only I could hold onto him the same way. But the girls in town were noticing him, and he noticed them back. My friend was becoming something more than I'd realised he could ever be, and sometimes I felt him slipping from my grasp.

I wasn't the only girl he spent time with now and how long could I really expect him to remain this close to me? One day, he would turn away and he wouldn't come back. This summer might mark the last of them that were just ours. And a small part of me wondered if I could find a way to keep him, but it was a selfish, greedy piece of me that had no right to its desires.

I couldn't offer Harlon what he sought in other girls. I already tarred his reputation enough by the sole fact that I was the town outcast and he still spent time with me. What would happen when the girls he courted started whispering in his ear about me? Asking why he lent his affections to someone so odd. Someone who rarely tried to fit in and who scorned the Fae of her own age. I'd turned my back on all of them long ago, just as they had done to me. I didn't have room in my heart for offering affections to Harlon's pursuits, just as they had no room to offer me theirs.

But here, between the olive trees in a hidden grove upon a faraway hill, I wanted what I never allowed myself to want. I dared to hope that Harlon wanted it too, and though logic told me I would risk shattering this beautiful, fragile friendship between us, tonight, it felt worth risking everything for.

"Harl," I whispered, leaning even closer, tip-toeing as I clung to his broad shoulders.

"Ever," he whispered back.

I leaned in, my heart thrashing and skin alive with the frantic heat of my secret wants.

Our mouths almost touched, so close to ruining us that I couldn't draw a single breath.

Then Harlon pulled back, rupturing the moment and pulverising it with his following words, "We drank far too much ale."

He laughed uneasily, releasing me and dropping down to sit on the cloth we'd laid out on the hill. As if the sun knew the moment was over, it stole away the last of the light and left the sky in dusky blues.

I glanced down at my dusty bare feet, now cold despite the oppressive warmth. I was somewhere between humiliated and rejected, knowing I shouldn't be either because Harl and I were not meant to be more than friends. Perhaps he was right. The ale was to blame. And as I moved to sit beside him to watch Faelights ignite the streets of Castelorain, his hand closed around mine, squeezing once. An apology perhaps. Or maybe an omen. That we were not to be.

I blinked out of the bittersweet memory, focusing on the instructions the Reapers were giving at the lowest level of the Galaseum. They were describing how to cast concealment spells which could coax shadows into life to keep you hidden from enemy Fae. There were other spells they spoke of too, some of which could repel Fae from yourself, an object or room.

Such spells, when detected by other Fae, could make them desperately need to use the latrine, or forget what they were doing. Or they could be more vicious, the magic constructed to make any Fae who approached your concealed object be filled with the sudden urge to slit open their own veins or hurl themselves out the nearest window.

I'd had quite enough experience of being thrown out of a window to know I absolutely needed to learn how to cast these spells and how to undo them. But for now, we were focusing on the more simple ability to cloak yourself in shadow. With the memory of mine and Harlon's night on Sunfern Hill still clinging to me, a shadow started to seep through my skin of a much more loathsome memory. The kiss of a killer painting my lips in malevolence. His touches were nothing like Harlon's, his hands possessive, firm, toxic.

I forced him out of my head and made notes on my sheath of parchment, dipping my quill in ink and shooting an envious look at the girl next to me who had a perma-quill. The ink never ran out, and the feather seemed to be that of a peacock, the beautiful green and gold colouring making my dull grey feather look even duller by comparison.

Mine was a reminder of home though, the feather from a common fishing gull in Castelorain. My mama had gifted it to me some years ago along with the ink well which had belonged to my grandmother. It was a simple blue glass structure with the emblem of Typhon, the celestial sea serpent, curling around it.

My gaze slid over to the Flamebringers as I listened to the Reapers, my eyes moving across them, hunting for the one among them who ignited hellfire in my soul, losing my ability to focus again. Kaiser, for reasons best known to himself, had not given me up to the Reapers after our last encounter. A simple Cyclops interrogation could have proved his story true had he wished to see me punished – or perhaps even executed. I had been trying to kill him after all, and a murder had been announced the next morning too after the Sky Witch had left her mark there. I could have taken the fall for that. I very well came close to it if Kaiser had considered handing me over, and now I was left with the tormenting question of why he hadn't.

After much furious deliberation, I'd concluded that he simply saw me as such a little threat that he didn't care to see me executed for what I'd done.

Something had happened between us that night, and I was tormented wondering what exactly it was. Some magic had passed from me to him unbidden and had affected him in a way I couldn't even guess at. Fuck, it had made him angry though. I had thought him terrifying without a soul, but with one dipped in ire, he was an even more ominous target.

Despite my failure in killing him, I wasn't giving up. Success was only achieved through attempt. The number of attempts was unknown, but triers were renowned for getting what they wanted eventually. The key was rebounding quickly and realigning to my goal. I wasn't ready yet, that was clear. I could accept that. But the word to hold onto was *yet*.

By the time the Reapers dismissed us, I hadn't located Kaiser among the Flamebringers and my notes left a lot to be desired.

"Kaské," I cursed. *Shit.*

I couldn't let the distractions in my head mess with my studies. It was important that I mastered everything I was taught so that I could become a warrior great enough to destroy Kaiser Brimtheon and leave her mark on this world too.

If I did that, perhaps my father would see me in a different light, unable to deny the truth of my prowess as a warrior. He would beg for my forgiveness, remorseful that he hadn't seen that potential in me sooner, that he hadn't nurtured it like he had in Ransom. Then he would grovel and pour fat, gold coins in my hands and-

"You have a hole in your sleeve," the girl beside me pointed out, wrinkling her nose at it then gathering her things up and walking away towards the exit.

I pursed my lips at the offending hole. Between instructions in wielding my element and the private combat training I was forcing myself to complete, my clothes were getting worn through and they had already been re-stitched and patched up countless times.

I was running out of thread and the fact was, I needed some new wares. Winter was getting its claws into the Keep now, and my clothes were not up for the challenge of fighting off the icy wind that cut through the hallways here, let alone venturing outside for long periods.

I pulled on my hand-made gloves as I walked, the fleece lining snug against my hands and keeping me warm against the chill.

Wandershire would be at Obsidian Cove today and as the bells rang out for our food break, I pushed out of my seat, gathering up my things and shouldering my pack.

I'd managed to make a few more coins by offering out armour repairs, but most of the Raincarvers avoided me, not wanting to be associated with someone that Ransom Rake had declared a pariah.

Whenever it seemed people were forgetting about the tar to my name, Ransom made a point of showing me up, embarrassing or belittling me in any way he could to keep me from easily finding friends. His hatred of me apparently knew no end, and sometimes I wondered what it was about me that he despised so deeply. Why couldn't he let me be? Why was he so insistent on keeping me banished from the masses? It was a twisted little power play most likely, just a show of his strength and a reminder to him and the Raincarvers of his position in the world. The apple didn't fall far from the tree, I supposed. But I guessed my father had given my apple a hard kick into the ocean when I'd been born.

I took a fast pace across Never Keep, soon passing through the towering Night Gate and heading down the Escalade, the steep stone steps cleared of ice and snow by the Reapers. Otherwise, I was certain more than a few Fae would have tumbled to their deaths here.

The snow was no longer falling, but there was a heavy mist in the air and a promise of more to come, the stillness to the wind telling of a brewing storm.

The weather was a beast out here in the northern waters, nothing like the calm shores of Cascada. The few storms we had were more of a blessing than a curse from Pisces, but here, it was as though her rage lived between the waves and in the churning swirl of the storm clouds, lashing at the island as if it had offended her. As my star sign, I knew the turbulence of a Pisces' emotions. When we hurt, we were in torment, and when we smiled, we felt joy with the entirety of our hearts.

Wandershire stood waiting on the beach, the sprawling, tightly-packed rooftops now coated in a dusting of snow and swirls of smoke rising from the chimney tops. Fellow neophytes came and went, and I shared a glower with a Stonebreaker as I passed her on the stairs into the town, my hand dropping to the concealed hilt of my dagger while hers twitched with the promise of magic. It was always like this, this tension, this hostility. It brewed between the walls of the Keep, stoked by the kindling of our long-worn hatred.

I wound through the narrow streets of Wandershire, hunting for a more reasonably priced clothmaker than the one I had visited before. Or perhaps a store offering second-hand wares that were more in my range of affordability. But everything seemed to shine and gleam, the craftsmen of this place offering out fine goods that were priced accordingly.

I lingered by a window that had a display of stunning gowns, the kind fit for balls and courts, the sort of item I had never had use for in all my life. I eyed the plain pink taffeta of the one on the left, picturing rows of crystals stitched into the underskirt and silver thread sewn in delicate patterns across the bodice. It needed more life, more uniqueness than what the dressmaker had offered it. This dress was made to be worn by someone with as little personality as the gown itself. I could only imagine the Skyforgers wearing clothes such as these, gowns for their royal parties and prissy banquets.

Beyond the window display were clothes of all kinds, the mix of the four elemental styles together in one store, looking wholly at odds with each other. There were thin dresses, skirts, loose-fitting trousers, sandals and swimwear for the Raincarvers, swathes of furs, tunics and leathers for the Stonebreakers and the mix of fine shirts, fitted dresses, tailed coats and more casual cotton jerseys and jackets for the Flamebringers. There was a much wider selection of gowns for the Skyforgers too, but there were battle clothes as well, leather straps, gauntlets and brigandines. Whatever land you were from, I guessed you could find an outfit here.

I clucked my tongue as my gaze fell back on the boring pink dress in the window display, moving to leave but a hand came down on my shoulder at the same moment.

"Something irk you, doll?" Mavus Angelico purred and I turned to him, startled by his sudden appearance. He was dressed in a green fur coat today along with his top hat, his chest bare as it had been before, displaying his many amulets, and his pants were black with gold embroidery.

I shrugged his hand off my shoulder. "No, I was just wondering how many vapid customers have shown interest in this equally vapid gown?"

His eyes slid to the dress then back to me and he barked a laugh. "It does rather pale into the background. Unlike you, doll. What's ya name again?"

"I didn't tell you it before."

"Ah, that's right. I remember now. My cryptic little Raincarver. So what is it then? Janice? Consuela? Or, stars forbid, Jessica."

"What's wrong with the name Jessica?"

"Nothing, in principle. But a lass with that name once had me doing things I should never have been doing."

"Like what?" I frowned.

"Nothing so bad as your expression tells me you're thinking, lass. I wasn't fiddling dolphins or dicking crustaceans."

"I really, *really* wasn't thinking that."

"I did have a wandering eye for a manatee once," he mused, stroking his chin as he thought back on it. "It gets lonely out on them seas sometimes; my mind was addled by the madness of the open ocean. My cock did not go near any sea creatures, though, I assure you of that. But did I pleasure myself to the thoughts of one a time or two? Who can say?"

"I'm…gonna go." I side stepped past him, but his hand shot out to catch my wrist, halting me in my tracks and setting my hackles rising. "Release me."

He smiled that twisted smile of his, letting go and showing me the palm of his hand in innocence. "Forgive my insistence, but I have waited months for you to return to Wandershire and I saw not a hide nor a hair of you, lass, since that very first meeting. I have been waiting for you, and I don't have a fondness for waiting. I take it you are as poor and coinless as the first day of our encounter?"

I clenched my teeth, saying nothing in answer to that.

"I'll take your silence as a yes then, doll. No need to speak the words that shame you so. As I've said before, I know what it is to carry the burden of only buttons in your purse. Now come, I've been working on a speech for ya, lass, and I'd like to give it to ya in the privacy of me own bureau."

"I'm good." I tugged my arm out of his grip. "I'm not going somewhere private with a Stonebreaker."

He cocked his head to one side, looking slightly wounded. "I ain't no Stonebreaker, I told you before. I'm one and all. Neutral in nature and I have a proposal for you that you will not want to pass up, I promise you that."

"Your assurance means nothing to me. I don't know you," I said, stepping back warily.

"You *can* know me, though. How is anyone to know anyone if they don't give 'em the opportunity of kindling a friendship?"

"I'm not looking for friends, I'm looking for affordable wares. If you can point me to a trader who has cheaper cloth, then-"

"These. Are. Sublime," he declared, taking hold of my wrist again and lifting my hand up to admire the glove I wore, made from the material he had given me the last time I was here. "The stitching is a marvel in itself, and stars have mercy, the embroidery – Typhon, is it?"

I nodded, his praise stalling me in my tracks. "I can cast through them too," I admitted, that needy little part of me drinking in the attention. Compliments were a rare resource that I couldn't deny the sweetness of.

"How?" he demanded. "Show me."

I cast frost and the glimlock lacquer I had soaked the gloves in allowed my magic to slip through, leaving the material untouched so ice formed on its exterior.

"Would ya look at that..." he trailed off, turning my hand left and right to admire the craftmanship and pride slipped into my chest, nestling there like a bird in a warm nest. *Kaské*, I needed to get a grip.

"Right, what will it take for you to agree to escort me to my bureau, lass?" he asked, dropping my hand and lifting his chin as he stared down at me. "I have an offer you won't be able to refuse, but I won't be speaking it here for prying ears to hear."

"So cast a silencing shield," I said, folding my arms.

"Clever mouse," he said with a glint in his dark blue eyes. "But maybe I have a thing or two I wish to show you. Things I do not wish to be seen, if you catch my meaning."

"I don't catch your meaning, actually. In fact, it kinda sounds like you're going to take me somewhere and whip your dick out. And I promise you, if you do, I will cut it off and feed it to that amorous manatee you were so taken with."

Mavus raised his eyebrows then boomed a laugh, clapping me on the arm so hard I stumbled a step sideways. "You must think me quite the rogue to expect such a crass move, but I have Fae a-plenty in all ports across The Waning Lands awaiting my return so they can show me the full extent of their affections. I do not need to lure some unsuspecting neophyte into my quarters to get my cock serviced, lass. You think a man like me has trouble with such a thing?" He gestured to himself, and I gave him a dry look that did nothing to stroke his ego.

"Two gold karmas and a star deal that promises I will not 'whip my dick out' - as you so elegantly put it - during our business meeting." He offered me his hand, those two shining coins right there, ready and waiting for me like he'd known it would come to this.

I snatched them before he could rescind his offer, thinking of all the material I could buy with them and lost to the picture of what I planned on making before slapping my hand into his.

He repeated the promise and magic flared between us, binding both him and me to it under penalty of the stars doling out bad luck on either of us for seven years.

His face twisted into something darker, his hand tugging on mine as he guided me down the street, not releasing me until we were stepping through a fine oak door in the front of a stone belltower that rose higher than all the rest of the buildings.

Mavus led me up a narrow stairway to the highest room where arching windows looked out over Wandershire. The space was filled with trinkets, shelves overflowing with golden, bronze and silver objects that glinted with magic and the promise of mystery. His desk was a slab of a thing, covered in a chaotic disarray of maps that charted the waters and land passages between The Waning Lands as well as the most recent known locations for the flying islands of Stormfell, a large bronze compass lying in the centre of it all.

I wondered what it was like out there, traversing the deadly wastelands and the monster-filled oceans that divided the four nations. Mavus had probably seen more of this world than I ever would, and a strange, envious niggle rose in me for that. He was free, and as much as I craved the glory of battle, there was something about his life that made me jealous. He didn't have to answer to the call of kings or fear the clash of crowns. He could wander after the whims of his own desires, follow a fate painted by his own hand. I had never known a life like that was even possible, but here he was, claiming it for all the lands to witness.

"Did you train at Never Keep?" I asked curiously, moving through his bureau to take in the roiling ocean beyond the rooftops of Wandershire.

"No, not me, lass. I learned to fight though, just not how you neophytes do it. There was no discipline, no rules, only havoc."

I turned back to face him, finding him perching on the edge of his desk, gazing at me with a grimness in his eyes that spoke of something that disturbed him in his past.

"You have a way of saying things without really saying anything at all," I accused. "You want me to trust you, I think, but you haven't given me any reason to so far. Gold and gifts won't ever buy that from me."

He regarded me for a moment, nodding slowly as he absorbed my words. "There's a reason I keep moving port to port, shore to shore, never staying in one place too long. You see, I fear if I stop, the demons will catch up to me. Not literal ones, mind, but the demons of my past. I need change. I am here and then I am elsewhere, it suits me greatly. It is so very easy to forget the fire you were forged in when you are busy chasing prettier flames."

"There you go again," I sighed. "Saying something without saying anything at all."

He ran his tongue over his teeth. "Yeah, I have a talent for that. It seems you ain't buying my riddles like most Fae do. I shall add it to the reasons I have a fondness for you."

"By fondness for me, you mean for my value. You said before, you see something in me you want. So what is it?"

"Smart, lass." He nodded to the dagger at my hip. "You forge better than my most experienced blacksmiths. Where did you learn to make blades like that?"

"My mother taught me," I answered.

"Hm, and likely the stars blessed you too. The constellation of Orion is linked to you, I'd bet. Woven into the fibres of your soul, a talent for smithing as our hunter of the sky possesses so well."

"Orion is more closely linked to the earth element," I said, rejecting what he proposed. "My gifts are water made if they are even gifts at all."

"Oh, they're gifts alright. And you're bright but you're not bright enough. You can't see it, can you, lass? It's right there in front of you neophytes, but you deny it, every last one of ya." He gripped the amulets at his throat. "You forge with fire that feeds on air, your metal comes from the belly of the earth, you cool your blade with the water of the ocean. You cannot forge without the four elements. You cannot breathe, you cannot roam, you cannot live without them all."

"That's different," I hissed. "The world is made of the combined elements, but that doesn't mean I wield anything other than water."

"And what difference does magic make? Fire is fire. Earth is earth-"

"Enough," I snarled. "Tell me what you brought me here for." I took a step towards the door, deciding to leave if he kept spewing this blasphemy at me.

He sighed, resting his ringed hands on his legs. "If only you could see... well, I guess I'll cut to the chase then, doll. I want to employ your services. I want four blades a month from you. Swords, daggers, cutlasses, the works. If you can provide me that to the best of your abilities, then I will offer you any wares of your desires. On top of that, now I've seen the gift of your clothes-making, I want ten pairs of those gloves in five colours by the end of the month. Any other gifts you possess in crafting, I want. I will give you cloth and metal and the finest smithing tools in Wandershire. Anything you need, anything you simply want for the pure desire of it, it's yours. Take your pick from the traders, take that vapid pink gown and take the hat from me head if you so wish it – though I am rather attached to ol' Hatticus and I'll need a day or two to say me farewells."

I stood in the wake of his offer with shock leaving me stunned. "Anything?" I whispered the word as if the stars might hear me and snatch away the possibility of it.

"Anything." He grinned like a devil and a prickling feeling in my blood told me that making deals with this man was a bad, bad idea.

But there was no catch that I could see. It would be hard work, and the cost was in potentially taking my attention from my studies, but I could make it happen. I'd stay up later, I'd split my time accordingly so it didn't impact my training.

"I've already written up the contract." He slid it across his desk, the large parchment filled with tiny, curling lettering and a space at the bottom awaiting my signature. "It's binding magically and there's a lot of small print I'm sure you'll want to be reading through, but every one of my traders have signed on with me like this. They know what they're taking on, and if they don't fulfil their end of the bargain then, well, they just have to repay their debt to me one way or another and we call it square."

I moved to the desk, eyeing the contract and glancing up at him. "I'll need time to read over this."

"Take all the time you need, lass." He threw himself down in a leather chair and stacked his hands on his stomach.

I started reading but he piped up again.

"Don't be thinking small here, doll," he said in a low voice, leaning forward in his seat and splaying his hand beside mine on the contract. "When I say anything, I mean that word in all the literal ways I am able to mean it." He lowered his hand to a drawer in the desk, sliding it open and revealing jars of some pink, glittering substance, rows and rows of them placed neatly together inside.

"These are just some of my more...taboo wares."

"You mean illegal." I arched a brow at him, and he smiled innocently.

"Have you ever heard of battle stims, doll?"

My jaw tightened. "They're forbidden. People have died from taking them."

"They've improved a lot these past years, the best alchemists I know have been perfecting the recipe. I reckon one of these days, the Reapers might just make 'em legal."

"Bullshit," I scoffed. "They're dangerous."

"They're wildly effective too," he purred, taking hold of my left hand and turning it over, skimming his thumb across the scarred skin.

I snatched my hand back, but the damage was done. He'd seen it all too well.

"You can't cast with the hand, can ya doll?"

I stiffened, heat rising up the back of my neck as I glared at him.

"Your secret is safe with me." He mimed zipping his lips. "But word on the wind is…the latest batch of stims contain healing properties. Miraculous kinds of healing, lass. The kind not even a Reaper can cast. This here scar might just respond to the right dosage. Course, we'd need to do a little blood-tie if we were gonna delve into that kinda venture together."

"As in the blood ties you're strictly forbidden from doing with neophytes at Never Keep?" I arched a brow.

"Ah yes, absolutely. I wouldn't go breaking my oath to the Reapers. Unless…" He smiled in a way that said he was the particular brand of unhinged that was deadly.

My hand curled into a tight fist and I slammed the drawer of battle stimulants shut, nearly catching his fingers in it and making him curse.

"I'll take that as a no," he laughed, leaning back in his seat and cupping his hands behind his head, the muscles of his chest flexing and his golden curls falling against his shoulders. "Go on then, doll. Read it back to front, then front to back again. I'll be taking a nap in the meantime. Nemean Lion Order, me. That's my curse, I guess. Asleep at random hours of the day, but hell if it ain't my favourite indulgence second to only fucking." He closed his eyes and promptly fell asleep. I narrowed my eyes at him in case he was faking, then carried the contract to a seat by the window, laying it out on the small table there and started to read.

His Order made a whole lot of sense. Nemean Lions were known for their Charisma, a magical sort of charm their kind worked on people to get what they wanted. They were compelling, likeable, manipulative and oh-so-charming that falling for them could seem as simple as taking a breath of fresh air. So I needed to keep my wits about me if I was going to enter into this deal.

It took me over an hour to go through the contract and the quiet streets beyond the windows told me the neophytes were all gone and I was going to be seriously late returning to my next session with the Reapers. But with the offering of all the supplies I could ask for in reach, I couldn't wait to seize this opportunity. It would be weeks before Wandershire would be back at Never Keep.

Some of the contract was written in the kind of complex verbiage that had my head spinning, but there was nothing of real note that stood out. The small print stated that I would have to pay back whatever Mavus bestowed on me before my goods were delivered to him if I failed to produce them in time. I didn't see the harm in that, so I finally moved back to his desk, picking up a pink feathered quill and signing my name at the bottom, printing it there in large letters too. Magic rippled across the contract, golden rivulets shivering through it before falling still and I felt that same magic settling in my veins, binding me to it.

I kicked Mavus in the ankle and he jerked awake, finding the contract hovering in front of his face as I held it there. "Done."

"Everest Arcadia," he purred and I swear my name on his tongue sounded like he was declaring me as his latest acquisition. "Welcome to the fold."

I arrived in my quarters in Never Keep with my pack fit to bursting with cloth, fabric, metals and the supplies to build a proper forge in the fire in my quarters. I'd been gathering items here and there for it but had yet to complete the roughly-made structure, and now I wouldn't have to. I could make one as fine as my mother's forge, and I was so overjoyed with the prospect that I set to work immediately.

I'd missed the last session in the Galaseum, but I'd see if I could get notes from Galomp so I could catch up.

I was a few hours into building my forge by the time my grumbling stomach demanded I pay attention. I checked the pocket watch I'd claimed from Wandershire, feeling like a thief when Mavus had handed it over without taking anything for it. An astrological clock ringed the inside of it along with the hours of the day around the outer edges.

"Hia kaské," I swore. *Holy shit.*

It was almost midnight and I had no idea if the refectory would be open now, but I'd skipped lunch already and didn't want to miss the possibility of dinner. I pushed to my feet, my knees aching from how long I'd been in the same position on the floor in front of the fire grate.

I cursed myself for not having taken some food from Wandershire. There had been pastries the size of my face that I'd casually walked by as if they weren't the most tempting thing in the world. But it had felt all too strange filling up my pack with offering anything in return, and I hadn't wanted to overdo it. It wasn't free, I had to remember. I had a lot of work to do to keep up with the items Mavus wanted me to make for him.

Wandershire wouldn't be back until next month, and I needed to be ready to present Mavus with my crafts or else I'd be handing all of this shit back to him.

I put my boots on and headed for the door, slipping quietly into the passage beyond and stilling as one of those bone-shuddering screams carried from somewhere deep down in the caves beneath the Keep. There was no helping the unfortunate soul it was coming from, so I made my feet track towards the stairs and head up, away from the sounds of those awful screams, an uncomfortable knot tying in my chest.

Between the strange magic that had passed from me to Kaiser, and the way I seemed to make it through magical boundaries that I should never have been able to cross, I was left wondering what kind of power was brewing in me. I didn't think it was a coincidence either that I was the only one who seemed to hear the wails coming from the underbelly of Never Keep. There was a connection between all those things, some intangible magic that I couldn't take hold of no matter how much I tried. I wondered if it was some mysterious gift of my Order, but I'd made no progress in learning the ways of my kind. If I'd been more prepared, I might have thought to visit a book trader in Wandershire, and I made a mental note to do just that as soon as the town returned.

The passages were quiet as I made my way from the Vault of Frost into the heart of the Keep and on towards the refectory. The Keep had a life of its own, its presence forbidding, like it was holding a thousand wicked secrets. In the dead of night, I could almost hear the walls whispering of the bad deeds they had laid witness to over the years.

The arching wooden doors to the refectory were firmly closed, bolted shut with a finality that said there likely wasn't any food waiting beyond them even if I could find a way through. So, with my stomach grumbling irritably at me, I turned back, figuring I would have to wait for breakfast.

Tiredness tugged at me, the sound of the howling wind rattling the high windows my only company as I walked. Or so I thought until a flash of gold down a passage to my left made me halt.

The swish of a cloak told of a nearby Reaper and though my instincts urged me to keep moving, the sound of two voices made me remain there.

"She should be here already," a woman hissed and I recognised Reaper Lily's voice from my elemental instructions.

"Patience," a male voice growled. "She will do as she's told by the Grand Maester. She will not fail."

Silence pressed in on me and my right hand moved, wielding a silencing shield around me before I began foolishly moving towards the sound of those voices. Curiosity killed the cat, they said, so my ass was definitely on the line. But as usual, I was drawn to chaos instead of shying away from it.

The Reapers had stepped through an archway to the left opposite a long line of windows and I drew up close to the arch before shooting a look around it. This passage led to the Vault of Sky so it wasn't one I ever traversed, the guarded gates at the end of it marking the path into enemy territory.

The two Reapers were moving towards those gates and several alcoves between here and there would allow me access to easy hiding places. So I followed, silent and slightly terrified as I crept after the two gold-cloaked figures, wondering what kind of punishment I would face if I was caught eavesdropping on them.

I slipped into an alcove several paces away from them, tucking myself in beside a statue of Gemini, the two winged queens holding swords that were raised towards a window in the curved ceiling above me. A window which flipped open, making me stifle a gasp as a figure came leaping down through it.

A glimmer of pink hair in the depths of a hood made realisation dagger through me and before I knew why I was doing it, I slapped my hand to the Sky Witch's mouth and yanked her back into the alcove before the Reapers could see her.

Her elbow drove into my side, forcing me off of her and she whirled towards me, her blade coming to my throat so fast, I did nothing but hush her frantically, pushing my silencing shield out around her and hoping I gave her enough pause not to kill me. She frowned, hesitating then slowly lowering the blade.

"The Reapers are out there. They're up to something," I hissed, unsure what I expected her to say to that. But she didn't question me, instead moving carefully forward and peering out into the corridor to check for herself. She tucked herself swiftly back out of sight and our arms pressed close together as we squeezed in beside the Gemini statue.

"You've seen them doing something fucked up before," she stated and I couldn't believe of all the Fae in Never Keep that she was the one who clearly believed me on that.

"So have you," I hissed in realisation, certain that could be the only explanation for her trust in my word.

"Perhaps," she said cryptically, but there was no other reason she would hide with me here now.

The Reapers were revered. If she trusted them as implicitly as most of the neophytes did, then she wouldn't hesitate in walking out there. She knew something just like I knew something, and I damn well wanted to know what it was.

"Finally, Grey is here," Reaper Lily exhaled and I edged forward with the Sky Witch, chancing a look out at them and finding the gate opening, revealing another Reaper guiding an air conscript along beside him. There was no sign of the guards who should have been standing to attention at the gate and I frowned, knowing I had never passed by any of the Vaults without seeing them in place before.

The male neophyte seemed to be unconscious and I frowned as I recognised Ogden Breeze, the asshole who had been disparaging the Reapers in the refectory several weeks ago. In the low light, I could just make out his chest moving, assuring me he was alive, but what the fuck were these Reapers doing with him?

"Quickly, now," the male Reaper beside Lily hissed, taking hold of Ogden, casting away the air so he landed on the floor between them.

"Do it fast," Lily encouraged.

"Let's wake him first, let him see the creatures he scorned have come to reap justice from his bones," Grey said keenly, reaching forward to wake him and making my heart judder from what he'd said. This wasn't right. Why was Ogden being pulled out here in the middle of the night in secret? The Reapers' punishments were always public. What point was there to this?

Grey was a thin sort of man, his cheeks hollow and his eyes sunken, but the lifeless look to his face was lost as he forced Ogden to stir awake with a blast of air magic driving against his face. Ogden cried out, blinking up at the three Reapers in confusion as he started to scramble away.

The Sky Witch tensed beside me and I glanced at her, wondering if she was going to step out in aid of her fellow Skyforger, but I found only a stony hardness to her expression as she held her ground.

"For the Void," Reaper Lily said in reverence, kissing two of her fingers and painting some shape in the air. My mind jarred at that word. The Void? As in the weapon mentioned in the Elysium Prophecy? Was she just showing her devotion to it, or had there been more meaning to her words?

"What's happening? Where am I?" Ogden murmured, trying to get up but Grey knocked him down with a blast of air. He took a silver knife from his cloak and pounced on Ogden while the other two cast a combination of vines from earth magic and coils of air to hold him down. Ogden screamed as Grey drove the knife into his chest, once, twice, three times, blood splashing across his gold cloak and splattering the flagstones.

I stared at the brutal murder in shock, unable to understand why this was happening and shuddering as Ogden fell still beneath Grey. The Reaper stood, tipping his head back and murmuring words in such a low voice that I couldn't catch them, then the three of them began hurrying this way, leaving Ogden's bloody body by the gates.

The Sky Witch and I shrank back into the alcove as they passed and despite my silencing shield, I was sure both of us held our breaths until they were gone.

When we were certain they were far enough away, the two of us quietly stepped out into the passage and looked to the lifeless body of Ogden.

"Why?" I whispered, confounded and horrified by what I'd seen.

"The Reapers are hiding things. And Ogden was a non-believer," the Sky Witch answered in a low voice, glancing at me warily as I eyed her with equal concern.

Was she about to strike at me? The tension in her posture said she was on guard, but I didn't reach for my blade, a silent agreement passing between us before we slowly stepped away from each other, her towards the Vault of Sky and me in the other direction.

"Say nothing of this," she warned.

"I have no one to tell," I growled, though I regretted that admission the moment it left my lips.

"All the better then." She turned and strode for the gates, careful to avoid stepping in any of the blood and leaving Ogden to his fate on the floor.

He was long beyond help anyway, and he was no warrior of my land. I had no allegiance to him. But as I turned and rushed back in the direction of my own Vault, something didn't sit right with me about his death. It had been cold blooded, meaningless, and no matter what side of the war you stood on, most Fae hoped for a warrior's death. Ogden had had that stolen from him…but why?

VESPER

CHAPTER TWENTY SIX

The wind blew harshly through the Heliacal Courtyard where we all stood crammed into ranks of four divisions, the Raincarvers to our right, Flamebringers beyond them and Stonebreakers to our left.

I leaned against a carved bull depicting Taurus at the back of the line-up, with Moraine and Dalia stationed like a pair of demons on either side of me. Their eyes were flicking over the assembled Fae while the Reapers who were standing on the platform closest to the warmth of the Keep droned on and on about propriety and the ancient rules of this place.

"Any who cross the lines of bloodshed beneath this roof will answer to the stars and reap the fury of their justice," the Grand Maester boomed, fury lining every word.

I supposed that meant I was damned then as I had now

successfully carried out four assassinations on my prince's command. The list he had given me was thinning so much that I might have to ask him for more names just to keep my evenings active.

An explosion of brown hair shifted in the space to my right and I turned to look at the girl from last night as she caught the wall to stop herself from falling thanks to the shove of the big bastard beyond her.

Her desires stabbed at me as I probed for them. Revenge was pretty prevalent, along with seeing all those who doubted her fall to ruin, a need for glory...

I sighed and looked away. *You and me both, Everest.*

Of course I'd had to look into her after our late night rendezvous in the dark. Sharing secrets wasn't a strong suit of mine – the best secret keepers were the dead after all, but killing in this place didn't come without consequence and sufficient risk. Which the Reapers were clearly keen to remind us of in this frigid stone courtyard regardless of the blustering snow that swirled down on us.

The Flamebringers were melting whatever came close to them, the heat of their masses providing a touch of relief for those of us standing close enough to claim it, though as the snow melted, it was slowly soaking them through. Earth was faring little better and the Raincarvers were letting the rain drench them, looking like they enjoyed the touch of it. I shuddered at the thought while relishing the luxury of an air shield which I had constructed to protect the three of us from the blizzard. The little shelf of snow that was now piling up a foot above our heads made the smug bitch in me preen as many of our comrades shot jealous glances our way. We'd only been taught the magic a few days prior and not many had gotten a grip on it so quickly as my sisters and me.

"Just last night, we discovered a murder mere feet from the

entrance to the Vault of Sky," the Grand Maester went on, fury in every word and my eyes once again trailed to Everest Arcadia from Castelorain. There was little to discover about her apart from the fact that she was sired by one of the most fearsome commanders of Cascada, and there had been far more to find about all his other sons and daughters than her. I'd been in Castelorain once, a year ago. The land we had stolen from the town was quite beautiful and had made for a decent addition to Ironwraith's mass. Did she remember? Well, of course she would remember us stealing half of the town she grew up in, but did she remember me being there? I was notorious enough that my name would have been noted in any reports on the battle so it was likely she knew. But still, she hadn't struck at me there in the dark. Was it from fear? Or was it something else?

Everest found my gaze on her and didn't flinch from returning it. She was striking to look at, not least because she was dressed in a way which screamed 'look at me' with seashells clinging to every seam of her deep blue garments but because her expression screamed 'stay the fuck away' in complete contrast to it.

Dalia turned to see what I was looking at and I let my eyes slip seamlessly to a huge warrior three rows ahead of Everest.

"Do you think it'd be wet to fuck one of them?" she murmured.

"Wet?" I questioned.

"Yeah, like, would they splash you in the throes of passion and just squirt all over the place?"

I snorted a little too loudly, causing a ripple of heads to twist our way. A silencing shield would have been nice but we were forbidden from casting them when in the company of the Reapers.

The Grand Maester threw me a reproachful glower over the heads of my peers and I bowed my head in apology, not looking up again until he went on.

"On this occasion, a witness – their account confirmed via Cyclops interrogation – saw the murder play out and so we can remind you of the consequences of desecrating our sacred Awakening grounds with your feuds and bloodshed."

I resisted the urge to look at Everest again, though I could feel her bronze eyes boring into the side of my face. Instead I watched and waited, wondering if we were about to witness what happened when a Reaper betrayed their own rules.

I almost chastised myself for my own idiotic thoughts as they dragged a Fae out of the ranks of Flamebringers, her cries of protest echoing all over the courtyard.

Even her own kind fell silent as she was dragged up before us and heaved onto the platform with a whip of air magic.

"Kala Emberthorn, you have been found guilty of murdering a fellow neophyte within the walls of Never Keep," the Grand Maester boomed, her shrieks of denial ignored entirely as a rack was lifted onto the stage behind her.

I shifted my weight, my gaze roaming the hooded figures in gold for the three who were truly guilty of the crime, but I gave up on seeking them out as Kala's screams grew in pitch.

"They should burn her," Moraine suggested, amusement colouring her words. "See how much the Flamebringer likes fire when it gets that close."

I smiled darkly, but it felt painted onto my lips, the injustice of this act leaving an ashy taste in my gut even if the Fae being put to death was nothing but a random fireborn bitch.

My expression remained unmoving as the Reapers deftly strapped each of the Flamebringer's limbs to a different portion of the rack and

I watched in silence as the vines leashing her began to pull in opposite directions.

Kala's screams grew more frantic, pleas for help from her fellow conscripts falling on hardened expressions, though I noted a few of the Flamebringers seemed to be struggling to watch this play out. They had clasped hands, one girl with tears silently rolling down her cheeks. But they did nothing to stop it.

The snap of bones dislocating and breaking rent the sky apart and many Fae dropped their eyes to avoid watching the rest of it. I didn't though. I kept my gaze fixed on Kala as her limbs were torn free like the wings of a trapped butterfly. I listened to her pitchy screams until they finally fell silent and I watched as the Reapers hastily gathered up her broken pieces and retreated without another word.

Were they going to fix her back together the way they had The Cobra? Would they be able to use the secrets of their healing magic to bring a Fae back from that? And if they did, would it be for the benefit of whatever foul entity I had witnessed in their chambers before?

Questions, questions, but no answers.

All I knew for certain was that the Reapers were keeping secrets far more destructive than the power of healing, and if they did so under the guidance of the stars themselves, then I was afraid of what that meant for all of us who followed so piously in their paths.

I didn't look to Everest as the crowd began to depart but I sank into her desires once more, shoving aside those bolder needs and finding the slight twinge which indicated she required the use of a latrine.

A sharp yank had a gasp spilling from her lips and I turned to file out of the courtyard casually, catching sight of her wild hair disappearing through the crowd as she shoved her way out in hunt of somewhere to take a piss.

"I'll meet you in the Galaseum," I told Dalia and Moraine, offering them no further explanation and peeling away from the crowd who were all headed towards the Great Stair to join our scheduled lecture on aural illusions.

A few other Fae were hurrying towards the closest latrines and I huffed out an irritated breath, yanking on their needs and making them piss themselves before they could get there. One guy wailed in horror as he shit his pants and if it wasn't for the stench, I would have laughed.

Leaving them to run for their Vaults and get themselves cleaned up, I threw open the door to the latrines and casually moved along them, kicking open each door until I found the last one locked.

The sound of someone taking a piss came from within and I folded my arms as I leaned back against the wall to wait for her.

After another moment, Everest ripped the door open, her right fist coated in ice, the other bearing a stunning dagger, both of which she brandished at me.

"I'm not brawling with you until you wash your hands," I drawled, constructing both a silencing shield around us and placing a barrier of air magic at the door to make certain our conversation remained private.

"You did that," she accused, seeming to realise that the desperate need for a piss had originated with me.

I gave her a flat smile. "Succubus means sex to so many fools that they forget our power is actually desire. Lust is great fun and all, but there's nothing like making some asshole jump off of a bridge because he desperately wishes he could fly."

Everest glared for three seconds before her lips twitched, "Have you truly done that?"

I shrugged.

She smiled in full, though it was a savage kind of thing. "I know someone whose greatest desire is to shove their head right up the ass of their father – do you think you could make him act on it?"

The image almost summoned a smile from me too. "Most Fae don't like where they end up when they start asking me to flex my gifts. I'd consider who you're talking to before begging me to perform circus tricks."

Everest assessed me but it wasn't with the blazing fear so many got when they blinked their way through my allure and realised they were making fools of themselves. No, she wasn't blinded by me or what I was which suggested she had taken the time to look at me for long enough and gotten close often enough to be able to shake off the desire which made idiots of so many.

"So," she said, sheathing her dagger as if it was clear we weren't going to be needing weapons for this interaction and heading to the basin to wash her hands. "That was pretty fucked up out there."

"You have no taste for executions?"

"I've never bathed in the blood of my victims if that's what you're asking. Or danced naked on the corpses of my enemies. Or used the blood of others to dabble in the dark magic of ether."

"You've been asking about me," I accused.

"The rumours are rife – there's a new one every day in the refectory. I heard you even…" she trailed off but I had to hear it now.

"Go on. I haven't heard a fresh one in a while. Maybe you'll surprise me and land on something true."

Everest turned to face me, raising her chin and I wasn't sure if it was meant to show me that she wasn't afraid or remind me that she was over a head taller than I was at my total of five feet. Neither thing mattered much to me.

"They say you kill the Fae you fuck in sacrifice to the magic you claim from the essence of the world and…"

She trailed off as I yawned widely. "Yes, yes and the men I use for such nefarious gain are only too willing to be sacrificed as such because a night between my thighs is well worth dying for."

Again, Everest almost smiled and I blinked as I realised we were exchanging small talk instead of focusing on the point of this interaction.

"Tell me what you know of the Reapers' secrets," I demanded, my voice losing any semblance of friendliness.

"You first." Everest folded her arms and I noted the scar marring her left hand. I'd heard a few whispers about that injury while digging for information on her.

I considered her. She'd already shown her hand when admitting she had no one to discuss this with and I supposed it didn't hurt to offer up my knowledge in exchange for hers. It wasn't as if I planned to act on any of this anyway. I was simply…curious.

I recounted what I had witnessed within the Reapers' quarters and didn't fail to note the flare of interest my mention of their secret passages awakened in her. In turn, Everest told me of screams in the dark and a similar encounter with an unknown entity in the caverns far beneath the Keep.

We were both going to be late to the Galaseum but every word from her lips only awakened a deeper desire for the truth in me.

"This isn't the kind of secret which can be shared with others," I warned her and she scowled at me.

"I'm not a fucking idiot."

"Glad to hear it. So we keep this between us and…" I tilted my head, inspecting her as the obvious answer occurred to me, but the words stalled on my lips. She was a Raincarver. My sworn enemy. One day in the not-so-distant future, we would be standing on opposite sides of a battlefield, hungering for each other's deaths.

"This isn't an alliance," Everest said firmly, as though she were thinking the same thing.

"Obviously," I replied dryly. "You don't trust me and I don't trust you. But we can hold each other to this secret if you aren't afraid of a little blood?"

Everest sucked in a sharp breath, clearly understanding what I was offering and she shifted slightly into a fighting position as I took a hidden knife from my waistband and pricked my finger on the lethal tip.

I offered her the blade next and she hesitantly took it, clearly second guessing this choice as she restrained from cutting into her skin.

"What do you plan on binding me to?" she asked.

"We will swear not to kill one another by any means while we reside here at Never Keep – that includes selling each other out to the Reapers by the way – if one of us breaks it, our blood will fester in our veins and rot will claim our flesh."

"That's so poetic," Everest said lightly, pressing the blade to her finger, but hesitating again without drawing blood. "Make it not to kill *or* harm," she said. "That way you won't have to worry about me locking you up and torturing you."

I scoffed at the suggestion, nodding in agreement as she punctured the work around in my plan, leaving me a little impressed that she had seen it considering she clearly knew nothing about blood magic or the use of Ether in general.

She pricked her finger and I plucked the blade from her grip, our combined blood glistening on the metal.

I yanked the sleeve of my leathers back then smeared the blood onto my finger and used it to paint the jagged S-shaped rune of Eihwaz for trust followed by the large X of Gebo for building a relationship against my skin. Then I called on the dark power of Ether and summoned the bond into place, muttering the words which would seal it.

Everest gritted her teeth as I took her hand in mine and shoved her sleeve back too, repeating the process.

"And may our blood sour and flesh rot should we act against this deal," I finished darkly.

Everest sucked in a sharp breath as the runes painted onto her skin in bright blood blackened then sank into her flesh until they couldn't be seen at all.

She eyed me warily, but I simply hid my knife and strode from the room, letting my magic shatter as I left. I'd find her again when I needed her and in the meantime, it looked like I'd just made a pact with the enemy. May the stars have mercy on my villainous soul.

My invitation came, not as a gold-leafed, handwritten card like the one I stole from Cassandra's chambers to read for myself, but as a scrawled note in the claws of a raven. It was nothing more than a summons to attend the royal event as the property of the prince in question.

I crushed it in my fist as I took my seat in the Galaseum a week later, raising my chin and saying nothing while Moraine and Dalia gossiped like a pair of old fish wives to my left.

"We leave for Wrathborn tonight," I grunted at them, ignoring the curious looks they shot my way. A spit of land was being sent to ferry those with invitations back to the palace for the wedding and I wasn't going to attend without them regardless of whether or not their names had been noted on my instructions to return. They didn't need to know that.

"Were you actually invited or are we just gate crash-" Dalia began but Moraine elbowed her hard enough to make her cough out a breath and double over with a curse which sounded like it contained the word bitch.

I ignored them. Would I have gone regardless of Dragor's instructions on the matter? I frowned out at the Stonebreakers opposite us as I considered it. But no, I wouldn't have. Was I pleased that he had deigned to request my presence at the last minute? No, I couldn't say I was. I both wanted to see him with a feral desperation and despised the idea of ever having to endure his eyes on me again.

Cayde took his seat just before the Reapers arrived, his wings blessedly not present for once, though his thigh butted up against mine obnoxiously.

I ground my teeth, resisting the urge to thump his thigh hard enough to give him a dead leg and force him away from me.

"So is there a dress requirement, or-" Moraine began but I snapped my fingers at her, quieting her instantly.

"You treat your friends like dogs," Cayde commented as if his opinion had been called upon.

"They're not dogs; they're wolves. And they require a firm hand to keep them in line – me included."

"I was under the impression you answered to no one."

"Almost no one," I agreed, thinking of Dragor.

"I was invited to the wedding," he added as the silence dragged. "In case you thought I wasn't aware you would be attending."

I pursed my lips.

No doubt his family name warranted the invite - even if he was technically a Sinfair like me. Oh how I despised the nepotism rife within our kingdom.

"This silent treatment bullshit is growing really old," he drawled when I ignored him.

"If I have anything to say to you then I will do so," I sneered. "But I'm currently here to focus on whatever it is that the Reapers have to say."

As if my words had summoned them, the Reapers stepped out into the lowered area at the centre of the Galaseum.

"The Skyforger neophytes designated to take leave for the haloed moon event are to leave now," the Grand Maester said without looking at the other elementals, the instruction clear even if the timing was a surprise.

I pushed to my feet, pressing my hand to Dalia's shoulder and shoving her back down into her seat when she tried to take the lead.

More Reapers appeared at the exit to escort us out and I had to assume the change to the official plan was so that the other elementals couldn't interfere with the arrangements. Any information which might have been passed to their armies would have now been rendered useless too.

We collected our things – my luggage consisting of my fur cloak and my long sword – then headed back out through the Night Gate where the narrow isle of Rackmere was floating beyond the jutting spike of land.

I stomped through the thick snow, squinting as fat flakes were blasted into my face by the rush of air magic which Rackmere's turbines were kicking out thanks to the Wind Weavers commanding them, to keep the lump of dirt and stone airborne.

The stolen land had once belonged to the Fae of Avanis, its quarter mile of rugged earth coated in swathes of lush plants which I had never seen growing wild in Stormfell. Deep purple blooms fit for a tropical landscape looked even more out of place in this backdrop of snow and ice.

I schooled my features against any reaction as I found General Imona standing there with a skeleton crew of soldiers, awaiting our arrival.

Predictably, her sneer grew as her narrowed eyes fell on me but I gave her nothing of the contempt I felt in reply, simply bowing my head like a good lieutenant, as if her distaste for me had gone entirely unnoticed.

"We will be travelling at speed," she barked as the hundred or so of us selected for the questionable esteem of attending this event filed onto the island over a narrow plank of wood above the three-hundred foot drop to the beach below. "This is not a comfort cruise or sightseeing excursion. Find your places within the hold and stay there until we arrive. We don't need any of you getting underfoot."

My sisters in arms stayed close as we led the pack towards the near unnoticeable building at the centre of the small island, the door carved into a lump of dark rock which was coated almost entirely in the vines holding those purple blooms.

I pulled the door to the hold wide and took the steps beyond, heading down into the rock itself, descending within the island until the floor levelled out and a wide space opened up before us.

Low lighting illuminated the rows of bunks which clung to the walls, bolted down and dressed with thin blankets and thinner pillows. Windows punctured the walls every ten paces, allowing a restricted view of the world beyond them through the rocky underbelly of the island we rode within.

I kept going until we arrived at the prow of Rackmere, tugging my thick cloak off and tossing it onto the top bunk which sat closest to the window with the view out of the front before taking a seat on the lower bed.

Moraine and Dalia claimed the one on the other side of the window, silently sitting too and we waited until Rackmere jolted into motion.

I said nothing as the snow and ice gave way to iron grey waters, The Waning Lands passing by beneath us far faster than they ever did when we rode upon the battle isles such as Ironwraith.

Rackmere and those like it were intended for speed and stealth – transporting important Fae or spying on the enemies. As such, they were vulnerable, far easier to knock from the sky or overwhelm and often targeted, brought down by the other nations.

Travelling upon one of them was always far riskier than boarding a Sky Trader or Battle Island, but there was a thrill to the speed of their travel which I never grew tired of.

But this time, I didn't pay attention to the way my gut lurched at the sudden propulsion of the air turbines or stare at the land speeding by far below us. I simply let my eyes fall out of focus and tried not to think of the piercing blue eyes which would be waiting to inspect me the moment I disembarked, because I had never been able to hide anything from Dragor.

For once I didn't insist upon taking the lead as we disembarked Rackmere, taking my time fastening my cloak and lingering by the window looking out at the view where the spires of Wrathborn Palace pierced the sky.

Dalia and Moraine remained silent and I chose to ignore the burn of Cayde's eyes on me before he disembarked among the swarm of high-born conscripts who were no doubt headed straight to their families to begin primping and preening for the royal event.

I had systematically shredded the note Dragor had sent me demanding my presence, but I had each word memorised.

"I'm required to present myself before the prince," I told the others as I fastened the clasp of my fur cloak, avoiding their penetrating gazes in case there was anything more than curiosity in their eyes. They knew me too damn well.

A pause.

"I left a set of throwing daggers behind when we packed for Never Keep," Moraine said eventually. "And Dalia forgot her soul. We'd better go and grab them while we have the chance."

Dalia sniggered delightedly at the remark and I twitched a grin.

"I never knew you had a soul in the first place, Dalia," I said lightly as we headed for the exit together.

"It's a ragged, twisted thing – easily forgotten when there is so much cunning, talent and wickedness to pack as a priority," Dalia agreed. "That's why I have no space for beauty either – we can't all wield our faces as a weapon so masterfully as you, V."

I glanced at Dalia's square jaw and hard features, wondering if I should tell her that I found far more beauty in her face than my own. Sometimes, my skin felt like a mask painted into place by the masterful hand of my Order form. Yes, there was power in the way

I looked, but I could never take it off, never shift like other Fae and return to a body more my own. I missed the promise of the scar which Dragor had seen wiped from my skin – at least I would have earned that part of my appearance. There would have been a brutal kind of truth to it.

We fell silent as we climbed the rough steps and emerged on the lush land which topped Rackmere. General Imona stood sneering at us as we passed her by, but I simply bowed my head like a respectful lieutenant and kept walking.

Rackmere had docked just outside the city, the floating island now tethered to a set of sheer metal stairs which allowed those riding it to disembark and return to the ground via a flight of over four thousand stairs. The alternative was leaping and using air magic or a Windrider to make the journey far faster. Depending on the level of magic a Fae possessed, some weaker conscripts did opt for the stairs, but that was never going to be me.

I didn't waste time on goodbyes, not needing to address the fact that I had dragged my friends along on this expedition despite knowing there would be nothing for them to do here. They weren't invited to attend the wedding – hell, I didn't even know if *I* was invited to attend it, only that my presence was required at once.

My shoulder blades itched distractingly as I moved to the edge of Rackmere, the wind whipping my hair back from my face and my lungs filling with the crisp air of what I wanted to call home. And yet…this didn't feel like relishing the beauty of my homeland and bathing in the feeling of belonging. For the first time in a long time it felt like a cage just waiting to close around me.

I spread my arms wide, the rush of air magic in my veins enough to banish my sense of unease for a few moments at least and I let myself plummet from the edge in a rush of exhilaration.

Snow had come for Wrathbane, frost glittering on the white towers of the palace and glazing the sprawling city in sparkling white and silver. The sun was high in the bright blue sky, not a cloud to diminish the sprawling view of the mountain ranges and frozen lakes.

I sped across the city, finally one of the many bodies hurtling through the air above the rest after having watched those Awakened Fae with envy for my entire life and dreaming of joining them in the sky.

When I finally gave in to the demand of gravity, the weight of my own flesh seemed to triple with the cloying tension in my soul.

My boots touched down on the pristine cobbles right outside the palace gates where the snow had been cleared and the royal guards stood to attention with spears in hand. There were far more of them posted around the walls than usual, no doubt because of the event due to take place the next day. Terrorists from the opposing nations in the war often liked to target celebrations such as these. I'd struck in the midst of several myself, once tripling the body count at a lavish funeral in Cascada and removing an entire family line from the board of players.

I pushed my windswept hair out of my eyes then fell utterly still as I found myself already face to face with the man who owned me.

Prince Dragor looked even more captivating than usual, dressed in his court finest, a high-collared white jacket embroidered with silver decals clinging to his muscular form.

"Your progress is to be commended, lieutenant," he said in a bored tone. "I was informed that you were among the first to leap from the Pinnacle."

"I was," I agreed, my voice coming out on a ragged breath and giving away a scrap of my roiling feelings as I looked to him. I didn't miss the weight he placed on the words 'among the first.' He was displeased that I hadn't leapt alone and I instantly wished I hadn't brought Dalia and Moraine back here with me.

A loud crash almost made me flinch and I looked to the guards on my left as one of them fell back among the others, apologies falling from his lips for approaching me. I hadn't even noticed that he'd been closing in on me, my focus so firmly fixed on Dragor that the rest of the world had simply fallen away.

"The Sky Witch is off limits," Prince Dragor snarled, clearly the force behind the man's fall. "Imagine there is a wall placed around her which none can scale or the next time your head will make a far more forceful contact with the flagstones."

The guard stammered apologies, dropping to his knees but Dragor had already turned away, a sharp incline of his head beckoning me to follow.

And so I did.

I remained a pace behind, silent as I trailed him into the palace, taking the familiar turns towards his own wing, heading closer to my apartment within it with each step.

My mouth grew dry as I watched the back of his pale-haired head, hunting the side of his profile for some inkling of his mood. Of all the Fae I had ever known, I'd never struggled to get a grasp on any of them the way I did with Dragor. His desires were multifaceted, wants and needs tangled up into cravings for so many things that it was like trying to read a group of people instead of just one. It made him unpredictable, capricious, volatile. I couldn't play him the way I could so many others and that was no doubt why I was so intoxicated by him.

We made it to the door of my apartment and I swallowed thickly as he paused there, his hand reaching out to brush the wood.

I stilled, my pulse hammering, my gaze sliding to the door, the taste of lust coiling on my tongue. Not my own. His.

Did he want to open that door? Had he summoned me back here just to make use of my flesh before discarding me for the woman who had been deigned so much more worthy of a place at his side?

I wasn't a fool. Never had I so much as imagined the ridiculous fantasy of him making a bride of me. No, even in my wildest daydreams about the two of us, the best I had considered was to be an open secret. The kind no one spoke of but everyone knew about. Something of a scandal but nothing worse than countless others in his kind of position took part in regularly.

I was just the fool who had assumed he would remain as he was, without a wife at all. His sister and brothers had all been married off far younger after all, in their early twenties for the most part. Dragor was in his thirty-fourth year and undoubtably the prize of the family bloodline as the one most likely to claim the crown from his father when the time came. But he had never shown an inclination to wed or provide heirs of his own.

Not that he would have shared any such information with me, I reminded myself.

Was I so fucking naïve? Had I really compiled all those moments alone with him, his body too close to my own, his breath against my ear as he whispered dark commands for me, into something they had never been? He had kissed me though. I had tasted the sin on his lips and felt his hand between my thighs, his fingers slick with my arousal as he forced me to come for him so easily.

My skin prickled at the memory of the words he had hurled at me while giving me that orgasm, the accusation, the…jealousy?

I had been wholly offended by the insinuation at the time, determined to prove my loyalty to him upon my return to his company. But as we lingered by my door, the place where he had brought me to ruin for him and spat furious words in my face about Cayde, I couldn't help but remember being pinned beneath Cayde's weight just days ago, his mouth on mine, cock driving against me through the confines of our clothes.

I hated to admit it in the face of that spectacular rejection, but I wouldn't have stopped there. The hurt and betrayal I felt over Dragor's betrothal had lit a fire in me which I had wanted to pour fuel all over and let it burn me alive.

"There is someone who wishes to meet you," Dragor said finally, his hand falling from my door, his lust tempered by another desire, one which was hard to pinpoint but burned through him with a feral need.

I didn't dare pry too deeply with my gifts despite my curiosity. I was never certain of how aware other Fae might be of my power when I started clawing at their desires. Certainly once they were within my grasp, very few fought free of it or even acknowledged what was happening to them until they were released. But I wasn't fool enough to try and toy with my prince that way.

Dragor led me deeper into his wing of the palace, beyond his offices and reception rooms, past all of the places where I had ever been granted access before.

Guards bowed as we went and I noted the way they kept their gazes from us. At first I thought it was some mark of respect to the prince's privacy, but as I caught a spike of lust followed by the desperate desire to not be noticed from a guard who peeked out at me,

I realised they had been commanded to avert their eyes. Did that mean Dragor didn't want them falling prey to my spell?

My curiosity was dampened instantly as we turned into a grand reception room where a lone woman sat in a chair akin to a throne, sipping on a cup of tea with her little finger extended in a white satin glove.

I fell still while Dragor moved to greet her, my insides crawling with suspicion as the deep blue eyes of this pampered and clearly privileged stranger roamed over me.

No introductions were made, but as I took in her extravagantly designed blue dress, the copious jewels clinging to her neck, ears and wrists and the air of utter superiority which rolled from her, I was left with little doubt as to who she must be. But I was at a complete loss as to why I had been gifted a private meeting with her.

The doors were closed firmly behind me, leaving the three of us alone in the room with ceilings so high a small tree could have lived happily beneath them. There was a mural coating all three of the walls within my eyeline and no doubt the one at my back too, depicting the royal family from generations gone by, flying among the clouds and the stars like the fates' chosen few who we were all raised to believe in so firmly. The words of the Elysium Prophecy, known by all to foretell the end of the war had been painted within the clouds themselves.

War of the four, divided and torn asunder.
Flame, sky, rock and sea collide,
While the stars bless the valiant souls of battle.
Seek the Void, for it shall guide the victor to their glorious
path,

A weapon of purity, and the gift of null.
In a web of lies and cruelty, fate will favour the ruthless storm
of destiny,
And a bountiful empire shall be reborn under one all-powerful
rule,
Garnering the fortune and favour of the almighty sky.

"She does steal the breath somewhat," the woman observed, her eyes roaming over me critically, appreciatively, appraisingly.

Dragor smiled slightly, taking the seat on the other side of the small table and pouring himself a cup of tea. I was so surprised to see him doing so without the aid of a servant that it took me another moment to notice that no cup lay waiting for me and that there was no other chair present either. The round table between them was clearly large enough to seat four however, and I got the distinct impression that the additional seating which might usually have lain there had been removed in advance of this meeting.

Uncertain if I should say anything, I opted for silence and assessed this woman just as she was assessing me.

One look and I hated her. Hated every single thing about her. Not because I was the idiotic type of bitch who blamed the other woman for the man's betrayal. No – she wasn't to blame for Dragor choosing her. I hated her because she was everything I wasn't. Everything I could never be and all the reasons why it should have been so obvious that no matter what promises Dragor stole from my lips, it never would have been me sitting up there at his side. I was a creature intended for the shadows, never the limelight. A weapon to be wielded, a threat to be made, a body to make use of. I was no wife of a prince.

But this woman was. From the crown of braided mahogany hair

on her head to the upturned tilt of her too small nose and the slightly pursed look of distaste which appeared to sit permanently on her painted pink lips, she was precisely what I hated about the aristocracy.

This one clearly hadn't ever taken the trouble to train for battle, no doubt having siblings to take up the mantle of conscription while she was pruned like a delicate flower in preparation of fresh buds. There weren't many families wealthy enough to pre-select heirs for the role of marriage and childbirth, but those who could flaunted it. This woman was all soft where it counted for in skills of bloodshed, but hard as a diamond point where it came to the games of the court. I could see it in her murky brown eyes as they roamed over me. People like her saw everyone else as pieces on a chessboard, most of us pawns, some of us knights but none really mattering so much as the king and his queen.

"Turn around," she commanded, raising a single finger and spinning it as if I couldn't understand the plainly spoken words.

"No," I replied just as calmly, my sugar sweet smile causing her to blink as it contrasted with my words.

Dragor's lips twitched in clear amusement and when his fiancé turned to him for backup he only shrugged, obviously disinclined to intervene.

The woman exhaled irritably and I arched a brow, surprised by her boldness. I'd never known a woman to outwardly show her irritation toward the prince aside from me.

"I don't know your name," I said flatly, not that I cared to.

Again, the woman looked to Dragor, again he left her to fend for herself.

"I am Alexandrius Collingsdale. And I will be your queen one day. Were you not taught how to address your bet-"

"The king still lives and is yet to select a successor among his children," I cut her off, not caring to hear her sneering at me. "It is treason to speculate upon his decision or to conspire to influence it."

Alexandrius gave me a crocodile's smile and tittered an utterly false, bullshit court laugh. "Of course I would never do such a thing. If you had listened attentively you would have heard me finish that I am one of four candidates who holds the potential to become the next queen. Or at least I will be by this time tomorrow. So you should address me with the proper-"

"Why am I here?" I asked Dragor, taking a step closer to him then stopping abruptly.

His icy gaze roamed from the tips of my weather-worn boots to the top of my windswept, pink hair before he shrugged.

"Alexandrius requested honesty within our union. She holds no objection to me claiming a…well, we haven't discussed your preferred term. Concubine? Courtesan? Mistress?"

A fist of ice gripped the back of my neck and squeezed so tightly that all words failed me for what may have been the first time in all my life. I swallowed thickly, forcing my face to remain blank just as I had through countless horrors in war, just as I had when the Fae fighting near me had fallen, my own death screaming closer by the moment, just as I had through every sneer and jibe and catcall about my weak blood until no one dared taunt me so brazenly again. But hidden beneath that mask, something was cracking within me as the prince continued to speak, his fiancée assessing me not as competition but as a piece of the estate she was about to inherit.

"Might we share her?" Alexandrius asked and my upper lip pulled back as my hand curled into a fist. I wasn't some fucking toy to be passed between the hands of these people.

"I'm a possessive creature," Prince Dragor replied, as if I weren't there, as if my opinion on it meant nothing. "I detest disloyalty and I have commanded hers without fault. She bows to me and me alone, don't you, Vesper?"

My name on his tongue was a slap to the face, the way he offered it to this stranger so casually when there were few to none who even knew it at all. It was somehow worse than him discussing the possibility of me becoming her plaything as well as his own.

Was this the man I had yearned after for so many years? Was this legend I had placed all of my faith in and bound my soul to unyieldingly, following him into death and combat with unwavering, unerring devotion for so many years that I couldn't even remember a time before his influence on my actions existed?

My silence rang through the room and Dragor chuckled to dispel it, but the look he gave me was pure warning.

"I do not think this arrangement will suit me," I said slowly, my voice dripping finality, my emotions and that cracking, splintering thing inside of me shoved deep, deep down into a vault within my chest where it would never see the light of day.

"Your loyalty is to me, your duty is to serve. Don't allow petty jealousy to make you sound like a fool, Vesper," Dragor sneered. "You have sworn yourself to me, have you not?"

"Yes."

"And you further vowed yourself to me too, didn't you? You swore that a wall would exist surrounding you which none barring I would hold the means to scale."

"Yes," I forced out though the word was quieter this time, the ringing truth of that stupid declaration echoing around me.

"Would you break a vow made to your sovereigns then? Would

you try to escape the binds of your own word?" Dragor sipped on his tea and I looked from him to Alexandrius, perhaps foolishly hoping to see some kind of comradery there, to find a common ground between us where we might at least agree that neither of us wanted my participation in any part of their union. But all I found in her murky eyes was hunger and when I dared to reach out to her with my gifts, the desire I found there was a feral, rabid beast.

Power. Oh how she longed for the throne which now dangled so closely before her. Her desire for Dragor was all-consuming, already at a level which required no boosting from me or my power. It wasn't so much lust for his flesh, though that was present too, but it was a want for all he was and all he represented. She would gladly let him fuck me every day for the rest of his life if he so wished. She'd watch, join in or ignore it entirely depending on what satisfied him, so long as it gained her what she wanted. A crown.

Though as her eyes roamed over mine, I found that lust which so many Fae fell prey to there too. She would push for the option she'd already suggested. She wanted to fuck a Succubus too. A mental image of that life, of myself at their beck and call while they rose to power and I became nothing more than their creature of sin slammed into my mind and I almost screamed at the path I found myself perched on.

"I'm a warrior, not a whore," I growled, forcing myself not to back up out of determination alone. I was still Dragor's sworn soldier, still his possession no matter his uses for me, but this would not be my fate.

"Ugh, my Prince, when you told me you were fucking the Succubus, I have to say I expected a little more from her," Alexandrius complained, wafting a silk-gloved hand in my direction like I was so disappointing.

"Technically, I haven't fucked her yet," Dragor drawled, leaning back in his chair and looking only to this woman who would wear a crown at his side. "I've been prolonging the anticipation. Besides, I want her begging for it."

I bristled, heat scalding my cheeks as I considered how close I had come to doing just that the last time he had had me alone. He'd seemed so big then, this legend given Fae form, this inaccessible, unattainable object of my most foolish desires. And yet now, as I looked at him drinking from that tiny fucking tea cup, tittering with this vapid woman he didn't even know and placing her at his side for nothing more than money and influence, I felt I was seeing him clearly at last. I was just a thing to him. I'd never been special. I was a toy to chew up and discard at will. A soldier to send to face her death time and again. Hooray if she succeeds, boohoo if she fails, shall we have another tiny cup of fucking tea?

"I assume I am not attending the ceremony tomorrow?" I ground out, my fingernails cutting into my palms as I held myself together, forcing my blood to calm.

Whatever else he was, Dragor was my prince and he was right; he did own me. I would serve him in battle and bloodshed until my very last breath and gladly die in the fight for the supremacy of Stormfell, but I would not become a trinket for his entertainment.

"What's your family name?" Alexandrius enquired.

I bit my tongue against the reply that I had none, that I was a Crossborn by both name and birth, and I was actually glad when Dragor spoke for me.

"It's of no significance. She won't be attending," he replied dismissively. I wondered if he didn't want his bride to know that I was nothing but a waifhouse brat with blood born of our enemies.

If it would crush the hunger now brewing in her expression as she watched me retreat, then I'd be certain to make sure she learned of it. "Enjoy the revelry in the city for a few days before your return to Never Keep, Vesper. No doubt your next attendance to court will allow for a longer interaction."

Somehow I forced myself not only to bow but to bite my tongue on any kind of reply to that and hurled myself from the room before letting so much as a scrap of what was burning inside of me escape before them.

The doors to the reception room banged closed at my back and I forced my feet one before the next. I kept going past my apartment, past the east wing of the palace and right on through the gates until the city swallowed me whole. And I hoped that by the time the day was done, it would devour me entirely and save me from this brutal twist of fate.

EVEREST

CHAPTER TWENTY SEVEN

"Where are you?" I murmured to myself, gazing out the window of the Library of Frost where a glimpse of the ragged island and the rough sea lay, thinking of Harlon.

"I am right here."

I whirled around at the male voice. "Fucking hell, Galomp," I exhaled, finding him shimmying his way between two closely-packed bookshelves.

He and I had formed something of an alliance. We didn't spend a whole lot of time together, but he was one of the few Fae in Never Keep who treated me like an equal, and I returned the favour in kind. I'd noticed he was a loner like me, hovering on the outskirts of society. I'd caught sight of him attempting conversation with a few groups of Fae only to see them turn from him, sniggering and whispering, leaving him on his own. His smiles never faltered though, and I wondered if he even noticed the rejection.

"What a nice day," he said with a smile, dropping into the chair opposite me. "I do like your clothes. They are very interesting. I like interesting things."

I glanced down at my newly made pale blue jersey which hugged my skin, the fleece inside it keeping me warm in the Keep at last. It had supple metal plates of ghoststeel stitched onto the shoulders and elbows, the natural white colour of them glimmering in the light. My trousers were snug and black with rainbows and schools of fish stitched into the pockets, plus a perfectly blended fold covered the dagger at my hip.

I was pretty sure no one had ever made such a nice comment about my clothes besides Harlon, and it brought a proud smile to my lips. "Thank you, Galomp. Really. That means a lot."

"Oh! I have a message for you from your brother. He speaks very loudly. I do not like his loud voice." Galomp tugged up his left sleeve and horror carved a hole in my chest as he showed me his inner forearm. "He wrote the message there with his blade so I would not forget. It is a little sore but the blood has stopped now. So that is good."

Two words stood out starkly on his skin, etched there just for me.

Courtyard. Now.

"Tan eskindo pishalé," I snarled, rising from my seat. *That fucking asshole.* "I'll make him pay for this," I swore to Galomp, but when had I ever been able to make Ransom pay for anything? He was twice my size, building muscle every day and his magical ability was turning out to be as great as our father's.

Why had Scorpio blessed *him* with his prowess? Why had Cancer given *him* the sharpness of her claws? He didn't deserve it. He was vile. And I was so done being pushed around by him.

"You are angry," Galomp said, rising too. "Did I do something bad?"

"No, it's Ransom. He shouldn't have hurt you. Did you even try and fight him off?"

He was an Icekian Polar Bear shifter for the stars' sake. He could probably eat Ransom's head if he tried.

Galomp frowned, considering that. "He said he did not have a quill."

"That's not a reason to allow him to hurt you." I stepped closer to him, feeling something for Galomp that I felt for very few Fae. He didn't deserve to be abused like this.

"Oh... yes, you are right, Miss Everest. It was not nice."

"No, it wasn't." I grabbed my pack, tossing the book on concealment spells I'd been reading into it before shouldering it and heading through the high stacks of bookshelves. I was on a murderous warpath. Ransom could not get away with this.

We were up on the highest level of the Library of Frost, a collection of spiralling stairways and ladders offering access to the various floors, balconies and hideaways that rose up through the chamber.

The railings and bookshelves glinted with frost, everything from the furniture to the fixings as white as snow, the lampshades made of clear ice with swirling blue patterns cast within them. Despite the theme, the library wasn't cold and the books were unaffected by the ice. There was an ancient hum of magic in here, cast by Reapers' hands many hundreds of years ago.

I led the way out of the library, moving down the stone passages at a fierce pace while Galomp hurried after me. When I made it to the triangular courtyard in the middle of the Vault, I stepped out from the stone shelter that ringed the expansive yard, my feet slowing to a halt as my gaze fell on my father. He wore his finest dark blue armour and Raincarvers were grouped around him working to catch his attention, but he only had eyes for Ransom opposite him, his hand resting firmly on my half-brother's shoulder.

I hesitated then raised my chin, walking forward to greet him, wondering if he might see how I had gained some muscle, how I was no longer too-thin and perhaps looked more like a warrior than before. Galomp stayed at my back, shadowing my footfalls as I went.

Father's brown eyes didn't slide to me until I was practically on his toes, my pulse erratic as I kept my gaze steadily on him.

"Father," I said, dipping my head in respect.

His hand slid from Ransom's shoulder and I felt my brother looking at me, but I refused to give anyone my attention but the commander. He had to see what I was now. I'd claimed my place here. I'd passed the trials and been deemed worthy of Never Keep. I was more than he'd ever thought I was, and he was about to acknowledge it.

"Ransom tells me you can cast with both hands," Father said, and was I just imagining it, or was there a hint of warmth to his voice?

"Yes," I lied quickly, trying out a smile.

He did not smile back.

"I see. Well I will have you know, I spoke with the Reapers upon my arrival."

Cold. Oh so cold were my bones. He knew. He fucking knew and he was dangling the truth over my head in front of Ransom and so many of the Raincarvers.

"Perhaps we can talk in private?" I asked in desperation, stepping even closer and giving my father an imploring look. *Please don't tell them.*

But it was then that I realised that Ransom was smiling. My eyes slid to him and icy fingers gripped my heart as if he was reaching into my chest and promising to destroy me. Father had already told him.

"Everest Arcadia is a one-handed caster, her left hand is a dud, scarred and useless," Ransom boomed so everyone in the courtyard could hear.

Mutters broke out through the crowd, and I heard Alina gasp dramatically, punctuating the sound of my soul fracturing ever deeper.

"She is a great caster," Galomp spoke behind me and I wished he hadn't because my father's unwelcoming eyes moved onto him.

"And who are you?" Father drawled.

"People call me Galomp," he said merrily, holding a hand past me in offering for my father to shake it. "It is nice to meet Miss Everest's dad. How do you do?"

I groaned internally. He did *not* just ask Commander Rake of the Aquin Legion 'how do you do?'.

Father's eyes moved back to me, a hardness to them that was an impenetrable barrier between us. "Keeping the company of halfwits, are you?"

"He's not a-" I started, bristling at him talking about Galomp that way but he cut over me.

"And lying to your fellow conscripts too. Pitiful behaviour. I hear the Reapers have asked you to sleep in the bowels of the Keep, even they could see that you were not worthy of a room here. Though why they allowed you to stay at all is beyond me."

"I proved myself worthy of my place," I insisted, my cheeks

heating from the stares that were driving into me from all sides.

"Did you now?" Father growled, then he pushed Ransom towards me. "Let's see how your elemental training has served you then. My boy will offer you a fair fight."

Ransom grinned hungrily, stalking closer to me as the crowd backed up to give us room.

"I shall take your pack and look after it well." Galomp pulled it from my shoulders and backed away, giving me a thumbs up, his confidence in me completely unfounded.

Ransom raised his hands, ice coating his palms as I readied to defend myself. Despite all the eyes on me, the ones I felt the most were Father's. This was my chance to prove to him what I could do, but with a beast like Ransom as my opponent, I doubted my chances against him. Still, I'd give it all I had.

Ransom blasted shards of ice at me and I leapt aside, melting any that came close to hitting me and sending a shot of water back at him. He diverted it, taking hold of my own cast and sending it splashing to the floor beside him while he stalked forward to try and get hold of me.

I ran, avoiding the swipe of his large arms and darting behind him, casting water beneath his feet and freezing it in an instant. He slipped once, then melted it, charging for me and reaching for my hair.

I leapt backwards, avoiding his outstretched hands once more, but he cast a whip of water, latching it around my throat and yanking on it hard. It cinched tight and he dragged me toward him by it, using so much force that I crashed to my knees beneath him.

I grabbed hold of his thighs as he choked away my air supply and I sent ice blasting along them, slamming into his balls.

He roared in pain, his fist connecting with my face in the next second and sending me plummeting to the hard stone ground. The tether of water around my throat tightened as he leapt on top of me, grabbing my head and cracking it against the ground, dazing me as I thrashed beneath him. His face was red with rage, my attack clearly having embarrassed him and he was not going to stop until he got his revenge for it. But he didn't have the wrath in him that lived in me.

I sent a surge of water rushing up at my back, using the power of it to flip us over so I was straddling him, throwing a fist of my own right into his nose. A satisfying crack brought a dark smile to my lips, but I was rewarded with two more lashes of water wrapping around my arms and yanking them behind my back. My head was getting fuzzy where I still couldn't draw breath, my vision blurring as Ransom cast more water tethers around my arms and made them lift me above him, my feet leaving the ground and kicking uselessly.

The crowd were chanting out Ransom's name, baying for my blood and Father's cool eyes remained set on me, his lips lifting just a little, like he was revelling in my suffering.

I didn't know why he scorned me so, but it hurt. It fucking hurt and I needed to prove him wrong. I wasn't a runt. I wasn't useless as a warrior. I was meant to be here.

I pushed my will into the water that was coursing around my throat and arms, working to take hold of it. Ransom snarled between his teeth as his own will butted up against mine. Without my focus on pretending to cast with my left hand, my attacks were stronger, more precise and I revelled in the bittersweet truth of that. Maybe I shouldn't have wasted so much time pretending for the sake of my pride.

Ransom might have had physical strength over me, but he didn't have the resilience I possessed. His power over the water cracked and

I shoved mine into its place, taking hold of his magic and releasing myself from his tethers. I sent them flying back at him in great whips as I hit the ground, stumbling but managing to stay upright. Ransom was thrown back from the strikes, nearly falling, but not quite.

He came at me like a charging bull, ice tearing up from the flagstones around me in a ring and trapping me inside it. I rose up on a pillar of water, racing for the gap of sky above, but I didn't have this style of casting perfected and my magic faltered, sending me crashing to my knees as the water collapsed beneath me.

Ransom's cage of ice closed above my head and I threw my fist at it, trying to break through, but all it did was start to grow thicker. The space around me thinned, the walls of ice closing in and starting to crush me in its grip.

I worked to get hold of Ransom's power once more, but he was ready for me this time, pouring more and more of his magic into the cast until I was packed tight into the space, my ribs bruising as the pressure mounted. The ice closed in around my head and panic rose as I realised he wasn't going to stop.

The ice was as clear as glass, but the crowd's faces were distorted by it, making them look like grimacing demons, their heckling becoming a dull echo that resounded through the ice and vibrated against my skin.

I pressed my right hand to the frozen cage, working to melt it, focusing on the strength I needed to do so, but Father stepped closer to the cage, his deep tenor reverberating through the ice as he spoke. "The runt yields."

"I don't!" I screamed. "I don't yield!"

"Then you will be crushed in there," Father said in a low voice just for me.

I felt him adding magic to the cage, the pressure amplifying, crushing me like a rabbit in a giant's fist.

"Stop," I rasped, unable to make more noise than that as my father toyed with my death, letting it be known how easily he could finish me.

"I yield," I gave in, but the pressure only increased. "Please... Father."

The ice turned abruptly to water and I fell to my hands and knees, gasping in a lungful of air, staring up at the man who had sired me, wondering how close he had come to killing me.

Ransom cried out in pain and Father wheeled towards him. The little blue lizard I had followed into the passages beneath the Keep was on Ransom's shoulder, biting into his neck. My half-brother grabbed it in his fist, throwing the creature to the ground and bringing up his foot, ready to stamp on its head.

"No!" I lunged forward, catching the lizard in a whip of water and retracting it fast, my own hand closing around the animal.

"It bit me," Ransom spat, striding towards me. "It dies for that."

I flexed my fingers, thinking fast and casting the best illusion I could create of the lizard and making it appear to leap from my hand and race across the courtyard. It was little more than a blur of blue scales, but it did the job because Ransom took chase with a battle cry and I shoved the real lizard quickly into my pocket.

Father turned his back on me and I sensed that was my cue to get the fuck out of here, turning and walking up to Galomp. He handed me my pack and I shouldered it as we headed inside, my pulse still wild and my defeat weighing heavily down on me while water dripped from my hair.

I didn't know where I was going, too furious to notice the mindless pounding of my feet turning down corridors left and right. "Father added his magic, how is that fair? I could have gotten out. The fight wasn't over. And then – *fuck* – I wasn't even – how could he? I'm his daughter too, but he acts like Ransom is the only Fae he ever sired. I can be more – he doesn't let me be more. He won't even try to see more. I'm more, Galomp. I'm *more*."

Galomp rested a hand on my arm. "I think you are more."

I looked up at him, my heart slowing a little at his warm smile. "Really?"

"Oh boy, I really do. Yes, I do." He gently drew the water magic from my soaked clothes and hair, carrying it away and depositing it into a stone fountain set into the wall.

"Thanks, Galomp," I breathed, unsure why he was so kind to me.

I reached into my pocket, taking out the lizard who chirruped happily, its little tongue whipping out to lick my left hand, reminding me of what everyone now knew about me. I had no doubt that Ransom would make sure the rest of the Fae in this place knew it too and the warmth in my chest fizzled out again.

"I'm so fucked," I whispered, looking at my scarred palm as the lizard went scrambling up my arm to perch on my shoulder. "Once everyone knows this about me, they'll think I'm useless."

"They think you are useless already," Galomp pointed out tactlessly and I pouted.

"Well, *more* useless."

"Yes, more useless. Oh bother, what will we do to make you seem less useless?" he said thoughtfully, really seeming to try and help me. "I cannot think of one thing."

"We?" I questioned, ignoring the last semi-insulting comment and quirking a brow at him.

"You, me and the small crocodile. Oh boy, I once saw a real crocodile, it was very big. I did not go swimming in that lake again. I did not want to be chomped."

I broke a laugh, looking to the lizard on my shoulder who seemed quite happy to stay there. "Crocodile, huh? I think he's more of a tiny dragon than a croc."

"Oh yes, I can see that now. He has wings. Dragons are not around anymore though. My uncle said they are all gone."

"Yeah…" I lifted a hand to scratch the lizard's chin. "What shall we call him?"

"He is blue so we could call him Blue."

"Simple enough," I said, looking to the lizard. "Do you like that name?"

The lizard chirruped, cocking his head as his big eyes stared into mine.

"Blue it is." I smiled.

Galomp patted his head with one finger. "Blue means you, small dragon. I do hope you remember that. Yes, oh boy. I think he likes it."

I slowed as I realised we'd arrived in the stairwell that led down to my quarters. I'd not brought anyone there before, the shame of it a bit too much to admit. Not that I'd had anyone to invite until now. But instead of asking Galomp to come and hang out, I found myself stepping away, withdrawing, my walls sliding up. He probably didn't want to come anyway. And I was better off keeping my guard high in this place.

"See you," I said vaguely, then turned and headed off into the dark, cold stairway that spiralled down into the unwelcoming depths of Never Keep.

"I see you too," Galomp called after me and I headed deeper into the stairway, leaving him behind, but his voice chased me anyway. "Now I do not see you."

Blue watched me work all evening, sitting close to the fire while I started on my newest blade. The forge was ready and I thrived in heating the metal until it was a beautiful sunburnt yellow, then shaping it on my new anvil, hammering it until both sides were even, the end tapering to a sharp point.

Then it was back in the fire before cooling again, repeating this process until the blade was ready for sanding. It was hard work, but it was one of my favourite parts, the rhythmic movement of the sandpaper against the metal smoothing out all the imperfections in the blade. It was so satisfying to be a part of. My magic rose in my skin and my heart beat to a melodic rhythm, my body never as calm as it was when doing this.

I soon had the makings of something beautiful, and I couldn't get Mavus's words out of mind while I worked, of how all the elements were at play here as I crafted the metal. I had always felt at home with fire despite it being the exact opposite of my element, but perhaps there was a balance in that. And now I was Awakened, I could coat my fingers in ice, keeping my skin from burning while being able to work the metal with even more precision.

Blue seemed fascinated by the process, moving closer to watch the movements of my hands before returning to snack on the pile of beans in a spicy sauce I'd brought him from the refectory. I had no damn idea what creatures like him ate, but he seemed pleased with the meal.

I pulled the blade from the fire once more and thrust it into the metal bucket I'd borrowed – okay stolen – from the servant's latrine. But it had just been sitting there with no use in mind and I'd needed it. It was full of winterseed oil, and a hiss sounded as the blazing metal met with it, quenching it and making the blade strong. My use of such oil was a method taught to me by my mama and was not the usual type used in forging. But her blades spoke for themselves in how effective it was.

That was enough for tonight. I had something else I needed to do. Something that I'd been planning for a while now. Since I'd found my way underneath the Keep and had made no progress in accessing that door again in the Poseidon Spa, I had taken to visiting the beaches that were accessible beyond Never Keep.

Apart from the Obsidian Cove, there were narrow, rocky, deadly as shit tracks that led to other beaches, and upon visiting one just west of the Vault of Frost, I'd seen something I wanted to investigate. A cave. Barely visible from the shore, further down the coast like a gaping mouth swallowing the tide. That underground river I'd discovered had to lead to the sea, and the boat there had proved it. So tonight, stupid, reckless and life-threatening as the idea was, I had decided to head to that cove and swim into that unholy motherfucker of a cave to see if it led where I hoped it did. Because if I could get back there, perhaps I could find Harlon and he could assure me he was safe from the terrible things I had seen. Or maybe he knew more about what I'd witnessed. Maybe he'd tell me I didn't need to worry. Maybe it would all just be okay if I could speak to him.

I thought back on the day we'd parted, his burning, hungry mouth against mine, and the words he'd spoken that I'd long ago hoped he would. That kiss had possibly shattered everything we had been in the past, and I was excited and terrified about what that meant. But I couldn't give myself to those hopes until I knew he was safe and well.

"I need to go somewhere," I told Blue, though why I was talking to a lizard, I didn't know. Maybe it was because I hadn't spoken in several hours and his company was the first I'd had down here since I'd arrived. "It's pretty dangerous. I might die actually, so you'd better stay here."

I stripped out of my clothes, changing into the fitted bathing suit I'd made from the waterproof material I'd taken from Wandershire. It had long arms and sleeves, the black suit like a second skin and the fabric soaked in blaze oil to offer me warmth out in the frigid ocean. I'd stitched Typhon curling up the back of it in silver thread along with curling patterns of water across it.

I was well on the way to making other new clothes, but this had taken up most of my time. The fabric I'd gotten from Wandershire was already cut into patterns ready to be sewn for my latest outfits. Maybe tomorrow I'd have time to finish one of the garments.

I pulled on the darkest clothes I owned over it and laced my boots onto my feet, finding Blue crawling out from under the tunic I'd tossed his way, flying up to land on my shoulder.

"You shouldn't come," I warned. "I have to swim tonight, I don't know if you can."

I took him from my shoulder, placing him on the furs on the floor that made up my bed.

"I'll be back later. Or not if, you know, the death thing happens. But I'll leave the door open a crack so you can get out."

I headed off, making my way up the endless stairs and through the Vault of Frost until I reached a window that looked over the barren, snow-covered land that separated this Vault from the Vault of Embers.

I pushed the window open, climbing out and a little blue lizard flew past my head.

"Blue," I cursed, but he flew on, his tail lighting up in a red glow as I raced to catch him. "Put that out, someone could spot us."

The glow stuttered out and I frowned, wondering if he had actually understood or if it was just a coincidence. I took the lead, Blue coming to land on my shoulder and staying firmly there despite my protests, but I guessed he could fly away if he got in any trouble in the water. I picked my way across the jagged black rocks that were laden with snow, careful not to slip and cut myself on them.

It was an arduous journey but I managed to make it to the far cliff where the small animal track wound down towards the black beach below. The wind dragged at me, the sea spray blowing off the waves to pepper my cheeks. Storm clouds were heavy in the air, no sign of the stars or the moon tonight to guide my way. But since my Order had Emerged, my eyesight was keen in the dark, and as I willed my eyes to change fully, they shifted into that of my Leopard Order.

I finally made it down to the beach, kicking my shoes off and peeling my clothes from my body so I was left in my bathing suit. Blue waited on a rock, watching me closely before taking to the air when I started for the dark waves.

I had grown up with warnings of riptides and strong currents drilled into me, but with my water element humming in my veins, I didn't have to fear those now. I could turn the water to my will, or at least, I hoped I could, because the ocean didn't feel all that welcoming as I waded into the freezing sea. When I was deep enough, I dove under, swimming beneath the turbulent waves and surfacing beyond them into calmer waters. Blue flew above, his tail igniting once more.

"There." I pointed at the cave and he flew in that direction, lighting my way forward. His glowing tail wasn't too bright so it was probably better to use it over a Faelight, in case anyone thought to look at this particular patch of sea from their bedroom window.

My arms carved through the water and even though it was as cold as all hell, it felt natural for me to be here – especially after so many elemental practise sessions spent out here.

I was growing used to wielding the turbulent ocean and my element helped me cleave the waves apart now, while pushing me along faster than I would normally be able to move. Soon, we came upon the cave and I gazed up at the giant stalagmites that hung from its roof like serrated teeth, hoping they were well fixed in place.

The cave was so dark that even my keener eyes couldn't pick out much in the gloom that stretched away into the abyss. The sound of my movements through the water echoed off the high black walls and I kept my gaze focused on Blue's gleaming tail, glad of his company in this stars-forsaken place.

His little light was a beacon that led me deeper and deeper into the mouth of the beast, the sound of the waves lost behind us. My ears filled with the steady drip, drip, drip of water falling from the ceiling above into the winding river I was swimming along. Despite the blaze oil in my bathing suit, the cold was getting its claws into me, driving into my very soul and making my limbs feel heavy in the water, but still, I kept moving, thinking of Harlon and nothing else. I needed to use more oil. The quantities hadn't been right, and I made a mental note to rectify it – if I didn't freeze my ass to death in here.

The roof slanted lower and lower above my head until the water dropped away beneath it, leaving not a breath of air above. Blue flew up into a crack in the wall, squeezing his way into it and disappearing out of sight. A bright chirrup echoed out from somewhere beyond the rocky wall. It sounded like he was in open space so, drawing in a deep breath, I swam beneath the waves, casting a Faelight ahead of me to light the way on.

The passage was as black as death and as narrow as a snake's asshole, but I made my way along it easily enough, used to exploring the coral reefs off the shores of Castelorain. Harlon and I had sought out hidden sea caves and hidden air pockets in long-sunken ships, so this was no real challenge for me.

It wasn't too long before my head broke the surface again and I found myself in an expansive cave once more with Blue hovering above me. I extinguished my Faelight, relying on his light again just in case my magic caught someone's attention up ahead.

I swam on and on, winding eternally down the river and just when my hopes were fading of finding that hidden dock, a low, pounding beat of a drum started in the tunnels ahead. I stilled in the water, listening as my heart rate picked up and Blue slowed to a hover, glancing back at me with a questioning chirrup.

"Toward the drums of doom we go," I whispered, swimming on and Blue flew lower beside me.

The drumming grew to a booming crescendo and chants joined the sound as I rounded a corner into a dead end. A high wall rose up far, far above me towards the cave roof and the faint glimmer of firelight called from a gap in the rocks. A doorway to something unknown.

Blue went flying up there, speeding away from me and promptly disappearing into the tunnel. I swore as I was plunged into near-darkness, nothing but that faint firelight way up above visible to me in the pressing gloom.

"Domerna sil oceania," I spoke the Cascalian words Harlon and I often echoed at each other when out in the waves together. *Tame the ocean.*

I coiled water around my legs, driving myself upwards, but the water elementals who had perfected this always used two hands to achieve the complex magic. I made it five feet before the water fell apart beneath me and I went plunging into the icy river with a splash that could definitely have drawn attention.

I kicked hard, resurfacing and finding Blue tearing back towards me from above. He landed on my head, nipping at my hair and I got the sense he was warning me because the sound of footfalls carried from the faraway tunnel.

I dove beneath the water, holding my breath and swimming as fast as possible back the way I'd come. I didn't surface again until I was sure I was out of sight and Blue chirruped, guiding me on as he flew ahead back through the tunnels.

Disappointment settled over me. I hadn't found my way to that underground dock. But I *had* discovered something. A different path to Harlon perhaps. But without me harnessing the ability to guide myself up there with water, how was I ever going to make it that high? It could take me weeks, even months to be adept enough to manage it.

The answer came to me, dangling there in offering, though I would have been a damn fool to choose that fate. So call me a damn fool I guess, because I was going to ask for help from the only other Fae in Never Keep who dared to suspect the Reapers as I did. The Sky Witch.

VESPER

CHAPTER TWENTY EIGHT

The prince and his new bride may have been under the impression that the entire city could think of nothing better to do than celebrate their loveless union, but I knew things about his precious Wrathbane which the prince in his pretty palace could never hope to understand.

It had taken long enough to navigate, first the vibrant and heavily decorated centre of the city, then the affluent merchants' quarters, and even the start of the roughs where those with the least lived crammed together. Once I had made it into the depths of the squalor - which all cities of this size held on their perimeters - I had found the truth of the peoples' hearts.

No one here gave a fuck which prince was marrying which pompous bitch in a castle built of stone that was cleaner than the clothes they wore on their backs. Of course they accepted the two days of revelry happily enough – though the ale in this part of the city was piss water compared to the wine supped at the stuffy wedding.

But I was good with piss water. And I was good with the house of sin I'd been loitering in for the last day and a half too.

I'd stolen a cloak which had fallen from the body of a Skyforger soldier getting his cock and balls sucked by a pair of rather flexible looking Fae and had hidden my face within the shadows of its hood not long after arriving.

So far, I had managed to keep it that way despite my own waning sobriety and the furiously rebellious part of me which kept whispering ideas of debauchery into my ears every time I heard a cry of pleasure or felt a stab of desire from the swarm of bodies surrounding me.

Far from the assumptions of those aristocratic ass wipes at the palace, a house of sin was not solely a place for fucking. Nope. It was a den of euphoria which could be claimed in many forms. So far the piss water ale had taken up most of my time, but I had sat among a cluster of Minotaurs while they smoked pipes filled with fogweed until the fumes made me laugh so much I was sick.

There was potentially some vomit on my boots now but that was the least of my concerns.

I was studying the blood which coated my split knuckles, trying to remember how many assholes I'd knocked out when I'd thrown myself into the fighting pit at the back of the house of sin, but I kept losing count at six because it rhymed with dicks. That shit was funny.

I snorted, drawing the attention of the Minotaur who slumped at the table beside mine, realising I'd returned to the fogweed corner.

"'S'cuse me," I grunted, patting him on the horn and making him moo in annoyance. But fuck him. Fuck his horns and fuck his little cow balls. "Come try your luck if you think you can manble it," I challenged but my voice was a lot sloppier than usual, my normal growl more of a grunt and, to be fair, he was shitfaced, so he didn't seem to have a clue what I was talking about anyway.

I flipped him off and stumbled away, almost tripping over my own feet as I set my gaze on the exit where the fresh air danced a merry tune and whispered my name.

It was cold as a penguin's asshole outside, snow clinging to my boots and threatening to make me slip with each step.

I took hold of the wall in my bloody fingers, letting it pull me along hand over hand until I was in the relative darkness of an alleyway outside the house of sin.

Someone was getting laid inside, the wall vibrating with repetitive thumps which ricocheted through my body as I leaned against it. The moans sounded kinda faked to me so I reached out with my gifts and tugged on the desire I found there.

"Ahh!" a man yelled.

"What is it?" a woman cried in reply.

"Oh please, Venus no, no!" he gasped, the thumping stopping as a small part of my brain realised I was boosting his desire to take a shit instead of his lust.

I scrunched my face up, trying to stop what I was doing but the horrified cries from both Fae within the room told me it was too late to undo it and the woman started screaming about him shitting on her leg.

I thought it best to make my escape and stumbled a little further down the alley, letting my hood fall back at last as I lifted my face to the stars and glared up at them through the narrow crack between buildings.

"What the fuck did I ever do to you?" I hissed. "Wasn't it enough to give me weak blood? Didn't I suffer through the waifhouses? Didn't I prove myself at every fucking challenge? You, Libra, you fucking ballsack, you know this shit doesn't balance out. I've paid my dues. I've fucking paid…"

I looked down at my feet as something wet hit them, relived to find that I was just spilling ale over my boots from my forgotten tankard rather than pissing myself. Ah yes, what a marvellous victory – my bladder was still mine to command.

"So it is possible for you to look like shit," a deep voice drawled and I whirled around, dagger out, world spinning, ground aiming for my face and – I cursed like a cat in a water barrel as my own dagger sliced into my fucking leg and the ground made connection with my cheek.

Strong arms banded around my waist and though I tried to swing my dagger, I found it gone as the world flipped upside down and I was slung over the shoulder of an asshole with leathery wings which immediately slapped me in the face.

I kicked, spat, cursed and maybe even vomited a little, but Cayde ignored me entirely as he hauled me away from the house of sin, his fingers digging in to the backs of my thighs and his wing mostly obscuring my view of the world.

I wasn't sure how long he carried me for – there was definitely a spell of darkness and I was still deciding between there having been a tunnel or whether I'd simply closed my eyes – but eventually he dropped me.

Water closed over my head and I screamed, the last of my oxygen swirling away in a haze of bubbles before he fisted my pink hair and heaved me up to gasp down more.

I blinked freezing water out of my eyes, grasping the edge of the wooden water butt he'd hurled me into and opening and closing my mouth like a fish tossed to shore as the ice which had cracked when he tossed me through it bobbed around my waist.

"I knew you'd need me eventually," Cayde said, inspecting me like I was a piece of dirt on his boot. "I just never suspected you'd lose your shit quite so spectacularly over that pretentious asshole. We probably could have gotten to this point sooner if I'd just realised how deluded you were being and had enlightened you before now. Of course, I didn't expect the great Sky Witch to be quite so...gullible."

"What?" I hissed between chattering teeth, swiping my pink hair out of my eyes and sobering up far faster than I'd have liked.

"Here," Cayde grunted, offering me a brightener, the green pill imbued with magic that could heal away the effects of inebriation in minutes. All members of the army were required to carry them so that we could sober up instantly in the case of a surprise attack. I had a fuzzy recollection of tossing mine to a Dolphin shifter who had been swimming in a tank in the underground chambers of the house of sin around six tankards in to my first evening here.

"Who's attacking?" I asked, glaring at the pill.

"No one. But we've got about ten hours until we need to reboard Rackmere in the morning and despite how much I'd enjoy watching you humiliate yourself in front of all the other neophytes, I don't think it would be the best look for the Skyforgers as a whole, and that doesn't serve my purpose. Besides, I've decided I'm done with you hating me so I'm ready to make you fall for me instead."

I scoffed, ignoring the offered pill and heaving myself out of the water butt with some difficulty.

I pitched myself over the edge headfirst, the dirty cobbles rushing for my face and only Cayde's fist tightening in my belt saved me from another kiss with the ground.

He twisted me around, dumping me on my back where the frozen cobbles and half a snow drift made my wet clothes feel even colder against my skin.

I fought to escape him but he straddled me, his wings blocking out the sight of the sky above, while he gripped my face in his hand and forced my mouth open.

I struggled but my head was spinning and the best I managed was to bite down on his thumb as he forced the pill between my lips. Cayde swore, snatching his hand away then clamping it down over my mouth before I could spit the pill back out.

I glared at him as it dissolved on my tongue, not bothering to fight anymore as the rush of magic spun through my flesh, burning away the toxins I'd ingested and forcing my mind to snap into sharper focus than I was ready for.

It all came rushing in on me without the foggy filter of inebriation to drown its severe edges, every hour spent licking my wounds in that filthy house of sin where Fae fucked and gambled and took pleasure in all forms of depravity. I'd gone there seeking my own escape but all I'd really done was languish in self-pity.

"Do you plan on sitting on top of me for the duration of the evening?" I growled.

"Ah, there she is, the ill-tempered witch the world knows so well." He got to his feet, offering me a hand to haul me up, but I ignored him, gaining my feet and looking around for my lost dagger.

Cayde twisted it through his fingers casually and I used a whip of air to snatch it from his grasp then turned and stalked away from him.

"You plan to board Rackmere soaked to the skin and stinking of vomit and ale?" he questioned lightly.

"No," I snapped, stalking away from him towards the end of the alley, but his footsteps soon hounded my own.

"So you're returning to your apartment in the palace?" he asked.

"No," I grunted because I wasn't going anywhere near that place for as long as I could avoid it.

"I have a room in the city."

I kept walking.

"You're really that stubborn?" Cayde demanded, still following me like a damn shadow.

"I can buy myself a room and clean clothes. I don't need you. Don't need anyone. Never have, never will."

"Need and want don't have to be the same thing."

"Why would I want you?" I asked scathingly, making it to the end of the alley and pausing because I had no idea where the fuck I was. Everything looked the same in this part of the city and everything was constantly changing too. Badly built buildings collapsed and were re-built, streets blocked by travelling merchants for weeks at a time then freed up again without notice. I wasn't here nearly enough to recognise the grubby street I found myself standing in especially since my last visit had been in the summer when there was no snow heaped in corners, changing the landscape once again.

Cayde laughed beneath his breath but I ignored him, aiming my palms at the ground before hurling myself skyward to get my bearings.

The city opened up around me as the frigid air nipped at my wet flesh and I looked out over the sparkling lights which spread away in all directions. My jaw ticked as I realised my wandering had taken me far to the east of the city – the opposite side to Rackmere's dock. I could fly but I'd likely freeze to death before I made it there and my magic had a hollowness to it which reminded me that I'd been using far more of it than I'd been replenishing.

I threw myself through the sky for a few hundred feet, shivers jarring my body as the arctic wind assaulted me before I headed back down to land in a street which was bigger and bit more brightly lit than those surrounding it.

I gazed around in satisfaction as I found myself in a bustling marketplace, the evening crowd mostly looking for food, drinks and entertainment, but I knew I'd be able to get everything else I needed here too.

I pushed my way between the packed bodies, the scent of cooking wafting up around me and the density of the crowd at least helping me feel a little warmer as the wind was blocked.

I found a vendor selling clothes and pointed to a simple black dress, made from thick wool and designed to combat the low temperatures. He started trying to haggle with me but I gave him a hard look and he quickly dropped the bullshit, agreeing to ten karmas. But as I reached for my coin purse, I found only a wooden button filling my pocket.

I stilled, hunting my other pockets and coming up empty. I remembered that button. There had been a woman with snakes for hair, she'd been telling me it was lucky and I'd been grinning because her snakes looked like they were dancing and I was off my fucking head. Had I bought the button? Or had she robbed me while I was blind drunk and distracted?

I cursed, tossing the button to the dirt and leaning over the wooden counter to snarl at the vendor in demand.

"Do you recognise me?" I asked him.

His shrewd gaze assessed me but he shook his head.

"I'm the Sky Witch," I said, irritated at his lack of realisation, waiting for the penny to drop but he simply snorted.

"The Sky Witch is said to be the most beautiful woman in all of Wrathbane, Stormfell and beyond – one look at her can ensnare the hearts of a thousand men. One taste of her cherry lips can cause those hearts to stop beating from the poison in her veins and yet any who took such a taste would die with a smile on their lips. I assume *you're* that girl from Madam Hulie's who she is touting about the place for fifty karmas a ride. I'll admit you have a somewhat symmetrical face but she should have paid more for that pink mop of a wig. Go try your con on someone less gullible."

He tried to shoo me away and I slammed my fist down on the counter furiously, reaching for his desires with my gifts and finding nothing but greed for money which I couldn't provide.

"I need that dress," I snarled but three more assholes appeared from the depths of the shop and the garment in question was whipped away as if it had never existed at all.

"No money, no gown. Don't make me call the royal guard."

I was tempted to let him call them, to have the guard confirm my identity and force him to comply, but if that happened then the story of me being found in this part of the city, soaked to the bone and reeking of shame would spread. I refused to let Dragor find out about this. And gutting the stall owner and his family wasn't exactly inconspicuous either.

"Here." Cayde knocked me aside, tossing ten fat, gold karmas to the merchant without so much as explaining how he'd found me again.

I bit my tongue on the protest I wanted to make as the dress was wrapped and handed to him because I needed to get out of these freezing clothes and accepting his help was beginning to look like my only simple way of doing so.

The merchant was all smiles again as he waved us away and I only cursed once as Cayde took my hand and began dragging me through the crush of bodies.

"You're coming to my room," he told me and I was shivering too hard to even care anymore.

"How did you find me?" I asked, my fingers tingling from the heat of his hand wrapped around them, that small point of warmth like a lifeline to my frozen bones.

"I know how to move in the shadows and how to get the answers I need. You might have been trying to hide yourself away but a face like yours draws attention even from under a hood. And Fae such as the ones living here have loose tongues in the face of gold."

"I meant *why*," I replied because none of that was news to me – I'd utilised the same tactic plenty of times when looking for a target both in this land and the others. Money spoke and betrayal paid well.

"Dalia and Moraine were looking first. I simply decided to join the hunt – the wedding was a dull affair anyway," Cayde said, tugging me down the widening street and leading the way to an inn which stood on the corner, the large, grey building rising over four floors, its windows looking down on us.

"I'd have preferred them to find me."

"No shit."

He still hadn't answered my questions but my teeth were now chattering so badly that I couldn't summon the energy required to ask again.

We headed inside, passing a portly man whose narrowed eyes watched us from the door all the way to the stairs without comment.

The entrance hall was dimly lit with one lantern flickering morosely by the foot of the deep brown stairs which ascended into further darkness. A threadbare carpet in a pattern of red and blue covered the foyer and climbed the stairs too. The deep blue walls were coated in ugly oil paintings which seemed to be in a competition for the dullest subject matter; one of a tree stump, the next of an empty bowl, though I had to think the one of a lone napkin took the title.

Cayde said nothing, tugging me up the stairs behind him, my numb toes stubbing against more than one of the wooden steps as we climbed all the way to the fourth floor then headed to the room right at the end of the corridor.

He released me as we stepped inside, the door snapping shut behind us, the room only lit by the dying embers of the fire. A single bed took up almost all of the space though a patch of floor remained clear in front of the hearth, and an uncomfortable stool perched next to a wonky table beneath the window.

"Well, this is about as interesting as your personality," I drawled as I began to fight the straps of my leathers undone, the water and my frozen fingers making it harder than usual.

"And you're about as grateful as I expected you to be," Cayde replied in turn, throwing several logs on the fire and coaxing it back to life.

"I didn't ask you to come rescue me. I wasn't a damsel in distress. I was just a bitch on a path to destruction – which I would have thought suited you fine."

My jacket finally opened and I yanked it off, tossing it by my feet and beginning the battle with my belt next.

Cayde finished with the fire and kicked his boots off, dropping onto the bed and making himself comfortable with his fingers laced behind his head as he watched me struggling against my clothes.

"There's only one bed," I grunted.

"You didn't expect me to shell out for a second room, did you? Don't worry – you're small enough to fit there on the floor." He jerked his chin towards the wooden boards in front of the fire and I bit my tongue on a retort to that. I planned on kicking him out of the bed if there was only one but that could wait until I wasn't dripping all over the damn floor.

"You didn't have to dump me in that water barrel," I grumbled, shoving my pants down and forcing my boots off with them. I was left in my wet undergarments which were likely transparent anyway thanks to the water so I pulled them off too.

"I disagree," Cayde's eyes moved down my naked body slowly. "There's a washroom if you want privacy," he added, jerking his chin towards a door I hadn't noticed in the shadows beside the fire.

"Your timing with that information was spectacular," I deadpanned, turning my ass to him and stalking into the tiny room.

There was a bedpan on a stool which looked more precarious than the one by the window in the main room and a bowl of cold water next to a bar of waxy soap with about three square inches to turn around in.

I exhaled irritably then set to work scrubbing myself clean in the cold water, using the soap to remove the vomit from my hair and the blood from beneath my fingernails before dumping the cold water over my head to rinse it all off. A puddle formed on the floor, rolling towards the rear wall and I considered the lack of drain for a moment before grabbing the scratchy rag which appeared to be meant as a towel and quickly drying myself off.

The dress remained in the bedroom with Cayde so I was forced to return to him still as naked as the dawn.

My leathers and undergarments were gone along with the man in question, but my new dress was waiting on the bed.

I pulled it over my head, the material instantly proving itself too long for me while the neckline hung wide and low too. I caught a glimpse of myself in the windowpane, the reflection making me snort a laugh. If only Dragor could see me now, he'd truly know what he was missing.

I dropped down in front of the fire and tugged my knees up to my chest, letting the heat of the flames roll over me.

There were only so many ways I could internally berate myself for getting into this mess but I couldn't help but go over and over them, wondering how I might free myself from the promises I'd made.

The door sounded behind me and Cayde came to sit on the dusty floor beside me, a tray in his hands with two steaming bowls of vegetable soup and a pair of bread rolls. He placed them down between us and took a small jar of ointment from the tray.

"Let me see your leg," he said.

"It's fine." I made to grab my soup, but he took hold of my ankle and yanked so suddenly that I was knocked onto my back by the motion.

Cayde shoved the overlong material of my dress up to find the wound on my thigh from where I'd cut myself with my own damn dagger and I kicked him squarely in the jaw.

"Back off," I snapped, claiming a spoon as I made it upright again and pointed it at him in a threat.

"Seriously?" he asked, dark hair falling into his eyes as he massaged his jaw where I'd kicked him. "A spoon?"

"I could kill you with it in sixteen different ways without pausing for breath and you know it."

"Or you could just eat your fucking soup and act a little less deranged for once. Honestly, you've got more walls up then a Minotaur has in their labyrinth – it's exhausting."

"What do you want from me?" I asked, ignoring his assessment of my prickly nature because a pampered asshole like him could never even begin to understand what it was like to come up through the waifhouses, fighting every day to prove yourself while knowing deep down that nothing would ever be enough. I didn't fit in and I never would.

"Eat, let me tend to your leg, and I'll tell you."

"I'll tend to my own damn leg."

"Well I'm not spoon-feeding you."

By the stars, I hated him.

I glowered at him while hiking my dress up to reveal the slowly bleeding wound I'd managed to give myself on my upper thigh. It wasn't all that deep but my daggers were sharp as sin and the skin had taken a slice even through the protection of my leathers. I smeared the ointment over the wound, ignoring the sting of it as the yellowish substance clung to the injury, blood and all, stopping the persistent bleeding.

"Happy?" I asked, tossing the ointment aside.

"Not really, but at least you've stopped staining the upholstery."

I snorted a laugh then blinked at myself, cutting the sound of amusement short and looking into the fire resolutely.

Cayde picked up my bowl of soup and shoved it at me in clear demand.

"You're like some clucking old nurse maid," I chastised, taking the soup and starting on it. It was flavoursome and hearty, nothing like the finery they enjoyed in the palace, but I preferred simple, nutritional fare like this anyway.

"I know you hate me because of our rivalry," Cayde began,

earning a grunt of agreement from me. "And honestly, I hate you too, though not for all the reasons you cling to. I couldn't give a fuck if your birth was the product of a rooster from Pyros sticking its cock into a rat from Avanis and you hatched from an egg as a result wearing a crown of ice. You put too much weight on that shit. You think it's all everyone sees when they look at you."

"Bullshit," I replied. "I've worked damn hard to make certain that the last thing people see when they look at me is my weak blood."

"You want them to see the cruelty, the carnage, the bloodshed, the face – and yeah, sweetheart, I've noticed the face and the body and every fucking inch of you so don't go glaring at me like you weren't perfectly aware of it. You wear what you are like a shield and you trap the hearts of Fae in your grasp like they're toys to place in a glass jar and shake whenever the mood strikes you."

"I have no interest in capturing hearts," I sneered.

Cayde placed his own bowl of soup aside and leaned in closer to me, his eyes full of dark secrets which I was growing all too curious to unravel. "Liar, liar," he breathed.

"Are you claiming I've stolen yours?" I asked, not flinching from this game, turning my head so that the distance between us fell away and the depths of his honey brown eyes were all I could see.

"You don't even know how perfect you are," he replied, the words striking against that bruised and shattered lump in my chest which Prince Dragor had so swiftly crushed. "But the more I watch you, the more I see it. You are precisely what I've been looking for, Vesper."

My name on his lips coiled around me, tying me in knots and making my pulse race for all the wrong reasons.

He was looking at me like he was looking at *me*. And I wasn't certain if I had ever been seen so plainly in all of my life.

"Get to the point, Cayde," I said, though my words held less bite than they should have.

"The point..." he breathed a laugh, reaching out to brush a lock of my pale pink hair back over my shoulder. "The *point* is that I have come to realise your weakness, Vesper..."

That name. That fucking name which I had as close to discarded as possible. The one they had given me in the waifhouse for no reason beyond it being the next name on the list the Reapers had given the homes for the stray children who were born to the wrong nation and torn from their mothers' arms so that they could be raised among their own kind. Its meaning had always seemed like an odd twist of fate to me – the evening star or evening prayer, Venus at sunset – the name of the planet most associated with love offered out to me like a joke because if there was one thing I had never been, it was loved.

"I have no weaknesses," I countered because this was war even if it was of the kind I hadn't fought before. He was hunting for my blind spot, searching to take me down, and I couldn't allow him to discover it.

Cayde smiled, moving so close that I could taste him on the air, that there was nothing at all beyond him and me and I was the fucking fool flying too close to the sun.

"He doesn't deserve your pain, Vesper. He certainly doesn't deserve your loyalty," those rough words were spoken so close that they brushed across my lips, the offer there for me to take, the wall Dragor had forced me to construct crumbling with every moment when I refused to back away.

"I would never betray my kingdom," I growled, though it was more of a purr.

I didn't dare reach out to taste his desire, didn't know what I would do if I found it wasn't what I thought it was. Or worse, if it was exactly as I suspected.

"I'm not asking you to betray your loyalty to Stormfell," Cayde said, his hand cupping my cheek, fingers whispering into my hair. "I'm just asking if you're his property? I want to know if I'm crossing a line you don't want crossed – or if it's one Prince Dragor scrawled around you regardless of your own desires. Because I'm willing to defy that command if the award is your heart, Vesper. I think that would be a prize well worth claiming for my own."

My breath stalled in my lungs, my hurt, my devotion, everything I'd done to prove myself worthy all coming to this. Dragor wanted me just as I had secretly wished he would for far longer than I would have liked to admit. But he only wanted to own me like every other powerful bastard I had ever known. Why had I thought him better than that? Why had I held him to some standard above that of the rest of the aristocrats I despised so much? He wasn't better than them in that regard. He was just as ruthlessly cold and power-hungry as all the rest.

But as I looked into Cayde's tempestuous gaze, I found a hunger there which was for something far greater than the petty power of men. He wanted me, just as I was, broken edges and shattered pieces included. I didn't know why and truthfully, I didn't care either. Because I needed to be wanted more than I cared to admit to myself and if the cost of that want was treason, then perhaps the taste of him would be my death sentence. But I was okay with that.

I leaned forward and took Cayde's mouth captive with my own, the molten heat of him invigorating against my still chilled flesh.

Any control he'd been clinging to slipped at the press of my lips to his and he groaned hungrily, his hands shifting to my waist as he dragged me onto his lap.

"Say it," he growled against my lips. "Tell me it's me, Vesper. Spill your pretty heart and tell me that I'm the one you want bringing you to ruin. I want to hear you say it, I want you to remember the words whenever you think of this and know that your destruction was entirely what you desired."

My pulse thundered at the thought of doing as he was commanding, of crossing this line wholly and completely and breaking my word to my prince. But if there was one thing I knew about warfare, it was that no rules applied to the victorious. If I didn't want to allow Dragor to claim victory over me then I needed to launch my own battle. I needed to claim my own conquest and I didn't care if there was a cost to doing so because he'd struck at me first and I was nothing if not a creature built for war.

"Make me a traitor, Cayde," I demanded, my fingers clasping the nape of his neck, tangling in the strands of dark hair there, nails raking against his skin. "You're the damnation I choose for myself and if the stars will see me ruined for it then make sure it's fucking worth it."

Cayde smiled against my mouth, lunging forward and sinking his tongue between my lips as my back collided with the wooden floor. He knotted his fingers through mine, pinning my hand to the floor above my head and driving his weight down on top of me as he kissed me so deeply that my every inhale was his exhale, his sighs my moans.

The thick ridge of his cock ground against my clit though his battle leathers and the rough wool of my ill-fitting dress and I moaned louder, my spine arching against the hard floor, my gifts spilling free of my skin and lacing the room in sin.

His lust stoked the wild tempest of my power, the first tendrils of it sinking beneath my flesh before a rush of magic started to spill from his body into mine. Cayde's desires were a heady concoction, almost making me drunk again with the sensation of his flesh against mine only intensifying everything I felt from him.

Flashes of each and every way he wanted to fuck me flickered through my mind, his imagination only sparking my own desire as I caught a glimpse of each position, each fantasy. He was hungry for more than me, seeking power and recognition, bloodshed and honour – a beast so like myself that I couldn't believe I hadn't realised how potent a cocktail the two of us might be together. We were one and the same, our wants as in line as our lust and as a vision of me riding him hit me with a powerful wave of longing, I shoved him back, rolling us so that he was beneath me instead, bringing that fantasy to life.

Cayde pushed up onto his elbows as I tugged the ugly dress from my body, a groan of utter masculine need rolling up the back of his throat as I ran my hands over my breasts, toying with my nipples.

His hands gripped my ass, squeezing hard, rocking me so that my clit ground down over his cock, the rough leather of his pants a brutal, punishing pleasure.

"I should have known you'd be like this," he panted, rocking me over him again while I tugged at the straps of his leathers, wanting to reveal his body.

"Like what?" I panted, yanking the buckles apart and finally bearing the hard planes of his chest for my exploration.

"You need it, don't you? This...us..." his words trailed off as I shoved his pants down, my hand wrapping around the length of his cock and pumping it slowly.

Cayde watched me as I began to work him, my fingers twisting over the head of his cock while I rolled my tongue up the length of my other thumb then smeared the saliva over him next.

His muscles bunched as he looked at me, his wants growing feral, every soft intention turning to rough abandon and I gasped in delight when he finally cracked and lunged for me.

Cayde's mouth collided with mine once more, his hands tightening in their grip on my ass as he shoved to his feet, lifting me easily in his powerful arms.

My spine hit the wall beside the mantlepiece, his hips pinning me there as I kissed him deeper, his cock driving between my thighs and yet still not filling me.

"Fuck me," I commanded as he shrugged his leathers off with a roll of his shoulders and the sound of his pants falling to his ankles followed.

"I will, sweetheart. In every way I can think of."

His desire spiked with those words, the brutal demand for power merging with the carnal need for my body to bow to his.

A low growl rolled through him, his hands rough as they moved over my body, exploring every curve, his lust building to a level of desperation which had my breaths heaving in my chest.

I broke our kiss, looking at him, my hand skimming the sharp line of his jaw as I took in the savagery of him, so different to the superiority of the prince, so much better suited to the ragged truth of my soul.

He jerked his gaze from mine, looking over his shoulder to the bed and hauling me to it. He dropped me onto the thin mattress, looking down at me while kicking the last of his clothes off, revealing a body cut with hard muscle, decorated with the scars of a warrior.

I leaned back, my hands moving over my flesh seductively, toying with the heaviness of my breasts, tugging at my nipples and drawing a soft moan from my own lips.

He watched me as I slid a hand down my navel and between my thighs, but his restraint cracked before I could make any real show for him.

Cayde moved over my legs, his hungry gaze drinking in every curve of my flesh before he took hold of my hips and flipped me over.

With a sharp yank he tugged my knees higher, parting my thighs and lifting my ass. I fisted the sheets, need devouring me until Cayde drove his cock straight into my soaking cunt.

I cried out as he took hold of my hips, burying himself to the hilt and groaning in raw delight.

"By the love of Taurus, you're so fucking tight," he hissed through his teeth.

"Don't be soft with me now, Cayde," I growled, the delay making my heart riot in my chest, my need for release consuming me.

This was it. I had broken my vow to my prince. Committed treason against him for all intents and purposes. And yet the only thing I felt with Cayde's cock deep inside me was the overriding sense of freedom that came with claiming some part of my fate for my own.

His desires were like a flood of need consuming me, his want for me somehow enrapturing his want for all else, every deep and dark desire of his heart colliding and becoming one. I was the key to everything he wanted and the truth of that unravelled an aching, secret piece of me which I had never before dared to expose.

Cayde drew back slowly, the slide of his cock making me groan with need as I arched my spine further, knotting my fingers deeper within his sheets.

His thrust back into me stole my breath but this time he didn't pause, gripping my ass tightly, as he fucked me hard and rough, driving in and out with furious pumps of his hips which made me curse and cry out.

Sex was a rush which always consumed me, the truth of what I was relishing in the slap of flesh against flesh, the fullness of my cunt, the rasp of my skin against the sheets. My gifts stoked the pleasure in both of us, making it consume every piece of our bodies, each drive of our hips calling out to the promise of euphoria.

He was rough and furious in his claiming of me and I was just as feral and ferocious in my own right, the two of us this writhing, pounding collision of need.

I cursed as my body rushed closer to the edge and he fucked me harder, hissing commands for me to give in, to come for him and take all he had to give. My cry of release was buried into the sheets and Cayde swore loudly as my pussy tightened around him, forcing him to come too.

He slammed into me one final time, coming inside me, his fingers biting into my hips so brutally that I knew he was leaving bruises behind.

His weight fell over me and we collapsed, panting onto the sheets, still tangled in each other.

"You…that…," he rasped, finding the energy to roll onto his back beside me and I turned my head to look at him through knotted strands of pink.

"I know," I replied, not even pretending I wasn't smug as shit about it. "Welcome to your ruin," I taunted, and he breathed a ragged laugh.

"If that is what destruction tastes like, I'll gladly become a glutton for your poison."

I smiled to myself, letting my eyes fall closed with thoughts of Cayde running circles in my mind, the regret or guilt never surfacing because that hadn't felt like treason to me. It had felt like claiming my own destiny and I refused to be sorry for it. Maybe that meant I was damned, but as I let sleep have me, I had to admit that damnation didn't feel so very bad.

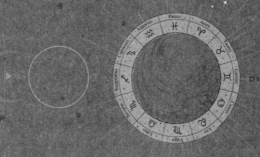

EVEREST

CHAPTER TWENTY NINE

Breakfast in the refectory was a special kind of carnage. Fae became more animal when they were hungry and regardless of the fact that there was plenty of food for everyone, brawls often broke out between elementals as they attempted to assert dominance.

This morning, I'd climbed up to perch on one of the large beams that spanned beneath the vaulted ceiling. I silently leapt from one to another, springing as easily as if I was in my Leopard form, certain my reflexes had sharpened further since my Order had Emerged.

I'd left my boots with Galomp then slipped away, climbing up in a darkened corner of the hall, practising the use of concealment magic as I made the shadows hug my figure.

Blue had run off the moment I'd opened my door this morning, and I wondered if he would return again or if that might be the last

I saw of him. He was a fickle little thing, but I enjoyed his company. It would be a shame to be alone again at night.

My target was at the far end of the hall where the Sky Witch sat with her friends, their return to the Keep having happened over three weeks ago now, rumours of a royal wedding rife. The refectory was still full of discussions about Stormfell's Prince Dragor now looking even likelier to claim the throne with heirs no doubt soon to follow, but it didn't matter much to me which rulers we fought against, so long as Cascada won.

I'd been trying to find a way to talk to the Sky Witch since her return, but there were always too many Fae around in the common areas, no one willing to walk alone in a space where your enemies all gathered. So I'd finally gotten sick of waiting for an opportunity to present itself and decided to create my own.

I continued on my way towards the Skyforgers, but as I landed on a beam above the heads of the Flamebringers, I paused. Kaiser and North were directly below me and from the excited looks and general overly touchy behaviour of the Fae packed in around them, I was pretty sure North's entire Werewolf pack were surrounding them.

North had grown the biggest pack in Never Keep and it hadn't gone without notice. He swept a hand through his messy brown hair that stuck out in all directions, revelling in the attention of his Wolves while Kaiser sat stoically beside him, unmoved by the keen yips and howls around him. They weren't even in their Wolf forms, yet they still acted like mutts.

Their tactile, too-friendly nature between one another was about as far from my own as you could get. But it looked like Kaiser was even further along that spectrum. The asshole was back to his usual impassive expression even as North started telling a loud, bragging story that drew all eyes to him.

"I got lost in Avanis once, had to go twelve days without food and I lived on nothing but the blood of the enemies I skewered with my blade." He pretended to draw a sword from his hip as he rose onto the wooden bench, fake stabbing at his friends' heads. "Tell them, Kai." He nudged Kaiser with his knee and the hollow man turned his black eyes upon his friend.

"It was four days and you spent most of it in that Stonebreaker's larder stuffing your face until I came and got you out," Kaiser said dryly and North cursed, his knee driving into Kaiser's shoulder again but with more force this time.

"Fuck off," North laughed. "You know it wasn't like that." He carved a hand down the back of his neck as his Wolves chuckled, looking to Kaiser instead of him. "Anyway, I didn't finish telling the story. On that particular little mission, I killed three Stonebreaker warriors, all Awakened - unlike me at the time."

"And how many did you kill, Kaiser?" a pretty female Wolf piped up, leaning toward him across the table.

"Nine," Kaiser answered flatly.

"Yeah, but I helped you with at least five of those," North insisted. "Oh, remember that time we were in Cascada and I set fire to those wheat fields? Bet those Raincarvers went hungry for weeks after that."

I noticed some mouse droppings on the wooden beam in front of me and as North sat down, picking up a cup of coffee, I flicked a few of the droppings over the edge, smiling as one landed in North's hair, another went down his collar and the third plopped into his drink.

Oops. There I go, accidently knocking tiny shits onto you.

Kaiser's head tipped back, his dark eyes aimed my way, and I tucked myself in tight against the beam, gathering the shadows around me more thickly. I stayed still a little longer before chancing a look back down, finding Kaiser gazing at his bowl of plain oatmeal and North still chattering mindlessly about his bloodthirsty achievements.

I moved into a crouch, ready to spring to the next beam ahead of me, and as I did so I sent another spray of mouse droppings down onto the Flamebringers. I didn't slow, smirking as North thanked one of his Wolves for adding raisins to his oats. With bursts of energy, I jumped from one beam to another, leaving the Flamebringers behind and finally arriving above the Skyforgers.

I crept along the length of the beam until I was right above the Sky Witch, two women flanking her and a man sitting opposite them whose eyes were pinned on my pink-haired target.

"Werewolves make so much fucking noise," the woman on the left with braided silver hair groaned, glaring over at the Flamebringers where North's pack were getting worked up into howls of laughter at whatever he was saying now. "I hardly got an ass crack of sleep last night."

The Sky Witch and the other woman with short, black hair sniggered.

"An ass crack of sleep? That's not a phrase," the man chipped in, but his lips were lifted in a grin.

"It's the perfect measurement actually, Cayde," the silver-haired woman tossed at him. "Take Dalia, for example, she has a wisp of an ass crack, basically not there at all. It starts far further down than you'd ever expect it to."

"What about your ass crack, Moraine?" Dalia threw back. "It's double the equator of mine with how much ass you have. If you're making a measurement out of ass cracks, they're not all as short as mine."

A laugh rose in my throat, but I quickly swallowed it, scowling instead as I remembered who I was listening to right now. Skyforgers were ferocious and they had left scars on my land that could never be healed.

The three women laughed and Cayde watched them, shaking his head as they all leaned into each other. My heart twisted in a pathetic sort of way as I realised I'd never known the kinship of female friends. I immediately hardened myself to the thought. I didn't need anyone anyway. Except maybe Harlon.

"She's got a point," the Sky Witch said. "Ass cracks aren't one and the same. You should have said you hardly got a Dalia's ass crack of sleep last night."

"What about you, V?" Moraine questioned. "Where would you fall in the ass crack equation?"

I arched a brow. V? Was that the Sky Witch's real name? Maybe it was, or more likely that was a nickname for something beginning with V. Verity? Valentina? Vagina? So many options…

"Don't tell me you're asking to see my ass, Moraine," the Sky Witch drawled. "You're the only one here who I thought I could rely on not to make a pass at me."

Moraine cackled while Dalia started yelling. "That isn't fair! You turned that shit on out of nowhere and caught me in the crosswinds!"

"You're not as irresistible as you like to think, sweetheart," Cayde replied.

My gaze was yanked to the Sky Witch and my lips parted a little as I found myself staring at her, admiring the curve of her lips, the roiling storm in her grey eyes, the way she-

"Cut it out, asshole!" Dalia punched the Sky Witch who may or may not have been called Vagina and the lure of her shattered as she snorted a laugh.

Cayde was gritting his jaw, leaning half way across the table towards her and as I glanced at the Fae on the surrounding tables, I noticed many of them either on their feet, moving towards her with outstretched hands or at least outright staring. One guy had drool dripping from his chin and another shrieked something about needing her to see his dick which was followed by many more similar demands.

Dalia slapped her hand down on the table and a gust of air magic tore from her, knocking them all back several steps. I guessed my efforts in making myself immune to the Sky Witch were paying off because I hadn't been tempted to hurl myself from the rafters or yell my desires at her, and I was glad to find she wasn't entirely impossible to resist.

I focused on what I'd come here to do, my gaze shifting to the Sky Witch's cup of tea as I willed my magic to connect with the liquid inside it. Gently, with such careful precision that I feared I would make a mistake at any moment, I froze her tea and wrote a message in the surface of the ice.

Meet me at midnight by the tapestry of Ursa Major.
It's five ass cracks away from the Night Gate.
-E

I waited as the Sky Witch went to take a sip then stilled, taking in the words. Her head twisted left and right as she sought me out. But I was gone, already slinking away across the beam before springing to another one, quietly journeying back across the refectory and hoping she might just take the bait.

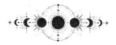

The wait was long as midnight approached and I wondered if the Sky Witch would come. Blue had been sleeping in my quarters after classes and he was now perched on my shoulder, seemingly determined not to leave my side any time soon. Which I was quietly glad of. His steady presence made me feel less alone in this place.

As I waited for the murderous Sky Witch to appear, my mind ripened with thoughts of the day the Skyforgers had come to Castelorain, ripping half the town away and taking plenty of the streets of my childhood with them. Alleys I'd known as well as my own skin, hills and hidden coves that were now lost forever. My grief over that had taken longer to surface, rising beneath the unimaginable weight of my mama's death. But it had left its wound on me all the same.

The Flamebringers had secured first place as my most hated nation, but the Skyforgers had easily fallen into second since that day. After that catastrophe, my father had led a battalion of Cascada's finest warriors to the land of Stormfell and made them pay in blood for their desecration of our town. But there was no retrieving what had been lost. The Endless War never gave, it only took. Land came at the price of graves. Gold came at the price of blood. There was always, always a price, and I had long ago learned it was never one worth paying. But pay it we did, every element, time and again, hurling our efforts into destroying one another so that one nation might finally come out victorious and achieve some semblance of peace.

Cascada had been prophesied to claim the final crown and so we strived ever on towards the day the stars placed it upon our heads. I hoped to be a part of that victory, painted in the glory of it all, my name earning its place in the mouths of Cascada's rulers. One day. One fucking divine day, I would know the taste of prestige and adoration, and no one would ever take it from me.

Blue scurried beneath the collar of my tunic and nestled himself under the back of my hair, his tickly feet making me fidget.

"Really?" I huffed, trying to get him out of there, but he didn't budge. As he stopped moving, I got used to the steady warmth of his body against my skin and decided to let him be. The little lizard got away with way too much when it came to me, his cuteness having a lot to do with it.

I got lost in the pretty daydream of my legendary status being secured, so much so that I didn't move fast enough to react to the shadow closing in on my left. I whirled, but the Sky Witch held no weapon as she stepped out of the gloom into the moonlight spilling through the window above.

"Edgy tonight, kitty cat," she purred.

"You don't frighten me," I said, taking in the black leathers she wore and the dagger concealed at her hip. "But death is an inconvenience that would get in the way of my life plans."

She breathed a laugh then flattened her lips, regarding me coolly. "What plans would those be exactly? Humiliating yourself in front of your father... again?"

I scowled, a growl rising in my throat at those cutting words.

"Word travels fast in Never Keep," she said, stepping closer, her taunt biting a little too deep as she lowered her voice to a whisper. "I know you're a one-handed caster. Pity, I thought you might pose more of a challenge than your every-day Raincarver, but it seems you're even more deficient than the rest of your kind."

In seconds, I had my dagger in my left hand, whipping it towards her throat while my right hand froze her boots to the flagstones so she couldn't run. She didn't move, did nothing but let me drive my dagger closer to her neck. It didn't strike her though, instead scraping against an air shield that was so tight against her body, it was like a second skin.

"One day, I will be strong enough to destroy you. So go ahead and underestimate me, Witch, because I will only delight more in proving you wrong on the battlefield," I hissed.

Her eyebrows lifted just a little and she took me in with keener eyes, something telling me she might just believe the words leaving my lips.

"Did you invite me here to make idle threats?" she asked, moving to place more distance between us but finding her feet frozen to the ground. She frowned, looking down, seeming mildly impressed that I'd managed the cast without her noticing.

"They're not idle. And no, that's not why I asked you here." I lowered my blade and melted the ice at her feet, figuring I would have to let my guard down if I was going to get her to go along with this. "I found a passage in a sea cave north of the Keep. I heard drums and chanting and I think it might lead somewhere important, but I can't reach it without…" I choked on the word, despising having to ask this from her. It was an admission of my weakness, my inability to be able to harness water well enough to rise that high yet.

"What?" she clipped.

"Air," I forced out. "It's too high."

She smiled wickedly. "Well why don't you just tell me exactly where this place is and I'll let you know if I find anything of interest."

"No," I snarled and she frowned.

"Why does this intrigue you so? What are you gaining from these investigations into the Reapers?"

"I'm looking for someone," I admitted, knowing lies wouldn't secure me any of her allegiance. I had a feeling she was used to seeing through false words. "A friend. He was Awakened with two elements and the Reapers took him away to become an acolyte."

"A friend," she mused.

"He's the only person I have in the world," I said, passion rising in me and spilling out. "He's been there for me through everything and after what I saw the Reapers doing, and after the lies they spewed in the Heliacal Courtyard before they murdered that Flamebringer, I'm afraid of what's happened to him. What he's being made to be a part of. We have always protected each other and I'm not going to abandon him, no matter what this costs me. I *will* find him. You think asking for your help is easy? You think I want to turn to my enemies for this? None of this is what I want, but for him, I would climb into the stars if that's where they've taken him."

Instead of chiding me like I half-expected her to do, she softened the slightest amount, almost imperceptibly. "Lead the way then, kitten."

I turned my back on her, knowing it was the most dangerous move I could make but I was placing my faith in her for one night only. I led her down the passages to a window that would lead out to the rocky land between the Vault of Frost and the Vault of Embers. Silently, I pushed it open and climbed outside, adjusting the pack on my shoulders as Blue let out a little grunt in his sleep.

The Sky Witch kept pace with me as we traversed across the frozen land, snow hiding pitfalls between the rocks, she even sent a blast of air out behind us to conceal our tracks.

Finally, we made it to the cliff, taking the winding animal track down to the beach where I slid my pack from my shoulders and took out the two bathing suits. One was newly made, black with pink embroidery across the chest, the letters SW written into the fabric with a twisting vortex of air curling around it and a gleaming silver sword I'd stitched within it all. The arms and legs were long like mine and it shimmered like a rainbow from the blaze oil I'd glazed it with. I'd added plenty of the oil and had soaked mine in it again too, making sure it would truly keep us warm out there this time.

"For you." I thrust it at her and she eyed the lettering in surprise.

Okay, maybe I'd gotten one percent carried away with making the item, but my creations were never half assed. I rarely made things for others, but the moment I'd set my attention to it, I had found my fingers stitching the patterns, my mind caught up on the essence of the Sky Witch and all she represented.

"I'll go without." She tossed it back at me.

I caught it and threw it back. "You'll freeze before we make it to the cave. The blaze oil in the suit will keep you warm."

The Sky Witch glanced at the choppy black waves then started stripping without another word.

I pulled off my clothes too, stuffing them in my pack and Blue finally crawled out from under my hair with a yawn.

"What the fuck is that?" The Sky Witch pointed.

"That's Blue. He's a...thing. I don't know what he is actually, but he stays."

"That better not be some asshole hiding in shifted form," she hissed, down to her undergarments now but she still looked just as fearsome.

"He's not," I insisted.

The Sky Witch slowly nodded, accepting that and we returned to changing into our swimwear. She fastened her belt back around it, a small pouch and three daggers clinging to it. I strapped my own dagger onto my hip too, a ripple of tension passing between us as we assessed each other for a second. But somehow, it passed.

We hid our clothes and my pack behind a large black rock that was capped in snow then took off towards the sea, the moonlight bright and painting the coal-coloured waves with tips of silver.

We waded out into the water while Blue hovered above me on his wings and my suit warmed with the heat of the blaze oil, fighting off the cold and working a thousand times better than it had before, the fact filling me with pride. I parted the sea as I walked while the Sky Witch got slapped in the face with a few waves then growled and dove under, swimming into calmer waters beyond. I sniggered, following her with more ease than she was having, wielding the water to push me to her side, then I led the way towards the gaping chasm of the sea cave.

Our journey was silent until we were deep within the cave system, swimming along the river beneath the red glow of Blue's tail, finally slowing as we reached the low cave roof that barred our way on. As before, Blue flew up and slipped away between a crack in the wall, but the only way forward for Vesper and I was under.

I cast a Faelight, readying to send it beneath the surface to guide the way along the submerged passage.

"Now what?" she demanded, treading water and gazing up at the cave wall barring our way forward.

"We have to swim under this. It's about ten feet."

The Sky Witch looked to the dark water then back up at the wall. "I think I'll find another way around."

"There's literally no other way. This is a dead end unless we go under."

"Uhuh." She eyed the tiny crack Blue had taken and I gave her a hollow look.

"You can't fit through there."

"Don't tell me what I'm not capable of," she growled.

"Are you scared?" I narrowed my eyes and she glared at me like I'd just given her the biggest insult of her life.

"I do not fear anything."

"Follow me then, Valery." I sent the Faelight under the water.

"That's not my name," she hissed, her grey eyes narrowing.

"Okay. Follow me then, Vorgash." I took a breath before swimming after my Faelight, sensing the Sky Witch on my heels.

I drove water behind us, forcing us through the passage at a wild pace so we were propelled out of it in a surging wave, breaching the surface once more.

The Sky Witch spluttered, cursing my element as I smirked, but her gaze spoke of vengeance as we swam on. "I'm not called fucking Vorgash."

"Well your name starts with a V, I heard your friends calling you that. So tell me what it is."

She remained silent, her lips pressed hard together and I shrugged, swimming on. "Vorgash it is then."

She said nothing, swimming on behind me and we finally rounded into the place the water met with the vast black wall that held a tunnel at its very peak.

"There," I pointed to it as Blue went whizzing up to the passage and disappeared into the dark. There was no pounding of drums tonight, no chanting or sound of anyone at all. I hoped that meant we would go undisturbed during our hunt.

"Oh that itty bitty climb?" the Sky Witch goaded, casting air to draw her up and out of the water, flying higher and higher before stepping into the tunnel.

"Hey – wait!" I called, swimming closer to the sheer wall.

The Sky Witch looked down at me in consideration like she was tempted to walk away.

"Help me up," I commanded.

"You look like a turd in a latrine down there," she called.

"You look like a turd hanging halfway out of an ass up there," I called back. "Now carry me up."

"Sure thing, kitten." She smiled viciously then cast air at the water, making it spin in a whirlpool before yanking me out of it by the leg. I was wheeled upside down, dragged at a terrifying speed skyward before coming to a violent halt dangling in front of her, hanging above the fifty-foot fall back to the water.

My Faelight faded as my connection to it was lost and the gloom pressed in a little thicker.

My pulse elevated as I cast a tether of water between us, lashing her waist to mine. "Drop me and you're coming with me, Witch."

"Touché." She tossed me haphazardly onto the rocky floor of the passage and I cursed, shoving myself upright. I cast ice beneath her feet and she went skidding violently forward, crashing into a wall.

She whipped around to glare at me and I glared back in kind, then a ripple of amusement passed through me and we both started smiling. In a flash, we both flattened the looks and I stalked on ahead, seeking out Blue as I walked into the dark.

The passage was tight and winding, the sconces on the walls void of fire and all quiet around us. I cast a silencing shield as a precaution in case we were closing in on any Reapers, but as we entered a vast chamber, I forgot about the possibility of danger as my gaze fell on a towering slab of stone on a raised dais in the centre of the circular space.

The stone slab was marked with silver writing, etched into its surface, the words of the Elysium Prophecy painted out before us. Only they weren't the words I knew. The ones that were hailed from every corner of Cascada, declaring our triumph in the Endless War was destined by the stars. These words were different, similar in ways, but wholly new in others.

> *War of the four, divided and torn asunder.*
> *Flame, sky, rock and sea collide,*
> *While the stars bless the valiant souls of heart and light.*
> *Seek the Void, for it shall guide the chosen ones to their glorious path,*
> *A weapon of purity, and the gift of null.*
> *In a web of lies and cruelty, fate will favour the peacemakers of destiny,*
> *And a bountiful empire shall be reborn under one united rule,*
> *Garnering the fortune and favour of the almighty sky.*

"The Elysium Prophecy spoke of Cascada's impending victory," I breathed, stepping closer to the stone epitaph in confusion.

"No, it spoke of Stormfell's victory." The Sky Witch shot me a confounded look then gazed back at the words written into the stone. "So what the fuck is this?"

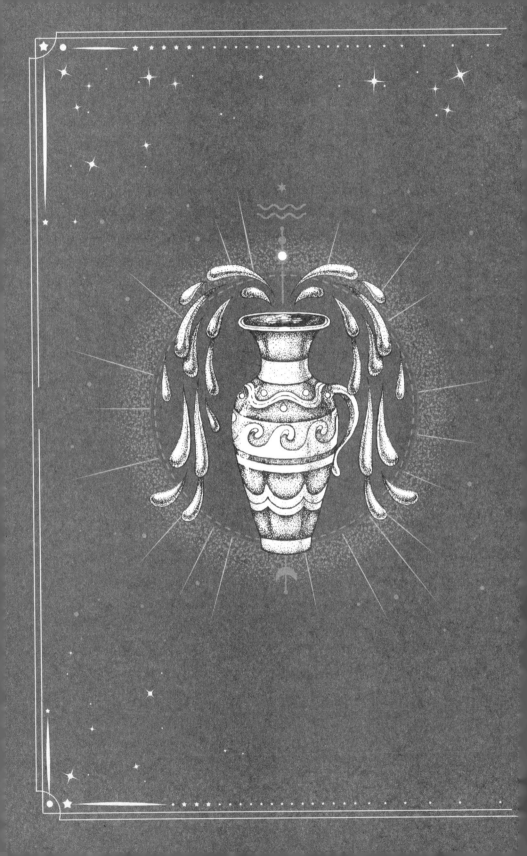

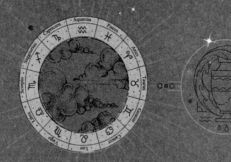

VESPER

CHAPTER THIRTY

"Why would they have a different version hidden away down here?" Everest frowned, stepping closer to the epitaph. "And why would our own nations declare their victory in the prophecies we've been told? Is it our leaders who decided that, or was it fed to them by the Reapers?"

"You ask a lot of questions for a girl who has no answers," I said coolly, taking in the words before me, unsure what to make of this.

"Don't you care?" she rounded on me. "This changes everything."

"It changes nothing. It's just another riddle without a solution."

"There's always a solution," she hissed. "Either our leaders lied to us or the Reapers did and judging by what I've seen of our oh so pious prophets lately, my bet is on them. But why?"

"Are you asking me or the stars? Because neither have much to say on the matter," I said stonily, tucking this information away for myself and letting her mind run rife with clueless guesses. Debating this wasn't going to offer us the truth.

The sound of something clattering to the ground made the two of us straighten, a tunnel which led further into the darkness echoing guiltily.

I exchanged a look with my co-conspirator before leading the way towards the noise.

"So you hear a scary noise and just walk straight towards it?" she asked, following close to my heels.

"I don't see you running away," I pointed out.

"It wasn't a criticism, just an observation," she replied.

We fell silent as we moved into the tunnel, the walls arching overhead, shifting from the rough rock to the perfectly hewn brick which made it clear this part of the caverns had been created by Fae.

I took my dagger from my belt as the dark consumed us, calling on my magic and igniting a pale Faelight to lead the way into the shadows. If someone was lurking ahead of us, I'd take the chance of alerting them to our presence over the risk of them leaping out unseen.

The tunnel climbed slowly, sconces hanging from the walls, unlit and without any sign that they recently had been. The cold whistled through this place but surprisingly, the outfit Everest had created for me fought it off. It fit me perfectly too which was something of a novelty considering my height – most items I purchased either had to be altered or made with me in mind. Clearly she had a good eye. Or perhaps she'd just spent that long studying my ass to know it by heart.

A room opened up ahead of us, the floor sloping into it to create a huge basin, though what it was designed to hold was unclear.

Something was slowly rotating on the ground several paces into the chamber, my Faelight casting flickering reflections across its metallic edges.

"Is that what fell?" Everest murmured as we looked at the goblet.

"I'm more concerned with what dropped it," I replied, my eyes moving up to the roof of the cave which was domed similarly to the floor. So more of a ball than a basin.

I pushed more magic into my Faelight, frowning as I took in the dull, grey colour of the walls. There were items strewn across the sloping floor, many of them collecting dust at the base of the bowl and each of them similarly lacking in colour almost as though the vibrancy had leaked out of them. The walls were marked with ragged fissures and cracks. There were lines like broken veins of black and grey creeping across the stone as if it had once been a living thing but now held nothing at all in its grasp.

Everest took a step forward as if meaning to move into the room, but I held a hand out to halt her, my eyes glued to my Faelight which had begun to sputter and crackle sporadically.

"You have to maintain a connection to the magic in it," Everest said as if the problem was with my cast.

"It's not my control that's causing that," I replied in a low voice. "There's something wrong with-" my words cut off in a gasp as the line of power which tethered me to the Faelight thrashed violently, a sharp jerk on it almost making me stumble into the room as if it truly were a rope lashing me to the magic.

I grabbed the wall to steady myself, cursing as I failed to cut my connection to it. Whatever was tugging on my power was getting a firmer grasp on it now, my breath stalling in my lungs as I fought to sever it.

Everest shouted at me, slapping me when I failed to react before finally blasting me with a rush of water which sent me crashing to the ground further back in the tunnel.

"What the fuck was that?" she demanded, advancing on me and I shook my head as I got to my feet.

"It was like something was...feeding on me, or draining me," I said, backing away from that room and whatever foul magic it held.

"You looked like you were about to leap in there."

"More like I was about to be dragged in," I said darkly, looking at this little kitty cat who might just have saved my life.

She seemed to realise it too, her eyebrows arching as she took it in, but I wasn't going to be thanking her. I was only here because she'd asked me to come.

I turned away, leading again as we made it back to the chamber with the unfamiliar prophecy and turning into the lone remaining tunnel.

This one, it turned out, was lit by everflames and we followed it as we climbed a set of tightly twisting stairs.

Everest muttered about me taking the lead but seemed to realise I wouldn't allow for any alternative and didn't force the issue.

Silence continued to press in on us and I couldn't help but wonder who had dropped that goblet. Or had it fallen of its own accord? Perhaps it was drawn into that chamber just as I had almost been?

"What was that back there?" Everest asked like I had any idea. "It was kind of like a stone amplification chamber. You know, like the ones in the Astral Sanctuaries which the Reapers use to talk to the stars."

"Those are underwater and have glass roofs," I pointed out. "To better allow the Reapers to attain prophecies from the stars. That thing was beneath the dirt and rock of Never Keep with a stone roof to match. I don't think it was seeking approval from the heavens."

Everest fell silent and I wasn't inclined to convince her into conversation again – I'd just felt a breath of fresh air upon my skin which tasted all too heavily of home.

"Do you hear the ocean?" Everest asked slowly. "Not the crashing of those violent waves we left back in that sea cave but the roll and pull of the ocean back…"

"I feel a cool wind on my face," I said, turning to her.

I looked at her and she looked at me, both of us acknowledging the fact that she no more felt the wind on her cheeks than I could hear the call of her precious ocean.

I wetted my lips, pausing for a moment as I considered the passage ahead.

"How much do you want to follow this path?" I asked, spinning my dagger between my fingers.

"I don't want to – I need to," she growled.

"Good. Then you won't mind bleeding for it." I held my hand out for hers and she predictably withdrew.

"What is it with you and blood magic? You know that shit isn't sanctioned by the stars, don't you?"

"What I know is that only those Fae most willing to sacrifice in the name of power can wield it," I replied. "And I know what it is to need power more than even you can imagine, kitten. Oh, I'm sure you had it rough as the least favoured child of Commander Rake but I crawled my way up from the waifhouse and I have sacrificed more than you could understand to have earned my reputation and the prospect of a true rank in the sky forged army. So yes, I offered up my soul to learn the arts of Ether and blood magic and no doubt I have done many things that would see your toes curl, but I'm standing here before you because of it. Now, if you want to know whether or not the path ahead holds a legion of Reapers just waiting to ambush us, give me your hand."

"I don't see why you can't use your own blood," Everest grumbled, offering up her left hand with clear reluctance.

"Because yours is so much sweeter, kitten. Besides, why waste mine when I have an alternative?" I took a moment to inspect the scars which marred her palm, causing her to growl irritably. Then I sliced into her finger with a shrug which didn't exactly declare my innocence but admitted to my curiosity.

"Want to trade war stories?" I asked, smearing her blood across my palm and drawing the rune Mannaz onto it for awareness before snatching a lock of her hair between my fingers and sheering a few stands off.

"Hey," she snapped, batting me away but I'd already dropped the hair onto my palm with the blood and was pulling a sprig of dill from the pouch at my belt for energy, tossing it into the mix.

I took a matchbook from the pouch last, glad to find it was as watertight as the Fae who had sold me it had claimed. I struck a match against the wall to light it before dropping it into my hand and setting the concoction ablaze with a low growl of command.

"Enlighten me."

I threw the burning mixture towards the tunnel before us, a jolt of Ether rocking through me as I connected to the power of the world and my awareness spun out ahead of us.

I couldn't actually see what awaited but I could feel the imprint of any souls who might be lingering out of sight, my senses expanding to comprehend the beating hearts of anyone who might be waiting in the dark, but I found nothing there.

"Looks like we chose the right night to come creeping about

down here," I said in satisfaction, ignoring the slightly disturbed look Everest was giving me.

"Your eyes went blank when you did that," she said. "Like you weren't even in there anymore."

"Maybe I wasn't," I agreed. "Maybe our bodies are simply shells for the impossible nature of our souls to hide within and true freedom comes when we're released from the confines of them."

Everest considered me for a long moment then shook her head. "Or maybe your mind has cracked from using too much of that dark magic."

"Spoken like a true Raincarver," I mocked. "So are you going to tell me what happened to your hand?"

Everest pursed her lips as we started walking onwards but she seemed to decide it wasn't such a secret that it had to remain hidden from me.

"A little over a year ago, Skyforgers attacked the town where I lived. You should remember it," she said, her voice cold, causing me to tighten my grip on my dagger as I cast a look back over my shoulder at her, but she didn't seem inclined to attack me just yet. "There was an explosion and my hand was burned with Basilisk Venom."

"Ah," I said.

"That's it?"

"I didn't set the explosion," I said plainly. "Though I doubt you'd believe me if I told you who did."

"I know precisely who it was," she growled. "And the Flamebringers' involvement in that day doesn't negate yours."

"We were only there because Cascada had kidnapped one of ours – or were you unaware that the Basilisk your people were milking for venom had been kidnapped and tortured, his venom drawn from him relentlessly for use as a biological weapon against his own people?"

Everest was silent for several minutes as we headed further into the tunnels beneath the Keep, the temperature growing and a scent of sulphur on the air.

"Sometimes this war is such bullshit," she snarled and I glanced at her, a single brow raised.

"Would you yield then?" I asked. "Concede defeat and see it done?"

"Never," she hissed.

"Then bullshit or not, we fight on."

This time, our discussion was cut short not because of our clear differences or the rivalry between our people, but because we had come to the end of the tunnel.

A wooden door stood ajar before us, the scent of sulphur rising from beyond it, that cool wind once again caressing my cheeks.

I stepped closer to the door, my fingers skidding across the rough wood as I slowly pushed it wide.

I wasn't certain what I had been expecting but the wide carven filled with at least twenty stone archways in a wide circle hadn't been it.

The flagstones lining the floor were so pale they were almost white, each of them carved with elemental symbols and likenesses of the various zodiac signs.

There was a stillness to the air which denied the possibility of that breeze I'd kept feeling from existence, but as I took a step into the chamber, I felt it again.

"Surely you hear the waves now?" Everest pushed but I shook my head in denial.

There were more wooden doors on the outer walls of the chamber suggesting that there were in fact six different routes to this place despite the difficult path we had followed to find it.

I crossed the chamber to the closest archway, tilting my head back to look up at the pale stones which were carved with runes and symbols alike. This one had been marked with the upside down triangle for water, a rivulet carved all the way through the stone beneath it which led from the ground, around the entire archway and back to the ground again.

I crouched low, my fingers brushing against the flagstone where the rivulet on the archway met with it and inspecting the low depression there marked with the rune Radio which appeared like a jagged R. Its meaning, as with all runes, could change somewhat depending on its use, but the one which came to mind was travel.

"Look at this," Everest called, drawing my attention to a bronze urn which sat in the centre of the room. It was almost as tall as me and marked with various carvings of Dragons and stars which seemed to be engaging in a dance. "The stuff inside is like black glitter."

I moved to stand at Everest's side, reaching into the urn and pulling out a handful of what looked like glittering grit but felt like something so much more, power whispering to me from it.

"Do you have tales of the lost Dragon shifters where you come from?" I asked in a low voice, my fingers closing around a handful of the mysterious substance.

"Some say the sea devoured them to punish them for their love of flames. Or I once heard a legend that they chose a life of unity on some hidden island, deciding to abandon the war to the rest of the Fae not unlike the Vampires," Everest said.

"I heard they had a way to travel through starlight," I breathed. "That they could disappear in the blink of an eye and reappear somewhere miles away instantly. The stars grew jealous of their power and the way they toyed with the magic of the heavens, so one day the starlight swallowed them and they were never seen again."

I took a step away from the urn, that cool wind brushing against my cheeks and lifting tendrils of my hair as I looked to an archway marked for air, the other symbols on it written in some ancient language I neither knew nor recognised, but I *did* recognise that rune.

Everest slipped into my shadow as I approached the archway, watching as I dropped to one knee and held my fist out over the depression at the base of it.

"This might go horribly wrong," I warned.

"Only one way to find out."

I nodded, releasing the fistful of grit and sucking in a sharp breath as the second it fell into the depression in the stone, the rune lit with magic and it was drawn into that rivulet, speeding through it until the archway was surrounded and a burst of light exploded from its centre.

The two of us lurched back, raising our weapons but as the light settled, we found a pool of glimmering white and silver rippling in the space within the archway.

"What is that?" Everest gasped.

"I think it's how the Dragons used to slip between the stars," I said, my pulse thundering in my chest as I took a step closer to it, reaching out with the tip of my blade and brushing it against the glimmering starlight.

I cursed as the blade was tugged forward, releasing my hold on it and staring in wonder as it was sucked into that pool of light, disappearing within it and leaving us behind.

"I'm going in there," I announced.

"You're insane," Everest replied.

"Are you staying behind?"

"Obviously not. I'm going first."

"Doubtful."

She tried to shove past me and I shoved her back in turn, the two of us scowling at each other before diving into the blazing pool of light together.

I swore loudly as something seemed to wrap its way around my entire being, my feet leaving the ground, the world spinning away from me and a thousand whispers starting up in my ears as the weight of untold eyes all whipped towards me. A swirl of stars and galaxies raced around me in twisting vortex and a scream lodged itself in my throat, that feeling of watchful eyes growing heavier, more interested. Just as suddenly as it had begun, I fell away from all of it, crashing to my knees on a sandstone floor.

I scrambled upright, staring first at Everest who looked even more wild than usual, her long brown hair having fallen into her face before she shoved it back again, then taking in the utterly new chamber we found ourselves in.

There was a torch burning in a distant sconce, its flickering light illuminating a passageway which was at once entirely familiar and totally foreign to me.

I looked at the pale walls, taking in the tapestries and decorations, knowing the style all too well. These was the markings of Stormfell. I had travelled all across the waning continent while playing spy and assassin and I knew the feel of each nation well. There was no doubt in me as I took in the impossibility of our new location – I was home.

I drew in a breath of fresh, skyborn air, my weight feeling more settled on this well-known ground and a wild terror dripped into me. This path was dangerous – catastrophic even if the other nations found out about it. We were somehow, impossibly, right in the heart of Stormfell without any fanfare or notice of our arrival. What if the other nations found out about this? What if they used this path to send their invading armies after us?

Panic welled in me and I lurched for my dagger as I spotted it on the ground, snatching it into my grasp and whirling to face Everest. If she knew where we were, if she figured it out then I needed to end her before she could tell a soul.

"What are you doing?" I barked, finding her on the other side of the low lit passageway, slipping between a set of massive iron bars which blocked the entrance to an even darker chamber – though they were so widely spaced that the only thing they would block from entrance was a cart or wagon, which seemed unlikely down here.

"I heard something," Everest replied because we were the head towards it types.

I stalked after her, my grip tightening on my dagger, magic prickling against my fingertips. Her end would equal my own thanks to the blood bond between us but if she knew where we were, if she had figured it out and could relay that information back to her father or any of the other Raincarvers then my death was a small price to pay to stop that.

She moved deeper into the shadows and I prowled after her, utterly silent, wondering if I was counting down my final heartbeats with this hunt.

"Do you see that?" Everest murmured, turning to look back at me and flinching as she found me in her shadow.

Our eyes met, the promise of death slinking closer, my predatory nature rising to strike but I didn't do it.

There was nothing victorious or cunning in her expression,

nothing cruel or eager to suggest that she knew where we were or what nation we were in. And why would she? By the stars, I couldn't even be truly certain myself – we were in a series of underground passages, not standing beneath the open air. We could be anywhere. Only my gut told me I was in my homeland. For all I knew, she might believe we were in hers.

A deep rumbling rolled through the surrounding space and I stilled as that sound set my instincts alight, whirling towards the green glow which Everest had pointed out.

Crystals jutted from the walls ahead of us, some deep power emanating from them which made my tongue stick to the roof of my mouth and two lines of unease score down my spine.

We crept towards the light, shadows seeming to shift around us as if they were stalking us into the chamber.

A warm breeze washed through the cavern, that rumbling sounding again, closer this time, except now I wasn't imagining a movement in the ground; now all I could picture were sharp claws and razor teeth.

I grasped Everest's arm, my heart pounding wildly and I threw a Faelight up above our heads, illuminating the enormous chamber and sending terror crashing through my soul.

A beast of myth and legend towered over us, its body larger than a fucking building, each taloned foot bigger than either of us and its beastly, silver eyes glaring down at us from a height of at least fifty feet over a row of deadly fangs.

Its scales were dull and cracked, great scars rent through them and four of those glowing green crystals puncturing them in a mimicry of a collar surrounding its neck.

"That's a...Dragon," Everest breathed in awe as the beast growled again, its talons cutting into the stone, chains rattling over the ground as it moved towards us.

My lips parted on nothing at all, no words coming for me as I stared up at this miraculous, terrifying beast and found my death shining in its cruel and haunted gaze.

I shoved Everest back, magic exploding from me as the Dragon lunged, its teeth crashing against my air shield as I threw myself to the ground to escape it.

The Dragon roared in fury, no sign of the Fae who lived within it shining in its animalistic gaze as it slammed into my shield and shattering it as it came for us again.

Everest dragged me to my feet, the two of us breaking into a sprint as we raced back the way we'd come, the Dragon's furious roars echoing off of every surface, alerting the entire world to its presence.

Heat seared across my spine and I called on my magic again, but Everest got there first, hurling an enormous wave of water up at our backs just as the beast blasted hellfire at us from its gaping jaws.

The water hissed and bubbled, turning to steam as we threw ourselves aside to avoid its burn, my air shield surrounding us to save us from it.

We raced on, the bars looming ahead, the Dragon's claws ripping at the stone as it chased us, the chain which held it rattling ominously across the ground and we weren't moving fast enough to escape it.

I only had to beat Everest to the door. It couldn't eat two of us at once. It could burn us both but I could shield myself from that. I glanced at her, the two of us keeping pace, but I could push myself faster, I could get ahead, I could...except for some unknown reason I just couldn't make myself do it.

With a curse, I shoved my dagger back into my belt, raised both hands and prayed to the stars that I hadn't just signed my own death warrant. *Come on, Libra, don't abandon me now.*

A rush of magic hurtled from me, whipping around the two of us and yanking us off of our feet as I threw us through the air towards the bars so fast that the world blurred around us.

The Dragon bellowed even louder as we skidded between the iron bars and hit the stone floor beyond, my eyes widening as an explosion of fire erupted from its mouth, far more than the last time, far more than either of us could hope to stop.

"Move!" Everest yelled and I twisted to find her grabbing a handful of that shimmering grit from an urn beside the empty archway and hurling it at the rune which would activate it.

Fire rushed for us and I could only throw myself at the open space within the stone archway, heat enveloping me as I slammed into Everest and knocked her through too.

Silver light erupted around us and we were snatched into the embrace of the stars once again, their whispers louder now, more engaged, so many eyes focused on us that I felt entirely naked beneath them.

We skidded out into the darkness of the gate chamber beneath Never Keep and I rolled onto my back, my hands raised with magic crackling against my palms as I stared at the archway which had fallen silent and empty once more.

I glanced at Everest, the two of us panting heavily, the scent of smoke clinging to our skin and a wildness to our expressions which didn't come close to enveloping the insanity of what we had just seen.

"What the fuck was that place?" Everest asked. "I mean, it wasn't in the Keep. And that Dragon was being held-"

I hushed her as the sound of voices pricked at my ears and her eyes widened in alarm as she heard them too.

We shoved to our feet, the low chanting of the Reapers coming from a doorway adjacent to the one we had used to get here all the way across the chamber.

Everest made to run that way but I'd been in enough of these types of situations to know that we didn't have time for that.

"Plan B," I hissed, jerking my chin and racing for the door closest to us instead. We might not have known where it led to but we did know that those voices were coming from the other direction.

Everest cursed as she whirled around and followed me, the two of us slipping through the door just as the Reapers entered the chamber from the other direction.

I hesitated, peering through the crack in the door and watching as around twenty of them filed into the space, chanting to the stars, their faces hidden within their golden cowls.

I was tempted to stay and watch more of what they were doing but the risk was too high and we needed to take our chance at escape.

We remained in silence as we hurried along the new passageway, finding a narrow, tightly curving staircase several paces into it and taking it upwards.

On and on it climbed, my thighs burning as we kept up a fast pace, the sounds of the Reapers fading below us until only our laboured breaths kept company with the darkness.

When we finally reached the peak of the stairs, we found ourselves in a narrow passageway similar to the one I had accessed through the shrine of Leo.

"I think the Reapers use these to traverse the Keep," I murmured, leading the way through the dark and pausing as I found a hole to peer through. "That's the refectory," I said, moving aside so that Everest could look too.

"I could eat," she said and I almost laughed.

"Seriously?"

"We just saw a fucking Dragon and were nearly burned alive. I have no words for what that was but I do know that we still have about twenty archways to investigate if we're going to find Harlon. I'll need my energy for that."

"You think they're keeping the acolytes through one of those doors?"

"Didn't you notice the carvings on them? Most were marked for the individual elements, but there were some which were different, carved with symbols for all four; water, air, earth and fire. Stands to reason that those are the ones which lead to more Reapers."

"I don't know what a cage for Dragons has to do with air," I said carefully, wondering if she was about to figure out what I was almost certain of about the location we had travelled to.

"Well, they can fly, right? I mean, that one looked like its wings were all fucked up so I doubt it could anymore but-"

"What are they doing with a Dragon anyway?" I growled, my throat thickening as I thought of the beast trapped and alone down there, the mention of its mutilated wings opening a searing burn within me.

"Those crystals in its neck must have been for something," Everest mused, the two of us moving on through the passage, hunting for a way out. "Maybe they control it – stop it from shifting back into Fae form?"

I frowned at that suggestion, wondering why anyone would want to cage a Dragon shifter. What purpose could it serve? Was it a prisoner down there or was there more to it? It couldn't be a coincidence that there were no Dragons left in the world and yet one was being chained below ground.

My fingers brushed against a raised edge and I felt around until I located a handle, twisting it sharply and opening a door in the back corner of the kitchens.

We stepped out into the pale moonlight which was filtering into the space through the windows and I shoved the door closed behind us with a sense of relief. A dull thud sounded within the wall as it sealed itself and Everest cursed as she tried and failed to find a way to open it again.

"We can't get back through there," she groaned and I gave her a few moments of assistance in trying to open it again before giving it up.

"They must have set it up that way to stop murderous neophytes from finding the secret ways between the Vaults." I shrugged.

"Which means we're stuck using the sea cave to get back there again," Everest sighed.

I said nothing because I was starting to wonder what the hell we'd been thinking by going down there. Whatever the Reapers were up to was none of our business. They were the few chosen to serve the stars. Wasn't working to discover their secrets something akin to sacrilege? Though I had to admit that I was more than a little curious to figure it out regardless.

We forced a window open and crept back across the blustering snowscape outside the Keep until we reached the spot where we had hidden our clothes and we changed into them quickly.

"Well, that was all kinds of fucked up," I announced. "Shall we get back to our beds before the Reapers come hunting for whoever pissed off their Dragon?"

Everest nodded, though I could tell she wanted to head back down there already. But the night was waning, the moon high above us and sleep beckoning.

Together we headed back to the Keep, my air magic erasing all signs of our passage across the snow and as we crept back inside, we exchanged a dark look.

"We need to continue investigating this," Everest said firmly.

That 'we' hung between us, a Skyforger and Raincarver. There should never be any sort of union between our kinds and yet here we stood. I inspected her desires, picking through them and finding only that desperate ache to find her friend and the prickling need for the answers which were driving at me too. There was nothing there about glory or ambition which I could link to her plotting to sell the secret of that passage to Stormfell to her superiors. But if we kept investigating those archways, wouldn't it soon become clear where at least some of them led?

Though on that thought, I might be able to discover a route into the other nations for my own kingdom. Perhaps finding out more about them would enable me to bring that information to Dragor, to prove my worth in all things military and barter for my freedom from his other desires. It wasn't much of a plan, but it was better than I'd had so far.

"We'll see," I said without committing to anything. I needed to sleep on this and figure out the best course before I would be making any more promises to a Fae outside of my kin.

Everest made to protest but I turned and walked away, letting the shadows have me as I sank into the darkness and headed back into the Vault of Sky.

I slipped into my room, the cold kiss of a blade finding my throat and a smile teasing over my lips as I recognised the shape of the man who had come to play with me.

Cayde's wings were flared wide at his back, blotting the light of the moon from the windows, casting the shape of them in silvery highlights.

"You shouldn't be here," I breathed.

"Why have you keyed your magical locks to let me in then?" he rumbled in reply, chest pressed to mine, breath laced with mint.

"Because I've been hoping you'd pluck up the nerve to come find me in the dark again," I replied, my fingers brushing against the door as I double checked the locks were in place, seeking out any sign of interference.

"Cassandra was asking me about you," he said, his knife pressing to my throat almost as firmly as his cock was driving against my waist.

"I didn't know she had a thing for me," I teased. "Tell her stuck-up little cunts with the sexual range of an overworked mule aren't my bag, but thanks for the offer."

"You laugh in the face of spies? You know she wasn't asking out of curiosity. She isn't the first I've heard speculating on who you take to your bed and the questions are too pointed for me to believe they're simple jealousy."

My gut lurched, pale blue eyes flashing within my mind. *I'm a jealous creature.*

What would Dragor do to me if he discovered what I'd done with Cayde back in Wrathbane? What would he do if he found out that I'd keyed my locks to let him come for me again? What about when this tension between us cracked and I stopped holding back? It had been weeks of near-casual touches, lingering looks, whispered insinuations and I was sick of feeling my own fingers between my thighs while relishing the memory of his cock.

It had been reckless and stupid and liberating in a way which I was desperate to re-capture. I knew it was madness, that it was treason, that there were a thousand reasons to deny myself of this petty rebellion and just give in to the fate Dragor had picked out for me but that didn't stop me wanting it.

"Are you afraid?" I taunted.

"Have you heard from the prince?" Cayde shot back.

My silence spoke for me and he withdrew.

"Not about you. He doesn't know."

Cayde moved to my desk and poured himself a measure of whiskey, knocking it back in a brutal hit.

"What did he say?" he asked as I made use of his distraction and tossed the bathing suit Everest had made for me behind my armoire.

"Nothing of importance."

"Show me the letter."

"No." I folded my arms and his expression softened, his eyes finding me in the darkened room.

"I'm afraid for you, Vesper. If we keep going in this direction then the prince will find out. I don't care what he might do to me but I need you. I can't lose you."

"Nothing to lose if you don't claim me in the first place," I countered.

Cayde looked at me and I could taste his lust in the air between us. This was ending one way and we both knew it. He hadn't come looking for me in the dead of night just to tell me we couldn't do this again. He'd come because he couldn't resist any longer.

"Where were you tonight?" he asked.

"Jealous?" I deflected. "I'm not yours to feel that over."

"Aren't you? Perhaps I haven't been clear enough then," he growled.

"Certainly not while you're standing on the other side of the room," I agreed.

Cayde looked at me, his desire rioting in the space between us and I bit down on my bottom lip as I waited for him to crack. He'd come this far. Weeks of this secret hanging between us, knowing it was still ours, that it could be ours again if only we dared risk it.

His attention moved to the mess of notes and letters on my desk and I straightened as he reached out and grabbed one, lifting it to read.

"What are you doing?" I demanded, my voice like ice.

"Is this a love letter to me?" he asked curiously before starting to read it. "Your cock is the biggest that I've ever seen, when I think of your body it feels like a dream-"

A surprised laugh spilled from my lips and he lifted his head from the letter which definitely said nothing of the sort, surprise marring his honeyed eyes.

"Are you...happy?"

"Oh fuck off. I don't do happy," I grumbled, making it to him and reaching for the letter. He deftly lifted it out of my reach but I lunged for it all the same, knocking him back into the desk and scattering everything which had been on it all over the floor.

"You're cleaning that up," I snarled but his mouth was on mine before I could make more of a complaint.

My ass hit the desk, his fingers biting into my flesh as he pushed me onto it, any pretence about what he was here for falling away as I moved myself back and made room for him to step between my thighs.

The letter he'd been holding tumbled to the floor with the rest of them as my lips parted for his tongue, our hands roaming in a frantic race to tear the clothes from each other with the most haste.

I yanked his jacket open, releasing the buckles on his shoulders where the material had joins to allow for his wings. It fell from him and I shoved his head back so that I could drop my mouth to his chest, licking and kissing my way across his sculpted muscles.

Cayde groaned, his head tipping back as he knotted his fingers in my hair and guided me lower. "Fuck, I want you on your knees for me," he panted, his words punctuated by a mental image of me beneath him, my lips wrapped around his cock as I brought him to ruin. I could sense how much he desired that power over me and I breathed a laugh against his skin.

"Still trying to conquer me, Cayde?" I taunted, pushing him back and shoving to my feet.

He conceded, backing up towards my bed, the two of us throwing a look towards the windows as we drew closer to them as if we imagined there might be someone out there to see us. It was supremely unlikely in this frozen tundra at the top of a tower but never impossible so I flicked my fingers at the shutters, slamming them firmly to negate the threat.

"This is going to get me killed," he muttered, not stalling for a second, dragging me with him towards the bed, and unbuckling his pants as he went.

"Backing out?" I asked, finishing the work of unfastening my jacket and shrugging out of it, my shirt following swiftly behind so that I was left topless before him.

"Never," he replied, eyes on my body.

I reached for his hand, lifting it to my mouth before biting down on the pad of his thumb. Cayde hissed, jerking his hand free and then fisting it in my hair, his eyes darkening with lust.

"On your knees, sweetheart," he commanded and I gave him a petulant smile before obeying, letting him have what he was desperate to claim from me and sinking to my knees before him.

Cayde shoved his pants down far enough to free his rigid cock and I leaned forward to run my tongue up the length of his shaft.

He cursed, both hands now knotting in my hair as he pulled me closer.

I wrapped my lips around his cock, making him groan with deep satisfaction as I took the full length of him into my mouth.

He drove his hips forward into the motion and I gripped his ass, my fingernails marking crescents into the firm flesh as he fucked my mouth and I moaned around the length of him.

His muscles tightened as I took control of him, my tongue flicking and working him, bringing him to the edge. My gifts thickened the air around us, the desire between us only growing more potent with it,

My flesh burned with need, the ache between my thighs desperate for relief and I moaned around his shaft, taking him closer to oblivion.

With a feral groan Cayde jerked back, hauling me into his arms and kissing me hard before turning me around and shoving me up against the wall.

The rough stone grazed my aching nipples and I hissed at him to hurry up as he wound his arms around me and he fought with the buckle on my belt. I leaned back against the solid plane of his chest, the heat of his flesh a heady contrast to the cold stone. Cayde kissed my neck, his fingers fumbling my belt buckle and I shoved his hands aside, jerking it off for him. My concealed dagger thumped to the floor as he dropped to his knees to drag my trousers off of me and a throaty moan spilled from my lips while I obligingly stepped free of them along with my boots.

I made a move to turn around but his hand pressed to the base of my spine, forcing me against the stone.

"Open your legs," he growled, his free hand roaming up the

inside of my ankle then passing my knee and trailing up to my soaked entrance where he groaned with approval as he began to toy with me.

"I should have done this sooner," he lamented, teasing me with his fingers, his other hand still pressed to my spine, holding me against the wall. "I should have seen that this was so much better than fighting you. So fucking sweet it hurts." He pushed two fingers into me and I moaned roughly, my palms pressing to the icy stone of the wall as I braced myself against it. "I love having you like this, bending you to my will, watching you fall for me with every touch, every word. Tell me, Vesper, are you mine?"

"I'm yours in the shadows," I panted, his fingers driving in and out of me, his thumb sweeping over my clit. "The only place that counts."

"Our secret reality," he agreed, his mouth brushing against my ass, laying kisses across my flesh before his teeth bit down hard enough to mark me.

I almost came as he drove his fingers into me with the motion, a noise of pure need escaping me which urged him to his feet.

"I can't go that long without this again," he growled in my ear and I could feel the desperation in those words, how much he had hungered for me since we had last crossed this line and how much he had fought against it, no doubt in an attempt to protect me from Dragor's wrath if he found out.

"So don't," I challenged because I didn't care if this was foolish and dangerous, possibly even lethal. Cayde had made me claim something entirely for myself for the first time in far too long. I didn't do anything for the pure pleasure of it. Every choice had a purpose until him, but this was pure, carnal, want and I hungered for more of it.

I turned around, pushing him back towards the bed and shoving him down onto it, his wings splaying beneath him, before climbing on top of him. Cayde's hands grasped my thighs, pushing them further apart as I settled over his hips and guided his cock into me, a heady groan slipping from him as he sank into my wet heat.

Cayde's fingers tangled with my own and he pressed my hands to the sheets either side of us, driving his hips up as I rolled mine, the two of us working up into a rhythm which struck to release this roiling tension.

He picked up speed quickly, losing control as he slammed into me from below and I met his every thrust with a roll of my hips and a gasp of pleasure.

"More," I panted, not wanting to hold back on any part of this and he smiled darkly as he complied.

I cried out as he took hold of my hips and started fucking me furiously, like every thrust was a point to prove, his cock aiming deeper, striking harder. My hands fell to his chest, tensing against his skin as I moved to meet his rhythm, sweat rolling down my spine while I chased that ungodly release.

Cayde thrust into me harder again and suddenly we were both coming undone with groans of release, my orgasm skittering through my skin while he tensed beneath me, his grip tight as he held me in place.

I met his eyes with a satisfied grin as I took in his ruin at my design.

Cayde released his hold on my hips, his fingers skimming along my thigh before taking possession of my hand, the gentle touch at odds with our rough claiming of one another.

"I'm losing myself when it comes to you," he said, his chest rising and falling heavily. "Since the moment we met I thought you were standing between me and what I wanted but I've started to see that you're the key to it, not a barrier in my way."

"Why?"

"Because there is no bypassing you, Vesper. I stalled the moment I laid eyes on you and have been struggling to recover ever since. But this…" he lifted our entwined hands to his mouth and kissed the back of mine. "This is perfection."

Something in his expression made my skin prickle with his words, my cheeks scoring with heat as I rolled off of him and fell down on my back at his side. No one had ever looked at me the way Cayde did.

There was more to it than simple lust and the thought of that terrified me because everything about this was insane. Twice now we'd defied the rules placed around me. Twice we'd gotten away with it. What we were doing was so much more than simply fucking, and the consequences for it coming to light could be catastrophic.

But as I watched Cayde dressing himself, each item of clothing hiding that beautiful body away piece by piece I only found myself wanting more. I bit my lip against asking him to stay. We both knew he couldn't. This had been dangerous enough and risking someone noticing him leaving in the morning wasn't an option.

He hesitated by the door, his eyes roaming over my naked body where I remained in the bed and I gave him a dark smile before he left me in silence.

I drew the comforter up over me, rolling onto my side and wrapping a lock of pink hair around my finger before watching as it sprung free again. We were playing with fire, but I couldn't help relishing the burn.

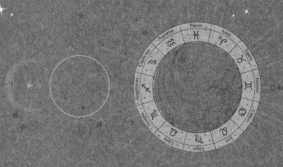

EVEREST

CHAPTER THIRTY ONE

My first completed outfit was proudly in place tonight and it would be perfect for sneaking about. My tunic was black with a snug lining that kept the chill in the air from licking my skin and I'd made golden bird wings out of velvet and lace, stitching them to the back of it, arching over my shoulder blades and down my spine.

There was golden trim on the sleeves to match and my fitted trousers paired well with the look. It was finished off with a leather skirt that strapped around my waist, hanging open at the front to reveal my trousers and hanging over my sides to conceal any weapons I wanted to carry. Which of course was my dagger of vengeance. I had plans to make some knee length boots, but I didn't have much of a skill for that yet, always having preferred the touch of my bare feet to the earth. But in this place, and out on the battlefield, bare feet wouldn't cut it.

Glances were being thrown at my new clothes from the surrounding Raincarvers in the refectory, and not all of them were sniggering at me. Some actually looked intrigued and one girl even came up to me and asked where I got them. I had been one seriously smug bitch when I'd told her I'd made them, and her eyes had widened in surprise. But when her friends had called out to her and asked why she was talking to the 'Rake reject', she'd blushed and run away like my social status was contagious. Still, I was taking it as a win. Albeit a pretty sour one.

I remained in the refectory all evening, waiting for the last of the Fae to leave, anxious to try and get through that door again. The Sky Witch had ignored my messages and without her help to reach the high passage in the sea cave, there was no point in me taking that route. Not until I perfected the cast over water which could carry me up there. And as every day I lost meant another one where I didn't know Harlon's fate, I wasn't willing to wait on her.

What we'd discovered through one of those doors had followed me into my dreams, the vivid image of that chained Dragon shifter leaving a chill in my soul. How long had it been kept there? What purpose did someone have in imprisoning it?

It seemed the Sky Witch and I had uncovered a secret that had been whispered about in the four nations since the Dragons' disappearance long before I was born. Were the Reapers responsible? Had they placed that beast there? Were there more hidden behind those other archways? And what about that strange prophecy which had been so like the one I had learned by heart in Cascada, yet so different in ways that truly mattered. It didn't point to my nation's victory. It spoke of favouring the 'peacemakers of destiny.' But who was that referring to?

Beyond all of those questions which festered in me like rot, was the possibility that Harlon could be hidden within one of those archways and sometimes my nightmares replaced the terrorised image of that Dragon with him. I saw him in chains, with those jagged green crystals lodged in his flesh and I woke gasping his name into the uncaring silence.

So now, I waited, toying with the butter knife beside my empty plate, my gaze skimming from one Fae to the next as I willed them to leave the hall. It was late and I wasn't certain exactly what time the Reapers would come to lock the doors, but I was banking on at least a few minutes alone in here before they appeared.

The room was growing quieter, the last of the Skyforgers heading out, closely followed by the remaining Raincarvers, leaving just a group of fierce-looking Stonebreakers and the infernal Flamebringers who invoked my ire.

Kaiser and North hung back as the Stonebreakers exited and North cast a silencing shield around them, his passion growing with whatever he was saying. He looked angry and if I wasn't entirely mistaken, he looked a little scared. Kaiser remained impassive as usual until North grabbed his arm and Kaiser caught him by the throat, shoving him up against the wall beside the exit.

I slid quietly beneath the table and crept forward, gathering shadows around me with a concealment spell as I watched, trying to work out what they were saying to each other. North was shouting now and Kaiser was talking back in short sentences, his facial expression flat as his friend grappled to get free of him.

Frustration burned through me at not being able to hear what they said, and as that thought crossed my mind, that strange, dark kind of magic stirred inside me. It was reaching out before I could stop it, unable to wrangle it under my control, but out of nowhere North's silencing shield shattered and his voice boomed out for me to hear.

Hia kaské.

"-either she set you a mission in secret and didn't have the courtesy to let me in on it, or you're up to something that could jeopardise her," he accused.

"I'd never jeopardise her," Kaiser said in a low tone.

"Then why are you sneaking around the Keep? What are you doing when you disappear at night?"

"My word is my bond."

"Your word to who?" North spat.

Kaiser said nothing but he lowered his hand from North's throat. The Werewolf lunged, gripping Kaiser's arms with affection instead of anger, his tone softening.

"We're brothers, you and I. Orphans raised by the same hands. She loves us equally, trusts us implicitly. Why am I not privy to this information if she set you some task?"

"Because your mouth runs away with you, North," Kaiser said plainly. "What I am doing cannot reach the ears of our enemies. I will not see your throat slit for this."

"By who?" North pressed. "The Stonebreakers? The Skyforgers? Who Kaiser? Who am I at risk from?"

"No one so long as you have no knowledge of my dealings," Kaiser answered.

North shook his head, stepping away and shoving his fingers into his brown hair. "We don't keep secrets from each other."

"I'm protecting you, North."

"I don't need protecting." North's eyes flashed dangerously. "I'm as strong as you."

Kaiser remained silent again and North scoffed irritably.

"You don't believe that, do you? You think I'm your lesser."

"Much more to the contrary, freyin," Kaiser said.

"Don't go calling me brother, you know she wants us speaking the universal tongue," North sighed.

"It was all you knew when she took you in. She understands its meaning to you - as do I," Kaiser said.

"Well fuck you for warming my heart." North smiled and it was a roguish thing. He was handsome in a carefree way, the effort put into his appearance minimal, but I doubted he needed to bother when those dimples and inviting green eyes did the work for him. Not that I could ever find a Flamebringer truly attractive.

"Anyway, what did you mean 'much more to the contrary'?" he demanded. "You're her favourite. You always have been."

"I will do what others will not and it does not leave a mark on my soul," Kaiser said darkly and my upper lip curled as my gaze slid over his villainous features, his looks like poison dipped in honey. One taste and your fate was sealed. "The Matriarch sets me the tasks that she knows will hurt the others. That would hurt *you*, in time. It has nothing to do with favourites."

"I can handle anything you can handle," North insisted.

"You have a life to make for yourself, freyin, that's what she wants for you. It's why she protects you. But I am what I am," Kaiser said. "A weapon, nothing more. She understands that. There is no future for me but one written in blood. I do not feel regret, I do not suffer in the wake of any atrocity I commit."

"We are all her weapons," North muttered, and I caught a subtle tone of bitterness.

"She loves you," Kaiser stated.

"She loves you more."

"North," Kaiser said, stepping closer to him. "There is not an ounce of truth to that. I would not waste my time on petty lies. What use would it serve me? The Matriarch fears losing you. All of you. But she knows what must be done, and if one of us must be sacrificed to this task, let it be the one without a heart."

"Kai," North sighed, gripping his friend's arm. "You have a heart. You care for me, don't you?"

"You're my brother," Kaiser answered hollowly, those words sounding rehearsed more than true but North smiled, taking them as an affirmation.

"Alright, keep your secrets, asshole," North said, a wicked grin spreading across his lips. "We'd better get going. We need to slip out of Never Keep before the Reapers-" He stalled, glancing around him, suddenly on edge. "Shit, my silencing shield is gone. I didn't think I lost concentration."

"It seems you did," Kaiser commented.

North pursed his lips before casting another one and the two them headed to the exit.

I hesitated, glancing at the wall where the hidden door might lead me to Harlon if only I could find a way to get through it again. But something was telling me to follow the Flamebringers. They were up to something, headed out of the Keep, and they didn't want the Reapers to know about it.

Plus, if Kaiser was headed somewhere out the boundaries of Never Keep, didn't that make his death fair game? I'd been training myself ragged since my last encounter with him, the memory of his rage still a thing that crossed my mind daily. I knew he was a formidable opponent and I knew what I was risking in pursuing this fight. But no part of me could let go of it. My mama was owed this. I would avenge her, no matter how much of my own blood I spilled in the process.

I was torn as I looked from the wall to the open wooden doors they had exited through. But despite my burning need for vengeance and the hunger in my soul for Kaiser's death, I had to find the man who meant more to me than that.

I hurried to the wall, scouring it until I was certain I'd found the hidden door, but before I could begin using my magic to try and open it, footsteps sounded from the corridor outside the refectory.

I leapt away from the hidden door just as a Reaper swept into the room with her long gold cloak trailing out behind her.

"The refectory is closing," she called. "Please return to your Vault." Her eyes found me and I walked towards her, bowing low and muttering, "Praise to the stars," to her before making my exit.

"Praise to those who tread their destined path," her words followed me out.

Well, I guessed my choice had been made for me, and I shot a silent thanks to Scorpio, wondering if he'd laid this fateful opportunity tonight.

Blue chirruped as he stuck his head out of my bag, yawning and blinking sleepily from his nap. He'd taken to doing that, staying with me most days and snuggling up in the soft fabric I'd stuffed in there. It was meant to be used to make a scarf, but he was so enamoured with the material that I couldn't bear to take it away from him.

I thought over what I'd heard North and Kaiser discussing as I hurried past the Great Stair, seeking them out and hoping I wasn't too late to catch them. At the end of this hallway, the passages diverged in several directions and if I didn't see which one they took, I doubted I'd find them again.

Kaiser was keeping secrets from his supposed brother and it sounded like The Matriarch herself – his adopted mother - had set him the task. That meant he was up to nothing good, and in fact, it was likely part of a deadly plot against one or several of the three nations. The Matriarch was one of the most feared Fae in the four lands and her bloody reputation spoke for itself. But if this private mission Kaiser was on was something she didn't even trust her other adopted children with, what in the ocean could it be?

I reached the Heliacal Courtyard, and my heart quickened at the sight of Kaiser and North slipping down the passage that led to the Vault of Embers. Casting a silencing shield of my own, I silently followed after them, keeping a healthy distance between us while Blue moved to perch on my shoulder.

North made a quick exit out of a window and Kaiser swiftly followed. I counted to fifty before slipping after them. It was pitch dark outside, the moon just a faint glow behind a mass of clouds that were threatening more snow, but as I shifted my eyes to that of my Leopard Order, I could pick out the faint shapes of the Flamebringers shrinking into the tundra.

I concealed myself against the snowy surroundings, working my magic to blend in with the ground as I kept low and followed them across the jagged rocks that were layered with snow.

They made a path for the western cliff then walked north, further and further while I remained at their backs, keeping fifty or more paces between us at all times.

After an hour of traversing the rock and ice, I noticed the Flamebringers slowing up ahead. We were far beyond the boundaries of the Keep now on a large, flat plain of snow that was protected from the wind. High rocks towered up around this place, concealing the view back to Never Keep and to the west, a cliff dropped away towards the dark sea. The cold was biting, but my new clothes were well prepared for this place, everything I made imbued with blaze oil to fight the chill. Though I was starting to run low on the stuff and would need to get more the next time Wandershire visited.

Faelights glinted into existence, rising up above the Flamebringers and more joined them, igniting the faces of five Stonebreakers opposite them. I knew their element from the look of them, the things they wore, the ink crawling across any exposed flesh. Three men, two women, outnumbering Kaiser and North. I hurried closer to a jutting boulder, climbing up it to peer over the ledge at my enemies, tucking myself in against the snow and drawing the shadows around me with concealment spells.

"I have waited a long time to challenge the Fury who The Matriarch hails as her most vicious prodigy," a woman at the front of the Stonebreakers bayed, the clear leader of their band. She had sharp features and dark hair, a brown fur ruff hanging from her shoulders and bronze armour beneath it. "I will send your head home to her wrapped in your Werewolf's hide." She gestured to North with her sword and he growled ferally, showing a glimpse of the beast that hid within his flesh.

"Your uncle butchered one of our sisters, Raya," North spat. "We're here to settle the score."

"My uncle will butcher the rest of your abnormal family and I intend to assist him in that plight this very night. True blood relatives have a bond that The Matriarch's orphan mutts could never know the depths of," Raya called and her group muttered their agreement, banding closer to her.

"Mutts?" North spat while Kaiser remained silent, taking the measure of his opponents, unperturbed by Raya's jibes. "I'll gut you for that word alone."

"Will The Matriarch even grieve a creature that didn't come from her own womb?" Raya mused. "Pity she cannot produce heirs of her own making, her body unable to bear fine crops, so she must settle for the chaff cut from withered wheat instead."

"My mother is the greatest Fae in the four nations," North snarled. "I'll slice your tongue from your mouth for speaking of her that way. She is a force of hellfire and she has instilled that very fire in us. Her children, her beasts, her finest warriors."

Kaiser shed the leather jacket from his shoulders, letting it fall in the snow behind him without taking his eyes off of his enemies. Beneath was a fitted white shirt that was short in the sleeves, revealing the thick muscles of his arms and the intricate design of a flock of magpies curling up his left one. Rings of teeth-marks were scarred on both of his arms just like the one I'd glimpsed on his side, the amber glow of the Faelights just brightening them enough to notice. He didn't unsheathe either of the swords at his hips, waiting patiently for the showboating to end, seeming unbothered as to when the fight might begin. It was clear he wasn't bothered by the cold, the fire in his veins keeping him warm just as all the Flamebringers were capable of. An enviable gift, I had to admit. Not even my blaze oil could truly banish the cold, but they were entirely immune to it. At least until their magic ran out.

"Ha," Raya scoffed at North. "You're fodder for the war. She's smart enough to brainwash you into serving her, adorning you with her name so you truly believe you are her family. But plenty of her orphan stock lie in graves – if they are even given such a privilege once their bodies have served their purpose."

"Shut your filthy mouth!" North roared, and at once he shifted, tearing out of his clothes and sending his sword falling to the snow.

His Werewolf form was huge, bigger than any I'd seen before, the beastly creature standing even taller than my father's warhorse. His fur was grey with white splashes across his chest, jaw and legs and he bayed a terrible howl as he raced toward his enemies.

My heart pounded as Raya swung her sword at his neck and North narrowly avoided it, leaping to the left then snatching her arm between his jaws and throwing her across the snow. Blood splattered, painting the white red, but Raya jumped up, rushing back into the fight without giving any attention to the wound. The other four Stonebreakers ignored their leader's struggle, drawing blades and running at Kaiser as a single unit.

Still, Kaiser didn't draw his swords. He watched them as calmly as an evening tide rolling in at his feet, his brutal good looks making him resemble the beautiful effigies of the hunter of the sky, Orion.

A mere moment before the Stonebreakers collided with him, his eyes flashed red. His three blood-red Fury hounds spilled into existence in front of him, leaping at the male Stonebreakers and as I braced for the savagery of teeth ripping into them, it didn't come. Instead, the three beasts disappeared into the men as if slipping directly into their bodies.

They came to an abrupt halt, their eyes turning red as Kaiser's Fury possession took root in them. I drew in a sharp inhale as they snatched hold of the female Stonebreaker between them, driving their swords into her in unison, killing their own without hesitation.

She screamed in horror as she hit the snow between them and they finished her with wicked twists of their blades. Kaiser cocked his head a little and the three men raised their swords to their own throats.

One of them whimpered in fear, another managing to cry out before the Fury forced them to swipe their own blades across their necks. I gritted my teeth, forcing myself to watch as they slumped to the snow, bleeding out at Kaiser's feet. And he hadn't even raised a single hand, hadn't taken one step forward to engage them.

He stood there without a drop of blood tarnishing him and he released a low whistle that called out to the Fury hounds, making them retreat from the bodies of the Stonebreakers and move to stand at his side. He petted their heads wordlessly then they disappeared as if they had never existed at all. Shock rolled through me at how easily death had been delivered by his mind alone, how he had shattered through the mental shields of those Stonebreakers within seconds and it had cost him no effort. No strain at all.

North pinned Raya beneath him and with a violent snap of his jaws, her cries fell quiet, blood pouring across the snow. He padded away, revealing her on the ground, her throat torn open and the furious look in her fading eyes. She choked on her own blood and the sword slipped from her fingers to lay uselessly out of reach.

My pulse thundered in my ears as North padded back to Kaiser, yapping his victory.

Kaiser raised a hand to briefly pet North's flank. "Head back to the Keep. I'll deal with the bodies and the remains of your clothes. You need to wash that blood off before you're seen."

North quickly licked Kaiser's cheek then picked up his sword between his teeth and raced off across the snow. I tucked myself in tight against the boulder, thickening the concealment spells around me as the giant Wolf went tearing by.

He didn't look my way though, and I watched as Kaiser started hauling the bodies towards the cliff edge with far too much ease, tossing them down into the hungry ocean, his hands only ever touching their clothes so they remained clean of blood.

I shimmied backwards down the boulder and prepared to make my escape. After what I'd seen him do, I knew I wasn't ready to face him. I had to ensure my mental shields were iron clad before I came head-to-head with him again. Because if he got possession of me, it was game over.

Blue nuzzled my neck, chirruping happily, unaware of the danger that lurked close by as I made a quick passage across the snow, rounding one of the hulking lumps of rock and setting my gaze on the faraway shadow of Never Keep in the distance. The wind was picking up, sweeping the snow around in great swirls and it would cover my tracks quick enough.

My mind kept replaying the moment those Stonebreakers had killed their own then turned their blades on themselves, the horror in their eyes speaking a thousand fear-fuelled words. Kaiser Brimtheon had caused a massacre without unsheathing a single blade and my heart was thumping erratically at what I now knew him to be capable of. I'd known he was strong, but this? It was terrifying.

I vowed to learn all I could about Furies and their weaknesses before I faced him again, but as my mind latched onto the warmth of a fire in my quarters, a cold and dreadful voice dripped over me from behind.

"I think it would be unwise of me to let an enemy spy run from me twice," Kaiser growled.

I twisted around, unsheathing my dagger in a flash, raising it in my left hand while jagged shards of frost grew against my right palm in warning.

"Stay back," I hissed venomously, mustering all of my hatred into those words.

He kept walking, his dominating form making me look up at him and his eyes flashed red in the dark, promising my end. I ducked low, slashing my dagger at his legs, but his boot came up and he kicked me square in the chest, sending me crashing away through the snow. I hit the jagged mound of rock that jutted up from the earth and one glance back showed me a gap I would just about fit into. I darted into it as he approached, crawling all the way to the back of it and rising to my feet.

He rested his hand to the rock, gazing in at me, his head tilting as he assessed me. He was too big to follow me in here, but that didn't mean I was any less trapped.

"Come here or I will set a fire that burns you out of there," he commanded, his fierce tone echoing through the rocks right into my soul.

"I will come out, but only if you agree to a fight. No Orders, just blades," I called, knowing it was insanity to ask it, but it looked like I was in the land of entirely fucked anyway. Might as well go down swinging.

Blue grunted in my ear like he was passing judgement on my madness.

"You're trying to bargain with me. What leverage do you possibly think you have? You have followed me to your death, silka la vin, and I doubt you told a soul at the Keep that you are here."

"Plenty of people know I'm here actually," I said fiercely.

"Liar. You hold no company. You slink in the shadows, going unnoticed, yet you dress to the contrary. A walking paradox. I know the cut of you, it is so glaringly obvious and tiresomely dull."

"And yet you noticed, and watched and made your assessment of me all the same," I growled, rage curling around my voice, fuelled by my utter hatred of this man. "So you must think I am a worthy opponent."

"Opponent," he echoed dismissively, shaking his head. "You are hardly that. You're just a rat that needs gutting."

"So I am worthy of a fight then?" I pushed.

"An extermination, nothing more."

"I demand more," I snarled.

"I am commanded by one woman and one woman only in this world. It is not you, and nor shall it ever be."

"I think those Stonebreakers had a point," I said lightly, though my heart was thrashing like it wanted to escape the confines of my chest. "The Matriarch has her claws in you so deep that you're just a mindless pawn serving a callous queen. She probably doesn't think of you beyond the victories you claim in her name."

I was aiming for a wound that might be there, hoping he would fight me on those words and be goaded into a duel with me. But as usual, he was unmoved.

"What is your Order?" he changed direction. "Speak it and perhaps I'll make your death swifter than I would prefer."

"Now who's driving bargains?" I scoffed.

"I have leverage, you do not." Fire crackled in his palms and he willed it into the narrow gap in the rockface, the flames blazing a path towards me then halting close to my feet. The heat was immediately stifling, the smoke filling up the small space fast.

"Out. Now," he commanded in that all-powerful tone of his.

"You want to know what magic I used on you last time, don't you? That's why you want to know my Order." I fought against a splutter as the smoke seeped into my throat, then sent a blast of water at the flames.

I doused them quickly, but he only cast more, letting them race along the walls and close in on me again. I swallowed them up with swathes of frost, sending it out in all directions to keep the fire at bay.

"Clever little cat. Now come here or I will send my hounds in after you." Terror knotted in my chest at the memory of those creatures taking me hostage, forcing me to relive my mother's death. The moment I felt it, Kaiser did too, drinking it in and letting it feed his magical power while stealing away mine.

"Mama-eskar," I hissed. *Motherfucker.*

"Your filthy mouth won't save you, silka la vin."

"You're under the impression that I don't have a back-up plan," I growled, sure that little nickname he had for me was nothing sweet.

"And there she goes, lying again. This has gone on too long." He sent a barrage of flames at me, but I cast lashes of water at his back, driving it up from the ground behind him and making them yank him down to the earth.

The second he hit the ground, I ran out of the narrow cave, leaping over the flames, landing on his chest heavily and kicking him in the face as I raced for freedom. His hand flew up, catching my ankle and I hit the ground hard, sending Blue flying from my shoulder to tumble away across the snow.

Adrenaline seared my veins as I kicked out, trying to get Kaiser's hand off of me, but he dragged me towards him with such force that there was no chance of escape. He flipped me over onto my back, his hands banding tight around my legs as he dragged me ever closer, reeling me in for slaughter.

His eyes flashed red and I knew what was coming, the seconds of my life ticking by with a screaming knowledge that they might just be my last. He was about to unleash his Order, about to grip me in his possession and end me as surely as he had ended those Stonebreakers.

I pushed my right hand into the snow, my connection to water spreading out all around me, reaching, tugging, trying to gather it all up to launch at him-

I felt a layer of ice beneath us, thick and near-impenetrable, arching over what seemed to be empty space.

Instead of fighting Kaiser off, I let him rear over me, let him grab my tunic in his fist and tug me up to face the wrath of the burning hot glow of his eyes. But really what I was doing was cracking the ice beneath us, shattering it all at once. With a rending, groaning roar, it collapsed and I cast a tether of water to catch me, hauling me away from him as he went crashing down into a pitch black cavern.

Breathless, I shoved myself to my feet, backing away from the gaping hole as ice and snow continued to cascade into the abyss. There was no sign of him, no sound, no hints of life at all. That fall had to be deadly, and as I peered into the gloom, waiting for a flash of fire to prove he was alive, hope rose in my chest.

Nothing.

I cast a Faelight in my hand, guiding it down into the endless cavern, falling, falling away lower and lower to where his face-down body lay. Kaiser didn't twitch, he didn't move at all, but he had to be dead. There was no glimpse of life in him.

Blue crept towards the ledge, blinking down at the corpse of my enemy below, letting out a low chirrup.

"I did it," I breathed, then joy exploded through my chest and I whipped Blue into the air, kissing him on the head. "I killed him!"

Movement in the chasm made me stall, shattering my dreams so very quickly. I lowered my hand while Blue remained perched in it, looking back down into the hole, my chest tightening as I found Kaiser rising to his feet. He glared up at me, and my Faelight picked out a glint of blood-red armour shining on his skin, some extension of his Order form clearly having saved him from that fall.

He strode towards the wall and started climbing, his gaze fixed on me and death pouring from his eyes. Eyes that were darkest red, staring into my soul and trying to tear through my mental shields so he could get possession of me.

I battled to keep him out of my head, stumbling away from the edge of the pit with a gasp, hesitating for one final second before running the fuck away. He was a beast set on ripping me to pieces and there would be no more games; if he caught me again, I would breathe the last of my breaths with his possession taking grip of me. He would claim me completely and make me suffer before he destroyed me.

I was used to fleeing, running from Ransom and his friends, but never in all my life had I felt so certain that if I slipped just once, my death was indisputable.

The slippery, snow-covered rocks and uneven ground made it hard to keep my footing, but I didn't slow, didn't dare hesitate as I fled across the frozen ground while Blue flew along by my ear.

One glance back sent my pulse into a tailspin. Kaiser was already heaving himself out of the chasm, rising up and fixing his gaze on me across the land.

Blue made a clicking noise at me that sounded like encouragement, like he knew what would happen if the wraith at my back caught me.

I ran until my lungs were burning, my thighs were screaming, and my heart was fit to burst.

Finally, I turned into the wide expanse of land between the Vault of Sky and Vault of Frost, aiming for my Vault and praying to Pisces that I could find an unlocked window.

I glanced back again, not seeing him, but that somehow only set me more on edge. My heart hammered as I made it to the first line of windows, figuring I'd just smash one if I had to, but on the third try, one swung open and I all but fell inside, hitting the flagstones hard and finding myself in a darkened latrine.

I shoved the window shut, locking it fast and staring out into the dark for half a second, seeking my purser but unable to see him. With relief scattering through me, I sprinted out of the communal latrine and made a quick path for the stairwell that led down to my quarters.

My breaths came raggedly as I arrived and hurried into the safety of my private space. Though as I shut the door and locked it tight, I had the sense that if Kaiser Brimtheon had finally decided on marking me for death, there would be no escaping. No path I could follow that wouldn't lead me to his rancour.

But as I sank down onto the furs laid out beside the fire grate, a manic kind of smile lifted my lips. Because I had just made him acknowledge me as a worthy adversary and yes, a monster he might be, but I was destined to slay him. I just had to buy myself time to learn how to kill a pestilent beast.

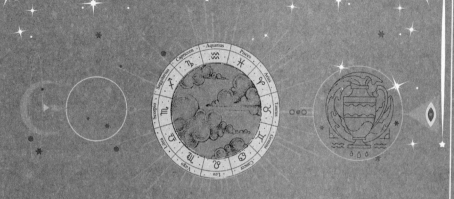

VESPER

CHAPTER THIRTY TWO

There's a legend carved into the walls of the Astral Sanctuary in Wrathbane. A place perched on a flying island all of its own, hidden in the sky surrounded by clouds and placed as close to the stars as any Fae can get. It whispers of a love so powerful it broke the world. Cracked it in two and then two again until the four continents of The Waning Lands were forged from the forgotten remnants of what came before.

It says that Layetaa, a cunning and beautiful fire born girl was due to marry Rishan, the prince of the earth lands. But one day, a foul wind caused a ship captained by the water warrior, Alrier, to wreck upon the shores of Layetaa's home.

Alrier was betrothed to Kiana, the heir of the air nation, a Fae beloved by her people for both her bravery and the sacrifices she had made for the welfare of her nation which had led to her face becoming scarred beyond recognition. Though the purity of her soul shone through all the brighter for her scars.

Layetaa took Alrier into her home under the pretence of nursing him back to health, but while she held him in her castle, she seduced and bewitched him with the treacherous nature of her fire magic. Alrier was a vain and wet minded male, easily tempted from his duty and the love of his betrothed by the cunning fire wielder, and so the two broke their betrothals and forged an alliance which defied the will of the stars themselves.

They ran from their responsibilities, stealing precious treasures from both the air and earth folk.

Rishan was a prideful man and his embarrassment over his betrothed's betrayal sparked a Great War between Avanis and Cascada. At first, those born of fire were uncertain of where to lay their alliance - should they support the selfish whims of Layetaa or hold to the promise made for her union and aid the Stonebreakers in their hunt for her?

Their procrastination cost the world more than a simple union of bloodlines. For a while they hesitated, Kiana, the heart of Stormfell urged her people of the air not to fight, but to hold true to peace and love. And in that strength of character, Layetaa and Alrier chose to see weakness which was never there.

They led an armada to attack the kingdom of the air wielders, claiming to be making the first strike in anticipation of one in return.

But they had been fooled into that belief. For there was no threat from Stormfell who believed in the teachings of their star signs and wished to follow in the ways of fairness and justice which Libra preached.

The Pyros warriors were predictably volatile, first backing the water born in their attack on air, then turning on them when Kiana tore the earth apart to save her people and launched the first of us into the sky, claiming a dominion beyond the reach of those of the inferior elements.

And so, the Skyforgers fled to save their people and The Waning Lands were changed for the first time. The Flamebringers took brutal damage at the wrath of the Stonebreakers and they sent an assassin to buy back peace with Layetaa's death.

But all that the head of the seductress bought them was war with Alrier who swore that every Raincarver born from that day forth would go without rest until they saw both Avanis and Pyros destroyed for the death of his beloved.

Earth blamed Fire for this response and Fire called Earth ungrateful. All while the people of Stormfell watched the world tear itself apart and created a sanctuary in the sky, coming to realise that peace would only ever return if they themselves won the war which would one day become known as Endless.

Eventually, the laws came to pass. No wielder of earth, sky, flame or flood should ever merge their blood with one who wasn't born of their element. And with the rise of the Reapers came the Elysium Prophecy, speaking of the day when peace might come at last on the wings of the Skyforgers who fought so valiantly to return the world to order.

I'd never understood why a story of love and betrayal could be so devastating as to start a war, but with the secret of my own duplicity hanging over me, I was starting to understand the weight such actions carried. And perhaps even realise why Fae fell into the trap of them anyway.

I just needed to make sure that Cayde and I remained secret.

Though from the pointed looks and muttered jibes I was enduring, I was fairly certain Moraine and Dalia knew. But the suspicions couldn't go beyond them.

The Sinfair were marked for war in a way that none of the other conscripts in this place were. Only the air kingdom doled out this label to the children born to shame, offering a chance at redemption through acts of valour and bloodshed.

That being the case, only the sixty or so of us from the Vault of Sky who had been branded Sinfair for the crimes of our bloodlines were actual soldiers in the war already. Every other conscript in this place had only been subjected to battle training of whatever variety their nation required during their lives so far.

None of them had actually seen war unless it happened to fall upon their doorsteps and had forced them into action. Regardless, they were never deployed, never spent years travelling away from their homeland, never slipped into the countries of their enemies and hunted prey in unfamiliar lands. I'd done all of that and more in the seven years since my service had started at fourteen years of age.

So when the call came for the Sinfair to join the warring forces at Rifarn where reinforcements were required to bolster our army, I wasn't surprised by it. I wasn't fool enough to believe that our training at Never Keep would shield us from being called out. But the looks on the faces of every Raincarver, Flamebringer and Stonebreaker we passed as we marched through the Heliacal Courtyard said they sure as shit were surprised.

I led the line with Dalia and Moraine on my left, Cayde on my right, his wings casting me in shadow, and making a chill cling to my skin. We were armed to the teeth, swords strapped at our waists, bows on our backs, lines of daggers hanging from belts. The other conscripts openly gawped at us as we strode through the ambling groups who had been enjoying an hour of free time before elemental training began.

The Night Gate loomed ahead of us, darkness clinging to it, bathing the space around it in shadow.

A Flamebringer lurched free of his group, moving into our way and spitting on the stones before us.

We fell still as one and I arched a brow at him, my fingers coiling around the hilt of my sword, but I didn't draw it.

"Move," I drawled. "Or you'll be as dead as those who come at me on the field today."

"My family fight at Rifarn," he growled.

"I'll be certain to send them your regards," I taunted, drawing a snigger from Dalia's lips.

More of the Flamebringers moved to join the first, a ripple of tension rolling through the ranks at my back, but I only sneered at the rabble of unarmed novices who thought to face us.

I didn't recognise any of them, meaning that none of them had done a single thing to take note of in the time I'd spent with them here. These were the grunts of Pyros's army, not the generals, and I wouldn't need a sword to strike a path through them.

"Enough," Reaper Tessa appeared from the Reapers' Quarters, a line of six more hooded servants of the stars following behind her as she strode into the tense space dividing us. "Never Keep is a place of learning, of devotion to the stars and sanctuary from war. The loyalties and commitments you hold outside of this place are your own business, but within the confines of the Keep, we will see no blood spilled nor battles fought. The Sinfair have made oaths to fight when called upon to do so, meaning that in times of need they are duty bound to leave the Keep and join the forces at play in the world beyond. The Flamebringers have no such arrangements with us and so have no need to be out here while they leave. Return to your Vault if you cannot control yourselves."

The Flamebringers continued to glare at us around the wall of Reapers and I took no small pleasure in watching as Reaper Tessa blasted them with air magic and sent them tumbling back towards the passage to their Vault.

I bowed my head in thanks to the Reapers as they turned to look at us and Tessa nodded her assessment of us before waving us towards the gate.

I didn't look back, though a prickling along my spine made me certain Tessa was watching us all the way to the exit. Watching me.

Could she suspect me? Memories of that chamber Everest and I had discovered rolled through me, of the iron bars and magical chains. What the fuck had we witnessed? Did Dragor know there were Dragons being held captive somewhere in his kingdom? Did the king know? Or had I stumbled upon a secret the Reapers were keeping even from the rulers of the elemental lands themselves?

I glanced at Dalia and Moraine to my left, once again wondering whether I should tell them. But there was danger to this secret, not least because we had stumbled across something we clearly weren't supposed to know about. But also because if the rest of those archways opened gateways to the other nations as I suspected, it meant that any of us could make use of them to launch an army directly into the stronghold of our enemies without a moment's notice for them to prepare.

If we marched into the hearts of their lands using those portals then the war might be won in a matter of days. It was a terrifying, exhilarating prospect and yet, if the king and the prince knew of it already, they hadn't acted. But if they didn't know then that meant the Reapers had constructed that potentially catastrophic pathway between the nations and it was only a matter of time before one of the warring lands discovered it. Whichever land that was would make use of it and very likely win this Endless War.

Could I risk holding my tongue in the hopes that the king and Dragor knew of it already and had it under control? Or should I bring this news to them immediately so that we could act upon it?

Hesitation cost lives. That was one of the first lessons I'd learned about this bloody carnage we lived among and since that day I had never waited to act upon anything. Every moment that slipped into days made a writhing knot grow in my gut, but I didn't know how to take action on this knowledge.

Worse was that Everest held it too. What if she had already written to the Raincarvers and told them about that place? What if the weapon of that knowledge had already passed on to our enemies and they were readying to use it against us?

We strode through the huge Night Gate and out onto the barren spit of land beyond it, Rackmere docked and waiting for us as before, though this time, our destination was far grimmer than the last.

A shimmer of movement caught my eye close to the summit of the Escalade which led down to Obsidian Cove, there, then gone again. Likely the wind shifting the snow across the boulders which were stacked on the beach. Then again...

I slipped out of formation, ignoring the curious looks my sisters in arms shot me as I moved away from Rackmere, leaving them to lead the rabble aboard. No one questioned me as I moved to stand at the summit of the cliff, my eyes roaming across the water below which was as petulant and grey as ever.

Air magic coiled through my fingers as I kept my gaze on the view and the sound of a low growl turned into a sharp curse as it snapped from my fingers and snared whoever had chosen to spy on us.

"Kaské."

I recognised that voice.

I released the hilt of my sword and stalked around the mound of boulders, finding a naked Everest pinned there by the cage of air magic I'd sent to snare her.

"I take it you were in your shifted form and not just out here for a nude stroll?" I mused, though honestly, I wouldn't put such habits past a Raincarver.

"And I take it you didn't know it was me before you attacked?" she hissed back.

I shrugged, releasing her from my magic and allowing her to stand. We were concealed for the most part, but I wasn't going to linger in her company while so many Fae lurked close at hand.

"Were you here for a reason or is this simply a twist of fate?" I asked.

"I needed to speak to you," she confirmed, her eyes moving warily over the many weapons I carried.

"Relax. I'm hunting Flamebringers today," I told her.

"And how long will that last?" she questioned.

"However long it takes for us to kill all of them."

"Or for you to die," she pointed out and I barked a laugh.

"You never know."

"Have you always been this…" She waved a hand at me as if uncertain of the correct word to choose.

"Confident?" I suggested.

"Arrogant," she corrected and I grinned.

"I've earned the right to be."

"Well, oh great and not-so-humble, Vikram, you can't leave. We have work to do here."

"Vikram?" I deadpanned. "You're clutching at straws now."

"Then tell me your real name or I'll settle on any V name I like. And Vageena is moving up the list."

I gave her a cool look and she offered me one right back.

"If your king called you to action would you deny him in favour of scurrying through the shadows with a Skyforger?" I asked.

"We don't have a king. We have a-"

"Semantics," I dismissed and though her jaw ticked, she dropped it.

"When will you be back?" she demanded. "I need to find-"

Everest cut herself off but there it was, the desperate need of her poor, lonely heart.

"I'm a creature who feasts on desire," I reminded her. "I see the face of your sweetheart every time you speak of discovering the secrets we chase. No need to try and hide him from me. I'm sure he's very...nice."

The word wasn't a compliment and Everest clearly didn't take it as one.

"Just don't die," she growled in command as if her will alone could prevent such a thing. "And hurry back."

She shifted into a white Leopard as if that was the final word to be had on the subject and my smile grew as I turned away from her.

"Careful, Everest. It's starting to sound like you care about me."

A feline growl came in reply, but I left her to her foray through the snow and boarded Rackmere without looking back again. Though

I was sure to stay on the edge of its cliff face until we had moved far enough from Never Keep for me to know that no Leopards could have leapt aboard. It seemed wildly unlikely that she would attempt it – what point would there be for a Raincarver to head into a battle between Fire and Air anyway – but Everest was nothing if not unpredictable. Yet another thing for me to fret over.

Rackmere set a fast pace towards Rifarn. It would have been five hours on a battle island like Ironwraith, but we were set to do it in two.

The incredible velocity had some of the Sinfair puking into buckets at the rear of the underground cabin. But I felt nothing but exhilaration as I stood by the window hidden within the underside of the island, looking out at the landscape of fire beneath us as we hurtled over it.

"Ten minutes to arrival," General Imona called from behind me but I didn't turn – I'd just spotted a riot of fire in the distance which marked the point of the battlefield. "We're close to victory already. You have been called to bolster numbers and nothing else. Prince Dragor's unit is closing in around the Tower of Nor where a prominent military target has gone to ground. Your only objective is to assist in the conquest of that tower. You are bodies in this battle. Not brains. So don't deviate from your commands."

I knew her eyes were on me, but I continued to watch the view ahead of us, movement on the wide and endless plains capturing my attention from below. The land of Pyros was lush with greenery thanks to the rich soil that was fed by the volcanic ash which was regularly scattered across the earth from the eruptions to the north.

The mounts of the deadliest volcanos in Pyros ringed the horizon in that direction, marking a barrier to the hollow basin where The Matriarch resided in her city of corruption. I wondered if she would be present on the battlefield today, her reputation a thing of savagery that sparked a curiosity in me which I couldn't deny.

An illusion fell apart beneath us, ten catapults already loaded with enormous flaming projectiles all firing at once, their target the small spit of land we all rode towards the battle and nothing more.

"Brace!" I bellowed, whirling around and knocking Moraine and Dalia away from the window, the three of us tumbling across the floor and grabbing hold of the metal bedframe bolted to the floor closest to us.

There was a flurry of movement as the Fae filling the belly of the island all dove to do the same, but the impact came almost instantly.

The world erupted around us, an explosion of noise ripping through the island, flames heating the space so violently that it felt like the whole world was on fire. I couldn't breathe for the intensity of it, my world narrowing to the place where I clutched the bedframe with a death grip.

Everything pitched wildly to the left, my legs swinging across the ground as Rackmere tumbled from the sky.

"Bail!" I roared as the flames stuttered out, revealing huge holes torn through the underbelly of the island, gaping patches of nothing where there had been bunks and warriors before.

I had no attention to spare beyond hunting for the three people closest to me aboard this doomed projectile and my heart raced in panic for several seconds before I spotted them.

Dalia and Moraine were scrambling upright beside me. Cayde was clinging to the wall next to one of the enormous holes through which the wind was now billowing relentlessly.

"Jump!" I ordered, grabbing Moraine's arm and shoving her ahead of me.

She sprinted for the closest hole where the ground outside was rushing closer with every passing heartbeat. We had to get outside and out from beneath the falling island before it hit the ground too.

Moraine shifted as she ran, her stunning silver wings erupting from her spine before she dove out into the air beyond our doomed island.

Dalia was at my side, the two of us sprinting for the jagged hole as one. Cayde met my eyes, nodding once before throwing himself out and taking to the sky on his wings too.

I cursed myself for not having brought my Windrider, knowing I could have moved thorough the sky more seamlessly on it but having expected to fight with my boots on the ground for the most part in this battle. I knew better than to rely on plans coming together.

Dalia whooped like a banshee as we leapt out of the hole in Rackmere's belly, hand in hand, wind tearing through our hair, adrenaline coursing through our veins.

My magic snatched us in its grasp, launching us out from beneath the falling island at a ferocious speed, our momentum forcing us to close in on the grassy plain below. My toes brushed the grass, Rackmere's shadow consuming us, but with a final jolt of motion, we were launched free of the crash site.

The resounding boom of our island hitting the ground made my skull rattle. A great wave of dust and debris exploded out from it and launched us even further away as we rode the wave of power back up into the sky.

I lost my grip on Dalia, her own magic taking hold of her as we were tossed aside by the blast, lost in a cloud of dirt.

I twisted my wrists, launching myself skyward on a plume of air magic, needing to get above the dirt and regain my view of the landscape and the enemies who were no doubt closing in.

I threw myself over the wreckage of Rackmere, speeding towards my best estimate of where those catapults had been and drawing my sword.

Flames blazed within the cloud of dust below and I dropped from the sky like a stone, catching myself at the last moment before landing lightly on the ground.

I dove towards the flames, casting air around me so that I opened passageways of sight through the cloud of dust.

A Flamebringer was revealed, fire blasting from him as he saw me, but my sword sailed straight through it, catching him in the chest and sending him to the ground.

I ran for him, snatching my sword from his corpse and lunging towards the Fae who stood around him. Four came at me at once and I threw the cloud of dust at them, blinding them while using an enhancing spell on my sense of hearing so I could track their movements in the dark.

I twisted between them, lurching from the dust and striking savagely with my sword, cutting them apart with violent swings of my blade then sinking into the cloud again before any of them could get a lock on me. Their screams soon gave way to silence and I launched myself into the sky once more.

Around fifty warriors had survived the crash – General Imona among them to my displeasure and she barked an order for us to advance on the distant battlefield.

Those with lower power levels broke into a race across the ground, conserving their magic for the fight ahead but I launched myself through the sky, bolstering my magic with the desire for bloodshed and glory pouring from the Fae surrounding me and hurtling towards the battle ahead of everyone else.

I spotted the Tower of Nor up ahead, its pale grey stone matching with the rest of the buildings in this small town, but its height rising far above the rest, a flat roof at its peak. I took in the scope of the battle surrounding the tower, seeing where our ranks were thinning beneath the forces of the Flamebringers where they battled for the upper hand.

Cayde raced after me, making it to my side with the power of his wings and grinning darkly at me before we threw ourselves into the dance of war.

Cries went up as we landed in the midst of the mele, Flamebringers screaming about the Sky Witch and begging for reinforcements.

The Sinfair were brutal in our attack, most of us all too familiar with the cost of our place in this war and all of us more than willing to pay it. We fought not just for the glory for our kingdom but for the right to claim our positions within our superior nation whether that be by reclaiming titles or simply carving out a place for our own like I planned to do.

I caught sight of Prince Dragor closing in on the tower door, his imposing figure impossible to miss in his white battle leathers, even amidst the chaos of the fight.

Fire blasted all around us, battles with the Flamebringers always so volatile though when air collided with their flames we could both bolster and extinguish them as suited our needs.

Cayde fell into place beside me, the two of us fighting seamlessly together, Fae falling all around us, blood splattering our clothes, our skin, our blades.

I lost myself in the fury of the fight, the rush of death surrounding me on all sides and the powerful movements of the man who battled beside me.

The crash of the tower door falling to our assault hailed like a victory, the screams of those inside ringing out over my own opponents' as they fell to the wrath of our prince.

When the last of our opponents fell before us, I had to shake the rush of battle from my limbs, my chest rising and falling to a ragged crescendo, my body alight with feral energy.

Cayde met my gaze, the lust in his expression clear and I took a single step towards him before remembering where we were.

I turned to face the tower as Prince Dragor stepped out of its broken doors, the head of his target clutched in his fist, blood spattering his white leathers and his feral gaze falling straight on me.

He said nothing as the cries of victory echoed out across the battlefield and the remainder of our enemy turned to retreat. He still said nothing as he tossed the head of his kill to the ground and strode away to board Ironwraith as though he hadn't seen me at all. But as he passed by close enough to touch me, I felt a stirring in the air, the sensation of a hand curling around my throat and the illusion of his breath against my ear.

"Do not forget your promise, Vesper."

And then he was gone.

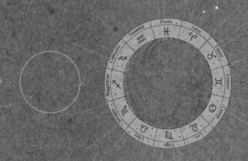

EVEREST

CHAPTER THIRTY THREE

I'd made several attempts at breaking through the hidden door in the refectory either just before the doors were closed at night or just after they opened at dawn, but I'd eventually had to accept, it was sealed tight with magic and I couldn't get through.

That left the path through the sea cave, and since the Sky Witch had returned from battle, she had gone back to ignoring my summons. It wasn't like I wanted to ask for help, in fact, doing so was starting to leave a bitter taste on my tongue. Especially with her continued refusals. So at every opportunity, I practised the cast on water I'd need to make the ascent into that high up tunnel in the underground caverns.

So far, the highest I'd gotten was around twenty feet before I'd lost my grip on the cast and had fallen down into the unforgiving ocean beyond the shore of Obsidian Cove. I was yet to make a new tiderunner to ride the waves, but the more time I spent in the wild waters out there, the more I realised I didn't need one anymore.

I could tame the waves and guide the swell beneath my feet, riding the frantic tide to shore. I might have been used to calmer waters, but I was growing fond of the ocean's temper here. And with the bathing suit I'd made to keep out the cold, there was little to fear out there now. Except perhaps the rumours of beasts and sea serpents writhing in the ocean's depths.

Today, I couldn't spend my food break out practising though, because Wandershire was set to return and I had a debt to pay.

I gathered up the blades I'd forged for Mavus and wrapped them in sheathes of leather, then I stacked the ten sets of gloves in my pack before making my way to Obsidian Cove.

Wandershire was waiting for me, the curved metal legs supporting the town digging deep into the black sand and delving into the murky abyss of the ocean at its furthest point. Plenty of neophytes were already onboard and I made a quick ascent up the stone steps and headed for the belltower at the centre of the town.

The door at the bottom was open, so I headed up the winding stairs to the entrance to Mavus's bureau, rapping my knuckles on the door.

"Enter," he called and I twisted the handle, pushing into the room and finding him standing by the window, buttoning up his yellow trousers. A man scrambled to his feet from his knees before him, glancing back at me with a blush lining his cheeks.

"Come back in an hour, Lucian," Mavus purred, scruffing the guy's dark hair. "Bring your wife too."

Lucian smiled, nodding and heading for the exit.

I tossed my selection of blades down onto Mavus's desk with a clatter the second he left.

"I'm going to choose to ignore the fact that you just finished getting your cock sucked and focus on business," I said lightly.

"Probably for the best, doll." He smirked, then looked me up and down, taking in the outfit I'd finished in the early hours of this morning. "Would ya look at you?"

I raised my chin a little higher as his dark blue eyes tracked over the gothic style navy overcoat I'd made, a pattern of silver fish scales on the shoulders and silver buttons to match. As I opened the long coat and tossed it onto a chair, Mavus let out an exhale as he took in my outfit underneath.

"Do me a twirl," he encouraged and I couldn't help soak up the attention as I did a slow spin for him.

The dress was no pretty thing made for dances and being courted, it was both practical, comfortable and – if I did say so myself - fucking striking. It was darkest green with a golden breast plate made into the shape of the bodice that fit me like a glove, yet was supple, allowing ease of movement. It was detailed with an emblem of the sun, its rays spilling down onto the symbols of Pisces, Scorpio and Cancer beneath it.

The skirt split at the front so I could wear matching trousers beneath, as was fast becoming my new favourite style, and there were plenty of concealed pockets and hidden sheaths for as many blades as I could possibly wish to carry.

"That's something, real something, lass," Mavus cooed. "The craftmanship, the colour, the detail. Fuck me, I think I'm getting hard for a dress."

I pursed my lips at him and he chuckled, proving he was joking and a smile tilted my lips.

"I still need new boots." I gestured to the old combat boots on my feet that were pretty scuffed up.

"Take any you like from me stores," he encouraged. "Assuming you have kept up your part of the deal?" His eyes moved to the blades on the table which were concealed by their leather sheathes.

"I'd prefer to make them, but I'm not much of a cobbler."

"I have no doubt that you'll figure it out, lass." He moved to a large green armchair, picking up a curling wooden pipe on a table beside it, and I couldn't help but revel in the faith he had in me.

Mavus struck a match and lit the dark substance in the pipe, puffing on the end of it and releasing a long line of smoke from his lips. "So what have you got for me? All the items I requested, I hope, or there'll just be the small matter of me ripping your soul from your body and keeping it in a jar forevermore."

"What?" I gasped and he boomed a laugh.

"A joke, lass. Just a little joke between friends. Come now, let's see what you've made for me. I'm dying of anticipation."

The scent of the smoke filling the air had a sweet kind of tang to it, notes of tobacco underlining it, but it was definitely more than just that.

I unfurled the leather sheath that held a cutlass, showing it to him and he curled a ringed finger to beckon me closer. I walked over to him, brandishing it in front of him and pointing it right at his heart. It had an amber hue and engravings of Venus in its hilt within a glittering cluster of stars, the blade made with the planet in mind. Venus represented beauty and love and this cutlass represented the darker side of those traits, like it held the soul of two lovers fated to die.

"Bless Cassiopeia," Mavus cooed. "What a deadly, pretty thing."

I smiled at the compliment, taking in the sheen of the blade, proud of what I'd forged, but when I glanced up at him, I found him looking at me, not the cutlass.

I scowled, flipping it over in my grip and offering the hilt to him. "Here."

He took it, rising to his feet with the pipe dangling from the corner of his lips as he tested the weight of it in his hand. "That'll fetch me a fair price. Have you shown me the best of your stock or are you building up to the grand finale?"

I shrugged innocently, moving back to the desk and taking out the twin Gemini swords next. They were bronze short swords which I'd made as twins of each other, half a Gemini symbol etched onto each hilt, so when brought together, they made one image.

I swung them in demonstration, carving them through the air in a lethal dance then twisting them around in my grip and offering the hilts to Mavus.

He placed his pipe in a stand shaped like a whale on the table beside his chair, laying the cutlass on the seat and taking the swords from me.

"Heavy," he commented.

"Almost pure bronze," I said with a nod.

"Almost?"

I smiled like a cat. "I tempered them with just a little ravensteel."

"That's used in construction, not blades," he scoffed.

I snatched one of the swords from his hand, launching it across the room to drive into a wooden beam on the far wall. The metal rang as it quivered, bending up and down in an undulating motion that showed the gift of the ravensteel. "It's shatterproof, and the flexibility in the metal means it can take even the fiercest of strikes. The bronze will ensure the blades do not corrode and I added a lacquer of glace oil too, making it resistant to fire."

"Bless the soil of the earth, you're making me a happy man, lass. Come now, let's see the last of them. You sure know how to edge a fella."

I unveiled the final blade, the small, wicked creation bringing another smile to my mouth. It was a sharp little combat knife which had a curved edge shaped like a crescent moon, the moon phases marked across the silver sheen of the smooth hilt. I was particularly fond of this one and it would be hard to part from it, but I wasn't about to go reneging on my deal for the sake of petty wants. Besides, I could forge myself another one once I had time.

"This is Lunalis – she was too beautiful not to name." I flicked her around in my hand, turning her between my fingers, the steel catching the sun and sending patterns of light dancing across the floorboards.

"I like her already," Mavus growled. "But she's small."

"Easily underestimated," I agreed then threw the blade with force, sending it flying past Mavus's ear, driving between the eyes of a painting of a seahorse on the wall.

Mavus turned to look at it, his eyes brightening as he tugged the knife out of the canvas.

"Stunning," he purred, turning Lunalis over in his palm and my chest expanded with his words.

"She's feather-light and the balance in the steel is so perfect that it aids precision in every throw," I explained.

"Anything else, doll?"

"She's charged with the energy of moonlight," I revealed a little smugly. "I bathed the steel in lune essence for a fortnight. Run your thumb over the moon phases and the blade will glow. If you throw it while it's glowing, your strike will be twice as powerful."

Mavus ran his thumb over the markings on the hilt and it lit up with a silver glow that reflected in his blue eyes. "I see why you left her 'til last. She's special. So special I'm almost tempted not to part with her."

"I felt the same," I admitted, and he looked at me in consideration, sharing my appreciation of fine weaponry.

He picked up his pipe, puffing on it again and moving to the desk, placing the knife on a pile of maps and blowing a coil of sweet smoke into the air. "I shouldn't be showing ya this, but I think you might be one of the few Fae I know who'll value it as I do."

He opened one of the drawers in his desk, taking out a vicious gold weapon that was curved with spikes ringing the top of it. Mavus slid his hand into a gap in the metal so the spikes sat along his knuckles. "I secured this on me last trip into the wilds. Do you know much of the Scorpius Pirates, doll?"

"They're nomads like the Vampires. They trade with them too, I've heard."

"It's a shaky alliance," Mavus agreed. "They're cutthroats mostly, seeking riches in all forms. Gold, sex, power. The usual suspects. They'd sell their own children for the right price."

"Sounds like someone I know." I gave him an accusing look and he chuckled low in his throat.

"Children's where I draw the line in me trades. There ain't nothing more innocent in this world and there are far too many evils out there waiting to corrupt 'em. I'd rather not add my name to that particular list. Anyway, as I was saying. I met in with a drove of the vicious bastards in the wilds and when I'd gutted the lot of them, I claimed myself this here prize. The rest of the loot can be found among the traders now, but this... this is special. More than what it appears."

"Knuckle dusters aren't that uncommon. What's so special about these?" I reached for the gold melee weapon, and he let me take it from his hand.

The gold was crafted well, the metal not one I preferred to work with considering its softness under pressure. But from the feel of it, this was hardened with something. Perhaps... I examined it closer, my pulse quickening.

"Dragon fire." I looked up at him in surprise, my thoughts wheeling to the Dragon the Sky Witch and I had discovered.

"Now how did a little Raincarver like you go recognising something as rare as that?" he purred, examining my expression closely.

"My mama taught me what to look for in case I ever stumbled across metal like this. That gold isn't gold anymore, it's draconia now that it's been altered with Dragon fire and likely imbued with the strength of a Dragon scale too if it's made in the ancient way."

"What else did your mama teach ya, Everest Arcadia? I'd like to meet this knowledgeable ol' biddy."

"She's not a biddy," I snarled, rage climbing through me, and his eyebrows lifted at my sudden sharpness. "And she's dead, so there's no meeting her. She was killed during a Skyforger raid over a year ago and two eskindo – *fucking* - Flamebringers snuck into our land during the distraction and set a blaze that murdered her in an acidic rain of Basilisk venom."

"Woah there, that's a lot to unpack in under a minute, doll. Let me digest that for a sec." He toked on his pipe, considering me while my heart rate slowed again.

A cloud of sweet smoke swept out around me and I wafted a hand to bat it away, pressing my lips together. "Watch where you're blowing your poison."

"Poison?" he balked, looking wounded. "This is the finest fogweed in the four nations. Premium cut with silk tobacco and-"

"And it's gross. So stop blowing it at me." I stalked to the window, shoving it open and he laughed.

"Alright, doll, I'll aim my poison elsewhere. But in the meantime, tell me more about this mama of yours. She sounds like a smart lass. I'll be betting you miss her something fierce."

I remained silent, that aching wound in my heart locked down tight beneath layers and layers of stubbornness, smothered by my refusal to let it rip open again. "I'm not here to talk about my mother. But I do have something I want to discuss with you."

"I'm all ears." He smiled that devil's smile and I once again doubted how much I could trust this Nemean Lion shifter. But he had access to potions, weapons and wares I probably didn't even know existed. So he might just be the right person to help me with the problem of my greatest enemy.

"I need to kill a Fury," I revealed, and I swear Mavus's pupils dilated like I'd just given him a hit of a drug he'd been craving.

"You do, do you?" he purred, stepping closer. "That wouldn't be Kaiser Brimtheon now, would it?"

My jaw tightened and I said nothing, but it was obvious enough. There weren't any other Furies I knew of and Kaiser's reputation as one of The Matriarch's orphan warriors had likely been of interest to this wandering Fae. Mavus no doubt picked up all the secrets of the world on the wind.

He started laughing, roaring with amusement at my expense. I snatched the silver combat knife off the table, rage bursting through my veins as I ran at him, slashing it across the side of his neck, leaving a slice in his skin that ran red in an instant. He grabbed my wrist in the next second, a vine slithering around my body and tightening like a leash as his earth magic poured out of him and his laughter turned to fury.

"You little wretch, now look what you've done." His vine snared my chest tighter then dragged me backwards, yanking me down onto the desk as thorns grew across it.

I snarled, cutting through it with Lunalis, and moving quickly onto my knees, ready to spring at him. But he was upon me in a flash, his hand gripping my tunic, throwing me flat on my back again with force, sending maps and objects flying off of it.

"You've gone and made me bleed," he seethed. "An eye for an eye, doll. I reap what others sow upon me." He snatched the silver knife from my hand, slicing a cut along my neck in the exact same place I'd marked him. "There now," he softened abruptly, stepping back and releasing me, leaving me panting on his desk. "It's best you learned this little lesson early on. A blessing really." He smiled, offering me a hand up but I shrank from it, sliding off the desk and eyeing him warily.

"Relax, lass. I don't hold grudges – well, alright, I do. But not against you. I like ya. Really. That fire in you is my favourite kind of flame, but I can't go letting ya get ideas about where you stand when it comes to me. I'm not the Mayor of Wandershire by pure chance. I'm a ruthless creature of the stars' design. A king who plays off of the chessboard, thinking outside the confines of the lines that have been drawn around him in this game of crowns and blood. My allies are the most fortunate souls in The Wandering Lands and I'm extending a hand to ya, offering you that rare position and mark my words when I tell ya, I don't offer it lightly, doll. I see you, Everest Arcadia, and I truly like what I see."

I touched the scratch on my neck, frowning at him, taking in his words. There was sense to them, I had to admit. And in light of his little power show, I found I liked him more. There weren't many Fae who looked at me at all, let alone saw the weight of my soul, but sometimes it felt like Mavus and I had a connection. Like we were cut from similar cloth.

He didn't let Fae walk over him, he delivered to them what they offered him, and I had the feeling that the same would be said of something good. A true friendship with him might just bring me advantages I couldn't dream up without him.

"Don't ever laugh at me again," I warned, pointing the silver knife at him.

"Noted," he said, etching a cross over his heart. "I swear not to make a mockery of ya twice."

"So when I say that Kaiser Brimtheon's death belongs to me, do you have anything to say to that?"

His lips twitched the slightest amount but he forcibly held back any more mirth and inclined his head. "His death is yours, lass."

I lowered the knife, placing it on the table then drawing my dagger from the concealed sheath at my hip. Reluctant as I was to open up to most Fae, I felt the need to do this. His interest in my blades and his obvious knowledge of their craft made me want this dagger to be witnessed for what it was.

"You asked me about this blade when we met," I said and he eyed it greedily.

"That I did, lass," he said.

"Well its purpose is vengeance. The name of my mother's killer is inlaid in the hilt." I showed it to him and his brows lowered as he took in Kaiser's name.

He nodded. "Well then." He wrapped his hand around mine, the roughened touch of his palm reminding me of the war-hardened men I had let ravish me between the back alleys of the taverns in Castelorain. Mavus reminded me of them sometimes, but I didn't think it was war that had made him into this twisted man of power and pride. But something had left a stain on his soul, blackening it until it matched the colour of mine. "Hunt him well, and reap from him what he sowed upon you, Everest."

I nodded as I withdrew, our eyes locking in a moment of understanding that went beyond the need for words. He had chased vengeance before, I held no doubt in that moment. And I had the feeling he might have secured it.

"So what was it you wanted to discuss about this marked Fury of yours, hm?" he asked, puffing on his pipe again.

I looked him over, from the tight golden curls of his hair that trailed over his shoulders to the bright hue of his green eyes and the sheen of his bare chest. Did I want to voice what I had been thinking of asking him? Did I really want to tread that path?

Since I'd met with Kaiser out in the tundra, I'd been careful to make sure he never found me alone. I had to keep my distance until I was prepared to face him again, because the next time we clashed, it was going to be life or death. He wouldn't be pulling punches anymore, dismissing me as someone unworthy of his swords. I would know the violence of them when we faced off once more.

"You have access to all kinds of knowledge...so I wondered if you might have a book or a secret or two stashed in that big head of yours about the weaknesses of the Fury Order."

He caressed the stubble on his chin. "Hmm, you want an advantage? I can give you an advantage." His gaze slid to the drawer that held his stash of illegal battle stims.

"No," I growled. "Not that."

"It'll unlock your mind, doll," he purred. "I've tried it myself. It's nirvana. No shackles on ya soul. No fears, no doubts, no more nightmares coiling through your mind. It'll free you from the traumas of your past and guide your feet into the most glorious of futures."

"I said no," I gritted out.

He raised his hands in innocence, letting his pipe dangle from his lips. "Alright, I meant no offence. It's just something to be considered." He strode to a bookshelf that was embedded in the wall, trailing his finger over the spines then pausing on one and tapping it. "Here." He drew it from the shelf, tossing it to me and I caught it, taking in the title.

The Intricacies of Fae.

"His Order might be detailed in there. There's many an Order discussed. And if not, it teaches games of the mind, how to spot the needs of one Fae to the next and how to push their buttons just so."

"You mean manipulate them," I said lightly, certain that was what he had used the knowledge in this book for.

He shrugged, turning to me with that roguish smile again. "I ain't the first person in the four nations to use knowledge to my advantage by a long shot, and I sure as shit won't be the last. Don't go casting judgement on me, lass."

"I'm not judging you, but I see you too Mavus," I purred, throwing back at him the same words he had spoken to me.

He barked a laugh. "You and me are the same, ain't we? Chasing the dark wants of our tainted hearts. So." He clapped his hands together, shattering the tension crackling through the air. "Let's see the rest of ya haul."

I took out the ten pairs of gloves from my pack, laying them on his desk. "Here. In all the colours you asked for."

Mavus smiled widely. "Thank you kindly. Now be off with ya. Fetch any wares you desire on your way. I'll be back in a full moon cycle as usual to collect. Four more blades and surprise me with an item of clothing or armour. Something that gives me the tingles."

"Sure. Pleasure doing business with you." I walked for the door and he was there in a flash, opening it for me and leaning low to whisper in my ear, leaving a skitter of goosebumps rolling across my skin.

"No, no. The pleasure was all mine, Everest Arcadia."

.

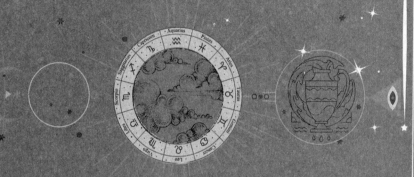

VESPER

CHAPTER THIRTY FOUR

The victory at Rifarn had sent the Skyforgers into a frenzy of celebrations - even though most of them hadn't been present and they openly sneered at the majority of the Sinfair who had been.

If it wasn't for the fact that I refused to let poor company ruin a good party, I would have bailed.

The Hall of Clouds, in the heart of the Vault of Sky had been decorated with golden flowers and shimmering swathes of gold fabric which clung to the white walls and gave the place an ethereal look as the light of the everflames flickered behind them.

Music rang through the wide space, the vaulted ceiling creating wonderful acoustics and making the entire place ring with the sounds of victory.

There was a feast laid out by one wall, a dance floor marked by a lack of furniture against the other, while the couches and chairs that were normally more spread out though the space had been clustered together to create a series of cosy seating arrangements.

We were late, which was of no surprise because I detested the small talk which took place at the beginning of such events.

Dalia and Moraine flanked me as always, and the sound of several thousand neophytes roaring their welcome to us made the walls vibrate as we were spotted.

We were war heroes yet again and though their distaste for our Sinfair legacy was apparent at most other times, all heroes were celebrated as if they were stars themselves when returning from a victorious battle. Tonight we would be beloved by all, tempted with pleasures and plied with gifts.

These affairs weren't like the formal balls held in the palaces and great houses of Stormfell by the aristocracy of the Wrathcourt. This would be a feast of debauchery and ruin, a celebration of our base nature and a host of sinful worship to thank the stars for their favour in our victory. No rules applied at a conquest reception and to make this night even more promising, there was going to be an eclipse tonight, when all Fae felt the sway of Venus in their veins and fell prey to their most base instincts. We were creatures at the beck and call of the heavens and the magic which swelled at such a prominent celestial event made the desires of our flesh more desperate than usual. The entire place would likely descend into something of an orgy before the night was out. My flesh was already heated with desire before I'd entered the hall and I was overwhelmed with the rush of lust that was gathering in all those around me as we headed deeper into the party.

The dress code for such a night was a far cry from the beautifully crafted suits and gowns of the formal affairs too – our bodies wrapped in slips of gossamer or silk, left vulnerable as a sign of our belief in our invincible nature. No blood could be shed at such an event unless you were willing to spit in the face of the stars who had blessed you with victory, but all other forms of debauchery were both expected and encouraged.

My dress was formed of two layers of fabric which were so thin that my flesh was almost visible beneath it, one swathe of gold, the other black, each starting at a shoulder then crossing over my breasts and falling into a skirt which held more slits than fabric. The rich bronze of my thighs peaked out between steps, revealing bare flesh then hiding it again with each movement of my body.

"By the stars, your company will be akin to hell tonight," Moraine groaned as heads turned our way, my lips lifting in amusement as, for once, I made no attempt to discourage the stares of my fellow Fae.

I was flaunting what I was tonight, my body exposed, my hair falling in a river of pale pink down my spine, my eyes lined in kohl and lips deepest red. The wall Dragor had erected still stood of course, but I planned on feasting on the sins of those around me and soaking myself in their magic as they offered it up for me to devour.

"I see no problem," Dalia disagreed, eyeing the hungry crowd as we moved into it. "V doesn't want to fuck any of them and there will be so much heat surrounding her that we can claim the fallout. I plan on drowning in the sin she attracts all night long."

I took a drink from the hand of a man whose mouth had fallen open as he stared, knocking it back and relishing the burn before thrusting it into his still raised palm while he blinked stupidly at me.

"I want to lick your-"

Moraine shoved him aside before he could complete that request and I grinned widely at Cassandra as she turned from her position on the dancefloor to see what had drawn everyone's attention.

Her eyes went cold as she found me before her, knowing she'd just lost her spotlight for the evening but she raised a glass in salute, even her hatred not enough to allow disrespect on a night such as this.

"To the victors!" she cried and her words were echoed all around.

I claimed another drink on my way to the dance floor, tossing the glass aside and causing a scuffle to ensue as three Fae fought over the honour of clearing it away for me.

Moraine and Dalia moved closer as the music twisted into a new rhythm and I tipped my head back and let it have me.

The three of us danced as one, their bodies shielding me from the cluster of Fae who were drawn closer with every move I made as I let my gifts unravel and began to stoke the desires of everyone around me.

The moon already had hearts pounding and lust mounting as it sank into its eclipse and the addition of my power had the entire Vault sinking into sin within minutes.

Gasps and soft moans filled the air as we danced, roaming hands sliding over half naked bodies, lips finding flesh, sighs of contentment and need punctuating our movements.

I let myself go in the midst of their pleasure, magic building in me as Fae all around gave in to their wants.

I spent so much of my time feeling the restrained desires of those surrounding me, feeding on needs which were stifled and unfulfilled, the rush of being surrounded by so many Fae finally claiming what they wanted made my head spin.

Hands found me between the masses, fingers trailing over my skin as the minutes turned into hours and the dancing descended into full debauchery.

Fae were pinned to walls by others, more still claiming couches and chairs together or finding questionable privacy in the shadows at the edges of the room.

I lost Moraine to a trio of Pegasus shifters who glittered with pleasure as their Order form crept up to the edges of their skin.

Sweat sheened my flesh, my hair clinging to my neck and spine as I danced within the writhing bodies, using the glut of magic I had stolen to push back any who got too close to me.

But my body was alive with need of its own, my skin burning, nipples tight and an ache between my thighs which cried out to be sated.

I blinked out of the fog of lust that surrounded me and as if I had known precisely where he would be, I found Cayde lurking in the darkness at the edge of the huge hall where swathes of decorative material created a layer of curtains fit for concealing wanting bodies.

I broke from Dalia, giving her a knowing smile as the two Minotaurs who had been vying for her attention gladly took my place dancing with her.

She mouthed the words *thank you* to me and I laughed as I slipped away.

Cayde was gone when I looked back across the room but the rampant pace of my heart and the ache in my flesh refused that answer.

I strode across the room, ignoring the eyes which hounded me and pushing aside a curtain of golden fabric, discovering nothing but a white wall behind it.

I pressed on, checking over my shoulder to make certain no one had followed me and grinning in satisfaction as I found myself alone.

I tugged another swathe of fabric aside, then another, frustration growing in me as I failed to find my prey.

I pushed a fifth curtain aside then a sixth, biting my lip in annoyance as I found an empty corner where I had expected to discover him.

I turned around to head back, gasping as I found him at my back, his eyes lit with hunger, hands falling to grasp my waist.

My spine hit the cold wall and his lips collided with mine in the next breath.

I moaned into his mouth, my burning skin a frenzy of wanton need where his hands dropped to the slits in my skirt and roamed up the edges of my thighs.

His chest was bare, the silk trousers he wore hanging low on his hips, making the strain of his cock all too obvious through the thin fabric.

"We'll be caught," I gasped as his hand pushed beneath my skirt, finding me bare.

Cayde groaned with need, his fingers sliding over my clit, discovering me wet and aching for him.

"Our chambers are too far away," he growled against my mouth, pushing two fingers inside me and making me moan for him. "And we're just as likely to be seen sneaking away to them."

"This is a bad idea," I panted, shoving his trousers down and moaning again as I took his cock into my hand.

"Then let's stop pretending we aren't acting on it and just focus on doing so before anyone finds us," Cayde growled.

I wanted to protest, wanted to warn him again of how dangerous this was for both of us but those words spilled away as his fingers tugged free of my core and I was left desperately aching with the need for release.

"Quickly," I agreed and with the feral lust that spiralled between us, I knew it would be that.

We were alone back here anyway and there were far more Fae bathing in their own sins than would be interested in discovering ours.

Cayde took hold of my hips and lifted me, my heels driving into his ass as I wrapped my legs around him and looked into his honey brown eyes, urging him closer as he pinned me to the wall. His gaze was dark with the intensity of his hunger and he speared me with his cock in a violent, desperate thrust.

I cried out as he drove into me, my body so tightly coiled that I almost fell apart with that single jerk of his hips.

My fingernails bit into his shoulder, my other hand finding one of the golden curtains above me and gripping it tightly to hold me up and he groaned as he relished the tight fit of his cock inside me.

Cayde ripped the sleeves of my dress down, revealing my breasts, my aching nipples peaked as I arched my spine against the cold stone at my back as he started to move.

He slammed his hips against mine, his cock driving into me at a furious pace as his mouth fell to claim my breast. The pull of the eclipse had my head spinning, the need in my flesh so rampant that I was almost undone already.

I met his thrusts with my own, our passion a messy, ruinous collision, our sounds of pleasure too loud, our hiding place too easily discovered, but my body demanded release and his clearly felt the same.

We were rabid in our claiming of each other, utterly reckless in our lust and the thrill of this stupidity had me falling even faster as we fucked like a pair of heathens in the dark, slaves to our desires, fools for the need of our flesh.

Faster, harder, my nails cutting into his skin, my spine bruising against the wall, his cock driving into me furiously, the two of us gasping for breath in the frenzy of it.

Cayde slammed into me in a clear demand and as a bellow of ecstasy fell from his lips, the intensity of his lust filling the air, I came apart with him, crying out with my own orgasm.

Movement caught my attention and I blinked through the heady release to the fluttering curtain behind Cayde, a chill racing down my spine as if someone had thrown cold water over me.

"Put me down," I hissed and Cayde released me, turning to look at the curtain too, following my focus to its movement.

I shoved past him, tugging the straps of my dress back up to conceal my flesh, following the fluttering trail through the curtains at a run until I stumbled out into the open again.

Fae moaned and sighed in the shadows surrounding me, all lost to their own lustful encounters on the sofas and tables which clustered in this part of the hall.

"Did you see anyone?" Cayde asked in a low tone, coming up behind me.

"No," I murmured, my eyes raking across the room, taking in Cassandra and her band of high born assholes, their eyes moving to me and making my skin prickle. But as I glanced away from them, I found more eyes on me, my power drawing attention just as it always did.

Fingers brushed my waist, a woman begging me to join her while a man feasted between her thighs and I slapped her hand away.

"No one saw," I said in a low voice, looking to Cayde.

He glanced around the hall once more, clearly as uncertain of that as I was, but there was little either of us could do about it now.

"Good," he replied softly, his fingers brushing against mine in the dark. And then he was gone.

I licked my lips slowly as I moved back towards the dancefloor, savouring the taste of him on them, relishing the rebellion against Dragor's leash. But even with the scent of Cayde clinging to my skin, the feel of his body a lingering impression against my own, I couldn't help but wonder how violently that rebellion might end. And whether I was sentencing him to death by giving him what I'd promised to none but a prince.

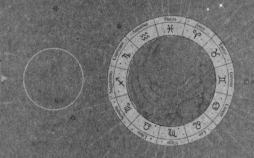

EVEREST

CHAPTER THIRTY FIVE

The gold fabric I'd claimed from my last visit to Wandershire had made a perfect mimicry of a Reaper's cloak and as I finished the last stitch, I stood up from the floor and shook it out to admire it. It was done. And there was no more time to squander. I swear I could hear Pisces whispering in my ear, urging me on, and Cancer clacking her claws in celebration of my achievement. Delphinus was cresting a wave, trilling out her good luck to me and I relished the sense of the stars looking out for me.

Or maybe I was semi-delusional and those sounds were more to do with the clunking of the pipes and the sloshing of the churning water above me in the glass tank. Either way, I was going to attempt something tonight that might end with my head on the chopping block, but I was done waiting on Sky Witches, wishing on stars and hoping for an opportunity to arise.

I had to forge my own opportunities, because Harlon could be beyond one of those archways and there wasn't anyone else in this world who was going to hunt for him.

I wrapped the cloak up in my pack along with Blue who was already asleep in there, tucking it in around him and making him chirrup softly in his sleep. I dressed plainly, my black clothes as simple as the ones the Reapers' wore beneath their cloaks, and I slipped on the dull shoes that I'd gotten from Wandershire, close enough to the Reapers' that they should go unnoticed.

I drew my hair back next, the full, flowing curls likely to draw attention if I didn't keep it out of sight. I braided it quickly, thinking of how my mama had tied it this way when I was a kid with a twist in my heart. It fell all the way down my back, the thick strands bound with a black ribbon, then I shouldered my pack and made for the door. My gaze fell on the book I had taken from Wandershire, the page folded where I'd read up to last night. Between forging and clothes making, I was hardly getting any time to study it, and so far I hadn't learned much about Furies or anything about my own Order. Maybe tomorrow I'd have more luck, but right now, I needed to get moving.

I was missing my final cardinal magic instruction of the day for this opportunity, figuring it would be easier to slip into the Reapers' Quarters unnoticed with fewer conscripts wandering about.

I reached the Heliacal Courtyard where an icy wind blew and snowflakes fluttered in the frosty air. The light of the sun was already fading, the days short and ending all too soon. Even in winter, Cascada had still had sun until the evening, but here, the winter held more power, darkness reigning far more often than light.

I headed past the wooden door that led into the Reapers' quarters, entirely unadorned as if trying to avoid attention and promising a whole host of secrets beyond. But this wouldn't be as simple as walking in there. My magical signature wouldn't open that door, so I needed someone to do it for me.

I walked up to the Taurus statue of a bull ready to charge which stood against the wall of the courtyard, slipping behind it and peering through its horns as I waited for a Reaper to appear. They came and went regularly enough, so it was only a few minutes until three of them stepped out from their quarters.

As fast as I could, I cast a sliver of ice into existence, sending it flying across the flagstones to drive right into the closing gap between the door and the jamb. It swung shut, trapping the ice and leaving it open the tiniest crack as the Reapers headed on their way, my magic going unnoticed.

I quickly pulled the gold cloak out of my pack and put it on. Blue stirred within the bag from his latest nap, jumping onto my hand and disappearing up my sleeve.

"I guess you're coming too then," I murmured, stashing the pack beneath the stone legs of the bull, gathering shadows around it with magic to conceal it from view.

With my heart starting up a wild rhythm in my chest, I made for the wooden door, keeping my head bowed a little to hide my face but walking with purpose, acting as if I belonged. I pushed through the door, hurrying inside and finding myself in a vast entrance hall with a grand stairway that swept away from me, leading down to a long hall below. My feet tracked across the blood red carpet that adorned the stairs, my fingers trailing over the mahogany banister, the grandeur in this place stealing the breath from my lungs.

Beautiful tapestries hung on the walls of the cavernous hall, depicting the zodiac signs in all their majesty, their eyes picked out with silver thread, catching the light of the candelabras above and making it seem as though they were watching me.

A doorway stood open at the far end of the hall and the sound of voices made my stomach knot, but I didn't slow, walking straight inside and hoping I went unnoticed.

The room appeared to be some sort of communal space for the Reapers, circular tables dotted around it, the décor gothic and macabre. There were paintings of skeletal beings on the walls laying on blood-soaked battlegrounds with the stars watching on from above, depicted as bright, unblinking eyes. One after another of the disturbing works showed death in all forms.

The attention of the Reapers milling around the room was captured as one of them threw her head back, her hood falling to her shoulders, revealing her face. Her eyes glazed, her hand reaching toward some unknown thing, and I couldn't help but stop to watch as she jerked back to attention.

"What did you *see?*" the Reapers asked her, gathering closer and I realised I had just witnessed a real-life Seer perceiving a star-gifted vision. A keenness filled me, and I felt so close to the voice of the stars in the presence of the Seer that it rattled my bones.

"It's time. The moment has come, are the acolytes prepared?" she asked excitedly and cries of joy broke out.

"I'll send word to the Grand Maester," a male Reaper raced across the room, hurrying to one of the gruesome paintings and flipping it open to reveal a passage beyond.

"The acolytes are cleansed and waiting to meet with fate and see which of them will survive their assessment," another man said keenly, making my blood run cold. What did he mean 'survive their assessment?' What the fuck were they going to put their acolytes through? "I'll check that they are well." He headed towards a painting of a woman being torn apart by some heinous, yellow-eyed beast. Dread twisted through me as he drew it open, striding away into the dark tunnel beyond, sconces illuminating as he went, then the painting swung shut behind him.

I was left with the rest of the Reapers in the room who were still clustered around the Seer, asking her questions, but her eyes glazed again and when she came back to herself, her face was contorted with horror.

"Blood. Fangs as sharp as blades. Monsters on the horizon," she gasped.

"When?" a man demanded.

The Seer frowned, her head shaking. "I cannot grasp more..." She looked tired, dropping into a seat at one of the tables.

An impulsive part of me urged me to follow on through that passage where the acolytes resided, but with so many Reapers here, I knew it would only draw attention. Instead, I backed away, slipping out of the room and breaking into a fast walk down the hall, rising up the stairs and pushing through the wooden gate back into the Heliacal Courtyard.

I had to cause a distraction, something that would draw the Reapers out of their hole and give me a chance to slip into that passage. Images tangled in my mind of that man tethered to an altar, naked and covered in runes in front of the Reapers, setting my soul alight with terror. I had to reach Harlon. I didn't know how I would stop his assessment, or what I was going to do when I found him at all, but I just had to find him. *Now.*

I rushed across the empty courtyard just as the bells rang to end the day. But no...it wasn't the right sound. Those bells kept ringing and ringing, the tone an ominous bellow that spoke of oncoming enemies. They had told us during our very first week here what the tolling of the bells meant, and that endless chiming told of only one thing. Never Keep was under attack.

I tore the gold cloak from my back, racing across the empty courtyard towards my bag as Blue clung tight to his perch on my shoulder. The sound of footsteps pounded this way and I shoved the cloak under the statue, thickening the shadows there and stepping back, abandoning my pack as a tide of neophytes came pouring into the courtyard with the Grand Maester and a line of Reapers at the forefront.

"Enemies approach!" a Reaper bellowed from beyond the Night Gate, their voice amplified by magic so it echoed out around the Keep, those words sending a shiver of dread through me. Who would dare attack a sacred place such as this?

My gaze locked on the Sky Witch just beyond the Reapers, she and her clique clustered tight together, the two women, Dalia with the short black hair and terrifying eyes, Moraine with her silver blades and murderous expression. And the man, Cayde, who looked like he was plotting death and carnage in every passing thought.

This was my chance. I knew it in my soul. Pisces was urging me on, encouraging me as if the perfection of this distraction had been borne into existence just for me. And with the challenge that faced me tonight, I wondered if the Sky Witch might just be tempted into the chaos of my plan.

I raced into the crowd, aiming straight for the Sky Witch, madness claiming me as I tossed a silencing shield around the two of us and explained what I'd heard in the Reapers' Quarters in a fast stream of words before telling her of my plan. "This fight will be our chance to get under the Keep again. While the Reapers face the attack along with the neophytes, we can get back there. I saw a way in."

"Are you insane?" she snapped, glancing at her friends who were staring at me in shock.

I'd just approached the Sky Witch in front of a whole crowd and I half-expected her to raise her blade against me, but for some reason she didn't.

"Probably," I admitted, throwing a glance towards the wooden door, hoping more Reapers would appear at any second and we could make it inside. "So, are you coming?"

I noticed the large, imposing form of Kaiser Brimtheon charting a path through the crowd with North and his pack at his heels, looking fit for war, but I ripped my eyes from him back to the pink-haired warrior before me. I couldn't get distracted by that monster right now. Harlon needed me.

"V?" Moraine called to the Sky Witch, the crowd surging past us as the Grand Maester called out for everyone to defend Never Keep. "What the fuck is going on?"

"Extend your silencing shield to include them," the Sky Witch said decisively, and I hesitated before allowing her three companions into the fold, laying everything on the line in the hopes that I could find Harlon tonight.

I could go without the Sky Witch, but in truth, I didn't want to. We had discovered a secret in the depths of this place and it was time we sought answers. Besides, whatever we faced down there would be better fronted together. If she refused, I'd be going either way.

"Vesper, explain," Cayde demanded, and I latched onto that name, finally claiming a piece of the Sky Witch's true identity.

"You are all going to trust this Raincarver for one night only," Vesper said sharply. "The Reapers are hiding something unimaginable at the Keep and it's time I showed you what it is."

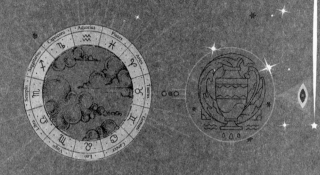

VESPER

CHAPTER THIRTY SIX

An explosion ripped through the air and I was knocked from my feet by the fury of the blast, Moraine colliding with me as all of us were sent skidding across the Heliacal Courtyard.

My leathers took the brunt of the impact and I rolled, throwing my hands up and casting an air shield over the five of us as the heat and flames of the explosion blasted through the air.

"Flamebringers," Dalia hissed, wiping the blood from her split lip across her chin with the back of her hand before digging into her boot and drawing a wicked dagger from the concealed sheath there.

"Why would they attack Never Keep?" I barked, my instincts telling me that this wasn't the Flamebringers, even though they were the obvious suspects.

"Maybe they want to wipe out the conscripts from the other

nations?" Everest suggested, a blade of ice forming in her fist as she kept her eyes on the billowing smoke which concealed the Night Gate.

Dalia cast the Raincarver a sneering look but said nothing, clearly not liking this tentative cease fire between me and our enemy.

"Moraine?" I barked, not taking my eyes from the smoke.

"I'm fine," she gritted out, her footsteps moving closer as she scrambled to join us.

"Cayde?"

"Right here, sweetheart," he said at my back and my pulse settled at the confirmation that my unit was secure.

"Let's see who's come to crash this party then," I said.

I lifted my hands before me, summoning a great wind into my fists as the cries of the wounded and confused punctured the air like the baying of babes in the night.

With a twist of my wrists, I released the power, the wind tearing from me and blasting the smoke, ash and debris back out of the Night Gate which had been blasted open by the explosion but still hung resolutely from its hinges.

My heart stalled in my chest as I took in the assailants moving towards us through the gate. Five of them in all – such a small force it should have been laughable, but terror rolled through me as I absorbed the sight of them.

The closest was tall with a dark skin and curling hair which hung to his chin, the sight of him jolting through me with a flare of recognition. I'd seen him before on the day of our Awakening.

"Vampires," I breathed, knowing that all five of them would hear me regardless, their senses heightened thanks to what they were.

The Vampires stayed out of our wars, coming close to the rest of the Fae only at Awakenings so that they could claim any of their kind who Emerged and steal them away to their hidden kingdom in the wastelands.

None who were claimed by them ever returned, abandoning all allegiance to their element and families and uniting with the terrible cruelty of their kind. If Fae were vicious then Vampires were the worst of us all, creatures of pure depravity who delighted in bloodshed beyond all other pleasures. Worse, they formed covens among themselves, like Werewolf packs only far deadlier. Their ferocious strength and speed - which were already far superior to all other Fae thanks to the gifts of their Order Form - were heightened by the bond they formed as a unit. It was said they could even communicate within each other's minds. They were formidable, monstrous and nigh on undefeatable in combat.

If the Vampires had breached the gate, this was going to be a bloodbath. The power of the covens they formed was insurmountable. Packs of five or six had been known to kill an army of a thousand, ripping through flesh like paper and moving like the wind itself.

There was a reason no one had ever tried to force them to conform to the laws of The Waning Lands. They were beasts who couldn't be controlled. Whatever fight they sought against the Keep would be bloody and vicious.

"Shield," I hissed and my sisters grasped my shoulders at once, their magic rushing towards me, colliding with mine through the barrier of our skin and combining in a vortex of raw, breath-taking power.

A shield sped from me, encircling the five of us with the considerable might of our magic and I swallowed against the lump in my throat as the Vampire to the right of the leader turned to look at us with a wide and threatening grin.

He was terrifying in his beauty, a creature surely carved by the hands of some vindictive deity who wanted to watch as his creation ensnared his victims through desire alone, but this Vampire did not tempt me with his wicked allure. I was a creature born of desire and I knew when it concealed a soul of evil because I wore that same mask myself.

The Vampire pushed strands of long, copper hair out of his eyes, the warmth to his complexion at stark contrast to the coldness of his gaze.

A blink and all five of them were gone.

I braced for the attack, knowing it was coming as a streak of movement, too fast for my eyes to track, shot straight for us.

The collision with our shield almost knocked me on my ass, a curse falling from my lips as the Vampire appeared a foot away, his fist slamming against my shield with such force that it took all of our combined power to resist him.

"At least our death has a pretty face," Dalia muttered, her tattooed fingers biting into my shoulder as she forced as much of her power into me as possible.

I gritted my teeth, fighting against the cracks which were beginning to splinter across the dome of magic that shielded us, my heels digging into the flagstones as I fought the urge to step back.

But the force of the Vampire's strength was unrelenting, his obvious glee in our defiance making my pulse race frantically. If he broke through, we were dead. The screams of the Stonebreakers who fought the other four Vampires were testament to that, their bodies crumpling in sprays of blood as the blurred forms of the Vampires raced between them, ripping out throats so fast they had no time to fight back.

Despite all of my effort, the cracks across my shield grew, the Vampire's excitement clear as he threw his fist against it again and again, the movement so fast I couldn't even see it, only the resounding booms of the collisions marking the strikes.

My power flared and faltered, my eyes meeting the feral gaze of our foe as I sought more magic from those close by and I locked onto his desires with an iron fist.

Revenge, blood, power, longing.

I took it all and I took it fast, ripping his magic from him and realising my mistake as his bloodlust grew from feral to insatiable.

An enormous crack splintered across our shield, Moraine gasping as she felt the moment of its demise closing in on us beneath his furious assault, and for the first time in as long as I could remember, fear found me in battle. Not for my own death but for the death of the two women who shared my soul and who deserved so much more than this from life.

A hand grasped mine in that final moment, unfamiliar power rushing towards me on a wave of ferocious magic.

I opened the floodgates to my own magic automatically, a tide of raw and foreign power slamming into me and stealing the breath from my lungs. It wasn't air magic but somehow, as the two forces within us collided, they merged, finding an impossible unity and becoming something that I could wield against all odds.

I threw Everest's power into the shield, the cracks sealing, the Vampire bellowing in frustration.

The shock of what we had just done crashed through me, but I had no time to consider it, my gaze whipping around as the wooden door to the Reapers' Quarters burst open and a tide of Reapers poured from the hidden passages there to intercept the Vampires.

The Vampire attacking us shot away without a moment's hesitation, racing towards his coven-mates and abandoning us as if we had been nothing but a petty challenge for him to conquer.

"Come on," Everest hissed, releasing my hand.

The others released me too, though I kept a shield around us as I looked to Everest, meeting her gaze.

"Band together!' Reaper Jaspin commanded. "Put aside your differences and fight as one for the good of the Keep!"

The Stonebreakers were fighting ferociously near the Night Gate, a band of Flamebringers throwing fireballs from their position closer to the entrance to the heart of the Keep, but they were in no way fighting as one.

"I'd sooner let those Vampires drain me than fight alongside our enemies," Dalia spat, echoing my own sentiments.

"This place belongs to the Reapers," I said. "So let them fight to protect it – it's no land of ours and those aren't our kin fighting."

Everest seemed uncertain of that assessment, but her eyes moved to that open door.

"I need to get to Harlon," she said firmly, the little blue lizard looking out at me from her shoulder beneath the wild tangle of her braided curls, half of them falling loose of its hold.

Cayde hesitated, his eyes roaming over the Stonebreakers where they fought a losing battle with the coven of Vampires but I grabbed his arm and steered him towards the door with us.

"You can test your prowess against a coven another time, Cayde. We have something else to do tonight."

His eyes met mine and he took a step closer, the violent heat burning between us as he leaned down to speak in my ear. "Let's see what you've been hiding then, Vesper. And it had better be as wicked as I've been hoping."

I flashed him a grin, turned my back on the Vampires and the Reapers who fought them then hounded after Everest as she slipped through the wooden door we were forbidden from entering and led us into the dark.

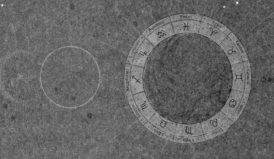

EVEREST

CHAPTER THIRTY SEVEN

We made it to the Reapers common room at a fast past, the sound of bloodcurdling screams still carrying to us from the Heliacal Courtyard, raising the hairs on the back of my neck. But my focus was all on Harlon now.

I moved to the painting of a woman who was being ripped apart by a beast and I pulled it open, revealing the passage beyond. The sconces were lit and I knew at least one Reaper might still be lurking down here, but I hoped all of them had been summoned to the defence of the Keep.

"Are you sure this is a good idea, V?" the one who I had figured out was Moraine hissed. "The Reapers might kill us if we're caught. They could make us face the wrath of the stars for defying their prophets."

"You keep watch then," I said sweetly, racing past her into the passage.

"What's with you and her?" Cayde growled at Vesper. "She's our enemy."

"If you dare breathe the word traitor at me, I'll gut you," Vesper warned as the four of them followed me into the passage. "You're going to want to see this and for now, we need the Raincarver, so just deal with it."

For now. Those two words made me feel as though I had just placed myself in front of a pack of bloodthirsty wolves. What was to say they wouldn't kill me the moment we reached those archways? What reason would they have not to?

I glanced back at them over my shoulder, drawing my dagger silently and quickening my pace. My focus had to remain on Harlon. Despite the danger I had put myself in with this chaotic plan, if it led me to him, it would be worth it. I'd figure out surviving the betrayal of the Sky Witch if that was what it came to. Though I supposed betrayal was a strong word. We had a fragile alliance at best, but now I was seeing that perhaps she had been using me after all.

We met a stairway and I gestured for the others to go ahead, but Cayde gave me a rough shove that sent me stumbling down a couple of steps. "Keep moving," he growled.

I moved back up the step, raising my dagger.

"I'm not your pawn to order around, Skyforger," I hissed. "Touch me again and I'll cut your fingers off."

Bells rang out again and we all looked around towards the entrance to the passage as the amplified voice of the Grand Maester echoed across the Keep.

"Two more covens approach! Defend the Keep! Answer the summons!"

Hia kaské. One coven was enough to rip this place apart, but three? Never Keep might just fall tonight.

I looked between the Skyforgers, wondering if they might turn back to face the fight, but Vesper's jaw just ticked with what appeared to be irritation as she turned towards the darkness of the passage with firm intention.

"I'll go first." She stepped past me and I eyed her warily as the two women followed, but Cayde remained, folding his arms and waiting for me to move.

I turned, not wasting any more precious time on arguing with him, though I didn't like the way it felt to have him breathing down my neck as I hurried on.

"By the ocean, are you breathing that loud to stake your claim over the air?" I clipped at him.

"Keep your mouth shut or I'll silence you permanently," he said in a low, threatening tone.

"Just don't suck up all the oxygen, yeah?" I muttered and the ferocious one with choppy black hair, Dalia, sniggered just ahead of me.

We made it to the bottom of the stairway arriving in yet another long passage, but as we started down it, a clash of noise sounded from the steps behind us.

I whirled around just as a huge male Vampire with dark skin and tightly curling hair collided with Cayde, driving him into the wall so his head cracked against it. Cayde snarled, air magic exploding from him and sending the Vampire flying into the opposite wall.

A blur of movement in the stairway made my heart stall as four more male Vampires raced out of the gloom with fangs bared, mouths bloody from recent kills and a look of utter savagery about them.

The silver haired one with bronze skin and tattoos crawling out from his cuffs and collars came for me in a blur and I brought my dagger up with a cry of fright, aiming for his heart, but he moved so fast that it slammed into his shoulder instead.

A clash of fighting rang out around me as the Skyforgers met with the violence of the other Vampires and I was thrown into the wall, pinned there by the impossible strength of my attacker's monstrous Order.

I stabbed at him again, slicing into his side while my right hand came up and blasted him back with water. He hit the opposite wall, touching the bloody wounds and shock filled me at the sight of him using healing magic, something only the Reapers were capable of, his injuries stitching over fast and offering him a full recovery.

"No," I gasped, raising my blade again.

Vesper, Moraine and Dalia were being forced further down the passage by three of the Vampires while Cayde grappled with one of his own, and my attacker sauntered back towards me with a vicious smile on his lips.

"Oh you're gonna pay for that, sugar," he purred.

I ran to meet him with a Leopard's growl in my throat, ice shooting out from my right hand in a cascade of shards, but he shot away in a flash of motion that defied all possibility. He was behind me in a heartbeat as my shards shattered against the wall, his hand coming tight around my neck. His fingers locked tight and forced my head sideways, baring my throat to him. I twisted my dagger in my grip, preparing to stab it into his side, but he caught my wrist with a dark chuckle in his throat, releasing my neck to capture my other arm too, his breath like a toxin against my skin.

"Stay still," he purred, immobilising me with the impossible strength of his Order, his mouth grazing my neck as he prepared to sink his fangs into my skin.

My heart lurched, my magic about to be immobilised by this asshole if he got his fangs into me, the venom in a Vampire's bite able to lock down my power. Ice scored out along my hand, travelling up his arm, but it wasn't moving fast enough-

Blue was there in a flash, his wings fluttering and his teeth gnashing into the Vampire's cheek.

The Vampire reared back in surprise, a snarl of anger tearing from him as he swatted the little lizard away, but Blue let out a shriek from his open jaws and a powerful blast of energy exploded from him, sending the Vampire smashing into the wall.

Surprise hit me as he crumpled to the flagstones and I raced forward to finish him with my blade, driving it down towards his chest. His hand shot up, capturing my hand and smiling grimly at me before yanking me close and digging his fangs into my wrist.

I screamed as the power of his venom immediately swept into me, locking down my magic as he drank my blood and began draining the well of power inside me, claiming it for himself.

I snatched my blade into my right hand and swung for his neck, but he shot away in a blur that left me dizzy. He was behind me once more, his hand closing tightly around my arm so I couldn't stab with my blade again. "Run rabbit, run. I adore the hunt."

"I'll never run." I whirled around, blasting a fist of water at him that crashed into his jaw so forcefully that he stumbled back, releasing me.

Cayde went flying past me as the huge Vampire he was fighting threw him full-bodily through the air. He hit the flagstones, his arms lined with bloody bites and his face a picture of rage as the Vampire ran to intercept him again.

The shouts and cries of battle sounded further down the passage, but I couldn't turn my attention to the Sky Witch and her friends because my own predator was drawing close again.

I raised my dagger, ice coating my right hand as I took in the hauntingly beautiful face of the Vampire before me.

"Your blood is mine," he declared, stepping closer with a glint of malice in his eyes.

"Come and get it then." I raised my blade higher, my teeth bared, my wrath awoken, but then a furious blast of air went crashing into my assailant and all five Vampires were thrown back into the stairwell.

I turned, finding Vesper power sharing with Dalia and Moraine, their magic forcing the Vampires back as a tempest roared down the passage then formed a barrier between us and them.

The five of them flung themselves at the wall of air, trying to break through, their eyes alight with hunger.

"We're coming for you," the one who had attacked me sang, a wildness to him that made my heart hammer. "Down in the warren with all the other bunnies. We'll hunt you like foxes and rip you apart."

"I'm quaking in my little bunny boots," Vesper drawled, looking entirely unimpressed despite the way her chest rose and fell rapidly and the blood that was splattered across her cheek. Was it all a mask she wore or was she really that cold to the core?

The Vampires threw themselves against the air shield again, but the magic held and Dalia grinned tauntingly at them like this was just a game to her.

"Move," Vesper barked and we turned our backs on the monstrous Fae who had come for our blood, charging off into the dark once more.

I stepped over Cayde who was yet to get his ass off the floor, my boot knocking into this chin as I went. He grunted irritably as he shoved to his feet, and Blue went flying over his shoulder, his wing slapping him in the face before he came to land on my hand.

"Good boy." I stroked his head, absorbing the fact that he held a fierce kind of power, one capable of knocking a Vampire on his back.

"What is that thing?" Cayde demanded from behind me, but I didn't answer.

I didn't know anyway, and if I did, I wouldn't be imparting that knowledge to a cock of a Skyforger.

I touched the bite mark on my arm, frowning at the two bloody holes as we delved deeper into the tunnels, leaving the Vampires behind. But their taunts followed us, their promises to claim our blood making my skin prickle. If I knew one thing of their kind, it was that they lived for the hunt. And we had just made ourselves into a challenge they would be dying to rise to.

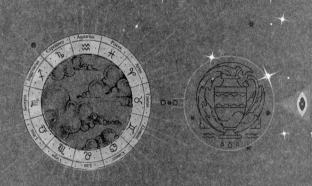

VESPER

CHAPTER THIRTY EIGHT

We ran on through the darkness, little knowledge to our direction aside from heading ever downward and hoping we might end up in our desired location. Everest's desire to find her man was rippling through the air, her magic continuously fuelling my own without me having to try and drain it. Her desires were what drove us on and I couldn't help but wonder why I was still pursuing them. But with the Vampires in the Keep and our route back upwards blocked by them, there weren't many alternatives to forging on regardless.

"Where is this Raincarver leading us?" Moraine growled, moving closer to me and hiding our words in a silencing shield as she narrowed her eyes at the back of Everest's head.

"The Reapers are keeping secrets in this place," I replied, looking from her to Cayde and Dalia who weren't at all subtle in their thirst for this information which I had been withholding for so long. "While I was investigating it, I came across her doing the same. I needed the information she'd gained and I offered her a blood pact to get it. I can't cause her harm or my own blood will rot."

"Why the fuck would you make that pact with a Raincarver?" Dalia hissed.

"Because she didn't seem important enough to kill and she's been useful in discovering the Reapers' secrets."

"Which are?" Cayde asked in a low voice.

"Something dark," Everest replied, glancing over her shoulder at us and making me startle as I realised my silencing shield had somehow vanished, leaving her to listen to all we said. "Something twisted and fucked up which they don't want us to know about. They've taken the acolytes somewhere and I just know that something isn't right about whatever they're doing with them."

Moraine arched a brow at me and I shrugged.

"Kitty cat has a little boyfriend who claimed two elements – she's all kinds of heartbroken over his disappearance."

Cayde snorted in amusement and Everest shot a dagger of ice at him which he only just shielded against in time.

"*You* might have a blood pact with her, but I don't," he growled, moving to step past me but I slammed my hand against his chest, halting him.

"Pretty sure one of you harming her on my behalf would trigger the blood pact too, asshole," I hissed, forcing him to back down.

"So she's here for her boyfriend," Dalia said as we took another set of stairs downwards. "But why are you so interested in the Reapers' private business, V?"

"Because I'm sick of being manipulated," I said in a low voice as a cool breeze drifted over me from the passage ahead and I inhaled the fresh air of home. "And I want to know what they're up to."

I upped my pace, moving ahead of them and glancing at Everest as I passed her too. We said nothing, but the look confirmed our tentative alliance still stood.

I moved to the front of the group just as we turned a final corner in the passage and recognition filled me as I found a heavy wooden door barring the way on. It wasn't the entrance we had used to reach this place before, but I knew before opening it that we had found our way back to the caverns lined with archways to the unknown.

I swallowed thickly and pushed the door wide, a shiver rolling down my spine as I led the way into the room.

Everest scurried forward, moving into the centre of the space, running her fingers over one archway then another, inspecting and dismissing them in turn.

"What is this place?" Dalia asked, walking up to the closest archway, decorated with the symbols for fire, and stepping through it to no effect.

I glanced between the three of them, the weight of this secret feeling heavier than before as I wondered about trusting them with it. But Dalia and Moraine had been my sisters for as far back as I could remember. And Cayde had unlocked my heart and stolen my trust alongside it since we'd been at Never Keep, earning his own level of faith. Besides, we were all loyal to the kingdom of air, all sworn to the same sovereign and all just as certain to protect it at any cost.

I glanced at Everest as I constructed a new silencing shield, making sure she was too far from us to overhear my words even if the shield somehow failed again.

"That urn contains the means to open these archways and create gates between places," I said in a low voice.

"What?" Moraine asked, her brow furrowing.

"When we came here before, I opened one of them and it took us to an underground hall decorated in the colours and style of our kingdom where the air tasted of home and my feet felt more firmly weighted on the ground than they ever have anywhere else."

"Home?" Dalia asked in confusion. "But we're a thousand miles from Stormfell. There's no way-"

"There is," I said firmly, looking to Cayde whose brows had creased, his expression stony as he took in what I was saying.

"You travelled to Stormfell via one of these archways?" he confirmed. "As simply as walking from one room to the next?"

"Yes," I confirmed. "But *she* didn't realise that," I said, nodding towards Everest. "She had no idea where we were. I could just…tell." I shrugged, knowing that sounded insane but the looks the three of them gave me said they trusted my word on it.

"Where do the rest of them lead?" Cayde asked, looking at the symbol for fire on the closest archway.

"We had to run before investigating further but my bet is that the rest lead to the other nations based on those symbols. You understand the risk of that, don't you? If the Reapers have created this secret network for moving around The Waning Lands at speed, it's only a matter of time before one of the nations discovers it and turns it to their advantage. Imagine an army passing through these archways and appearing without notice in the heart of an enemy city? This could be the key to the end of the war."

"Who have you told about this?" Cayde demanded, his glare shifting to Everest again and I stiffened.

"I told you, she hasn't figured it out," I growled. "She's just looking for that man she lost. She has no idea."

"And V's life is tied to hers so stop eyeing her like you're planning where to stab first," Moraine hissed in warning and Cayde's eyes flashed with anger at the suggestion.

"It's this one," Everest called, turning to beckon us closer from across the cavern and I gave the others a stern look before striding over to join her, taking a fistful of that sparkling grit from the urn and dumping it into my pocket as I went.

"How do you know?" I demanded, moving to stand beside Everest where she looked up at an archway marked with all four elemental symbols. It was one of at least six which held the same markings, but the certainty on her face said she knew without a doubt that her boyfriend lay beyond this one.

"I can...feel him. It's hard to explain but I can taste salt on my lips from the ocean where we always swam together as I stand here. I can smell the lime and sea air which always clung to his skin and almost hear a breath of his laughter... He's here. I know it."

Something twisted in my chest as I looked at the desperate longing written into her features, the pull of that desire untying a knot within in me, her need to find this Fae so intense that I couldn't even summon a quip or joke at her expense.

"Alright." I dug into my pocket, taking the glittering grit from it and moving to the depression marked with the rune for travel before dropping it into place.

Bright light sped into the rivulet which curved over the archway, rushing through it before erupting across the open space at its centre and once again opening a door to the unknown.

A foreign whoop of victory shattered the silence and I whirled around as a door on the far side of the cavern burst open, my eyes widening as the Vampires tore through it with cries of delight at finding their prey.

"Vesper!" Moraine yelled in alarm, drawing her daggers while Cayde and Dalia whipped up a storm of air to defend themselves.

I turned to Everest whose eyes were wide with terror.

"Go find him, kitten." I gave her a dark smile before shoving her straight into the blazing light and sending her into the questionable safety beyond the archway.

Air blasted from me as one of the Vampires shot straight towards us, but my smile only widened as he came for me, the thrill of the fight lighting a blaze in my veins while Everest sped into the unknown. And despite all the reasons I had to hate her for what and who she was, I couldn't help but hope that she found her copper-eyed Fae beyond that door because I'd tasted her desire and it had been so fucking sweet, it hurt.

EVEREST

CHAPTER THIRTY NINE

I twisted around, the shimmering archway at my back emptying in an instant and stranding me here. Fuck, I hadn't brought a scrap of that glittering grit with me and those Vampires were descending on all of them back there. There was no way to help. And maybe I didn't give a shit about the others, but Vesper... I didn't know why but leaving her to that fate didn't sit right with me. But there was nothing I could do now.

My fingers flexed as I turned to take in my surroundings, the walls rough and shimmering silver like they were imbued with metal. I could no longer sense Harlon's presence, but he had to be this way. I'd felt him back in that chamber, had been so sure he was beyond that particular archway. So I wasn't going to falter now.

I crept through the silent cavern as a low humming sound grew in the atmosphere, the noise pulsing, strong then weak, a sense of power building in the air around me. It didn't feel like any magic I had encountered before, the root of it dark and forbidding, drawing my blood to the very edges of my skin.

Closer and closer I came to the source of that sound, the passage winding along before opening out into a chamber that domed overhead. I stilled at the sight of a strange, dark liquid coiling across the ceiling, thrumming and writhing in time with the pulsing, humming noise. Beneath it in a wide circle were around twenty of this year's acolytes, all tethered upright to stone pillars by gleaming silver chains.

My gaze fell on Harlon like my body was magnetised to his, drawing me to him and pulling a desperate noise from my lips.

I ran, tearing across the chamber toward him, my heart cleaving in two at the sight of the runes cut into his bare chest. His head sagged forward, his body limp and his hair was falling into his eyes, that golden stripe at the front caressing his cheek.

I gripped his jaw in a panic, lifting his head and searching his face for signs of life, my chest thick with fear. He was warm, his pulse skipping beneath my fingers as I touched my other hand to his throat and I let out a breath of relief.

"Harl, it's me. Wake up," I urged, my voice cracking the smallest amount, but I couldn't break in the face of seeing him like this. I had to help him. Had to free him. I didn't know what was set to happen here, but I didn't want him to have any part in it.

"Harlon," I growled more firmly, shaking him as I let his head fall forward again.

I focused on the chains instead, gripping them and trying to tug them loose, but they were wrapped around him without an end. No lock at all. So that left one option.

I focused on freezing the chains, trying to figure out what kind of metal they were made of, but I didn't recognise it. True silver would be weak enough to shatter when frozen well enough, but my ice magic was having no effect on it.

"I'm not giving up on you," I swore just in case he could hear me. "I'm here and I'm not leaving without you."

The pulsing thrum of that unholy, dark mass above me was growing in urgency, the power crackling through the air and making my lungs weigh like anchors in my chest. I didn't look at it, ignoring its presence and fighting to break through Harlon's chains, determination burning through me.

I will not leave you here.

I will get you free.

I unsheathed my dagger, jamming it between the frozen chain and the stone pillar, wrenching backwards to see if it would give. My blade groaned, pushed to its limits as I poured all of my strength into levering it backwards, my muscles protesting, screaming at me to stop. But I didn't, pushing myself to breaking point and demanding these chains release him to me. No matter the effort I used, they didn't break and I was forced to give up, panting from exertion.

I tugged the blade loose, looking around for some magical answer that would help me free him, my soul frantic.

"Ever?" Harlon murmured and I gasped, cupping his cheek as his head lifted.

His copper eyes were heavily hooded, whatever spell he was under already working to steal him away from me again.

"Stay with me," I demanded. "I'm here. I'm getting you out. How do I release these chains?"

"*Run*," he rasped, terror sparking in his gaze and weaving dread into my bones. "Get out of here."

"No, I'm not leaving you," I swore, clinging to his arms, trying to pull him from the chains and hating that I couldn't find a way to save him. "Tell me how to break these. Is there a lock I can't see? A key somewhere? Please, Harl. Stay awake. Tell me how to get you out."

"You can't," he said, his voice fading, his eyes blinking heavily. His fingers moved, trying to reach for me and I took his hand, resting my forehead to his.

"Fight it," I begged, my heart aching. "Whatever they've done to you, swear you'll fight your way free of it."

"No escape," he croaked. "Run, Ever. Never stop running." He groaned, then lost consciousness again and I reared back from him with a roar of anger leaving me.

I clawed at the chains, trying to break them with water and ice and all the Cardinal Magics I knew. But nothing affected them, nothing released him into my hold.

That power was growing unbearably thick in the air and I felt it creeping closer from above. I didn't want to look, but I forced my eyes that way to face what I was denying. The writhing mass of darkness shuddered and the sconces on the wall flickered out like a gust of air from the mouth of a beast had just snuffed them from existence.

My throat thickened and I placed myself in front of Harlon, raising my blade. The whole chamber shuddered and the sound of something heavy hit the ground before me. Something that made the atmosphere shiver and fear score a line across my chest.

"Blue," I whispered for him. "Light your tail," I urged, knowing I needed to see whatever was here if I was going to have a hope of surviving it. But Blue didn't answer, and I couldn't sense a single claw of his or the light weight of him on my body anymore.

He was gone.

A guttural breath rasped from the jaws of some unknown being before me and I steadied my hand around my dagger, my pulse hammering as I awaited its approach.

Power roiled and scattered from the being, racing out around the chamber and a few of the Fae in chains awoke and started screaming. At least, I assumed it was them because no one else was here and the roars and cries of utter terror set my nerve endings on fire.

I held my breath, trying not to draw attention as a terrible sound filled my ears. Crunching bones and ripping flesh, screams like no other flooding the air and branding themselves inside my skull. Whatever monster was here was feeding on the acolytes and I was terrified for the man at my back as those screams slowly quieted, the wet slap of body parts and spill of blood making my chest clog with terror.

The scent of it was everywhere, death like a tangible thing that was moving this way, about to dig its claws into me too.

I felt it move closer, the power of this thing beyond anything I could imagine, its presence so consuming that it felt foolish to hold my blade against it. No weapon, no magic could halt this entity and as its cold, lifeless breath washed over my cheeks, I felt the weight of its gaze settle on me.

"I'm Everest Arcadia," I spoke, not knowing why only those words came to my lips and I simply let them pour free. "Daughter of Kaylina Arcadia and Commander Abraham Rake, Raincarver of the mighty Cascada, neophyte of Never Keep, and one day I will be a warrior who is feared across the four lands. I don't know what you are, but I know that my fate does not end here. I am destined for *more*."

That dark and terrible power slammed against me all at once and I cried out, my knees hitting the floor as the being took control of my mind, rooting through everything I was and ever wished I could be. It saw me as a dirty-kneed child with a bloody nose and my back against the wall of an alley while Ransom and his friends closed in on me.

It saw me bleed and saw me fail time again. But then it saw me rising too. It saw me love and burn and ache and want. Oh the desperate wants of me, it saw them all. The crux of my being, the root of my desires and it examined each one like placing worth upon it, deciding its value. I didn't know if I'd passed its assessment until it released me, that unbearable weight of its magic retreating from my body and leaving me panting beneath it.

Then it was gone, so abruptly that I was still quivering on the floor when the sconces flushed back to life and I found a Reaper striding into the chamber with rage pouring from his eyes. Three of the acolytes had been ripped apart, their pillars red with blood and pieces of their bodies strewn across the stone floor. But the rest of them remained unconscious, unharmed.

"Blaspheme!" the Reaper spat. "You are not chosen. You do not belong here!" He cast huge vines in his hand, slashing them at me in great whips and I was too slow to recover, still shaken to my core from what that being had done to me.

I was dragged to the centre of the chamber by his earth power, those whips striking at me, tearing into my clothes and biting through my skin. I cried out as pain ripped through me and more vines gripped my arms and legs, yanking on my limbs then pulling, laying me out for punishment. I stared up at the writhing mass of darkness on the cavern ceiling with fear clamouring in my chest as those whips struck at me again.

Agony raced through me, the Reaper's whips slashing across my legs and stomach, making me scream. I sent ice flooding over me in a shield, thickening it as the whips lashed down again, trying to shatter it.

"You will bleed for your crimes," the Reaper hissed. "You will be sacrificed to the Void and your pain shall be the first payment."

The word 'Void' echoed in my skull. That strange entity must have been what he was referring to. They had found the weapon the Elysium Prophecy spoke of. And that knowledge would die with me here if I couldn't escape.

Another whip struck me so hard that the pain of it had me baying like a wounded animal. I was a girl on her back beneath her mother's screaming form again, rendered useless by the cruelty of others. And my mind cracked and split apart, my fear turning to a blinding rage at the injustice of it all. I thought of my half-brother pushing me in the dirt, calling me freak, nothing, worthless. I heard the laughter of all the Fae who had dismissed me, and it awoke something so brutal and cold inside me that I fell into the darkest spaces between the fractured pieces of my soul. All of it brewed and boiled and burst from me at once and a roar of refusal left me, rejecting my fate as a girl who was *nothing*.

Power spewed from me in an unimaginable wave, that darkness inside me spilling onto the outside and eating through the Reaper's binds at once until they were dust.

I rose to my feet, blood soaking down my thighs, stomach and arms from his strikes and my upper lip peeled back in a sneer.

"Wh-what are you?" he stammered, backing up, raising his hands but no power came for me. He was too afraid to cast against me again, and I revelled in the high I got from that.

"Your death," I whispered, shifting my eyes into that of my Leopard's before sending a blast of water out around the room, plunging us into the dark. But without that thick presence clogging the air, the being returned to that strange coiling liquid above us, I could see and the Reaper could not. And I prepared to punish the devil who had hurt me.

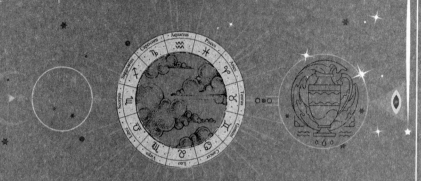

VESPER

CHAPTER FORTY

The collision of magic and blades echoed ferociously throughout the chamber, our fight with the Vampires a chaos of brutal attacks and desperate defence.

I'd never been on the back foot in a fight like this, never found myself scrambling for cover and relying on shields instead of attacking.

I threw my power at a blur of motion who was racing towards me, an explosion of air magic hitting the Vampire hard enough to send him crashing into the far wall, a cascade of grit tumbling down where he fell. But he was up and shooting back into the fight before I could make any attempt at advancing.

I'd given up fighting with my blades, all of my focus on the weight of my magic which I was forced to replenish as quickly as I was using it, my gifts locked onto the Vampires, their desire for blood and love of the hunt fuelling me continuously.

But as I replenished myself with their power, my gifts only stoked the flames of those desires, making their hunger increase, their attacks growing more reckless, more volatile, more deadly.

Cayde cursed as the one who I had assumed to be the leader with the curls which hung to his jaw took him to the ground, fangs snapping at his throat. He swung a heavy punch into the Vampire's jaw, knocking him off again before his teeth could make contact and rage poured through me.

I blasted magic at them, hurling the Vampire away before Dalia's scream of pain had me whipping around once more.

Terror sped through me as I found her pinned to the ground with two Vampires feasting on her blood, their teeth deep in either side of her throat as they drank and her thrashing limbs lost momentum.

"Moraine!" I cried as I sprinted for our sister, another of the Vampires racing to take me on.

Moraine shifted into her Harpy Order form, revealing her silver wings and launching herself into the air, out of reach of the monstrous beasts. She wrapped me in a fist of her air magic as the Vampire shot for me, whipping me towards the cavern roof and hurling me towards Dalia with a cry of effort.

I took control of my descent, blasting the Vampires off of my friend and dropping down before her as she scrambled to sit up, clutching at her bleeding throat.

"Fisherman!" I bellowed, naming one of the attack formations the three of us had been perfecting during our hours of battle training and I met Moraine's gaze across the room as she nodded in confirmation.

Cayde still wrestled with the lead Vampire, the two of them locked in a fit of furious blows and my pulse thundered with the need to get to him, but I focused on the plan first, trusting him to hold his own until I could get there.

I threw my fist out, blasting a wall of air magic into existence behind the three Vampires who had rushed to join with one another in the centre of the chamber before using a whip of power to claim a measure of that glittering grit from the urn behind them.

Moraine's magic met with mine from the other side and the two of us threw our power into the Vampires. We caught them in our net, hurling them towards an archway marked for earth just as I dropped the measure of grit I had collected into the depression at its base and opened it.

The three of them were thrown through the archway into the unknown, our combined power blasting at the wall of glimmering light until it faded away, leaving them on the far side of it and reducing our enemies to two.

I broke into a run, my eyes on Cayde whose fight with the Vampire was turning more brutal, the beastly leader of the coven fighting with such force and speed that I could hear bones crunching from the impact of his blows.

Panic threatened to envelop me and I didn't think twice before hurling myself at the pair of them, colliding with the Vampire and knocking him off of the man I had claimed for my own.

A flash of light caught my attention from across the cavern but I couldn't spare any attention to look for it.

We rolled across the hard floor, my head hitting the stone of an archway so hard that for a moment only darkness called to me.

And a moment was all the leader of the Vampires needed.

My curse of fury ripped through the air as he tore into my throat, his venom immobilising my hold over my magic as he began to drink furiously, a sickening sucking sensation overtaking me as he drew my power out of my body and into his own.

I scrambled for a weapon, my hands clawing at his back and finding the hilt of a battle axe he had strapped there.

I fought beneath his weight, tugging at the axe as the sound of the others fighting the final Vampire in their desperation to get to me filled my ears.

The world flickered around me as every drop of magic was torn from my limbs, the blood loss making my vision darken as the feral desire for blood consumed the beast on top of me.

He wasn't going to stop. My magic hadn't been enough to sate him. His vicious desires would only climax in my death.

I tugged the axe free of its sheath but it was too heavy in my leaden arms, falling with a clang to the stone beside us as my boots kicked feebly at the flagstones.

Death was a sweet caress against my cheeks, the Ferryman drawing closer, ready to guide me beyond The Veil, the echo of his paddle dipping into the waters of ruin echoing in my ears…

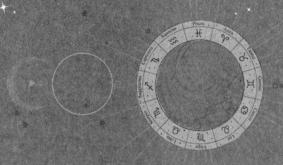

EVEREST

CHAPTER FORTY ONE

I had the Reaper pinned beneath me, my knife to his throat as he whimpered in terror, still not using his magic on me. But he wasn't getting the message, his answers to my questions only driving more rage into me with every passing second.

"What is that thing?" I demanded, slicing my blade into his shoulder and making him scream.

"Stars bless me. Save me from this accursed soul," he pleaded.

"They're not coming to save you," I hissed. "Now tell me how to release those chains!"

I slashed another line into his shoulder and he wailed like a newborn babe, cowering from me and only fuelling my ire.

"Tell me," I hissed like a wraith, becoming a being of darkness who would not rest until Harlon was free.

"You c-cannot release the acolytes. The Grand Maester cast the chains into existence. Only he can undo them when the ritual is d-done," he stammered, raising a hand to try and cast at me, but his fingers only flexed strangely instead.

"There must be a way," I insisted.

"There is not," he snarled.

I drove my dagger into his arm, making him scream once more.

"I'll cut you to pieces if you don't give me an answer," I snapped, my blood rising as I glanced back at Harlon's unconscious form. What would I do if this Reaper's words were true? I was in some unknown place with a Reaper who had been bloodied by my hands. I had no way of freeing him and a thousand crimes now tarnished my name.

Fire bloomed in my periphery and I turned sharply to look, my pulse stalling at the sight of the man standing there.

Kaiser was formidable in his full Fury form, his chest bare to reveal reams of blood-red armour coating his skin from the waist up above a pair of black trousers, the thick scales moulding to his body. Two curved black horns curled up from his head, sharpening to points, and his eyes burned deepest red.

"How are you here?" I gasped in horror, raising my right hand to defend myself.

Blue coiled between Kaiser's fingers then scurried up his arm to perch on his shoulder with a purring chirrup as he nuzzled his cheek.

I stared at the little creature in confusion as he watched me from my enemy's shoulder.

"My sayer dragon, Calcifiend, led me here, I had to sneak past the Sky Witch and her little clan of Skyforgers who are fully engaged in fighting the Vampires out there. You have been keeping the company of at least one of them, now more? What a traitor you are turning out to be, silka la vin," Kaiser said in a dark tone. "And here you are with a Reaper pinned beneath you in a chamber designed for some unholy devices."

He regarded it all with vague intrigue, taking in the gore left behind by that terrible being, before his destructive eyes fell on me again.

"Calcifiend?" I breathed, staring from the traitorous little lizard to Kaiser. The creature had been visiting me for months, coming and going at will, but I'd never thought for even a second that he was heading off to keep the company of a monster.

The Reaper thrashed beneath me and I pressed my blade to his throat again in warning.

"Stay still," I hissed, my mind skipping from one thought to the next as I tried to figure out my next move.

My enemy had followed me to this place. He knew all of my crimes. Was he going to try and save this Reaper and force me to face execution by the prophets of the stars? And if so, why hadn't he fucking moved to do it yet?

"What has she done to you?" Kaiser asked the Reaper, seeming at ease. There was no hint of surprise in his eyes at finding this revered Fae on his back beneath me, wet with his own blood.

"My magic. I cannot cast it," he rasped and I stared down at him in shock, taking in the truth in his eyes and trying to understand it.

"What do you mean?" I whispered, my voice a soft whisper in comparison to the harsh rage I had aimed at him before.

"He means you are what I suspected you are," Kaiser said flatly, and my eyes whipped to him again.

"And what is that exactly?" I demanded.

"Only I will be the keeper of that knowledge," Kaiser growled then flung his hand out, a tiny blade scoring through the air and slamming into the Reaper's throat.

I lurched backwards as he spluttered, pulling out the blade only to release spurts of blood.

Kaiser strode towards me, ignoring the dying Reaper and I scrambled to my feet in alarm, lifting my blade and preparing to cast.

"I'll kill you," I vowed, side stepping as Kaiser strode forward to engage me, not bothering to unsheathe either of his swords.

"You don't have control over that power in you. You don't even know what it is, do you? But I am certain of it now I've seen you render a Reaper powerless."

He stepped forward and I stepped back, the two of us moving in a dance that could only end in blood. I didn't know how much time I had left. If the Reapers managed to secure a victory over the Vampires, they could return here at any moment. But I couldn't leave without Harlon. And it looked like I wasn't going to get out at all unless I killed Kaiser Brimtheon.

I raised my chin, accepting the fight that fate was offering me and readying my magic for attack.

"Yos sala ki mintil," I vowed. *Your death is mine.*

"Delusional as usual," he drawled then three dark red beasts came into existence at his back, the hounds snarling and snapping at me as they drew closer.

I blasted water at Kaiser's face, trying to blind those vicious eyes as his hounds came racing toward me, but he turned it to steam with a forceful heated flame rising from his hand.

I braced myself for the dogs' attack, slashing my knife at the face of the first and striking its muzzle. But it was no true thing, the knife passing through its head just before its jaws latched around my arm. I cried out in agony, the beast able to hurt me but I couldn't hurt it in return. As Kaiser's eyes flashed, its bite deepened, pulling me towards its master.

Blue chirruped angrily on Kaiser's shoulder, biting at him, but he ignored the lizard's chattering, the other two hounds nipping at my legs, driving me towards their master.

I blasted ice at Kaiser, my fingers flexing and sending shards of deadly ice at his face, but again he melted them away within a rippling barrier of heat that radiated from him.

As the hounds forced me in front of him, I thrust my dagger up, aiming for his heart and crashing against the metallic armour of his chest. Cursing, I drew my arm back as a wave of oppressive heat poured from him, surrounding me like a cage. I winced against the stifling burn, stabbing at him again and trying to cut through the metallic red plates of his chest. He watched me struggle to claim his death, raising no hand to me even now, his mouth a flat line and his expression unchanged.

"On your knees where you belong." His dogs caught my arms again, dragging me down and rage snared me as I thrashed against them.

Kaiser drew his sword at last. I glared at it, realising he had selected my mother's blade, disguised as the pair to his other. He intended to destroy me with her blade and I balked against the idea of it.

The pain in my arms burrowed deeper but that dark power of mine rippled through my chest and doused my soul in hope. It lay there in offering for me to use, and I sent it out from my body in an uncontrollable wave. The force of my mysterious magic slammed into Kaiser's hounds and they vanished in an instant. Triumph made me raise my chin, my gaze set on my enemy. I didn't know exactly how I'd taken hold of that power and I still didn't know what it was, but I was damn thankful for it.

Kaiser frowned in surprise as I leapt up, aiming for his throat which was bare of armour, slashing my dagger with all the wildness I contained, demanding his death from all the deities of the sky.

His sword came up, barring the blow at the last second and I staggered back, but a smile lifted my lips. He was engaging me now. A true fight. Blade on blade. And that was exactly how I wanted it.

"Come then," he conceded. "Show me what you can do with that dagger, silka la vin."

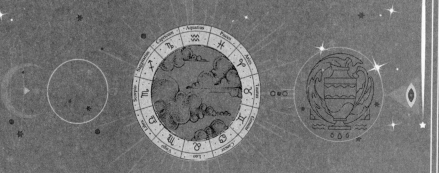

VESPER

CHAPTER FORTY TWO

The dark was deep and restful, a silence held within it which promised a calm that I had never known in life and I was tempted, oh so tempted to let that silence have me.

But my friends had other ideas for my fate.

Dalia bellowed as she threw herself on top of me and the Vampire who had come to claim my death, the flash of her dagger a blinding light in the darkness which had come for me before she slammed it home between the Vampire's shoulder blades.

The Vampire tore his teeth from my throat with a howl of pure agony as she tore the blade free and stabbed him again and again, a rain of blood coating both of us as she ripped him from this world with a brutal, terrorising force.

A cry of utter agony poured from the throat of the other Vampire in the chamber and I caught sight of his wild, grief-stricken eyes. He stared at me and Dalia, the corpse of his brethren sagging between us, horror written into his features.

The copper-haired Vampire made to lunge for us, but Moraine was faster, blasting him away with a lash of air magic. He slammed into the wall then shot to his feet, throwing one final, hateful gaze at the four of us before shooting from the room at such speed that I lost sight of him entirely.

Dalia hissed in pain as she half fell off of me, gripping the closest archway and hauling herself to her feet with clear difficulty.

Moraine strode for us, her silver wings rustling at her back as she tucked them close to her spine and kicked the corpse of the Vampire off of me.

I offered her a grim smile as she heaved me to my feet, taking hold of the battle axe belonging to the dead Vampire and hefting the weapon into my grip. I'd fought many battles without magic before, but the hollowness in my chest now that my power had been stolen left me feeling vulnerable in a way I never had before knowing it.

I looked beyond my friends for Cayde, my heart rate settling as I found him stalking closer, his neck bloody and eyes hard with a powerful hatred which reminded me of exactly how terrifying he could be on the battlefield.

I met the darkness of his eyes over Moraine's shoulder, a smile lifting my lips which wasn't savage or wicked or any of the things I normally offered the world. It was pure, and honest, and spoke of the way my heart pounded harder just for him, of the secret we shared and how desperately I ached to make my claim on him known to all the world.

Moraine's pained cry was a soft caress against my ears, her dark eyes widening in shock and understanding while I stared at her in uncomprehending confusion.

Her hand grasped for the sliver of silver which protruded from her chest, the tip of a bloody knife jutting from her heart before being ripped away so fast I wasn't certain I'd seen it at all.

I lunged for her, catching her weight as she fell on me, her eyes holding mine in a brutal realisation which tore through me with agonising clarity as the light faded from them so fast, I could barely capture the memory of it in my palm.

"Moraine," I gasped, my knees buckling with her weight, the shadow of Cayde's body moving closer, his expression driving through me just as forcefully as the knife that had pierced my sister's flesh. All I could do was stare at him in horrified shock.

I blinked at the man I had offered my blackened heart to, a mask seeming to slip from his features as he looked at me with feral hatred, his desires lashing against me with the bloodthirsty need for death.

My lips parted on words which wouldn't come, devastation and agony rooting me in place beneath the dead weight of the woman who I loved far more dearly than my own rotten soul deserved.

"*Moraine,*" I choked out again, my muscles shaking with her weight as I tried to hold her up, her head falling against my shoulder, the heat of her blood pooling against my chest through the thick material of my leathers.

I couldn't comprehend a universe without her sinful wit and acidic tongue, her slow temper and brutal power. She was a guiding force in my world, a bright light in an otherwise dark existence and there was no truth to me without her. She was one of only two people who truly knew me, truly saw the woman I was beneath the legacy I had built to mask myself. What was I without her?

A cry poured from my lips so brutal and raw that I couldn't draw another breath beyond it, my fingers grasping the back of her head, knotting in her braids as I begged the stars to take it back, to change their minds.

Me. It should have been me, not her. He was my failure, the demon with the eyes of sin who I had distrusted from the first but had somehow slipped into my confidence. I had brought him here. And as he came to send me into the after behind my sister, I found I couldn't move to stop him. I couldn't release her. It was my fault. I deserved death for causing hers.

Cayde lunged for me, but Dalia was suddenly there, throwing herself between us with a ragged command spilling from her lips.

"Run, V!" she snarled, her eyes wild with agony as she looked to Moraine in my arms, an acceptance in her eyes which I refused with all that remained of my ragged, ruined soul.

"No!" I bellowed.

Moraine fell from my grasp as I lurched for Dalia instead, the blade which had been aimed at me cutting deep into her throat as she threw herself between me and the man who I had given myself to completely like a fucking fool. I had caused this. It was all on me and yet now both of my sisters were going to pay the fatal price of my stupidity.

I screamed as the three of us fell beneath the force of Cayde's strike, his feral cry of murderous rage echoing off of the walls as he ripped his blade free of my sister's throat and Dalia's blood splattered my face.

"Dalia!" I screamed, reality catching up to me as he swung for her again, my boot catching on the body beneath me which I refused to admit was Moraine.

I swung the stolen axe, the weapon heavy and cumbersome, but

Dalia threw herself between us once more, clutching at her bleeding throat while aiming a dagger at Cayde in her final moments, her boot swinging out to strike me in the chest and knock me back.

Agony tore through my heart with such potency that I barely felt it as I hit the ground, my body reacting on instinct as I rolled to my feet again in time to see Cayde throw Dalia's body to the floor with a solid thump.

Her eyes stared glassily up at me, her fingers falling lax around her throat as her blood pooled in a great river from her body. Impossibly, I found myself staring at the three people who I had truly had in this cruel world, two dead at the hands of the third, the scene before me making no kind of sense at all.

"Why?" I gasped, backing up as my head swum from blood loss, and my fingers gripped the blade of the axe like it was a lifeline. But what life did I even have without my sisters to cling to? "I don't... Cayde...?"

I stared at the man who I had offered my heart and soul to, searching his piercing gaze for some sign that this wasn't truly him, some explanation for the horror before me which I could make sense out of.

"You made it so fucking easy, Vesper," he purred, advancing on me with that dagger in his hand, the blood of the two people I loved most in this world staining it in grim proof of what he had done. "I thought you were what stood between me and the prince but you weren't, were you? You were so fucking desperate for love that the moment I offered you a hint of it, you were mine. And you never even questioned it, did you?"

"Dragor?" I breathed, trying to make sense of his words as he stalked me between the archways, my friends' blood smearing across the floor in his bloody boot prints, their empty eyes watching us. Dalia's command echoed through my mind, but how could I run? How could I abandon them here?

"Well I hardly went to all this effort for a waifhouse brat, did I?" Cayde growled, contempt marring the face I had once found so alluring. "But now I have a prize far better than the head of a prince to offer my sovereign. You just gave me a path right into the heart of your nation and all the others besides. I'll be praised above every warrior in Avanis for winning this war for him. And to think, all it took was a few turns between your thighs to have you spilling your secrets for me. I'd expected a creature built for seduction to be more wary of it."

The horror which had taken hold of me shattered with those words, a sickening, terrifying truth peeling their way free of them as he stalked after me, my death shining in those honey brown eyes which had concealed so much from me with every look.

"You're a Stonebreaker," I accused and his smile darkened as he flexed his fingers, the ground beneath my feet quaking in reply to the call of his magic.

"I saw you wield air," I said, shaking my head. "You can't wield both. Only the Reapers-"

"Do you think you were the first Fae to ever wonder at the secrets the Reapers keep from the rest of us? Clever, suspicious little Vesper? Of course you weren't. You're just a nosy bitch leashed to the will of a monster. The Stonebreakers have been figuring out the Reapers' secrets for years and you don't have to attend Never Keep for the stars to Awaken your power."

Shock rolled through me at that admission, but Cayde was clearly done basking in his own betrayal and the stupidity of the succubus who had fallen for her own game.

Vines ripped from the flagstones at my feet, coiling around my legs with ferocious strength and yanking me to the ground.

The blood loss made me slower to react than usual, my grief marring my reflexes, but I refused to fall at the feet of the bastard who had stolen my entire world from me. I refused to leave this world without avenging the only two women who had ever made living in it mean a fucking thing to me.

Cayde lunged for me but I swung my axe, forcing him back and cleaving through the vines with a furious blow.

I tried to steal his magic with my gifts but his desire for my death and the power he would soon claim in Avanis wasn't enough to fill my reserves as quickly as I needed it.

A pathetic blast of air sprung from my fingers, knocking him back a single step and only buying me enough time to regain my feet.

The ground bucked beneath me as he lunged at me with his dagger, my axe deflecting the blow but only just; the cumbersome weapon slowing me down.

He forced me back. Then again. My boots stumbled over the ground as it rioted beneath me, the pain in my soul making it hard to focus on anything beyond the furious desire to reap vengeance upon his tarnished soul.

Tears stained my cheeks as he forced me to back up again and again, reality sinking in as my head spun with dizziness. He was fucking toying with me.

"I told you I was watching you train so that I could learn your weaknesses, Vesper," he growled, meeting my next blow with ease. "I know your habits, your preferences, the moves you hold back in reserve. And I never gave you the chance to learn mine."

He was right. How many times had he watched me train with Moraine and Dalia, never once accepting the offer to join us, taunting me with the suggestion that he was hunting for my weaknesses? It didn't matter if he hadn't found any. He knew how I moved and with my magic gone and the blood loss slowing me, he had the advantage he'd been working to gain.

My back struck one of the archways and the scent of home washed over my cheeks, cold against the wetness of my tears.

I deflected another strike of his blade as a second scent moulded with the first and an idea came to me, one fit for nothing short of suicide, but I had little left to live for now anyway.

I yelled out as I swung my axe for him in a savage blow, forcing him back at last, my free hand scrambling for the dregs of grit that remained in my pocket and taking hold of a paltry handful.

I hurled it at the rune to activate the archway, leaping back as Cayde lunged for me, his dagger opening a wound across my bicep, tearing through my leathers.

But as he came at me again, a blinding light erupted at my spine and I hurled myself into the clutches of the stars with one wild, desperate hope fluttering through my mind. Not for my survival. But for the vengeance owed to my sisters.

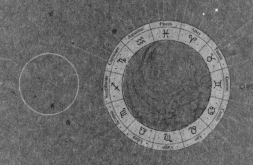

EVEREST

CHAPTER FORTY THREE

Our blades clashed time and again, Kaiser parrying each of my blows and pushing me onto the back foot. He was unyielding, tireless and worst of all, I suspected he was calling upon just a fraction of his energy to keep up this tirade. Calcifiend grunted at us, fluttering around Kaiser's head, but he batted him away and the sayer dragon flew to sit on one of the stone pillars, watching us and clicking his tongue.

My arms were aching from countering the powerful strikes of Kaiser's sword, and his deflections of my dagger always sent me stumbling from the ferocity he used.

"If you came to kill me, why don't you engage me properly?" I snapped. "Why keep pushing me back?"

"Because I did not come here to kill you," Kaiser stated, swinging his blade so hard that it connected with mine and nearly tore it from my grip. He swung for me with his free hand, trying to get hold of me, but I slipped away, attacking from the side and driving my dagger at his kidney. I hit his armour, the reverberation resounding up my arms and making me curse as I jolted back from the impact.

"Why did you come then?" I snarled, throwing a brief glance at Harlon and wondering how I would ever be able to get him out of here.

"I came to see if my suspicions were true and it seems they are," he said, the threat in his words dripping over me.

"What are your suspicions?" I demanded, swinging a punch at his head, magic glittering in my right hand as I coated it in ice, driving my dagger up beneath his jaw. His red eyes snared me, our gazes meeting and I faltered, his possession slamming into my mental shields.

So much power, so much terrible, terrible power lived in this beast, and I felt my shields cracking, giving in to all that potent magic. I fought to keep him out with everything I had, my shields stronger than before, and a surge of triumph spilled through my chest when they held. But he only tipped his head a little and his eyes flashed brighter red, the resulting explosion of strength that met with my mind like the violent collision of an anvil against my skull.

"*No*," I gritted out, wincing at the almighty power he threw against me.

I was helpless to stop him getting through. My mental shields cracked then fell, and I gasped as he claimed my mind, shuddering as I was forced to stand motionless before him, my dagger lowering to hang uselessly between my fingertips.

He took the blade from me, making my chest crush with a furious loathing. I realised I still had control over my tongue, so nothing stopped me speaking my mind. "You're a blight to me. A plague of rot in my bones," I spat.

"Do I truly effect you so deeply?" he mused, examining my dagger and taking in his name on the hilt before looking to me, assessing, perhaps a little stumped by me.

"You killed my mother!" I screamed, the pain of her loss breaking free inside me, spilling into every part of my being and making me hurt so fucking bad.

Never rest, Everest.

Her parting words and my promise to keep them scraped through my mind like jagged fingernails. I was failing her, just as I had failed Harlon, just as I had failed myself. This soulless Fae had disarmed me with hardly any effort at all and my vow to destroy him might have continued to hack at my heart, but what use were petty words?

Maybe it was right that I was scoffed at for this desire, maybe I would never be strong enough to kill him, maybe I was lying to myself so deeply that I couldn't see the starkness of the truth right in front of me. But even in the face of it, I cringed back, refusing to accept it, not allowing it to permeate my skin like a toxin. If I fell into those beliefs, my mama would never be avenged, Harlon would never be saved. They needed me, even if they deserved better than I could offer. I would throw everything I had into trying to be enough, into keeping my promises.

I fought against Kaiser's unholy power, desperate to move, to strike, to *kill.*

"Give me that back," I hissed venomously.

He held the dagger's tip under my chin, almost pricking my skin. "You cannot wield that power in you. You do not know how."

"What power? What do you know about it?" I growled, trying to force that dark, twisted magic in me to the surface once more, but it was not so easily guided. Like it had a mind of its own.

"You are not a threat, but when you figure it out..." He regarded me. "You will be."

Those words breathed life into my flesh, the promise of them weaving a beautiful craving inside me that I needed to sate. I would be powerful, he believed that. He knew something of this power in me that told him to beware, and there was nothing I needed to hear more than that right now.

"Then I will learn it well and turn it upon you," I swore. "I will make you fear me before I let you die."

My vows of his death did little to perturb him, and I continued to battle his mental control, desperate to fight it off. I cursed his name as he regarded me without any fear in his eyes at all, but one day, that would change. His words had brought on a wild resilience in me, because he saw what I could become. He knew I could claim his life given time. But if that was true, why hadn't he killed me yet? He had me at his mercy. He could strike at me with my own blade but still, he left me breathing, and I couldn't fathom why.

"Death would save us all from you," he murmured and fear raced through me, and I felt him feeding on it, drawing my magic away into his veins. "But that would mean your gifts would be wasted."

"Get away from me," I hissed.

"Would Mirelle see you dead or have you chained?" he mused to himself. Mirelle. As in Mirelle Brimtheon, The Matriarch. That woman's name set a chime of dread echoing though my soul and Kaiser fed on that note of terror, drawing more of my power into his reserves.

I wasn't going to allow either of those things to happen to me, and as his possession dug deeper into my mind, rage splintered through my body.

I hated this man. I hated him with all the fires in all the burning stars of this universe and I would not let him decide my fate this day. It was mine for the taking. My moment in the sun.

That dark, twisting power rose its head inside me and I snatched it into my grasp with a jolt of fervour, forcing it out of me, out and out towards the hellion who had his claws in my mind.

It slammed into him, making him stumble back a step, my dagger falling from his fingers as his hand flew to his chest in shock.

His head bowed, his breaths coming heavily and that beautiful red armour began to recede like the tide across his upper body. It spilled away from his skin, rippling then lost, revealing his bare chest beneath, the line of the scar I had left on him from hip to shoulder and the other scars that marked him.

"Void," Kaiser growled, that word like the voice of fate calling my name as the words of the Elysium Prophecy tumbled through my mind. *Seek the Void, for it shall guide the victor to their glorious path, a weapon of purity, and the gift of null.*

"That is what you are," he swore. "That is the power you possess."

I stared at him, unable to believe that absurd accusation because it was purely impossible. The Elysium Prophecy was the greatest prophecy of the four lands; it was written in a thousand books, etched onto the sacred walls of the Astral Sanctuaries, hailed from the holiest and most revered tongues of the greatest Fae to ever walk in our world.

The weapon of the Void had been sought for centuries, it was fabled, little more than legend that was weighted with a million hopes of our people. *All* people. It was nothing more than ridiculous to claim I was that weapon, that I possessed a power so venerable it was practically a myth.

"You're wrong. That thing, that monstrous being they keep in this place is the Void. I heard that Reaper say it himself." I glanced up at the ceiling, that strange, writhing liquid still rippling there but holding no sign of the terrifying presence within it now. Though as I looked back at Kaiser, he was still bowed forward, struggling with whatever my magic had done to him and I wasn't sure he was listening.

He groaned then took his hand from his chest, his face twisting into rage, confusion and most of all, violence. I willed my dark power to take him, having some semblance of control over it now and able to drive it deeper into his body. He shook his head, horrors flashing in his eyes as their red glow dimmed to coldest black.

"Stop!" he bellowed, a vortex of rage spewing from his gaze.

I strode towards him, watching him struggle with this unknown force inside him, but then my grip over the power slipped from my grasp. It tumbled away from me as surely as the night gave way to day, irreversible until it decided upon its return. I was left with a furious-looking Kaiser, and the loss of strength in my blood made me feel all too exposed in front of his hellish state. If I'd thought he was indifferent to me, it didn't seem so now. There was true hostility aimed at me, a desire to punish me for whatever I'd done to him.

Fire flared hot in his hands, brightest red then changing and darkening until the flames were as black as his soul. He lashed out with the great chains of the ebony fire, snaring me in it and dragging me towards him. Despite the heat of the flames, they didn't burn, they bound, tethering my limbs to his and coiling around me like a serpent.

"Let go!" I screamed, sending ice out to fight off the shackles, but the flames were unmoved by my power.

"Nightfire is a gift of Furies," Kaiser said darkly, lifting his hand to grip my chin and make me look into those eyes of blazing crimson.

His possession rocked through my mind before I could do anything to stop it and I took a shuddering breath as his will took hold of mine. "It's not a weapon. It has a single purpose. One sole use. And it is not something my kind wield lightly, for we can only do so once."

He didn't let me speak in reply, my body belonging to him in every way. He could make me do anything he pleased and it awoke a true kind of terror in me. This total dominion over my body was an invasion I couldn't bear, and whatever this Nightfire was, I feared it to my core.

"I can select one Fae in this forsaken world to be mine. Wholly mine. To the very root of your soul, you will belong to me," Kaiser announced, those words rattling me as I fought to escape his mind control, but there was no way out. "And I have chosen you."

My soul thrashed at that terrifying assertion. I couldn't let this happen. Inside my head I was screaming, but outside, I could only stand and watch this monster cast this merciless fate upon me.

"Everest Arcadia, I claim you as my Fearsire," he stated, magic snapping through the air as those words fell upon my soul. I didn't know what that declaration meant, but I felt it crawling beneath my skin, whispering of sins and sorrows.

"You will serve me in all the ways my Order demands. You will feed me your most haunting fears, you will suffer so that I might thrive, and you will offer me your nightmares in any form I require," he stated as the black Nightfire coiled tighter around us both, sinking into our flesh with a flicker and hiss of spitting flames until there was no sign of it anymore. It writhed through my blood, but no pain found me. All I felt was the heavy, heated weight of those fiery tethers snaking into my skin and settling there irrevocably. "And know this. You cannot ever kill me; this soul-tie will not allow it."

Of all the things this power could do to me, that was the worst. He was taking away my free will, and I felt him feeding on the fear that stoked in me.

"The darkest pieces of our souls will unite as one, silka la vin." He moved his face close to mine, his cruelty palpable, toxic. "There is no fighting it. No reneging on this power. It is as old as the stars and as binding as destiny. You will not be able to fight my possession again. If I will you to do something, you will do it. I can summon you with a single desire, and if you refuse my call or go against this soul-tie in any way, you will face the burn of the Nightfire."

His grip on my arms became bruising as he forced me to submit to the magic woven into existence by his Order. It rushed into me, and I would have buckled to my knees had he not been holding me there, the pressure of the soul-tie setting the air alight and blinding me with its unwavering strength.

"There is only one way to seal this magic," Kaiser hissed, that anger in him still there, no longer hidden behind a veil, and it was entirely aimed at me now. "With a kiss."

I couldn't move, my feet rooted in place as he pressed his despicable mouth to mine, his lips a furnace against my own. He stole that kiss from me, soaked in his depravity, but it was laced with my own hatred too, marking him as he marked me in return.

There were whispers in the air for a moment, as if the stars were leaning close to witness the carnage we were forging between us, shocking me that they cared for the fates of two simple Fae. But perhaps it was because two enemies being bound like this would rock the foundations of what the four lands stood for. We were meant to stand on opposite sides of the war, our souls should never have been tangled in this way. And my fate reeked of bad omens because of it.

As he withdrew, the hard press of my enemy's mouth finally relinquishing mine, the Nightfire blazed inside me, heating me through and making me burn. I could feel him tugging on the darkness in me, the most haunted parts of my soul rising to the surface of my skin. The need to give them to him racked my being, leaving me tainted. But even as the magic pulsed through me, forging some deep, unbreakable connection between us, I knew that desire wasn't really mine. I could feel my truth clashing with the soul-tie and screaming to be released, but there was no power in this universe that would listen to my pleas. I didn't know what this tether to him would truly lead to, what demands it would make of me, but I knew it was nothing good.

He released me from his possession, allowing me to move and I realised hot tears were slowly rolling down my cheeks. My soul was no longer my own. It belonged to my nemesis.

"There are requirements to this soul-tie," Kaiser said darkly, his eyes speaking of the horrors I was yet to face. "I will tell you of them soon, but now, we must leave this place."

"No," I breathed, shrinking from him, the Nightfire burning hotter beneath my skin and demanding I listen to his commands instead. The commands of mother's killer, the man I had vowed upon all the celestial beings that I would destroy. It was as if my full focus had been shifted onto him, like he was my north star, guiding me across a dark ocean and following him was the only path to salvation. But that was a filthy lie, sewn into my essence by the magic of his Order.

"You cannot chain me!" I roared, dropping to the floor to grab my dagger then bringing it up with a determination that rocked the foundations of my being and yanked on the soul-tie that Kaiser Brimtheon had stitched between us.

A scorching burn rose in my chest and I yanked my arm back as the possibility of his death brought the Nightfire to life. It burned me from the inside and I screamed, stumbling away from him as my hand shook around the hilt of my dagger, the pain only easing when my intention to strike at him subsided.

I couldn't kill him. The Nightfire ensured it, just as he'd said.

"Why did you do this to me?" I whispered, shattered, broken and trembling as he reached out to caress my cheek, gazing at me like that ire in him had lessened in light of this barbaric connection between us.

"Because the Void has to be delivered to Pyros, silka la vin. You must belong to me. It will make it all the easier to bring you to The Matriarch once our time at Never Keep is done, and it will ensure you do not slip from my grasp in the meantime, nor tell a soul of what you are."

"I am not what you think I am," I said in disbelief. "I'm not the Void. It's insanity. How can you really believe that?"

"I know what I saw," he said firmly. "You are the weapon the Elysium Prophecy speaks of, and for now, you are *my* secret to keep. And you will not tell anyone that truth."

The Nightfire ignited inside me, binding me to that command. I hissed between my teeth as the heat of the flames roared within my veins, and I was sure they would devour me if I uttered those words to anyone but him.

"Start walking," he growled. "We mustn't be found here when the Reapers return."

I looked back at Harlon, desperation clawing through me as I stood before the monster who had declared me as his. Who had placed a leash upon me which I had no idea how to break.

"I'm not leaving without him." I ran for Harlon, but Kaiser

somehow tugged on the Nightfire inside me and he possessed my mind and body as simply as that. There was no mental shield in this world that could keep him out. And it was a frightful truth to be faced with.

"You are leaving now and you are leaving with me alone," he commanded, and my legs moved, willed along by his possession as he turned me from Harlon and forced me to abandon him.

"I won't," I growled, my voice full of raw fear for what might happen to Harlon if I left him with the Reapers. What if that monstrous entity returned here to feast on the rest of the acolytes? What if Harlon was next to be torn to pieces by it?

Kaiser slowed, looking back at the man who was the only Fae in this wretched world I cared for. I loved him. I didn't know exactly what kind of love it was, but it was the only pure, good thing I had left. I couldn't abandon him when he needed me most.

As I resisted the demands of Kaiser's possession, the Nightfire burned hotter inside me, forcing me to bow to his whims and a groan of agony left me.

Kaiser's brows drew together as he stared at Harlon, and for a fleeting moment I could have sworn there was something akin to envy in his eyes. But it was darker than that, more volatile, something that perhaps had to do with the soul-tie.

He tore his gaze from Harlon back to me and the look he gave me made the hairs raise on the back of my neck. "His fate is set. He's destined to be a Reaper. There is no freeing him from that path, even if I were inclined to try and break his chains. Forget him."

"I could no sooner forget the beating of my own heart," I hissed, my arms shaking with exertion as I fought to go back to Harlon.

Kaiser sneered, his gaze moving across the acolytes like he would have no hesitation in gutting them all, but I was confused as to why. "It's too late for him. He's already one of them."

He turned, forcing me to walk after him and using his possession to seal my lips shut, leaving me unable to voice a word against this awful thing he was making me do. He had taken my power from me, but worse than that, so much fucking worse, he was taking Harlon from me. Making me abandon him to the heinous intentions of the Reapers. I had lost my faith in them. I'd unveiled too many of their secrets, seen beneath their lies, but I still had no idea of their dark purposes.

Kaiser set a fire in the chamber, burning the dead Reaper's body in a blaze so hot that he was reduced to ash in mere moments.

Calcifiend flew over from his perch on one of the stone pillars and landed on the Fury's shoulder, looking down at me with a soft chirrup, like he felt sorry for me, but the creature was just a traitor. Another being in this world not to be trusted.

I was forced to follow Kaiser down the passage that led to the archway, and he took a measure of that glittering grit from his pocket, ensuring we could make it back to the Keep.

A true kind of terror took hold of me as my enemy's hand slid around mine and crushed my fingers tight in his, because at his touch, I sensed the darkest pieces of his soul rising to meet with mine. They tugged on the chains of the power that tied me to this villainous Fae and told me in no uncertain terms, that I now belonged to him.

BASTIAN

CHAPTER FORTY FOUR

Pain splintered through my every movement, my enormous, scaled body cramped in this dank cavern, my neck bowed low from being unable to fully extend it for so long.

My whole world existed in a glow of green light emanating from the jagged lumps of crystal which were driven into my flesh, the agony of them punctuating each lingering moment of my existence.

A distant thumping pricked at my ears, my eyes cracking open as the sound drew closer, a ragged gasp falling from the unwitting lips of the Fae who approached.

The dark consumed me here, but the light of the passage beyond the bars winked in the distance, the silhouette of a Fae with pale pink hair passing through them, a sob rattling her chest.

I inhaled deeply, the raw scent of life which clung to her awakening the beast in me, even as the fog of my own thoughts threatened to drown me again. I was dying. I had been dying in this place for hundreds of years. Ever since I had emerged as a Dragon and been presented to the Reapers as a miracle by my father. His tremendous claim to much of the green lands of Avanis, alongside his countless victories in battle had made him believe the stars favoured him above all other warlords. And in his arrogance, he had believed that my Emergence as a Dragon was a symbol of that supremacy.

I could still smell the burning of his flesh, the screams of my family, the pleas for it to end.

I scoffed at my family name. Bastian Carderrin. Some Heir to the Crown of Bones I'd turned out to be – more like Heir to Decay and Ruin.

A second figure emerged beyond the bars, a second set of footsteps pounding into my lowly domain, this one a male, far larger than the first, reeking of bloodlust and spoiled earth.

My lips pulled back on a snarl, my claws flexing against the rocks beneath me, Dragon Fire growing in my chest.

Gold glinted in the fist of the woman as she raced into the darkness before me, an axe clasped in her grip which sang to me in a melody at once unfamiliar and utterly devastating.

Magic clawed through my veins with every step she took, the treasure awakening a power inside me which I had almost forgotten in my years festering in this cavern at the mercy of the Reapers.

Fire rolled up the back of my throat, my eyes on the pair of figures who dared disturb my torturous existence.

I bared my teeth, the glow of molten fire shining through them, illuminating the dark cavern and making the man stumble over his own feet, a choked curse escaping him.

But my attention didn't linger on the male. My focus fell to the female who didn't check her stride as she ran for me, her hair knotted and clinging to the blood which splattered her skin.

I met her storm grey eyes and in them I found a river of agony so like the pain I had come to call home. A bolt of energy surged between us in that look, like a spear of light driving into my chest and cracking it open. She was wild and furious, devastating in her beauty and ruinous in her suffering. She was a creature born of the same torment which lived in me and the taste of her death would be the sweetest tonic to my suffering.

A roar broke from my lips, loud enough to shake the dank walls of the cavern I was chained within. And as my gaze stayed locked with hers, I let hellfire spew from my lips with the hopes that it would burn this pain right out of me and take every piece of suffering in her tempestuous eyes with it.

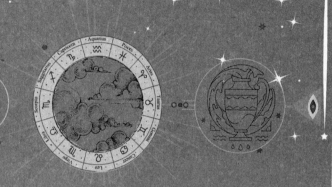

VESPER

CHAPTER FORTY FIVE

The Dragon towered over me, its eyes filled with a furious contempt for the world and all that surrounded it as it took in the sight of me running for it, axe raised and a demon charging at my back.

Cayde was closing in on me, my injuries slowing me down, but I only had to make it a few more paces. The mistake he'd made was in thinking I wouldn't welcome death. But I had nothing left to lose now and my own mortality was a simple price to pay for his annihilation.

The roar which escaped the Dragon made the walls rattle around us, the fire which blasted from its jaws blinding with its light.

I threw myself into a dive as flames exploded from its mouth, the heat stealing the air from the world, scorching my lungs, scalding my flesh.

I rolled, careful to keep the axe in my fist from cutting me open and as I slammed into something hard and hot, I peeled my eyes open.

The scales of the Dragon's steel grey foot were at once rough and silken against my palm as I steadied myself against it. Talons the size of my entire body punctured the stone beneath us and a great, iron manacle was clamped around its ankle.

Cayde released a battle cry at my back and I twisted to look at him, crouched behind an air shield which had splintered and cracked beneath the onslaught of Dragon Fire.

The Dragon roared again, talons digging further into the stone as it strained against the length of chain which held it, snapping ferocious jaws at the motherfucker who had stolen so much from me.

I craned my neck to look up at the chest of the enormous beast above me as it expanded on an inhale, heat emanating from its scarred scales as fire once again lit within its core.

"More secrets, Vesper?!" Cayde roared at me, his honeyed eyes blazing with hatred as I raised my axe above my head. His expression shifted from hostility to horror as he took in my position, the chain taut between us, a snarl upon my lips.

"Don't!" Cayde bellowed as I swung with all my might, a scream of defiant malevolence tearing from me as my grief threatened to consume every piece of my heart.

The chain broke with the force of my strike, the golden axe embedding itself in the stone beneath as the Dragon lurched forward with an earth-shattering roar.

I backed up as Cayde cried out in terror, the cavern trembling with the movements of the monstrous creature as it lunged for him, its four powerful legs pounding the ground around me as it tore over my head.

The strike of its tail caught me in the gut, hurling me from my feet into the dank stone wall at the back of the cavern, my head cracking against the stone.

Cayde was yelling curses at me, the walls cleaving apart as I shoved myself upright again and took my last weapon from my belt, the dagger feeling impossibly small in my fist.

I cursed as a huge lump of stone fell from the cavern roof, throwing myself away from it then launching myself aside as the Dragon's tail swept across the ground once more while it lurched around in the confined space, chasing after Cayde.

My eyes widened in horror as the wall of the cavern cracked in two, the world appearing to tear along its seams as rock and dirt tumbled through the fissure which Cayde was creating with his earth magic.

The Dragon lunged for him, its jaws snapping mere inches from his flesh as he threw himself into that crack in the stone and began to climb.

"No," I gasped, seeing his plan, realising what he was doing, how he was going to escape the vengeance he was owed.

I broke into a run, my chest hollow with emptiness where my magic should have resided, my lone dagger all I had left to secure his demise as he scrambled up into that crack in the stone, faint starlight appearing at its peak, signalling his liberation.

I ran my thumb over the dagger's tip, slicing my skin open and letting my blood roll down the metal.

"Don't run from this you fucking coward!" I roared but the Dragon's tail struck me again as it threw itself at the crack in the stone and started tearing great chunks from it with its powerful claws.

I blinked at the beast from my position on the ground. The dim starlight illuminated countless scars cut through its steel grey scales, the wing which hung limp and broken at its side and yet none of that diminished the majestic power of this creature of legend.

Cayde threw one contemptuous look back over his shoulder as the Dragon summoned hellfire to its jaws once again, his eyes meeting mine with a predatory enmity.

I scrambled to my feet and hurled my dagger at Cayde with a cry which tore my throat to ribbons, all of the pain he had delivered to me with the deaths of my beloved sisters ripping from me in that wretched, broken sound.

He threw his weight upwards right as the blade escaped my fingers, the sharp point skimming his thigh instead of imbedding in his spine as I had intended.

Panic captured me as he reached for the sky above him, an air shield glimmering into place beneath his feet, set to save him from the flames of the Dragon once more.

But I had his blood.

Ether rushed for me like never before, the force of it almost knocking me from my feet as I dropped to my knees beneath the onslaught. I smeared my fingers through the blood of my sisters which still coated my skin, their sacrifices for me rife with power.

Cayde jerked to a halt as I tugged on the blood in his veins, stopping his ascent just as Dragon Fire erupted from the mouth of the terrifying creature beneath him.

My head spun with the weight of my injuries, the intensity of my connection to the Ether almost too much to bear as darkness closed in around my eyes.

I couldn't hold it for long enough to rip Cayde's blood from him, and the reality of that struck me like a blow to the heart, Dalia and Moraine seeming to slip further from me at the thought of his survival.

But I wouldn't simply let him run.

A cry spilled from my lips as I pressed my shaking fingers to the ground, my body racked with agony as the darkness pushed in closer. Only Dragon Fire illuminated my world and the symbol I painted onto the unforgiving stone in the blood of my dearest friends. A curse fell from my tongue, latching itself to Cayde's soul while I fought to maintain my hold on him long enough for it to take root. The cost to wielding this dark magic was far greater than any I had ever paid before, but I gave all I had to see it done, to seal the spell and force the poison of my words to fester in his blood.

More rocks broke from the cavern roof, my head spinning with darkness as I pitched forwards, consciousness eluding me for several agonising moments before I forced myself back into my body.

"The Veil beckons, Vesper," Cayde spat, his words lashing against the open wounds of my grief. "No doubt I'll meet you again beyond it one day." And then he was gone, heaving himself up out of that gap between the rocks and disappearing into the star-lit world beyond.

The world was falling apart all around me, the starlight growing brighter though I was swathed in shadow.

Enormous rocks fell to the ground as the Dragon clawed at the gap Cayde had created to escape this hellish place and my lips parted as I realised what was happening. The Dragon was ripping the cavern open through brute strength alone, forcing that passage to the sky to widen and taking the roof down as it went.

I looked up as a tremendous boom broke the stone apart above my head, not flinching as I found the sky caving in on me, promising my death on swift wings.

I turned my hands palm up and inhaled deeply, allowing my eyes to fall closed as I called out to my sisters on their journey to The Veil, begging them to wait for me so that we might cross into death as one.

But I was not greeted with the beauty of their embrace or even the icy chill of the river of death. My end did not snatch me away on the wings of the wind, or in the clutches of the Ferryman's bony hand.

The world fell apart around me, the crash of the roof caving in and the rush of grit and dust washing over me, but there was no crack of stone against flesh, no crushing weight nor sudden demise.

My lips parted as I opened my eyes once more and found the Dragon standing over me, his body bowed and wings tucked close where he had taken the force of that blow, shielding me from the impact beneath him.

He pushed himself upright, boulders and jagged lumps of rock falling from his scaled hide, revealing deep gashes across his body and torn into his wings.

I scrambled to my feet and backed up, looking into the savage gaze of this king of beasts, this legend given life and offered nothing but suffering, who had just saved my worthless soul from death.

"You should have let me die," I choked out, my boots catching on broken stone as I backed up enough to meet his stare.

A low growl sounded in his throat and he dipped his head, expelling a cloud of smoke which sent my hair flying over my shoulders.

My heart stilled as I stared into his eyes, something within me calling out to this broken creature as if I could feel the agony he had suffered just as he could taste mine. A moment of affinity passed between our battered souls, an understanding which went deeper than the bones in our broken bodies and speared out into the world around us and the sky above.

Then he was gone.

And I was just a broken girl watching as he leapt out of this dank hole in the ground and scrambled across the rubble until making a break for the promise of freedom beyond.

I forced myself to follow, my battered body barely able to grip the fractured stone and make the climb towards the watching stars, but I did it. I needed to go after Cayde. I couldn't let this vengeance lie.

But when I finally made it to the frigid world above the crater which had once been the cavernous jail of a Dragon, I found nothing in the barren landscape beyond.

There was no sign of Cayde anywhere and the hulking form of the Dragon was already little more than a distant strike of shadow across the horizon.

I turned as that familiar wind pulled on my hair and fresh tears blurred my eyes as I looked out over the distant castle of Wrathbane.

I was home.

And yet I knew in my soul that I would never be home again.

The Sky Witch was dead and I was simply the shell who lingered in her wake, with nothing but the promise of retribution to keep me breathing.

AUTHOR NOTE

Soooo that was…admittedly a little brutal. Now if you're there crying and cursing us, staring on in horror at the horizon, wondering why we would do such a thing and perhaps considering hunting us down to gain some level of vengeance then please, PLEASE remember this:

We have a very specific set of skills.

We are really good at hiding and you won't find us easily.

We have a small dog and two feral children at our disposal who will gladly hurl poop at you should you manage to track us down regardless.

We can't fix it if you kill us.*

Starting something new is always daunting and setting out on a brand new journey in the same world as Solaria, set completely apart from all of the characters many of you know and love so dearly from Zodiac Academy (including us) was even more daunting than usual. So despite the pain, grief, and hurt you may have experienced while delving into the vaulted halls of Never Keep, we do hope that you found enough light to guide you onwards in this chaotic journey of reading that we have prepared for you.

There is always light waiting to break the darkest of nights and at the very least we promise you some inappropriate humour mixed in with your heartache in the rest of this series. So buckle up, get ready, hold onto your socks (lest they get blown off) and prepare yourself for book two because there are storms blowing in and this boat won't just coast through calm waters forever.

As always, we love and appreciate every one of you who is reading this and has read our work – none of this would be possible without you and we can never fully express how much you all mean to us.

Love Susanne and Caroline XOXO

*Fixing it is not guaranteed - we need readers' tears for sustenance and to grow the bitter lemons on our lemon tree of doom which is all we eat while writing these soul-destroying stories.

DISCOVER MORE FROM

CAROLINE PECKHAM

&

SUSANNE VALENTI

To find out more, grab yourself some freebies, merchandise, and special signed editions or to join their reader group, scan the QR code below.